PRAISE FOR JOHN WILLIAMS

'John Williams could form a literary triumvirate with Bateman and Welsh . . . this is a world of dope, docks and prostitution, a culture that is part-Cardiff and part-Caribbean. And while everyone is looking for a big score, few characters actually want to leave. Whether this is love or inertia, Williams does not say. But he has a talent for depicting both, especially love. *Five Pubs* is everything one would hope from as keen a critic of neo-noir as Williams'
Observer

'A cocktail of the breezy and lugubrious . . . although *Five Pubs* is littered with small-time gangsters, drug dealers, bent local government officials and prostitutes on awaydays, it is a surprisingly genial affair. At its best, it tends towards an unsentimental melancholy, a yearning for elsewhere that is touching'
Independent on Sunday

'Begins and ends with two of the most stylishly executed stings this side of a Tarantino film . . . this is literature as urban graffiti: bright, vibrant, fiercely individual'
Sunday Times

'*Trainspotting* transplanted to Cardiff, Williams' stories of a tough part of town where drugs, prostitution and multi-racial gangster warfare are part of everyday life are by turns blackly comic and true-to-life . . . a great page-turner'
Scotsman

The Cardiff Trilogy

By the Same Author

fiction
Faithless
Temperance Town

non-fiction
Into the Badlands
Bloody Valentine

edited
Wales Half Welsh

The Cardiff Trilogy

John Williams

BLOOMSBURY

Author's Note

This trilogy is set in a city called Cardiff that broadly resembles the real one, but it isn't a guidebook; now and again history and geography are played around with for fictional purposes. Anyone who knows the city may be surprised to find assorted landmarks – The Casablanca Club, The Custom House – that no longer exist in Cardiff today. And of course the people who inhabit this fictional Cardiff should not be confused with the fine upstanding citizens of the real one. All the events depicted herein are entirely fictional.

This paperback edition published 2006
Copyright © 2006 by John Williams

Five Pubs, Two Bars and a Nightclub first published 1999
Copyright © 1999 by John Williams

'The North Star' first appeared in slightly different form in *Fresh Blood 2* (Do-Not Press, 1997) edited by Maxim Jakubowski and Mike Ripley. 'The Glastonbury Arms' appeared in slightly different form (and under the title 'Supposed To Be A Funeral') in *Blue Lightning* (Slow Dancer, 1998), edited by John Harvey.

Cardiff Dead first published 2000
Copyright © 2000 by John Williams

The Prince of Wales first published 2003
Copyright © 2003 by John Williams

The moral right of the author has been asserted

Bloomsbury Publishing Plc, 36 Soho Square, London W1D 3QY

A CIP catalogue record for this book is available from the British Library

ISBN 0 7475 8122 3
9780747581222

10 9 8 7 6 5 4 3 2 1

All papers used by Bloomsbury Publishing are natural, recyclable products made from wood grown in well-managed forests. The manufacturing processes conform to the environmental regulations of the country of origin.

Typeset by Hewer Text UK Ltd, Edinburgh
Printed in Great Britain by Clays Ltd, St Ives Plc

www.bloomsbury.com/johnwilliams

Contents

Five Pubs, Two Bars and a Nightclub

Acknowledgements

Thanks to Abner Stein for seeing a book where I saw a short story. Thanks to Maxim Jakubowski for commissioning that first story. Thanks to John Harvey for commissioning a second story. Thanks also to Peter Ayrton and Philip John for their support and encouragement. Thanks to my editor Matthew Hamilton for his faith and perception, and to my copy-editor Sarah-Jane Forder for a job well done. Thanks, finally to Charlotte Greig for everything.

Contents

For Henry

Black Caesar's

The day they were due to finish building the mosque, Kenny Ibadulla was sitting in his front room with the curtains closed, watching the rugby. Wales were playing Ireland at home. Didn't know why he bothered watching it, really. You could just open the back door and, if the wind was blowing the right way, you could hear the roar from the Arms Park.

Always put him in a bad mood too. That's why he didn't like people knowing about it, knowing he still watched it. Everyone knew he used to play; it was part of the Kenny Ibadulla legend – the best outside centre Cardiff Boys ever had, at sixteen the biggest, fastest, meanest back the coach had ever seen.

'Course then he'd gone to prison, even if he was only sixteen, and that had been the end of that. And of course he hadn't given a shit, because when he came out he was the man. And he was still the man, fifteen years on. Which was why he didn't specially want people to see him throwing things at the telly when Wales's latest pathetic excuse for a centre knocked the ball on one more time.

So he was half furious and half relieved when the phone rang just as they were coming out for the second half. He picked it up and listened for a minute, then said, 'Fucking hell, not that thieving cunt. I'll be there in five, all right.'

Then he picked up his leather jacket, XXX Large and it was

still pretty snug across his shoulders, ran his hand over the stubble on his head, checking the barber had cropped it evenly, walked through to the kitchen where Melanie was chatting to her mate Lorraine, bent to kiss Melanie on the cheek and told her he was going down the club.

Out on the street he wondered, not for the first time, if building a mosque was really worth the hassle. Seeing as there was a perfectly good one in Butetown already. But then black Muslims and regular Muslims were hardly the same thing, and what Kenny was building was Cardiff's first outpost of Louis Farrakhan's Nation of Islam.

The other worry was whether it was really all right to build your mosque on the ground floor of a nightclub. Still, the club, Black Caesar's, was the only building Kenny owned, and he'd never been able to do much with the downstairs. He'd run it as a wine bar for a bit but Kenny's clientele weren't exactly wine drinkers, and the business types who were down the docks in the daytime never used it either, so he'd given that up. Then he'd tried turning it into a shop selling sports-wear and stuff. He'd had the whole Soul II Soul range in but then Soul II Soul had gone down the toilet and so had the shop. Docks boys didn't believe the gear was kosher unless they were buying it down Queen Street from some white man's store.

It had been brooding on this particular question that had led Kenny to his recent spiritual conversion. He'd been up in London, Harlesden way, doing a little bit of business, and the guys he was dealing with had taken him round the Final Call bookshop there. Nearly burst out laughing at first, sight of all these guys standing around in their black suits with the red bow ties, but when they got to talking a bit, it started to make sense. Specially all the stuff about setting up black businesses in black areas.

The way Kenny saw it, he was a community leader, yet he didn't get any credit for it. He had a business already, of course; in fact he had several, but they weren't exactly respectable. That was the way it worked – people didn't mind a black man selling draw and coke. They could just about handle a black man running a club. But a black man opens a clothes shop, and the punters fuck off up town and buy their gear there. Ignorant fuckers.

So Kenny had come back a bit inspired, like. He'd done his best to explain it all to the boys, and they'd gone along with it. Which wasn't surprising given that most of them were shit scared of him, but still, most of them knew about Minister Farrakhan already, so it wasn't too difficult, once they'd customised the approach for the local conditions.

He'd thought about changing his name, calling himself El-Haji Malik or something, but then Melanie had pointed out that he already had a Muslim name. Which was true enough, of course, and his grandad had actually been a Muslim, though his dad hadn't bothered with it, specially not after he met Kenny's mum, who was a fierce bloody Baptist and the one person Kenny was not looking forward to telling about his religious conversion.

Kenny's club, Black Caesar's, was on West Bute Street, right in the old commercial heart of the docks. On a Saturday afternoon, though, the street was almost completely dead. The only faint sign of life Kenny could see came from three of his guys – Col, Neville and Mark – sat in line along the pavement outside the club, holding cans of Carlsberg. Fuckers had been raiding the upstairs bar again.

3

'So where is he then?' asked Kenny.

Col jerked his thumb towards the building. 'Inside, boss. Checking the wiring, he said.'

'Fucking hell, Col, you don't want to leave that thieving cunt on his own,' said Kenny, and he headed into the club in search of Barry Myers, planning officer of the Docks Development Authority.

He found him downstairs in the back room, now the business part of the mosque, looking at the pulpit.

'Jesus, butt,' said Myers as Kenny approached, 'looks just like the one they used to have down the Swedish church.'

'Hmm,' said Kenny.

'Didn't know they had pulpits in mosques, Ken.'

'Yeah, it's called the mimbar,' said Kenny, and was pleased to see a look of surprise flash across Myers's smug face.

'Oh,' said Myers after a moment, 'the mimbar, I was wondering where you kept the booze,' and he started laughing.

Kenny didn't join in, just stood there wishing he could get away with decking the bastard. But he couldn't, he knew the form and he knew a hint when he heard one. 'Fancy a drink then, Barry?'

'Don't mind if I do, Ken, don't mind at all. Just check everything's shipshape down here first.'

So the two of them went through the motions of looking around the downstairs and Kenny had to admit his boys had done a decent job. The temple itself was all painted white and was furnished with some pews and the pulpit – mimbar – all of which, as Barry had pointed out, bore a pretty fair resemblance to the fittings in the old Swedish church. Best thing was, the back wall was even facing Mecca. It was just right, Kenny thought. Serious.

The front room still had some of the display cases left over from the clothes shop, but now they held copies of the *Final Call* and a few books on black history, plus a couple of videos of Farrakhan in action, and one of the Million Man March.

There were separate entrances outside for the mosque and the club but Kenny opened a side door and led Myers upstairs. The lights were already on around the bar, and there was the unmistakable smell of draw hanging in the air. The boys had clearly popped up to relax earlier on. Myers sniffed the air too, but didn't say anything. Kenny walked round the bar and dug out a bottle of Glenfiddich, poured a large one and handed it to Myers, then cracked open a Coke for himself.

'Missing the match then, Barry?'

'Oh yes,' said the planning officer. 'Tell you the truth, Ken, I can't stand the fucking game. When the ball's not stuck in the fucking scrum, they're kicking it into touch. Give me the ice hockey any day. You been down there, see the Devils, Ken?'

Kenny nodded. He'd been a couple of times. Nice to see Cardiff doing well at something. And a lot of young boys now were into it. But far as Kenny was concerned, you were stuck with the sport you grew up with. And suddenly he felt aggrieved that this parasite Myers was dragging him away from watching it. Time to get on with the business.

'So, Barry mate, what can I do for you?' he said, putting his drink down next to Myers and folding his arms, letting a little menace creep into the air.

But Myers didn't seem to register the threat. 'Well, Kenny,' he said, 'I've been studying the records, and this kind of change of use is highly irregular. You have to think about the whole make-up of a neighbourhood, and a church – sorry, a

5

mosque – and a nightclub in the same building . . . Well, there's a lot of ethical issues . . .'

'How much, Barry?'

Myers looked around, then shrugged, like he figured that there were a lot of things Kenny Ibadulla was capable of, but wearing a wire wasn't one of them.

'Oh, a grand up front and a ton a week should do it.'

Kenny just looked at him. The logistics of killing him flashed through his mind. The deed itself would be no problem, whip the baseball bat out from behind the bar, strike one and it would be over. Dump the body in the foundations of one of the building sites his boys were looking after. Perfect. Proper gangster business. Then he sighed inwardly and accepted that wasn't the way things worked down here.

'Fuck the grand, Barry. I've got three hundred here in my pocket. Take it or leave it. You comes back and asks for more, I breaks your fucking legs and I'll laugh while I'm doing it.' By the end of this little speech he had his face about three inches from Barry's and that seemed to do the trick.

The weasel didn't piss himself or pass out but the smile certainly disappeared. He stepped back, hacked out a laugh and said, 'Yeah, well, Ken, like I say, it'll be a tricky one to get through the committee, but three hundred'll be all right. Long as there's no complaints.'

Kenny handed over the money and Myers downed his drink and was out of the club in seconds. Kenny headed past the dance floor and opened the door to his office, turned on the TV just in time to see Wales concede a late try to Ireland and lose a match they should have won comfortably. He switched the TV off again and headed back out to the street, the urge to deck someone growing ever stronger.

He was cheered up, though, when he saw Col halfway up a ladder carefully stencilling in the outlines of the letters prior to painting the words 'Nation of Islam' over the door.

'Nice,' said Kenny, 'gonna be nice. So we'll be ready for tomorrow, then?'

'Yeah, Ken,' said Col, not turning around from his painting, 'easy. You go on home, give the missis one. See you down the Pilot later, yeah, you can sort out my bonus.'

Kenny laughed, said, 'Pay your hospital bill more like, you don't get it done,' and headed back towards Loudoun Square wondering what else he had to get sorted for tomorrow.

Tomorrow, Sunday, was set to be the mosque's grand opening. Way Kenny saw it, things would kick off about three. Have a couple of stalls and stuff out on the street, bit of music. Open the mosque up for anyone wanted to have a look, stick a video player in there running the Farrakhan tapes. Open the club up and get the disco going around six. Make it a little community dance thing.

Kenny was so wrapped up in thinking through his plans as he cut round the side of the real mosque – as he couldn't help thinking of it – that he didn't notice the noise of movement in the bushes next to him. Then there was a sudden whoop and Kenny spun round. If he hadn't checked himself just in time he would have taken the head off seven-year-old little Mikey, who had launched himself off a tree in the direction of Kenny's broad back.

'Gotcha,' said Kenny, catching the little boy and making to throw him back into the undergrowth where a couple of his mates were watching.

'C'mon then,' he said to them. 'Aren't you lot going to help your mate?' And so seconds later Kenny was buried under a heap of junior-school banditos. He played with the little gang for another five minutes or so before chasing them back in the direction of Mikey senior's flat, and then he carried on home with a positive spring in his step. Feeling well in the mood to do as Col suggested, the second he got indoors with Melanie.

That idea flew out of his head pretty quickly when the first thing Melanie said was that he'd had a phone call. Bloke with an American accent, said he was from the Nation of Islam, and he'd be coming down tomorrow, to the opening.

'Shit,' said Kenny, and sat down heavily on the sofa. This he hadn't been expecting. Of course he'd told the people up in London what he was planning. He'd bought all the videos and books and stuff from them. And they'd spoken to head office or whatever in Chicago and got the go-ahead for a new branch. But he'd thought that would have been that. He'd told the London boys about his opening, of course, and if a couple of them had wanted to come down, well that would have been no problem. But an American? Fuck.

Kenny started to work through a mental checklist. The mosque was fine, the boys had really done a good job with it. He'd got all the literature and stuff sorted out front. Got a fine-looking sister called Stephanie to work out front too. He'd got security. In fact that had all worked out very well indeed. All the guys who worked on the door for him and stuff already had the black bouncer suits. All he'd needed to do was get a consignment of red bow ties and he'd got the uniform sorted.

Then it hit him. The one thing he didn't have was a minister. He'd been so much in charge of it all that no one had mentioned who was going to be the preacher. Maybe everyone was expecting him to do it. Well, perhaps he could do it, at that.

'Mel,' he said, 'you reckon I'd make a good minister? For the mosque, like.'

Melanie looked at him for a moment, then burst out laughing.

'What's so fucking funny?' said Kenny.

'Kenny,' she said, 'when did you last say two sentences without the word fuck in them, eh?'

Kenny shook his head, then laughed too. It was true. He'd always had a filthy mouth, and it was worse when he was nervous. And, frankly, the thought of standing up in front of all his people pretending to be some kind of minister scared the shit out of him.

What he needed was someone with a bit of front and a lot of bullshit. It didn't take long for a name to spring to mind. Mikey Thompson. He hadn't spoken to Mikey since he'd heard the little bastard had started doing a bit of freelance dealing for Billy Pinto. But what the hell, Kenny Ibadulla was a big enough man to forgive and forget; he'd give Mikey a chance to redeem himself.

He picked the phone up and called Mikey's number. Tina answered.

'Who wants him?' she asked.

'Me. Kenny.'

'Oh, sorry, Ken, he's been out all day. I'll tell him you called, like.'

'No, he fucking hasn't,' growled Kenny, 'I knows he's

there. It's fucking *Blind Date* on now, innit? Telling me Mikey's missing his *Blind Date*?'

Tina didn't say anything, just put the phone down and, a few seconds later, Mikey's voice came on the line. 'Sorry, Ken, just got in, like. Whassup?'

Kenny laid things out for Mikey. Option one, he signed on as temporary minister in Kenny's mosque. Option two, Kenny broke several of Mikey's bones, just like he should have done months ago when he found out he was freelancing for fucking Billy Pinto. Didn't take Mikey too long to choose option one. So Kenny told him to come down the Pilot around nine, they'd have a chat before the club opened.

Relieved, Kenny put the phone down and went into the kitchen where Melanie was starting to sort out the tea. He put his arms round her and was just letting them start to wander up towards her breasts when the back door blew open and in piled his three little girls and a couple of their mates.

Nine o'clock, Kenny walked up to the club, checked everything was ready for the night, and headed over to the Ship and Pilot. The boys were all there in the pool-room already. Mikey and Col were on the table, laughing and passing a spliff back and forth.

'Mikey,' said Kenny, 'you still got your suit?'

'Yeah, sure,' said Mikey. 'You want me on the door tonight, boss?' Mikey loved working the door, perfect chance to check out the talent coming in, and make his mark early. Couple of jokes as he's helping them to the cloakroom, then later in the evening, when most of the blokes are too pissed to function, Mikey leaves the door, comes into the club, and eases on in. Sweet. Once in a while it even worked out.

'Nah,' said Kenny, 'least I don't think so – check it with

Col. No, Mikey, you'll need the suit for the minister number. I'll sort you out with the bow tie and the fez, like.'

'Fucking 'ell, Ken, I thought you were joking.'

'Wish I was, Mikey, wish I was.'

'But why me, Ken? You've got a bunch of boys all into this stuff good and proper. Why can't one of them do it?'

Kenny shook his head. 'They're all fucking kids, Mikey. Need a bit of experience for this job.' Kenny paused for a moment then decided to give Mikey the full story. 'See, thing is, what I need is a bullshitter. There's some Yank coming down tomorrow, from head office, like, in Chicago, wants to see we're doing things right. I need someone can give him a bit of a show.'

'Tomorrow, Ken? You're joking.'

'Tell you what, Mikey. Best thing, we go over the mosque and I show you the stuff.'

And so it was that Mikey ended up spending his evening not hitting on the sweetest young things in Cardiff, but closeted in front of the VCR watching Minister Farrakhan in action, and frantically reading back issues of the *Final Call*.

Next day, Sunday, the festivities weren't due to start till three, but the inner circle got together at the club around one. Kenny was a bear with a sore head. Hadn't got to bed till five. Kids had woken him early, and now some fucking Yank was going to come and rain on his parade.

Still, everything seemed to be coming together pretty well. The band had just showed up, on their truck. They were just going to set up in the street outside and play. Brought their own generator and everything. Like Kenny, the boys all had their black suits and red bow ties on; looked damn serious when there was a bunch of you together. Stephanie he'd seen in the front of the mosque, looking absolutely gorgeous. The cleaners had been into the club already and it was looking pretty tidy. Col was busy blowing up balloons and tying them to everything in sight. In fact it all seemed pretty damn kosher, for want of a more appropriate word.

Then the major problem came back to him. 'Where's Mikey?' he asked.

'Christ, boss, haven't you seen him?' said Mark. 'He's inside the bloody temple pretending to be Malcolm X, like.'

And indeed he was. Kenny found Mikey standing at the mimbar waving his hands around and spouting bullshit, wearing a pair of sunglasses so dark that he didn't even notice Kenny coming in. Though, Kenny being the size he was, it didn't take too long for his shadow to register on Mikey's radar. '*Salaam aleikum*, boss,' he said, whipping his glasses off.

'*Aleikum salaam*,' said Kenny without even thinking about it. It was still a greeting you heard all the time around Butetown. 'So, you ready to go, Mikey?'

'I don't know, Ken. I thought I'd just, like, welcome everyone and then read out this introduction, like,' he said, waving one of the pamphlets Kenny had brought down.

'Yeah, fine,' said Kenny, 'just go for it,' and he headed upstairs to sort out the music for the disco later on.

By three o'clock there was already a reasonable crowd built up, practically all locals, plus a few social-worker types and a photographer who said she'd try and sell some pictures to the *Echo*.

The band got going a few minutes after, running through a few Bob Marley tunes to warm everybody up. There was a steady stream of people having a look at the mosque, even a few of the elders from the regular mosque, acting like they were just passing by accidentally. The home-made patties and samosas and fruit punch were all starting to tick over nicely and the vibe was just nice, Kenny reckoned, when the limousine drew up.

The limousine was indubitably the business. Some kind of American stretch with tinted windows. It pulled up on the edge of the crowd and double-parked neatly in the middle of the street. The passenger-side front door opened first, shortly to be followed by the two back doors and finally the driver's door. Out of each door emerged a shaven-headed character in an immaculate black suit and a red bow tie. Then, a moment later, a fifth person came out, a slighter figure with the suit and bow tie and also a fez. Evidently the boss-man.

The band kept on playing regardless, chugging through Stevie Wonder's 'Isn't She Lovely', but all other activity seemed to stop as everyone stared at the new arrivals.

Kenny nodded his head quickly to a couple of his guys and they followed in his wake as he moved through the crowd towards the out-of-towners.

'*Salaam aleikum*,' he said as he approached.

'*Aleikum salaam*,' said the guy in the fez, with a pronounced New York accent.

'So you're from, like, head office,' said Kenny.

'Kamal al-Mohammed. From Chicago, yes,' said the American, cold as anything.

'Well,' said Kenny, unaccustomedly nervous in the face of this skinny Yank, 'this is the mosque here and, as you can see, we're having a bit of an opening do, like.'

Al-Mohammed inclined his head slightly. The four other guys – bodyguards or whatever they were – didn't say a word.

Kenny wasn't sure even whether they were British or American. He waited for the guy to say something and for a few seconds they were just stood there staring at each other. Then the guy shook his head irritably and said, 'So. Show me.'

'All right, butt,' said Kenny and turned to lead the way, muttering under his breath, 'I'll fucking show you then.'

The people parted to let through what was by now quite an impressive Muslim cortège, what with Kenny and his boys and the American's crew. But before they could enter the mosque al-Mohammed stopped, surveyed the crowd and then stared at Kenny before saying, 'This is a mixed event.'

Kenny didn't know what he was on about for a moment. Thought maybe al-Mohammed meant it ought to be a men-only event. Then he realised it was racial mixing he meant.

'Yeah,' he said, 'reaching out, you knows what I mean?'

Al-Mohammed didn't look too impressed but he carried on into the front part of the mosque where Stephanie was looking beautiful behind the counter. She should cheer the old sourface up, thought Kenny, but no, not a bit of it. Al-Mohammed took one look at her crop-top and said, 'Inappropriate dress for a Muslim woman.'

Stephanie just looked at him like she was watching something really unusual on TV. Kenny stayed silent and opened the door into the mosque proper. And he wasn't sure, but he reckoned his face probably fell a mile when the first person he saw in the room, standing by the mimbar, was Mark, looking impeccable in his suit and bow tie, his hair cropped to the bone, but obviously as white as can be.

'Mr Ibadulla,' said the American after a brief, painful silence, 'have you read any of the Nation's literature?'

Kenny nodded.

'Have you read perhaps our program of belief?'

'Uh,' said Kenny, but before he could go on the American cut in.

'Well, I suggest you re-read it.'

Kenny felt like he was a kid at school again. Only difference was, none of Kenny's teachers ever dared speak like that to him, at least not after what happened when he was thirteen with that science teacher.

Back out on the street, al-Mohammed took up a position at the back of the crowd looking at the band. Behind him his comrades lined up in a row, all standing with their arms folded in front of them.

When Kenny came up alongside al-Mohammed, the American turned to him and said, 'So. When will the educational part of the proceedings start?'

Christ, thought Kenny, realising it was now up to Mikey to save the day. But he smiled and said, 'Yes, indeed, brother Waqar el-Faid will be talking in just a little while, like.'

He found Mikey in the shop giving Stephanie the full charm offensive. 'C'mon,' he said, 'you're on.'

Kenny climbed up on to the band's truck with Mikey right behind him. They stood on the side of the makeshift stage till the band finished a reggaed-up 'Wonderful Tonight', and then Kenny went to the mike.

'Ladies and gentlemen,' he said, 'and all the rest of you lot. *Salaam aleikum*, and welcome to the opening of Cardiff's first Nation of Islam mosque. I'd also like to welcome our special guest, Mr al-Mohammed from Chicago. And now we're going to have a few words about the Nation of Islam from a man you all knows.' Kenny ground to a halt, wondering whether he could get away with introducing Mikey as Waqar el-Faid. He decided against it and just waved his arm in Mikey's direction before jumping off the front of the stage.

Immediately there was a muttering from certain sections of the crowd. No one had quite seen Mikey as a spiritual teacher before. The real trouble, though, it quickly became clear, was that neither had Mikey.

Mikey's speech was basically just a matter of reading out the pamphlet he'd found, but with every sentence it was falling flatter and flatter. Mikey Thompson delivering a lecture on living a clean life and running your own business was just too ridiculous. They might have taken it from an American, but from Mikey? Then he said something about the importance of respecting your women, and a voice shouted, 'You should bloody know, Mikey,' and suddenly the whole crowd was creased with laughter. Mikey just dried up. For a moment Kenny thought he might be about to burst into tears. But then Mikey started talking again.

'Listen,' he said, 'like all of you, I'm new to this Muslim bit. But you shouldn't laugh at it just 'cause it's me talking.' He paused for another couple of seconds and started again. 'I've been thinking about my little boy, little Mikey. He's seven, right, just started junior school. And I was thinking about when I was at junior school, just down the road here, same place as most of you. And I was thinking about how I didn't know I was black then.'

A woman laughed.

Mikey put his hand up. 'No, I'm not saying I was blind, love, but I didn't know what it meant to be black. Down here, down the docks, it seemed like we were all together, right. Then, when I was eleven, I went to secondary over Fitzalan, and I found out what it meant. Nah mean?'

A rumble of agreement came from the crowd.

'What I found out, right, was that the rest of the people out there think they knows what you are if you come from Butetown. Right. So what I'm saying, and I'm going to shut up now, so don't worry, is that if we're going to make something of our lives, we've got to do it ourselves. And that's why I say that, whatever you think about Kenny here – and I know a lot of you may have had your troubles with Kenny – you've got to respect what he's doing.' And with that he too jumped off the stage.

The applause Mikey got wasn't exactly wild, but still, when he came down into the crowd, several people clapped him on the back and said well done. One or two of the sisters gave him 'Mikey, I never knew you were so sensitive'-type looks, which he returned with his most sensitive wink. Kenny walked over and clapped him on the back too, then turned round to see what his guests had made of it.

He found them standing in formation once more, this time outside the entrance to the club.

'What's this, brother Ibadulla?' asked al-Mohammed, pointing at the sign saying 'Black Caesar's Dancing and Dining'.

'It's a club,' said Kenny.

Al-Mohammed looked at his coterie and then looked back at Kenny. 'You're going to place Allah's temple underneath a nightclub, brother Ibadulla?'

'Well, there are separate entrances,' said Kenny, sounding feeble even to himself.

Al-Mohammed shook his head. 'Show us inside,' he said.

Kenny looked at his watch. Half five. The club was due to open in thirty minutes. That would probably be the last straw for these guys. He had to get them in and out and fast, before people started banging on the doors. So he sighed, opened the door and led the way upstairs into the club. Lloyd the barman was busy washing glasses but otherwise the place was deserted. Al-Mohammed just looked at the bar, shook his head once more and uttered the one word 'alcohol' before saying, 'Mr Ibadulla, let's go into your office. We have much to discuss.'

Kenny shrugged, thinking to himself, this is the thanks you get for trying to put something back into the community. He unlocked the office door, ushering the visitors inside.

The last man in shut the door behind him, and in an instant Kenny found himself looking straight down the barrel of a gun.

Al-Mohammed was the man holding the gun, and once Kenny had registered its presence he started talking again, only this time his voice had no trace of a New York accent. Instead it was pure Brummie.

'All right, Kenny mate. Had you going there, eh!'

Kenny shook his head in absolute and total disbelief. He'd let the Handsworth crew jerk him about like a prize bloody twat.

The Handsworth crew were evidently of the same mind. Two of the bodyguards were shaking with suppressed laughter. 'Inappropriate dress for a Muslim woman,' said one of them. The other grinned and rolled his eyes and, for a moment, Kenny thought he might have an opening.

The leader, however, kept his gun firmly trained on Kenny and said, 'Now, Mr Ibadulla, how about you open your safe and we have a look, see if there's anything we like in there.'

Kenny was a pro. He didn't do anything stupid. Just swore under his breath at his gullibility and tried to remember just how much he was holding in the safe. Around seven and a bit, he figured, and sighed as he opened up.

The former al-Mohammed kept his gun steadily on Kenny as his cohorts loaded the contents into a couple of black canvas bags. One of them then stepped behind Kenny, who wondered for a moment whether he was about to die, before a voice said, '*Salaam aleikum*, mate', and unconsciousness hit him like a freight train.

When Kenny came to, ten minutes later, after being given a good shaking by Col and Mikey, he discovered what had happened next. The Brummies had held a gun on Lloyd behind the bar, then knocked him out too. Then they'd walked downstairs and out of the club, back in character, shaking their heads and acting disgusted by what they'd found. The crowd had parted to let them make their way to the limo. A couple of the youth had catcalled them as they drove away, but that was that. The band had launched into Seal's 'Crazy' and it had taken a few minutes for anyone to wonder why Kenny hadn't come back down.

'Shit,' said Mikey, when Kenny told him what had happened. 'Don't know about you, Ken, but I don't think we're cut out for the religious life.'

The North Star

The baby, Jamal, woke up at eight. Maria rolled over once, buried her head in the pillow and tried to ignore him but it was no good, so she fetched him from his cot and brought him into the bed with her. There was plenty of room. Bobby must have left some time in the middle of the night. Though when they'd got to bed it had been late enough already, couldn't have been before four.

Anyway, Jamal went back to sleep for an hour, so she did too, and by then it was nine o'clock and Donna was up and played with him for a couple of hours so she managed to kip on and off till eleven, which was a result. It had been a hard night.

Maria got up, dug out a fresh pair of black jeans and a pink blouse, then rifled through last night's pockets to see how much money she had left. Forty quid. She was sure she'd taken at least a hundred yesterday. Where had it gone?

Looking at her face in the bathroom mirror, even after a good long shower, she could still trace where most of it had gone. Her eyes were bloodshot from the booze, her pupils dilated from the coke – or at least what Bobby swore blind was coke, tasted more like weak sulphate – her whole face puffy from the tranks she'd taken to get to sleep. Fifty quids' worth of hangover, any way you looked at it.

Still, she was only twenty-two, she could handle it. And she was a mother too and she could handle that, not like some people she knew.

Jamal was sitting in his highchair with a yoghurt pot in front of him and most of its contents around his mouth. Donna was watching *Richard and Judy*. Maria kissed Jamal and ruffled his black hair and made a cup of tea. Drank that with four paracetamols and she felt halfway human. Sitting on the sofa with Jamal on her knee watching a cooking show, she could feel a memory nagging at her. Something from last night. It wasn't something she'd done, there was none of that guilt or embarrassment lurking there; it was something good, but what?

Getting Jamal ready to go out, zipping him into his miniature puffa, she remembered. It was one of the ship boys, a German boy in from Rotterdam, in the club last night. A little bit of smuggling business he needed a hand with. Her and Bobby had looked at each other, lightbulbs popping up in bubbles on top of their heads. Both thinking the same thing, you better believe it.

Walking down Bute Street with Jamal in his pushchair, she tried to recall the details but they obstinately refused to come. So halfway down she stopped at the phone and called Bobby. Bobby sounded half asleep, but brightened when Maria mentioned the ship guy, and suggested they meet up at the Hayes Café in a couple of hours, when Maria had done her shopping.

So Maria carried on walking, happy to be out and about on a fine sunny May day. Stopped every couple of minutes for her mates to admire Jamal. Even the old biddies who wouldn't talk to her would stop and have a look at Jamal, who was so sweet with his blue eyes and golden-brown face, and they could see she looked after him well.

She wondered if his eyes would stay blue. He was eighteen months now, so she supposed they probably would. Weird, but nice; showed there was a lot of her there.

Passing the Custom House, she saw John the landlord bringing in a couple of crates of Hooch. He waved and dashed inside, came out with a lollipop for Jamal.

'Col must be proud of him, eh?'

Col was her baby's father. And he was a nice bloke, as it went, though full of all this Twelve Tribes bollocks. His main contribution to Jamal's upbringing was to come round and make sure she wasn't feeding him any pork. Not that he'd been coming round much at all lately; he couldn't really handle her scene with Bobby.

'Yeah. He thinks you're pretty safe, don't he,' she said, tickling Jamal under his chin.

'Yeah, well, give him my regards, tell him to stop by if you see him.'

Oh right, she thought, running a little low on the ganja, are we? Still, you had to hand it to Col. He'd been going on about all this back-to-the-land shit for years and now he was doing a tidy little business with this hydroponic gear.

She carried on under the bridge, past the Golden Cross, exchanged 'hiya love's with one of Col's aunties and thought about going into Toys'R'Us for a moment. Then she pictured the mountain of toys Jamal already had that he couldn't play with yet. Still, what was the use of having some money if you couldn't spend it on your kid? So she carried on to Mothercare, bought him a couple of new outfits, went into the St David's Centre and mucked about in Boots for a while, buying some nice stuff for herself. Just had a few minutes to get a carton of cheap fags and a bit of food from the market, and it was time to meet Bobby.

The Hayes Island Snack Bar looked like an old park caff that had been accidentally dropped slap bang in the city centre. Bobby was sitting at one of the tables over near the public toilets, a cup of coffee in front of her, brazenly staring down the passers-by.

'All right, girl,' said Bobby, and Maria's heart leapt. She could swear it really did jump inside her as she looked at Bobby, this stocky black girl with the short locks who was the strongest person she'd ever met. Sat there in a black Adidas tracksuit looking for all the world like a fourteen-year-old boy, though she must be thirty at least. Maria just wanted to throw herself at her. She wanted to eat her.

Bobby was her pimp.

Bobby insisted on that. 'I'm a pimp, me,' she'd say, flashing her gold tooth. 'Top pimp.'

Maria gave Bobby money.

But it wasn't like Bobby had some stable of bitches, like they say in the down-in-the-hood movies. Bobby was Maria's girl. It's just that that's how it is when you hustle. Someone who shares their life with a hustler, they're a pimp. Maria buys a can of baked beans and gives half to Bobby. Immoral earnings. Hey, one day, Maria thought, she'd like to see someone who had some moral earnings. Colliers. Yeah, right. At least with what she did you knew you were getting fucked.

And Bobby had respect. All the lesbians – Christ, she didn't like that word – the lesbian pimps on the scene had respect. The men, though, that was another story. They couldn't handle it. Couldn't handle their woman hustling. Sure, they'd take the money all right, but then they'd disrespect you. It pissed her off. She knew she was fit, she knew how men looked at her before they knew, and she saw how they looked at her after. Weaklings. Not like Bobby.

Bobby picked Jamal out of his pushchair. Bobby loved Jamal, was always criticising the way Maria dealt with him. Half the time, people who didn't know saw them together, they'd swear Bobby was Jamal's big brother. Same colouring. Bobby never talked about her mam and dad; she'd talked about a home, though. Surprise.

'You remember the guy, then, last night,' Maria said once she'd got herself a tuna sandwich and a piece of toast for Jamal.

'Yeah,' said Bobby, 'so you going to do it or what?'

The ship guy had told Maria, back in the North Star, luxuriating in the aftermath of the blowjob she'd given him in the car-park, that he had a k of the good stuff, prime coke, on the boat. But he was hinky about bringing it on shore and double hinky about who to sell it to. He was young – no more than nineteen, she figured – and she could see that this was a boy jumping out of his depth and hoping he could swim. Mind the sharks, boy, she felt like saying, but naturally didn't. Instead she listened to his worries about getting past the checkpoints on and off the boat, and told him it was no problem, bring a girl on and they'll turn a blind eye.

Really, he'd said. Yeah, really, she'd said, been doing it long enough.

'But who am I going to deal with?' he'd asked. 'I don't know this town.' Like he knew anywhere.

'Relax,' she'd said, 'I'll bring the gear out for you, and sort you out with a deal, you just cut me a little taste,' and she'd squeezed his dick and half an hour later she'd done him again in the back of a car. When the North Star closed he was almost begging her to meet him again.

'All right,' she'd said, 'see you here, midnight tomorrow. We'll sort your little problem out.'

'Yeah,' she said to Bobby, 'he'll be easy.'

Bobby laughed and contorted her face into a parody of sexual ecstasy. Jamal saw her and laughed too, shouting Bobby's name and clapping his hands together.

Coffee finished, Bobby wanted to buy some new trainers, so they trekked round Queen Street checking out the options before Bobby went for a pair of Adidas, white stripes on black to match her tracksuit, in a boy's size. By then Jamal was hungry again so they dined at the sign of the Golden Arches and then headed back towards Butetown, making plans for the night ahead.

Bobby peeled off at the Custom House to play pool with the other pimps and the girls on the afternoon shift. Maria kind of missed the afternoon shift. For a start, you were less vulnerable in daylight and for seconds you really felt like you were putting one over on the poor stiffs sweating in McDonald's, spending your afternoons drinking and shooting pool and smoking with just the odd couple of minutes behind Aspro Travel Agents to earn your wedge.

Still, it worked pretty well for her now too. She could spend all day with Jamal and just go out to work once she'd put him to bed. Donna was always there to babysit. Donna was the only girl she knew that used to pretend to be a hustler, 'cause it made it sound like she had a sex life. It wasn't that she was ugly, really – well she was, but that never had much to do with anything, you should see some of the girls out there on the beat and they did all right. It was just she was such an ignorant mouthy cunt. Still, she was good to Jamal.

Eight o'clock, Jamal was asleep and Maria spent the last of her money on a cab down to the Custom House. Bobby wasn't there, must have gone back home for her tea, so Maria cadged her first can of Breaker off Paula, a big girl from up the valleys somewhere who was already starting to show. 'Only three months,' she said, pissed off.

Half an hour later there was still no sign of Bobby, so Maria thought fuck it and went out on the beat, shared a spliff with a couple of girls and was just getting fed up with waiting around when a carload of Asians showed up. Normally she wasn't too keen on bulk deals but she'd never had any trouble with Asians. Bloody mainstay of the trade, they were; poor geezers over from God knows where to work in some cousin's restaurant for fifty quid a week. No chance of an arranged marriage till they got their own balti house, hardly surprising they came down here for a quick one.

So she bent down to the window and bargained a bit. Made a deal. For eighty quid she'd take the four of them back to the flat and do them all.

She was just doing number two when Bobby burst in, blue in the face, saying she needed a word. Poor bloke inside her didn't know where to put himself, so she told Bobby to fucking behave and wait outside, got number two back in the saddle and off in two minutes flat, which wasn't bad going as it goes. Then she went out to the living-room and found numbers one, three and four looking fed up while Bobby gave Donna a hard time about something or other. Not keeping Jamal's toys tidy enough, probably.

'Now,' said Bobby, 'I've got to talk to you *now*.' So Maria had a quick word with Donna, got her to do number three for a twenty-quid rake-off. Sent numbers one, two and four out to the chip shop, and once all the doors had closed asked Bobby what the fuck she was playing at.

'No,' said Bobby, crowding her into a corner like she was a tough guy, which was comical, really, as Maria was a good three inches taller than her, but, still, she let Bobby have her fun. 'It's what you've been playing at. Who you've been talking to.'

'What?'

'Kenny Ibadulla knows about tonight.'

'Shit.'

'So how comes, eh? How comes Kenny knows my business, you stupid slag?'

'I'm sorry, Bob,' said Maria, realising what had happened and compensating by letting the tears start. She was always a great crier, Maria.

Bobby was a pushover. She stepped back, said, 'All right, love, who did you tell?'

'Terry. Fucking Terry. Except I never told him, he was just sitting next to me and Hansi.'

'Hansi?'

'The sailor, right, and Terry was there, but I thought he was too out of it to notice what was going on, and anyway I didn't think he was talking to Kenny.'

'Yeah, well, maybe this is Terry's way of getting back in the good books.'

Then the bell rang and Maria let in the three punters who sat down and politely offered their chips around. Number three was still in with Donna – must have been a good eight minutes, which outraged Maria's professional soul – so she ate one more chip and took number four into her room and had him back out again just as number three came out of Donna's.

'Any time, boys,' she said as she closed the door on the blokes. Bunged twenty to Donna and then sat down with Bobby to figure out what the hell to do about Kenny Ibadulla.

Quarter to twelve, they went over to the North Star. No sign of Terry or Kenny, though it was unlikely Kenny would show in person. Kenny was a gangster, all right, but these days he thought he was too good to hang around with hustlers.

Around ten past twelve, Bobby was just lighting up a spliff and Maria was dancing with one of the Barry girls to an old Chaka Khan record when Hansi the sailor came in. He was about five nine, dark-haired with a rather sorry-looking tache. He was with three other blokes from the ship, looked like they were probably German as well.

They stood in the centre of the room for a moment, eyes adjusting to the gloom, checking the place out. Hansi saw Maria on the dance floor and waved. Then one of his mates, a six-foot redhead, went over to Maria and the Barry girl and asked them if they wanted a drink. They both said yeah and soon they were all sat around a table drinking cans of Pils. The North Star didn't run to draught beer, which was probably just as well, the amount Stevo behind the bar bothered with keeping the place clean.

Bobby sat at the bar, smoking her spliff, watching them. After a while she went over to another couple of girls, Sue from Merthyr and Big Lesley, and told them the sailors were loaded and in the mood to go back to the ship for a party.

Around one, everyone seemed to be having a good time and the German boys were definitely in the mood for action.

So Maria led the way out of the club and, linking arms with Hansi, headed for the hulk of the *Queen of Liberia.*

Out in the open, it was obvious that Hansi was nervous as shit but, when Maria pulled him closer and whispered in his ear what she was going to do to him when they got to the ship, he brightened up.

As predicted, there was no problem with security when they got to the ship. The watchman was out for the count, a telltale can of Tennent's Super on his desk. On board ship, they piled into an empty mess-room, started passing around a bottle of vodka one of the Germans produced and some spliff that Big Lesley had rolled up. Maria began to notice that Hansi wasn't really all that friendly with the other guys. 'Ozzie,' they called him, and from the way he reacted she could tell it was a nickname and not a friendly one.

So, after twenty minutes or so, she said, 'Let's go back to your cabin,' and it was with obvious relief that Hansi agreed.

'Some problem with your mates?' she asked, worried that they might have wind of Hansi's deal.

'No,' he said, 'they just don't like me because I'm from the East.'

'Oh right,' she said, and started rubbing the front of his jeans to get his mind back on track.

In his cabin she started taking his jeans off while detailing what she was going to do for him. Experience had told her that talking up her act in advance was just as effective and a lot easier than actually running through her bag of tricks. And so it proved with Hansi. By the time she had him in her mouth, he was primed and ready. Thirty seconds later she was rinsing her mouth out in the basin and he was sitting back on his bunk looking a little crestfallen.

'Five minutes,' he said, 'five minutes and we go again, yes?'

At his age, she thought, he probably wasn't joking. It was time to get things moving on. 'Plenty of time later for that,' she said, giving his hair a quick ruffle, 'but if we're going to get out of here while your mates are still busy, we'd better be going.' He nodded and stood up. She hoped to hell he was understanding everything she said.

'You wait outside,' he said, and he shooed her out of the cabin. A minute later he came out too, a little black canvas bag over his shoulder.

'Let's go,' he said, and they headed back off the ship. This time there were a couple of official types standing by the watchman's office. They looked dubiously at Maria and Hansi for a moment and said something in German to Hansi, but Maria started licking Hansi's ear and he did a creditable impersonation of a drunken sailor walking his girl back to shore, and after a brief hard stare one of the officer types waved them by.

Back in the North Star, Bobby was waiting for them. As Maria and Hansi came in, she ushered them to a table at the back where the darkness was almost total. 'Is that it?' she said, prodding the bag Hansi held clasped between his knees.

He nodded and she hefted it, testing it for weight, though Hansi never let go of the bag. Then he proffered it to Bobby and she dipped a finger in and took a taste from the top, which was all she could get at. Tasted good to her.

'Yeah, that'll do,' she said. 'Now, how much d'you want for it?'

'Fifty thousand marks,' he said, puffing himself up a little but his eyes giving him away, nervously looking around the room, realising how little control he had over the situation.

'Yeah, what's that in pounds?'

Neither Bobby nor Maria had much of a clue about exchange rates, but they knew what a k of Charlie went for and, when Hansi came back with, 'Twenty thousand,' after thinking for a moment Bobby almost found herself nodding.

'Fuck off,' she said. 'Five grand, tops.'

'OK,' said Hansi, smiling now.

'Half an hour,' said Bobby. 'You stay here with Maria, I'll be back with the money.'

Forty minutes later, Bobby was back, ten grand in her jacket after a rendezvous with Billy Pinto, who she knew was looking for a decent score, let him take a bit of Kenny's market. Billy had jumped at the deal. Turn the k into rocks, and he'd be doing some serious business. And 'cause he lived over Ely, with a bit of luck Kenny would never figure out who sold him the gear.

'Hansi,' she said, 'fucker beat me down to four grand.' And she started discreetly counting out the money.

Hansi suddenly looked harder and older than before. A lock-knife appeared below table height, jabbing into Maria's leg.

'You want me to cut your girlfriend here? By this artery?' he said. 'Or you want to pay me my money?'

'Christ,' said Bobby, 'calm down, mate. Only trying it on.' And she kept on counting till she got to four grand, then dipped her hand into her pocket and pulled out another wedge. 'Here's your five grand, like I said.'

Hansi had the money inside his leather jacket before Bobby had time to blink. He stood up, the knife still held inside his sleeve, bowed slightly to Maria and a moment later he was gone.

'Shit,' said Maria.

'Don't worry, girl,' said Bobby, and leaned closer to her and told her how much money they'd cleared.

Maria said nothing for a moment, just thought about the changes five grand could make to her life. 'C'mon,' she said, 'let's get back to the flat.'

They were almost at the flat door when they heard the footsteps behind them, coming up the stairs. Maria had the door open and Bobby was half through it when, for the second time in ten minutes, Maria felt a knife pressing against her flesh. It was Billy Pinto holding the knife and neither he nor his two associates looked too well pleased with life.

Bobby and Maria were bundled into the flat. Billy made them sit next to each other on the couch and then got right down in Bobby's face. 'What the fuck,' he said, 'what the fuck d'you think you're doing, trying to rip me off like that?'

'What?' said Bobby.

'That kilo of crap you sold me. Coke on the top; fuck knows what underneath. I wants my money back, girl.'

'Shit,' said Bobby, looking at Maria.

Maria shook her head in genuine disbelief. She really couldn't credit that Hansi had had it in him to pull off a stunt like this. No wonder he'd looked nervous.

'So where's my money?' said Billy.

'Bill,' said Bobby, 'it's not our deal. It's this sailor. He's the one who's ripped you off.'

'I don't think so, Bob,' said Billy, 'I don't think it was no sailor came round my house, told me she had a kilo of gear. It wasn't no sailor took my ten grand.' He paused for a moment and stared at Bobby. 'And I'll bet it wasn't no sailor got the ten grand either. How much you holding, Bob?'

Bobby considered holding out for about a millisecond. Then she sighed and said, 'I've got five, Billy, take that and we'll get you the other five back. Just let go of us, right.'

Billy walked over, took the five grand from Bobby's pocket. 'Yeah, you'll pay it back, all right, but first you're going to have to learn a lesson.'

'Not here,' said Maria, the first thing she'd said since things went to hell. 'My boy's sleeping. Not here.'

Billy nodded. 'All right, I knows just the place.'

Billy led the way down the stairs, Bobby and Maria following, Billy's guys right behind them.

Halfway down the second flight, Maria suddenly clutched her stomach and collapsed to the ground. 'Fuck,' she said, 'the baby.'

It worked a treat. Billy and his guys stopped as one, looks of horror on their faces. Bobby whipped the legs from under the guy nearest to her, sent him tumbling down the stairs. A second later she had her own knife out and started swinging it in an arc in front of her, keeping Billy and the other guy away. Meanwhile Maria was back on her feet and kicking the guy who'd fallen downstairs hard in the face before he could get back up. And then the two women were off, flying down the remaining stairs into the lobby.

And smack into the ample frame of Kenny Ibadulla. There was Kenny and Terry and another bloke standing there, Kenny with a gun in his hand. Billy and his boys arrived on the scene a second or two later and Kenny shifted around so the gun was pointed squarely at Billy. And then everyone started talking at once. Five minutes later everyone had some idea what the situation was, and it was clear that it was up to Kenny, as the man with the gun, to dictate what happened next.

'Billy,' he said, 'you fuck off out of this. You want to be some big-time dealer, boy, you stay up in fucking Ely and do it there. Now fuck off. You'll get your money.'

And, at that, Billy and his boys slunk off, doing their best to look like it was their own decision.

Then Kenny turned to Bobby and Maria. 'Now, Bob,' he said, 'I got to pay Billy five grand. And you know what that means?'

Bobby nodded.

'Right, that means you owe me five grand. And how are you going to get that for me? Your girlfriend going to make it for me? Lying on her back? Or you got some better idea?'

'The ship guy,' Bobby said.

'Right,' said Kenny, 'the ship guy. He's the one to blame, inne? But he's not my problem.' By now Kenny was virtually standing on top of Bobby, letting his size and weight work for him. Then he turned and pulled back. 'You've got till daylight. You haven't got my five grand back by then, you'll be working for me.'

And so Kenny and his boys left, and Maria and Bobby sat together on the stairs for a moment, holding each other and shaking. Maria thought she was going to hyperventilate. The prospect of owing Kenny Ibadulla didn't bear thinking about. Christ knows what the interest payment on five grand would be – a hundred a week, at least. Working for herself and Bobby and Jamal was one thing: working for that arrogant bastard was something else entirely, specially as he most likely wouldn't pay Billy the money anyway.

'Shit. Shit. Shit,' she said. Then she had an idea.

'C'mon,' she said to Bobby. 'We've got to get back to the North Star.'

It was four o'clock, closing time in the North Star; but luck was with Maria when a couple of sailors came out with Lorna, one of the Barry girls. It was no trouble for Maria to join the party, and ten minutes later she was back on board the ship. Five minutes of wrestling in another mess-room with a drunken sailor, and she was able to beg off to find a toilet. Ten more minutes of floundering around the ship and she found Hansi's cabin. Took a deep breath and knocked.

He looked horrified at first, but Maria pretended not to notice and stuck to her script like the trouper she was. 'Hansi, baby, I've come back to celebrate, I would have come straight back with you but I had to dump that dyke Bobby.' And before his brain could start functioning, she carried straight on into, 'Hansi, I need you inside me,' and started pulling his clothes off.

And it worked. He let her. He let himself believe that he was such a slick piece of work that he could screw the girl over the deal and still screw her all night long with no come-back. Just sail away in the morning.

She had to do it twice, but the second time she got her result. He fell asleep. It didn't take long to search the cabin. First thing she found was a washbag that weighed far too much. Inside it was another kilo of white stuff. God alone knew whether this one was real or fake, but she scooped it up anyway and a moment later she found the five grand stuffed in a sock.

Five minutes later, she was starting to panic. The boat was a total bloody maze. Once she'd found herself in the rec room they'd all been in earlier, but she must have taken the wrong exit, 'cause where the hell she was now she had no idea, except the cabins were looking a bit posher.

She could have sworn she must have walked down the same corridor three times, when what she was dreading finally happened. A door opened and she walked slap bang into one of the handsomest men she'd ever seen in her life. She had him pinned instantly as a type, the Latin lover. Fair enough in private life, but a pain in the arse in her professional life. They'd spend hours trying to get you to look like you were doing it for fun not fifty quid. Anyway, last thing she needed right now, Casanova in his boxers.

'Uh,' she said, 'I was looking for . . .'

'Yes?' he said, his eyes giving her the old up and down. 'You were looking for something?' There was a pause. 'A man maybe?'

Jesus, thought Maria, here we go, and started to shake her head.

' 'Cause you come to the wrong place here, darling,' he said, and Maria actually did sigh with relief.

'No,' she said, 'I was just looking for the way out.'

'No problem, sweetie,' said the bloke, and popped back into his room for a dressing-gown. Maria followed, dumb with gratitude, as the guy swished his way up a flight of stairs, along a couple of corridors and out to the gangway. The face of the guard on duty was a picture when he saw who it was, waving Maria goodbye off the ship.

Bobby was waiting for her in the car-park and Maria just collapsed in her arms. Bobby wrinkled her nose for a moment at the smell of her, but never let go.

Six thirty a.m., Bobby knocked on Kenny's door. Woke his wife up, who shouted at her to get her perverted black arse out of there, but then Kenny came to the door and let her in. She handed him the coke, Kenny tasted it, from the top, the bottom and the middle, nodded and told Bobby she was cool.

'And what about Billy?' said Bobby.

Kenny laughed, said, 'Billy's my problem. Be cool.'

Coke talking, thought Bobby. Everyone's a superman with coke. And walked back up to Maria's place.

Maria's already celebrating, got a bottle of champagne from round Bab's. Opens it as Bobby comes in the door, stuff sprays everywhere, must have been warm as fuck. Jamal's jumping up and down with excitement.

'Tell you what,' says Bobby, 'why don't we go for a little holiday? Just the three of us, like.'

'Yeah,' says Maria, 'you serious?', her eyes going wide, like it's the biggest treat anyone's ever offered her, like it wasn't her got the five grand that's sitting on the table.

'Yeah,' says Bobby, 'let's just get a cab out the airport. We'll get the first plane going somewhere hot.' And Maria jumped up and threw her arms round Bobby, hugging her hard. Jamal did the same to her knees, and for a moment Bobby felt like it was more than her heart could stand. A couple of minutes later, she picked up the money and carefully put it into the inside pocket of her jacket.

Six o'clock that evening, Bobby, Maria and Jamal were in Tenerife.

Two weeks later they came back.

Week after that, Maria was back outside the Custom House and Bobby was playing pool inside. You know what they say – you have to hustle in this life.

The Four Ways

Mikey felt it was time he got in on the pimping game. Doing the shops had done him fine over the years, apart from the once, but there came a time when you knew you were pushing your luck. He'd tried dealing. He wasn't exactly giving up on that either – if you wanted to buy something, little bit of weed, a couple of Es, well he could sort you out, no trouble at all – but moving up in that world was a problem. Some well heavy geezers in that world. For instance, the thing that happened with Deandra's cousin, down from Birmingham there. Mikey had told him he had a line on some serious Charlie, fresh off the boat. It had just been the brew talking, but a week later the guy's back down in Cardiff saying, 'Mikey, I'm in the market – now set me up.'

So Mikey had acted like he was the man and called Kenny, who'd told him to fuck off, no way he was dealing with no Brummies. So then he'd called Billy Pinto over in Ely there, and Billy had only come to the meet with a fucking shotgun, and the guy from Edgbaston or Handsworth, or whatever balti-house place he came from, had freaked out and opened up with some joker pistol, looked like his grandad had brought it back from World War Two, and Mikey had done the only sensible thing and legged it, and now the Pintoes were out for his blood for setting them up with some Brummie psycho, and the Brummie psycho was threatening all kinds of shit, and frankly drugs were fine but Mikey was looking for something a little less dangerous.

So, Wednesday morning, Mikey decided to get up early. First step was to get out of the house without any bother from Tina. Best way to do that, he'd found, was to say he'd take little Mikey to school. That way Tina didn't get her fat arse out of bed and, once Mikey was out of the house, that was the hard part done. So he was up at eight thirty. Little Mikey was already sitting in the living-room with a bowl of cereal next to him. *The Big Breakfast* was on the TV, but little Mikey wasn't watching it; instead he was bent over a picture he was drawing – Spiderman fighting some villain or other. Spidey was swinging up the side of a building, little Mikey concentrating hard on getting the web right.

Mikey had a quick hit of Lucozade Sport from the fridge, checked his hair carefully in the mirror and wondered, as he often had the last few months, whether he should go for a total skinhead like a lot of the boys these days. But he knew that looking hard was tricky when you were five foot four so, splashing on a spot of aftershave, he decided to stick with the flat-top do, gave him an extra inch or so on top.

Quarter to nine, he had little Mikey out of the house, wearing his coat even in May because Tina was terrified about his asthma. It was only five minutes down to the school, but Mikey made a habit of getting there a little early. Lot of fit women taking their kids into school. And taking your own seven-year-old in was perfect camouflage, showed you were a nice guy. Wolf in sheep's clothing – that's the way Mikey liked to think about himself. Being small helped too, he thought, meant they didn't take him seriously till it was too late.

So, as they got to the playground, he shooed little Mikey

in, to play football with the boys, and stood around chatting with Tina's mate Lesley and her friend Ruth-Ann, who was wearing some kind of Lycra sports top that had Mikey's attention pretty well occupied at eye level. Ruth-Ann was out of the question, though; he knew who she was seeing and no way was he going sniffing round that yard. So, after a moment or two, he let his eyes wander away from Ruth-Ann's chest and let them alight on a girl named Tyra.

Tyra, he thought, might be a prospect. So he made a couple of lewd suggestions to Lesley and Ruth-Ann, laughed as they made to batter him, and waved goodbye. Then timed things nicely so he brushed up against Tyra as they squeezed out of the school gate.

'Whassup, girl?'

'Nothing,' said Tyra, who was long, tall and light-skinned. She'd been in school with Mikey, a couple of years younger, ran with Mikey's sister Lisa for a bit, but she never gave him the time of day. Never had since either, never went for his bullshit at all, never laughed at it like you were supposed to. Fucking stuck-up piece, in fact, if you asked Mikey, but she'd come down with a bump lately, what he'd heard. Two kids in school, and now her man inside, little matter of armed robbery over a bookie's in Canton. What Mikey'd heard was Tyra had been seen out hustling. She had to be a prospect, just a matter of getting the pitch right.

'Sorry to hear 'bout Tony.'

'Long fucking time you waited to tell me that.'

'Yeah, well I was thinking, maybe you could do with a few new clothes, for the kids, like.'

Tyra kept walking but betrayed her interest by not saying anything. You see, Mikey's talent was pretty well known – it was generally agreed around Butetown that no one could shoplift like Mikey. You wanted some tasty Stone Island jacket you'd seen up town? Ask Mikey. You fancied some sharp gear for the kids – Gap, Next, decent stuff – have a word with Mikey. One third the price on the tag, give or take, and it was yours.

Trouble was, Mikey's reputation had been spreading a little too far and wide lately. There'd been a close one with the store detective out of David Morgan's the other week; Mikey'd lost him in the St David's Centre, but not by much, and at the time he'd thought he should give it a rest for a while. But he didn't mind going on one more little shopping trip, if that's what it took to hook Tyra up.

'What d' you want?' she said after a moment. 'You think you're going to get a little piece now my man's inside? That what you thinking, Mikey?'

Mikey put up his hands like that was the furthest thing from his mind. 'No, no. You got to pay for the clothes, you know.'

Tyra snorted and said, 'Yeah, what with?'

Mikey went on quickly, 'But no need to worry 'bout paying for it now. When's Tony gonna reach up from jail?'

Tyra stared at him. 'A year minimum, the brief says. You gonna wait a year for your money, Mikey?'

Mikey spread his hands out. 'Yeah, well. Relax, sister, we can work something out.'

'I'm not your damn sister,' said Tyra, but she didn't say anything about the working things out, let it hang there. Mikey moved in.

'I'll check you round lunchtime, OK, bring some stuff to show you.'

Tyra nodded, then walked on fast.

★   ★   ★

Mikey's shoplifting technique was a simple but effective one. Misdirection was at the heart of it. Essentially it involved him carrying on as he always did. Take this Wednesday morning. Around eleven Mikey walked into Gap. You wouldn't have thought it looked too promising – hardly any punters, two women working there, one on the till, one on the floor.

'Hiya, sweetness, how's it going?' he said to the Greek-looking girl sat behind the cash desk. 'You got a boyfriend still?'

'Yeah, and he catch you chatting me up there'd be trouble.'

'Yeah?' said Mikey. 'Yeah, well I bet he's not sweet like me. He buy you presents, girl? Let's see that chain.'

And so Nicky on the cash desk found herself pulling out the long chain her fiancé had given her for her last birthday, and then, when she caught Mikey ogling her breasts, wishing she hadn't. And so, for the rest of his time in the store, she averted her eyes from him, and acted like she was busy with some till business.

One down, one to go, thought Mikey, and moved in on the only other visible member of staff, a natural blonde about nineteen, seriously fit, who was rearranging piles of T-shirts.

'How 'bout you, darlin',' he called out. 'You got a boyfriend?'

The girl turned round, looked at Mikey, and smiled. That's what generally happened. Growing up, Mikey hadn't been too pleased to be short and bug-eyed and funny looking, but over the years he'd learned to make it work for him.

'So what do they call you, blondie?'

'Lucy,' she said.

Mikey decided to go for it straight off.

'So, Lucy,' he said, coming closer to her and affecting to

study her face, 'let me see, have you got a little Jamaican in you?'

'No,' said Lucy, bemused, evidently not a Lenny Henry fan.

'Well, any time, girl, any time!' said Mikey, cracking up as he watched Lucy put it together, and then blush furiously. A crap joke, but it worked every time. Shame his dad's people came from Anguilla, but still.

'Don't worry, girl,' he said, 'I don't bite,' at which he opened his mouth wide and then let his tongue just fractionally dart out. Mikey loved these uptown shop girls. Try and pull this kind of stunt in Butetown, he'd have been smacked upside the head by now. Not this Lucy, she just sort of smiled and looked at him the way you might at a cute dog that had suddenly morphed into a Doberman or something.

'So where's the kids' gear?' Mikey asked.

'Oh, right,' said Lucy and, as she started to turn round to lead him towards the back of the store, he blatantly let his eyes drop to her arse, looking nice in a pair of tight jeans. Lucy stared firmly ahead and Mikey grinned. Two out of two. From that moment on, there might as well have been a sign up – 'Help yourself, Mikey'.

And so the morning went on: Mikey's bullshit worked its magic in two out of three stores he tried. Third one, Next, it worked too well. Girl called Lorraine with a bad perm and a big bum just wouldn't leave him be, ended up making him promise to take her out on the weekend. Which was a result too. Mikey had absolutely nothing against big bums. So he was in a very good mood indeed as he headed back up to Butetown.

He made a couple of stops on the way. First in the Big

Asteys, by the bus station. Just sat at a table in the corner with a can of Pepsi Max and waited for business. Sold a couple of blouses and a pair of those kids' dungarees straight off. Took an order for a pair of Versace jeans in white and then, seeing as it was half twelve, ambled round to the Custom House.

Lot of the boys wouldn't go in the Custom House. Didn't approve of the hustlers. Even the ones didn't mind taking the girls' money, they'd still chat on about those dirty women. But Mikey was all right with the hustlers. Thing about Mikey was he really liked women, enjoyed their company a lot more than he liked going round with some bunch of geezers always making funny-ha-fucking-ha jokes about him being small and shit, treating him as some kind of mascot.

There were a couple of girls out on the street, down the side of the pub. Dayshift girls down from the valleys, doing it for their kids, like. Mikey hated the bloody valleys, full of blokes sitting round smoking draw, bollocksing on about how they used to be miners, never done a week's work between them. And all the time their wives — just off to work, dear, down the computer factory. Straight down on the train to town, outside the Custom House for the lunchtime trade. Blokes carry on pretending they didn't know. Good day on the assembly line, darlin'? Yeah, right.

Inside the pub Bobby was playing pool with some new girl, hardly looked eighteen, pretty enough, even if she'd got that white-faced 'I live on chips and speed, me' look. Mikey would have tried making a move on her if she'd been on her own, but he wasn't any too keen to go up against Bobby. A lover not a fighter, Mikey, way he saw it. Still, there were a couple more awayday girls sitting over at one of the tables by the bar, so Mikey bought a quick brandy, then went over and did a little more clothes business. One thing about hustlers, they were always ready to lay out a bit for the kids. Then he started to feel Bobby's dirty looks boring into his back and he headed out the side door.

Out in the street, he nearly bounced into a black girl called Bernice who was heading in. She was some kind of cousin of his, just got out of care.

'All right, Mikey?'

'Yeah, whassup?'

'Usual shit. You got any draw?'

'Yeah,' said Mikey, and they walked round to the car-park to spliff up, Mikey making a deal to sell her a quarter later on, when she'd made a little money.

'Listen,' he said after a moment, 'you know a girl name Tyra?'

Bernice thought for a moment. 'Y'mean the fat girl works down the health centre?'

'No,' said Mikey, 'the other one, Tyra Davies, tall girl, use to play on the basketball team, got the kids for Tony.'

Bernice nodded.

'You seen her working?' Mikey's eyes indicated the street.

'No,' said Bernice. 'Wait, I dunno, maybe someone said they'd seen her working over Riverside. Why? You looking for business?' She burst out in a peal of stoned laughter. Then, when she'd calmed down, 'You could ask Bobby.'

'Nah,' said Mikey, 'it don't matter. I'll check you later, right.'

Tyra, washing up in the kitchen, saw Mikey coming as he cut through her back yard and she had the kitchen door open before he could knock.

'What's a matter, darlin'?' said Mikey. 'Afraid the neighbours are going to see me coming round? Think you've got a little t'ing going on.'

Tyra didn't say anything, Mikey looked around him. The kitchen ran into the living-room and took up the whole ground floor. Tyra kept it tidy, he could see. Walls looked like they'd been painted recently, pictures hanging up – Robert Nesta on black velvet, big studio photo of Tony next to him. Mikey couldn't help feeling a little guilty when he looked at the photo, Tony smiling out like he didn't have a care in the world.

'Brought you some stuff,' said Mikey, moving over to the sofa in front of the TV, which was showing *Knots Landing* with the sound off. Mikey thought about asking her to turn the sound back up for a moment.

'Let's see then,' said Tyra, sitting down on the far side of the coffee table from Mikey.

Mikey brought out the gear, good stuff from Gap and Next, and even a couple of kids'-size Adidas tracksuits. When Tyra started picking the stuff up, he was sure he had her.

'So, how much?'

'For all of it?'

'Yeah.'

'Twenty,' he said, which was about half what he'd normally get for that much decent gear, but he wanted her to see what a nice guy he was.

Tyra didn't say anything for a moment. Then she sighed and said, 'OK,' and disappeared upstairs before coming back down with two tenners in her hand.

Shit, thought Mikey, wasn't supposed to go like this. 'Sure

you can spare that much, darlin'?' he said. 'Don't want to be taking the food out of your kids' mouths.'

'It's OK,' said Tyra, giving nothing away.

'You sure? You're not working, are you?'

Something flickered in Tyra's green eyes. 'What you mean, working?'

Well, this was the crunch, Mikey thought, and one of those moments when he wouldn't mind being a little bigger. Tyra had a good three inches on him, and those basketball muscles still. He moved on to the balls of his feet as he said, 'Well, I'd heard maybe you was doing a little business.'

She didn't hit him. She looked like she was thinking of spitting at him, but instead she turned away and said, 'Fuck off, Mikey. Take the money and fuck off and get your nose out of my business.'

Mikey shrugged; he wasn't a man to waste time on things that weren't working. He put his hands up. 'Easy, sister, your business is your business. But, listen, you have any trouble, you need a little management, call me, y'hear?'

Tyra kissed her teeth derisively and Mikey headed out the back, figuring that that was that then.

He spent the next week not getting much further with the career move. After an embarrassing episode outside the North Star, when some sixteen-year-old ended up hitting him with one of her shoes, he started to think that maybe he should stick with shoplifting, just do the odd awayday to Swansea or Bristol where they didn't know him.

Plus, there were more perks with the shoplifting. He'd seen that Lorraine from Next on the Saturday. Saw her down Chicago's in town so Tina wouldn't get on the warpath. Saw her again on Tuesday. Well up for it, she was. Maybe, if he left it a little while, he might get her to think about peddling a little on the side, like. She wasn't getting rich doing two days a week casual.

It was Thursday night. Mikey and Tina were just finishing off a pizza and watching some piece of shit video with Julia Roberts in it – still, worth it if it got her in the mood – when the phone rang. Luckily, she was well wrapped up in it, so it was Mikey got the phone. Tina didn't take kindly to women phoning up her husband, he had the bruises to prove it.

'Mikey,' said a woman's voice, sounding frantic.

'Yeah,' he said, wondering who the hell.

'It's Tyra.'

'Yeah,' he said again, keeping his voice gruff for Tina's benefit.

'Y'know you said you could give me some help if I needed it?'

Mikey didn't exactly remember offering help – 'management' was the word he'd used, he was pretty sure – but still he gave a vaguely affirmative grunt.

'Yeah, well I needs some help. Now, like.'

'Where are you?'

'The Four Ways.'

Mikey paused. The Four Ways was a prostitutes' pub over Riverside. Tyra must have got in a bit of bother. Taking someone else's beat, most likely. Probably some girl getting heavy with her. Well, if he was going to move into this line of business, that was the kind of shit you had to deal with.

'All right,' he said, 'I'll be right over.' She started to say something but the pips went and the phone cut out.

Tina was still watching her vid so Mikey just called out that he was stepping out for a minute – 'Bit of business.' He was out the door before the message had time to cut through Tina's focus on Julia's big love scene. Mikey wasn't too fussed, all mouth and no arse.

Down the stairs at the end of the block and into Loudoun Square, looked for the car and couldn't see it. Walked round to the Paddle Steamer, and there was cousin Del sitting outside in the motor drinking a brandy and listening to some jazz-funk tape. Mikey opened the passenger door.

'Del,' he said. 'Here's a couple of quid. Get inside the pub and get a drink. I've got to get over Riverside.'

Del, whose pupils indicated a current residence in outer space, nodded eventually, closed his hand over the money and shambled into the pub. Mikey shifted over to the driver's seat and kicked the Datsun into action.

Just as he was heading out towards Bute Street, a car flashed him. Mikey looked over to see the driver. Fucking Jim Fairfax, went to school with him over Fitzalan. Used to go down City together. Biggest damn hooligan of the lot, Jimmy Fairfax. No wonder he ended up in the police. Probably heading over the Paddle, have a couple with the boys, on the house like.

Driving over Grangetown Bridge, Mikey fingered his lock-knife as he wondered what was waiting for him over the Four Ways. Most likely some pissed-off girl from Ely with a Stanley on her, that kind of business. Well, he could handle that. 'Course there could be a pimp involved, maybe one of those Newport guys, been bringing the under-age girls over. Still, what he'd heard, they'd been chased out a week or two back, told not to come back if they didn't fancy getting Kenny's baseball bat up their arses. One thing about Kenny Ibadulla, cunt that he was, he had some standards. Well, sod it, thought Mikey, one way to find out.

He parked the car down the side of the pub, near the embankment. Hardly come to a halt when some girl in a white mini-skirt bent down to the window, asked if he was looking for business.

'No, honey, ah'm looking for love,' Mikey said in his best Eddie Murphy, and she told him to shag off and look somewhere else.

He turned the lights off and then had a quick look in the glove box, case Del had left anything there, might be useful. He smiled as his hand made contact with something, and then, held between his thumb and forefinger, he pulled out a little newspaper wrap. Del must have been so out of it he'd forgotten it. Only question was what was inside. No call for downers at a moment like this. He grinned again when he opened it up and saw white powder. Stuck in his finger and took a little taste on his tongue. Coke. Well, it could have been speed but, if Mikey had been selling, it would have been coke, all right. Either way, it was just what the doctor ordered. He speedily laid out a line on a 1978 AA yearbook he found in the passenger door, hoovered it up, put the wrap in his pocket and sauntered into the pub just as the buzz hit, ready for anything.

Well, ready for most things, anyway. He cut his eyes right as soon as he came in, towards the pool table where the hard boys hung out. Sure enough, there were a couple of the Ibadullas there, both sporting the family haircut, shaved right to the bone. They didn't look too interested in Mikey, though. One of them, Danny, raised his hand, and Mikey did likewise. He was just looking left towards where the girls usually sat when Tyra appeared right in front of him, threw her arms round him and kissed him on the mouth.

Momentarily stunned, Mikey was just about to ask where the emergency was when Tyra hissed, 'Don't say anything,' in his ear. Then she temporarily let go of him before grabbing his hand and leading him over to where she was sitting.

There were a couple of other girls around the table, Bernice and a white girl called Lynsey or something from Llanederyn, plus an older man, a guy called Charlie, used to be a boxer around when Mikey was born, had a lot of respect back then.

'All right, ladies!' said Mikey. 'How ya doing, Charlie?' ducking his head a little, making a jokey little boxing move.

'All right, man,' said Charlie, half getting up so he could reach over and tap fists with Mikey. 'All right. Now, how long you been seeing my daughter, you bad boy.'

Mikey didn't get it for a moment. He just grinned and shook his head as if responding to somebody saying something funny. Then, as he pulled up a chair, he figured it. Charlie was Tyra's old man. He supposed he'd probably always known that, but it wasn't like he'd ever lived with Tyra's mum, not since Mikey could remember, so it was hardly surprising he'd forgotten.

And then he saw the rest of it. Tyra must have been down on the beat, come in here for a warm-up with a couple of the girls, and who should she clap eyes on but her old man having a few rum and Cokes? So she must have given him some bullshit line about meeting her boyfriend here. And who should she think of but Mr Loverman himself, Mikey Dread, as they used to call him?

Mikey was both pissed off and relieved to find out that it was this kind of total foolishness that had brought him over to the Four Ways. Far as he could see, it wasn't like Charlie was in such a good state himself that he was going to pass judgement on his daughter. Can of Special outside the book-ie's, that was about what Charlie ran to these days, far as Mikey knew. Still, family was family, and anyway now he was here he might as well have a little fun.

'Yeah, man,' he said, pulling his chair right up close to Tyra and putting his hand dangerously high up on her leg, 'you got one sweet daughter here.'

Tyra let it lie for a second, then stood up and said, 'Get you a drink then, Mikey?'

'Yeah, sweetness,' he said. 'Make it a Diamond White and a brandy chaser.'

A moment later, Tyra motioned to him to give her a hand at the bar. 'Touch my leg again and you're dead,' she said.

Mikey just laughed, put his arm around her waist and pulled her to him, letting his shoulder rub against her breast. 'C'mon, darlin',' he said. 'That's not the way to talk to your new boyfriend.'

Tyra gave him one seriously cold look, and Mikey backed off a fraction. Back at the table, Bernice and Lynsey were whispering to each other and Charlie was looking at them a little askance, like he was figuring out what was really going on here.

Mikey handled it. A stream of crap jokes, lots of 'Didn't I see your auntie over town last week?' and 'How's your cousin getting on in the Rugby League there?', a string of bullshit about Prince Naz – 'You'd have taken him easy, man, easy' – to keep the old man sweet, and after half an hour or so everyone was sweet, and Mikey had his left hand practically in Tyra's knickers.

Lynsey and Bernice cried off about ten thirty, said they wanted to get home before the pubs shut. Wanted to be out on the beat for the closing-time rush, more like, but Charlie didn't seem to clock it. Instead he started talking about Mikey's dad, which Mikey thought he could do without, but was nice, really, turned out Charlie had known the old man pretty well. 'Devil for the women, ol' Lester,' he said, before looking at Mikey and Tyra and laughing.

'Damn bloody shame,' he said a little later. 'Someone should have sued the bloody shipping line.' Lester had died in some kind of accident at sea when Mikey was thirteen. This time it was Tyra who put her hand on Mikey's knee.

It was half midnight before they finally made it out of the pub. Charlie was three sheets to the wind by then, so Tyra put him in a minicab back to Ely.

Mikey and Tyra walked round to the car. There were still a couple of girls out. No sign of Bernice, but Lynsey was there smoking a fag and looking cold. Tyra stopped for a quick word and Mikey walked round to unlock the car. He got into the driver's seat, then leaned over to open the door for Tyra.

As he did so, he saw a bloke walk up, an obvious punter. He looked quickly at Tyra and Lynsey then said something to Tyra. Mikey couldn't hear what exactly, but it wasn't hard to figure. Tyra looked round, caught Mikey's eyes.

Mikey looked back. But he couldn't say anything. In the end he bottled out. His big pimp chance gone. He called to Tyra, 'C'mon, doll.' She walked to the car, smiling. The punter walked off, shaking his head. Lynsey walked after the punter, shouting out something.

'Mikey,' said Tyra, 'you're all right.'

Mikey just inclined his head slightly and started driving, but he felt good. Felt even better when they got back to Tyra's. Even when Tina gave him a serious beating after he got home at four in the morning, left him with a bleeding nose and a couple of ribs he'd have sworn were broken, he still felt good.

Shit, he thought, as he lay there on the sofa, wondering how bad he was going to hurt in the morning, he might not be much of a villain, but he certainly got a lot of action for a little guy.

The Packet

Monday morning, and Kim had a headache. She was sitting in the weekly ideas meeting and, to be honest, she was feeling like shit. Mostly it was a hangover; why anyone had parties on a Sunday night, she couldn't imagine. She didn't have the ghost of an idea for the meeting and it was going to be her turn next. Still, she'd been in the job three months now and they hadn't looked twice at any of the ideas she'd come up with so far, so big deal, really.

'Kim,' said Huw, the director. 'Any thoughts? Or should I fetch you a couple of paracetamol?'

'No thanks,' she said, thinking 'bastard'. She was doing her best to fancy Huw; it was part of the makeover she was trying to effect on her so-called life. She'd started wearing black all the time; that was a given, if you were going to be a media chick. She'd had her long wavy brown hair cut short, bobbed and hennaed. She'd stopped wearing heels so she didn't tower over her midget boss. Her accent was getting snottier and less Cardiff every day, so her mam said, and now she was working on upgrading her class of boyfriend. No more PT instructors. That was her New Year's resolution. But, God knows, jerks like Huw weren't making it easy.

'So, Kim? What have you got for us? Any tales from Cardiff clubland to follow up? Sex, drugs, rock and roll – that kind of thing?'

Kim closed her eyes for a moment. Opened them again pretty quickly when everything swirled about behind her eyelids. And in her brain too, come to that.

'Drugs,' she said all of a sudden.

'Sorry, Kim,' said Huw, 'can't oblige, I'm afraid. Paracetamol's best I can do.' He turned round to his pals, Sian the producer and a scary woman named Anne whose job Kim hadn't yet figured out, and they laughed dutifully.

Which suited Kim fine, as in that instant something popped into her brain.

'Cocaine wars,' she said.

'What?' said Huw.

'Yeah,' said Kim, dredging her memory for a conversation her mate had been having with some bloke at God knows what time the night before. 'What I've heard is there's this kind of turf war, yeah, between these cocaine dealers down the docks and some people from out of town.'

'Really,' said Huw, and looked round to his cronies with his eyebrows raised, but swivelled back again quickly when he saw that Sian's attention was firmly focused on Kim.

'Great,' said Sian, 'that sounds really interesting.'

Kim was excited. No point in pretending not to be. She'd slaved in the PR department, brown-nosing every twat that passed in front of her, for too long not to be excited, now she'd finally got her break as a researcher on *Wednesday Week*. With a chance to present too, if the right story came along. That's what they said at the interview, anyway, believe it when she saw it. And now maybe she'd finally got it. The right idea.

Huw popped out of his office and over to her cubicle just before lunch. 'Kim,' he said, 'this drugs-war thing. You know it's all a load of bullshit, don't you?'

'What?' she said.

'Yeah,' he said, 'I've got a couple of very good sources in the police. They keep me informed if anything's going on.'

'Oh,' she said. 'Well, it's just what I . . .'

Huw held his hand up. 'Yes, yes, I'm sure, but people do talk a lot of crap in nightclubs, don't they?'

Apparently that was it. Huw turned round and headed for his office. Kim couldn't resist flicking a V-sign at the back of his Next blazer as it disappeared down the corridor. She only just got her fingers down in time as he spun round again and said, 'Don't look so disappointed, dear. Tell you what, I'll just call one of my sources, check there's nothing in it.'

Ten minutes later, Huw came out again, his coat on now on top of his blazer.

'Well,' he said to Kim, 'I've had a word with my contacts and, you know what, you may be on to something. Fancy coming for lunch?'

And that's how it started.

It was his brief told Mikey about the documentary. Said he'd had a call from some bloke on *Wednesday Week*, the BBC thing.

'Wants to know all about the drugs war, Mikey.'

Mikey laughed, so did the brief, Terry – Mr Richards – who was a decent bloke all in all, down to earth, like, and had one lovely receptionist, Donna, which meant that Mikey didn't mind walking into town even for a little matter like this one. Some bollocks about wanting him to testify in court. One of the hustlers said he was a witness to some foolishness with a knife, happened outside the North Star a couple of weeks back.

'Drugs war, Terry? You heard of any drugs war?'

Terry shook his head. 'Huw, the TV bloke, sounded serious about it, though. Someone gave him Kenny's name, told him Kenny's going to war with some Birmingham Yardies, and they're all excited.'

Mikey raised his eyebrows, didn't comment.

'Anyway, they're looking for someone from the docks to help them out, be their researcher. Show 'em the lie of the land.'

Mikey raised his eyebrows again. 'Money in it, Terr?'

Terry shrugged. 'I'm not your agent, Mikey. The TV guy's name is Huw. Huw Jarvis. Now, what's this North Star business about?'

'Nothing, Terry, believe me, couple of girls got a bit aereated outside the club, Tina got a knife out, the other girl, don't even know her name, had a Stanley in her bag. Tina got a little cut on her arm, bled all over the place, fat as she is.'

'What's that, Mikey, girls fighting over you again?' The voice came from behind him, Donna bringing in a pile of papers.

'That's right, darlin',' he said, 'they don't like me seeing so much of you.'

Donna kissed her teeth. 'Well, feast your eyes, Mikey, 'cause this is all you're seeing.'

Ten minutes later, Mikey was back on the street and in a good mood. Terry had told what he already knew – sit tight and the odds of the court case coming off were practically nil. The last thing any of the girls wanted to do was sit around all day in court when they could be out earning a living. Then Donna had turned him down three times for a drink, but that was all right too. Mikey was a great believer in the drip-drip theory of seduction.

He didn't think about the TV guy again till late on in the evening having a quiet game of pool down the Avondale with a couple of the valleys boys, come down to pick up some supplies for Col. Skunk was going through the roof. Couldn't get enough of it in Ponty, by all accounts.

Col didn't even show till half eleven, which was typical. Lucky it was the Avondale; just had to knock on the side door and you were in for as long as you or Bryn the barman could hack it. Anyway, Col had the merchandise, which calmed down the valleys boys. One of them rolled up a sampler straight off, which was another user-friendly feature of the Avondale.

'Shit,' said Col a little while later, after the valleys boys had saddled up their ancient Sierra and headed home.

'What?' said Mikey.

'That's the end of the skunk for this year. 'Cept mi personal supplies, like. Got to find another little job.'

'Don't Kenny have anything for you?'

'Nah, little bit of door here, bit of bar there. 'Less I want to get into his gangster business and I'm getting too old for that shit.'

Mikey nodded in sympathy, then thought of something. 'How d'you fancy working for a TV company?'

Col just looked at him, like he was waiting for the punch-line, but Mikey carried on and told him about what Terry had said. When he finished Col said, 'Yeah. Let's have a laugh with them.'

Next lunchtime, around two o'clock, there they all were sitting round a table at the back of the Packet. Mikey and Col, and Huw and Kim from the TV, three of them on the Labatt's, Huw on the Brains Light.

They'd been sat there for half an hour or so. Col had hardly said a word, just sat back looking moody while Mikey rattled out his usual bullshit, probably have had his tongue in Kim's ear if he'd sat any closer to her. Finally, in the microscopic pause between a couple of Mikey's stories, Huw leaned forward and said in a half whisper, 'Is it safe to talk?'

Col nearly burst out laughing. There wasn't a soul within twenty feet of them, and the boys hardly ever used the Packet anyway, that's why they'd picked it for the meet. But Mikey was evidently made of sterner stuff, and he made a show of looking around the pub cautiously before starting to talk very quietly so that everyone else had to lean forward, and, in Kim's case, brush up next to him.

'So,' he said, 'you people have heard about the drugs war we're having down here.'

'Well,' said Huw, looking pleased to be such an in-the-know sort of cat, 'we've heard some rumours . . .'

'Rumours,' said Mikey. 'What sort of rumours?'

Huw looked around even more carefully, like he thought someone might be bugging the fireplace. 'We've heard Kenny Ibadulla's involved.'

Mikey nodded seriously, as if every kid in kindergarten didn't know Kenny Ibadulla was a gangster.

'And the Yardies,' added Kim, smiling like she was the goose laying the golden egg, and Mikey turned to give her a big grin as if she'd said something really on the button. Yardies! Fucking hell. Put any three black guys together on the street after lunchtime and, far as Mr and Mrs General Public were concerned, you had a gang of Yardies. Never mind the closest they've been to Jamaica's a day trip down Porthcawl.

'Yeah,' he said, 'there's some well heavy geezers around. Isn't it, Col?'

Col's attention had been elsewhere, fighting the urge to nip outside and fire up some skunk, leave these idiots to it. So he just nodded and instinctively repeated Mikey's words. 'Well heavy,' he said.

The table fell silent for a moment as everyone present ruminated on the heaviness of Yardies.

'So where've you been hearing this?' asked Mikey.

Huw and Kim looked at each other, and Huw was just starting to say something about sources and confidentiality when Kim cut in and said, 'The police. We had a briefing from the chief constable. He's worried about, quote, Cardiff becoming a major staging post on the cocaine trail, un-quote.'

This provoked Col and Mikey to look at each other. Mikey raised his eyebrows and Col shrugged in a 'search me' kind of way.

'Look,' said Mikey. 'You got any idea what you're getting on to here?'

Huw and Kim nodded, rather nervously.

' 'Cause, like I say, there are some well heavy geezers involved. Innit, Col?'

Col nodded microscopically while staring heavy-lidded at the TV people, as if measuring them for toughness. Then he suddenly leaned forward. 'Tell you what, you say you want to do this thing proper?'

Huw and Kim nodded again, both feeling slightly foolish and increasingly out of their depth.

'Right,' said Col. 'Best thing, you go undercover. You got some expenses?'

'Mmm,' said Kim. Huw was about to wade in with some sort of mealy-mouthed qualification but Col cut him off.

'OK, we'll set you up with a buy. Everyone knows you media people like a bit of Charlie, yeah. So we'll see you in the Cantonese over Riverside, nine o'clock tonight, all right. And no camera business, yeah. This is just the start.'

And, before Huw or Kim could say anything, he stood up and Mikey did likewise.

'See you at nine,' said Mikey to Kim, holding on to her hand a good couple of seconds too long.

'All right,' said Kim, flustered, looking at Huw for some kind of sign that it would be all right.

Nine o'clock. Mikey, Col, Col's baby mother Maria, and Mikey's mate Darren, who was just back from a little sojourn down Dartmoor, were all sat in the front bar of the Tudor Arms, smack opposite the Cantonese. Around ten past a rather tasty-looking Honda Accord drew up outside the restaurant and out come Huw and Kim. They both looked around warily, as if they were going to spot a bunch of Brummie Yardies waiting in ambush, then ducked into the restaurant.

'Give 'em half an hour to start shitting it,' said Mikey, and the others laughed, though in fact it was only about ten minutes before Maria said she was bloody starving and Col said he was too and all, and they headed over the road.

Inside the Cantonese, the head-waiter guy gave them a bit of a look till one of the other waiters came up to Col and said, 'All right, butt.'

Col said, 'Yeah, how's it going, Ricky,' and clashed fists with the guy, much to the head–waiter's disapproval.

Mikey caught Kim's eye. She was sat over at a corner table as far away from the window as possible. She raised her hand in a small wave. Mikey walked over and ushered her and Huw to a big round table slap in front of the window. Col ordered up a top–of–the–line set meal for everybody. Peking duck, crispy seaweed, the whole works. He gave a meaningful nod towards Huw as he did so. Huw correctly interpreted the nod as meaning 'this one's on the BBC', and did his best to look relaxed as he nodded back.

Meanwhile Mikey started making the introductions. Maria he introduced as Maria. Darren, however, he introduced as 'um, Paulo', leaving no one in any doubt that this was not in fact his real name. Darren looked about as much like a Paulo as Cardiff City looked like Barcelona.

For the first half hour or so, conversation was a little strained. The TV duo were nervous, Col was his usual low–key self, Darren seemed completely freaked by the whole situation, and Maria was still pissed off with Mikey over a little misunderstanding outside the Custom House a while back. So it was left to Mikey to single–handedly keep things going.

After a couple of rounds of lager, things livened up a bit and Mikey finally scored a hit when he asked Kim if the things people said about a couple of daytime TV presenters were true. So Kim took the chance to deliver a few choice nuggets of TV–world gossip. That and the Peking duck being passed round, and soon you could almost have mistaken the table for a social gathering.

Then, as the last traces of pancake, plum jam and duck were being mopped up, Col leaned over to Huw and said quietly,

'Give Kim there a ton, tell her to follow Maria into the toilet next time she goes. She's the one.'

'Maria?'

Col nodded.

'Not Paulo?'

Col widened his eyes in a disgusted kind of way and leant even closer to Huw. 'Paulo isn't going to be holding, is he? He's only been out of Dartmoor for a week.'

Huw nodded quickly, then he turned away, tapped Kim on the shoulder and made a spectacularly clumsy job of surreptitiously passing her the money while whispering in her ear.

A couple of minutes later Maria headed for the ladies', and Kim, as instructed by Huw, followed suit. After ten minutes the two women emerged. You didn't need a sniffer dog to suspect that they might have been having a little tasting session back there.

Next morning, Kim had another serious hangover. She counted her blessings first. She was in her own bed, by herself. She was indubitably alive, or her head wouldn't be hurting so much, and she'd made sure he'd used a condom, so she didn't have to worry. Whether that was a blessing or just a not-curse, she couldn't quite decide. Well, in her state, she felt you took blessings where you could find them.

She'd done it with Mikey, of course. She supposed she'd known she was going to. She'd fancied Col a lot more, from the off, but you could tell that Mikey was the one who'd put the work in. Col she'd have had to chase and, to give her her due, she wasn't reduced to that yet. Mikey started chasing the moment he clapped eyes on her, and by four o'clock in the morning, or whatever time it had been they got back to that flat – Maria's, she supposed it was – well, she didn't like to see a man put in that much running for nothing.

And it had been fun, she thought, what she remembered of it. God, weren't drugs great! She looked at the clock, saw it was still only eight o'clock, figured that the only reason she didn't feel worse than she did was that she must still be half cut, and decided to take another half-hour's nap. She curled up, her hand between her legs, and was just drifting off when she was assailed by the memory of a nipple between her lips. For a moment, she thought it was just some kind of student flashback, but then the image broadened out and suddenly she was lying on her front, biting the pillow and thumping her fist against the mattress as she shook with laughter. Maria and her in Maria's surprisingly big, nice bathroom, snorting up a couple of huge lines of coke off the edge of the bath, then all of a sudden snogging each other. And stuff.

'And stuff – you dirty cow,' Kim said to herself, and then, once again, aren't drugs great! With that, she turned over again, and next thing she knew it was a quarter to ten and she was an hour late for work, but what the hell. Her hangover seemed to have disappeared and she felt totally bloody excellent.

She was still feeling fine at eleven oh five when she finally made it to the BBC offices out in Llandaff North. Felt fine as Jo on reception took the piss. Felt fine as she got a cup of coffee from the machine and sat down in her blissfully quiet cubicle with the *Western Mail*. Didn't feel quite so fine five minutes later when Huw came out of his office, sat down right opposite her and just gave her this look. Kind of look that had her wanting to check there wasn't a white stain on her skirt or a little bit of coke crusted under her nose.

'So,' he said, 'somebody had a good time last night.'

Kim didn't say anything, waiting to see how Huw wanted to play it.

'Well, you're sure you're not too exhausted after your exertions . . .' Huw tailed off. Kim could see he was dying to ask her just what she had got up to. Meanwhile she was desperately trying to remember how long he'd stuck around. After the meal they'd all piled into Huw's car and driven back down the docks. Gone down the Casablanca first. All of them nipping in and out of the toilets every ten minutes. All except Huw, of course; BBC producers on a fast track couldn't take that kind of risk but, fair play to him, he'd turned a blind eye.

After the Casa closed, around two, Col had suggested they all go round to Kenny Ibadulla's place – Black Caesar's – said it'd be open another hour or so, be a good chance to get their faces seen around town. She thought she could remember Huw being there then – but she couldn't remember him leaving. All she could remember about Caesar's was dancing with Mikey, trying to do some kind of a ragga move, Mikey round behind her, rubbing up against her bum, obviously very pleased to see her. Shit, she hoped Huw had gone by then.

And then, with a sudden flash of hungover genius, she spotted that the best form of defence of her conduct had got to be attack.

'Huw,' she said, leaning forward, 'you should have stuck around. Just wait till you hear what I found out.'

Huw raised his eyebrows.

'I know when the next big shipment's coming into town.'

'Uh, huh.' Bastard doing his best not to look impressed.

'Yeah, it'll be coming by boat.'

'Yeah?'

'Yeah.'

'That's not it, is it, Kim? I think we could all figure out that a boat is the best way of bringing stuff into Cardiff Docks. Your sources happen to mention which boat?'

'Mmm,' said Kim, desperately trying to think where boats might come from into Cardiff. Then she shook her head. 'No, it's gone. I just can't remember anything with this hangover.'

She thought Huw was about to explode as she waited a couple of seconds before carrying on. 'Do me a favour, Huw, and stop looking at me like you've never seen a person with a hangover before. Of course I can remember which boat it is.'

Huw forced a grin on to his face and said, 'Sorry, Kim.'

'Yeah, well,' she said, 'the boat is coming from . . .' Suddenly she remembered a boat story she'd worked on back when she first started on the show. 'The boat's coming from St Helena.'

Even as the words were out of her mouth, she started to regret them. As far as she could remember, St Helena was in the middle of absolutely bloody nowhere.

'St Helena,' said Huw, a note not quite of incredulity but definitely of surprise in his voice. 'Isn't that in the middle of nowhere?'

'Yeah . . . that's the whole point. Apparently it's like a crossroads between Africa and South America and that, and no one expects anything to be coming in from there. All the boats from the West Indies and stuff are more dangerous to use.'

'Oh,' said Huw. 'Right. Makes sense, I guess. So how often do the boats run?'

Kim knew the answer to this one. 'Every three months. Twenty days' sailing time.'

'Christ,' said Huw, starting to look excited. 'So d'you know how they smuggle it in? Not that it matters at this stage.'

'Tuna,' said Kim, 'big tins of tuna. It's about the only thing they export.'

So, a little later that afternoon, Kim found herself a quiet little office and settled down to make some phone calls, one to the lawyer, Terry Richards, to get Mikey's number. One to Mikey, which got a very frosty reception from a woman with the strongest Cardiff accent Kim had ever heard in all her years of living in the city. Then one to the Avondale where, it had grudgingly been conceded, Mikey might be. No joy there, though, and Kim was starting to sweat, wondering what would happen if Huw got hold of Mikey or Col first, asked them about St bloody Helena.

Col. She couldn't believe she was being so dumb. She dug around in her bag till she found a scrap of paper with a mobile number on it.

Col answered straight away and she set up a meet in the Packet, six o'clock. Then she went to see Huw, put him off coming. That was easy enough. He was busy filling forms in triplicate justifying the money he'd spent already, and was happy enough to stay out when she told him it would be better if she went on her own. They'd talk more in front of a woman, they'll let things slip to me, things they wouldn't if you were around. Huw nodded seriously, and told her to be careful.

Mikey was the first into the pub. Getting out past Tina had been a nightmare. He'd come in from doing a little bit of business around four, picked little Mikey up from school on the way. The second little Mikey was sat in front of his programmes, she'd started in. Some posh tart had phoned up for him, said she was from the BBC, how stupid did he think she was, like the fucking BBC would be phoning you up.

'Calm down, woman,' Mikey said, 'it's the truth. Terry gave her my number. I told you yesterday.'

'Yeah, and I believed you. Like a twat. Then you come in at five in the fucking morning.'

Bollocks, Mikey thought. He was sure he'd got in without her noticing the time. Now he knew whatever he said there was going to be trouble.

'Yeah, well,' he said. 'They wanted to go down Kenny's club, check out the scene, y'know what I mean?'

Tina looked at Mikey for a moment, standing there in the kitchen while she made some cheese on toast for her son, smiling this bullshit smile at her, and she snapped. Threw the frying pan straight at him and, when he dodged left to get out of the way of it, she caught him with a kick to the shin and whipped her fingernails hard across his cheek, feeling them cut into the flesh.

'Fuck,' said Mikey, and 'fuck' again as he raised his hand to his cheek and found wetness there. Tina just stood stock still, transfixed for a moment by the sight of the blood on Mikey's cheek. He seized the chance to shake his head and say you're well out of order and scarper to the bathroom.

Spot of Savlon on the cuts and a couple of minutes getting his hair right, and he came out cautiously. When Tina didn't immediately return to the attack, he reckoned she must be feeling guilty so he walked into the kitchen. He found her standing next to the cooker crying, the smell of burnt cheese pervading the air.

'I'm going out,' he said. 'TV business.'

Sitting with his brandy at the bar of the Packet, he thought to himself that he had to stop letting women beat him up. Second time in a fortnight this was: first his girlfriend, now his wife. He'd mentioned to Lorraine, the girl from Next, that she might like to try using her talents in the pro leagues. And she'd responded with one hell of a straight right that made him wonder if she might not have a real sporting future, if they ever get women's boxing off the ground proper. Women were his Achilles' heel, he couldn't help feeling.

On which note Kim walked in. He let her buy him another brandy, a Labatt's for herself, shaking her head saying it had been a hell of a day.

Then she looked at Mikey properly, ready to say something nice about what had happened the night before, but instead came out with, 'What the hell happened to your face?'

Mikey put his hand up to his cheek, laughed and said, 'You should see the other guy.'

Kim laughed and said, 'Yeah, I certainly should. Must have some set of fingernails. You been fighting with a transvestite then?'

Mikey looked at her hard for the first time, gave her a real look, the one he gave people who lived in his world. She held it, looked straight back at him. Mikey cracked first, started laughing, then she laughed too. Kim, he decided, was cool.

He was convinced of it when they sat down at the back of the pub and she told him what she'd told Huw, especially when she got to the punchline.

'St Helena?' he said. 'You told him St Helena?' and he started to laugh.

'Yeah,' she said, grinning herself.

'And he went for it?'

'Yeah,' she said, now laughing too. 'Hook, line and bloody sinker.'

Just then Col arrived, clashed fists with Mikey, nodded to Kim. She didn't think Col liked her much. Mikey seemed oblivious, though.

'St Helena, Col,' he repeated. 'Isn't that the funniest fucking thing you ever heard? There's only the one boat ever goes there, coming or going. They'd have to smuggle the stuff there, then smuggle it back out again.'

Col did his best to look unamused but after a few seconds a smile broke out and he sat down.

'Well,' he said. 'So how's that fit into your drugs war, then?'

'Oh,' said Kim, 'that's what we're paying you guys for, tell us things like that.'

It was Col's turn now to look long and hard at Kim. 'So you've sold your boss some bullshit about this gear coming in from St Helena and now you want us to tell you some bullshit about how that fits into this drugs war?'

Kim nodded, let a smile start to show on her face.

'This drugs war, right,' Col went on. 'You know it's all crap?'

Kim nodded again.

'But I don't suppose that matters to you TV people – whether it's crap or not?'

Kim nodded yet again but Col carried on.

'Leastwise,' he said. 'I don't reckon you mind whether it's

kosher or not. Your boss Huw, he probably cares, right?' He waited for Kim's nod. 'But if we set up a little situation that looked good on film, he probably wouldn't ask too many questions, right?'

The St Helena boat came in at ten o'clock on a Sunday night. The next morning Tony the cameraman was in place at six, hiding out in an old warehouse, his long lens trained on the boat. Around half past eleven, he'd just got off his mobile for the third time, telling Huw to call him back to the office, he had better things to do than freeze his bollocks off out here. That's when he saw the two guys he'd been told about, a tall Rasta and a short guy.

Tony got the footage of the two of them walking on to the boat, and half an hour later he got them coming off again. This time the short guy was carrying a holdall and he seemed to be laughing. Tony whistled to himself at the arrogance of the guy. Walking off a boat in plain daylight carrying God knows how much coke in a holdall and laughing about it. He started tingling, knowing full well how good the tight close-up he was getting would look. A shame, though, he thought, that they had no way of picking up what the guys were saying to each other.

'Christ,' Col was saying to Mikey, 'stop bloody smiling. You're supposed to have a load of coke in the bag, you should look like you're shitting yourself.'

'Yeah, sorry, Col,' said Mikey, and shifted the holdall from one hand to the other, trying to make it look heavy.

Later on they filmed a bit more round Col's brother's place, a couple of the boys done up as Yardies – gold, big trainers, dark glasses – and that was it, a done deal. One of those times everybody's happy. Kim forked over the expenses to Mikey and Col, and back in the editing suite she was well and truly belle of the ball.

'Remarkable documentary footage,' somebody said and everyone agreed.

'And no questions asked,' said Huw, tapping the side of his nose.

Kim looked him straight in the eye and he held the look. Maybe he wasn't such a bad bloke after all, she thought.

The Paddle Steamer

Mandy liked a little drama in her life. It was the only way she could explain it, stupid situations she'd get herself into. Not that this wasn't the best yet. Leaving Neville to go out with a cop, for Christ's sake. And now they were both going to be coming down the Paddle tonight, listen to her playing records.

'What d'you reckon I should do, Linz?' she asked, sitting round the childminder's having a cup of tea and a smoke, ten o'clock that morning.

'Leave the bloody country, love,' said Linsey, big and florid and bottle-blonde, where Mandy was wiry and neat, her naturally wavy dirty-blonde hair drawn back tightly into a short ponytail. Then she spluttered with laughter, looking at Mandy's crestfallen face. 'Nah, leave 'em to it. Jimmy can look after himself.'

'It's not Jimmy I'm worried about. It's Neville. He starts giving Jimmy grief . . .'

Linsey shook her head. 'You're right, he was always mental, Jimmy Fairfax. Remember at school?'

Mandy laughed too, didn't say anything.

'Seriously, though, love,' Linsey went on. 'Why don't you?'

'Why don't I what?'

'Leave the country. Go and stay with your dad. He sounds well set up over there.'

Mandy stiffened slightly, as she tried to remember what she'd told Linsey about her dad lately. Usually she said he was in Florida. She always said he'd made his money in the construction business, she knew she stuck to that, but the other day she'd been watching some vid with a couple of mates, set in Los Angeles, and she'd suddenly come out with it, 'Oh, my dad lives there.' Silly cow she was. Still, maybe he could have two homes, one in Florida, one in LA. That sounded good.

'Yeah, well,' she said, 'I've got my responsibilities here, you know . . .'

Just then Linsey's little boy, Jordan, whacked Mandy's youngest, Emma, in the back, sending her tumbling towards the TV. Linsey plunged forward just in time to stop her putting her head through the screen but not soon enough to stop her bursting into explosive screams, and Mandy decided it was time to go.

'Ta-ra now, Linz,' she said, putting her mug down by the sink and nipping out the back door before the childminder had a chance to say anything.

Back out on the street, she checked her watch. Still only quarter past ten, plenty of time to walk down Spiller's, pick up a couple of singles before she had to be in the pub at twelve. Cope with the lunchtime rush. Ha ha.

Walking down the back way, along Angelina Street, she started to worry again. Jimmy Fairfax, what in hell's name was she doing with Jimmy Fairfax?

It had started a couple of months ago. She'd finally had it with Nev, taken off with the kids down her sister's in Newport. Stayed there for a couple of weeks, giving Nev time to cool off, like, then she'd come back to Butetown.

Moved in with her mum down the bottom there. And after a couple of days she'd gone back to work, left the kids with Linz, all just like before except no Nev giving her grief.

Then, Friday afternoon after the lunch shift, she goes to pick up the kids and they're not there. Linz says, 'Oh, Neville came and picked them up.' Stupid cow just went and let him.

'Course she'd completely freaked. It was embarrassing, really. She'd had a couple of brandies over lunchtime and, anyway, next thing she knew she was calling up the local TV, saying her kids had been kidnapped and their dad was going to smuggle them out of the country.

Must have been a quiet day or something 'cause in no time they had her up in the studio pleading for the public to help her get her kids back. She hadn't been meaning to get the police involved, just wanted to freak Nev out, basically, but the TV people called them in anyway, and she couldn't believe it who should they send up the studio to talk to her. Fucking Jimmy Fairfax. Last time she remembered having anything to do with him, they'd both been sent out of class – different classes, she'd never been that thick – and he'd tried to feel her tits in the corridor. Twat. But, fifteen years later, she had to admit he'd changed.

Anyway, she'd gone for it when they got to the studio. Tears, the whole bit, and they'd done a nice job with the make-up and all, and Jimmy had gone on after her, appealing for anyone who knew where the kids might be to phone in. Then, after she'd been waiting for the TV people to call her a cab, Jimmy said he'd drop her back down, said he was living in one of the new places over the marina there.

So they were chatting a bit in his car – one of those Mazda 323s – and she had to say she fancied him like hell. So they were almost back down the docks when she gave it another bit of the old waterworks, said she couldn't face being alone, would he mind going for a drink with her, keep her company for a little bit. So they went down the Wharf there on the marina, which should have been no problem except it was only Leanne's sister behind the bar, gave them a bit of a look.

Still, they were only having a drink and she was a free woman, wasn't she, and after a couple she was telling Jimmy how much she appreciated his support and she had her hand on his leg and she reckoned he was getting the message, except she looked at the clock and saw it was ten past eight and she should have been in work at half seven. So he drops her back over the Paddle and gives her his phone number – let him know if there are any developments, like – and she says ta and walks in the pub and there's Neville and the kids waiting for her, Neville looking like blue bloody murder.

So, anyway, next day she'd given Jimmy a bell and told him she'd got the kids back, gave him some bollocks about catching them at Neville's cousin's place with the passports all ready and everything. And then she started crying, telling him how Neville had slapped her and all – which he had, though nothing much. So Jimmy had been all concerned and he'd come round to see her and she had a nice big bruise on her cheek, she always bruised easy, and he'd asked her if she wanted him to sort the bastard out and she'd said no but gave him a bit of a hug and, well, one thing had led to a bit of the other, really.

It had been going on for a month or so now. She hadn't meant it to, but the thing was, Jimmy was just so bloody keen on her that . . . Well, it drove her mad, really, but still she liked it, Christ knows she'd had little enough of that with Nev the last couple of years. Jimmy was mad for her so . . .

The main thing was she'd kept it from Neville so far. Bruise he'd given her the last time would be nothing what'd happen he found out about Jimmy. Not that Jimmy couldn't sort him out – Jimmy had muscles on his muscles – but that would be that then, restraining orders and all that. Most likely have to move out her flat. And she'd be stuck with Jimmy big time then, and frankly she wasn't sure about that at all. Not at all. And, far as she could see, she'd better make her mind up by tonight. Shit, she thought, why can't life be a little more simple? And she was just cursing her luck when she realised she had a dirty great smile on her face. She couldn't help it. Like she said, she was a right old drama queen.

She spent half an hour in Spiller's chatting up the bloke with the long hair and picking up some chart stuff for the disco. Spiller's was the best place for that; must be a chart return shop, she reckoned, they had all the special offers. Then she went down the arcade to pick up a couple of house tunes, even though she doubted there'd be much demand, crowd she'd be playing to tonight.

The rest of the day was pure same old same old – work in the pub, pick the kids up from Linz, give them their tea, took them round her mum's for the night, back home, quick change and cart her records over the Paddle.

By nine o'clock she was enjoying herself, pumping out some solid house tunes, smoking some serious skunk, just her and a couple of mates in the back bar so far. 'Course she knew it was the lull before the storm and all, but she was enjoying it anyway.

It was Neville showed up first, around ten, and it could

hardly have been worse. He came in with Kenny and Col. Neville on the right, Col on the left, like a pair of bookends with Kenny in the middle. Kenny was really the last person she wanted to see in this situation. Not that she didn't get on with him all right. He was some kind of cousin of hers and he'd always looked out for her when they were kids, even though he was a few years older and all, but the thing about Kenny was he really hated the police. Just the sight of Jimmy would get him going. Let alone finding out Jimmy was knocking off his mate's woman. Way he would see it, she knew. Nothing for it, she had to get rid of them.

First thing she thought of was driving them out with music. She knew Kenny was like her when it came to music, took it serious. A lot of the boys were still living in the past when it came to tunes – play the Gap Band all night, they'd be happy – but Kenny was house and garage all the way. Well, she hated to do it but there was nothing else for it, so she dug under the table she had the decks on and found the box of singles she kept for children's parties, and there it was, right at the front. 2 Unlimited.

Whoa oh. Whoa whoa oh oh there's no limit.

Perfect, a whole bunch of people drifted on to the dance floor, unable to resist the Pavlovian simplicity of the beat. Normally that would piss Mandy off royally, like playing records to a bunch of sheep, but this time she had her whole attention focused on Kenny and his face had turned gratifyingly dark.

Then, bollocks, Col leaned over to say something to Kenny and he started laughing and they just stood there at the bar chatting away as the record played. Neville even gave her a smile and a wave. Shit, she thought, and dug deep into the kiddy record box, flicking through the records furiously before her eyes seized on something.

And so 2 Unlimited's floor–filling 'No Limit' was followed by Culturebeat's likewise floor–filling 'Mr Vain', and this time Kenny could take it no longer. He walked over to the decks.

'All right, Mand,' he said. 'What are you playing this shit for?'

Mandy just shook her head. 'I know, Ken, I know.' Then she shrugged in the direction of the heaving dance floor and said, 'But what can you do, Ken? They love this shit, and Peter told me to give them what they want.'

This was bollocks, of course; Peter the landlord wouldn't know 2 Unlimited from James Brown, but Kenny seemed to buy it. 'Yeah, well,' he said, 'I better be going down the club. See you later, Mand.'

Mandy just smiled and said, 'Yeah, later, Ken.'

The big man headed back to the bar, collected Col, and was gone before the track finished. Mandy just managed to restrain herself from whipping it off the second she saw his broad back pass through the door.

An hour later there was still no sign of Jimmy, and Mandy was feeling pretty relaxed about things, so relaxed that when Neville came over while she was playing some Mary J. Blige tune, and asked her if she fancied a dance, she said, 'Yeah, why not.' And, without even thinking about it, she started rubbing up against him as they moved, letting the music take over.

Later still, five to midnight, last tune of the night, just like always, Phyllis Nelson's 'Move Closer' – didn't finish with that in the Paddle, you were dead meat – Neville was taking the words to heart. Moved any closer, she'd be in serious danger of pregnancy. Well, she wouldn't actually; after her youngest, Brittany, was born she'd gone down the clinic got herself a coil. No way you could trust the docks boys to use a condom: like standing in the shower with your coat on, Neville used to say. Wanker, but, still, right now, him holding her tight, she couldn't help remembering why she liked him in the first place.

She closed her eyes for a second, let everything go but the moment. Then she opened them again, thinking it'd be just her luck if Jimmy Fairfax came in right now.

He didn't, though. Didn't turn up even when she was packing the records away, and getting ready to go. No, what he did was he rang on her bell, half past one in the morning, her and Neville lying in bed together having a friendly fag, like, after giving each other a fair-old going-over.

Ding bloody dong went the door chime which normally she liked, spent ages in Do It All testing out the different rings.

'Who the fuck's that?' said Neville.

'No one I wants to see,' said Mandy.

'You want me to go down, tell 'em to fuck off?'

'No, leave it, Nev, they'll piss off in a minute.'

But the bell rang again, and then again, and Mandy, sighing, got out of bed and pulled a big T-shirt on. Neville started to get up too, but Mandy motioned to him to stay put. 'Could be the law, I don't want them knowing my business.'

Neville nodded.

Downstairs, Mandy opened the door, saw Jimmy Fairfax standing there just as large as grief, put her finger to her lips before he could say anything and smartly ushered him into the front room.

Five more seconds of her standing there like a lemon,

absolutely unable to think of anything sensible to say, he obviously thinks she's playing some kind of game and he's over to her. Mouth on her mouth, freezing cold hands up the back of her T-shirt, pushing the whole T-shirt up above her waist, pushing her towards the sofa, like they're going to do it right here and now. Idiot's been watching too many videos.

'Stop it,' she said, attempting to giggle very quietly. 'The kids.'

'Kids are fast asleep, Mand,' he said, 'come on,' and went back on the attack, biting her neck now. She wasn't sure whether to laugh or knee him in the balls. Part of her even thought, sod it, what the hell.

But then, all of a sudden, he stopped of his own accord, shot bolt upright and stood back a pace, letting go of Mandy in the process. Mandy looked at him surprised and then saw that he was looking straight past her. She whirled round and thought for an instant she was going to have a heart attack. Neville was standing right there in the doorway, wearing a pair of boxer shorts.

Mandy was rooted to the spot, unable even to figure out whose safety she was most worried about. Probably her own. If Neville got rid of Jimmy, she knew she'd be next in line for some serious licks. But, as for the words that would simply defuse the situation, she couldn't begin to think what they might be.

Then a small miracle occurred. Neville just said, 'Oh. All right, Jim?' like they were just saying hello in the street.

'Yeah, all right, Nev,' said Jimmy, and then, 'Paisley, eh, I'd have thought you were more of a polka-dot type.' Neville looked down at his boxers and laughed. Mandy sat down, bewildered, but not so bewildered that she didn't catch what happened next between Jimmy and Neville – a quick silent exchange that consisted of an inquisitive eyebrow-raise from Neville and a short affirmative nod from Jimmy.

Then Jimmy turned to her. 'Well,' he said, 'he come round to nick the kids again, has he? Take 'em back to St Lucia. Or was it Splott?' This time a little edge in the voice.

Mandy looked down at her hands, wondering how the hell she was expected to play this scene, feeling thoroughly rumbled. But then Jimmy laughed and said, 'Well, he is your husband, love.'

Then he switched tone and suddenly sounded businesslike. 'Listen,' he said, 'why don't you two put some clothes on and come back down, we've got some things to sort out.'

Mandy and Neville did as they were told, walked back upstairs, put some clothes on, didn't exchange a word. Mandy was furiously trying to make sense of the situation, trying to find her place in the web of guilt and misbehaviour. Any way she looked at it, she'd got to be in the wrong, but that didn't normally stop her apportioning blame elsewhere. Well, never explain never apologise, that was her motto, and as she walked back down the stairs she was feeling a little tingle of anticipation.

That's when Jimmy's mobile rang.

'All right,' said Jimmy, then, 'Shit,' then, 'Wait, just wait.' Then he clicked the phone off and didn't say anything at all for a few seconds.

'That was Mark,' he said eventually, and Mandy wondered who the hell he was talking about till she realised he wasn't talking to her at all but to Neville.

Neville didn't say anything, just waited for Jimmy to continue.

'Silly cunt's broken down up by St Mellons, like.'

'Serious?'

'Yeah, said the engine just cut out. Smoke coming out the front.'

Mandy switched off. She couldn't fucking believe it. She was just getting ready for a big fucking drama and, be honest, she was looking forward to it. Two blokes ready to go to war over her. But now she was written out of the damn script. Instead she was back watching a little play she'd seen too many times already. Seemed like she'd spent half her life sitting in kitchens with men who couldn't even manage to be proper villains. She knew what would happen next. The two of them would go out. Neville would borrow a van off someone – Wayne Ibadulla, probably – and then he'd go up to St Mellons and pick up whatever it was. Something electrical, most likely. God knows what Jimmy was going to do: ride shotgun in a fucking squad car for all she knew. Or cared. 'Cause suddenly she was sick of it. It wasn't Neville; she'd always known what he was like and she'd still gone for him, silly cow that she was. She'd even believed him when he gave her the old sob stuff about how there was nothing else out there for him 'cept a bit of thieving. But Jimmy, that was something else. Jimmy, he'd found something else, and now he was shitting on it.

'Get out,' she said.

They both turned and looked at her, and for a moment she couldn't tell them apart, the black guy and the white guy, so identical were their expressions, shocked but already figuring the odds.

'Both of you,' she said. And she wished she could keep and bottle whatever it was she had in her voice because there wasn't a peep. They got up and left like little lambs. And she knew it would be a while before either of them were back in her yard.

The Ship and Pilot

The way Col remembered it, the pirate radio station was mostly Ozzie's idea. OK, it was T-Bird who was the front-man, but it was Ozzie's idea in the first place, Col was sure. He'd first heard about it when he took his old lady down the community centre for some curry goat. She'd bought him a Dragon stout, but the sound of Harry calling the bingo numbers in the hall next door had been driving him mad, so he'd wandered off into the other room and found himself in the middle of some kind of meeting.

Mrs Harris and Leila from the school had been there. T-Bird had been sitting at the back sprawled across three seats keeping his eye on some little girl looked like she was from the paper. And Ozzie was near the front talking.

Now, Col's general reaction on seeing Ozzie was to duck out of the way. Ozzie had been his social worker back when Col was about fifteen, and they'd got on OK, but now Ozzie seemed to have some kind of mission to set Col on the straight and narrow. Either that or get him to join some protest or other.

But, before he could turn and leave, T-Bird spotted him, waved him over and grasped Col's hands in both of his like they were blood. Not that Col minded T-Bird — he was a mouthy fucker, but at least he had a bit of get up and go — it was just that he was a London geezer, been down here a couple of years, all right, but it still made a difference. Different rhythm down here.

Anyway, he was just leaning over to T–Bird, telling him he had to shoot, when Ozzie, still talking, turned round to survey his audience.

'Well,' said Ozzie, his ponytail flapping around behind him as he turned fully to face T–Bird and Col, 'good to see that this is an issue that gets the whole community interested.'

Cheeky bastard, thought Col, what did he mean by that? But he didn't say anything, not having a clue what the issue was. Didn't have to wait long to find out, though.

'So,' said Ozzie, 'you have some ideas for a community radio station then, Colin?'

'Nah, man, no,' said Col, 'I was just waiting to hear what you had to say, like.'

For his part, Ozzie was well pleased to see Col out there in the audience. Trouble with these kinds of initiatives, the ones aimed at the street–level guys, was that half the time the guys never knew you were taking the initiative in the first place.

Still, T–Bird had said he'd put the word out, get some of the brothers along, and it looked like this time the guy had delivered. Maybe it was to do with T–Bird being a Londoner like Ozzie, not that Ozzie had lived there in twenty years now, but he seemed to have a bit more ambition than a lot of the guys down here. Gave off a vibe as though things could happen.

So tonight, when Col asked him what his ideas were about the radio station, Ozzie got carried away and launched into a spiel that went beyond the usual multi–culti bullshit the councillors all wanted to hear. Instead he found himself making a speech that finally blossomed into a call for rebel radio – the true sound of the Cardiff Underground.

The moment he finished and turned round to look at the committee members, he knew he'd blown it. Renegade drum and bass was not what the council had been promised – more like gardening tips and the occasional Bob Marley record. Gardening tips! He couldn't believe some woman on the broadcasting sub-committee had actually said that to him. He wondered if the stupid cow had ever been to Butetown. Lot of use gardening tips are when you're living twelve floors up.

Of course the members didn't come right out and say it there and then. Ozzie got the usual polite round of applause when he finished talking, but he was sure he saw Don the local councillor roll his eyes at Mrs Harris, the so-called bloody community leader. And, sure enough, a moment later Mrs Harris was nodding to one of her cronies sat out in the audience, inviting her for her thoughts – which were the usual blather of well-meaning stuff about educating the kids and giving them a sense of pride. Ozzie wondered why she didn't just break into 'The Greatest Love of All' and have done with it.

Of course it all went down a storm and Mrs Ernestine Harris couldn't restrain herself from giving him a smirk, like you come down here telling black people what they want, well you don't know anything. What we want is gardening tips and self-improvement. Well, maybe she was right. Then he found himself looking at Col and nearly burst out laughing as he thought that there was a man could offer Butetown a few gardening tips. Col's hydroponic half hour.

The formal part of the meeting wound up pretty quickly after that, thank Christ, and Ozzie headed straight for the bar, elbowing the bingo-sated pensioners out of the way as he ordered up a pint of SA. He'd just taken the first gulp when he saw T-Bird and Col waving to him from the corner of the bar.

'That was great, man,' said T-Bird, putting his hand out and pulling Ozzie into a soul shake. 'Yeah, you had them jumping there, my man.'

Ozzie shook his head. 'No,' he said, 'I totally blew it. I should have just told them the bollocks they want to hear and got the station up and running.'

'You reckon?' said T-Bird.

'Yeah,' replied Ozzie. No way that bunch are interested in doing something radical.'

'So?' said T-Bird.

'So, what?' said Ozzie.

'So, what are you gonna do about it?'

Ozzie shrugged. 'Not much I can do, man. Just keep plugging away.'

'How about going pirate? That's what we need, a real rebel radio station. Innit, Col?'

Col, who was only half listening, nodded his head.

And that's how it started.

'Rainbow Radio,' said T-Bird. 'That's what we gotta call it.'

Ozzie and Col looked at each other and rolled their eyes; sounded exactly the sort of crap name Mrs Harris and her crew would have come up with. Still T-Bird chuntered on regardless.

'Soul and swing in the morning, bit of reggae round lunchtime, get things moving in the afternoon, garage and house, then get serious in the evenings. Time this city joined the 1990s, you know what I mean?'

Amens to that all round and a couple more drinks while they roughed out a programming schedule. Next morning, though, it seemed to Ozzie like one of those things you get excited about over a few beers but never do anything about.

So he was surprised a couple of days later, when opening his office post, to find a photocopied sheet inviting him to the first planning session for Rainbow Radio. ATTENDANCE BY INVITATION ONLY. The meeting was set for nine o'clock that night, the back bar in the Ship and Pilot.

And so that evening, after putting his daughter to bed and wolfing down a quick plate of tagliatelle, he was ready to go the minute his partner, Bethan, got in from her evening class. She laughed when he told her he was going down the docks to set up a pirate radio station, asked if he was sure the docks people really wanted to listen to Grateful Dead records. That was the trouble with living with someone fifteen years younger than you; they didn't always appreciate just what a long strange trip it had been. And didn't quite believe that a person could be forty-five years old and be able to get their head around speed garage as well as Garcia and Grisman.

Ozzie jumped on the bus on North Road, took it as far as the bus station, looked around for the docks bus, didn't see one and decided to start walking. It still gave him a buzz walking away from the town centre and under the bridge into Butetown. It was over twenty years ago now, but there was still a thrill attached to passing under a bridge you'd personally once blown up.

God knows, he wouldn't want to do another two years inside, but there still weren't many days went by without Ozzie missing that time, the early seventies, when you could talk about revolution and people didn't laugh at you. Now he was as keen as anyone to avoid all that 'those were the days – kids today are apathetic good-for-nothings who've never read a word of Trotsky' bullshit. But, still, it had been a time and he had been there. Not that running the youth centre wasn't worthwhile, serious, committed, blah, blah. But, anyway, the minute T-Bird had said the word 'pirate', well something in Ozzie's soul had stirred. And, hallelujah, there was a bus stopping right in front of him, saving him the long, windy walk up Bute Street.

It was five past nine when Ozzie arrived at the pub, and he wasn't entirely surprised to find himself the first one there. So he bought a drink and sat at the bar chatting to the barmaid, a cute little thing, name of Sarita, whose dad, it turned out, was one of the guys who'd run the Casablanca way back when, which reminded Ozzie just how old he was.

Around twenty past T-Bird turned up, cracking on about her indoors letting him off the leash. And, by half past, three more people had turned up. First of all Col. Ozzie still couldn't figure out Col, even though he had known him for nearly twenty years, for God's sake, since the days Col was a pissed-off kid and Ozzie had come out of prison and just started as a social worker – working for the man, way he used to look at it. The other two were women: a girl named Mandy, another one Ozzie had known since she was a kid, and who he'd seen DJing around the clubs, and with her was a dark, stocky girl with short locks. No one introduced her so he figured she was probably just Mandy's mate, brought along to have someone to chat to in the ladies.'

Ozzie ended up getting the drinks in, couple of K ciders for the girls, pint of Extra for T-Bird, orange juice for Col who was on some kind of martial-arts diet, least that's what he said.

Then they were all sat down and Ozzie was waiting for T-Bird or Col to get things going, seeing as it was one of them had called the meeting, but after a minute or two he figured that they were all waiting for him to start. So he did.

'Right,' he said, 'you've all heard about this community-radio thing that's being talked about? OK. Well, I know you two' – nodding at Col and T-Bird – 'realise that what's going on is a farce. A bunch of happy-clappy bollocks. So what T-Bird has suggested . . .'

Ozzie paused, aware that, although he had started talking to the group as a whole, he was now addressing Mandy almost exclusively. She had leaned in towards him the moment he started talking, while the others had leaned back. And when he'd said the word 'suggested', he could have sworn he'd seen her tongue dart out from between her small perfect teeth and run along her lips.

What was he thinking of? Quite apart from the fact he was committed elsewhere, the girl was young enough to be his daughter. Or was she? He did some rapid mental arithmetic: if he was forty-five and had met her fifteen years ago, when she was sixteen or so . . . Christ, that made her thirty. She probably had kids and stuff herself. It happened all the time: he'd seen kids grow up, have a family, screw up, have another family, all in the blink of an eye, while his own life drifted quietly along.

'So,' he returned to the plot, 'so T-Bird here has suggested we ignore all that local-government funding crap and set up our own station, a pirate station.'

'Yeah,' said everyone, more or less at once, and in the ensuing pause Ozzie realised that this wasn't going to be debated endlessly, it was a simple flat-out decision. All that remained was to get on with it.

'So, anybody know about the equipment side of things?'

'Yeah, man,' said T-Bird. 'Back up in the smoke I used to run with some brothers used to do a pirate thing.'

'So what do we need?'

'Well, turntables and a decent Mike, for starters.'

'We can use mine,' offered Mandy, and there was a chorus of approving grunts.

'What else?'

'Just a transmitter, really,' said T-Bird, 'plus a few leads and stuff you can pick up from Tandy's.'

'How about the transmitter?' asked Ozzie. 'Anyone know how much one of them costs?'

T-Bird shook his head, but then Col cut in. 'About four hundred and fifty to five hundred pounds, far as I knows. Bloke over Bristol might let us have one cheaper.'

'How much?'

'Well,' said Col, slightly embarrassed, 'I was thinking of doing a little bit of trade with the guy, you knows what I mean.'

'Well, great,' said Ozzie. 'Great. Thanks.'

'Yeah, but I'd still be out of pocket, like,' murmured Col.

'Oh, yeah, sure, about how much are we talking about then?' asked Ozzie.

''Bout a couple of hundred sounds right,' replied Col.

'I'll sort it.'

Ozzie glanced round in surprise. The black girl who'd come with Mandy had spoken. He looked at her closely for the first time. She was a small butch person. He couldn't quite decide whether he'd seen her before or not. The odd thing was the reaction her offer was getting. Col just stared at her, looking pissed off. T-Bird suddenly seemed preoccupied with what was going on on the pool table. Only Mandy looked enthusiastic, reaching over, squeezing the other girl's knee, saying, 'Nice one, Bobby.'

Then Ozzie got who she was: Bobby Ranger. Something of a legend in social services circles ever since she broke her social worker's arm when she was fifteen. That bastard Frank Evans had come into work, his arm in a sling. The whole place had nearly erupted in applause. If you'd ever seen the way he behaved with any teenage girl who looked all right, you'd know why. The creep never put in a complaint, transferred out to Carmarthen a couple of months later. Be ministering to the sheep now, they let him get close enough. That was Bobby Ranger. Ran with the City crew for a while back then too, he'd heard from some of the football boys he'd been working with.

'Just tell Maria how much, like,' Bobby added, speaking directly to Col. There followed a couple of seconds of really evil silence before Ozzie stepped in.

'Thanks for the offer, Bobby – it's Bobby, yeah? – but I can probably find the money in the centre's budget somewhere, if that'd help.'

A rapid series of nods indicated that it would indeed help. Bobby stood up, glowered at Col, and said she needed to go check on how her business was running, and that was more or less that.

The next couple of weeks, things moved along nicely. Col picked up the transmitter from Bristol. T-Bird produced a guy named Little Steve who actually understood how it all worked. Sitting in T-Bird's front room halfway up the Loudoun Square flats, he managed to connect the transmitter up to Mandy's turntables and Ozzie's old CD player for a quick trial blast.

Meanwhile the group met each Wednesday in the Ship and Pilot to plan things out and they decided to broadcast non-stop every weekend from Friday lunchtime to Sunday night.

Another fortnight, and the big day arrived. The transmitter was stuck on top of the flats, and the studio was set up in an empty flat a couple of floors from the top, which one of Col's brothers had the keys to. Word had been put round the community that 105.2 FM would be the place to be twelve noon on Saturday, and by half eleven, amazingly enough, there they all were. Ozzie, Col, T-Bird and Bobby. Mandy was due along later, around four, to take over from T-Bird.

It was around ten to that Ozzie said, innocently enough, 'Shouldn't we have some jingles?' and suddenly everyone realised they still didn't have a name for the station, let alone any jingles. T-Bird had been pushing for Rainbow Radio, which had drawn snorts of derision, but no one had come up with anything much better – Rebel Radio, Roots Radio, Bay FM, blah, blah. Around two minutes to twelve Bobby suddenly said TSOB – The Sound of Butetown – and everyone agreed just like that.

And then it was happening. T-Bird took the first shift. On the stroke of twelve he stuck McFadden and Whitehead's immortal 'Ain't No Stopping Us Now' on turntable one. At five minutes past twelve he said, 'Welcome to TSOB, your main man T-Bird here on the wheels of steel. That's the T-Bird in your area and, like the car, bra, I'm long, sleek and black.'

First time he said it, everyone in the studio cracked up. By four o'clock, though, when he'd said the same thing after every other bloody record, they were close to strangling him.

But, still, the bottles were being poured, the draw was making the rounds and there was a constant stream of visitors popping in to say they were picking the show up loud and clear.

At four there was something of a changing of the guard. A kid called Marcus came in to do a rap and swing session and he brought his own posse of teenagers with him. For Ozzie, at least, it was time to make a move.

Walking back home, he felt pleasantly out of it and well pleased with the way the station was shaping up. Next morning, however, he hurried to get to the studio at ten to present his own show – Back to the Old Skool with Count Ozzie', as he was billing it – and was a bit less than impressed to find the place deserted. According to the schedule they'd drawn up, someone called Mikey was supposed to have been presenting the Sunday morning champagne breakfast show. But, whoever this Mikey was, it didn't look like he'd made it out of bed.

Still, Ozzie pushed the faders up, stuck Elmore James's 'Dust My Broom' on the turntable and just enjoyed himself for the next four hours. He played everything from the blues to Salif Keita to a whole set of old-school hip-hop tunes. He played the funky Meters from New Orleans and segued them straight into the funky Red Beans and Rice from Cardiff. He played Billie Holiday and Dinah Washington and, in between records, he talked about the things that were on his mind. He read out bits from the Sunday papers, went on a bit about the bay development and the latest stupid plans. He was on the point of trying out a competition, just to see if there was anyone out there listening, when he realised that there wasn't a phone number anyone could ring. Have to get a mobile for the station, he decided.

The long and short of it was Ozzie was having the time of his life. He loved doing the radio, the time flew by and, when T-Bird showed up just before two, he felt oddly reluctant to hand over. Still, he stuck a Bill Withers tune on the deck, said goodbye and see you next week to the imaginary people at the other end of the microphone, and made space for T-Bird.

As he left the studio the last words he heard were, 'This is the T-Bird – like the car, bra, long, sleek and black – coming atcha with the sounds of the Prodigy, and a big shout out to all you good, good people down at Caesar's last night.'

Ozzie fled. If there was one thing he couldn't stand, it was the goddamn Prodigy. Back home, though, he was on a high. Bethan and a couple of mates were waiting for him and everyone loved the show and blah, blah, blah.

Over the next week, though, Ozzie's high turned to anxiety as he wondered whether anyone apart from the presenters' mates was listening to the station.

On Wednesday they had the usual meeting in the Ship, and Ozzie persuaded everyone that a mobile phone would be a good idea, which wasn't difficult once he said he'd be finding the money again.

Friday, though, T-Bird tried it out. He announced a competition on the air and gave out the phone number. Not a single person called.

So Ozzie was worrying a little as to whether the station would ever take off when, Friday night, his pub night, he went down the Oak. First person he saw was a six-foot-four old hippy with a great mane of long grey hair who everyone called the Colonel. The Colonel had his own personal spot at the corner of the bar, from which he propositioned every woman foolish enough to come within his orbit, but was held in a certain amount of respect as the pub's undisputed quiz-night king. As Ozzie approached the bar, the Colonel walked over, clapped him on the back and said, 'Brilliant show, butt, fucking brilliant.'

'Cheers,' said Ozzie, suddenly warming to the bloke. 'Thanks a lot. You all right for a drink?'

'Pint of Dark, butt, cheers. Tell you what would be good, though.'

'What?'

'Bit of racing.'

'You what?'

'Yeah, bit of racing news, a tip of the week, that kind of thing. People likes a flutter down the docks.'

Ozzie knew this was true.

'Colonel,' he said, 'you remember Andy I used to work with?'

The Colonel shook his head.

'Mr Serious, from up north. Most humourless Trot on the block.'

The Colonel shook his head again. 'Sorry, butt, got a memory for names but not faces. What too many mushrooms does for you.'

'Anyway,' said Ozzie, 'this guy Andy is out selling papers every Saturday morning, a rag called *Fight Racism, Fight Imperialism*. And he's doing the docks beat. Fair play to him, he's gone round every one of the flats there, all the way up to the stop of Loudoun Square. And most of the people who haven't threatened to set the dog on him have slammed the door in his face.

'And he's really thinking of jacking it in when, bingo, ninth floor, this sweet old lady, old Mrs Pinto, real old-school docks lady, never got over them knocking the old streets down, she opens the door, gives him a big smile. Andy says, "*Fight Racism, Fight Imperialism*, madam," and he can't believe she says, "All right, son, how much is it?" He's so overjoyed he just gives her it. She smiles again, wishes him all the best and God's blessing and all and, just as she shuts the door, she says, "Oh yes, I buys all the racing papers, me." '

The Colonel laughed. 'See what I mean? You got to go for it. You going to be on Sunday morning again?'

'No,' said Ozzie, 'I'm doing Saturday afternoons from now on.'

'Perfect,' said the Colonel. 'I'll bring along my tip of the day and give you a little bit of football chat too. Just tell us where to show up.' As if hypnotised, Ozzie complied, and with that the Colonel belched hugely and wandered off towards the music-room.

And so it came to pass that Saturday afternoon, quarter to three, just as Ozzie placed Curtis Mayfield's 'Pusherman' in the CD player, there was a clanking noise outside the studio door. Seconds later the Colonel entered, his long grey hair bound up in a ponytail, clutching a carrier bag full of bottles of Brains Dark in one hand, and a *Daily Mirror* and a copy of Bruce Springsteen's *Born to Run* in the other.

'All right, butt?' he said, and dragged a chair over close enough for Ozzie to savour the unmistakable smell of a man who's been in the pub since opening time.

'Got a mike for me then?'

Ozzie shook his head.

'Never mind, we'll just have to share. You introduce me and I'll shift over.'

Ozzie did as he was told. 'That was Curtis Mayfield,' he said, 'and any of you out there who haven't checked out the man's *New World Order* album should do so right now. One of the true greats. And now I've got a guest in the studio – he paused for a moment. Did the Colonel have a real name? Christ knows. Christ knew why they called him the Colonel, come to that – 'come to talk about today's sport and racing. Here's the Colonel.'

There was a distinct pause and several heavy clunks were to be heard as Ozzie shifted out of his chair and the Colonel moved in, and after a long pause the old hippy bent his frame down to the mike and started talking.

'How you doing, boys and girls? Anyone out there want to get rich this afternoon? Well, stay tuned for the Colonel's Saturday Best. I'll tell you now, it's running in the four o'clock at Doncaster, but you'll have to listen to me slagging off the City for a while before I'll tell you its name, and before that you'll have to listen to a few words from God.' At which point listeners were confronted with another lengthy pause as the Colonel unpacked his Bruce Springsteen album and handed it to Ozzie with instructions to play track one, side one. 'Thunder Road'.

Ozzie was dying inside. He couldn't believe he'd let this idiot rock fan come in and ruin his show. No one round here was tuning in to listen to Bruce the Boss Springsteen.

Things went from bad to worse when, after the song finally finished, the Colonel launched into what seemed to Ozzie to be a completely incomprehensible rant about the failings of

Cardiff City and its players, management, chairman, caterers, even the poor bloody car-parking attendants.

At the end of the rant, the Colonel reached over before a stunned Ozzie could stop him, and plonked the needle down so hard it bounced a couple of times before settling down to play another bloody Bruce Springsteen track. As the tune started playing, Ozzie turned the microphone off and said, in a tone that barely stopped short of hostility, that that was enough.

'Hey,' said the Colonel, 'what about my racing tip?'

'OK, give them the racing tip, and then hand back to me.' He took a deep breath. The Colonel was a big bloke, and there was no point in antagonising him. 'You've done a great job.'

'Yeah?' said the Colonel, pleased. 'It's a good laugh, butt. Tell you what, why don't I ask if anyone wants to phone in, have a chat about what I was saying.'

'Fine,' said Ozzie, figuring that the ensuing silence should deflate the Colonel efficiently enough.

So, as the anthemic strains of 'Born to Run' faded away, the Colonel stuck the faders up, announced that today's finger-lickin'-good selection from the Colonel was Mahatma Coat in the four o'clock at Doncaster — 'Put your shirt on it' — and then handed back to Ozzie with the words, 'Take it easy, but make sure you take it.'

Ozzie thanked the Colonel, cursing himself for sounding like Smashy and Nicey as he did so, and then gave out the phone number, 'for anyone interested in having a chat with the Colonel about sporting matters'. And he was frankly astonished when, fifteen seconds later, just as the intro to the next record started, the phone rang.

It was a bloke wanting to argue the toss about the City manager. Ozzie had no choice but to stick the mike back up and pass him over to the Colonel. And, while they seemed to be talking a foreign language to Ozzie, who had a pretty thoroughgoing contempt for all forms of sport, the Colonel was clearly handling it like a pro.

After that the phone rang two or three more times. It was remarkable. To be honest, Ozzie had always found the Colonel a borderline-annoying drunk and drink cadger, and now he turned out to be a fast, witty conversationalist. More than that, it had to be said the Colonel's full-on Cardiff accent gave him a natural advantage as a local broadcaster over Ozzie's flattened-out middle-class vowels.

Wednesday night, TSOB's founding crew had their regular get-together in the Ship and Pilot, chance to discuss how things were going. T-Bird arrived just at the same time as Ozzie.

'Great show on Saturday, man,' he said as Ozzie was getting the drinks in. ''Specially your mate the Colonel.'

'Oh,' said Ozzie, who'd been expecting to get a bit of a hard time for letting some bloke come in and play Springsteen records. 'Didn't figure you were much of a Bruce fan.'

'No,' said T-Bird, looking at him blankly, 'I was talking about his Saturday tip, Mahatma Coat. Fourteen to one, man. I was sitting at home, right, chilling, listening to your show, and then this geezer comes on. Mate of yours, so I figure he knows what he's talking about, and I thought fuck it and went round the bookie's. Fiver on the nose, seventy quid, mate.'

Col turned up ten minutes later and went through the same routine more or less word for word. Except he'd stuck a tenner on, which struck Ozzie as a rather excessive gesture of faith in the Colonel but had clearly paid off handsomely. Then Bobby showed up and said how much she liked the bloke who'd given the City some stick, and Ozzie started to feel half like a proud parent and half pissed off that nobody had anything to say about the rest of his show.

Next week it was even worse. Saturday, the calls had started practically as soon as the Colonel showed up, a copy of *The River* with him this time. Apparently the listeners kept on phoning till halfway through Mandy's swing and rap show that evening, pissing her off considerably, as sport was not one of her big interests. By then the Colonel's tip, a ten-to-one shot called Nova Express, had steamed in at Wincanton, and it sounded like half Butetown had got in on the bet.

Come the following Wednesday, Ozzie had had a call from T-Bird suggesting he bring along 'my man the Colonel' to the Ship, so the rest of the crew could have a little chat with the geezer, y'know what I mean.

Ozzie certainly did know what he meant when he and the Colonel showed up at nine to find Col and T-Bird already sitting at the bar, a copy of the *Sporting Life* sitting on the bar in between them.

T-Bird had the Colonel's hand clasped in a soul shake before he could get his coat off, and Col had him a pint of Guinness in record time.

'So, big man,' said T-Bird as they sat down in the corner table, 'you getting rich then?'

The Colonel shook his head. 'No, butt, I spent too long making the bookies rich. I just make the tips these days.'

T-Bird laughed. 'Your loss, man. You got a gift for it, far as I can see.'

'Nah,' said the Colonel, 'just on a little bit of a roll. Got to stop soon.'

'Yeah, well,' said T-Bird and then, doing his best to sound casual but failing horribly, 'so, you got any ideas about tomorrow's races, then? Me and Col were just looking over the form a little . . .'

'Yeah,' said the Colonel. 'Go for a Yankee. Miles of Aisles in the two fifteen at Ripon. Hey Jude in the three o'clock at Doncaster and Interzone in the four fifteen back at Ripon.'

'Yeah,' said T-Bird, whipping out a pen, 'could you give us that again?'

'I could,' said the Colonel, 'but I won't 'cause it was bollocks. One tip a week. Saturday afternoon, that's all I can manage.' He stopped and held his head between his hands. 'I got to ration the power.'

T-Bird laughed, aiming for friendly but coming off as mildly irritated. 'I hear you, man. Saturday's fine.'

Ozzie was racking his brains for something to change the subject to. He could see that the Colonel was getting a little annoyed at being taken for a freak show. And seeing as he was a) the station's golden goose and b) a seriously big bloke, it would be best all round if he was calmed down. But before Ozzie could say anything, Mandy chipped in.

'Why'd they call you the Colonel?'

It was an obvious question, and one Ozzie himself didn't know the answer to, so he leaned forward to hear the big man's answer. But the Colonel shrugged and said, 'Just a nickname the guys gave me years ago.'

Then Bobby jumped in. 'Fucking hell,' she said, 'I knows who you are. You used to play for the City, is it?'

The Colonel shook his head, but there was a half smile round his mouth.

'Yeah,' she went on, 'I remember you, you were like the first sweeper the City ever had back when I was a kid. Ronnie something, isn't it?'

The Colonel put his hand up. 'Yeah. OK, OK. Less of the Ronnie, please.'

'You were great,' said Bobby and turned to address the others. 'He was brilliant. It was like having Franz bloody Beckenbauer in the team. That's why they called you the Colonel, 'cause they used to call him the General.'

The Colonel looked embarrassed. 'Yeah, well, maybe, love. Anyway, you can't hardly have been old enough . . .'

'Nah,' she said. 'Older than I look, me. I must have been nine or ten I saw you playing. And I've got some videos . . .' She tailed off, realising that everyone was staring at her now. 'Yeah, well, bit of an anorak me, you know what I mean? Anyway, what happened? You only played a couple of years. Seventy five, six – around then, wasn't it?'

The Colonel laughed. 'Bit of a problem with the old recreational substances. I was teaching a few of the boys how to relax before a game, like, and the manager, miserable Scots git always chopsing on about getting my hair cut, walked in the boot-room and, bang, I was fucking out of there. Joke of it was our left wing used to have four pints in the pub before he went out to play. Couldn't see where the touchline was half the time, manager never said a dicky bird. I could have gone somewhere else, I suppose, but, be honest, I was never that bothered about playing professional.'

'So what d'you do then, mate?' asked T-Bird.

'Went to work for my brother-in-law, on the cars, like. Respray work and stuff.'

'Didn't you play any more football?'

'Played one game for my mate's works team. Halfway through the first half, bloke clattered me, broke my leg. I thought, fuck that for a game of soldiers. Last time I touched a ball, apart from in the park with my kids, like.'

'So you don't fancy turning out for a little team we got down here then, mate?'

'Christ, T–Bird, leave the man alone,' said Col.

'Yeah,' chipped in Bobby, 'leave the man alone. He wants to play football, he'll play it, won't he?'

T–Bird put his hands up. 'Hey, no offence,' he said, and then, 'What was that music you were playing last week? The last thing you played before the tip?'

Ozzie almost sighed out loud with relief. The Colonel had shown signs of beginning to get pissed off. And, though he'd never seen it for himself, he'd heard stories about what happened when the Colonel lost his temper. This was six foot three and fifteen stone of hippy you didn't want to enrage.

The rest of the evening passed off amiably enough. Next Saturday, the Colonel showed up right on cue with a copy of *Lucky Town* – 'the most underrated album the Boss ever made' – and a hot tip. The hot tip – a nag called Dead Fingers Talk running in the four o'clock at Catterick – duly strolled home at twelve to one.

At least it was twelve to one every place in the British Isles except Butetown. Way Col told it to Ozzie later, what happened was a sight to see. Two o'clock, there's a whole bloody line-up of people queuing up outside the bookie's.

No one's inside watching the racing on TV, everyone's outside, transistor radios clutched to their heads waiting for the Colonel's tip. And it's not just the usual bookie's crowd either: the old geezers in their pork-pie hats. Today there's grandmothers in their Sunday go-to-church dresses, and mums with pushchairs, and they're all asking how to fill the forms in, and all it needed was a bloody hot-dog van to make a street party of it, with Bruce Springsteen providing the soundtrack.

'Course it was obvious, really, what was going to happen next. First four people in, making the same bet on a horse the bookie's never even heard of. It puts the wind up him, 'specially when he sees the queue coming through the door. He calls head office. The odds go down to six to one, and then down to two to one. And after a few minutes, they have to call the police because it looks like there's going to be a riot out there, people screaming about how they were told it was twelve to one.

Not that Col saw that bit because, the second him and T-Bird clocked the queue, they'd run over to Col's motor and hammered it over City Road way, found a nice empty bookie's and put their money down there.

Still, Col's brother Roy had been down the bookie's in Butetown, and he said it had been touch and go for a moment. But the police showed up before anyone could trash the bookie's like they were threatening to, and then, when it got to about half three, a lot of the boys decided to try and find another bookie's as well. No use arguing the toss after the race was run.

By the next week, though, things were crazy. Col was arranging to call his cousin up in Birmingham to put some money on there. T-Bird had the same kind of deal with his mum back up London.

'Don't you worry he might pick a loser?' Ozzie asked Col at the Wednesday-night meeting.

'Hasn't yet, has he?' chipped in T-Bird before Col could answer.

'Yeah, but, Christ, it's just a lucky streak – three out of three. All the more likely it's going to come to an end next time.'

Col looked at T-Bird. T-Bird looked at Col, who spoke up. 'You've got to be a gambler to feel it, boss. Sometimes you just knows things are going your way. You don't know why but you don't question it. The man's on a roll.'

'Yeah,' said T-Bird. 'Where is he, by the way?'

Ten minutes later the question was answered. The Colonel walked into the pub looking like Daddy Cool. Well, the Colonel looked like he always did. Tight jeans, big old leather jacket, long frizzy grey hair. What made him look like Daddy Cool were the women hanging off each of his arms. On his left was a girl named Stephanie, worked in Black Caesar's and was one seriously fit individual. As was the girl on his right arm, Bernice.

'Fucking hell,' said T-Bird reverently.

'Man's on a roll, all right,' said Col.

Saturday afternoon, the studio was a zoo. The Colonel showed up with a half-empty bottle of brandy in one hand, a bumper-sized spliff in the other, and a full-scale posse in attendance. Four or five girls plus a couple of Ibadulla cousins plus a couple of old guys from the Oak: a boxing trainer name of Bernie and an old middleweight used to be a big deal in the fifties, Charlie something. Every single person there seemed to be carrying a mobile.

III

Ozzie was finding it almost impossible to think. He'd lined up a terrific little segment. Working back and back from Mase to Bootsy's Rubber Band to James Brown and then spinning off via Miles's *Bitches Brew* to a couple of cuts from the Sun Ra singles set. The secret history of the funk with Count Ozzie, he was billing it as, but delivering it in the midst of half a dozen people shouting at each other and down their phones was no fun at all.

Then it was time for the Colonel. Ozzie was half expecting him to show up this time with Shabba's *Trailer Load of Girls* and have done with it. But no, the attention had clearly not driven the Boss from his place next to the Colonel's heart. He plonked himself down on the seat next to Ozzie, who moved over to allow him to put a copy of *Darkness at the Edge of Town* on the turntable, and stuck on the desperately mournful 'Racing in the Street'.

Ozzie looked at the Colonel. All of a sudden, he could see the man looked tired, going on exhausted.

'Christ, man,' said the Colonel, dragging heavily on the spliff before passing it to Ozzie, 'I'm getting too old for this shit.'

Ozzie shook his head, smiling, the smile starting to disappear as he smelt something acrid behind him. He turned to see one of the Ibadulla boys firing up a rock. Ozzie spun round in his chair, said, 'Oi, mate, what do you think you're doing? This is a pirate radio station. Chances are the police are sussing out where we are right now. 'Specially as half the bloody world's already here. Look, the police show up, not only will they haul off all our equipment, but they'll bust you and most probably me and the Colonel as well. So leave it out, right.'

Even as the words were coming out of his mouth, he

couldn't believe he was saying them. Veteran anarchist like himself telling people not to take drugs 'cause the police might bust them. Still, there was something about the dumb bloody arrogance of the way the kid was carrying on in what – he couldn't help it – felt like his studio that had enraged him.

The guy stood up, also clearly unable to believe that some social-worker twat would get in his face about a little rock, and the situation was well on the way to bad news when the record stopped.

The Colonel said, 'Afternoon, everyone, that was the Boss with the greatest of all his car songs, you take my word for it. I'm the Colonel and I'm not going to hang about this afternoon, my top tip is running in just half an hour's time in the two thirty at Exeter, and it's a fifteen-to-one shot – a filly name of Yage, that's Y-A-G-E, Yage.'

Suddenly all thoughts of violence disappeared as everyone except Ozzie and the Colonel reached for their mobile phones.

Ozzie decided that discretion was the better part of valour and took the chance to gather up his records and head out the door. As he left he clapped the Colonel on the shoulder and the old hippy turned round, waved and mouthed the words, 'Sorry, man,' just as he raised the faders on 'Badlands'. At the time Ozzie thought he was talking about the chaos in the studio.

The horse won, of course. Ozzie heard about it in the Old Arcade. He stopped off there for a pint on his way home, try and take the edge off his mood before he returned to his family. Seemed like half the pub had had money on Yage, but no one had managed to get fifteen to one. The bookies had her down to evens by the time the race started. And they'd still put money on. Ozzie could scarcely credit it. Who did they think the Colonel was?

It was at the Wednesday meeting that Ozzie suspected something was up. T–Bird didn't show and neither did the Colonel. Even then, Ozzie wouldn't have made much of it if Col hadn't been so uncharacteristically agitated.

'Something's going on, boss,' he said. 'Bobby saw T–Bird coming out the community centre with Ernestine, didn't you, Bob?'

Bobby nodded. Ozzie was more bewildered by the fact that Bobby and Col were speaking to each other than anything else. T–Bird had explained the tension between them, the little matter of Col's baby mother Maria being with Bobby.

'You got to ask some questions, boss,' said Bobby, her big brown eyes focused firmly on Ozzie. 'Ask them council people what's going on.'

'Yeah,' said Col and Mandy in chorus, and Ozzie realised that what was motivating them all was a real concern for the station.

'OK,' said Ozzie, 'no problem. I'll have a few words. But I shouldn't worry too much. The council never decided anything in less than a decade.'

'Thanks, boss,' said Col, 'and if you've got a chance, like, why don't you go see your man, the Colonel. Fucking T–Bird we can live without, but we needs the Colonel.'

Ozzie nodded again. 'Do what I can.'

So, Friday night, Ozzie went up the Oak, as per usual. He wasn't sure if the Colonel would be there or not. And if he was there he was half expecting him to come complete with entourage.

As it turned out, though, the Colonel was there, all right. But he wasn't at his usual perch on the bar. Instead he was sitting alone at a table in the corner with a great pile of newspapers and form guides in front of him. On seeing Ozzie, though, he realised an arm and waved him over.

'Ozzie, man,' he said, 'I've lost it.'

'Lost what?'

'The knack, mate, the gift.'

Ozzie just stared at him, still not quite sure what he was talking about.

'My Saturday tip, man, I haven't got a clue what it's going to be.'

'Oh,' said Ozzie, 'isn't that what you've got all this stuff for?' waving at the pile of papers.

'No,' said the Colonel, 'you don't get it. The last few weeks I've just known. I've looked at the day's racing and something's just jumped out at me. Don't ask me why, but I've just known those horses were going to do it. This week – nothing.'

'Yeah, well, don't worry. You've had an incredible run. People have got to understand you can't be right every time.'

The Colonel shook his head. ' 'Course that's what they should think, but they don't. They think four out of four the Colonel's the magic man. Tomorrow half Cardiff's going to go and bet on whatever sodding horse I say. And, when it limps in bloody fifth, they're all going to want to kill me. What am I going to do, Oz?'

'Just don't give them a tip, then. Tell 'em you just don't know.'

'No good. They'll think I'm just keeping it to myself or

giving it to some syndicate. People'll probably storm the bloody station. It's madness out there, Oz, madness.'

Oz rolled his eyes, did the only helpful thing he could think of, which was to supply the Colonel with another pint of Dark, and then left the big man to his fevered studies.

Just as he was leaving, though, he stopped by the Colonel's table again and said, 'I could always tell them you're sick, man, if you don't want to come in.'

'No,' said the Colonel, 'I'll be there.'

And so he was. In fact he turned up about an hour earlier than usual, just about a half hour into Ozzie's show. Ozzie was doing a little subliminal broadcasting, segueing Barbara Lynn's 'You'll Lose a Good Thing' into Doris Duke's 'I'm a Loser' into Harold Melvin's 'The Love I Lost'.

The Colonel was on his own again. And not so much as a can of lager on his person, just a copy of Springsteen's *Nebraska*, the mournful acoustic one, in a carrier bag.

He just sat there for a while, listening to Ozzie play records and chat about this and that, but hardly saying a word. Finally, around half one, he leaned over to Ozzie, handed him the album and said, 'Tell you what, Oz, d'you mind playing all of side one?'

Ozzie gulped, then shrugged. On TSOB the Colonel got what the Colonel wanted. A couple of times, as the record played, he tried to engage the Colonel in conversation, but he just shook his head, wrapped in contemplation of the music, far as Ozzie could tell.

The last track on the side had just started, and Ozzie was wondering what the Colonel was going to do next, as he hardly seemed in the mood to talk about football, when all hell broke loose.

From the outer room there was the unmistakable sound of sledgehammer hitting door. Ozzie, moving quickly, with a rush of adrenalin that took him back to the old days, just had time to grab his own record boxes and stick them in a cupboard, then stick up the fader and shout, 'We'll be going off air in a moment, the studio's being raided,' before the room was full of police.

They were there for about an hour. Dismantling equipment and bundling it up, in between while taking the chance to have a bloody good sniff around for any sign of drugs. Thankfully there was nothing around. Even the Colonel seemed to have showed up clean. So, after a bit of huffing and puffing, and once they realised that Ozzie was a vaguely respectable member of society, they decided not to bother taking them down the station, just took names and addresses and told them to piss off.

Walking down the stairs, the Colonel laughed for the first time that day. 'Tell you what, Oz,' he said, 'every single fucking one of those coppers must have asked me what my tip of the day was.'

'So, d'you tell them?'

'Oh yes, I told them, all right. Gave 'em some three-legged nag running at Aintree, be a miracle if it even finishes the damn race.' And he laughed again.

Outside the flats, they ran into a welcoming committee: Col, Bobby and Mandy. All of them looking madder than hell.

Mandy spoke first. 'T–Bird,' she said.

'What?' said Ozzie.

'He was there,' said Mandy. 'I came over second I heard you on the radio. Two minutes I must have been there. Police tried to stop me, told them I was visiting my nan up the top. And he was there, outside the flat. Tried to keep out of sight, but I clocked him. The big yellow streak of piss was trying to hide by the lift but I clocked him. Bastard must have showed them where to go.'

'Oh well,' said Ozzie, with a sidelong glance at the Colonel, 'least the bookies will be happy.'

No one managed a laugh. Instead they all headed round the Ship for a drink. Which was a bad idea too. People kept coming by their table to say how great the station was, and they didn't just happen to know today's tip, did they? Even Kenny Ibadulla came over to have a word. When he heard what had happened, he offered to hold a fundraiser in the club, pay for some new gear. But really it felt to Ozzie like all they were doing was huffing and puffing.

Back on the street that afternoon, it was almost comical. Ozzie and the Colonel walked back together through town and everywhere they went there were people fiddling with their radios, trying to tune into TSOB. Then, just as they were heading for home, he picked up a copy of the *Echo*. And there it was, page three. A story about the police busting the radio station. A couple of paras of the usual party-line police bullshit, a ho-ho para about the Colonel and the bookies would be celebrating tonight. And then this:

Plans are afoot to launch a brand-new community station for the Cardiff Docks. To be known as Rainbow Radio, the service is scheduled to go on air in just two weeks' time, according to Community Radio Trust chair Ernestine Harris. Rainbow Radio's managing director will be the well-known local DJ, Darrell 'T-Bird'

Simpson. One question remains – will the Colonel, scourge of the Cardiff bookies, return to the airwaves?

Ozzie looked at the Colonel. 'How the hell did they know that? The raid only happened a couple of hours ago and the story's there already. Fucker must have told them it was happening.'

He waited for the Colonel to join in slagging off the long, sleek and black one. But instead he saw the Colonel's face contract into an expression of pure misery.

'Christ,' he said then, 'it was you too, Colonel. You were in on it, weren't you?'

Slowly, the Colonel nodded. 'I couldn't do it, Oz, I couldn't let everyone down, like. I was just going to say there was no tip today. Then I got a call from T–Bird, like, sounding me out, whether I wanted to join his station. So I says yes, thinking I'd find out what was going on. And he gives me the spiel – all be just the same 'cept I'll be getting paid for it. And then he says it might be an idea not to show up at the station today.'

Ozzie shook his head, puzzled. 'Then what's the problem, Colonel, you weren't in with him, were you?'

'No, but I should have said something – maybe we could have moved the gear. Truth is, I wanted them bastards to come in, save me screwing up on my tip. My fault, boss.'

The two of them stayed silent for a little while, walking back past the prison now and on into Adamsdown.

'One thing, though,' said the Colonel.

'What?'

'T–Bird was bugging me for my tip of the day. Said they'd

given him some upfront development money and he was planning on investing it. So I gave him the tip, all right.'

Ozzie started laughing. 'Came last, yeah?'

The Colonel started laughing too. 'No, mate,' he said, 'what d'you take me for? It won, didn't it.'

And that was the last anyone saw of T–Bird.

The Glastonbury Arms

After the radio station was closed down, Col and Ozzie used to meet up from time to time for a drink. At first it was mostly just to run down T-Bird, speculate on how much money he got away with and to wonder why on earth anyone would have trusted a guy like that, a line of thought that tended to peter out when they realised that they'd both trusted the guy.

Then they would meet for the ostensible purpose of Col supplying some grade-A hydroponic homegrown for Ozzie's domestic consumption. But basically what it was was that, after twenty years of knowing each other, since Col had been a bad boy and Ozzie a trainee social worker, they'd finally found it easy enough to be in one another's company. So they would meet up, sometimes in the Ship and sometimes right on the edge of town in the Glastonbury, which used, Col remembered, to be full of hippies and bikers but had lately been done up in order to attract the suit-and-tie brigade.

And it was in here one night that Col finally got round to asking Ozzie the question he'd always wanted to ask.

'Ozzie,' he said, 'did you really blow up the Butetown bridge back in the seventies?'

Ozzie laughed, put his hands up in surrender. 'Yes, your honour, but I'm a reformed character now. 'Course I did, don't you remember?'

'No,' said Col. 'Well, I remember something happening

about the bridge but I was just a kid. Didn't pay no attention. What happened?'

'It's a long story.'

'There's no hurry on, man, far as I can see. Take your time.'

'All right, then,' said Ozzie, and he got up and got a couple more pints in before settling down in his seat and saying, 'OK, first thing you should know, I was a member of a group called – don't laugh – the White Panthers. It was a group started by some guy in Detroit as, like, a white support group for the Black Panthers. Anyway, there were a bunch of us in Cardiff, we were well into it. You've got to remember this was the early seventies, the Angry Brigade were blowing stuff up, the IRA were blowing stuff up. Basically, you wanted to be taken seriously, you had to blow something up.'

A Saturday morning in the summer of 1976, Ozzie left the dynamite at home while he went out to get the paper. He would have been back in five minutes easy if he hadn't stopped to look in the guitar-shop window. There was a Fender Jaguar bass in there, and he knew it was hardly a revolutionary priority, but he coveted it. Trying to sound like the MC5 with a tinny little piece of shit bass like he had at the moment wasn't easy.

Anyway, he was only looking, but it was while he was standing there that old T-Bone came up to him.

'All right, mi brethren,' said T-Bone, and Ozzie couldn't help but be pleased. He knew that T-Bone was putting him on, but still it was a slight worry for Ozzie and the rest of the Cardiff chapter of the White Panthers that they sometimes seemed a little, well, isolated from the local black people.

'So, I check you at the funeral this afternoon. Rastaman?'

Ozzie had not quite come to grips with this Rasta business. The last year or two, it seemed to have caught on. Some kind of religious thing. Far as he could see, T-Bone calling him Rastaman was just taking the piss because he had long hair. So he grinned and nodded and bent his long skinny frame down towards the stocky T-Bone and asked, 'What funeral?'

T-Bone stood back in an attitude of exaggerated shock. 'Mi brethren, mi good, good brethren, Louis Hammer. He died last Monday.'

'Oh shit, man,' said Ozzie. He knew who the Hammer was, of course. Anyone who was out and about on the Cardiff pub scene did. The Hammer was this blind blues guy. He'd always be wearing a suit and a hat and dark glasses, played a big old semi-acoustic, would just set up in the corner of a pub and start playing. Wasn't exactly Ozzie's cup of tea, to be honest. When it came down to it, Ozzie pretty much thought the Cream had got the blues down. There was something a bit too countrified about the Hammer. But, still, he was the real thing.

'Shit,' he said again. 'The Hammer was the real thing, man.'

T-Bone nodded, said, 'Yes indeed. And we're going to send the brother off, big time, down the bay. Be a marching band, the whole deal. Start outside the Casablanca, two o'clock. So, I check you later?'

Ozzie nodded, said, 'Sure,' already wondering what that was going to do to their plan. Christ, it could be perfect. 'Later,' he said then, wondering whether T-Bone was going to engage him in one of those complicated handshake rituals. But T-Bone just touched his tam and said, 'Later, man. Seen.'

Ozzie stood still for a moment, pondering. Then he headed back past the post office to the phone box.

Half an hour later, and he was round at Terry's place over in Grangetown, smoking a joint. It kind of went without saying that if you were round at Terry's you would be smoking a joint. Terry wasn't even dressed yet. He was just sitting there on the edge of the bed, his black hair, normally puffed up into an Afro, collapsed on one side from sleep, his skinny white hands shaking slightly as he skinned up. His lady was in the kitchen making some breakfast for them all.

'A funeral procession. Man, that's perfect,' Terry said after a while. 'We wait till it's coming down Bute Street and then we go for it.'

'Yeah,' said Ozzie, 'great.' And then he paused for a moment. 'Only thing was, I thought it would be good if we went to the funeral. Put in a presence, y'know what I mean. It's going to be a big day for the black community and, y'know, there's a lot of people don't know about what we're doing.'

Terry didn't say anything, just toked deeply on the joint a couple of times, then he shouted through to the kitchen that he was starving and took a couple more tokes.

'You're right. Let's get all the cadres out on the streets for the funeral. Full dress. Then it's up to one of us from the operational cell to do the other thing. And then they'll know about us, all right.'

The operational cell was comprised of precisely two people: Ozzie and Terry. The thing that they were planning to do, the thing that was going to launch the Cardiff chapter of the White Panthers into the big time, was that they were going to blow up the Bute Street bridge, cutting off the railway line from London to Cardiff and commemorating the first British race riots, which happened in Cardiff back in 1919, fifty-seven years ago that day.

'All right,' said Ozzie, 'which one of us is going to do the thing?'

They were very careful, Ozzie and Terry, not to come right out and say what the thing was. It was an article of faith that the state was listening to your every word.

'Toss a coin,' said Ozzie facetiously.

'May as well,' said Terry, after a moment, and so they did.

Ozzie called tails and he was wrong. Terry looked pensive, and then said, 'Great, well, I'll take care of the business. You go round up the cadres and we'll meet at your place around one. You've got the, uh, provisions, ready?'

Ozzie nodded and Terry said, 'Cool,' and he genuinely seemed relaxed about the whole thing. Ozzie, on the other hand, was feeling so tense that, despite the dope, he couldn't sit still. 'Right,' he said, 'I'll get moving,' and with that he stood up and headed for the door. As he left, he could see Terry getting up and walking into the kitchen in search of his fried egg, joint swinging in his left hand.

Outside, Ozzie took a couple of deep breaths and decided which of the cadres to round up first. It didn't take long. Gwyneth was easily the most appealing option. For starters, she would be awake by now and, further to that, Ozzie's crush on her was getting to the point where even he realised it was resembling dog-like devotion and that, if he didn't do something about it soon, it was going to get pitiful. Today was a big day already, may as well go for it.

That, at least, was the plan. And, as Ozzie walked round to the house in Roath where Gwyneth lived with a couple of other members of the Women's Action Group, he could feel the rightness of it swelling in his chest. Found himself making crap jokes to himself along the lines of two big bangs on the same day.

Got to the front door, rang on the bell and one of the kids, a little boy, opened up. Ozzie said hello and walked upstairs to Gwyneth's room. As he approached the door, he heard a groan, but he kept going and knocked on the door and was just about to open it when he heard a strained female voice shout, 'Go away,' and then a man laugh and then the unmistakable sounds of a man and a woman doing the thing they do.

Abashed, not to say thoroughly pissed off, Ozzie retreated downstairs to the kitchen. A woman called Lilac was there chopping up vegetables on the big wooden table. The kettle was on so Ozzie accepted a cup of tea and then he spent the next fifteen minutes being quizzed about football teams by the little boy who, Ozzie supposed, must have been a bit starved of male company, living in this house with three women and his little sister. Though there was a man there at the moment, all right.

A little while later he found out who the man was. Gwyneth came downstairs first, long dirty-blonde hair piled up on top of her head, wearing some kind of loose-fitting ethnic dress, with, as far as Ozzie could tell, and he was doing his best, nothing underneath it. She put the kettle back on, said hello and, 'Oh, when did you come round? I didn't hear you,' to Ozzie, who prevented himself from grinding his teeth. An act of self-denial he had to repeat a minute or so later when Gwyneth's bloke came downstairs and proved to be none other than Red Mike, another White Panther cadre.

'Fookin' 'ell,' said Red Mike, as was his wont, 'look what the cat dragged in.'

Ozzie somehow raised a smile and then looked at Gwyneth and said, 'D'you think we could have a word?' nodding his head towards the door.

'Yeah, OK, sure,' said Gwyneth, and she led the way to the front room, Ozzie and Red Mike behind. Red Mike was rolling his eyes towards Gwyneth, and then doing everything but raising his fist and going 'Phwhorrrr!' but Ozzie affected not to notice.

In the front room, which was freezing even on a summer's day like this, Ozzie did his best to take charge of the situation. Told the other two about the funeral and that they needed to meet up at his at one. 'Shit,' he said, looking at his watch, 'it's half eleven now.'

Gwyneth said she would fetch Rose and bring her round. Red Mike reckoned he could get hold of Ken and Dafydd. 'Be in the pub by now, I know those two daft bastards,' he said. Ozzie said that would be great, he had a couple of things to get together. And then, he couldn't resist adding, there might be a bit of a surprise later on; just to remind the others that he was an operational cadre and worthy of respect.

Shit, he said to himself as he waited at the bus stop outside Gwyneth's. Red Mike, how could she go for that carrot-topped northern twat?

Walking back up Neville Street, he was faintly relieved to see it was still there. The flat was in one of two buildings that had been built to fill in one of Hitler's little holes, and Ozzie was a tad nervous that having a dozen sticks of gelignite stuck in his fridge might lead to a kind of repeat performance.

Still, it was hard to believe it was really going to happen. The White Panthers' Cardiff chapter was finally going to put itself on the world map.

Back in the flat, he gingerly checked the fridge, then headed into the front room where he stuck a Traffic album on the record player and sat down to check through the instructions in *The Anarchists' Cookbook* one more time.

Over the next half hour the rest of the chapter showed up, Gwyneth and Rose first. Before Rose – small and dark in some kind of gypsy outfit – could finish rolling up or Ozzie could make the tea, Terry was there wearing his greatcoat over jeans and a T-shirt, carrying the constituent parts of the group's banner.

'All right, girls,' he said as came into the front room, 'you two mind putting this together,' depositing the banner on the floor. 'Ozzie and me just got a couple of things to talk over.'

So Terry and Ozzie went into the bedroom. Terry produced a couple of fuses from the depths of his greatcoat. Ozzie dug out the holdall he was going to carry the dynamite in. Terry nodded his approval and Ozzie went to the fridge. A couple of minutes later, Ozzie had his greatcoat on too, and Terry was telling Gwyneth and Rose to wait at the flat for Red Mike and the others and they'd see them in the Glendower, the freaks' pub at the bottom of Bute Street, in an hour or so, as soon as they'd done their little bit of business.

It was only a ten-minute walk up to Tudor Road across the bridge and over to the station, but it felt a lot longer to Ozzie carrying a bag full of dynamite. Still, nothing untoward happened and soon the two hippies were walking along platform seven past the buffet and toilets and the signs telling travellers to go no further. At the end of the platform they jumped down next to the track and kept on walking for another thirty yards or so till they were on top of the railway bridge. It was a routine they'd done several times before. It was amazing how few people there were on the station on a Saturday lunchtime. On the wall next to the tracks you could see the signs of their previous visits, big white slogans – THE FIRE NEXT TIME, KICK OUT THE JAMS, FREE THE ANGRY BRIGADE. Terry had been planning on using the prime southern wall of the bridge for today's graffito but was annoyed to see he'd been beaten to it.

'Fuckin' IMG,' he said, surveying the words CHILE – VENCEREMOS. Then he walked a couple of yards further along, took out his aerosol can and began work on today's message – the one that would make the headlines. He began with a big R.

Meanwhile Ozzie walked up to the little coalhole-type structure they'd noticed on a previous spray-painting expedition, pulled open the wooden cover and found nothing there apart from a couple of dirty mags. Probably some railwayman's stash, thought Ozzie, as he deposited the dynamite on top of them. He waited for a moment till Terry finished his slogan, and the two of them walked back on to the platform just as one of the little valley's trains started to nose out of the station. No one appeared to have noticed a thing.

They were on to their second pint in the Glendower before the others turned up. Everyone in the pub was talking about the funeral. You'd think the Hammer had been some kind of spiritual leader to the assembled longhairs, not just that old blind black geezer used to play in the pubs and nobody paid him much notice.

'You hear it's going to be a New Orleans job?' someone asked Ozzie.

Ozzie nodded.

'Yeah. it's a local tradition,' said the guy, who had glasses and a hefty moustache and worked for some community film project, Ozzie thought, a suspicion confirmed a minute or two later when the guy said he had to shoot off and join his crew.

'Looks like there's going to be a film,' Ozzie said to Terry, striving to keep his voice neutral.

The others arrived in a cluster. Ozzie was pleased to see that Gwyneth had enough self-respect to keep her distance from Red Mike in public. Maybe it was just a one-nighter, he speculated, before catching himself in this train of excessively bourgeois sexual-jealousy bullshit.

Half an hour later – you didn't get Dafydd and Ken out of a pub in under half an hour – they were walking down Bute Street heading for the Casablanca. They had made it as far as the shops near Loudoun Square when Terry turned to Gwyneth and said, 'Where's the banner?'

Gwyneth looked quickly at Rose, then looked at Terry. 'Well, me and Rose were talking, we thought this isn't a march, right? It's supposed to be a funeral and maybe people wouldn't be too pleased seeing us with a banner. I mean, it's not a demo, is it?'

Terry looked mountainously pissed off for a moment but then he shrugged and said, 'No, you're right, wouldn't want to antagonise the community.'

It was half past two before they made it to the Casablanca, an old church turned reggae dancehall right down in the docks, but they were evidently in little danger of being late. There were a couple of big old hearses parked outside the club and a crowd of people milling about. Inside the Casablanca, the sound of a big jazz band tuning up could be heard. Ozzie wandered in to have a look. In the centre of the room were a bunch of white guys he recognised as the trad jazzers who played at the Inn on the River, Sunday lunchtimes. Their leader, a fat, white, bearded trombonist, was counting in the inevitable 'When the Saints Go Marching In', focusing his attention on a group of schoolkids carrying a motley assortment of recorders, triangles, a violin and a couple of guitars.

'Just try and keep the beat. Don't worry too much about the tune,' he was exhorting desperately. Ozzie stuck around for a couple more run-throughs, and the sound was becoming marginally less painful when the warm-up was interrupted by a thunderous noise. In through the open door of the Casablanca came four black men dressed in African robes, their hair in dreadlocks, carrying big African drums and beating them with sticks.

The lead drummer came over to the trombonist.

'All right, Bev?' he said in a startlingly incongruous Cardiff accent.

'Aye,' said the trombonist. 'All right, Barry, but what's with the Zulu war drums?'

'Come to join the band, haven't we, Bev. Don't worry, bra, you just keep with the jazz shit and we'll fit in.'

Bev shuddered but was just about to start things off one more time when another party of new arrivals came in through the door – evidently a local church choir. Bev looked about ready to have a nervous breakdown. Ozzie slipped outside where he found Terry in conversation with the film bloke and a local so-called community leader, name of Big George.

'I thought these funerals were a local tradition,' said Ozzie, 'but it doesn't look like they've got a clue what's going on in there.'

'Local tradition, man!' hooted Big George. 'Nah, man, some of the boys were in the Pilot the other night and they were talking about that James Bond thing, you know *Live and Let Die*. Wicked funeral at the beginning, seen. Thought the Hammer would have liked one of them.'

Ozzie could see the film guy backing off from the line of conversation, tuning it out. Local tradition was what he wanted, so a local tradition this funeral was going to be.

It was nearly four when the parade, now a couple of hundred strong, finally started moving. The drummers took the lead and, as the cortège wound through Mount Stuart Square, that was all you could hear, a huge growling beat. Then, as they came into James Street, the brass joined in, still playing 'When the Saints' but mutating it now to fit in with the drums. Bev had clearly reasoned that, with the drums, the rest of the band had to adapt or die. By the time they hit the long straight line of Bute Street, heading north towards the city centre, the schoolkids and the choir were in too and, while it was a bit of a racket, it was undeniably a mighty racket.

The procession was loosely split into mostly black locals at the front, and mostly white hippies and music lovers at the back. The South Wales Jazz Preservation Society was out in force, passing flagons of Brains Dark amongst themselves. The White Panthers were in the middle of things, forming a kind of flying wedge around the substantial figures of Dafydd and Ken, two blokes who, if you didn't know them to be a couple of harmless pissheads, looked like a pair of very mean bikers indeed. Ozzie was on the left of the wedge next to the diminutive blonde figure of Terry's old lady, Angie. Terry himself had already gone ahead on his mission.

Around halfway down the road, Ozzie began to get nervous. The band was playing a cacophonous but exhilarating version of 'The Rivers of Babylon', joints were being freely passed around from the front of the parade and bottles of beer from the back. The whole thing was starting to resemble a crazed seaside outing, but Ozzie couldn't keep his mind on it.

He and Terry had gone out to the Brecon Beacons a couple of weeks before and tried out setting off one stick of dynamite, using a fuse, and that had worked fine. Thirty seconds, just as it said in the *Cookbook*, plenty of time to get out of the way of the blast. But then the original plan had been to blow up the bridge in the middle of the night when no one was around, so a few seconds here or there wouldn't make much difference.

Now, however, Terry was going to try to time it so the bridge blew up in full view of the film camera. The risks suddenly looked huge. The bridge might come down on the marchers – almost impossible to justify, even with the most advanced revolutionary rhetoric – or it might take out an incoming train – which was also a little further than Ozzie was prepared to go.

Soon the bridge drew into sight, but the size of the procession – it had now swelled to nearly a thousand people – meant that it was just inching along the road. Ozzie could hardly bear it. At one point Gwyneth came over and asked if he was all right. 'Fine,' he said, 'fine, maybe a little too much reefer and booze in the sun.' She nodded and went back to Red Mike, who looked like he really was suffering from the sun and the booze, his face looking redder than his hair.

Fifty yards from the bridge, and Ozzie's nerves were at

screaming point. 'Do it now, you daft bastard,' he was inwardly shouting. 'How close do you want us to be?'

Twenty yards away from the bridge, and he was wondering whether he should run to the front of the parade and tell everyone to stop. As if they'd take any notice.

And then the front of the parade was under the bridge. Ozzie and the Panthers were still a further fifty yards behind, but Ozzie was starting to shake uncontrollably just waiting for the explosion. The question running through his mind was: 'Should I tell Gwyneth? Should I tell Gwyneth?'

He was just about to do so, he'd tapped her on the shoulder and was about to say something, when he realised it was already too late. They were under the bridge now.

Still, Gwyneth turned to him. 'What?'

'Oh,' he said, 'I was wondering if you'd seen Terry.'

'No,' she said, looking puzzled, 'I thought you knew where he was.'

'Yeah, well,' said Ozzie, weakly, 'I thought he'd be back by now.'

And that was it, they were through the bridge. Ozzie held his breath for a moment or two longer, waiting for the blast of rubble to hit them from behind as they carried on towards the town centre, but nothing happened. A train rumbled over the bridge and still nothing happened, and then Ozzie started to worry in earnest about Terry's whereabouts. Maybe he'd been nicked sneaking on to the bridge. Or maybe he'd just bottled the whole thing and headed for the pub.

And then Ozzie's attention was firmly dragged away from this line of thinking. Standing ahead of the funeral procession, a hundred yards or so beyond the bridge, near the beginning of the city's shopping centre, stood a line of police.

As the drummers approached the police Ozzie could see one of the policemen walk forward with his hand raised in the air, and start to talk.

Ozzie pushed forward so he could hear what was being said. The policeman was saying something about how there was no way an unlicensed demonstration could come into the city centre.

The lead drummer, the one named Barry, said, 'This ain't no demonstration. Supposed to be a funeral, man.'

The policeman just shook his head and said something Ozzie couldn't hear.

Barry turned around to the rest of the procession, which had grown ominously quiet since the band had stopped playing and the hearses hushed their motors.

Soon there was an angry muttering amongst the crowd that quietened only when the priest, a big red-faced rugby-playing type, walked forward to talk to the police. He spoke for a moment or two, started waving his arms around and then came back looking gloomy. He was about to say something when the first stone whistled past him and struck a copper right on the head.

Chaos broke out immediately. The police started forward, pulling out their truncheons. More stones were thrown, women clustered around the hearse started shrieking, and the scene looked set to get very ugly indeed, when there was a huge bang.

Everyone paused and looked back towards the noise. The sight that greeted their eyes was the Bute Street bridge slowly collapsing to the ground and, as the smoke and rubble cleared, there, on the far wall, now the only remaining part of the bridge, was the slogan 'Remember 1919'.

'Fookin' hell,' said the unmistakable voice of Red Mike in Ozzie's ear, 'nice one,' and suddenly they were running back towards the bombsite, ignoring the shouts of the police for everyone to remain calm and stay where they were. And it wasn't only Ozzie and the White Panthers who were running. Most of the Butetown youth were coming too, racing towards the rubble, clambering through it and over it, and into what suddenly seemed like the sanctuary of Butetown itself.

That evening the White Panthers got together at Gwyneth's house to watch it on the telly. There was no local news programme, this being a Saturday, but there it was, third story on the national news. First some shots of the aftermath and an interview with a couple of policemen condemning this reckless act of terrorism. Trains were indefinitely cancelled from Cardiff, passengers would have to use alternative bus services.

'Any idea who might be responsible?' the presenter asked. The camera focused in on the slogan 'Remember 1919'. No one seemed to have a clue what it meant. Somebody speculated that it indicated some kind of Welsh Nat solidarity with the Irish, and they'd got the date of the Easter Rising wrong. Terry swore and said they'd better get a communiqué out quickly.

'Any idea how the bomb was detonated?' the presenter asked. 'Yes,' said a policeman. 'A crude device, left somewhere on the bridge. The perpetrator or perpetrators would appear to have escaped by going further along the railway line and dropping down into some builders' yards via a rope.'

'Got that bit right at least,' grunted Terry.

They got the communiqué out to the papers on Monday morning. None of the nationals seemed to take it seriously at first. But then a bloke named Randall on the *South Wales Echo* picked it up and made it a front-page splash, and by Tuesday lunchtime the Cardiff White Panthers were famous.

It was odd, really. Tuesday night, they all got together at what they called the Safe House, Ken's senile old uncle's place in Roath. They watched their news coverage and cheered, but they were basically terrified, sure the police would be through the door any second. Membership of the Panthers was meant to be kind of covert, but still it was hardly a secret amongst the people they knew. The next few days they stayed cooped up in the house, living on tins of tuna and driving each other mad.

Friday, Gwyneth had had enough and headed up to some cottage near Usk with one of the sisters. Saturday, Red Mike disappeared around six o'clock. Came back at two in the morning completely pissed. Said they'd been buying him drinks all night in the pub.

And by the next week they all gradually let their lives return to normal, as it became increasingly obvious that the Cardiff cops hadn't a clue how to go about catching a bunch of student revolutionaries.

Another month, and it was clear that they'd got away with it. Events in Ireland had long since blown the Panthers' exploit out of the news. The police had evidently given up and life returned imperceptibly to normal.

Some time in the summer they read a communiqué from Detroit: the American White Panthers had renounced violence. The group were horrified at first, but Ozzie was pretty sure he wasn't the only one who was secretly a little relieved that his career of terrorism looked to have come to a sudden end.

Still, they didn't give up activism, and, on a Friday night in late August, the six of them were out with spray cans on the Crwys Road bridge busily painting up the month's slogan – Carnival '76 Kick Out the Jams – when a single policeman, no more than nineteen years old, with an expression of utter terror on his face, walked up and told them they were breaking the law and he was putting them under arrest.

Red Mike laughed out loud, turned to the copper and said, 'Does your mother know you're out, son?' He was all set to deck the poor kid when Terry stepped in.

'No, Mike,' he said. 'Non-violence, remember.' Then he turned to the copper and said, 'OK, we're under arrest. Now, where d'you want to take us?'

'And that was the end of that,' said Ozzie.

Col laughed and shook his head and later on they walked outside and sat in the moonlight in the WNO car-park looking back at the bridge, sharing a smoke. After a while Ozzie laughed and Col looked round at him.

'Different times, man,' said Ozzie. 'Different times.'

The Casablanca

Tony Pinto came out of prison on a fine spring morning, wearing the same blue go-to-court suit he'd had on the day they convicted him. He came out the front door, turned right and crossed over the road to the lawyers' pub, Rumpoles. He knew Danny Jenkins, his so-called brief, would be in there. And so he was.

Tony went straight up to him, picked up a pint of lager from the table and tipped it over Danny's head. 'Start watching your back, Danny,' he said and walked out. No one said a thing.

Tony kept on going, into town, pleased that he could at least tick off item one from the checklist of things to do he'd built up over a year inside. And putting the fear of God into Danny Jenkins had had to be near the top. It was the principle of the thing. It wasn't that he'd expected Danny to get him off. God knows, he'd been caught bang to rights. But he'd thought a suspended wasn't out of the question, and if Danny had done the bare minimum – like showing up in court on time – then he might just have got that. Instead he ended up drawing two years, serving one.

A year, it was a weird length, just long enough for everything to change but not long enough for anything to look different. Walking into town now, it was like he'd never been away, and yet he knew nothing would be the same. He walked into a club, it wouldn't be the right club. He went to buy some new trainers, he wouldn't be sure which were the right ones. He went back to see his woman, he didn't know if she'd have him.

Tyra hadn't come to see him once while he'd been inside. She'd let his auntie come with the kids, she wasn't that heartless. But she had not been to see him once. It was his fault, of course; he'd broken something in her – in them – when he did the last stupid thing. After all the never evers he'd given her, all the times he'd promised no more bad-man business. And still he'd gone into the bookie's with his cousin. Billy waving a replica around like they were the sodding James Gang.

In no time he was at the corner of Bute Street. Question of whether to head on under the bridge, or into town. There was no reason to be in town, just the chance to be in a place full of people walking where they wanted, buying what they wanted, a place full of stuff. Not prison.

He decided it would probably just depress him, to be surrounded by citizens, so he took a deep breath and headed south under the bridge, to Butetown.

He was just passing the Custom House when out came a bloke, a hard, young bloke, and nearly bumped into him. Tony was ready in an instant. Bumping into people in prison was something you didn't do lightly. Then the guy spun and was halfway through saying sorry, boss, when they recognised each other. It was Mark, another of Tony's endless supply of cousins.

' 'Kin' 'ell, blood, you're out,' he said, clasping Tony's hand. 'You told Auntie Pearl?'

'No,' said Tony, 'thought I'd surprise her, like. Otherwise she'd have been down the prison waiting for me.'

Mark shook his head. 'Yeah, well.' Then he nodded towards the open door of the Custom House. 'Buy you a drink, bra?'

Tony shrugged. Why not, it had been a year since his last one. It wasn't that you couldn't get a drink inside, but he'd gone on a health kick the minute they banged him up. Just made it worse getting pissed inside.

They stood at the bar drinking bottles of Pils. There were just a handful of girls sitting inside, mostly the ones who were too old to make much of a go on the street, in the broad daylight anyway, just hung about in the Custom House for the company. Bobby was on the pool table as per. Some places, time really did seem to stand still.

'Like the new image,' said Mark.

Tony looked at himself in the mirror behind the bar. He'd lost a bit of excess weight while he'd been inside, his five-foot-ten frame looked lean and hard. He'd cropped his hair back to the bone and grown a little goatee, part of the Muslim kick. He hadn't gone for it all the way, but it was another thing to keep you sane inside. Still, seeing his reflection staring back at him, he was surprised to realise what a serious bastard he looked, 'specially wearing his suit, just needed a pair of little round glasses to complete the picture.

'So,' said Tony, after a little while, 'you seen Tyra?' He did his best to make it sound casual, but it obviously wasn't and Mark took a second before replying.

'Yeah, I seen her around. Picking up the kids from school, down the shop, them kind of places. She don't want much to do with me, though.'

Tony nodded; that figured.

'She's not been out clubbing or anything,' Mark went on. 'She's straight, your missis.'

Tony nodded again. That's why he didn't believe what he'd heard inside. He knew it was none of his business what she did anyway, way he'd let her down. But still he knew Tyra and he reckoned she'd wait till he was out before she started seeing anyone else. She liked things to be in the open. That was why he didn't believe what he'd heard about her and Mikey having a little scene. Fucking Mikey, he wouldn't put it past him to come sniffing round her yard, that's the way he was. Mate or not didn't mean nothing to Mikey, he thought he might get in there. But he couldn't see Tyra going for the little bastard.

'Least she's not been in here,' said Mark, and Tony wished he'd leave it alone. Of course Tyra wouldn't have been in the Custom House, she wasn't a hustler. It was time to move on, see what kind of a life he had left. He clashed fists with Mark and headed back out into the thin lunchtime sun.

Time to get it over with, go see Auntie Pearl. Auntie Pearl was his dad's sister and he'd lived with her after his mum had pissed off, back when he was ten. Twenty-three years ago now. They'd moved her into one of the new houses, right down in the docks past Techniquest, a good couple of years before he went inside, but it still felt odd to him, seeing her there.

She was thrilled to see him, of course, and he settled in and spent the afternoon, let her cook for him, put up with the stream of neighbours popping by to welcome him home. Relished them, really, because it meant that it was nearly six before there was a temporary lull and they were alone together, so Pearl could give him the third degree.

'I don't know,' he kept saying as Pearl asked him what he was going to do about Tyra. 'You don't know what she's like.'

Pearl was old-school stand by your man. Your man went to prison, you shrugged and cursed and got on with it and praised the lord when he came back out. You didn't bar the door to him. 'Go on,' she said, 'just go round there and ring on the door. The kids see you, she'll never throw you out.'

Christ, but old people were ruthless. 'No,' he said, 'I can't do that to her. She wants me back, I'll be back, I'm not going to force her. I'll see her tomorrow, when the kids are in school.'

'You stay here tonight?'

'Yes, Pearl,' he said, 'thanks,' and he got up, went over and hugged the old lady. It was a shock to realise it, but Pearl really was getting old now. 'I'll take a walk out now. Go see a few of the boys.'

'Oh,' she said, just as he was leaving, 'your cousin Billy called this afternoon. Wants you to call him back.' She paused a moment. 'You going to call him?'

Tony shook his head. 'Got nothing to say to him, Pearl.'

Pearl nodded and smiled, pleased.

Tony headed back up to James Street, thinking he might call in on Col, see what was happening. He cut up West Bute Street and then came to a stop outside Black Caesar's. He was meaning to have a look in the window of Kenny's clothes shop, and was staggered to see it had turned into a Nation of Islam mosque.

There'd been a lot of it about inside, a lot of the London brothers in particular, guys he'd hung around with when they'd had him down in Dartmoor for a while, they were well into it. But Kenny starting up a mosque, that was a career move and a half. Assuming this was Kenny's place, of course. The shop part at the front was closed but there was a light on out back so Tony leant on the bell for a little while. A minute later, there was Kenny himself, bigger than life as ever. Thing was, the moment Kenny caught sight of him, Tony could see his face tighten for a second. But then he opened the door and it was all how's it going, bra, when d'you get out?

After a moment Kenny stood back and looked at Tony. 'So, you checking the Nation of Islam?'

Tony gave a half-assenting shrug, and Kenny ushered him into the building. Showed him round the mosque which, to be honest, looked about three-quarters finished. Then they headed upstairs to the club, Kenny flicked a couple of lights on, brought a couple of beers from behind the bar and started boxing up a spliff.

'So, Ken, you got a lot of the boys coming down your mosque?'

Kenny shook his head. 'Long story, bra, long story. Thing is, I've got the mosque but we need a preacher.' The big man spluttered with laughter. 'You won't believe who we had try out preaching.'

Tony waited for the punchline.

'Mikey,' said Kenny, 'fucking Mikey Thompson. And, fair play to him, he gave it his best shot.' Then Kenny's mood seemed to darken. 'You seen your cousin?' he asked Tony.

'Which one?'

'Billy.'

Tony shook his head but Kenny carried on. 'I don't know what you've heard, but Billy's been a long way out of order.'

Tony raised his hands. 'Kenny, leave it. I don't want to know. I don't want to know anything about Billy. Last time I saw the cunt, I ended up in prison.' The irony of the thing was that, though the whole stupid business had been Billy's idea from start to finish, and though it had been Billy waving the damn replica around, it was Tony had ended up doing the time. Billy had walked 'cause some stupid fucking copper had compromised the identification. His witness, on the stand no less, had mentioned she'd had no trouble picking out Billy after the nice copper showed her his photo beforehand, 'just to jog my memory'. Far as Tony was concerned, though, Kenny could do what he liked with Billy.

Kenny leant forward, handed Tony the spliff.

'Safe,' said Tony, and the two of them sat there for another hour or so, talking about when they were kids. They were the same age, Kenny and Tony, and they'd played rugby together on the school team for a while – Kenny at centre, Tony at fly half – before Kenny got too good and went to play for Cardiff boys, and Tony got keener on chasing girls than standing round in the middle of a freezing bloody park, waiting to be clattered by some valleys retard as wide as he was high. Christ, it all seemed a long time ago now. And by the time they were eighteen, they'd both fucked up big time: Kenny had already been inside, and Tony had three kids by two different girls and was well into the hustling life.

Funny how they'd gone along in parallel, though: back then they'd both had dreadlocks, and now they were both wandering around looking like Malcolm X.

'Michael X,' said Tony, out of nowhere.

'Malcolm, you tosser,' said Kenny.

'No, no, there was a guy called Michael as well,' said

Tony. 'Trinidad fella, he was, like, the first British black Muslim.'

'Yeah?'

'Yeah, my dad knew him. He was on the boats, used to stay here sometimes.'

'Fuck,' said Kenny, and was quiet for a moment. 'What d'you reckon, I call it the Michael X Mosque?'

'Nice,' said Tony. 'Nice.'

Just then there was another blast on the bell and Kenny walked off to return a minute later with a middle-aged white guy.

'Tony,' he said, 'this is Bernie Walters.'

The guy stuck his hand out and Tony stood up to shake. He was one of those well-preserved specimens, looked fifty but was probably a good sixty, with a perma tan and a lot of gold, round his neck, on his fingers, though the sharp blue suit was classier than the rest of him.

Thing was, though, you looked hard at Bernie Walters and the word 'bent' came fast back at you. Tony decided to leave them to it. 'Ta for the drink, Ken,' he said, and Kenny just waved, already busy talking to Walters. Something to do with hiring exotic dancers for the lunchtime trade. Tony wasn't sure what Walters's involvement was; the last words he heard him say were, 'Not like the old days, Ken, remember the girl with the snake?'

Tony walked out, holding a laugh back. The girl with the snake had to be his Auntie Deandra. She'd been something else when he was a kid. Been an extra in Tiger Bay when she was just a kid herself and showbiz had certainly got in the blood. Times he remembered seeing her, she was always wearing a fur coat, and he had thought she was a film star. But there was shame and scandal in the family, he remembered that. Long time till he found out why. The original exotic dancer – Deandra and the snake. Christ.

Out on the street, he realised he'd been longer than he thought in Black Caesar's, it was getting on for nine now. He hurried round to Col's place but there was no one in. He carried on to the Paddle and it was deader than ever, just a handful of old-timers watching TV; he ducked out again before any of them could collar him, and wondered where to go next. He was just heading down Angelina Street, thinking to give Mikey a call, when he realised he was passing Mandy's place.

On the spur of the moment, he rang on the bell and seconds later there she was, her dark-blonde hair dragged back from her forehead and held in a ponytail, looking trim as ever, never an extra pound on her. He remembered when she was a kid she was always winning the long-distance running prizes.

'Christ,' she said, 'look what the cat dragged in.' Then she got up on tiptoe and threw her arms round him.

'You seen Pearl yet?' she said after a moment.

Why did everyone keep asking him that? 'Yeah,' he said, 'I just escaped now.'

They laughed together. That was their bond. Pearl had taken them both in as kids, Tony as a ten-year-old after his mum left and his dad couldn't cope with him on his own. Then Mandy a couple of years later, after her dad fucked off wherever it was he fucked off to and her mum went to pieces. So she'd been like a kid sister to him for a time.

Sitting down in the front room, he played with the two little girls, Emma and Brittany, for a while before Mandy packed them off to bed.

Mandy boxed a draw then and Tony lay back on the sofa, his eyes idly resting on *Friends* on the TV, savouring the sensation of not being in prison.

'How's your love life then, Mand?' he asked eventually.

Mandy made a face. 'Don't ask,' she said, and then, before Tony had more than an instant in which not to ask, she told him anyway. 'You won't believe who I had a scene with, Tone.'

Tony raised his eyebrows obligingly.

'Only Jim Fairfax, you remember Jimmy?'

'You talking about the Jimmy Fairfax that's in the police?'

Mandy nodded.

'Fuckin' hell, Neville must have been pleased.'

'That's what I thought, Tone. I was busy running round trying to hide it – turns out Neville and Jimmy are best fucking mates, you know what I mean. Doing a little bit of business.'

Tony whistled, shook his head.

'I'm sick of it, Tone. You know what I'd like, one time in my life, see some bloke you don't spend your whole time wondering when the police are going to come round middle of the night, kick your door in.'

She broke off. Tony had put his hands in the air. 'Ah, sorry, Tone,' she said. 'How'd it go this time, anyway?'

'No,' he said, 'you're right, I've had enough of it and all.'

'Yeah, well,' said Mandy, and fetched a couple of cans of Coke from the fridge. They sat for a while in amiable silence watching one of those American sitcoms where some glamorous blonde runs around pretending her life's in a mess when it obviously isn't.

Next thing Tony knew, it must have been about midnight.

He woke up from a vivid dream about being back in prison and felt a sense of exquisite joy to find himself lying on Mandy's sofa with a blanket over him. The TV was still on but Mandy didn't seem to be watching it. She had her nose in a library book, one of those old-time tales of plucky mill girls and orphan boys.

He watched her for a moment, his eyes just barely open, then stretched and sat up and said, 'Mand, did Pearl ever tell you where my mum went?'

'No,' said Mandy, 'don't think I ever heard her say anything 'bout your mum, except to curse her now and again. Didn't she run away to be a big star?'

Tony reached over for his can of Coke, swirled it around a bit before taking a sip, and then said, 'Yeah, something like that.'

'What was her name?'

'Fatima.'

'No, her singing name.'

'April,' said Tony after a while, 'April Angel. Stupid, yeah?'

'No,' said Mandy, 'I think it sounds good.' Then she went quiet a moment before saying, 'Tell you what, Tone, I've an idea who might know something.'

'Who?'

'This bloke runs clubs, he's been running clubs for ever. He's going partners with Kenny Ibadulla, doing up the Casablanca.'

'Oh yeah, what's his name?'

'Bernie. Bernie Walters.'

'Shit, I seen him today.'

'How come?'

'I was round Caesar's with Kenny. Bloke with a lot of rope,

looks like he lives under a sunbed, comes in. That's the guy, yeah?'

Mandy nodded.

'So what's he want with the Casa?'

'Want to open it up again, put bands on and stuff, get the students down.'

'So what's he want with Kenny?'

'Well, Kenny's the man, case you hadn't noticed. He does all right with Caesar's, and I suppose Bernie needs him for security and that, saves paying him to do it, anyway Kenny comes in as a partner.'

Tony nodded. That made sense. It had been one of Kenny's main rackets for years, charging anyone opened up down the docks for a bit of security. Security from Kenny mostly. Few of the boys didn't mind causing a little trouble, Kenny asked them to nicely, like. So, yeah, he could see it made sense, bring Kenny in the front door for a change, save him knocking your back door down with a baseball bat.

'And this Bernie, how d'you know him?'

'DJing. Been playing records one of his clubs in town, the Los Angeles. Been playing out there every Thursday. You should come down, like, few of the boys, show up most nights. But, Tone, what's this about your mum anyway?'

'Nah, nothing, Mand, just prison bollocks. Too much time staring at the wall.'

'What, you been thinking 'bout trying to contact her?'

'No,' said Tony. 'Leave it, Mand, really.'

'All right,' she said. 'Still, tell you what, tomorrow night there's going to be special benefit night down the Casa, they're opening up for one night only, some kind of charity thing before they open it up proper next month. I'll be playing there, and Delroy, and there's some guys meant to be coming down from London. And Bernie'll be there. Got to be there, Tony. Back on the scene.'

'Maybe I have, Mand, or maybe I don't.'

'What's that supposed to mean?'

'Wish I knew, Mand. Wish I knew.' And, with that, Tony, his mood suddenly plummeting, got up and headed back to Aunt Pearl's. He hesitated for a moment outside Caesar's, then thought sod it, he'd see everyone tomorrow.

Next morning was a blow-out. He'd been planning to go over to see Tyra while the kids were at school, but like a twat he'd forgotten it was a Saturday, so he belled her instead and it was like talking to an iceberg. I'm out, he'd said, like she might be pleased. I know, she'd said, and it had gone downhill from there. Eventually she said he could come round Monday morning, like it was some big favour.

He didn't even dare ask about the kids, and after he put the phone down he just sat there for a while in Auntie Pearl's front room, grateful that the old lady had gone off up town shopping, sat there doing his very best to think of nothing at all.

Then he shook himself out of it and picked up the phone again. Called Mikey at home and got Tina, who was in a decent mood for once, gave him a mobile number. Couple of tries and he got Mikey himself, sounding like he was talking from the middle of a building site. And he wasn't sure whether it was the line or not, but he could have sworn he heard a note of fear in Mikey's voice when he realised it was Tony. Anyway, Mikey said he'd see him down the Ship about one.

Tony was halfway through his first pint when Mikey showed up, which was par for the course.

'How's it going, bra?' said Mikey, sitting himself down, no sign of the nervousness Tony thought he'd detected over the phone. 'Christ, you turned into a Jehovah's Witness or what?'

Tony laughed: for some reason he'd put a suit on again today. He'd just stared at the pile of Nike stuff lying in his room round at Pearl's and it had suddenly struck him that all that wasn't him any more. Walking round advertising some Babylonian corporation. So he'd suited up.

'Yeah, well,' he said, 'I hear you've turned preacher and all, Mikey.'

'One time, bra, one time only, and only that time 'cause Kenny would have ripped my throat out I said no. Never felt such a twat in my whole life. You hear about what happened?'

Tony nodded.

Mikey laughed. 'You should have seen Kenny's face, man, he realised those Brummies had put that one over him. Thought he was going to explode.' Then Mikey's tone changed. 'You've heard about your cousin?'

Tony shook his head.

'Your cousin Billy, he's heading for a war with Kenny, and Kenny's been so pissed off since then, he's most likely going to give him one.'

'What?'

'Yeah. Billy's started thinking he's Mister Untouchable ever since he got off that bookie's thing with you – reckons he can get away with anything if he can get away with waving a shooter in a bookie's.'

'Fake shooter,' said Tony.

'Yeah, well, ever since then he reckons he's the ranking don in person. You hear about him waving a shooter around in the street some other Birmingham crew came down?'

'I haven't heard nothing, Mikey. I've been inside, you hadn't noticed.'

'Yeah, well, being inside doesn't mean you don't hear things.'

There was a sudden silence, as Tony recalled what he had heard inside. Tyra and Mikey. He still didn't believe it, but the little man was looking mighty shifty again.

'So where've you been this morning?' asked Tony, by way of changing the subject.

'Nowhere much, just a little bit of work for Kenny getting the Casa ready for tonight. You hear about tonight?'

'Yeah.'

'Coming down?'

'Yeah.'

'Cool, bra,' said Mikey, standing up, 'I'll check you later then.' Then, as he was leaving, he turned and added, 'You know Billy's put the word out. Wants you to get in touch. Urgent, like.'

'Yeah, yeah,' said Tony.

Tony sat there for a while longer. Momentarily he felt at a complete and utter loss. The world had been spinning for a full year while he had been staring at the walls and doing push-ups on the floor, and now the speed of the spin was too much. He'd been here before, of course. This had been the fourth time he'd been inside. Fucking good thing he wasn't in California or they'd have thrown away the key. 'Course, they'd been in California, cousin Billy would have been waving a real shooter and . . .

And it didn't bear thinking about. But he had to think about Billy. Had to find out what kind of war Billy was planning with Kenny before he got caught in the middle of it.

And it might as well be now, he thought, fuck all else to do Saturday afternoon, every other bastard out shopping with the missis. Good a time as any for a trip out to Ely. Billy would be in, he was sure; Billy wasn't the shopping type. Leastways, not unless he was carrying a sawed-off.

Out of the pub, Tony decided to walk to the bus station. Passed Kenny's mosque on the way. The shop was open this time and a fit-looking sister inside reading something called *Men Are From Mars*. She looked up and waved when she saw Tony, and Tony waved back but didn't go in, seemed like his motor wasn't running yet. Instead he studied a notice pinned to the window, promising a meeting two p.m. tomorrow, Sunday, with Cyrus talking about Black Men and Nature: the Hidden Truth.

It started to rain, a sudden quick shower, as he walked down Bute Street. Suited Tony fine, meant every old biddy with nothing better to do didn't stop and talk to him and make him promise to never do anything bad again 'less he wanted to see Auntie Pearl in her grave. That, and it was just a pleasure to be out in the weather, feel the rain on your face.

Bus station, he picked up a *Mirror* and sat on the bus reading the football pages while he waited for it to get moving. Twenty minutes later, the bus dumped him on Cowbridge Road, just opposite the big snooker club, and he walked up on to Grand Avenue. Christ, there was something so fucking depressing about Ely. The houses were all grey pebbledash, and way it was stuck up on the hillside made the wind whip though it like a buzzsaw. About two shops in the whole place, shopkeepers behind full-length security grilles, and everywhere you looked bored youth just checking for something or someone to do. He was just coming up to Billy's place, right on Grand Avenue, and a couple of kids, couldn't have been more than eighteen, stared at him.

'Oi, cunt,' the fat one said. And was about to follow up when Tony turned into Billy's yard.

'Oh sorry, mate,' the porker said then. 'Didn't know you were –'

'Were what?'

'Friend of Billy's.'

Tony didn't say anything, just gave them the old prison stare. Christ, it was worrying, though, little twats like that didn't give you any respect. Then he looked down at himself, kept forgetting he was wearing a suit.

Tony knocked on the door and Billy's woman, Stacey, opened up. She was a washed-out-looking blonde; Tony knew for a fact she couldn't be more than twenty-five, but she'd have passed for forty any day. What living with Billy Pinto did for you.

Billy was in the front room watching Sky Sports with the curtains drawn, Simply Red playing on the sound system.

He half turned at the sound of a newcomer, then leapt up when he saw who it was.

Billy gave the situation all the necessary. How sorry he was it had all screwed up, how it should have been Tony got off and not him, blah, blah, blah. Tony felt like he'd floated out of his body and was just up there on the ceiling, watching this go on.

'Want one of these?' said Billy after a bit, pointing at a pile of boxed PlayStations in the corner of the room. 'Go on, bra, take one.'

Tony shook his head. Billy looked at him bemused, suddenly registering Tony's suit.

'Whassup, Tone, you gone Muslim? Allah told you fucking computer games are no good for the soul?'

'Billy,' said Tony, suddenly tired, 'what's happening with you and Kenny?'

Billy stepped back, all trace of the geniality gone now. Actually, Tony preferred him that way. He'd known his cousin was a psycho since they were kids, and he'd always hated dealing with nice-guy Billy 'cause you spent the whole time waiting for bad-boy Billy to come out. Least once he was like that you knew where you were.

'Who you been talking to, Tone?' he asked now.

'Kenny.'

'Fuck you talking to Kenny for?'

'He's my mate, butt, been my mate since we were kids. Been your mate too. Last thing I knew, before I went down the bookie's for a year, you were still mates. I comes out. I walks past his mosque, which is another thing I'm not expecting, and I sees Kenny, and he calls me in, boxes a draw and we talk about this and that. He says you're going to war with him. And now I comes here to find out what's going on before you dump me in it again.'

Billy stared at Tony. 'Money, Tone, money. What d'you think it's about? Kenny's had it all his own way too long. Just 'cause he's big he thinks he's bad, and all the other clowns follow along behind him. Kenny tells them to walk like an Egyptian, they'll all be wearing fezzes, you know what I mean. And it's like there's a ton of gear coming through Cardiff at the moment; the boat comes in from Trinidad, there's more fucking Charlie than bananas on it, like.

'And it's time someone else got a piece of the action. Load of the stuff goes straight up to London. Some firm comes down, sorts it out, it's all locked down tight. But there's enough other shit around, and I'm sick of buying it all off Kenny. I've got the business round here,' he waved out the window, 'Kenny knows that, but long as I'm buying off him he's laughing anyway. Time Kenny moved over, let someone else have a share.'

'And how are you going to do that? Kenny got a lot of boys he can call on. Who you got?'

'Got a few boys up here, don't mind getting stuck in. Got some friends up Birmingham interested in making a deal, guys don't like Kenny one little bit. There's a boat coming in next week. Wednesday night. That's when it's going to happen, Tone. That's when I'm going to let Kenny know the rules have changed. And now I've got my cousin Tony, back out of prison. Only brer I ever seen Kenny back off a fight with.'

'That's 'cause I had a knife and he didn't.'

'Wouldn't stop Kenny most times, most people don't know how to use a blade, Tone.'

'Yeah, well, that's not me any more.'

Tony turned away as Billy shot him a sour look. 'Oh sorry, Tone, forgot you'd turned into Louis fucking Farrakhan since you been inside.'

'Anyway, what I hear, Kenny's going legit. This club business and all. Taking over the Casa. You heard about this business guy he's going in with?'

'Who's that?'

'Bloke name Bernie Walters.'

'Bernie Walters,' said Billy slowly, his eyes narrowing. 'I heard that name.'

'Yeah, well, he's supposed to own some club up town.'

'No, that's not it. It was a long time ago. Bernie Walters. Something my mum told me. He's an old guy, yeah?'

'Yeah,' said Tony. 'Anyway, forget Bernie Walters, Billy, and forget hauling me into your thing with Kenny. You want to play ranking gangsters with big Ken, go on. Just leave me out.'

'Yeah.'

'Yeah,' said Tony, and got up to go.

As he was leaving, Billy shouted after him, 'I'll be seeing you, Tone. Ask your missis. Ask your missis what Kenny made her do. Then tell me you're staying out of it. Wednesday night, Tone. Wednesday night.'

Tony kept on walking, like he never heard a word.

Tony made it to the Casablanca around midnight. He'd come out of Billy's house with his head reeling, just thinking it was time to get out of Cardiff, to get out of his life. And then his mind started running round in circles. Sure he could get out of Cardiff, 'cept he'd have to leave his woman, leave the kids, leave Auntie Pearl. And of course he could go up to London and stay with some of the friends he'd made inside. Friends he'd made inside — he repeated that to himself, letting the implications sink in. Yeah, he could go up to London and find himself in the same gangster business he was running away from down here. Fucking Billy, fucking Kenny, why couldn't people just let you live your life? He was seriously thinking of going to work on the boats by the time he got back to Auntie Pearl's.

He'd gone out that evening in a filthy bloody mood, but the strange thing was he'd been having a really good time. Played some pool in the Avondale with a few of the boys. Little drink, little smoke, and Tony was feeling just nicely blocked up as he walked into the Casa.

The Casablanca was an old church down in Mount Stuart Square, right in the heart of the docks' business district. It had been a dancehall as long as Tony could remember, except for being closed the last five years or so.

Walking in the door, it was like a violent attack of déjà vu. Here was Mikey on the door, done up in his tux the way he always used to, looking like that little bloke from the Stylistics. Standing in the lobby talking to Mikey, who looked a lot more chipper than he had done at lunchtime, he could have sworn he heard some serious dub playing inside. Remembered different times, the late seventies, early eighties, him and Mikey and Kenny and Billy and all the rest, just kids all of them, trying to grow locks. Mikey had the best; later on he had them piled up high in a tam, made him look taller. Reckoned that was a lot of the charm of Rastafari for Mikey – big hair and a staff and all the draw you could take. Dancing with Tyra to lovers' tunes. 'Caught You In a Lie.'

Where did the time go? He shook his head. He knew it was all bullshit; there never were any good old days. Pushed open the door into the main hall and came sharply back into the present. Hardstep drum and bass all the way. Room full of kids like he used to be, youth trying to look tough, girls trying to look tough and sweet at the same time.

Trouble with this hardstep shit, Tony thought, was you couldn't dance to it. All you could do was pose to it. Sounded all right – in fact sounded great – in the car, driving round with the big bass speakers making the whole motor shake and old ladies cover their ears. But in a club on a Saturday night, you wanted something a little sweeter.

'All right, Tone,' said a voice at his ear. Mandy. 'Tyra not coming down with you?'

He bent down, shouted in her ear, 'No, haven't seen her yet.'

Mandy mimed disappointment, then pointed over at the decks. 'Time I did some work. Later on, Tony.'

He nodded, walked over to the bar, where the sound was a little less ear-splitting. Col was there, and he and Tony clashed fists and bullshitted around a little, talking about the Glastonbury Wars.

The Glastonbury Festival for years had been like Christmas to the Butetown boys. You could sell whatever you could get your hands on to the million students in the mud. By the end of the weekend you'd be selling aspirins, Beechams Powders, bags of toffees, anything you could lay your hands on looked remotely like a controlled substance. Or at least looked like one to someone who'd spent the last three days discovering whether scrumpy and acid really are the perfect match.

First few years it had been great, they'd had the place virtually to themselves. Lately it had got like strategic warfare. Crews from all over the country were trying to get in on the action, people turning up days beforehand staking out their territory, shooters everywhere. Free-market economics and no mistake.

After a while Col headed off into a corner to do a little bit of business and Tony drifted back into the main hall. The mood had got mellower since Mandy took over the decks, mixing in some deep house and garage with a little swing to keep the girls happy. She caught Tony's eye as he walked across the floor; he nodded back, noticing a little jolt of excitement that went through him at her smile. Just then he caught sight of Kenny heading towards the backstage area. Tony raised an arm and Kenny waved him over. Made a follow-me sign and headed backstage.

There was nothing much there, a shambolic space full of bits of old speakers and similar crap, a little bathroom cum dressing-room over in the corner and a table at the back. Sitting at the table were Bernie Walters and another white guy, a heavy-set thirtyish type in a suit, looked like he might be ex-army. Respectable-looking type, but respectable muscle is still muscle and that's what this guy was, you could see it a mile off. 'Come on, Tone,' said Kenny, 'say hello to the gents.'

'Bernie,' he said, 'this is Tony Pinto, feller I was telling you about, said hello to you in Caesar's yesterday.'

Tony nodded like an idiot, as if he was confirming his own existence. Christ, he was thinking, was that only yesterday?

'Good to meet you again, son,' said Bernie, standing up to shake Tony's hand. 'Been hearing good things about you from Ken here.'

Tony nodded again, his mind racing through a fog of drink and smoke, wondering what the hell this was all about.

'Tell you what,' said Bernie, seemingly impervious to Tony's silence, 'here's my card. How about you come and have lunch with me Monday? I've got a proposal you might be interested in. One o'clock OK?'

Tony stayed silent for a moment longer. This simply wasn't how things were done in his world. People didn't make lunch appointments with you. Still, God knows he had nothing to lose. 'All right,' he said.

'Good,' said Bernie, 'I'll see you then,' and then he turned and started talking to Kenny. After a moment Tony realised he'd been dismissed and headed back into the dancehall.

Delroy was at the controls now and Tony saw that the crowd had changed. There seemed to be fewer young people around and more of the old crew. Delroy was pumping out classic funk tunes. The big synth bass of 'Just Be Good to Me' boomed out and Mandy was there tapping him on the arm. 'Fancy a dance then?'

Suddenly it was three in the morning and Tony was walking out of the Casablanca, with Mandy, walking her home. But the weather had cleared and it was a glorious spring night, and instead they headed down to the waterfront, through the midst of the bay development. Stood together for a while by the Norwegian church talking about the way it had all been when they were kids. The places that weren't there any more and the things that had replaced them. The usual nostalgic shit. At one point they had their heads right together leaning over the sea wall and Tony felt the urge to kiss her but he pulled back. Like a sister to him, that kind of feeling. Thing people always said when they meant they didn't fancy someone, but this time it was true.

Tony slept right through to lunchtime. Woke up momentarily at half six, opened his eyes for long enough to register he wasn't in prison any more, and shut them again. Next thing he knew, it was half one and he could hear Auntie Pearl and a couple of the church ladies having lunch in the next room.

They were still there when he emerged half an hour later, wearing the grey suit he'd bought for Tyra's sister's wedding. Nice suit but he'd hardly worn it since. It was becoming a thing for him, though, he realised, not to get back into the sports. Wasn't the way he wanted to be any more. What was, though? That was the question.

The old ladies were thrilled, of course, started talking about the old days, you never saw a man except in a suit. He sat down with them for a while, ate some rice and peas, then, when he could stand it no longer, he remembered something. 'See you later, ladies,' he said, 'I've got a meeting to go to.'

There were half a dozen people inside the mosque when he got there, waiting for Cyrus's talk. A couple of old dreads, Clyde and Paulie, Twelve Tribes brethren. Tony wasn't sure whether they were checking out the competition or what. A couple of younger guys, maybe he'd seen them around, he wasn't sure; they both looked keen, one of them had brought his girlfriend, who looked anything but. And there in the corner, talking to Cyrus himself, was Col. Tony raised his fist in greeting but didn't go over. Cyrus was one of those people you didn't want to get stuck with. He was an older bloke; hard to say how old but he'd known Tony's dad and he'd been the first person Tony remembered seeing around with locks. Weird thing was he'd always tell you he wasn't a Rastafarian, some kind of mutant Christian instead. Anyway, he was always wandering round the pubs testifying about this and that and he was all right, but you had to be in the mood for him.

Still, he was taking the lecture seriously. Three o'clock precisely, he closed the door, moved to the front of the room, stepped up behind the lectern – Tony couldn't help laughing at the thought of Kenny shopping around for a lectern – and started talking. Black men and nature was his subject and it was one he rapidly warmed to.

Tony'd heard it all before, but he didn't mind; there was something relaxing about listening to the old dread explain that black men were essentially a higher, more physically evolved species than white men, a point illustrated by the potent comparison between the achievements of Butetown's own world-beating Colin Jackson and those of the entire Welsh rugby team. The scientific rationale for this revolved around an extra gland found in black men but not white men, Cyrus explained.

Tony couldn't help wondering what that meant for most of the people in Butetown who, like him, were mixed race. He didn't have to wait long for an answer, though; Cyrus had clearly been asked this enough times. 'The white gene is a recessive gene,' he boomed. 'If black and white mix, the black wins out. Nah true?'

All present were happy enough to say amen to that, and Cyrus moved on to the second part of his thesis, which was that black men were not just better fitted out by nature but also had a closer relationship to nature. Whole thing built up to the usual exhortation to return to Africa and farm the ancestral soil, and Tony smiled and nodded and drifted away under the influence of Col's wickedly strong homegrown. He was transported to his kitchen back when he was a kid, listening to his dad and his mates sit around with a few bottles of the Export Guinness, the Nigerian stuff, setting the world to rights.

Seemed like a different life, thinking about it now: that kid, a lanky ten-year-old who played rugby, for Christ's sake, a different kid. His mum – still there. His dad – still alive.

Wandering off after the meeting, he found himself thinking about his mum again. Trying to figure out what the hell happened. A woman walks out one day, never comes back. The weird thing, thinking about it now, was that he'd never asked where she went. No one talked about her at all. His dad and Auntie Pearl, they'd done it on purpose, he supposed; had the idea it was best not to talk about her.

Before long he found himself back at Mandy's place. She was there with a friend, girl named Gail, four kids running round the house causing mayhem. Mandy was pleased to see him, though, and they ended up taking the kids out for a little walk down the playground. It was the wrong thing to do, really. Seeing Mandy was good, but playing with other people's kids just brought it home how much he'd thrown away. And he didn't stay long, headed back to Auntie Pearl and an evening watching TV, little glass of rum before bedtime. Billy called a couple of times but Pearl told him Tony was out. Apparently he'd been calling all day.

Next morning he was round to Tyra's by ten. She opened the door, looked at him, her expression giving nothing away, and ushered him into her front room – *their* front room last time he'd been in it. He just stood there looking round, staring at the children's toys scattered around the place, and suddenly Tyra came to him, pulled him to her, threw her arms around his neck. And they stood there hugging for what seemed like minutes. Then she broke off and without a word headed for the bathroom. He waited five minutes – he was watching the clock this time – and she came out, and he sensed the difference immediately. Pure chill was radiating at him now. They sat down, him on the sofa, her on the chair.

'What are you going to do now, Tony?' she asked. 'Go see cousin Billy, see if he's got another little job for you?'

'No,' he said, 'I . . .'

'You what? You're going to stop messing about the gangster business, come back here, be a real dad to your kids? You going to get a job? You wouldn't know where to start. You know where the job centre is, Tony? You goes into town, it's on Charles Street, big fucking orange place. You goes in there, they gives you a job working in the petrol station, two fifty an hour. 'Cept they won't let you do it 'cause they'd think you'd rip off the fucking till. And they'd be right.'

Tony just sat there, his head bowed, taking it. He knew what other people would do, what they'd say. Tell him to give her a slap. Not just men, that's what women told you too. Don't take that shit, give her a smack. Got to make her respect you. What his dad believed, all right. Shit, something he didn't want to think about snagged on the corner of his mind and receded again. Whatever, it wasn't him; he couldn't lay a finger on Tyra. He didn't feel good about it, knew he'd hurt her already worse than any slap. So he just sat there taking it.

'Look at you,' she said. 'You comes in here wearing a suit. You know the last man came round here wearing a damn suit?'

Tony shook his head.

'A fucking bailiff, that's who it was. He was going to take the TV, the video right under the kids' faces.'

'What d'you do?' asked Tony.

'I called my man, didn't I? 'Cept he was in Dartmoor. What d'you think I did? Asked the man how much, then I called Kenny. Kenny comes round, gives the guy two hundred. And then I owed Kenny. Then I owed fucking Kenny.'

She lost it then, threw herself across the room at Tony, started hitting him, drumming her fists on his chest. Then, just as suddenly, she stopped, went to the bathroom again, this time for no more than a minute. She didn't sit down again when she came out.

'Just go now,' she said. And Tony, feeling numb, just stood up, straightened his jacket.

He looked straight at Tyra for a moment, thought about saying something like I'm sorry and rejected it, thinking it sounded pathetic. Instead he just headed for the door.

'Don't you want to see your kids, then?'

Tony turned and looked at her again. He still couldn't make any words come out. Finally he managed to make himself nod.

'All right,' she said, 'I'll bring 'em round your auntie's, tomorrow after school.'

Walking away, Tony felt a sudden wave of anger, an onrush of how-dare-the-bitch-talk-to-me-like-that fury. And, just as suddenly, that too receded, to be replaced by something too near to despair for Tony to want to look at it too closely. Instead he concentrated on putting one foot in front of the other, heading back to Auntie Pearl's until he remembered he had a lunch appointment.

Bernie Walters's office turned out to be right in the middle of town, the top end of St Mary Street, one of the big old Gothic buildings there. Downstairs was a coffee importer's. Bernie's office was on the first floor. Seemed like a pretty minimal operation to Tony: a secretary in the front office, a couple of accountant types in the middle office, then Bernie himself in a great big office looking out over the street. Bernie was putting his coat on as Tony entered.

'You're late, son.'

Tony shrugged, like he could care less, morning he'd had. Anyway, he'd seen the time in the secretary's office. Ten past. Guy should see late some time.

'You asks me to come here, I'm here. You wants me to go, I'll go.'

'No,' said Bernie, shaking his head. 'Sorry, son, just been one of those days so far. Let's go and eat.'

They walked together up to the top of St Mary Street and round the corner to the little strip where a bunch of restaurants had started putting tables outside on the pavement. Bernie bypassed the first couple of places, then turned into the next one, some kind of Italian joint. Tony followed him in, watched as Bernie went through a backslapping routine with the guy with the are–you–serious Italian accent by the bar, and then they headed to a booth right at the back.

Even then, they didn't get down to business. Instead Bernie started fussing about with the menu, talking to Tony as if he'd never eaten in a bloody restaurant before, ordering a bottle of wine then looking pissed off when Tony asked for a Coke.

'What's this all about?' Tony asked, once the waiter had finally disappeared and the drinks arrived.

'Look,' said Bernie, 'what I do is I run clubs. Been running clubs around town since the fifties when I was a kid myself.'

Tony nodded.

'Right then,' Bernie went on, 'then you've probably heard. I'm going into business with Kenny Ibadulla, get the Casablanca going again.'

Tony nodded once more and switched off while Bernie went into a spiel about what a great asset to the bloody community it would be having the Casa open again. For a moment Tony thought he was going to ask him to invest in the damn place. 'What's it to do with me?' he asked finally, as Bernie started to slow up.

'Well,' said Bernie, 'me and Kenny have been thinking.

We need someone to manage the club. Kenny's got Caesar's to look after and I'm all over the place, so we need someone on the spot. Someone knows how things work, and we can trust not to stick all the money in their own pocket.' Bernie paused and smiled a smile that didn't even think about reaching his eyes. 'And let's just say that you come highly recommended.'

Tony sat back for a moment, tried to get his head round this, then leaned forward again. 'Bullshit,' he said, 'I just got out of prison Friday, turning over a bookie's. Now you want me managing your club. Don't even nearly add up.'

Bernie leant back now but he was smooth, Tony couldn't read what was going on behind his eyes. 'Yes,' he said finally. 'I heard about that. Kenny told me you'd been in trouble. And I took the liberty of looking into it a bit. Line of work like mine, you make a few contacts in the police force, as you can imagine.' He paused for a moment for Tony to imagine the kind of police contacts Bernie was talking about. The kind of contacts showed up at your club in the afternoon asking for a bag of money to make sure the health and safety don't look too hard, or you don't get busted for under-age drinkers or drugs in the toilets. Contacts. Made the world go round.

'Anyway,' Bernie carried on, 'I made a couple of calls. And I found out something rather interesting. Let me ask you this, Tony. Did you ever wonder why you ended up doing time and not your cousin Billy who, after all, as I understand it, was the one with the gun?'

'Replica,' said Tony automatically.

'Replica, then. Didn't you ever wonder why he didn't get sent down?'

Tony looked at Bernie hard, seeing exactly what he was

suggesting. 'Police screwed up the case, didn't they? Their witness fucked them up on the stand. Otherwise he'd been doing five years at least.'

'Hmm,' said Bernie, 'convenient that, wasn't it, witness screwing up like that.'

'Look,' said Tony, 'stop pissing about. You telling me Billy grassed me up? Don't see it myself. They'd have had me anyway. Didn't need to give him anything.'

'Yeah, well, Tony, sorry to tell you this, but what my sources say is your cousin Billy talks to the trees on a regular basis, right old whispering grass.'

Tony sat back for a moment, trying to let this compute. Did he believe it? Maybe. Billy was a cunt any way you looked at him, and a lying cunt at that, always had been. Question was, though, who cared? 'So what?' he said to Bernie. 'What's any of this to do with you?'

'Well,' said Bernie, 'I don't think it'll be news to a bright boy like you if I tell you that your cousin Billy and my associate Mr Ibadulla are not on the best of terms. In fact I'm reliably informed that Billy is planning to attempt to move in on Kenny's, shall we say, private business. You follow me?'

Tony nodded. ' 'Course I follow you. Thing I don't see is what it's got to do with me. I got nothing to do with Billy.'

'Not exactly what I've heard, Tony.'

Tony stared at him.

'What I heard, Tony, you went to see cousin Billy on Saturday afternoon.'

Christ, thought Tony, how the hell could he have known that? And started to realise that whatever was going on was a sight more serious than he was used to. Mostly, people he knew had business disagreements, or whatever the likes of

Bernie Walters would call it, they went round each other's yard with a shotgun. They didn't have spies ringing them up and telling them who's been visiting the other guy.

'Yeah, that's right,' he said, 'I went round to see Billy on Saturday. And you know why I went round there? I went round to tell him I'm out of the life. He wants to go up against Kenny, that's his business. And that's the same thing I'm telling you. It's not what I'm into now.'

Tony started to get up from the table but Bernie waved him back down.

'I appreciate that, Tony, and I admire that. Just the qualities that make me think you'd be ideal for the job I was talking about. And I'm serious about that. Don't matter to me you've been inside. I've been in this business long as I have 'cause I like to think I have instincts about people, and you're all right, son, I can see that. And, let's face it, there aren't a lot of jobs around.' Here the words trailed off and Bernie looked Tony square in the eyes.

Tony stared back thinking, I should just get up now and keep walking. But he didn't. Bernie was right. What choice did he have?

'What do you want?' he said.

'Just the word, Tony, just a word. You go see your cousin Billy, and tell him you need a little earner, whatever, get back on side with him, and when he tells you what he's planning, you tip uncle Bernie the good word. And that's it.'

'Right,' said Tony. 'That's all, is it? Sell out my cousin to some bloke buys me a plate of spaghetti, tells me my cousin's a grass.' He shook his head.

'Tell you what,' said Bernie. 'Why don't you think it over, ask about a bit and then let me know? I'll be there till eight.

That's when the offer closes.' Bernie stood up, put a couple of twenties down on the table and started out of the restaurant. Tony was going to let him go, but then something occurred to him and he got up too and caught Bernie up as they emerged on to the street.

'Did you ever know a singer called April Angel?' he asked.

Bernie came to a dead halt. 'Jesus,' he said, 'I haven't heard that name in thirty years. April Angel. Christ. Tell you what, son, I've been working in clubs my whole bloody life and I never saw another girl like that. April Angel. So what made you ask that?'

'She's my mother,' said Tony.

It wasn't something you saw often, someone with an orange tan as fervent as Bernie Walters's go completely white, but that's what happened then. 'Oh my God,' he said after a moment. 'You're April's son.'

'What I said,' said Tony, wondering what the hell was going on.

Bernie stared at him, his colour gradually returning. 'Tell you what, son, whatever you decide, come back to my office later, round seven o'clock. You and me better have a chat.' And before Tony could say anything more, Bernie was off, moving fast through the shoppers.

Tony headed back towards Butetown, his head overloading. He hadn't gone far when he realised he needed a drink and a piss, so he stopped into the Custom House. He had a word with Wariq behind the bar, a game of pool with Bobby who beat him on the black which showed his concentration had gone, and then sat down by himself for a while, trying to figure out where the hell to go from here.

Way he saw it, he was trapped like a lab rat. Whatever he

did, he was screwed. No way he was going to grass up his cousin Billy on the one side. Family got to mean something, and Bernie's story about Billy could be true but was most likely just hot air. Other hand, though, God knows he could do with that job, if that wasn't bullshit as well. Only chance he had, far as he could see, to get Tyra back: get a decent job, show her he could do it. But he didn't turn Billy over – no fucking job. Life, he thought, total crock of shit. For a moment he even thought fondly of being inside. Least you didn't have crap choices like this to make.

He finished his drink and walked back out into the afternoon sun, absolutely no clearer as to what he should do. His feet led him automatically down Crichton Street and left into East Canal Wharf, taking the back way into Butetown. Distracted as he was, it took him a second or two to register the car coming up slowly behind him, and, before he could properly react, a side door had opened and a guy jumped out and pressed a blade against Tony's back.

The guy was a total amateur; Tony threw himself forward and down, away from the blade, causing the knife-man to lose his balance. As Tony fell, he twisted and kicked backwards, tripping the guy. Tony was on his feet in two seconds flat and his left foot stamped down on the knife-man's hand. Two more seconds, and the knife was in Tony's hand, the other hand holding on to the guy's throat.

Tony had never seen the guy he was holding on to before, but by now the driver had got out of the car and Tony knew him all right. Gary something or other, one of Billy's Ely boys. Gary kept his distance. He knew better than to come anywhere near Tony, any time he had a knife in his hand.

'Fuck's going on, Gary?' said Tony, ignoring the kid –

that's all he was, some stupid kid in a Calvin Klein jacket thought he was about ten times harder than he actually was.

'Nothing, Tone. Billy just wanted a word, that's all.'

'And that's what he thinks he needs to do, have a word with me? Send some YTS villain round to stick a penknife in my back. Fuck's sake.' Suddenly Tony brought his head down hard on the kid's nose. Blood started flowing at once and Tony pushed the kid away. 'Fuck off now,' he said, 'back to the playground.'

The kid did as he was told, walked off towards town, fast as he could go without looking like he was running.

'Come on then,' said Tony. 'Let's go and see Billy, he wants a word with me.'

Gary shrugged, said, 'That's what I told him, Tone. But Billy's a bit hyper, like, at the moment and that lad Kelvin's looking to impress him, and that's what you get, this kind of situation. A cock-up.'

Tony just shook his head and the rest of the drive up to Ely passed off in silence.

Billy must have been watching for the car, as the door opened as soon as Tony got out.

'Sorted out Kelvin then,' he said, apparently cheery as ever.

Tony stared at him but Billy carried on. 'Thought I'd give him a taste of playing the big leagues, like.'

'Fuck you, Billy.'

'Yeah, well, thought you might take it like that. Come on in.'

'No,' said Tony, 'you send Gary in, then you and me can get in the car and have a little drive back down town, drop me off there.'

Billy shrugged. 'Your call, Tony. What you think, I've got

an ambush waiting for you inside? Got Stacey there with a shotgun?'

'Wouldn't know, Billy, would I?' said Tony.

Billy shrugged again, motioned for Gary to get inside. Gary tossed him the car keys and the cousins got into the car.

'You grass me up, Billy?' said Tony once they'd turned into Cowbridge Road.

'That what he told you, this Bernie Walters fella?'

Tony nodded.

'Bollocks, Tony. Police screwed the case up fair and simple. You think they're going to make themselves look that stupid just to let me off, when they had me red-handed? Don't think so, Tone. Thanks for giving me Walters's name, though. Knew Kenny was hooked up with someone but I didn't know who. So what's he want, Tony? What's he talking to you about?'

'Nothing. Same old bullshit you're giving me. Kenny and him wants me, you wants me, every fucker wants me. How many times I got to tell you all I'm out of it?'

'Yeah?'

'Yeah?'

Billy shook his head. 'I'm surprised, Tony. You ain't seen Tyra yet?'

'Yeah, this morning.'

'Didn't she tell you 'bout Kenny?'

'Said she borrowed some money off him, yeah.'

'Tell you how she paid him back?'

There was a silence. Tony stared at Billy, then he said, 'Billy, you better be telling me something real. ' 'Cause you lie to me now, I'll cut your face off.'

Billy raised his hands from the steering wheel momentarily,

held them up pacifyingly. 'Tone, this is what I've heard. Can't swear I seen it myself, 'cause I haven't, but it's what I heard, right. You know how it goes, you borrow off Kenny. Two hundred, that's twenty a week; four hundred, that's forty. You miss one week, pay double next week. You miss two weeks, you're screwed. Yeah?'

Tony nodded.

'Yeah, well, Tyra don't have the money, do she? So what's she going to do to get it? Get a job. Sure, I bet she tried, but with the kids and all it's not easy. And she's a good-looking woman, Tone, always has been.'

'What're you saying, Billy?'

'What I'm saying, Tone, is that Kenny, your old mate, gave your woman so much grief 'bout this little two hundred pound, she ends up out hustling over Riverside.'

Tony had seen it coming but he still wasn't prepared. As Billy spoke, a white mist came down, blurring his vision. For a moment he thought he might start crying, but he bit his lip and rocked back and forward in his seat and kept the tears back, let the anger course through his veins instead.

'Who told you?'

'Don't matter who told me, Tone.'

'I asked you a fucking question. Who told you?'

Billy shrugged. 'What it's worth, Tone, it was a girl called Pauline, friend of Stacey's, works down there from time to time. Told Stacey she'd seen Tyra on the beat. Sorry, Tone.'

Tony didn't say a word. Just sat there in the passenger seat, staring blindly out at the shoppers on Clare Street, feeling like he was ready to explode with anger, but unable to decide where to go with it.

Kenny was looking favourite for it, if what Billy was telling him was true. Which was still a pretty big if. 'Cept it explained why Tyra was so angry with him. Christ. Thing he couldn't escape, though, was that, even if it was true, then maybe it wasn't Kenny's fault. Tyra certainly didn't think so. She wasn't blaming Kenny; you borrowed off Kenny, you knew what you were doing. She just hadn't had a choice. And why hadn't she had a choice? 'Cause of him, 'cause he'd been sitting in jail like a twat. And why had he been in jail? 'Cause he'd gone along with the idiot sitting next to him.

'So you going to come in with me, bra?' said Billy. 'Give Kenny a piece of what he deserves.' They were in Butetown now; Billy stopped the car across the way from Pearl's place. Tony just opened the door and was about to get out without saying anything, but, as he got up from his seat, Billy leaned over and said, 'Wednesday night, bra, that's when the boat comes in.'

Tony walked away from the car without a word, heading for Pearl's. But as he saw Billy pull a U-turn and head back over the Grangetown bridge, he switched direction and headed for Tyra's place. His place. He came round the back door. Most people did. Front door was for official visits.

He got as far as the yard gate and then he stopped. The kitchen light was on and he could see Tyra in there – making the kids' tea, he supposed. It was dark enough now, though, at six o'clock, that there was little chance she could see him standing out there. Which was lucky, as he suddenly realised he couldn't move. Couldn't step forward or back; he was just stuck there, rooted to the spot, contemplating what he'd done to the best person he knew. He wanted, he wanted with every fibre of his being to blame someone else. He had the knife – Christ, he had the knife gripped in his hand – and he knew if he saw Kenny right that moment he would probably go for him. But he couldn't sustain it, couldn't keep the blame anywhere except on his own head.

He might have stood there all night if he hadn't heard footsteps after a while and seen old Mrs Watkins from next door coming his way. Tony turned on his heel then and headed back towards Bute Street. Checking his watch, he saw it was half six; half an hour must have gone by as he stood staring through the window. It was time to pay another visit to Bernie Walters.

He hadn't seen it before, but this time it was the first thing he noticed in Bernie's office, the framed ten-by-eight glossy of April Angel. It was right there on the wall next to the picture of Bernie with one arm round George Mr Speaker Thomas, and the other round a fixer named Jack Brooks, sunny Jim Callaghan's right-hand man, ended up as Lord Splott or something. In fact, you looked closely, the room was plastered in pictures of Cardiff's movers and shakers over the last forty years. There was John Toshack handing Bernie a copy of his book, *Gosh, It's Tosh*, William Hague looking about twelve handing Bernie some kind of award, Ray Reardon handing him a snooker cue, too many opera singers and rugby players to count. And of course there was a picture of Shirley Bassey. How could there not be?

'I booked her at the beginning, you know,' said Bernie.

'Who? My mum?'

'No, well, I did book your mum, of course. But I was talking about Shirley. She had it right from the start, you know. Little girl from Butetown, knew she was ready to take on the world. 'Course she'd already been up to London, been in a couple of shows by the time I worked with her. I put her on at the Capitol. Packed. Could have sold it three times over, really got me started in the industry. You remember the Capitol, Tony?'

Tony nodded, 'course he remembered the Capitol. First big show he ever went to, Earth, Wind and Fire at the Capitol, seventy-five or -six. Went with Debbie, his first kid's mum. She was pregnant then. She was nineteen, he was only fifteen. Christ, weird when you thought about it now; the kid, Lorraine, she must be grown up by now. Hadn't seen her since she was six; Debbie buggered off to Swindon, married some RAF guy. He didn't blame her, never had.

'No, butt,' he said finally, 'I don't remember the Capitol or the bloody trolley buses or the sodding Kardomah, or the bloody Casablanca, come to that. I just came here 'cause you said you knew something about my mum, so let's have it.'

Bernie raised his hand. 'Take it easy, son,' he said. 'Have a drink.' He got up from behind his desk and walked over to a cocktail cabinet topped by a picture of the cricketer Tony Lewis, took out a half-empty bottle of flash-looking whisky and poured Tony a whacking great glass of the stuff.

'Right then,' he said, once he'd returned to his own drink. 'What d'you want to know about April, then? Or I suppose you think of her as Fatima, do you?'

'No,' said Tony, 'I think of her as Mum.'

'You know it was me came up with the name,' said Bernie, rattling on oblivious. 'April 'cause that's when her birthday was, Angel because that's the first thing I ever said to her. You sing like an angel, I said to her down the old Ocean Club, and she laughed and laughed at me but after that I just used to say "Hiya, angel" when I saw her and it kind of stuck. She was one of the best, you know, your mum. Back then there weren't a lot of girls could sing the American stuff; you know, the rhythm and blues. GIs used to come down to Butetown every weekend, brought their records – great stuff, you know, all those vocal groups, the Moonglows and the Five Satins and those dance records, Ivory Joe Hunter, Ray Brown. You could hear all that stuff down Butetown no one else ever heard of till the sixties. And all the singers down here had a go. Shirley even did a few, but it was always show tunes she liked. Lorne Lesley wasn't bad either, but your mum was the best. Took her up to London, must have been 1959, signed her up to Decca, you ever hear that record she made?'

Tony shook his head.

' "In the Still of the Night". You know that song?' Suddenly Bernie launched into a couple of bars. 'Anyway, she did it fabulous and then they stuck this horrible bloody orchestra on it and screwed the whole thing up. I was absolutely bloody tamping mad about it at the time. Funny thing was, your mum didn't seem to care that much. 'Course it wasn't long after that you came along and I, we . . .'

Bernie came to a pause and Tony could sense rapid calculation going on behind his eyes.

'Yeah, well,' he went on. 'One thing or another, I didn't see much of April after you were born. I was up in London most of the sixties. Fantastic time, the sixties, never be another like it. Anyway, your mum kept busy doing the club circuit down here, far as I know, and I didn't hear from her at all. Not for a long time.'

Bernie stood up, walked over to the drinks cabinet. All of a sudden, Tony noticed he'd started to sweat. 'Another drink?' Bernie said, pouring himself a tumblerful of pure Scotch. Tony shook his head.

'So you heard from her again?' prompted Tony after a while, as Bernie sat back behind his desk and went to work on the whisky.

'Oh yes. I heard from her once more.'

'When?'

'1970, I think it was, thereabouts anyway. I remember it was the week the Beatles split up. You like the Beatles, Tony? I never thought they were much, to be honest.'

'1970,' Tony cut in, trying to get the increasingly drunk Walters back on track, 'that's when she left us.'

'Yeah, son, I know that. Look, there isn't an easy way to tell you this. But here goes. That's why your mum called me up, she wanted to get out and she'd heard I'd been booking acts abroad. Cruises and resorts and stuff. So she asked me if I could get her something, anything really, she said, long as it was out of the country. I made a few calls and I got her a nice little cruise job, round the Med.'

'That's why she left us, to go on a cruise?'

'Hardly, son; no, that was the only thing going. What I heard was after that she went to Marbella, got a residency in one of the clubs there, in the yacht place they have down there, Puerto something or other. You ever been out there, Tony?'

'Get lost,' said Tony. 'Why did she go, then? Did she tell you that?'

Once again Bernie hesitated before talking, and poured another large one. 'Your dad,' he said then. 'He's dead now, right?'

Tony nodded, wondering why Bernie would have known that.

'Well, your dad was a jealous man. And, I mean, who could

blame him? He was married to a woman like April, beautiful and out there singing in the clubs with men hitting on her all the time, and your dad he was off at sea a lot of the time. Not surprising he was jealous. But round the time you were born, he started getting really bad. That was the real reason I stopped working with your mum, you want to know the truth, 'cause Everton, your dad, told her to get rid of me, he was going to be her manager. Which, between you and me, if you bear in mind that he didn't know a thing about the business, is why your mum spent the sixties playing the Trafalgar Club, Caerphilly when she should have been at the London Palladium.'

Suddenly Bernie came to a full stop, and when he started talking again it was like he was talking to himself. 'I loved her, you know,' he said. 'But it was different back then, the fifties, my family would have killed me.'

'You've lost me now, boss,' said Tony. 'What I want to know is, you've got any idea where she is now?'

For a while it was as if Bernie was too wrapped up in memory to have heard him but then he shook himself and said, 'No idea, son. But you never know, I might know a man who does. Give me a couple of days and I'll see what I can do. And how about you, son, you thought about what we talked about? You going to help Kenny out with your cousin?'

'Tomorrow,' said Tony, 'I'll talk to you tomorrow.' And, with that, he stood up. As he walked through the darkened outer office, he turned his head slightly to catch sight of Bernie Walters going over to the whisky bottle once more.

Heading back up towards Butetown, Tony felt overwhelmed by a sense of dread. It had started that morning with Tyra when she'd been giving him all that grief. Thinking about his dad. Memories coming back. His dad shouting. The way the house would be just before his dad was due back from sea. Frightened. Shit, he didn't want any of this. Not many things he knew in life, but he knew his dad had loved him. His dad had stayed with them, hadn't he? His dad hadn't gone off on no cruise ship, had he? But, shit. His mother crying.

Without conscious thought, his feet had taken him to Mandy's place. She widened her eyes when she saw him, then led him into the kitchen where she was preparing some pasta.

'Kids in bed?' he asked.

'Yeah,' she said. 'What's up with you? You look like you've seen a ghost.'

'Near enough,' he said, and, as she added more tagliatelle to the saucepan, cooked it up and served it out for the two of them, he told her about his meeting with Bernie Walters.

'Whoo,' said Mandy when he finished. 'You don't think he's your dad, do you?'

'What?' said Tony, completely blindsided.

'Bernie Walters. You don't think he could be your dad, do you? I mean, what he was saying about your dad being jealous around when you were born, and Bernie pissing off to London. You don't think —'

'Nah, Christ's sake, Mand, he's a white guy, isn't he?'

'Yeah, well,' said Mandy, shrugging and backing off.

Tony stayed silent for a moment. It was true he was light-skinned, but then so was his mum. He'd just assumed he took after her, but that could work both ways . . . Then he shook his head firmly. No way. 'Hell of a thing to say, Mand, you know that.'

She put her hands up. 'Yeah, sorry, Tone, I just got caught up in the story. Reading too many of them Catherine Cooksons, you know what I mean. Always turns out people's dads aren't who they're supposed to be.'

'Yeah, well,' he said. 'Anyway, it's the least of my problems, really, all that crap. Real question is what am I going to do about Kenny and Billy?' He shook his head. 'Shit, Mand, I swear it's doing my head in, stuff's being going on today. Billy told me Tyra been hustling while I was inside. Did you know that?'

Mandy frowned. 'First I've heard of it, Tone. But' — and her voice was harder now — 'that's the kind of thing happens, your man goes away. Tone, you've got to keep out of this shit with Kenny and Billy. Don't matter who done what to who, you get involved it's going to be you who gets screwed again. Best thing you can do for Tyra and the kids, keep out of it.'

Tony stood up. 'Yeah, you're right,' he said. 'I better get back to Pearl's. I've got the kids tomorrow after school, you want to meet up?'

'Maybe. Call me. And remember what I said. Stay out of it.'

Tony just managed to keep his eyes open long enough to watch *News at Ten* with Pearl before he crashed into bed. The night seemed to go on for ever. Dream after dream assailed him. In one he was in a nightclub. Tyra and the children were there somewhere, he knew it, so he went upstairs. There was an empty dance floor there and he walked to the edge to see if he could find them. Suddenly he realised there was no floor in this part of the room, just a fragile latticework of thin metal strips that didn't look like they'd support the weight of a cat.

He jumped on to the window sill only to find there was no glass and he was swaying out over the lights of the city. The only way to safety was across the metal latticework. Nothing for it: he had to walk across it, had to push forward off each strand as it collapsed beneath him. And somehow he did it, made it back to the empty dance floor. When he woke up from this one, his heart was going like a steam hammer.

After that he stayed awake for hours trying to make some sense of that overload of information he'd been receiving. When he came out of prison, he'd at least believed he knew who his family were. Now his wife – and he couldn't blame her – wanted shot of him, and some damn golf-club guy seemed to know more about his own parents than he did.

One way or another, then, Tony didn't feel much like getting up come morning. Instead he just lay in bed and smoked and tried to construct some kind of plan. Around lunchtime it came to him.

First thing he did was bell Mikey and arrange to see him round the Ship. Mikey was half an hour late, as per usual, but he looked a lot more relaxed this time. Which left him completely unprepared for Tony's first words.

'I hear you've been messing round with my woman while I was inside.'

Tony was staring straight at Mikey as he said it, and he knew at once from the horror on Mikey's face that it was true. Funny thing was, he wasn't that bothered. It was like he'd already accepted that Tyra was gone from him, so what she did was her own business. He wasn't going to let Mikey know that, though. Mikey was going to suffer.

Mikey bullshitted and burbled away. 'Wasn't like you think, Tone. Only one time, bra. I'd . . . I'd helped her out, like, and she was grateful and lonely, you know, Tone. And, Christ, you knows what I'm like. But it's you she cares about, Tone, you know what I mean.'

Tony just sat there, giving Mikey the stare, letting him imagine the beating he was going to get. Then he leaned forward and said, 'Mikey. Shut up.'

Mikey shut up.

'You know what you done, I should fuck you up.'

Mikey nodded, his eyes moving swiftly round the room looking for potential allies.

'But I got a better idea. You're going to give me a bit of help, like.'

Mikey nodded again, his eyes narrowing this time. Then Tony leaned in close to him and told him what he wanted. As he finished, Mikey's head started to shake but then he saw the look Tony was giving him and abandoned the movement. Instead he said, 'What's in it for me, bra?'

'Ten per cent, off the top, and your dick gets to stay attached to the rest of your body.'

Mikey shook his head once again. 'Better pray to fuck this works, Tone, or none of us are going to be putting it round much any more.' Then, Mikey being Mikey, he brightened. 'Anyway, you been getting any since you been out? Tyra have you back yet?'

Tony stood up. 'Leave it,' he said, 'just leave it. And be there tomorrow, all right?'

Tony just had time to get back to the house and warm up some stew Pearl had left on the stove when Tyra brought the kids round. Tyra herself was gone the second the words 'Bring them back by seven' were out of her mouth, but seeing the kids, Jermaine and Emily, was enough to take the bitterness out of the situation. Emily, who was five, just threw herself at Tony, leaped up into his arms, while seven-year-old Jermaine stood there trying to look cool but with a huge grin across his face, so Tony scooped him up too.

For the next ten minutes or so they sat there, wrestling on Auntie Pearl's sofa, just happy to be together. But then, just as suddenly, the kids' mood seemed to change, like they'd seen enough of Dad now and it was time to go home. Tony realised he'd better do something with them. He looked out the window and properly registered for the first time that it was a beautiful day out there. A plan came to him. A quick phone call, and it was put into action.

He herded the kids out of the house and down the road, cutting through Mount Stuart Square and along to Mandy's place. Mandy had her two kids ready to go and the six of them squeezed into Mandy's car, an ageing Sierra, coming round the clock for the second time.

Fifteen minutes later, they were in Roath Park, an Edwardian oasis in the suburban north-east of the city.

'Any of you kids ever been in a boat before?' Tony asked.

The kids all shook their heads and Tony felt a swell of enthusiasm for life as he led the way alongside the boating lake to the boathouse itself. A little while later, and the whole troupe were waterborne and all laughing at Tony as he turned the boat in a complete circle and crashed back into the dock, trying to remember how to row. Still, a bit of perseverance and he got the hang of it, and then, out in the middle of the lake, the spring sun as hot as he could remember it in April, his kids beside him and a woman he loved opposite. Jesus, he thought to himself, woman he loved, where did that come from? It was Mandy opposite him. Like a sister to him; Christ, she was still a young girl. He pulled himself up again, thought about it for a moment. If he was thirty-six, that made Mandy thirty-one. Christ, but the years creep up on you. 'Specially if you make a habit of spending them in prison.

They circled round the little wooded island in the middle of the lake and the kids started clamouring to get off and explore. Tony looked at Mandy, who smiled and shrugged back at him, so he nosed the row boat in as close as he could and the kids took off their shoes and socks, rolled up their tracksuit bottoms and waded on to the island. Mandy stood up and moved over to sit next to Tony. Tony was about to say something fatuous, like nice day for it, but before the words were out of his mouth Mandy said shhh, and then her lips were on his and then her tongue snaking between them, and then suddenly both their mouths opened and they were doing their best to devour each other.

'Christ,' said Tony, as they came up for air. It was all he could say, caught up as he was in a rush of excitement and alarm. The excitement of the first kiss coupled with a sense of horror that she was virtually his sister, and worse yet the realisation that that only made it more exciting. Thank God for the virtually, really.

He leaned back a little and twisted his head round to look at Mandy and was relieved to see that she was grinning like the cat with the cream. 'Shit, Tone,' she said, 'if you knew how long I'd wanted to do that.'

And then the kids were back, almost tipping the boat over as they clambered back on.

'So who fancies an icecream then?' said Tony, and four little voices assented and Tony put his back into rowing them back to the boathouse. Cones of Thayers chocolate were duly dispensed all round and the return home passed in a blur. The only thing to stick in Tony's mind being Mandy's lips close to his ear saying 'Come round later' as she dropped him and the kids off back at Pearl's.

Tony walked the kids round to Tyra's, hoping to hell they hadn't seen him kissing Mandy, last thing he wanted Tyra to know. Or maybe it wasn't, maybe he didn't care. Shit, what was happening to his life? You spent all those days in prison where no fucking thing happened, the nearest thing to excitement when he won the table-tennis tournament on his block, and now the world seemed to be rushing at him, keeping him permanently off balance.

Tyra didn't ask him in or anything but she gave him a little bit of a smile, which was something, and asked if he'd like to see them again on Friday and he said yes. And it was only as he turned and left, after giving the kids one last hug, that he realised it was a lie. No way he was going to be seeing his kids on Friday if what he was planning went off right. Or went off wrong, come to that. Likelihood was he wouldn't be seeing anyone on Friday, it went off wrong.

Walking back to Pearl's, he was too preoccupied to register at first that Pearl was talking to someone. Col was sitting there in the living-room chatting away with the old lady about the latest things going on with the bay development. A lot of the old-timers couldn't see anything good about the way things were going, spent their whole time reminiscing about the old bay. Pearl, however, was a more realistic soul and had little nostalgia for living in a slum, and she was excited by all the new stuff springing up now. So she and Col were talking away, apparently oblivious, when Tony walked in.

It was obvious, though, that there was only one reason for Col to be there, and so it proved.

'Let's go for a drink,' said Col, after a couple more minutes' chat with the old lady. 'Kenny's over the Ship.'

Tony shrugged, said, 'Why not?' and headed out into the night with Col, wondering what the hell he was walking into.

Tony needn't have worried; he played it perfectly. Yes, he told Kenny, he'd met Bernie. Yes, he'd heard about Billy. No, he couldn't believe what the bastard had done to him. Yes, Billy had approached him. Yes, Billy was planning something tomorrow night. Yes, he, Tony, would be happy to play along with Billy and then sell him out to Kenny when the time came.

Kenny was happy, Kenny was thrilled. Kenny let Tony in on the plans. The drugs were indeed coming in on the Trinidad boat tomorrow night. The deal was going to go down in the Casablanca at nine. All Tony had to do was tell Billy the wrong time. Tell him to be there at eight o'clock, then Kenny and his guys could ambush the ambushers. Simple.

Couple more drinks, then, to seal the deal, and Kenny headed over to Caesar's. Col and Tony sat over their drinks a little while longer.

'How's it with Tyra?' Col asked.

Tony shook his head. 'Seriously pissed off with me, bra.' There was more he wanted to say but realised he couldn't. He wanted to know if Col had known about Kenny and Tyra's loan, but he couldn't risk sounding critical of Kenny. The other thing he felt like asking was about Col's baby mother, Maria. She was a hustler. He wondered now how Col had handled that. But it wasn't, to be honest, the kind of thing guys like him talked about. He was starting to wonder a little about that. Wondering why he'd spent so much of his life learning to be so damn hard. Still, that would have to wait; next couple of days he was going to have to be every bit as hard as they come if he wanted to walk out the other side. So he changed the subject, laughed and joked a little, then told Col he had to go.

Col laughed and said, 'You got a woman waiting,' and Tony laughed too and said, 'Yeah, man,' and clashed fists with Col and walked back into the night, letting the cool air sober him up as he headed round to Mandy's place.

Later he would wonder if it was just the tension of his whole situation, the total chaos that was engulfing his life, that made what happened next feel so powerful. There was no question about what was going down from the moment he opened the door. It was dark and quiet in the house, the kids were in bed asleep, Mandy was in a nightdress and her bedroom was lit by candles. What happened next was just the usual stuff that happens when a man and a woman get together in a bedroom in the candlelight, but for both of them it was the same but different, the same but better, the same but so good that it left both of them close to tears afterwards.

Somewhere towards morning, Tony asked Mandy a question.

'What'd you say to going to Spain for a while, you and me and the kids?'

'Spain,' she said sleepily. 'What's in Spain?'

'My mum, maybe.'

'Oh,' she said, 'yeah, sounds nice,' and wrapped her arm round him.

'Seriously,' he said. 'Let's go to Spain.'

'Mmmm.'

'Tomorrow.'

'What?' said Mandy. 'Better wait till the holidays,' a faint note of anxiety coming into her voice. Tony decided to leave it, turned round again to face her and stopped talking, let his finger trace a line from her collarbone to her nipple.

In the morning Tony dozed fitfully while Mandy got the kids ready for school and nursery. By the time she came back, though, he was up and dressed and they had a little breakfast together before Mandy had to be in work, over the pub.

Tony walked out with her and kissed her long and hard goodbye, but was by then actually relieved to be on his own. He had a lot to think about, he was going to make it through to the end of the day.

First he made a phone call to a London number, one he'd acquired in prison. Then, satisfied with the ensuing conversation, he took the bus out to Ely, walked round to Billy's place. He did exactly what Kenny had told him to do. Told Billy he was prepared to help him ambush Kenny. Billy smiled big. Then Tony told Billy what he wanted. A quarter share off the top, whatever they got away with.

Billy said no problem, cuz, no problem. So what's the plan? Simple, Tony told him, the deal goes down in the Casa. Be round the back at eight o'clock. I'll open the back door for you. Come in fast and hard and it's all yours.

Billy wanted Tony to hang around, smoke a little draw – or something a little stronger if you're up for it, bra, get you up big time.

Tony shook his head, said he'd better get back, didn't want Kenny getting suspicious. So Billy had Gary drive Tony back into town, dropped him off by the ice rink, just over from the Bute Street bridge. But Tony didn't head on into Butetown, like he told Gary he was going to do. Instead he waited till Gary had pulled a Uey across the six lanes of traffic and headed back up to Ely, then he walked round to the bus station. There he went into the café, got a coffee and sat down at a window table on the side looking out at Wood Street. A half hour later, almost exactly on three o'clock, he saw a black Saab 900 with London plates pull up on the double yellow lines and, when the window wound down to reveal a familiar face, Tony walked out of the café and got into the car.

At six o'clock Tony met up with Col, Kenny and one of Kenny's cousins, a hard boy named Darrell, in the Ship.

'All set, boss,' said Tony.

Kenny didn't say anything, just raised his giant fist and clashed it against Tony's.

'Billy'll be coming round the back around eight,' Tony went on.

'Any idea how many?'

Tony shook his head. 'Gary, I expect. Maybe this kid called Kelvin. Dunno who else, could be any of the Ely boys. Don't reckon more than a carful, though, if they're going to try to sneak up quiet, like.'

'Don't matter, we'll be ready for them. Won't forget this, bra.'

Col stood up then. 'Going up town,' he announced. 'Little bit of business. You fancy coming along, bra?' he said to Tony.

Before Tony could answer, Kenny cut in. 'You'll be staying here, see how things work out, won't you, Tone.'

He didn't put any menace in it. That was the thing with

Kenny: he didn't have to come on like a thug all the time; you just had to look at him to know you didn't want to cross him, and evidently what Kenny wanted was to keep Tony where he could see him. Suited Tony too, but he let a glimmer of irritation cross his face, like he couldn't believe Kenny didn't trust him.

'You're not staying around yourself then?' he said to Col.

'Nah, too old for this business, man. Stick to mi retail activities, you know what I'm saying.' And, with that, he was off.

Tony stayed in the pub for another half hour, then Kenny led the way over to the Casa. They went in through the front door, and Kenny locked it behind them before ushering them over to a table by the bar. Over the next half hour four more of Kenny's guys showed up. Younger faces that Tony knew, but wouldn't have thought ready for this kind of serious business. But that's what a year out of circulation could do. Made you lose your sense of who's who. Some boys grew up quick in the bad-man business. They all said hello to Tony and he was pleased to see they gave him a little bit of respect, though there was none of the fear there he used to get off guys who'd seen him in action.

But then two of the guys at least had shooters, and Tony had never been comfortable around shooters. Partly for the obvious reason. Shooters killed people, even if you weren't trying to. Not like a knife, where you could use a bit of judgement. And where you needed a bit of skill and a bit of courage. Going up against someone with a knife was an art. Any twelve-year-old could pull a trigger. Other thing was if you got shooters involved, they threw away the key, turned a one-year sentence into five. He couldn't stop himself from letting out a sigh. Christ, he hoped he'd get through this one. Cops showed up, he didn't know what he'd do. Still, one thing about working with Kenny, chances were the cops were squared away.

Between seven and eight the tension level in the room mounted steadily. The chit-chat had died out almost completely when, all of a sudden, Kenny said to Tony, 'Got a message for you, bra, from Bernie.'

'Oh yeah.'

'Yeah, it's about your mum. Bernie reckons he knows where she is.'

'Where?'

'Somewhere in Spain, bra. Porto something, I think, fucked if I can remember. But Bernie got the details. Christ, I thought your mum was dead.'

'No,' said Tony. 'Looks like she's alive.'

The room relapsed into silence after that till around quarter to. Then everyone took up their positions. Kenny and Tony sat round a table under the only light that was turned on in the whole place. They had a couple of bags out on the table. The bags were empty but anyone bursting in the back door would assume that this is where the deal was going down. With a bit of luck they wouldn't notice the four guys waiting in the shadows. The worry Tony had was that Billy's boys would just steam in shooting and that would be the end of him and Kenny. But he didn't really believe it. That wasn't the way things happened down here.

They all heard the car arrive round the back of the Casa. They all heard the doors open and then somebody curse as he tripped over some of the crap lying around in the back yard. They didn't so much charge through the back door as stumble into it. There were four of them: Billy and Gary plus two others Tony didn't know. The kid Kelvin wasn't there. Tony hoped he'd realised he wasn't cut out for the life, but suspected he'd probably just shot himself in the foot when they were tooling up.

In fact Billy looked to be the only one who was armed. He was swinging an evil-looking sawn-off and, to give him his due, he at least made a go at carrying the thing off proper. Second he saw Kenny sat at the table with someone, he swung the shotgun up and told them not to move. As he advanced, though, and saw it was Tony there, he couldn't resist giving his cousin a wink and saying, 'Nice one, bra.' And as he did so his posture relaxed slightly and he never even noticed Kenny's boy Darrell come up behind him till it was far too late. All he could do was half turn before Darrell's baseball bat caught him across the neck and shoulders.

Billy went down hard, the way blokes who've been hit with baseball bats tend to go, and within seconds the rest of Billy's gang all found themselves looking down gun barrels, courtesy of the young guys, all of whom, Tony had to say, looked impressively calm.

That was it. About two minutes start to finish and Billy's master plan was fucked. Tony wasn't surprised: it wasn't like the raid on the bookie's had been a clockwork success either. Face it: cousin Billy was, like 99 per cent of all known villains, completely crap.

Tony stood up and walked over to where Billy was lying. For a second he was worried that Billy was lying too still, thought maybe the baseball bat had caught him on the temple or something. But then Billy writhed a little and Tony stepped back and just watched as Kenny organised the tying up of

Billy and his three guys, then packed them off into the storeroom with Darrell to watch over them, carrying Billy's own shotgun.

'Sort you cunts out later,' said Kenny.

Then it was back to the waiting. This time Tony found it almost unbearable. The others were more relaxed, figuring they'd done the hard bit, but, by the time the drug guys from the ship turned up, Tony felt like he was about to explode.

There were two of them. The one you'd remember was a white guy, who had to be one of the three or four biggest people Tony had ever seen in his life. Not many people made Kenny look small but this feller did. The other guy was a wiry type who was completely unreadable. Could have been any age from thirty to fifty and could have come from any nation on earth. Neither of them looked too worried, despite the fact that the big guy was carrying three kilos of coke. Still, way Tony saw it, they must have done the risky stuff already, getting the gear off the boat. It wasn't likely Kenny was going to try and rip them off, not if he wanted to do any more business. No sense in cutting off your own supply.

In fact they were in and out of the Casa in fifteen minutes flat. Quick hellos between Kenny and the wiry guy, Kenny had a look at the merchandise, a little taste from a couple of bags, pronounced it good and produced a briefcase full of fifties, counted out thirty grand. A little bit more chat then, a quiet word between Kenny and the guy. Setting up the next deal, Tony supposed, and they were off. The big guy never said a word the whole time.

Things went perfectly after that, far as Tony was concerned. First thing was – he'd hoped for it, but hardly believed it would happen – Kenny and the boys decided to have a little tasting session. Tony, hanging back, looking like he was waiting his turn, was the only one who heard the faint sound of a car door opening somewhere out the back.

Tony exhaled with relief. That meant Mikey had done his stuff. Seconds later they were in there, the three London guys. And the lead guy, Trey, the one Tony had roomed with down Dartmoor, was carrying an automatic pistol. Tony thought it might have been a Glock but he wasn't sure. He didn't know shit about guns.

Anyway, it did the business. Kenny and his boys were caught completely off guard, noses in the trough. Trey kept his gun on Kenny. The second guy, a tall fella with a shaven head, grabbed Tony by the throat and held a gun to his temple. The third guy, a cheerful-looking bloke with a beard, opened up a holdall and swiftly scooped the money and drugs inside. Kenny half moved forward and Tony thought for a moment that he was so angry he might charge the gun. But he didn't; instead he slunk back down in his seat when Trey started shouting.

'Move another inch, I'll fucking kill you. We're going out now and, if any of you move a muscle, your mate here' – he pointed at Tony – 'he's dead. We're taking him with us. So don't none of yow move.' At the end there Trey even remembered to put on his best Brummie accent, the way Tony had told him to.

And, with that, the three guys moved backwards towards the door. One with the loot. One with the gun trained on Kenny and the boys. The other pushing Tony in front of him, gun to the back of Tony's head.

It was going perfectly. They were almost at the door. And then a voice came out of the shadows.

'Stop it right there.'

It was Darrell. Fuck. Tony had forgotten that Darrell had been in the storeroom guarding Billy and the boys.

It was a stand-off. Darrell came out of the shadows with the shotgun. Trey kept his gun on Kenny. Tony tensed up again. There seemed to be only two ways this was likely to go. Either they all stood there together for ever, or everyone was going to start firing and it was going to be a sodding blood-bath.

And then a miracle happened. Darrell's head was suddenly whipped back and a choking noise came from his throat. It was Billy. He'd come round. And now he had a piece of rope pulled tight round Darrell's neck. Then he chopped hard down on Darrell's arm and the shotgun fell to the floor.

The London guys didn't hesitate; the three of them and Tony were out of the back door in seconds. They all piled into the Saab and the driver had them moving out of there just as the first shot sounded from inside the Casa, Kenny and Billy going head to head.

'Fucking hell, bra, that sounded a bit close,' said the driver, as he screeched the Saab into a right turn past the police station and into Dumballs Road. Tony realised with mild surprise that it was Mikey, a baseball cap pulled low over his face, doing the driving. He'd rather thought that Mikey would have legged it once he'd done what Tony asked him to, shown the London guys where and when to hit the Casa. He'd probably hung around to make sure he got his share. Tony said nothing, just shook his head, waiting for his heartbeat to return to an acceptable level.

A couple of minutes later they were pulled up next to Mikey's old Datsun, round the back of a warehouse, right down the far end of Dumballs Road. The split was simple. Trey and the London guys took the coke and ten grand of the cash. Tony took the other twenty grand. Mikey got two grand from Tony's end and a baggie full of coke. Then the London guys were gone, heading straight out to the M4, and Tony and Mikey got into the Datsun.

'What the hell happened inside?' asked Mikey.

Tony ran through the edited highlights and Mikey whistled, said, 'He always did have a hard head, Billy.'

'Yeah, well,' said Tony. 'Be lucky to have a head at all by now, I should reckon.'

Mikey shrugged. 'Nah, once they realise the money and the drugs are gone, they'll probably calm down. Be too busy trying to chase after your mates there. Nice boys too, by the way. Now it's time I got home, put me feet up by the TV before Kenny gets the idea I might know something. And how about you, what you going to do? You think Kenny bought the hostage thing?'

'God knows. Don't worry 'bout me, Mikey. Tell you what, just drop me off by the Monument. And, listen, one thing you can do for me.'

'Yeah?' Mikey's tone was instantly guarded.

'Yeah.' Tony took an envelope out of his inside pocket and stuffed five grand or so into it. 'Next day or two take this round Tyra's, tell her I won it on the horses.' He stared at Mikey. 'And don't start thinking of ripping it off. I don't hear from Tyra she got it, you're dead.'

Mikey nodded, no problem, and, as the car pulled up to the lights, corner of Penarth Road and St Mary Street, Tony jumped out.

'Hey.' Mikey was leaning over, winding down the window. He raised his fist and Tony bent down and clashed fists. 'Take care, man,' said Mikey.

Tony scanned the road carefully for any sign of big Kenny's Land Rover and then sprinted across, and into Bernie's building.

Bernie was there in his office, glass of whisky next to his right hand.

'Tony,' he said, 'the very man.' Then he said it again. 'Tony, the very man.'

The state he was in, Tony wondered if he'd been sitting there drinking non-stop since the last time he'd seen him.

'My mum,' he said, 'Kenny says you know where my mum is.'

'No rush, son,' said Bernie, 'have a drink,' and he waved Tony towards a seat. In doing so, though, he must have caught a glimpse of the wildness in Tony's eyes, because then he said, 'Shit, where is it?' and started scrabbling around on his desk, evidently looking for a piece of paper. Eventually he came up with it. An envelope with an address jotted down on it. Tony leant over and took it from Bernie's hand.

'Sure you won't stay for a drink?'

'No thanks,' said Tony, looking down at the address which was indeed in Spain, a place called Sitges. 'Got a plane to catch.' And he turned to go.

'Wait,' said Bernie, suddenly sharper. 'You're going to see her?'

Tony nodded.

'Listen, then. You better know what happened. In fact, you coming in here like this, it's like a recur, a recurring, shit, I can't think of the word . . . Anyway, it's the same thing. I was sitting in this same office – what, getting on for thirty years ago – and she came in . . .'

'You told me she phoned you.'

'No, she came in. Listen. She came in and she looked like a ghost, she was so pale. She'd come straight from the hospital, she told me. He'd stabbed her.'

'Who had?'

'Your dad, of course. With a knife. Had a bit of a reputation, you know, Everton. With a knife.'

Bernie paused and Tony just stood there with his eyes squeezed tight shut wishing it would all go away. Then Bernie started talking again.

'That's why she went, Tony. She was in fear of her life. I told her to get a lawyer, but she just laughed, told me I didn't know him, didn't know what I was talking about. Then I said to her what about the kid and she said, quite calmly, like she'd been thinking about it, she said the kid will be fine. He loves Tony now.'

Bernie paused again and Tony was trembling all over. He was going to ask Bernie what he meant by that 'now'. Had his dad not loved him before? Was his dad even his dad? But before he could get a question out, he heard a noise from downstairs. Tony had pulled the downstairs door closed behind him, but there was a furious banging going on. Kenny. It had to be Kenny. He looked at Bernie and Bernie pointed a finger upwards and Tony said thanks and rushed up the stairs just as Bernie walked down them shouting, 'Calm down, who the hell's there?'

As Tony climbed the stairs, the successive storeys got shabbier and shabbier. The floor above Bernie's was just barely functional; a photocopied piece of paper stuck to a door proclaimed the existence of Raju Secretarial Services. The next floor, though, had clearly been unoccupied for years and he began to be aware of a strange noise – not coming from below, where he could hear a raised voice that sounded like Kenny, but from above.

He slowed down now, both trying to be quiet and because there was no light at all on this level. He gingerly felt his way up the stairs once more. Suddenly something brushed against his face and it was all he could do not to scream. Then another thing brushed his face, and another. Birds. There were birds flapping all around him.

As the staircase turned one last corner, there began to be a little more light. He could see the sky through the gaping holes in the roof above the next floor and there were birds absolutely everywhere, hundreds of them all flapping around in the confined space. The noise was incredible now and the smell of birdshit overpowering. He was looking frantically around for a way to climb up and out when he saw a side door. To get to it he fought his way through a phalanx of angrily flapping pigeons, but it was worth it when he opened the door and found himself on a roof terrace. He walked out and assessed his options.

There was a building on either side of him, but neither looked promising. The one to the right was easily accessible but it was the end of the line, the last building in the street. Still, Tony resolved to give it a try. He pulled himself up the six feet on to the next-door roof and wandered around looking for a fire escape or a way down inside. All he found was a firmly closed skylight and then a fire escape which went right down the front of the building. If Kenny was indeed in with Bernie, and he came back out on the street while Tony was climbing down, he'd be a sitting duck. He shook his head and jumped back down on the roof terrace he'd originally emerged on to. He'd have to try the other way.

One problem: there was a narrow alley, one he couldn't remember ever noticing at ground level, running between the two buildings. It was no more than six feet across and the other building was slightly lower down. So it was a simple enough jump. Except it would be difficult to build up much momentum, and, to be honest, heights were never Tony's thing. And, if he missed it, he died.

But then there was a sudden terrible sound of fluttering from the floor below and Tony figured someone was coming up the stairs. So he shut his mind down and went for it. And made it. Hurt his knee and scraped a load of skin off his right hand, but he made it. And, glory be, he was able to scuttle quickly along four more roofs in succession without having to climb or jump.

Then his progress came to a stop. He was three-quarters of the way along the block, and there were more rooftops ahead of him, but in between there was a valley. He looked down to see what was in the valley. Of course. It was the Wyndham Arcade, one of the many Edwardian shopping arcades that criss-crossed the city centre. Its glass-topped roof was a good storey lower than the buildings on either side of it. For a moment Tony thought he'd reached the end of his luck, then he noticed a little metal ladder going down the side of his building towards the glass roof. He climbed down and, just at the level of the glass roof, discovered a little walkway, running alongside it. He followed it to the northern end of the arcade where the walkway dead-ended in a door. Locked.

No problem. Tony gave the door the hearty shove of a

desperate man and it flew open. Down two flights of stairs and through an unmarked door, and he found himself in between the kitchen and toilets of the very same Italian restaurant he'd been in with Bernie just a day or two before.

Thanking God with all his heart, and looking around very carefully for Kenny's Land Rover, Tony crabbed his way past the Marriott and over into East Canal Wharf, kept to the shadows and in ten minutes found himself at Mandy's back door.

Mandy took one look at Tony and had him in and the door shut behind him before any of the neighbours could have blinked. She'd seen that kind of wild expression on too many men at her kitchen door not to recognise it for what it was. The face of someone hoping to hell they'd got away with something. And it was always followed by more visits — the police, more villains — it made little difference.

'What've you done?' she asked as Tony slumped down at her kitchen table.

He didn't say anything, just held out his arms to her, and, like a fool, like a lover, she succumbed, went to him, let him hold her. And was unutterably distressed to hear, for the first time in her life, the sound of Tony Pinto crying.

They stayed there for a while, her stroking his wiry hair while he sobbed into her breast. And then, just as suddenly as he'd started crying, he stopped. Held her a little way away from him so he could see her face and said, 'Come to Spain with me, Mand. I've got to see my mum.'

'What?' she said, joking. 'Tonight?'

'Yeah,' he said. 'Tonight.'

'You're crazy, man, what about the kids? You remember I have kids?'

'Bring 'em too.'

'Yeah, right,' she said. 'What about school? What about money?'

'Christ, Mand, they're only babies – won't matter if they miss school a few weeks. And I've got money, Mand. Don't worry about that.'

'What?' she said. 'What are you telling me not to worry about? Where'd you get the money, Tone?'

'Don't matter,' said Tony. 'Some people owed me and I collected, that's all. But we got to go now. Pack up the stuff and the kids, let's get out to the airport. There's a plane tonight. Midnight. Straight to Barcelona, Mand.'

Mandy just looked at him, not quite believing what was going on. And then suddenly she was swept up in it. Why the hell not? Wasn't this what she'd spent her life daydreaming about, getting out of this shithole? She'd got the passports and everything a few months back. When she'd told Linz she was going to take the kids out to see her dad in the States. Crazy cow she was, she almost believed it herself by now. Believed her dad was some millionaire in Florida or Hollywood or one of them places, not stuck up in Aberdeen where he'd gone to work on the rigs twenty years ago and never come back.

So she did it. She threw her stuff and the kids' stuff in a couple of bags. Woke the kids up and dressed them and loaded them in the back of the car. And half an hour later they were at Cardiff Airport, out past Barry.

It was standing in the ticket line, with her kids asking what was going on, that she came to her senses. Suddenly stood back from herself for a moment and saw what she was doing. Taking her children on a plane with a man who had – she just knew it – ripped off some money. She'd sworn she'd never do it again, never let her life be dominated by some man who would expose her to those dangers. She'd dumped Neville and she'd dumped fucking Jimmy Fairfax just to get out of that world, and now this . . .

Thing was, Tony was sweeter than the pair of them and what hurt was she was sure he could do better. And for another moment she let herself dream that maybe this was it, this was the start of Tony's new life and hers. Then she shook her head. Maybe if it had just been her, but not her kids too.

'Tony,' she said, 'I'm not going.'

The hurt on his face was painful to see.

'Mandy,' he said, 'you can't.' And he faltered. 'Mand,' he said, and she was sure he'd never in his hard life said his next words before; never in earnest, at least. 'I love you, Mand.'

'I know,' she said, but suddenly she was strong. She pulled him to her, kissed him hard and long, gave it everything she had. And then she said, 'Phone me, Tone. Phone me or write me from Spain. You get a life sorted out, out there – a legal life – you call me and I'll come. 'Cause you're not coming back, are you, Tone?'

'No,' he said, 'I'm not coming back.'

'Then send for me, Tony,' she said, and turned and led her children out of the airport and back to the car. The last thing Tony heard: the older kid Brittany asking, 'Where's he going, Mum? Where's that man going?'

CARDIFF DEAD

ACKNOWLEDGEMENTS

Thanks to Abner Stein for help, advice and lunch well above and beyond. Thanks to Matthew Hamilton for his faith and editorial perception. Thanks to Sarah-Jane Forder for fine copy-editing. I would also like to gratefully acknowledge the financial assistance offered by a Writing Bursary from the Arts Council of Wales. Thanks to Phil John, Mike Parker, Mary Bruton, Rosemarie Buckman, Pete Ayrton, Carlton B. Morgan and Richard Thomas, and to a mystery Australian surfer for the dead dog. Thanks finally to Charlotte, as ever.

For my sister, Sophie Athanasiadis

I'm Cardiff born and Cardiff bred
And when I dies I'll be Cardiff dead

Frank Hennessey

I

THE CUSTOM HOUSE

1999

Mazz was riding the ghost train. The 125 from Paddington to Cardiff. Ghosts everywhere. Ghosts behind him in London. Susie the night before – this must be the last time. Ghosts of Camden Town this morning, walking through the market. Thirty-nine years old and feeling like his time was done and gone, walking through a sea of teenage Goths. Ghosts ahead of him in Wales. His family, what was left of it, up in the valleys, his mam long gone and passed away, his dad a ghost for years, haunting every pub that'd have him from Newbridge to Newport. Ghosts in Cardiff. Ghosts he didn't even want to think about. And Charlie. A ghost now for sure, Charlie dead and gone.

He was standing in the bar drinking cans of Stella with a couple of squaddies from out Ammanford way and, as the train pulled out of Bristol Parkway, he started telling them about Charlie.

'You boys ever hear of Charlie Unger?' Mazz asked, getting the answer he expected: a couple of shaken heads.

'Not into the boxing, then?'

This time one of the squaddies, a big lad named Bren, said he used to box a bit himself, in the army, like, and his mate's mate was a mate of Joe Calzaghe's, or some such regulation bullshit.

'Joe Calzaghe?' said Mazz. 'Charlie would have taken him one-handed. What's Calzaghe – QVC champion of the world? WBX? Christ, when

Charlie was fighting, back in the fifties, he was just plain world champion; there weren't half a dozen of them all swanning about exclusively on Sky Sports.'

'Yeah?' said Bren. 'What weight was he then?'

'Lightweight, least that's what he was when he was champion. Later on he went up to middle.'

'Lightweight.' Bren scratched his head a bit and squinted. 'Yeah,' he said again after a little while, 'no one remembers a lightweight. Comes to boxing, it's heavyweight or nothing really, isnit?'

Mazz shook his head. It was true. No one remembers a lightweight. No one remembered the Wurriyas either, the ska band that had brought Mazz and Charlie Unger together, twenty years ago when Charlie was already on the long slide down and Mazz was on the way up. The way up to this. Mazz Marshall, guitar player for hire. Heavyweight or nothing. Never a truer word.

Suddenly Mazz couldn't stand the squaddies any more. Didn't want to talk about rugby or where they were planning to go on their big night out in Cardiff. The train went into the Severn Tunnel and Mazz said he needed a fag and headed for the smoking carriage.

Other side of the tunnel, back in Wales, Mazz stubbed out his fag and looked out left at the Llanwern steelworks. One of the last hold-outs of Welsh heavy industry. He wondered if his cousin Gav was still working there. Probably, you didn't give up a job like that lightly these days. Man's work. Not a lot of it about.

Course it had seemed like there was plenty of it about when he was growing up, mind; man's work. Been the main reason he'd got the hell out of the valleys soon as he could.

Train was coming into Newport now. Newport. A couple of years ago some idiot rock writer called it the new Seattle. Just cause it had one decent rock club, TJ's, and a couple of bands looked briefly like they might be the new Oasis. He'd played TJ's a year or two back, done a tour with these bad-tempered Scottish brothers, indie legends for about ten minutes back in the eighties. Last time he'd seen his dad too, over in the Engineers just by the railway line.

Newport: when he was a kid it had seemed like some place, capital of the Gwent Valleys; now it looked like the town time left behind. And suddenly he had a fierce pang of nostalgia and before he knew what he was doing he was picking up his bag and getting off the train.

And as quickly as it had come the impulse passed and he was left looking at the departing train thinking, Newport, what the hell am I going to do in Newport? The answer was obvious – do what you always did in Newport. Go for a drink.

Same time Mazz was in Le Pub, cursing the jukebox, getting nowhere with the barmaid, Tyra Unger was down the gym. She had an hour there every day before picking the kids up from school. This had been her New Year's resolution. Stop going round her mates for a coffee and a smoke, start getting into shape. Thirty-six you had to start working at things. And right now, in the days after her dad's death, she was damn grateful for every routine she had.

And she liked it. Hadn't been looking forward to it beforehand. The place would be full of teenage bodybuilders, that's what her friend Linz had said, but the time of day Tyra went it was fine. Guy did the inductions, Mark, seen him round over the years, he was nice, took her through the machines properly, didn't try to feel her up, another thing Linz said. Sad, really, but the fact was she was a little bit disappointed. Not like she was interested or anything, but way she saw it you spent half your life complaining about blokes trying it on, and the rest of it complaining 'cause they didn't, too busy giving the eye to some little sister hasn't even screwed up her GCSEs yet.

Anyway, it was a nice little routine she had there. Saw the same faces most days. This dread Col she'd known for ever, been in the band together even, he was there pretty much every time. Col worked with Kenny Ibadulla now and again but she didn't hold it against him. Col brought his ghetto-blaster down too, played the music she liked – old seventies and eighties funk, bit of reggae. Nothing she liked better in this life just at the moment than pumping some iron, SOS band kicking into 'Just Be Good to Me'; you could just feel the chemicals get busy inside your body, endorphins or whatever. Course now and again some kid would come in with his own sound system, start blasting out this garage stuff they liked these days. Look from Col was usually enough. Carried a bit of respect with him, Col.

Been a good three or four months now she'd been seeing Col in there every day more or less, so God knows why it was today she said it but there it was.

'You fancy taking a girl out for a drink later on?' she said.

Bit pushy maybe, but at thirty-six you can't waste time waiting for blokes to ask you out and her mum could have the kids easy enough and frankly all this working out was great but it didn't make you forget there were other ways to work out, in fact it got you right up for it. Course that wasn't what she was suggesting. Col was a mate, they saw each other every day. No reason she couldn't have a drink with him. Not like he was married either. His baby mother was a lesbian now, and a hustler what Tyra heard. As for Tyra, her kids' father had fucked off to God knows where right after he came out of prison the last time, so there wasn't no armchair keeping warm round her place. Length of time Col took to answer, she had space to think all these things.

'Yeah, girl,' he said, 'see you down the Baltimore. Nine o'clock.'

And that was that. Col picked up his bag and went off to shower. Tyra worked on her pecs for a bit, pushing her chest out hard as she could. And then stopped suddenly, laughing at herself. Got a date.

'You reckon? You reckon that's a good fucking band? Mazz was on his fourth or fifth by now, been in Le Pub all the time but now he was sat at a corner table with a couple of little indie girls. 'Sounds like bloody Queen to me. And what's the bloke on about anyway? Paranoid android? It's just shit, what's that mean to anyone? Only two kinds of songs in this world, you know.' He looked at the girls expectantly.

'Oh, yeah, what are they then?' said the Asian one.

'Love songs and novelty songs. If it's not a love song, it's just some piece of shit made up to make students feel like they're on to something. You two students?'

'Art college,' said the dyed-blonde one, Emma she'd said. Anita he thought the other girl had said. Was that an Asian name? Fuck knows.

'What, here in Newport?'

'Yeah.'

For a moment Mazz was lost in reverie. Art college in Newport. A vision of a life path not taken. A memory of his art teacher back in Cross Keys Tertiary, when he was pissing about pretending to do A levels. Mr Hughes thought he was good, Mazz doing all these cut-up collage things, stuff he'd read about in the *NME*, told him he should go to art college, Newport. Bloke was hip enough, as it goes. Told him Joe Strummer had been there, like that would be the clincher for Mazz. Nearly was too, but playing guitar was the only thing he'd given a shit about then. Well, that and getting his leg over. And at the time the two seemed to go hand in hand.

Now, well he frankly didn't know if he'd care if he never picked up a guitar again, all the good it had done him over the years. He was still keen enough on the other thing, though, idly figuring out which of the two girls in front of him was the better prospect, but still he couldn't help wondering how things might have worked out, if he'd gone to art school. Mate of his worked in animation, he was doing all right. He'd known a few designers over the years; mostly the work was bollocks – designing fucking brochures for electronics companies and shit – but the money was there all right. Not like for some people.

Mazz had five hundred quid in his pocket, less the train fare and the drinks. More money than he'd had in one go for a while, but he'd practically had to beg to get it out of the fat American junkie and his evil Jap wife who'd been his last employers. Backing them up on a totally shit tour of Italy, the pair of them fighting every second they weren't sticking needles in each other and only unanimous on one thing: let's not pay Mazz what we told him we'd pay him. Fuckers had made him beg. Made him meet them in the departure lounge at Heathrow to get the money. But at least he had it now. Wouldn't last long, though, even in Cardiff. But still, beneath it all, Mazz wasn't worried; he'd survived too long to worry. Something usually turned up. Usually a girl, as it went.

'So,' he said, winking extravagantly, 'you two fancy a little toot?'

Back at the house making the kids' tea, Tyra figured it was the routines got you through a time like this. Her dad dying. Her dad was dead. Charlie was dead. Weird, when he was alive she called him Charlie like everyone else did. After all, at his best he was just like some uncle came round and brought you sweets. Wasn't like he ever lived with them. Uncle Charlie would have been about right, but he wasn't. He was her dad. Later on, when she grew up, he'd been better. Well, better and worse. She'd seen him for what he was and she'd loved him, she supposed. Everyone loved Charlie Unger. Least they did till the drinking and the gambling took him down. And she hadn't been much better than the rest. Hardly saw him at all the last couple of years. Charlie was just another man, just another loser to her by then, and she'd had it with all of them. But he shouldn't have died like that. Left there for a week before anyone noticed. Her dad.

Thing that made her sick, though, was the way everyone was getting all pious about it. Now Charlie was dead everybody cared like hell about him. The funeral was going to be a circus. It made her feel ill really, and guilty too.

At least the gym had been good and now, taking the peanut butter sandwiches into the front room where Jermaine and Emily were watching *Nickelodeon*, she felt like her kids were the only things anchoring her to the planet. Worst thing – well, not the worst thing but the oddest thing – was she felt so horny. It was embarrassing really. Got any worse she'd be rubbing herself up against the furniture.

'Mum,' said Jermaine, 'more peanut butter.'

She took his proffered plate automatically, not even bothering to tell him to say please.

Mazz woke up feeling like shit. Which was nothing new and wasn't it Tony Curtis who said that the worst thing about being teetotal must be waking up in the morning knowing that's the best you're going to feel all day? Sounded like it ought to be Dean Martin or one of those big-name boozers but Mazz was pretty sure it was Tony Curtis. Anyway, whatever, time to survey the situation.

He was in a strange bedroom in an unknown building; he was by himself lying under an opened-out sleeping bag and a blanket. There was a bookshelf near his head which contained what looked like a bunch of student textbooks and an ashtray complete with the butt ends of several joints, smoked right down to the roach. By the side of the bed there was a pile of clothes – his – and a couple of CDs, the Manics and something else – not his. He raised his head and looked around the bed and floor a little more carefully, sniffing as he did so. No sign of any vomit. Always a plus. On the wall there was a poster advertising a Howard Marks gig. He'd obviously landed up in some kind of student lair. What was it with students and dope these days?

Mazz wasn't really bothered about dope either way: if someone was smoking a joint he'd smoke some too, just to be friendly, like, but it'd never occur to him to go out and buy some. These days, though, far as he could see, it had turned into an interest in itself. People made records about smoking dope, read books about smoking dope and even went to gigs where they sat down on the floor smoking dope listening to some old reprobate talk about how he used to be a dope smuggler. People funny, boy.

Next question was what the hell had happened. First off, had he scored? He ran his brain through the faulty memory program marked 'last night', not once but repeatedly, and still there was absolutely nothing of a carnal nature in there. Bollocks, the rest of it was starting to come back. The hours in Le Pub, the coke in the toilets with the indie girls, the movement on to some other pub, the quick visit to the takeaway, the walk to a third pub, and – bollocks again – the arrival of the indie girls' boyfriends. Actually – it really was starting to get clearer now – he hadn't minded that much. It had already been feeling like more effort than he was up to, going through the final ritual-seduction part of the night, and the blokes had been all right, as it went. Some more drinking then someone saying you want to crash at ours then, mate, and that must have been what happened.

Try as he did, he still couldn't conjure up any memory of the walk back from the pub or club or whatever, or the cup of tea and the joint that must have been passed round, or the undressing and getting into bed that had evidently taken place, but still he reckoned he had the measure of it now and it wasn't too bad. Nothing broken.

'All right, mate.' He was out of the bedroom now and standing in the living-room. The person who'd spoken was a bloke sitting at a table drinking a cup of tea and leafing through a Richer Sounds catalogue. He looked vaguely familiar, presumably one of the boyfriends.

'All right,' said Mazz and kept on going, heading for the door that looked most likely to offer a route to the outside world. Mazz was getting too old for small talk this time of the morning.

'You want a cup of tea?' said the bloke, his eyes not moving from the catalogue.

'No, ta,' said Mazz, 'better get going.'

'All right,' said the bloke.

'All right,' said Mazz, 'and thanks, yeah.'

Out on the street he still didn't have much of a clue where he was. Looked left and saw what seemed like a bigger street and headed that way. On the bigger street the sight of a bus going the other way with the word Caerleon on the front helped him figure out he was on the Caerleon road over the river from the station. A bus came but he ignored it. Walk would do him good, he reckoned.

He'd just made it over the bridge and was skirting the town centre when he walked into his dad. It was pitiful really, his dad stood outside the boozer waiting for opening time. A can of Special in his hand already, wearing the same ancient camel-coloured coat he'd been wearing two years ago, last time Mazz saw him.

Mazz shook his head in the vain hope the apparition might go away. When he was younger he'd have laughed, seen his dad's steady plunge into the drinking pro-leagues as a laugh. These days it looked a lot too close for comfort. Mazz's old man had been a miner once, and was happy enough to remind you of the fact. That was a while back now, though. He hadn't worked since 1971, if Mazz remembered it right. Not 'cause of the pit closures or the strikes – he'd been gone before all that got going, he'd been on the permanent sick. Black lung Mazz had always thought it was when he was a kid, the way his dad would point at his lungs and cough theatrically if anyone asked why he wasn't working. Most of his childhood Mazz was waiting for him to keel over dead at any minute. He'd been in his twenties before his mam told him the truth. It was his nerves, that was all she'd said even then. Claustrophobia or sheer bloody terror; Mazz didn't know and couldn't blame him anyway. One thing he'd known from as far back as he could remember, he wasn't going down no big hole in the ground to work. Course that nice Mrs Thatcher had made sure there was no question of that.

It took a moment for the old man to focus on him but, as soon as he did, to be fair he did his best, stuck the hand with the can in it behind his back, gave Mazz a smile of genuine pleasure.

'Fuckin' hell, butt. It's been a while.'

'Yeah,' said Mazz.

'Where you been then? Travelling the world?'

'Yeah, well,' said Mazz. Oh yes, the rock'n'roll lifestyle; after a while it was like a cross between being a long-distance lorry driver and an itinerant brickie. No fate more glamorous than to trek round Italy in the back of a minibus with a fat American singer passed out across the back seats, his evil Jap wife bitching about Mazz smoking, and bloody Massive Attack playing for the eight zillionth time on the stereo.

'Lot of girls, eh?'

Christ, thought Mazz, the old feller must be well gone. 'Yeah,' he repeated, 'lot of girls.'

And it was true, of course. Particularly this last tour, to be honest. One thing to be said for the fat American, he pulled a lot of nice little Italian Goth girls to his gigs. They'd all show up expecting him to look like the skinny dude with the cheekbones he'd been on his first album cover. Then they'd discover him to be a fat asshole with a scary wife and more than a few would have the good sense to turn their attention to Mazz, whose cheekbones were at least still visible.

That seemed to have exhausted the old man's conversational gambits so they just stood there for a moment staring at each other until the welcome sound of the pub door being unlocked broke the silence.

'Fancy a quick one, then?' said Mazz's dad.

Tyra woke up crying. Six in the morning, Emily and Jermaine in the bed with her. Every morning they came in and God knows she loved to see them there. Course one of these mornings there'd be someone else there with her and God knows what they'd make of that. Fact was she'd been half thinking it might have been this morning, thought it would have been all right, Col being there. Would have been better than this anyway, them seeing her blubbing her eyes out 'cause she'd dreamed about Charlie again.

'What's the matter, Mum?' said Jermaine, doing his eight-year-old man-of-the-house bit.

'Nothing, love,' she said, pulling him close. 'I'm just sad about Granddad dying, that's all.'

'Don't worry, Mum,' he said, 'you're not dying.' She smiled and patted his head and soon the two kids had drifted back off to sleep.

The night before hadn't turned out the way she planned – the absence of Col in her bed was clear enough evidence of that – but still, lying there in the early-morning light, Tyra found herself smiling at the memory of it. They'd been sat downstairs in the Balti for a while, her and Col, both being awkward as anything. Tyra couldn't work out whether it was he didn't fancy her or whether he thought maybe she was only after a shoulder to cry on and he made a move she'd freak. So they just sat there chatting about this and that and what a great bloke Charlie had been, which he had been, you weren't his daughter. The pub was dead as anything downstairs, just a couple of old-timers watching the Sky news, and she'd almost been feeling like saying sod it and going home when Col said why didn't they pop upstairs, got the karaoke up there, might be a laugh.

And it was. First off there were a bunch of gay guys sat round a table at the front, all doing the maddest songs you could imagine – Shirley Bassey and Blur and all sorts – before this little guy with a dodgy peroxide job did 'The Greatest Love of All' and Tyra couldn't help it, found herself tearing up.

Col started looking at her, all concerned like, and she was on the point of saying she had to go when the trainee barman, some teenage fat boy from Ely, came out from behind the bar, walked up to the tiny stage and launched into 'Bat Out of Hell'. And you'd have had to have had your whole family massacred before your eyes in the previous half hour not to have laughed. It wasn't that he was crap at it; quite the reverse, the kid was brilliant, bellowing out the lyrics like old Meat himself, dropping to one knee with the passion of it all. The whole mood of the room switched in an instant – the old fellas with their long slow pints started to perk up, the gay guys started whooping and hollering – and by the second time the bloke launched into the chorus Tyra was shaking with laughter.

The guy, Lee his name was they found out later, got the whole place stamping and clapping when he finished, so he did another one, 'Tainted Love', had everyone shouting out the chorus. Things calmed down a bit then as a couple of young girls made a bit of a mess of the All Saints thing, 'Never Ever', and Gary the doorman did his usual balls-up of 'Satisfaction'. Every week he did it, and every week he screwed the timing up at the exact same place, but what could you do? Gary wasn't exactly the kind of fella welcomed constructive criticism.

Still Tyra's mood stayed with her; she nudged Col's leg under the table as Gary did his thing and Col nudged back. The end of the song Tyra marched straight up the front, had a little word in the DJ's ear. He nodded, rooted around a little in his collection of tunes and came out with the one he was looking for. He slipped it in the karaoke machine and drew Tyra's attention to the video screen where the words came up. Tyra just shook her head, smiled, walked a couple of steps forward and closed her eyes, letting the first few chords of the song wash over her, then the backing vocals. If you don't know me by now, they refrained, and then Tyra came in with the first line. 'We've all got our own funny moves/You've got yours and I've got mine,' she sang and opened her eyes to stare straight at Col.

And Col, bless him, was up to it. He smiled back, let her finish the first verse and get straight into the chorus, and then he was there beside her, took the second verse himself, and if he wasn't much of a singer, his piano-player's phrasing carried the day. Then they did the big chorus together and Tyra wasn't the only one there reckoned something was happening.

The end of the song, though, they walked back to the table and Col let her have it.

'Sweetheart,' he said, 'you and me, we known each other for ever, right?'

Tyra nodded.

'We been in school together, right?'

Tyra nodded again.

'We been in the band together, right?'

Tyra carried on nodding.

'Had the hit single and stayed in plenty of hotels together, right?'

'Yeah.'

'We been living round the corner from each other all the time since. You knows my kid, I knows your kids. I knows your Tony fucked off. To Spain from what I hear. You knows my Maria and you got the good grace not to talk to me about what's happened to her.'

Tyra nodded one last time, suddenly aware of where all this was leading.

'Well that's how it is: you knows me and I knows you and I loves you like a sister, you know what I'm saying? But something else was going to happen it would have happened long time ago. What's happening now you need a friend and you got one here, sister. So let's have a good time, yeah, little drink, little smoke and who knows, maybe we'll both get lucky before too long. You cool?'

Tyra smiled weakly, trying to ignore an errant tear forcing its way down her cheek. 'I'm cool,' she said.

And funny thing was a little while later it was true. She was cool. Did a couple more numbers, old Motown things, yelling out 'Heatwave' at the top of her voice, flashing back on the Wurriyas, the craziest year of her life. Playing bass and shouting out the backing vocals. Col to one side playing keyboards, her dad on the right playing his congas, and Bobby and Mazz in front. Mazz. Damn, the memories you keep buried inside you, the things that seem like they happened to someone else, they have so little to do with the way you live now.

Mazz was proud of himself. He'd got out of the pub after having just the one. Bought his dad a next drink and then scarpered, saying he had a train to catch. It was an achievement really. There's something so seductive about a pub in the late morning. There are no illusions left. You're not a successful young professional popping in for a quick one on the way to the theatre; everyone's hardcore at eleven-thirty in the morning. And in a good mood too. You've got twelve hours' drinking time ahead of you, a pint on the bar ready for you, a little sunlight poking in through a window, and the barman watching *Richard and Judy* on the TV. It's a time to savour life and your lack of a part in it. And leaving that behind, walking out of there at twelve, that first pint of Guinness still warming its way around your body, makes you feel pretentious, absurd, like you think the world cares what you do.

And if that wasn't a triumph, maintaining that he did have a purpose in the face of overwhelming worldly indifference, Mazz didn't know what was. His sense of purpose carried him easily through the fifteen-minute wait at Newport Station, through the ten-minute journey to Cardiff, and the five-minute walk past the monument and under the Bute Street bridge. It dissipated the moment he walked through the door of the Custom House, went up to the bar and ordered what he suspected would still be the only safe thing to drink in the place: a can of Breaker. It was twelve-forty-five.

'Bobby around?' he asked the barmaid, a new one to him, motherly type from up the Rhondda somewhere, he reckoned.

She looked at him closely. 'Not yet,' she said and glanced at the clock. 'Won't be long, though, I expect.'

Mazz smiled his thanks, sat back on his barstool and surveyed his surroundings.

The Custom House was a dump. Actually, it was somewhere way beyond being a dump. In fact it was a legendary dump. It had been the prostitutes' pub since time immemorial. And for some reason neither the brewery nor the landlord ever seemed to reckon that the girls needed horse brasses or carpet or shelves of fake books or ciabatta rolls or stripped-wood floors, or even a new coat of paint more than once a century. Instead what you had was as basic a boozer as ever existed: a bar along one wall, a handful of scarred tables and matching slashed plastic seats, a pool table near the door and a raucous jukebox stocked exclusively with the kind of tunes only ever listened to by very drunk people. Of which there was never any shortage in the Custom House. 'Cause just as the real football fans one hears so much about are mostly one and the same as the football-hooligan element one also hears so much about, so too are the kind of drinkers you get down the Custom House the real drinkers.

Troubling thing for Mazz was he seemed to be fitting in perfectly. Sitting there on his stool, he wasn't attracting as much as a flicker of interest. Didn't know who they thought he was. Not police, not a pimp either; way he heard it hardly none of the girls ever dealt with white guys. White girls, yeah, most of them were lesbians in their private life and Mazz couldn't exactly argue with that – he wouldn't want to listen to the kind of music he played for a living either. Course they might think he was a punter, but then he'd expect the odd look. The way he was being ignored, it was plain the girls had him marked down as one more lost soul, come home to roost.

He watched the action on the pool table: an Italian-looking girl with hard sharp features was playing a younger girl with acne and a feather cut dyed blonde on the top. The blonde girl was winning, least she had more balls down, but then she missed an easyish cut into the centre pocket and Mazz knew from the way the Italian girl smiled it was over. And so it was, four straight reds and the black arrogantly doubled into the corner.

Mazz got off his stool and walked over to the table, fifty-pence piece held between thumb and forefinger.

'Game?' he said to the Italian girl, nodding at the table.

'No, mate' said the Italian girl. 'Got to wait your turn.'

Mazz looked around, scanning first the table for a row of coins, then the blackboard for a list of names, then the room for a sign of anyone else acting like they were waiting for a game of pool.

The Italian girl just watched him then laughed dismissively in his face.

'Me and her, see,' she said, 'we're having a little tournament, like. Best of nineteen. Like the snooker. Two nil to me, now. You want to watch?' She rolled her eyes theatrically at the blonde as she delivered this last line and her mate obliged by laughing derisively.

'Yeah, mate,' she chipped in, her voice already slurring at lunchtime, 'you like watching, do you?'

Mazz just shook his head, refusing to be intimidated by a couple of pissed girls, and walked over to the jukebox, determined to find something they'd really hate.

Moments later he sat back at the bar listening to the opening strains of the Furey Brothers' 'When I Was Sweet Sixteen', and smiled inwardly as the two pool players looked at each other aghast. For a moment he thought the Italian girl was actually going to come over and get in his face when the door opened and in walked Bobby Ranger.

'All right, Treez,' she said to the Italian girl. 'How's it going, beauty?' she said to the blonde girl. And then she noticed Mazz.

'Good Christ,' she said, standing stock still for a second. Then she came over and hugged him hard. 'Christ,' she said again after a moment. 'You've come for Charlie, haven't you?'

'Yeah,' said Mazz, his voice, much to his surprise, choking slightly, 'I've come for Charlie.'

'Nice,' said Bobby. 'Charlie would have appreciated it. You met my girls then?' She pointed at the Italian and the blonde.

Mazz smiled and said, 'Well, we haven't been introduced, like.'

'Hey,' she said. 'You girls remember I told you 'bout that record I made? Well this is the fella I done it with. Mazz.'

The girls just looked totally unimpressed, mumbled a couple of quick hiyas and went back to their game.

'Drink?' she said to Mazz. He nodded and pointed to the can of Breaker in his hand. She ordered two more off Dianne and led Mazz over to a table in the far corner.

'Welcome to the office,' she said and he smiled again. 'So what's happening? How's the music business?'

She could see him gearing up to bullshit her about how great it all was, but then he caught her looking at him and shook his head. 'Shit, Bobby,' he said. 'Be honest with you, it's pure fucking shit.'

Bobby didn't say anything. What was she supposed to be? Sorry for him? They sat back in silence, Bobby watching Mazz kill off his drink with two huge swallows. Then he dug in his pocket for a packet of Camels.

'Fag, Bob?' he said, holding them towards her. She shook her head and he lit himself one.

'You see any of the others, Bob?'

'Others?'

'Out of the group.'

The group, the Wurriyas. The one shot they'd all had of getting out of Cardiff.

'Col,' she said. 'I sees him now and again. He does a little bit of business. You likes a little draw still?'

Mazz shrugged.

'Well, you want some, Col'll sort you out. Charlie you knows about.'

Mazz nodded.

'And Emyr I 'spect you know more about than I do.'

Mazz shook his head.

'But I 'spect you don't care much about any of the rest of us. It's Tyra you wants to know about, isn't it?'

Mazz couldn't help the blush coming to his face.

'Not just Charlie you've come back for, eh?'

Mazz wanted to deny it, didn't know if he could.

2

GRASSROOTS

1980

First time Mazz clapped eyes on Tyra, be honest, he didn't think anything of it. Tall skinny girl came down to a rehearsal with her dad. Had his mind on other things then. Had the world at his feet. Hard to recapture, to even imagine now, the excitement of that first year in Cardiff.

Mazz came down to Cardiff in the summer of '79, nineteen years old. The second he arrived, moved into a room in a mate's flat in Riverside, he wondered why the hell he'd waited so long. He should have come at sixteen, instead of spending two years pissing around in Cross Keys Tertiary screwing up his A levels and then another year pissing around 'cause he didn't want to leave Gaynor behind. Gaynor he'd have dumped in a day if he'd known the girls he'd find in Cardiff.

Only things Mazz brought with him were a bag of clothes and a Fender Telecaster. He came down in his cousin Stevo's van on a Thursday morning and he played his first gig, jamming with some hard-rock boys from Merthyr down the New Moon, on the Saturday night. Wasn't his scene, the New Moon back then, all bikers and beer on the floor. Took him a few days to find where the punk rockers hung out, down Grassroots.

Grassroots was his base for a while; you could hang out there all day and no one hassled you. Free rehearsal space too, so you got to meet all the bands. Used to have meetings there every Tuesday night with some boys from Splott who were trying to put out a Cardiff compilation album of all the local bands. Got to meet girls too, least you did if you were Mazz. First one he ever went out with in Cardiff was a sixteen-year-old Italian girl from Rumney who always wore a jacket with a big picture of Siouxsie Sioux on the back. First time he ever saw her without it was the first time they went to bed together, middle of the afternoon back in Riverside. She was wild, Maria, used to like doing it in the bath – which was going it some when you lived in a house full of bedsits, communal bathroom down the hall – but what the fuck, Mazz had never suffered much from modesty.

It was around the same time, two three weeks into living in Cardiff, he joined his first band proper. First time he met Jason Flaherty and all. It was a Friday afternoon, pissing down outside. Mazz was sitting in Grassroots reading a copy of the *NME* someone left lying around, waiting for Maria to finish school and get down there. In walked this huge bloke.

Jason Flaherty can only have been a year or two older than Mazz but the size of him always made the age gap seem greater. That and the fact you were scared of him. Size he was some of it had to be fat but enough of it was pure blood muscle you didn't ever cross him you had a choice about it. Anyway, Jason Flaherty walked into Grassroots wearing this giant Crombie, looked around, had a word with Linda behind the counter and went over to Mazz.

'You play guitar,' he'd said to Mazz, and Mazz had agreed and Jason had taken him off in his Triumph Stag, looked like it would collapse under his weight, round to a house off Richmond Road just by the railway line where this band were waiting. They were called Venomous and they were basically just a rock band who speeded up their songs enough to pretend to be a punk band. The singer had green hair which was still a bit of a novelty then but you could see he was a good five years too old for it. All of them were. Took Mazz a while to figure it out because at first he was impressed – these guys were serious, they rehearsed hard, they had gigs lined up; he didn't know the signs of desperation back then, the old lags tarting themselves up one more time to try and make it on the latest bandwagon.

Best thing about Venomous – at least at the time he'd thought it was the best thing – was they introduced him to speed. Mazz had this idea that everyone had a drug that was theirs – one that worked utterly for them – and with him it was speed. He loved it, loved everything about it – the unmistakable taste in the back of your mouth, the minutes when you think it's not working and suddenly realise you're talking like a machine gun, the way you could keep going all night – yeah, with whatever. First time him and Maria took some speed together, Christ, they nearly tore his room apart.

Venomous didn't last long, though. One single paid for by Jason, got a bunch of snotty reviews from the music papers – 'warmed-over speeded-up brain-dead pub rock' was what the man from *Sounds* said. A bunch of support gigs with the Lurkers and then Jason pulled the plug, told them they were a bunch of losers and kicked them out of the house in Roath.

Mazz wasn't bothered; he was a quick study and it hadn't taken him long to figure the emptiness of the band. Hadn't been pushed, he would have left anyway. Next couple of months he just went back to hanging in Grassroots, played with a student band trying to do some arty Talking Heads kind of thing, spent more time worrying about getting their slide show right than rehearsing the songs, but still it got Mazz launched on his student phase – Kate, Michelle, Bethan. He loved them. Specially 'cause they didn't have psycho brothers living round the corner like Maria had. They came after Mazz one time with a bicycle chain cause Maria heard what Mazz had been up to on tour with Venomous. After that they wouldn't let Maria anywhere near Mazz which frankly was fine by him in the circs.

It was with Kate he found out about the ska thing. They were up in London for the weekend, staying with Kate's brother who was a student up there. Ended up going to see the Specials. Place was going utterly wild and the audience was different. Loads of young kids, loads of girls and a lot more black kids than Mazz had ever seen at a gig before. Black guys in the band too – couple of older guys looked like they'd been in reggae bands for years and had hooked up with this bunch of punky white boys – doing old Prince Buster tunes, mixed in with their own stuff. Straight away, and for the only time in his life, Mazz could see that this was a new scene, one that was going to be big, and if he jumped in now he could be a part of it.

Back in Cardiff, Mazz got to work. Went down Kelly's secondhand stall in the market, picked up all the old ska stuff he could find, which wasn't much. But it gave him something to start with. Days on end Mazz sat in the flat completely rethinking his guitar playing – just working on getting those chicken-scratch rhythm chords together, letting the syncopation enter his soul. He started checking all the groups in Grassroots carefully, looking for musicians to steal. Only possibility was a kid called Emyr, an angel-faced skinhead looked about twelve and played the drums like a whirlwind in a band called Smegma, the absolute worst bunch of punk-rock losers you could imagine. It was pure racket but underneath Mazz could feel Emyr's time was faultless.

A Wednesday morning walking back from town after signing on, Mazz went into the junkshop at the end of his road, Frankie Johnson's place. There were a couple of cardboard boxes of records balanced on top of a three-piece suite and Mazz headed for them, pulled along by the sight of an album cover with a picture of a black girl wrapped in a snake. He picked it up – *Tighten Up* it was called – and, as Mazz suspected, it was a collection of early rocksteady tunes. He delved further into the box. And discovered he'd found a regular gold mine: three albums by Lee Perry's Upsetters, a couple of Prince Buster singles on the old Blue Beat label, *Guns of Navarone* by the Skatalites, a couple more things by people he'd never heard of but sounded like they were probably the right stuff. Mazz dug in his pockets, figured he could spend a couple of quid, and gathered together ten likely-looking singles and one of the Lee Perry albums, *The Return of Django*.

The black guy who ran the place looked at him with mild surprise. 'You like this old stuff, son?'

'Yeah,' said Mazz. 'You got any more, like?'

'Maybe,' said the guy. 'I knows the feller brought this lot in, I'll ask him he's got any more.'

Mazz said ta and thought no more about it. The records were great, though, so when his next dole cheque showed up on the Friday he headed back down the shop. This time he was hardly in the door when the guy called him over. 'Hey, Prince Buster! Over here, man.'

The guy was sat at a little table at the back of the shop playing cards with another feller, a wiry middle-aged black man. 'Hey,' said the shop guy, 'Charlie, this is who bought all your records.'

And that was how Mazz came to meet Charlie Unger. Ten minutes later Charlie had Mazz spending some more of his dole cheque on pints of

Guinness over the Four Ways. Hour or so after that Mazz was telling Charlie about the band he was planning and Charlie said he played percussion, bongos, congas, that kind of thing, and he knew a load of docks boys played and all. Mazz smiled and said yeah, that would be cool and left Charlie in the company of a couple of old geezers wanted to talk boxing and thought little more of it.

Couple of days later, though, he was walking past the secondhand store again, carrying his guitar, on the way over to Grassroots, and the cry went out, 'Hey, boss,' and Mazz turned and there was Charlie emerging from the gloom wearing a neat sixties suit, porkpie hat perched on his head.

A couple of weeks later and things were starting to move; the first rehearsal was set up at Grassroots. Mazz got there early. Emyr the drummer arrived more or less on time and Charlie showed up, with a young dread called Col who played keyboards, a full hour and a half late, which wasn't too bad as by then Mazz had got Emyr more or less familiar with the basic rhythms. Charlie kept up a constant patter, stories from his boxing days – which was the first Mazz had heard that Charlie used to be the lightweight champion – interspersed with little riffs aimed at any girls who stopped in front of the stage for more than two seconds.

After three or four hours of hard work they'd figured out the rudiments of two Prince Buster songs and 'The Return of Django' and then Charlie called a time out and they all trooped out the back door into the deserted building site for a quick spliff. 'So two things we need,' said Charlie, 'a singer and a bass player. You know any bass players?'

Mazz and Emyr looked at each other then shook their heads. 'None worth speaking of, like,' said Mazz.

Charlie thought for a little while then smiled. 'Well,' he said, 'maybe I've got an idea 'bout that. Now, either of you boys sing?'

Mazz and Emyr looked at each other once again. Mazz shook his head firmly; Emyr shrugged and said, 'A bit, like, but if I'm playing the drums . . .'

'Fair enough,' said Charlie. 'You and me can do the backing vocals, then, but we need a singer. Best thing you put an advert out there, son,' he said, looking at Mazz. Mazz wondered what was happening to the chain of command here but shrugged again and said yeah, he'd get on to it.

What Mazz did was put up a poster in Grassroots asking anyone interested in singing in a new ska band to show up the next Wednesday at six.

Once again he and Emyr were the first ones there and it was Mazz who had to deal with the unlikely gaggle of misfits interested in being the singer. Emyr wanted to wait for Col and Charlie to arrive but Mazz decided to get on with it so Emyr got behind his kit and Mazz asked bloke number one, some kid with green hair called Frog hung around a lot, what he wanted to sing. Frog said he wanted to sing something by Crass, Mazz told him to fuck off so the bloke said how about something by the Pistols then and Mazz powered into 'God Save the Queen' and Emyr started hammering at the kit and Frog started yelling his head off and it was quite all right for about half a minute at which point it quickly became clear that Frog couldn't sing a note.

The next bloke was even worse – some student type with a bit of an attitude. Demanded they played 'Honky Tonk Woman' and started bunny-hopping round the stage in the worst Mick Jagger impersonation you could conceive of. Half a minute of that and Mazz waved to Emyr to stop and told the bloke to fuck off and die.

This had the side effect of causing the other two blokes hanging round to disappear as well and Mazz was starting to feel a bit of an idiot when this little mixed-race skinhead girl came up and said was it all right she had a go.

Mazz said OK and the girl hopped on stage and asked if they knew that Specials song that was in the charts, like – 'Gangsters' – and Mazz and Emyr cranked it out as it was basically just the old rhythm from Prince Buster's 'Al Capone', and the girl – you could see she was nervous as hell but at the same time she had an energy there – gave it a go. It wasn't great or anything, but compared to the idiots they'd just tried out she looked like a godsend.

'What's your name?' Mazz said after the song stumbled to halt. 'I've seen you round, haven't I?'

'Yeah,' said the girl, 'I'm Bobby. They calls you Mazz, don't they?'

'Yeah,' agreed Mazz and right then Col and Charlie walked in accompanied by a tall light-skinned black girl, around Mazz's age, a long serious face, maybe a little Somali in there, and her hair up in very short locks. All three of the newcomers were carrying musical equipment.

'How's it going, boss?' said Charlie to Mazz. 'Meet my daughter, Tyra; she plays the bass.'

'Hiya,' said Mazz, not needing to adjust his line of vision up or down to look her in the eye.

'Hiya,' said Tyra back, holding Mazz's look but not giving it anything. Just then another figure appeared, a black guy with glasses and an Afro, bit on the overweight side.

'And this is Delroy,' said Charlie, 'my little girl's boyfriend and bass teacher, like. Delroy plays with Radical Roots, yeah.'

Mazz nodded. Radical Roots were like *the* Cardiff reggae band, which wasn't saying much. He felt pissed off really; why hadn't Charlie talked this guy into playing in the band instead of his daughter probably on lesson two? He shook Delroy's hand quickly and then said, 'Right, let's get on with it.' Col and Charlie got on the stage and started setting up, Delroy and Tyra went into a corner and Mazz's heart sank as he saw Delroy tune the bass for her. Then he fetched Bobby from over by the coffee bar and introduced her to the rest of the crew. Col and Charlie both gave her looks that were a little short of enthusiastic, Mazz couldn't help noticing.

And that was how it all started, really. The rehearsal wasn't great; Tyra was obviously not that good, fluffed her parts a few times but her time was OK which is the crucial thing with a bass player and Emyr seemed happy enough to play with her. On the upside, too, Bobby came on with leaps and bounds. After a little while she was bouncing around the stage belting out the old Desmond Dekker thing, '007', which was the one song they all seemed to know well enough. She didn't have much range but she had a big strong tone and that love for the limelight that Mazz had realised was the main requirement for pop success.

Fast-forward a couple of months and the band was ready for the first gig. They now had a name – the Wurriyas – from a Somali greeting 'Hey, wurriya', meant brother as far as Mazz knew. Hanging out with Charlie in Butetown he'd heard people use it and it kind of stuck in his head. Wurriya – halfway between worrier and warrior – suited Mazz down to the ground. They had a dozen numbers – ten ska classics and a couple of Mazz's own songs, one of them with a few changes made by Bobby – made it more of a girl's song, like.

Couple of days before the first gig, a semi-private kind of thing in Grassroots, Mazz went on a demo. What happened was, the night before, Saturday night, he'd got off with Kate again. Hadn't seen her for a couple of months, and then he'd been at this party and she'd been at this party and all of a sudden they were in some bedroom with a bottle of wine, locked the door, chucked the big pile of coats on the floor and got to it. People kept banging on the door trying to come in and get their coats while Kate and Mazz just laughed and laughed. Eventually they emerged, nicked a couple more bottles of wine and went back to hers.

Next morning Mazz was all for staying in bed all day. But around twelve Kate started getting up and told Mazz he had to go on this demo. Some Irish thing, this IRA guy called Bobby Sands was on hunger strike about something or other and it was their duty to go and support him. 'Imagine, Mazz,' she said, 'this guy's been living in this cell covered in his own shit and not eaten for thirty days. Have you ever heard of anything so heroic?'

Be honest, Mazz thought he'd heard all the heroic stories he needed to growing up in the valleys, living through the miners' strike. But it was one of the things he was getting used to, student politics. Freaked him out first time he'd heard someone going on about supporting the IRA; now he knew the form, knew the words to mouth; anti-imperialist struggle, not about religion about civil rights, the Birmingham pub bombings were carried out by MI5 and what about Bloody Sunday, eh?

And of course as a Welsh nationalist it was just the comradely thing to do, lend one's support to our Celtic brothers across the sea. Not of course that Mazz had ever thought about Welsh nationalism for two consecutive seconds before he came to Cardiff. Not beyond the sporting chauvinism level anyway. Course since then he'd met all these nice student girls from Canterbury and Leamington Spa, who had all learned about three words of Welsh and were well into it, and who was Mazz to play down his Celtic roots? So fine, he'd said, and pulled on last night's jeans and last night's wine-stained white shirt.

In the end, though, they'd had another quick one before they made it out of the door and the demo was just about moving off when they arrived at the rallying point in Splott Park. Kate immediately joined her student mates in the WRP, all gathered around their trophy member, some tough old girl from Ely they'd discovered on a housing protest. Mazz nipped into the newsagent's and by the time he came out the march was fifty yards up the road and he had to jog forward to catch up.

Suddenly he realised he was standing next to Tyra. She was walking along with a couple of other girls: a serious-looking Indian and a beefy white girl carrying a placard. Mazz quickly scanned the placard to find out what brand of revolutionary Tyra was hanging out with and nodded to himself when he saw it was the SWP. Girl had obviously been recruited at one of their Rock Against Racism things.

Just then Tyra turned her head and noticed him there. 'Oh,' she said. 'Hiya.'

'Hiya,' said Mazz. 'Didn't know you were into politics, like.'

Tyra blushed. He was sure of it. It hadn't really occurred to him that black people could blush – be honest, black people had hardly occurred to him at all, growing up in Newbridge – and he felt oddly touched.

'Well,' she said, 'I don't really know much, but Leila' – she inclined her head towards the Asian girl – 'got me to come along.'

'Yeah, well same with me really,' said Mazz, stopping short of mentioning Kate. 'Some mates of mine in the WRP got me to come. Don't think they get on with your lot.' He nodded at the SWP banner up ahead.

Tyra quickly glanced around to check no one was paying attention the looked at Mazz and rolled her eyes. 'Mad, isn't it?'

Mazz smiled back. 'Hey,' he said, 'how are you enjoying the music, like?'

'Great,' said Tyra.

'Must be a bit weird being in the band with your dad.'

She frowned. 'No. It's all right. Charlie's never been . . . Well he never lived with us, like, so he's . . . I dunno. Being in the band with him . . . it's like if I was a boy he'd have taken me out fishing with him or taken me boxing like he did. Now playing music's something we can share. Get to know each other, like.'

'Right,' said Mazz, not really sure what she was saying, but again oddly touched by the way she was talking to him. Just straight ahead. 'Looking forward to the gig?'

'Terrified, to be honest with you,' she said and smiled again, this time a real teeth-and-all grin.

'Your first time is it?'

'Yeah . . . no . . . well, I've done a few things in school. In the orchestra.'

'Oh,' said Mazz, 'right.' And they walked on for a little while, then Tyra's friend Leila started talking to her and Mazz decided it was time he moved forward a bit and found Kate.

Later on Mazz and Kate had a bit of a row. After the demo had finished over City Hall with the usual speeches and a little bit of excitement when a couple of dozen NF types made a half-hearted attempt to get at the marchers, Mazz had gone back with Kate and her WRP mates to their local guru's house. His name was Tony, some kind of lecturer as far as Mazz could gather, and frankly the whole scene was positively creepy. All these little student girls were coming up to Tony telling him how many newspapers they'd sold that week and he would nod approvingly or give them this saddened look of reproach.

And all the time these people were being terribly nice to Mazz. Took him a little while to figure out why. Eventually some girl – Helen, he thought her name was – came over and told him he must meet Tony. Tony was really keen to meet him. Telling him this like Mazz was really honoured. So Mazz shrugged and followed her over to Tony who was stood with a couple of little girls, and he shooed them all away and gave Mazz a serious look and then let the cat out of the bag straight away.

'So good to have some working-class comrades getting involved.' Course it was Mazz's accent had this lot wetting their knickers – hey, look, we've got a genuine prole here.

So this Tony gave Mazz the whole spiel. Up the miners, down with Maggie. Irish struggle is our struggle, troops out, Trots in. Wasn't a bad pitch, as it went; guy had probably made a great timeshare salesman in later life, but he'd read Mazz wrong. Had enough of that up-the-miners shit from his dad. Didn't want to hear it down in Cardiff from some smooth fucker like Tony.

'Yeah, mate, right on,' he said, the first moment Tony paused for air, and wandered off in search of a drink.

Kate was furious with him.

'How could you do that to me?' she yelled, the minute they got back to her place.

'What?' said Mazz.

'Humiliate me like that.'

'What?' said Mazz again, genuinely baffled.

'Talking to Tony like that. Don't you know who he is?'

'Yeah, he's . . .' Mazz paused. Even drunk as he by now was, he could figure that if he uttered the words 'a boring cunt' his chances of getting anywhere with Kate that night were fucked so he bit his lip and said, 'He's your leader, like, in the Party.'

'He's not a leader, Mazz, he's our most prominent intellectual theorist.' Like she was reading off the back of a book. 'He's written two books and he's met all these revolutionaries round the world and I can't believe you could act like that.'

'Like what?'

'Like such a wanker, after all he's done for you people.'

Fuck, thought Mazz, as those last two words just hung there. *You people.* To be fair, Kate realised what she'd said and did her best to apologise, but like with most apologies only made it worse. Sober, Mazz might have let her get away with it – just one of the hazards of screwing students, getting patronised once in a while – but on this night, drunk, he wouldn't have it. He came back at her with a ferocity that surprised him, all the frustrations of his year in Cardiff pouring out, then left her there crying.

Walking back across town to Riverside, Mazz realised he still had a copy of the paper stuck in his jacket pocket. He was about to chuck it in the nearest bin, when for want of anything better to do he started reading the cover story.

It was all about this Bobby Sands feller. And cynical as Mazz was, he couldn't help but be impressed by the guts of the man, this IRA activist who was well on the way to starving himself to death if the government didn't give in to his demand to be treated as a political prisoner. Seemed obvious enough to Mazz. If it wasn't political what the IRA did, what the hell was it? You didn't have to agree with their politics to see that.

The rest of the paper was all bollocks, though, and it found its way into a bin on the corner of Queen Street. Somewhere between the castle and the bridge, a distance of a hundred yards or so, a song popped into his head, fully formed. First the chorus then the first verse. Nothing to do with Bobby Sands, or arguing with your girlfriend – well, maybe a bit more the latter – but basically it was just a nonsense pop song with a ska beat. The chorus mostly consisted of repeating the words 'lick her down' over and over. It would be variously lauded as a joyous piece of sexual liberation and damned as a hymn to male violence and it was to be the Wurriyas' one and only hit.

Mazz brought it along to the rehearsal the next day. Embarrassed as hell actually. Songwriting wasn't his thing, and particularly those rare songs that just came out of nowhere – you were never sure if they were great or whether it was just something you'd heard on the radio when you weren't paying attention and your subconscious had just rehashed it. No problem this time, though. The arrangement came together as easily as the song and, once Bobby had taken the thirty seconds necessary to learn the words, the sight of her singing, 'Lick her down, lick her down, you better lick her down,' with her tongue rolling lasciviously out of her mouth was frankly hysterical.

It was also the moment Mazz realised Bobby was a lesbian. Obvious now but back then, be honest, lesbians were a bit of a novelty. You kind of knew they existed but it was mostly something blokes shouted at girls who wouldn't go out with them, not something anyone Mazz knew actually did.

The gig went well. Not that that meant too much. First gigs tended to go well in Mazz's experience. All your mates would come down and say it was great even if it was shit. Then again, playing ska you couldn't go too far wrong, not this year anyway. Long as you got the beat halfway right, there were a load of kids out there, happy to have their first local ska band on the scene . . .

Afterwards, eleven o'clock, the gear all packed away, Mazz was cursing the licensing laws, meant it was too late to get a celebratory drink.

'Don't worry about that, man,' said Charlie. 'We'll go to a little blues thing, down the docks.'

Mazz looked at the others. Col and Emyr, the sinsemilla twins, gave their customary stoned nods of acceptance.

Bobby shook her head. 'Kenny's place? Nah. Well, maybe later. I got someone to see first.'

Bobby winked at Mazz and he nearly laughed out loud. 'How about you, Tyra?' he said then. 'You and Delroy coming?'

Delroy, who was as ever sitting in the corner with Tyra, frowned. 'No, man, we got things to do.'

'No we haven't.' That was Tyra and Mazz took an involuntary step backwards. First time he'd heard Tyra argue with anything Delroy said.

Delroy took Tyra by the arm and they walked over to the far end of the room, by the coffee bar. A conversation followed, conducted in angry whispers and culminating in a bout of finger pointing. Then Delroy walked back fast past the members of the band and out the back door. Tyra came slowly over towards them, giving them a don't-you-dare-mention-any-of-that look.

Half an hour later, Mazz, Charlie, Tyra, Emyr and Col were getting out of a cab in West Bute Street by the Dowlais. Charlie led the way down the alley by the side of the pub and stopped at an unmarked door on the left. He rang on the bell and almost immediately a hugely built young man with short dreads opened the door.

'All right, Charlie,' he said. 'Tyra. Col. Who are these boys then?' Angling his head towards Mazz and Emyr.

'Boys from the ska band I been telling you about. Mazz, Emyr, this is Kenny.'

Mazz stuck his hand out and felt like an idiot when the fella called Kenny just turned his back and led the way up two flights of stairs into what looked like a fair-sized living-room with a little bar stuck in one corner and a DJ system in another.

The DJ, a rasta with waist-length locks and dark glasses on in what was already a pretty dark room, was playing some lovers' rock, all big dirty basslines with South London schoolgirls warbling off-key over the top. Charlie nodded to the guy who nodded fractionally back and then Charlie went over to the bar.

Little while later on, Charlie was off talking to Kenny, Emyr and Col were in the corner spliffing up, for a change, like, which left Mazz and Tyra standing by the bar. Mazz was drinking from a bottle of pale ale; Tyra had a glass of an unlikely mixture of Guinness and orange juice. Conversation had come to a halt when Charlie moved off, so Mazz had a go at reigniting it.

'You were good tonight,' he said.

'Yeah, thanks,' said Tyra, distracted.

'No, really. You and Emyr, you got the groove there.'

'Mmm.'

'You got trouble with your boyfriend, then? You want to talk about it?'

Tyra looked at him then, forced a smile on to her face. 'Not really.'

They fell silent again after that, Tyra sipping her drink, Mazz scanning the room for likely talent. He was just sizing up a blonde piece standing over by the DJ when a scary-looking guy with a couple of gold teeth, and a scar on his left cheek serious enough to be visible even in this light from across the room, walked over and casually put his arm round the blonde. Mazz figured it was probably best to wait a little, check out the runnings, before making a move in a place like this. So he was just drifting off, moving unconsciously to the music which was now some upbeat Dennis Brown thing, when he was jolted out of his reverie by Tyra pulling on his sleeve.

'You want to dance?'

Mazz shrugged, smiled, stuck his pale ale on the bar next to Tyra's murky concoction, and moved on to the floor.

Blame what happened next on the beat. There probably is a way to dance to reggae that isn't blatantly sexual but Mazz hadn't come across it, nor had any of the other people in the room. Nor Tyra. She was winding up her waist with the best of them and as Mazz danced with her he was struck with surprise as he realised first that she was interested, and second that he was too.

Mazz, for once, was disconcerted, blindsided, a little unnerved by knowing this girl already. Usually that didn't happen; the sex thing came first or not at all. Which made it easy. There is a thing girls say – which like a lot of things girls say sounds nice but is essentially shit – about how they want to be friends, how they want to get to know a boy before they can really fancy them. Bollocks, only reason people really fancy each other, way Mazz saw it, was 'cause they didn't know each other. Getting to know people took the shine off matters fast as anything. You didn't want to find out all that same old shit: bloke lives in a pigsty, girl has fluffy animals on her bed. You wanted to get down to doing the in-bed on-the-floor in-the-bath stuff a.s.a.p.

Now this – Mazz realised in those first seconds of dancing together, catching Tyra's eyes shining as she looked at him – was going to be harder. Already he knew more than he cared to know about a girl. He knew her old boyfriend and her dad. Her dad, for Christ's sake. And of course ticking in the back of his brain he supposed there was always the other thing. The black thing.

But, for the moment, in that moment in Kenny's blues, there was just music and dancing and two young people, neither of them yet twenty years old, looking at each other and laughing and leaving the dance floor together, on a shared smile, to get a drink at the bar.

'Hot,' she said after a minute, rolling her drink across her forehead to cool down.

'Hot,' Mazz agreed. 'You want to get some air?'

Tyra looked at Mazz hard, like she was searching for something in his face, then she smiled. 'Yeah,' she said, 'come with me.'

Tyra led the way back across the room. Charlie was engrossed in conversation with some tattooed white guy, looked like another ex-boxer, and Mazz was relieved not to catch his eye. On their way out the door, Mazz heard a hiss from behind him. He turned and saw a couple of hard young black guys, looking less than impressed by the sight of Mazz and Tyra leaving together. Mazz was about to move towards them when Tyra tugged on his shirt and pulled him after her out on to the landing.

Mazz started down the stairs but quickly realised Tyra wasn't behind him. Instead she inclined her head upwards, and Mazz followed her up two more flights of stairs to a semi-derelict attic floor. Tyra opened a door and suddenly they were out on the roof, looking up at a three-quarter moon.

Mazz closed the deal right away. Lot of blokes would have blown a situation like this, started jabbering away about what a nice night it was, all that bollocks, making themselves nervous, making the girl nervous too. Mazz didn't say a word, just leaned his back against the wall and pulled Tyra to him. And his lips were on her lips, his hands up the back of her shirt before she had time to think let alone speak.

And it was nice, she was nice, gave the kiss back hard. He liked her basketball muscles, her big eyes, laughed at the way she pulled his hand forward to rub her tits, but slapped that same hand away when it wandered near her carefully arranged hair.

A little while later they were lying on the ground on top of Mazz's coat, getting seriously intimate with each other, when Tyra said the first semi-coherent words either of them had uttered since they got on to the roof.

'You got any . . . you know?'

'No,' said Mazz. 'You taking . . .'

Tyra shook her head and Mazz said the words men tend to say in those particular situations: 'It'll be all right.' And kept on moving his fingers just where he'd been moving them for the last minute or two, and Tyra sighed and spread herself for him.

And it was good. Course it was. Nothing to beat it. Could have gone on a bit longer, Mazz had to admit, but that was the first time for you. And afterwards, be honest, she seemed a little down, but that was another thing Mazz had noticed, lot of girls went funny after sex. Guilt kicking in, he reckoned. Still, it was a bit of a chicken-and-egg thing far as he could see: it was the guilt that got you right up for it in the first place, and it was the guilt made you sad after, rough with the smooth, like.

And Mazz was a gent, he took Tyra back to her place after. Sneaking past the blues which was still going, making sure Charlie didn't spot them. Tyra lived on Angelina Street, at the town end of Butetown, so Mazz walked her there through the empty streets, kissed her on the street corner, quickly 'cause he could tell she was nervous about being spotted, and said he'd see her at rehearsal tomorrow. He walked back along the embankment to Riverside, whistling most of the way.

3

THE ROYAL OAK

1999

Tyra had an appointment. Twelve-thirty round the police station. Copper there Jimmy Fairfax, who she knew from school as it happened, wanted to see her. Something about her dad. Returning some effects of his. Walking over there she realised she'd not paid much attention to the details. She'd just felt so guilty when she'd heard. Charlie, her dad, dead in his flat, been there a week and nobody noticed. She'd just felt so like shit she hadn't even asked what happened. Suspected heart attack they'd said and that had sounded about right. Amount Charlie had smoked and drank, and all those years of boxing couldn't have helped. Now, though, she thought she'd better ask this Jimmy Fairfax, who she hoped to God had changed from the little hooligan he'd been in school, what exactly the state of play was.

Thing was he didn't seem to know too much either.

Fact was, and it was kind of funny really, he spent most of the time she was in the station just looking at her. Yeah, yeah, that look, the 'I want to get next to you' look, not the 'Oh I'm sorry about your dear old dad' look. And the awful thing was, though she was starting to get used to it now, she felt like saying, 'All right, let's get down to it right here in this little interview cubicle.' She didn't, of course, even though to be fair Jimmy Fairfax looked a whole lot better than she remembered from school, worked out a bit obviously and wearing a decent-looking suit. Bit embarrassed about it he was in fact, said he'd just been in court, but she liked to see a man in a nice suit.

'Nothing else to do then is there?' she said after Jimmy had handed her a bag containing the things they'd found in Charlie's pockets. His wallet, his lighter, couple of betting slips. She didn't look at the wallet – knew there'd be a picture of her in there and the second she saw it the waterworks would start and she didn't want that, not there in that room.

'Not as far as we're concerned, love,' he said. 'There'll be the inquest tomorrow. No need for you to come; it's just a formality, like. I mean, it's not like anyone would have murdered him, is it?'

'Nah,' said Tyra, though fleetingly the absurd fantasy came into her head that one of the betting slips might have been a big winner or maybe a lottery ticket . . . Nah, hardly, her dad never had that kind of luck.

Tyra just stared at the little plastic bag full of her dad's relics and for a moment Jimmy just sat there too. Then after a little while he stood up, moved over to her and with surprising gentleness put his hand on her shoulder, sending another shaft of unwanted electricity right through her.

'You all right?' he said. 'Yourself, like?'

'Yes,' she said, 'I'm fine, uh, Jimmy,' she said, finding it odd the sound of his name on her lips. If she'd ever spoken to him before it was probably just a 'Fuck off, Fairfax' in the playground. She stood up quickly, losing his hand in the process.

'Thanks,' she said, 'thanks for asking, though.'

He showed her out on to James Street and, as she was just walking off, called after her. 'When's the funeral then?'

'Friday,' she said. 'St Cuthbert's. Twelve o'clock.'

'Right,' he said, 'I'll see you there then, like, pay my respects to the old man.'

She turned then to face him. 'You knew Charlie?'

'Oh yeah,' he said, 'everyone knew your dad,' and he smiled and suddenly she had the sense that he was holding something back, but before she could follow up he had said goodbye and was back into the station, leaving her standing on James Street, frowning.

Mazz didn't stay much longer in the Custom House. Had a game of pool with Bobby for old times' sake and got beaten with contemptuous ease, so he said he'd see her around and headed out on to Bute Street. As the fresh air hit him he realised the first thing he had to do was find somewhere to stay. He stopped for a moment to think. He had enough money to stay in a guest house somewhere he supposed, but he'd sooner not. God knows how long the five hundred pounds was going to have to last him. And, anyway, guest houses just evoked the depression of those endless bloody tours, playing in bands who were always on the way up or the way down, never at the bloody top. No, best thing was to find someone to crash with. He dug into his shoulder bag and pulled out an ancient black notebook. Then he headed back under the bridge and into the Golden Cross to make a few calls.

Leafing through the address book in the corner of the bar, he had a sudden awful sense of just how much time had gone by since he'd lived in this place. Almost twenty years and yet here they still were, all these phone numbers from yesteryear. Michelle, Emma, Kate. Three students all lived in the same house; he'd got off with Michelle and Kate, never got anywhere with Emma. Likelihood they'd all stayed living in the same bedsits for the next two decades? Less than zero. More girls' numbers: Lucy, Gail, Bethan. Bethan? She'd lived with her parents; maybe they'd still be in the same place, and . . . And what? Hey, remember me? I'm Mazz, we had a one-night stand back in 1980. You were really keen but I never bothered to call you again. How about I come and stay with you and your husband and your three teenage kids up in Radyr? Yeah, that'd work. Christ, he started to wonder as he went through the ancient pencil-marked numbers, had he had any male friends at all, or just spent his whole time chasing girls? Then he found one: Lawrence.

Lawrence with an ancient biro address and then over the top of it a felt-tipped phone number 'cause he'd run into him up in London a couple of years back.

Lawrence had been the coolest person Mazz had ever met back when he first came to Cardiff. He was the DJ in the club they always went to, Mel's down in the docks. Tall thin guy with locks, though he was never really a rasta far as Mazz knew. Been Lawrence who'd introduced Mazz to reggae, and helped him find the old stuff: the Prince Buster tunes and that that had been the basis of the Wurriyas. Mazz found himself grinning at the memory, then he recalled the last time he'd seen Lawrence up in London, still charming but frayed around the edges, and he was put in mind that it was Lawrence who'd introduced him to a lot of other stuff too. Drugs and that.

Whatever, thought Mazz, he wasn't overburdened with options, so he reached for the phone on the edge of the bar and rang Lawrence's number.

The phone was picked up on the first ring. 'Danny,' said the voice at the other end of the line.

'No,' said Mazz. 'It's Mazz here. Is that you, Lawrence?'

'Oh,' said the voice, then there was a pause as Mazz could sense a hand being placed over the receiver and then heard a voice – Lawrence he was sure – shouting, 'No, it's not him, it's just some guy.' Then Lawrence came back on the line. 'Hey, Mazz, whassup, bra?'

'I'm down in Cardiff. I was thinking of coming to see you.'

Another pause, then, 'Great, yeah. Listen, where are you now, man?'

'Town.'

'Tell you what, I've got a little bit of business to sort out. Give us a couple of hours, and come round. You know the place?'

'No, just got your number.'

'All right, 110 Constellation Street, over Adamsdown. Later then, man,' and with that Lawrence hung up, leaving Mazz standing there at the bar with the receiver in his hand and foreboding in his heart, wearily sure what the scene would be round Lawrence's place.

Suddenly tired of drinking, Mazz left his half-finished pint on the bar and headed out into the late-afternoon sunshine. He walked past the ice rink into town, pausing briefly to mourn the passing of the Salutation, his regular drinker in the old days, now part of the foundations of Toys 'R' us. He kept moving into the Hayes, went into Spillers Records simply because it was a surviving landmark, not 'cause he had the remotest intention of buying anything. Like most of the musicians he knew, Mazz didn't even possess a CD player and had hardly bought any music since the early eighties. Only time he ever heard anything new was the stuff whatever woman he was with would play, and most of the time that would be some hideous indie dance bullshit that simply confirmed him in his prejudice. Still, it would be even worse if he was one of those sad bastard ponytails who ran around trying to be part of fucking Britpop.

Back on the street he kept walking for another hundred yards then stopped at the open-air snack bar, once again more out of familiarity than necessity, though once he'd sat down with a cup of tea and a tuna sandwich he realised he was starving and ended up eating three more sandwiches.

A quick shufti round the shops and a leisurely stroll eastwards past the prison and he made it over to Adamsdown almost exactly two hours after he'd phoned Lawrence.

The scene in Constellation Street was precisely as expected. A spectral redhead opened the door and ushered Mazz into the front room, which contained an old sofa, three bean bags, a TV showing *Hollyoaks* and precious little else.

'He's upstairs,' she said. 'I'll just go and get him for you.'

An hour passed; the phone rang three times. Mazz dozed off briefly, woke up towards the end of the Channel Four news. Still no sign of Lawrence or the redhead. He stood up, went into the kitchen, checked the fridge for beer and found it wanting, wrote a note in felt tip saying, 'Back later, maybe,' and walked back out into Adamsdown.

He kept on walking away from town, past Clifton Street with its despairing discount furniture stores and great Italian caff. No more Patrice's Grill, though: the place you used to be able to drink all night long as you ordered a portion of chips had finally bitten the dust. He carried on along Broadway, past the snooker hall and the studio the band went into once, and finally arrived at the Royal Oak.

The Oak was one of the last reminders of the old Cardiff. Three bars plus a snug and a skittle alley. One bar for the hippies, one bar for the R&B bands, and the big public bar full of boxing mementoes for anyone and everyone. There was a boxing gym upstairs where they all used to train – Peerless Jim Driscoll, Joey Erskine, Randolph Turpin, Charlie Unger – and their pictures and yellowed cuttings were everywhere downstairs.

Mazz walked into the public bar; five years at least since he'd last set foot in there but no one seemed to have moved a muscle since he first went in there twenty years ago. Same old geezers in the corner with their personal mugs drinking the SA from the wood that you couldn't get in any other pub in the known world; same old parties of three generations of raucous girls whooping it up beneath the TV screen – that was new, to be fair, the big Sky Sports apparatus, but the same phone was next to it and he was sure, he looked careful at the piece of wood next to the phone he'd find the numbers he'd scribbled down there: Michelle, Kate, Tyra . . .

No Charlie Unger, though. It hadn't been Charlie's regular, the Oak – too far from where he lived – but he loved to come down here once in a while, get a little respect, a little affirmation of who he used to be.

Mazz stood at the bar, drinking a pint of dark. After a while he saw the bloke standing along the bar from him – tall old hippy with a grey ponytail – had finished with his *Echo* so Mazz begged it off him. When he handed it back ten minutes later, he looked at the bloke closely and the bloke looked at him. Then the bloke smiled and said, 'Hey, how you doing, butt?'

Mazz was still none the wiser. 'Good,' he said. 'Good to be back in here, anyway. I've been away, like,' he trailed off and the bloke nodded sympathetically. 'How about you?' he added in the hope that the answer might shake loose some recognition.

'Yeah, you know, the usual, like,' said the bloke completely unhelpfully, then burst out laughing. 'You don't have a fucking clue who I am, butt, do you?'

'No, sorry, mate,' said Mazz, raising his glass and smiling too.

'The Colonel,' said the bloke, 'that's me. You remembering now, or you swallowed too many mushrooms since last time?'

'Christ,' said Mazz, scanning frantically through the memory banks and then striking gold, 'the Colonel. You were the bloke on *Mastermind*. Years ago, answered questions on Bruce Springsteen and the Civil War or something.'

'Yeah,' said the Colonel, 'that was me.'

'They had a little party for you in here and we played in the back room.'

'That's right, mate,' said the Colonel, 'and I came up and asked you if you could play "Born to Run" and I'd sing and you told me to fuck off.'

'And you nearly broke my fucking nose, you bastard,' said Mazz, finishing off the story.

'Yeah, well, I was wondering when you'd remember that bit,' said the Colonel. 'Have another drink, butt, least I can do for you.'

Mazz raised his near-empty pint of dark, signalling his readiness for another one.

Couple of hours down the line, Mazz and the Colonel were getting on like a house on fire. They were just standing out in the back yard of the pub, near the toilets, sharing a spliff when the Colonel said, 'Fancy a game of pool?' And Mazz said why not and next thing they were in the back of a cab and another ten minutes or so they were getting out outside what had to be the dodgiest-looking pub in Penarth – the faded Edwardian resort across the far side of Cardiff Bay, and a place longer on nursing homes than dodgy pubs. This one, though, was called The Royal and it was smack opposite the only middle-rise council blocks in town, on top of the hill looking back over the bay.

Inside it was unnervingly brightly lit and populated by a mixture of old geezers, a few lads and a bunch of long-bearded old hippies congregated next to the bar. Mazz and the Colonel were at home from the off.

The Colonel walked up to the bar, ordered up a couple of pints of something called Bullmastiff, then led the way round to the back room which sported a great big gaudy mural of the sort more usually found in youth clubs, depicting what Mazz took to be the pub's regulars, and a pool table.

The Colonel stuck fifty pence in the slot and racked up the balls.

'Break?' he said to Mazz, who nodded, walked round to the end of the table and just smashed the cue ball as hard as he could. Two reds and a yellow went down, and Mazz could see he was in luck; three more reds had ended up around the centre pockets and Mazz picked them off easily. A tricky long red into the corner pocket followed and then a bit of luck as the cue ball just kept on rolling, casually sorting out the little cluster of balls around the back as it did so, and leaving a nice easy angle on the last red back into the centre. Just the black left; another nice straight shot into the corner. Mazz found himself breaking into a smile as he lined the shot up. Only once or twice he'd ever done that – run all the balls in straight from the break. He stopped himself in mid-shot, looked over at the Colonel and winked. The Colonel winked back and Mazz returned to his shot. He rolled the black nicely into the pocket and watched disbelievingly as the cue ball seemed once again to suddenly gather momentum, and dropped straight after the black into the same pocket.

'Hard luck, mate,' said the Colonel straight-faced, and Mazz looked at him aghast. Then the Colonel burst out laughing and Mazz did the same.

'Luck like that, butt, I shouldn't show my face out of doors.'

Mazz shrugged and laughed again, but would have sworn he was cursed the way things went over the next four games of pool. Every time he seemed to have the frame in his pocket and every time something screwed up absurdly. Then, thankfully, the last orders bell rang and they returned to the bar, two more pints with double whisky chasers, and it was only when the Colonel suggested heading round the corner to some late-night drinker that Mazz realised he didn't have anywhere else to go.

Walking round to the drinker, a half-baked nightclub above a shoe shop in the high street, Mazz brought the subject up.

'There any hotels round here?' He asked.

'What,' said the Colonel, 'you need somewhere to stay? Don't worry about that, mate, stay at mine. Plenty of room.'

So that was that settled. The dodgy nightclub had two floors, one playing horrible eighties music. The other one was OK, though; just a bar, basically, with a karaoke machine on the go, anyone was interested. The Colonel got the drinks in then went over to the bloke operating the machine, and even as he walked over the bloke was digging in his CD box looking for something. Moments later the karaoke machine was blasting out the opening bars to Bruce Springsteen's 'Born to Run' and then the Colonel was giving it some welly. Total sincerity and completely out of tune, it was riveting in a disconcerting kind of way. The whole place gave the Colonel a round of applause when he finished. The Colonel walked over to Mazz and said, 'Well, they expect me to do it, like. You going to have a go, butt?'

Mazz was momentarily tempted. One of the more surreal incidents in his life had occurred in a pub up in far North London, somewhere where they were having an eighties-themed karaoke night, and on came Mazz's hit as played by some bunch of session men and then this secretary type can hardly have been born when it came out stepped out and started singing it. Weirder than hell. And drunk and exhausted as he was, there seemed something appealingly grim about going up to the DJ and asking if he had a copy of his own record so he could sing it to a bunch of uninterested pissheads. Momentary was all it was, though.

'No, mate,' he said to the Colonel. 'Be honest, I'm starting to feel totally knackered.'

'C'mon then,' said the Colonel, downing most of a pint of cider in one go, 'let's get out of here.'

Back on the street Mazz started across the road, instinctively surmising that the Colonel lived in one of the little terraces running up the hill: few bits of fabric across the windows for curtains and an old dog for company. Sofa in the front room for Mazz, no doubt — comfortable enough if you didn't let your mind focus on the stains. How many years had Mazz spent crashing in places like this?

'Hang on, butt,' said the Colonel and Mazz aborted his road-crossing. Instead he followed the Colonel down towards the seafront and then left just before the steep incline down, into a very classy-looking street of detached Tudor-Gothic piles. To Mazz's considerable amazement, the Colonel strolled to one of these, halfway along on the right, inserted his key in the lock and, as he entered the porch, started taking his shoes off and motioned for Mazz to do the same.

'Christ,' said Mazz, surveying the immaculate interior of the place, 'you win the lottery?'

'Yeah,' said the Colonel, 'well, in a manner of speaking anyway.' Then he gave Mazz a nod and a wink and changed the subject. 'You hungry, butt?' he asked.

'Yeah,' said Mazz, suddenly ravenous. 'If you've got anything lying around, like.'

'See what we can do,' said the Colonel and led the way into the kitchen. 'Here, butt,' he said, 'you sit here,' pointing Mazz at the breakfast bar, 'and I'll see what I can find. Just hang on a sec while I see if Nat's still about. Drinks in the fridge, you want one.'

Mazz sat down, his head spinning from tiredness, drunkenness and surprise. Hell was the Colonel doing in a place like this? Couple of minutes later, when the Colonel still hadn't come back, he got off his stool, went prospecting in the fridge. Looked inside and it was like peering into Tesco's gourmet-selection cabinet, box of little French beers at the bottom. Mazz pulled one out, twisted the top off and was halfway through drinking it when the Colonel reappeared, behind him a woman wearing overalls and holding a chisel.

'Mazz,' said the Colonel, 'this is Nat.'

'Hiya, love,' said Mazz, suddenly feeling energised. 'Bit late for the old DIY, isn't it?'

'I'm a sculptor,' she replied frostily before turning her head to the Colonel and rolling her eyes in a Christ-who-is-this-drunken-arsehole-you've-brought-back kind of way. Which was when Mazz started to think he recognised her. Nat, Natalie. He was sure he remembered a Natalie some-where along the line. At the end, maybe, after Tyra . . .

Shit, he was paralysed for a moment by a wave of total shame and self-loathing. The things you do, the cruelty you're capable of, when you're young. Yes, he was sure it had been a Natalie that night. Awful thing was he couldn't say for the life of him whether it was this Natalie standing in front of him now. He had this frisson of familiarity but nothing specific, and she wasn't exactly giving him the fond-remembrance look. Not that she would be even if she was the same Natalie. In fact last thing she'd be giving him probably. Or maybe she'd forgotten him too. Either way, there didn't seem a lot of mileage in asking her so he decided to play it straight.

'Yeah, sorry,' he said, giving his accent a bit more valleys; your artist types liked a nice working-class boy. 'Only joking, like.'

'You're a musician,' she said, fixing him with a distinctly inscrutable look, which he held, allowing him to check her out. No make-up, black hair with a dramatic streak of grey all scraped back and tied up in an impromptu ponytail, little bit of weakness round the mouth. Could be a real artist, could be just another flake pushing forty looking for something to do with her life in between aromatherapy sessions. Interesting, though. Christ, there he went again. One thing Mazz knew: he was a bloke and he met Mazz he wouldn't introduce him to his girlfriend. Mazz was sorry about it, but there it was. He didn't have any way of pulling back from it.

'Yeah,' he said, 'well, it's what I do, anyway.'

'Ronnie says you were in a band here a long time ago, said you had a hit.'

For a moment Mazz was totally flummoxed – who the hell was Ronnie? – before logic told him it had to be the Colonel. Ronnie, eh?

'Yeah,' he said, 'that's right,' then picked up his beer and drained it off. 'So what were you called?'

'The Wurriyas,' he said, smiling, figuring she must be the Natalie he half-remembered, joking with him now, flirting a little maybe.

But she didn't respond, just looked blankly at him for a moment then said, 'Oh right, well, nice to meet you, I'm sure Ronnie will show you the guest room.' And with that she was gone.

It was midnight and Tyra knew she should be going to bed. Long day coming up and all that, funeral to sort out. But here she was sitting in the front room drinking – nearly got through the whole bottle of white wine – and listening to records, things she hadn't heard in years.

She'd been going through the stuff in the cupboards, looking for anything of her dad's. Instead she'd found this box of records and tapes, all the stuff she used to listen to: Michael Jackson, Stevie Wonder, Elton John, *Supremes Greatest Hits*, *Rumours*, David Essex – yeah, well, she couldn't have been more than twelve when she bought that one. Awful thing was he'd been in panto in town just last Christmas, lot of the girls she was in school with had gone to see him. Tragic, apparently – same old hairstyle except thinning like mad and a little old man underneath it. Never a good idea to see people you used to fancy.

Last hour or so she'd been listening to all the real girly stuff. Joan Armatrading singing 'Love and Affection'. Tyra remembered seeing her on telly, *Magpie*, the show with the white bloke with the Afro you were meant to fancy, Mick something. Anyway, there she was, this little black girl with a proper Afro, looking terrified and singing this lovely song, just sounded so grown-up. Followed that up with her favourite Diana Ross album, the one all the older girls had in school, *Touch Me In the Morning*. Bet every girl she knew had run home and played that one first time they'd done it. She knew she had. Though she'd been a good couple of years older than most of her mates when she got round to doing it. Her mum drilling it into her. You're not going the same way I did, girl, having a kid when you're sixteen. Her dad just the same. Hypocrisy of it with him took your breath away. Knocked off half Cardiff you could believe his boasting but when it came to his own dear daughter she was expected to be a bloody nun. Well, she'd shown him in the end all right. She'd actually devised a plan to piss off her father, she could hardly have done it better.

But she didn't want to think about him, her first time, now. She wanted to go back to those early teenage years, the *Jackie* years, the basketball team years, school dances when she'd be the tallest one there practically, taller than all the girls and most of the boys. Sitting on the back of the bus singing Bay City Rollers songs – yeah, well, you can laugh now but it was fun then and how old were they anyway? Eleven? Michael Jackson pictures on the wall; funny now if you thought about it, but apart from anything else he was the only black boy you ever saw in the pin-up mags. Christ, it was different back then. Now all the little girls, black or white, were wetting themselves over some obvious badman like R Kelly or those fucking rap guys she couldn't even be bothered to remember; back then you got your gran calling to watch the telly cause Hot Chocolate were on *Top of the Pops*. They were good, though. Not just that *Full Monty* one; she loved those slow ones. *Emma Emmeline* – she knew she had it somewhere – *gonna make you the biggest star this world has ever seen.* Dreams you have when you're a kid. Christ, she was definitely getting drunk now.

4

THE ASSEMBLY

1999

As it turned out, the funeral was the same day they launched the Assembly. Wasn't planned like that or anything, just the day suited the crematorium.

Tyra didn't know whether she was coming or going. The arrangements should have been down to her but somehow she'd lost control of the situation. This feller Big George – community leader they'd call him whenever he turned up in the *Echo*, which was as often as he could manage; you know, objecting to this or that bit of the bay development, demanding more local boys got jobs on the sites. All fair enough stuff, like, except you couldn't help feeling like the main thing was getting in the papers not getting anything done. Anyway, this feller comes round saying how he was Charlie's best mate and how this local developer feller wants to shell out for a big funeral for Charlie, big procession and all just like the old days, and Tyra really wanted to say fuck off. But she supposed it was just guilt that made her say yes. Like, she hadn't paid enough attention to Charlie while he was alive, so how could she deny him a big send-off now he was dead?

So that was the start of it and somehow George seemed to have taken over everything, to the point that on the morning of her father's funeral, Tyra was standing around in her own front room wondering what the hell she was supposed to be doing. When the hearse arrived at eleven she was sitting on the sofa, arms round the kids watching *Nickelodeon*, trying to shut out the noise of her mum fussing round in the kitchen.

She realised the dress she was wearing – her only black one – was a bit too sexy when the undertaker started peering down her front even as he was asking if they were ready to come to the church now.

'OK,' said Tyra, gathered her mum and the kids and got into the back of the hearse, feeling weirdly disconnected from everything.

Felt weird for starters sitting in this huge great car just to travel a hundred yards round the corner. As soon as they got close she could see it was going to be a circus. There were people milling around all over James Street. There were police, photographers, even a TV crew, plus a bunch of Kenny Ibadulla's Nation of Islam boys stood around in their bow ties.

'Mum,' said Tyra, 'did you know about this?'

Her mum, Celeste, didn't say anything. Tyra turned round to look at her and, to her amazement, saw tears streaming down her face. She didn't think she'd ever seen her mum cry before. Not even when Tyra came back from Bristol all those years ago. Just shouted at her then for bringing shame on the family. But she was crying all right now and Tyra couldn't believe it. In fact it made her bloody furious. Her mum had never had a nice word to say about her dad her whole bloody life growing up, not one nice word, and now here she was sobbing her heart out before they even made it to the church.

Then the car pulled up outside the church and the undertaker came round to open the door and Tyra stepped out and it was pure craziness, flashes going off, TV cameras coming up close like it was the Queen bloody Mother had died and not Charlie Unger who everyone cared about so much they'd left him there to rot for a bloody week. Her included, her the worst of the lot, but then it wasn't her making a big bloody pantomime out of his funeral. Hypocrites, stinking bloody hypocrites.

The service passed in a blur. Few old boys got up to say a few words; reverend who can't have seen Charlie in church in thirty years got up to say the usual shit. Big George got up and made a bloody political speech about the development, had people muttering shame well before he finished. They'd asked Tyra to say a few words, and she'd said no thanks, but suddenly she couldn't stand it and, just as George finished, and the reverend was about to announce the final hymn, she got up and walked to the front of the church, whole place suddenly buzzing with whispers.

'Look,' she said, 'it's nice of you all to come but who are we kidding? We didn't look after Charlie when he was alive and it's too late now. So let's just say goodbye to him and get out of here.' Then she almost ran back to her pew, the sobs welling up in her throat, determined not to cry in front of these vultures.

It was only walking out of the church, following the rev, the kids next to her, that she started to notice some of the people who'd shown up. Gave her a start to see some of them: Bobby Ranger, Kenny Ibadulla, for fuck's sake. Still didn't prepare her for the shock of seeing him, right at the back, like he was trying to hide behind a pillar. Mazz. Bloody Mazz, large as life and twice as pale. She knew it was nothing to do with seeing him, just the whole occasion, but she almost fainted on the spot. Felt her legs start to go but somehow caught herself. Willed herself out of the building and into the waiting car. Christ, you try to bury a man and there's no one there but ghosts.

Afterwards the car went to the cemetery and some words were said and someone pressed the little button that commended Charlie's body to the incinerator and Tyra stood outside in the spring sunshine feeling utterly numb, her mum next to her sobbing continuously. All the old aunties and church women came up to Celeste then and hugged her but it was like Tyra had a force field around her. People smiled nervously towards her, mumbled about how sorry they were and what a lovely man Charlie had been – not that most of them would have let him into their houses state he'd been in this last ten years, but still. And it was like she was just floating up above it all, watching.

'Will you be wanting the car to take you to the wake?' The undertaker's voice startled her. All of a sudden she realised it was just her, her mum and the kids standing there.

'Wake?' she said, turning to her mum. 'You know anything about a wake?'

'Course there's a wake, what's the matter with you, girl? Mr Ibadulla kindly offered to have it.'

'Mr Ibadulla, Mum? When did you start calling Kenny Mr Ibadulla?'

'Never you mind how I speak, girl. Now, we getting in the car?'

Tyra nodded and sat back in the hearse, her head spinning. Hell did Kenny Ibadulla care for Charlie, these last years, or for her come to that? Less than a year ago he'd been threatening to take her TV away over some poxy little loan. Money she owed while Tony was in prison the last time.

Tony. All of a sudden the tears came. Tears for Tony. Took her dad's funeral to cry for Tony. And he wasn't even dead. Just gone. Gone to Spain, she'd heard. Looking for his mum. And why had he gone? 'Cause she'd kicked him out. The father of her kids. Christ knows, she'd had her reasons but right now she missed him. Oh God, she missed him. What she wouldn't give to have him there now, his arms round her, taking her home. She had the kids, of course, had her arms round them now, even as she was crying. Poor little things, their mum going to pieces in front of their eyes. And that was it. She was tired of being strong for everyone else. Why couldn't anyone ever have been strong for her?

Mazz didn't go straight to the wake. He'd bumped into Col, coming out of the church, and been amazed how pleased they were to see each other. So they went over the Baltimore for a quick one before heading up the road to the do.

'So what's happening, bra?' said Col once they were sat in the corner with a couple of pints of Guinness.

'Same old, same old,' said Mazz.

'Still in the music business, yeah?'

'Yeah,' said Mazz, 'twenty years' hard guitar-playing served.'

'You're not playing in the thing tonight then?'

'What thing?'

'The Assembly concert. Just in the bay by here. Didn't you see the security? Serious business, bra. Shirley Bassey, Tom Jones, all of them, and some of them rock boys, Stereophonics and that, I expect.'

'No,' said Mazz, 'didn't know a thing about it.'

'Charlotte Church, that little girl, you know sings opera.'

'Jesus.'

'Nah, man, she's lovely. Her dad used to play in bands, you know.'

Mazz shook his head. 'Dunno. How about you, you still playing?'

'Yeah, well little bit. Was playing with this little girl-band thing Mikey put together. You remember Mikey?'

Mazz shook his head again, feeling jaded and out of touch. He picked up his pint, took a good long pull on it. 'You see much of Charlie then, these last few years?'

Col went quiet. 'Yeah, well, now and again, like,' he said eventually. 'It wasn't good, Mazz, way he went.'

'No, I heard.'

'Yeah, well. Thing about Charlie, you asking me, is he was always someone. He was a boxer, he was a musician. All the way up to our band, like, he always had something going, had a bit of respect. After that, though, y'know, what happened, well he wasn't the same really. Just another old geezer goes down the bookie's, goes down the pub, chopsing on about the old days. Young brers now they didn't know who he was, didn't give a fuck either. Y'know what I'm saying?'

Mazz nodded. 'None of us getting younger.'

'That's the truth, bra,' laughed Col, his hand going instinctively to his greying locks. 'But with Charlie, it was like he was shrinking.'

They sat there is silence for a while, both contemplating the abyss, then Mazz shook himself, lit up a fag and said, 'You ever see anything of Emyr?'

Col laughed. 'Ed, not since long time. Year or so after the band maybe, he'd come by, have a little smoke and a chat, but then he got into his rock'n'roll thing and . . . Nah, how's he doing these days?'

'What, you haven't heard?'

'Heard what?'

'Christ,' said Mazz, shaking his head, and launched into the whole strange tale of how Emyr, onetime drummer in the Wurriyas, had over the years transformed himself into an indie icon and now a rock'n'roll lost boy. After the band had split Emyr and Mazz had both headed up to London and tried to work together, but too much bad feeling remained and they went their different ways. Couple of years later Mazz had been stunned to see a picture of Emyr in the *NME*, no longer a drummer but a guitar player in some post-Smiths bunch of indie miserabilists. The band had been nothing much, far as Mazz could see, but Emyr with his blond hair grown and his puppy fat gone was an undeniable icon. His celebrity started outstripping the rest of the band; you'd see him modelling clothes in the *Face* or on the front of Japanese teen magazines, always with that look like he wasn't really there. Mazz just assumed it was 'cause he was still as stoned as ever, but sixteen-year-old Goth girls the world over seemed to see it as a sign of spiritual depth. Eventually he moved to Berlin and started making solo albums – Nick Cave without the sense of humour you asked Mazz – but still the Goth girls lapped it up.

And then he disappeared. Walked out of a sound check in Utrecht one day saying he was going to get a packet of fags and never came back. Made the cover of the *NME* three weeks running. People said he'd committed suicide, lot of stories about a blond man seen walking to the end of the pier in the Hague. Claims on the net that he'd ODed in his hotel room and the record company had hidden his body to create a mystery. Meanwhile there were sightings of him everywhere from Barry Island to Bali.

'Emyr?' said Col, looking utterly bewildered as Mazz wound up the tale. 'What d'you reckon happened, then?'

'Christ knows.'

'I saw him,' Col said suddenly.

'What?' said Mazz, stunned. 'Recently?'

'No,' said Col, 'couple of years ago easy. I'm down by Mount Stuart Square, having a little drink, just standing on the pavement outside the Ship, talking to a couple of little girls, like, and you can see there's a band playing at the Coal Exchange, couple of trucks unloading gear and that, and there's this blond feller, thin, wearing the whole black-leather thing. Thought to myself he reminded me of Emyr. Might have gone over to check him out that fat fuck hadn't been there.'

'Which fat fuck?'

'Flaherty. Jason fucking Flaherty.'

'Oh,' said Mazz, laughing, 'that fat fuck.'

Col stood up. 'Let's go to the wake, boss. Have one on Charlie.'

The wake was being held in Black Caesar's, Kenny Ibadulla's club in West Bute Street. There was a Nation of Islam mosque and storefront downstairs, window full of pictures of Louis Farrakhan and Muhammad Ali, while the other two floors of the building were firmly devoted to Mammon. The contradiction summed up Kenny Ibadulla perfectly. He wasn't a gangster with a heart of gold, but he was a gangster with a philosophy of life. And that philosophy was simple enough: it's a jungle out there and if a black man wants to prosper in the jungle he'd better work hard, not sample his own product, and carry a damn big stick.

Which was pretty much the opposite of the way Charlie Unger had lived his life, so what the hell Kenny was doing hosting the wake was something Charlie's daughter Tyra found hard to figure out.

And being a direct kind of girl herself, it was the first thing she said when she walked into the club and found it rammed with everyone she'd ever met in her life, drinking Kenny's booze and eating rice and peas and patties and chicken on paper plates.

'What you doing this for, Ken?' she asked, right up in his face.

'Easy now, sister,' said Kenny, his palms raised to pacify her. 'Just showing a little respect. Your dad was one of the guys, you know, back in the day.'

'Don't bullshit me, Kenny,' said Tyra. 'Last few years you wouldn't have crossed the road to piss on him. None of you would,' raising her voice now, waving her arm to indicate the crowd around them.

'Hey, sister,' said Kenny, his voice sounding genuinely sympathetic. 'We all' – and he held her eyes with his as he said *all* – 'know what happened to Charlie the last few years. But that don't mean we forget how he used to be.' He put his hand on Tyra's shoulder then and she felt ashamed. Felt like all she was thinking about was herself, forgetting about her dad.

'All right, Ken,' she said, 'and thanks.'

A little while later Tyra found herself in the middle of the packed club, completely alone. Her mum was still playing the role of chief mourner surrounded by all the old-timers, bursting into sobs at regular intervals and – if you asked Tyra – having the time of her life. These were probably the happiest moments she'd ever had with Charlie, least in Tyra's memory. The kids were running around with their friends, stuffing their faces with crisps, and Tyra was standing alone, an untouched glass of white wine in her hand, scanning the room for any sign of Col.

Unable to see him anywhere, she walked over to the bar to change her wine for a glass of water. Lloyd was there, pouring out a couple of bottles of wine into glasses, started saying how sorry he was and all that. Tyra waved his condolences away.

'Must be costing Kenny a fortune, this,' she said, as he dug out a warm bottle of Perrier from a dusty shelf.

'Yeah, well,' said Lloyd, 'it's not Kenny paying for it, is it.'

'What?' said Tyra.

'Nah,' said Lloyd, 'I'd have thought you knew. It's this developer guy, you know paid for the church and that and he's paying for this and all. Knew Charlie from the old days, I suppose.'

Tyra shook her head. 'He got a name, this developer?'

'Yeah,' said Lloyd. 'Flaherty, they call him, Jason, big feller.'

'Oh,' said Tyra, 'right, thanks,' and turned back towards the room, feeling more confused than ever. Jason Flaherty. She couldn't figure it at all. Far as she knew, last time Charlie had seen Flaherty was the same as her, the day the Wurriyas split up.

Just then she spotted Col over by the entrance and she was three-quarters of the way across the room towards him before she noticed who he was with, and by then Col had seen her and it was too late.

'All right, girl,' said Col, folding her in a hug. Then he stepped back and said, 'Look what the cat dragged in.'

'Mazz,' said Tyra.

'Yeah,' said Mazz, and they stood there for a couple of seconds in silence.

'Well fucking hell,' said Mazz then and he stepped towards her and hugged her too, quickly but firmly.

What was the matter with her? It was all Tyra could do not to grind up against him. Up against Mazz after what he'd done to her and all these years gone by. Your mind's saying fine, say hello, he was a friend of your dad's after all, it's nice he's here, now say goodbye and walk away, any luck you won't see him again for another eighteen years. Eighteen years . . . she'd had the baby, he'd be in college now – she knew it was a he, they'd told her after the abortion. All right then, really what her mind was saying was screw you for what you did. But her body was singing a different tune.

She was proud of herself how she coped, though. 'Good of you to come,' she said, cold as you like, 'Charlie would have appreciated it, I'm sure.'

'Yeah, well,' said Mazz, 'I'm sorry I haven't seen him in so long, like.' He paused. 'I loved your dad, you know.'

Tyra softened a little; she couldn't help it. 'Yeah,' she said, 'I know.' Then she saw that Mazz's attention was distracted; he was looking past her at someone. Tyra turned to see who it was.

It was Jason Flaherty, walking through the middle of the room, deep in conversation with Big George, who, by comparison with the behemoth Flaherty had become, looked more like Medium-Large George.

'What's he doing here?' asked Mazz.

'I dunno,' said Tyra, 'Lloyd told me he was paying for all this.' She turned to Col. 'You heard that?'

'Yeah,' said Col, 'I heard that. Dunno if it's true but it's what I hears people saying.'

'What,' said Mazz, 'old Jase got religion, has he?'

'No,' said Col, 'not what I heard. He's made a lot of money, mind. Lot of the new stuff you sees down the bay, those are Flaherty sites. But I ain't heard he's doing a lot for charity, like. He seen a lot of your old man these last few years, has he?'

'No,' said Tyra. 'I don't know what the fuck's going on. I'll go and ask him.' And with that she walked off towards Jason Flaherty who was by now settled at the bar, book-ended by the only slightly less imposing figures of Big George and Kenny Ibadulla.

Mazz and Col watched Tyra go, Mazz happy to see she still walked as upright and purposeful as he remembered, back then when he used to think of her as his girl. He watched her go right into Jason's face, saw Jason smile then frown then smile again, a big bullshitter's smile that said don't worry, little girl, I'm just a nice friendly old wolf out for your best interests. Saw Tyra shake her head and walk away, heading for the toilets until she was intercepted by Jermaine and Emily.

'Who are the kids?' Mazz asked Col.

'Hers, innit. Hers and Tony's.'

'Christ, she's married.'

'Nah, well he's not around. You ever meet Tony?'

'Don't think so.'

'Docks boy. Used to come to the gigs, like. Tall, skinny guy, Kenny's mate.'

'Oh,' said Mazz, vaguely conjuring up the image of a dangerous-looking guy with shortish dreads. 'He's not around, though?'

'No,' said Col, 'and he's not a name to mention too much these days, specially not around Kenny.'

'And two kids,' said Mazz.

'Yeah, well,' said Col, 'life goes on, you knows what I mean. You goes away for ten years or twenty years or whatever, it don't all stay the same waiting for you to come back, like. You got any kids yourself?'

'No,' said Mazz, 'not as far as I know. How about you?'

'Well,' said Col, 'two that I knows about. A boy from when I was young – he's nearly grown now – and another little one with another girl, live round the corner.'

'Shit,' said Mazz, shaking his head.

'Yeah,' said Col, laughing and lighting up a spliff.

Mazz shared the draw with Col and then Col moved off doing his rounds and Mazz found a space at the bar and leaned there for a while just watching the people and wondering how it might have been if he'd made a life there with Tyra.

Couple of people came by and said hello. Bobby and her girlfriend, then Jason Flaherty. He acted amazed to see Mazz there, but somehow Mazz felt like Jason knew already. Anyway he was friendly and asked Mazz to drop by the office sometime, have some lunch, catch up. Yeah, said Mazz, sure.

He was just about ready to call it a day when another ghost from the past slipped in beside him at the bar.

'Man, how you doing? Listen, I'm sorry about last night. Business, you know.'

It was Lawrence. He looked different, though it took Mazz a minute to figure out what it was. Well, partly he didn't have locks any more, had a little goatee and round glasses, his hair cropped short. But the way that the new look combined with the jaundiced complexion of the heroin aficionado meant that instead of looking mixed race going on black, he now looked mixed race going on white.

'Lawrence, man, what are you drinking?'

'Brandy, man, with a little bit of soda. Don't let them fill up the whole glass, though. No ice neither. So how are you doing, Brer Mazz?'

'Yeah, good,' said Mazz, waving to get the barman's attention and weary of retelling his tale of rock'n'roll woes.

'Good, good. Old Charlie, eh?'

'Yeah,' said Mazz, 'Charlie.' And was about to leave it there but then decided to go on with what seemed to be a ritual exchange: Did you see much of him lately? No. You? No. Shame, eh? So Mazz kicked it off. 'See much of him lately?'

'No,' said Lawrence, right on cue, but then he went on, 'Didn't see much of him, but I did see him lately. Just a couple of weeks ago, as it happens.'

'Yeah?'

'Yeah, it was Charlie, the big man over there, Flaherty, and another guy coming out of the snooker club on Broadway. Late, you know, I was just in the all-night garage over the road, buying some fags, and I saw them come out. Remember thinking old Charlie was starting to look his age. Had a big coat on but he looked cold.'

'Strange,' said Mazz.

'Yeah, what I thought,' said Lawrence. 'Flaherty's a big man these days and Charlie, well you know Charlie hadn't been too good for a while – not that I'm like, one to talk. Anyway, s'pose I just figured Charlie was after him for a loan or something.'

'Yeah,' said Mazz, 'sounds about right.' And with that they dropped the subject, started on the catch-up questions. Few minutes of that and Lawrence started looking uncomfortable.

'Tell you what, man,' he said. 'You mind if we step outside for a bit? Don't like to be in a room with so many people.'

'Sure,' said Mazz, feeling about ready to head off anyway.

Outside, West Bute Street was alive with people. Which was strange as usually by this time, seven or so, of an evening the commercial part of the docks was generally as dead as anything. Instead it was full of people walking purposefully towards the bay.

'Ah shit, man,' said Lawrence, 'it's this Assembly business.'

'Oh yeah,' said Mazz. 'You want to check it out?'

Lawrence shrugged and they started to walk down towards James Street. Lawrence pulled a spliff out of his pocket and lit it up and they passed it back and forth in companionable silence till they reached the edge of what turned out to be a huge crowd assembled in the bay.

There were two stages and a giant TV screen set up in the vacant lot where Lawrence told Mazz they were meant to be putting the Assembly building. In front of the bigger stage there must have been a good thirty thousand people. And there on the stage – you had to see it to believe it – was Shirley Bassey wearing a dress that appeared to be made out of the Welsh flag.

Don't know which one of them started laughing first, Mazz or Lawrence, but after a moment they were both in hysterics, holding on to each other to keep from falling over. Then they started to notice the dirty looks they were getting from all the born-again Welsh patriots around them and that just made things worse. Finally Shirley stopped singing and swept offstage just in time to save Mazz and Lawrence from a good kicking from a bunch of rugby boys.

Mazz inclined his head back away from the crowd and Lawrence nodded and a couple of minutes later they were sat in the Packet still shaking with laughter.

Inside, surreally enough, the shebang was on the TV and there were a good twenty or so people clustered around it watching, even though they could be seeing it for real simply by walking out the door.

The next couple of hours Mazz just couldn't stop laughing, watching this absurdist panoply of Welsh cultural life unfolding in front of him. Tom Jones of course. Well, at least big Tom knows he's funny these days. But still, 'The Green, Green Grass of Home' – if the sight of Wales welcoming the brave new world to the sound of 'Green, Green Grass' didn't make you laugh, your kitsch bullshit detector had to be well out of order. And the rest of the stuff – well, it was hard to choose between the ghastly reading of *Under Milk Wood* by some terrible old ham and the bunch of, ahem, hip Welsh actors making complete tits of themselves doing some kind of rock poetry, until the outright winner came along in the shape of the bloke with the big hair from the Alarm doing some kind of cod folk song with a male-voice choir backing him. And then came the grand finale, the whole bloody lot of them singing 'Every day I Thank the Lord I'm Welsh', which Mazz had kind of assumed was meant to be funny more or less but was here being done in deadly earnest.

'Fuckin' hell, butt,' said Mazz once he'd recovered himself. 'Glad to be Welsh then?'

'*Was ist das?*' said Lawrence in a dumb German accent and Mazz started laughing again.

'Christ,' he said eventually, 'great to know you've got a culture boils down to one famous play, two sixties cabaret stars, a male-voice choir and a twelve-year-old opera singer, innit?'

'Should have got the Wurriyas back together again for it, mate. Legends of Welsh ska, you could have done "Cwm Rhondda".'

Mazz made to punch Lawrence who ducked then came up frowning.

'Hey,' he said. 'That's who that guy was.'

'Which guy?'

'The other guy. You know I told you I saw Charlie with Flaherty and another guy? Now I remember who the other guy was. It's just he looked different, but it was that guy from your band.'

'Which guy?' said Mazz, quickly taking an inventory of who'd been in the Wurriyas – the only guys were him, Charlie, Col and Emyr. 'Col?'

'No, the drummer guy.'

'Ed. Can't have been.'

'Why not?'

'He's vanished. It's been all over the papers and that. Missing rock star Emyr.'

'Shit, that's the same Emyr? The missing guy?'

'Yeah, what I said.'

Lawrence frowned, then scratched his head. 'It was him, though, I'm sure. He's got long hair. Really white blond. Looks a bit like that albino guitar-player guy.'

'Johnny Winter.'

'Yeah, yeah. Wearing, like, surfer clothes, you know, those baggy trousers and a Hawaiian shirt, I remember, looked weird in the middle of the night.'

Mazz nodded non-committally. Sounded possible. One thing about Emyr was he had a knack of looking, like Chandler said of Moose Malloy in Mazz's favourite road book, 'about as inconspicuous as a tarantula on a slab of angel cake'. And a Hawaiian shirt on a cold spring night in Splott sounded about right to Mazz. But what would he have been doing with Flaherty and Charlie?

It was late and Tyra was drunk. She was walking down the street, holding her heels in one hand, weaving between the cans and bottles strewn around the place in the aftermath of the Assembly do. Her mum had taken the kids off hours ago, must have sensed what was coming. After she'd talked to Jason Flaherty, who'd just brushed her off with some bullshit about what an inspiration Charlie had been and how it was the least he could do, she'd just thought fuck it, grabbed a bottle of wine and a glass from the bar, sat at a table in the corner and started drinking. It's what her dad would have wanted. Hah!

So she'd been sitting there thinking bad thoughts about everyone in the room, and about Charlie and about herself too, don't worry, when Bobby Ranger came over.

They hadn't had much to do with each other, all the years since the band. Tyra'd gone one way – jobs, husband, children; Bobby'd gone the other way – into the life. She'd been hanging round with the Custom House girls even back then. Tyra'd supposed you were a lesbian you didn't have much choice. Not the kind of lesbian Bob was anyway, wasn't a student lefty like the other lesbians Tyra knew; Bobby was just a little hooligan from Ely. So, yeah, it wasn't surprising Bobby ended up in the life, pimping and that. Tyra didn't know the details but she knew enough.

And Tyra, well, after the first year or two when she'd gone to pieces, she'd done her best to stay on the straight and narrow. Wasn't easy being married to Tony but, whatever he'd done, she'd been straight and she was proud of that and she did her best to keep herself and her children away from the life.

Bobby she'd see once in a while maybe walking into town or at the carnival, but it was a surprise when she came over and sat herself down next to Tyra.

'All right, girl?' she said.

'No, not really,' said Tyra.

'Nah,' said Bobby, 's'pose you wouldn't be.' She paused for a moment. 'Me either, really. I loved your dad, you know.'

'Yeah,' said Tyra, remembering then how close Bobby and Charlie had been in the band. 'Yeah, well he liked you too. In fact,' she said, and where the hell was this coming from, 'I used to think he liked you better than me. Like you were the kind of daughter he wanted.'

Bobby went very quiet, made a kind of choking noise in her throat. Christ, thought Tyra, what's that about? Then it struck her: of course Bobby grew up in a home – or bunch of homes more like. Didn't have a clue who her dad was.

'Sorry,' said Tyra. 'Didn't mean . . .'

'No,' said Bobby, putting her hand on Tyra's knee and squeezing. 'Not your fault. It's just, like, you're right. I used to think, you know, what it would be like if Charlie was my dad. He was the right age and everything . . .' Bobby sniffed hard and straightened up. 'Fuckin' hell, Bob, pull yourself together.'

Then Bobby'd gone and grabbed another bottle of wine and they'd sat there, the two of them getting drunker and drunker, and suddenly Tyra was able to talk about Charlie and funny thing was it was a cliché but it was true talking did make her feel better and after a bit she'd been up and dancing with Bobby. People probably saying all sorts about her blind drunk dancing with Bobby Ranger but fuck 'em. Least Bobby was straight with you.

And after that it had all got a bit blurry and now here she was, no shoes on, walking down James Street with a car slowing down and drawing up just behind her.

She turned round ready to give whatever kerb–crawling slimeball it was a good slagging when she saw it was a police car. Great, bloody great, going to spend the night of her father's funeral banged up drunk in the cells.

Jimmy Fairfax got out of the car, walked over to her and took her gently by the arm.

'You all right, love?' he said.

'Fine,' said Tyra.

'Yeah,' he said, looking at her and smiling, 'I can see that. C'mon, let me give you a lift home.' And he guided Tyra into the passenger seat, Tyra showing the first signs of making a fuss then subsiding.

What happened next she could piece together approximately. She must have fallen asleep on the brief ride home. Then she distinctly recalled inviting Jimmy in. And then what she wasn't too sure. But when she woke up about four in the morning desperate for a pee and a glass of water, she was fully clothed and lying on the sofa so it couldn't have been anything too outrageous.

Christ, though, she felt miserable the next morning. Couldn't believe it. Her dad's funeral and what does she do but get pissed and dance around like an idiot with Bobby Ranger. She called her mum to ask her to bring the kids round. Her mum sounded typically bloody snotty, said they were happy watching the Saturday cartoons and she'd bring them over a bit later. Tyra put the phone down and started crying the way you do over nothing when you're hungover.

Then the bell rang. Tyra walked over and opened the door thinking her mum wasn't so bad after all. But it wasn't her mum and the kids; it was Mazz. She just stood there staring at him for a moment, her mouth open.

'Can I come in?' he said eventually.

'Yeah,' she said, 'all right.' Then, 'How d'you know where I live?' She knew even as the words left her mouth that this was a stupid question. Nothing was secret in Butetown; ask anyone they'd tell you where she lived. People, the police and that, used to talk about a wall of silence any time there was crime they couldn't solve. Bollocks, the real problem you had round here was too many people chatting at you, all getting it wrong.

'Oh,' said Mazz vaguely, 'Col.'

Tyra led the way into the kitchen and Mazz, looking, she noticed now, no better than she felt, collapsed on a stool by the breakfast bar.

5

THE COTTAGE

1980

A Tuesday lunchtime Mazz was walking through town, just been to Kelly's in the market and picked up a couple more compilation albums looked quite decent, and he was just about to go into the Hayes Island Snack Bar when Kate spotted him.

Minutes later they were sat down, egg sandwich for her, bacon roll for him, and she was doing her best to jerk him about.

First she said the black thing, like she understood his urge to check out some jungle pussy. All he could do not to chuck his tea in her face; only thing that stopped him was he wasn't quite sure who she was being more offensive to – him or Tyra. Anyway she must have noticed that this didn't go down too well 'cause she changed the subject for a bit, asking about the band and that, using this snotty tone like oh yes, your amusing band, course we all know which one of us is going to end up with the money in the bank. But he sat there and listened to it, taking the path of least resistance, then she went back to her favourite subject – obviously smarted like hell seeing Mazz with Tyra.

'Oh,' she said, 'I was talking to Margot. From the SWP, yeah.'

'Mmm,' said Mazz, vaguely.

'Tall girl, spiky hair.'

'Mmm,' said Mazz again, vaguer still.

'Well anyway, we were having a little chat and she was telling me about your girlfriend.'

'Yeah,' said Mazz in a tone of complete disinterest that might have told a more sensitive or less determined soul to drop the subject now.

'Yeah,' said Kate. 'You know she's a lesbian, of course?'

Mazz, to his credit, didn't react at all for a moment, just carried on letting his eyes follow the passers-by. Then he stood, picked up the last of his bacon roll and popped it in his mouth, said 'See you then' to Kate and walked off up the Hayes towards Bridge Street.

Kate's words came back into Mazz's head, though, when he was in bed with Tyra again, Thursday night after the rehearsal. They'd all gone down the Panorama after. Emyr and Col wanted to go over to Monty's next, meet up with a couple of nurses. Tyra said she was tired and Mazz said he'd walk her home. Which he did, but his home not hers. And . . . and it was the same again really. The sex was fine, no complaints there. But afterwards, Christ, she just looked so miserable, and that's when the lesbian thing popped back into Mazz's brain. Was obvious something was bothering her to do with sex anyway. He was wondering whether he should bring it up when she started to talk.

'I'm sorry,' she said.

'What for?' said Mazz, turning towards her and stroking her back, something she accepted for a couple of seconds before rolling away.

'It's just,' she said, faltering, 'it's just afterwards I feel so . . .'

'Guilty?' offered Mazz.

'Yeah, well, I was going to say miserable,' she said, half smiling, 'but guilty, yeah. I suppose that's it. It's like my mother's in the room watching me. You ever feel like that?'

'No,' said Mazz, laughing and shuddering at the same time.

They lay there in silence for a little while, easier now than they had been together. Mazz lit the traditional fag and passed it to Tyra who took it gratefully.

'You had a lot of boyfriends then?' he asked, casually as he could.

'No,' said Tyra, turning to look him straight in the eye, 'a couple, like. Delroy was the longest.'

Mazz stared at her, raised his eyebrows in an interrogative kind of way.

'Six months,' she said, 'something like that.'

'And before him?' Mazz asked, idly now, drifting towards sleep.

'Before that,' said Tyra slowly, 'before that I was going with a girl, like.'

'Oh yeah,' said Mazz, no longer heading for sleep.

'Yeah,' said Tyra, 'Maggie, Mags. We was in school together. She's in the Party. You remember that march? You might have seen her there.'

'Hmmm,' said Mazz non-committally, half wanting to drop the subject utterly, half wanting to know every detail. Part of him, to be honest, wanting to smack her one, like she was making a fool out of him.

'You think about him at all?' said Tyra suddenly.

'Who?' asked Mazz, wondering what the hell she was going to drop on him next.

'Bobby Sands, the feller on hunger strike.'

'Yeah,' said Mazz, surprising himself, 'yeah, I had a dream about him the other night.' It was true; he'd forgotten it but it came back to him now. He'd been in this recording studio and suddenly he'd realised the walls were covered in shit and then it wasn't a recording studio at all, it was Bobby Sands' cell in the H Blocks, and at first he'd thought he was going to throw up but then Bobby Sands was talking to him and he didn't notice the smell any more – good thing about dreams, really, you couldn't smell too much – and Bobby Sands was telling him to be careful what he signed. They'll stick all kinds of pieces of paper in front of you and expect you to sign them but don't, he said. Don't let them take your name away from you, he'd said, and then Mazz had woken up, or maybe the dream had gone some place else, but anyway that was the end of the Bobby Sands bit of the dream.

'Me too,' said Tyra, 'I think about him a lot. Sitting in that cell covered in his own shit, starving himself to death. And all you read in the papers here is how he's just a common criminal. That make sense to you?'

'No,' said Mazz, who never read the front part of the paper much, and then Tyra turned towards him and let him take her in his arms and they said nothing for a bit till Mazz realised she'd gone to sleep. He didn't move for a little while, made sure she was soundly out, then carefully extricated his arm from underneath her head and lay there, not sleeping just staring up at the ceiling, thinking about the future, suddenly filled with a conviction that the Wurriyas were going somewhere.

Mazz woke at six to find Tyra getting dressed. He half-heartedly offered to walk her home but didn't protest when she said she'd be fine. As she left she wrote down a number on a piece of paper. My mum's, she said. Call me tomorrow, maybe we could go out. Great, said Mazz, and was asleep before she was out the front door.

He was having a bath later that morning when the lesbian thing came back into his mind. His first thought was he should be angry about it; she was taking the piss. But really he couldn't get angry about it . . . Came down to it, he couldn't see much difference – old boyfriend, old girlfriend, what did it matter who your girlfriend's exes were – so long as they weren't still seeing them. Thing was, too, and he couldn't explain it really but there it was, it didn't seem like such a big deal, a girl copping off with another girl. Two blokes were at it together, well, that was that, you were a queer any way you looked at it, and, be honest again, Mazz knew you weren't meant to mind and everything but he still didn't feel at all comfortable around queers. Two girls, though, it didn't seem too bad. He didn't mean like he wanted to watch or any of that crap, it just, well – when it came down to it he couldn't take it that seriously he supposed. And, anyway, he hadn't come down to Cardiff for everything to be just the same as the valleys, had he?

Saturday afternoon Mazz called the number Tyra had given him. It rang half a dozen times, then a woman with a strong West Indian accent picked up the phone.

''Scuse me, is Tyra there, please?' said Mazz.

'She's gone out,' said the woman.

'Oh right, thanks,' said Mazz and was about to put the phone down.

'Hold on now,' said the voice. 'They call you Mazz?'

'Yes,' said Mazz.

'Right, well she leave me a message. She wants you to come round at eight o'clock.'

Mazz turned up at the house around ten past eight. This time of a Saturday evening Angelina Street was full of people, all of whom seemed to be staring at him. A couple of teenage rastas on the corner started to say something to him but stopped when they saw him heading purposefully towards Tyra's place. He knocked on the door and immediately saw the front-room curtains twitch and two girls' faces, looked about twelve, peered out at him, giggled, and closed the curtains again. Another thirty seconds or so passed, Mazz sure the whole street was staring at him now, wondering when bailiffs started dressing like that, and then, finally, the door opened.

A tall fortyish woman in an African print dress, the spit of Tyra only a little darker complected, was standing there. She looked Mazz up and down – literally started off looking at his face, let her eyes travel all the way down to the DMs on his feet and then come back up. She didn't bother to look anything but unimpressed, didn't say a word, just turned back into the house and shouted.

'Tyra, girl, someone here for you.' Then she walked off, leaving Mazz still stranded on the doorstep.

Another thirty seconds passed and Mazz was on the point of saying fuck it and going, when Tyra came down the stairs wearing pedal pushers and a white Fred Perry, her hair up and wrapped in a towel and looking like the finest thing Mazz had ever seen. Suddenly, just like that. Up to that point he hadn't really thought too much about how she looked. Well, he wasn't blind, he knew she was a good-looking woman all right, but seeing her then he just thought fucking hell she's beautiful, almost said it out loud which would have been just a bit embarrassing . . .

Tyra saw Mazz standing on the front step and her face darkened instantly.

'Mum,' she yelled, 'what are you doing leaving him standing outside?'

'I don't know, girl,' came the reply, 'who you wants to bring in my house and who you don't.'

Tyra shook her head furiously, grabbed Mazz by the hand and pulled him through the hall and upstairs after her. As they turned the bend in the stairs, the two girls Mazz had seen looking out the window popped out of the front room and peered up at him.

'He your new boyfriend?' said the skinnier one to Tyra.

Tyra sighed. 'Mazz,' she said, 'this is my little sister Corinne and this is her friend Gemma.' The two girls giggled some more and Mazz waved at them. Tyra waited a couple of seconds then said, 'Piss off, you two, I'm getting ready to go out.'

With that she led Mazz into her bedroom. She pulled out a chair for Mazz to sit on, said, 'Sorry about this, I'll just be a sec,' and turned on the hair dryer. Mazz looked around the room. It was spotlessly neat. He checked the bed for any sign of piles of cuddly animals and was relieved to see none. He checked the posters on the walls – Bob Marley, of course, one from the big Rock Against Racism Carnival, an abstract art thing from some exhibition at the museum, Joan Miró, didn't mean much to Mazz. He looked around a little more, spotted a picture on the mantelpiece, a fifties portrait of a young boxer holding up a Lonsdale belt – Charlie in his prime.

Tyra stopped the dryer for a moment. 'Put a record on if you like,' she said.

Mazz stood up and walked over to the music centre, perched on the window ledge. Next to it was a pile of albums. He started flicking through them. Took him aback slightly. Didn't know what he was expecting – a load of reggae and funk records he'd never heard of maybe – but actually she just had a typical girl's record collection – that's typical white girl, he supposed. All present and correct were Fleetwood Mac's *Rumours*, lying there, the disc out of its sleeve and scratched all over, the usual thing; three Elton John albums; Stevie Wonder's *Talking Book*, which he thought he'd put on if nothing better showed up; the first Jam album, felt-tip scrawl on the front, must have got one of them to sign it; Joan Armatrading, the one with 'Love and Affection' – was it, like, compulsory to have that record if you were a girl? – and, yep, there it was, Cat Stevens' *Tea For the Tillerman*. Then he got to a bunch of classical records and he gave up, pulled out the Stevie Wonder, checked he'd got the side which didn't have 'You Are the Sunshine of My Life' on and stuck it on the record player.

Moments later Tyra stopped drying her hair, checked herself in the mirror, then leaned over and kissed Mazz hard and deep as the strains of 'Maybe Your Baby Done Found Somebody New' burbled away in the background.

'Right,' she said, coming up for air one and a half songs later and removing Mazz's hands from under her Fred Perry, 'time we were going out.'

'Mmm,' said Mazz, giving every indication he was quite happy staying in.

Tyra stood up, straightened her clothing. 'No, really, we should have been in the pub half an hour ago.'

'Oh yeah,' said Mazz. 'Where are we going?'

'Oh,' said Tyra, 'didn't I tell you? There's a benefit night for the Party on, over in Roath somewhere. I said we'd meet some of the others in the Cottage before.'

'Oh,' said Mazz, a little less than fully enthusiastic, but still happy enough just to be close to Tyra at the moment.

It took another half hour to get out past Tyra's over-excited little sister and blatantly disapproving mother, who wanted them to get a cab into town, but Tyra thankfully told her not to be stupid, it would be quicker to walk. Which it would have been if they hadn't kept stopping every hundred yards or so to get some serious snogging in.

In the pub they met half a dozen of Tyra's Party comrades sat round a table in the quiet front bar. There was the Indian girl Mazz had seen on the march, a bloke in a leather jacket sitting next to her, a couple of obvious students in matching glasses – looked like the most boring couple on earth – a big jolly-looking girl with tons of frizzy hair, and next to her a small intense-looking girl with cropped bright red hair, looked natural to Mazz.

'Hiya, darling,' said Tyra to the red-headed girl and bent down to kiss her, something in Mazz's experience Tyra generally didn't do. 'Mazz,' she said then, 'meet Maggie.'

Mazz was smiling and sticking his hand out before the information computed. This was Tyra's girlfriend. Ex-girlfriend. Funny thing was, even as he was realising this and ready to be thoroughly fucked off, Maggie was smiling back at him and shaking his hand firmly and his first reaction was he liked her.

An hour or so later they were all in the upstairs room of a pub on City Road. A bloke in full skinhead Harrington and crop was behind the record decks playing a mixture of old ska tunes, early James Brown and a bit of Motown. Mazz went over to have a word, ask him what one of the ska tunes was, and was gratified to find that the bloke, Nicky, had seen the Wurriyas at the University.

'Fucking great, man,' he told him repeatedly and suggested the band should play at the Rock Against Racism thing the Party was organising next month. Mazz said sure, sounded good to him.

Nicky was not the only one there who had seen the Wurriyas. All evening people kept coming up to Mazz telling him how good the band was or asking when they were going to be playing next. In fact he was having a thoroughly good time, showing off, feeling like life was going his way. He could see Tyra was feeling the same; she was mostly off with her crowd of mates but now and again their eyes would meet across the room and she'd give him this smile sent shivers down his spine. Christ, he thought, he was close to losing it over this girl.

Then, just as the night was building up nicely, someone turned the lights on. Literally. No way you could trust Trotskyists to run a proper party. Coming up to midnight on a Saturday night, room full of young people getting stuck in to each other, and what d'you do – bring up the house lights and make a speech. The weird, if not downright creepy, thing was, far as Mazz was concerned, that everyone clapped in what seemed to be genuine enthusiasm when this fortyish bloke, with John Lennon glasses, a high forehead and long hair round the sides and back, stood up and started talking.

'That's Derek,' whispered Tyra, who'd suddenly materialised at Mazz's side.

Derek waffled on for about ten minutes about how, thanks to the Party, the British State was on the point of collapse. The riots in St Paul's showed how the conditions for revolution were ripe – everyone stomped and cheered at this bit – and then he went on to say that next Sunday's hunger-strike support march had been called off – puzzled grunts from the audience – because the hunger strike had been called off! Bobby Sands has won! – cheers from everyone – the British State – now faltering on its last legs – has made historic concessions – he didn't say what they might be but it didn't matter – the whole room was cheering and hugging each other now. Mazz turned to clutch Tyra and was a little put out to find her already gripped in a fierce embrace by Maggie.

Then the music started up again. DJ put on 'The Whip' by the Ethiopians – the number that always stuck in Mazz's mind in the years after as the absolute archetypal ska dance tune – and suddenly everyone was dancing, Tyra and Maggie right in the centre of the floor together.

And Mazz was cool about it. He could give Tyra her space. Maggie seemed like a nice enough person, your regular fiery young Irish lefty. So Mazz headed over to the bar, got himself a pint and a whisky, chatted to a couple of girls came up asking about the band. Cool.

He hardly even understood it himself when forty minutes later, after the do had finished and everyone had hugged everyone else in sight, and Mazz and Tyra were walking back through town heading for his place, he suddenly went for her. What the fuck she think she was doing showing him up like that? Like what? she said, her face cheery enough at first, like he was just playing around. Like, like dancing with your fucking lezzo girlfriend right under my nose. Tyra tried to laugh at this, show him how ridiculous he was being, make it go away. But instead something – the whisky, his bad self – was infuriated by her laughter.

'Fuck's so funny?'

'Nothing,' said Tyra, her face falling now.

'You think it's funny, make me look like a dickhead? Your lefty mates laughing at me 'cause I'm the only one doesn't know what's going on? You think that's funny?'

Tyra just shook her head and picked up her pace. Mazz speeded up too. Caught Tyra by the shoulders, pulled her round to look at him.

'I asked you a question. You think I'm a joke or what?'

Tyra stepped back smartly, disentangling herself from Mazz in the process. Angry now, as well as visibly upset.

'Don't you put your hands on me,' she said. 'And don't give me this shit, you hypocrite. Like, I'm expected to have been a bloody nun but you, every time we go out you're rubbing my face in it, all these stupid girls going "Ooh, Mazz, you haven't phoned; Ooh, Mazz, your guitar playing's really great; ooh, Mazz could you teach me to play guitar." '

She stopped in mid-rant, suddenly overcome, then she stepped back another couple of paces, pointed at him and said, 'I thought you were better than this but you're not. You're just full of shit.' Then her voice broke, she looked around wildly, saw they were outside the castle and, instead of carrying on towards Riverside and Mazz's place, she just ran across Castle Street, not even glancing around to see if there was any traffic heading for St Mary Street and the way home to Butetown.

Mazz stood then, half stunned, half still angry, and watched her go, heading up St Mary Street past a few drunken office types coming out of Bananas. He shrugged his shoulders, straightened his jacket round his shoulders and headed for home. Fucking bitch going into one like that, who did she think he was?

He was on the Taff bridge, stopped for a moment looking down at the water, when his attention was gripped by a couple of dossers sitting down almost underneath the bridge sharing a couple of cans of lager, and for an instant he had a presentiment of himself there in years to come. A total screw-up. And in that same instant he realised that he was screwing up right there and then. And he turned and he ran.

Ran back across the bridge past the Post House Hotel. Ran over Westgate Street and turned right at the Angel, down past the Arms Park till he got to the new burger bar. He turned left there and cut back up to St Mary Street, running slightly slower now, scanning the late-night stragglers as they came out of Les Croupiers and Qui Qui's. He saw her just past the Taurus Steak House, and caught up with her by the monument outside the Central Hotel, just about to head under the railway.

She heard his footsteps first, running footsteps right behind her, and turned fearfully, a girl alone on the streets at night. She started to smile when she saw it was Mazz then almost instantly set her face into a frown.

'Sorry,' he said, 'sorry, sorry, sorry.'

'Yeah,' she said, looking at him hard. 'So you're sorry. I'm going home.' And she turned and walked on under the bridge.

Mazz paused for a moment then ran after her again. 'I said I'm sorry,' he said when he caught up with her once more, on East Canal Wharf now.

'I know,' she said, 'I heard you and I'm going home.' Then she softened a little. 'Listen, we'll talk about it tomorrow, yeah.'

'No,' said Mazz, a new tone creeping into his voice. 'No, please. I'm sorry I was being a dickhead. I was just, just . . . jealous.' It surprised him as the words came out of his mouth. He'd never been jealous before, not so he could remember anyway. It surprised Tyra too, he could see. She had stopped now and was looking at him closely. Still it didn't surprise either of them half as much as what he said next.

'It's 'cause I love you.'

The words just hung there for a few moments. Mazz shook his head, amazed at himself. Tyra whistled, then she moved towards Mazz, touched his face tentatively like she was seeing him for the first time, like she was a blind girl looking to know him by feel.

'You mean it?' she said softly, in a voice apparently devoid of emotion.

'Yeah,' said Mazz, and suddenly Tyra was all over him, and he her.

A little while later Tyra looked around her and then pulled Mazz by the hand towards the railway arches, Mazz wondering what the hell was going on. Most of the arches were bricked or boarded up, a couple had the inevitable car-related activities, but Tyra made for one said City Skates and sported a very badly painted mural of a skateboarder daubed across its doors. Getting close to it, Tyra suddenly ducked down and examined the wall to the side of the arch. Seconds later she removed a loose half brick, felt around behind it and pulled out a key. Mazz started to ask something but Tyra put her finger to his lips and smiled. Moments later they were inside the skateboard shop and Tyra was laying a big roll of plastic down on the floor. Precious few seconds after that she was naked beneath Mazz, pulling him on to her.

Three times they did it before they left the skate shop, and when they left Mazz had a chain of love-bites on the right side of his neck and blood and skin from Tyra's back beneath his fingernails.

For her part, Tyra was pregnant, but they didn't know that till later.

6

TECHNIQUEST

1999

Mazz couldn't stop staring at Tyra. Stood there making the tea wearing a faded old dressing gown, she still just looked great. It's weird seeing people you've slept with twenty years ago, and haven't seen since. On the one hand there's these flashes of intimate memory, skin on skin, all of that; on the other hand there's the here and now and a person you just don't know any more. So close and so far. Even the memories seem hardly more real than dreams or fantasies, things from another lifetime. Which is what it felt like now to Mazz, that time in Cardiff, separated from the present Cardiff by year after year of Camden rehearsal rooms, mid-American Holiday Inns, Transit vans and tour buses, floors in Krakow, pensiones in Italy and those weird French motorway hotels where you don't ever see a living person, just get a key card from a machine, spend the night in a box, about the right size for a battery human.

And Tyra? He didn't know, couldn't guess. Was staying here all this time just as weird as leaving? Growing into kids and husband just as strange as running as fast as you can just to tread water in the music business? Seemed to him she was different, like she was – well, not exactly blacker 'cause that sounded terrible – more docks, he supposed. Like when they met he knew she lived in the docks and that but he supposed he'd seen her as just another student-type serious girl, only a bit more streetwise and that. But now, seeing her in her own house, her kids' toys around the place, and having heard the stories about her man Tony, some gangster who'd fled the country, he could see she'd grown up into a life he didn't really comprehend at all.

Still, you get older you can handle these situations easier. So they sat there both nursing their hangovers and talking about nothing for a few minutes before Mazz decided to broach the reason he'd come. Apart from the chance to feast his eyes on Tyra one more time.

Mazz had been up most of the night. After the pub he'd phoned the Colonel and dragged Lawrence over to the late-night drinker in Penarth. And over the next few hours, aided by drink and the last of Mazz's cocaine, they'd worked Lawrence's alleged sighting of Charlie, Emyr and Jason together into an epic conspiracy theory. Why would Charlie have been seeing Flaherty? Jason wouldn't have given the time of day to Charlie these days. What had Charlie got that Jason wanted? Or was Charlie blackmailing Jason? The Colonel said Jason was getting to be a big man in the city and God knew he must have enough skeletons in his closet. And Emyr – if it was Emyr – something strange had to be going on there.

Mazz woke up on the Colonel's spare bed at nine unable to go back to sleep and filled with a sense of purpose he hadn't felt in . . . years? He was going to dig a little. May not have done much for Charlie while he was alive but the least he could do now was follow this thing up.

He hadn't been so hungover, he'd have tried to introduce the subject sensitively into the conversation. As it was he just blurted it out into the silence as he sat there dipping a digestive in his tea.

'You thing there was anything funny about Charlie's death?'

'Funny!' For a moment Mazz thought Tyra was going to hit the roof. Then she caught herself and stared at him. 'What d'you mean, funny?'

'I dunno,' said Mazz. 'It's just there's a few things seem a bit strange about Charlie's last few weeks. I mean, he wasn't in too good a state these last few years, that's right?'

'Yeah,' she said, and he could see her wondering if she had the energy to have a go at him but instead she just shook her head wearily. 'Not too good at all.'

'Well,' said Mazz, 'you got any idea what he'd been doing with Jason Flaherty lately? Two different people have told me they saw them together the last few weeks.'

Tyra frowned and hesitated, then she said, 'He paid for the funeral too, you know. And the wake. I thought that was weird myself. But so what?'

'I dunno. It's just it seems really kind of odd. And I tell you the strangest thing. Someone told me they saw Charlie, Jason and Emyr together.'

'Emyr the drummer?' Tyra said. 'Isn't he meant to have vanished?'

'Yeah,' said Mazz. 'You knew that already?' He looked at her closely. 'You still interested in music then?'

Tyra smiled – the first time he'd seen her smile. 'Yeah, you know, old stuff mostly. But there was a documentary about him a little while back. I saw that. Couldn't believe it really. Emyr. She smiled again. 'Dark horse that one, wasn't he?'

'Yeah,' said Mazz, 'a dark horse, or a pale horse, more like.'

'Well, that's weird too,' she said, 'but I still don't see . . .'

'Me either,' said Mazz. 'But still I don't know, the way he died and everything, that was all straightforward, wasn't it?'

Tyra frowned. 'I think so. They had an inquest the other day so it must have been all right or the police would have said, I s'pose.'

'You haven't seen it then?'

'What?'

'The autopsy report.'

'No.'

'Might be worth just having a look, you know.'

Tyra shivered at the prospect of reading the details of her father's death and decay. 'Christ,' she said, 'no thanks.'

'Oh sure, sorry.' Mazz fell silent.

Tyra shrugged. 'Tell you what, I'll have a word with the police, find out if there was anything strange about it.'

'Great,' said Mazz, and they both lapsed into silence now. Before either of them could break it there was a knock on the front door.

'Oh Christ,' said Tyra. 'That'll be my mum.'

Mazz considered jumping into a cupboard for a moment but, tired as he was, opted for just staying put. Tyra opened the door and in walked Celeste accompanied by a couple of kids, a boy and a girl, who yelled perfunctory hiyas before disappearing into the front room. Celeste stayed in the hall talking to Tyra, and Mazz thought he might escape unobserved. But just as she was preparing to go Celeste's eyes swivelled right into the kitchen and she caught sight of him. Gave Mazz a look that instantly made him feel nineteen again.

Celeste turned to Tyra. 'What's he doing here?'

'Nothing, Mum,' said Tyra, sounding like a teenager again too. 'He just came for Dad's funeral. Just came round this morning for a cup of coffee.'

'Mmm hmm,' said Celeste and moved towards the door. 'You call me later on, girl,' she ordered as she left.

Mazz and Tyra waited a few seconds then looked at each other and burst out laughing. Both nineteen again and together, just for a moment.

'Oh God,' said Mazz eventually, 'she always liked me, didn't she?' They both cracked up again, but then Mazz could see Tyra's face tighten up, sure he could read what was going on behind her eyes, something along the lines of 'And she was damn right to mistrust you'. He leaned forward and said, 'Sorry.'

It hung there in the air.

'Sorry,' she repeated, 'yeah, sorry . . . Look, Mazz, just leave it, OK? Long time ago. Different people, you know what I'm saying?'

She stood up, made it clear it was time for him to go. At the door she said. 'Thanks for coming round. Give me your number and I'll let you know about the autopsy. OK?'

Mazz nodded, smiled weakly, scribbled the Colonel's number on the back of a bus ticket and headed off towards the bay.

Monday morning and Tyra had pulled herself together. All weekend she'd been weepy as hell. Just anything would set her off. The kids, the telly, her book, some blind lady walking down the street. Kids didn't seem to notice much, thank God; you worry you're going to disturb them or something but mostly they don't pay any attention. One time Emily saw her in the living-room sobbing in front of the afternoon film, she was sweet as anything, came up and said, 'You sad about Charlie dying?' – everyone called him Charlie, even his grandkids – and when Tyra nodded she just hugged her and said, 'Don't worry, Mum, he's in heaven now.'

Which must have been her own mum's influence – the heaven bit not the Charlie bit.

Anyway it was Monday now and the kids were off at school and she was feeling, well, not great but better. And she'd been thinking about what Mazz had said about Charlie and Jason. Well, she was sure it was nothing but it didn't hurt checking it out a bit, did it? Yeah, well, she knew it was her own guilt really and to be honest she wasn't sure if it would make her feel better or worse if he had been murdered. Murdered? What the hell was she talking about?

So she'd called Jimmy Fairfax. And maybe that's what it was all about, maybe she was just after Jimmy Fairfax. Way she was feeling at the moment, sobbing one moment, horny as hell the next, she didn't trust herself an inch. So, yeah, so she'd spoken to Jimmy and he was nice enough, but sounded like he was in a bit of a hurry. Told her to come down the station at twelve, they'd have a chat.

He was waiting for her by the desk when she came in.

'All right,' he said, 'nice day out there so I'm told.' He turned and winked at the chubby blonde on the phones. 'Fancy a little walk?'

Tyra nodded and they crossed the road and headed down towards Techniquest.

'Uh, the other night . . .' Tyra started.

'Don't worry,' said Jimmy. 'Got your key in the door, over to the sofa and out like a light.'

'Yeah?' she said.

'No, not really. You had me on the go all night long.'

Tyra looked at him, speechless for a second, then he started laughing and she said, 'Bastard.'

'Yeah, sorry,' said Jimmy, not looking a bit sorry, 'couldn't resist it. Still, like I said before, sorry about your dad.'

'Yeah,' said Tyra, 'so the inquest or whatever – all right, was it?'

'Well, no big surprises, like. Be honest, someone's been dead a week like that, there's not a hell of a lot you can be sure about.'

Tyra swallowed.

'Sorry,' said Jimmy, 'but you did ask. You sure you want to hear any more?'

Tyra nodded.

'All right, well there were a few little things. There was a certain amount of bruising on his arms and body, but it's impossible to say how long before he died it was inflicted and, be honest, the way Charlie was the last . . .'

'Few years, yeah. Could have happened any time.'

'Yeah, well, sorry again, but that's the truth. Other funny thing is – and, look, again I'm sorry – did you know your dad to take much cocaine?'

'Cocaine? Hardly. His pension barely covered the Special Brew.'

'Yeah, that's what I thought, but the doc reckoned he'd taken a good bit shortly before he died.'

Tyra frowned. 'Doesn't make sense, that.'

Jimmy shrugged. 'Someone must have given him some, I suppose.'

They walked on together in silence for a while past Techniquest and the Sports Café till they came to the edge of the bay itself, still a gigantic rather ghostly mud-bath waiting for the barrage to come into operation and turn it into a bustling marina. Tyra pondered who might have given her dad some coke before he died. Far as she knew, he mostly just hung around with a bunch of fellow deadbeats doing the pub, bookie's, Spar shuffle. Then a thought hit her.

'You hear anything about Charlie hanging round with Jason Flaherty at all?'

Jimmy didn't answer the question, just fired one straight back. 'Where d'you hear that?'

'Oh I dunno, couple of people said they'd seen them together. And Jason paid for the funeral.'

'Yeah?' said Jimmy. 'Did he?' And his brow creased. Then he smiled. 'Course, Jason' – not Flaherty, she noticed, Jason – 'used to manage Charlie's band, that ska band, the Wurriyas, you remember?'

'Course I remember,' said Tyra, 'I was in it.'

'Christ, you were and all.' Jimmy turned round to stare at her. 'Course you were. It's just like . . . You ever think we were different people when we were younger?'

Tyra couldn't help laughing. 'You certainly were, Fairfax.'

'Yeah,' said Jimmy, smiling, 'that's what I was remembering. Went to see your band once down the Top Rank, whole bunch of us City boys went down, 'cause you had Bobby in the band, like. And a load of Bristol Rovers came over, terrible ruck.' He shook his head. 'And now look at me.'

Tyra smiled too, thinking of herself back then: short skirts, black tights and DMs, hair tied up in a polka-dot bow. And Mazz. She shook her head, trying to banish the thoughts of the old days. She couldn't believe seeing Mazz the other morning had been such a non-event. There he'd been in her kitchen and she wasn't angry, wasn't happy, wasn't anything. Same for him, far as she could see, and yet back then it had been wild, way she remembered it. Times she'd been out of control. And now nothing. That was passion for you, she supposed. And time.

Didn't know how long she'd drifted off on this train of thought but suddenly she was startled by Jimmy coughing.

'Look,' he said, 'got to get back to the station now. And sorry not to be more help, like, but anything I can do, yeah, just let me know.'

'Yeah,' said Tyra, 'thanks,' and smiled at Jimmy but didn't follow him back to James Street. Instead she stood there a while longer looking out at the bay wondering what to make of what Jimmy had told her. Three strange things. Charlie got beaten up before he died, Charlie took some cocaine before he died, Charlie met up with Jason Flaherty before he died. Any of them could be explained easily enough, but all three together? Maybe Mazz had a point; maybe there was something going on.

Later that evening Tyra was sitting at home, trying to take it easy. She'd got her feet up, the kids in bed, glass of wine in her hand watching *Who Wants to be a Millionaire?*. She was just up to thirty-two grand and was wondering whether to phone a friend to find out which American state somewhere called Cape Cod was in when someone came knocking on her back door.

She opened the door and there was Bobby Ranger standing there, gap-toothed grin in place, but a definite urgency about her stance.

'Hiya,' said Tyra. 'C'mon in.'

Inside she offered Bobby a glass of wine.

Bobby shook her head. 'Got some pop or something that'd be nice, though.'

Tyra went to fetch a glass of Coke from the fridge and when she came back Bobby was sat there in front of the TV shouting, 'Massachusetts, you silly cunt, Massachusetts.'

'Yeah,' said Tyra, 'you sure?'

'Course I'm sure,' said Bobby. 'Where the President and that goes for their holidays, Cape Cod.'

'Oh,' said Tyra and sat back in her chair with her drink.

They stayed there till the show finished, Tyra not saying anything much at all, Bobby calling out the answers, getting them right three times out of four, the fourth generally being very confidently wrong.

Tyra was sitting there watching Bobby, wondering why she was here. 'Bob,' she said when the credits started rolling and she'd turned down the sound with the remote, 'something I can do for you?'

'Nah,' said Bobby. 'Well, I was just wondering, like, if you've been through Charlie's flat yet.'

Tyra stared at her, perplexed. 'How d'you mean?'

'Through his things, like.'

Tyra was on the point of saying what's it got to do with you, but her curiosity got the better of her. 'Why? He got something of yours?'

'No,' said Bobby, 'it's not that. You haven't heard the rumours, then?'

'Rumours?'

'Yeah, that Charlie had something stashed away. Lot of the old-timers – Charlie's mates – been talking about it. Apparently Charlie was going on about it before, before he died, like, how he had this stuff stashed away. Being very mysterious about it, what it was exactly. No one thought much about it at the time, like, but now he's dead people are talking. Probably making it up as they go along, you know. But I'd tell you.'

Tyra frowned. 'First I've heard of it,' she said. 'Be honest with you, I've been putting it off, like, going round there. Seeing his stuff . . . And knowing he was lying there all that time . . .'

'Course,' said Bobby, 'course. I'll come round with you if you like.'

'Yeah?'

'Yeah, no problem. Do it tomorrow, yeah?'

Tyra nodded. It was agreed. Bobby stayed a little while longer then said she had to go pick her girl up from work. Tyra said all right she'd see her tomorrow then. Who was she to judge?

Mazz had spent a shitty night on Lawrence's sofa, after a long night out at the Oak, listening to Big Mo sing the blues. Eventually, around eight, he'd had enough, got off the couch, put his jeans on, rinsed his mouth out under the tap and headed out.

Walking into town, he clocked for the first time just how much the new rugby stadium was dominating the skyline, changing it radically from the cityscape he remembered. He shook his head, feeling like everything he knew and had hoped for in this city was long gone, while other people's dreams, the grand development dreams of the Jason Flahertys, carried on apace.

As if looking for reassurance that not everything had changed, his feet led him into the old Victorian covered market in town, past the fishmonger and through the ranks of haberdashers and cheese sellers, watch repairers and sweetshops and then up to the gallery and the cheapest greasiest breakfast left in captivity.

Sitting there over successive cups of sweet stewed tea, Mazz reviewed his options. He could go back to London. His stuff, what there was of it, was there, if Susie, his ex, hadn't thrown it out on the street yet. Probably she'd let him stay for a couple of weeks while he found another gig. Worst case he could eat humble pie and get back with the fat Yank. Or he could get a few guys together and call them the Wurriyas, go off and play the American ska circuit. Word was there was plenty of work to be had out there, specially since 'Lick Her Down' had been stuck on some *20 Ska Greats* CD lately. But that just felt too depressing. In fact all of option one sounded too damn depressing.

Option two then. Stay in Cardiff. And do what? Run some half-arsed investigation into why Charlie died. Uh huh, and for whose benefit would that be? Certainly not Charlie's. Charlie was dead. For Tyra then. He didn't want to go there at all. But . . . but, but, but. He did want to know what had happened. What had happened to Charlie, what had happened to Emyr.

Face it, he thought, mournfully eyeing the world from behind the remains of a bacon roll, he wanted to know what had happened to himself, brought him to this stage in his life with so little to anchor him to the world. And unbidden he found himself humming the theme to *Whatever Happened to the Likely Lads?*.

He smiled and stood up. Decision made. He was going to hang about. Next question: where to start? Didn't take long to figure that out. There was one man seemed to be most involved in whatever it was that was going on, and that same man was the one person Mazz knew in Cardiff who might have some work for him. His old mate and manager Jason Flaherty.

Bobby came round about twelve. Tyra asked it she wanted a drink but Bob shook her head and said why didn't they get on with it, which was nice of her – she could probably see how nervous Tyra was. Stupid, really, it was only a couple of hundred yards and she must have walked them about a billion times but today she was dreading every inch of it.

Charlie's flat was on James Street just above a newsagent's. Horrible flat at the best of times. She'd hardly ever been there; too depressing to see how far her dad had fallen. There was a street door next to the shop and Charlie's flat was on the first floor. She dug out the keys he'd given her, years ago when he first moved in there, and opened the door. The light wasn't working inside so she picked her way up the filthy stairs, round the bend and on to the first-floor landing. No light here either and Tyra fumbled about for a minute before she got her key in the lock. She opened the door, turned the light on in the hall with a sigh of relief when it worked, then walked into the front room.

'Oh my God,' she said as she looked around the place.

'Fucking hell,' said Bobby as she pushed in beside her.

The room was trashed. It wasn't like Charlie had been Mr Houseproud or anything but this was different. The ratty old sofa was tipped upside down, the cushions slashed on the floor next to it. The pictures were off the walls, frames smashed; the table he ate on and kept his bills and stuff on was upturned and the papers all over the place; the back was hanging off the TV. His stash of racing form guides were scattered around by the fireplace. God knows what the rest of the chaos was.

Tyra couldn't take it; she just sank to the floor and started sobbing.

'C'mon,' said Bobby, sitting down next to her, putting her arms round her, 'c'mon,' and after a while Tyra's sobs subsided.

She turned to Bobby and said, 'What's going on, Bob?'

Bobby shook her head. 'Dunno, girl.' She frowned then looked up. 'Tell you what, I knows the girls live upstairs. Why don't I go up, have a little word, see if they know anything about it?'

'All right,' said Tyra. 'But, Bob . . . don't be long, yeah? Place is giving me the creeps.'

Bobby went upstairs and Tyra took a deep breath then started exploring the rest of the flat. Same story in the kitchen and the bedroom – totally ransacked. The bathroom even: they'd ripped the top off the toilet, pulled off the cladding round the bath. No getting round it, someone had been searching the place for something.

What? And had they found it? No way of knowing, though she supposed the fact they'd ransacked the whole place, instead of stopping halfway through, suggested that maybe they hadn't. What the hell they could be looking for she couldn't imagine. It beggared belief that Charlie had hold of anything worth having. Anything Charlie'd had had been sold off years ago. Records, boxing mementoes, you name it. Still, you didn't go to these kind of lengths to find someone's last bottle of White Lightning. Maybe he had had that winning lottery ticket after all. She almost laughed then stopped herself, realising how close she was to total hysteria.

'Bobby,' she called, walking out on to the landing. 'Bobby!'

'Just coming, doll,' shouted Bobby from the floor above, and Tyra went back into the living-room and started aimlessly tidying things up, drop-in-the-ocean time, till Bobby reappeared.

'Say they don't know nothing about the break-in,' said Bob, 'but I dunno. Pair of lying fucking slags, you ask me. One thing they did say, though, was the landlord wouldn't be pleased. And you know who he is?'

'Who?' said Tyra.

'Nichols, Vernon Nichols,' said Bobby. 'You know him?'

'Know the name,' said Tyra. She'd known it most of her life, in fact. These days he was some big developer. Any of these big buildings – the stadium, the Assembly – people'd mention him. But she'd known his name for longer than that.

'Yeah,' she said, 'my dad knew him, something to do with the boxing. He used to be a promoter or something. S'pose that's why Charlie was living her, a favour from some old boxing guy.'

'Mmm,' said Bobby, 'maybe. Though, what I hear, Vernon Nichols doesn't do a lot of favours. Anyway, what're we going to do about all this shit? You think they found anything?'

Tyra looked around helplessly. 'I dunno, Bob. If they did they made a hell of a mess doing it.'

'Yeah, you know where he kept his papers and stuff?'

'On the table by the window.' Tyra pointed at the upturned table and the pile of crap surrounding it. Then a thought stuck her. 'And he had a box he kept a lot of his precious stuff in. His boxing things, old photos . . .'

'What sort of box?'

'Just an old shoebox.'

'Any idea where he kept it?'

'I dunno. In the bedroom, maybe?'

The two women walked into the bedroom and looked around. Tyra gingerly lifted up piles of clothes. Nothing. Then Bobby opened up the cupboard and there it was: an upturned shoebox and a bunch of papers underneath it. Bobby picked them up carefully then went over to the bed and sat down. She started looking through them with an eagerness and care that surprised Tyra.

'What you searching for, Bob?'

Bobby looked up, startled. 'I dunno, nothing really . . . Just, you know, something might explain what's going on here.'

Tyra sat down next to her and had a quick shufti but it was just a bunch of old papers, a building society bank book that hadn't been touched in years, his NHS card, a few boxing certificates. It was all Tyra could do not to start crying at the pathetic sight of it all.

'C'mon,' she said. 'Better go and report this to the police.'

*　　*　　*

Jason's office was on Windsor Terrace, a classy little street just off the city centre, Italian restaurants at one end, lawyers at the other. Jason had a whole building, a discreet brownstone halfway up on the left. The foyer was expensively minimalist, dominated by a hugely blown-up photo of the Cardiff Docklands. Building sites all over the place, and big red circles round many of them. Jason's sites, Mazz supposed.

The receptionist, a good-looking blonde Mazz's age but doing her best not to seem it, took his name and gave him a look that sent him over to examine his reflection in the mirror, while she murmured something into a phone. Unshaven, red-eyed, clothes he'd slept in, probably whiffed a bit you got up close. Probably too you could smell the couple of pints he'd had already this morning waiting for half twelve when Jason had said he could see him. But Mazz knew he still had what it took. Outlaw charisma.

He straightened his hair in the mirror, turned to the receptionist and winked. 'Hard night last night,' he said.

'Oh,' she said, like she could really, really give a shit.

'Yeah,' he said. Then, his attention suddenly caught by a gold disc on the wall behind her, he asked, 'Whose is that?'

The receptionist ignored him. Mazz walked round her and peered at the record himself. It was one of Emyr's albums, a gold disc for Japanese sales presented to JPF Management Services. Mazz scratched his head; he didn't know Jason still managed Emyr.

'Mr Flaherty will see you now,' said the receptionist, sounding surprised and slightly offended at the news. 'Take the lift to the third floor.'

Mazz did as he was told, passed through a secretary's antechamber and found himself in Jason's office, a huge great space equal parts corporate intimidating and lads rec room. There was a dirty great desk with a computer and flat-screen monitor that must have cost a fortune, but Jason wasn't behind it: he was over by the window bending over a pool table.

'Mazz!' he said like it was an amazing surprise to find Mazz standing in his office. 'Coffee, tea? Something stronger?'

'Yeah,' said Mazz, 'OK.'

Jason walked over to the bar in the corner of the room, opened a bottle of Bell's, poured out a large one and handed it to Mazz. Mazz stood there waiting for Jason to pour himself one; when he didn't he shrugged and knocked back a healthy swallow. What did he care if Jason Flaherty thought he was an alky?

'So, Mazz,' said Jason, looking amused like Mazz was some kind of standup comic wheeled into the room for his benefit, 'how's the rock'n'roll game?'

Mazz shrugged, drank off some more of the whisky.

'Like that, yeah?' said Jason. 'Tough business, all right. So what can I do for you, assuming you're not here just to shoot the shit with your old mucker Jason?'

'No,' said Mazz. 'I was thinking of staying back in town, like, for a bit and I was wondering . . .'

'If your old Uncle Jase could sort you out with some work. That it?'

'Yeah, well,' said Mazz, trying to stop himself from shuffling.

'You an architect then?'

'Mazz shook his head.

'A hod carrier, crane operator? Didn't think so. Or did you think maybe I was looking for a forty-year-old guitar player, so's I could turn him into the new Eric Clapton? No? Well, you're right there. Christ.' Jason paused. 'He was in here too a month or so back.'

'Who?' said Mazz.

'Charlie. Came in, asked me if I needed any security. Thought he was trying to shake me down for a minute, which would have been a laugh. Then I realised he seriously thought I was going to hire a sixty-year-old alky to work security for me.'

'So what d'you tell him?'

'Told him to fuck off, of course. Same way I'm going to tell you to fuck off soon as you finish drinking my whisky.'

Mazz stood there immobile wondering what the hell he was supposed to say to that, but then Jason carried on.

''Cept one thing I told him, and I may as well tell you the same thing. I've had one or two people asking me questions about your old band. Asking if you ever thought about getting back together, like.'

'Oh,' said Mazz.

'Yeah, incredible, isn't it? Twenty years on.'

'Yeah,' said Mazz, not laughing, 'Not going to happen now, is it?'

Jason looked at him quizzically, if a man that big can ever look quizzical.

'Charlie's dead, you know. You paid for his bloody funeral.' Whisky before lunchtime; is there anyone it doesn't put in a fighting mood?

'Yeah,' said Jason. 'Poor Charlie, couldn't help feeling a bit guilty in the end there, like. But, be honest with you, Mazz, it's not Charlie you'd need to get the band back together. Feller that would make the difference would be Emyr.'

Mazz looked at Jason disbelievingly. 'Emyr? What the fuck would Emyr want to do that for? Anyway isn't he meant to have topped himself?'

Jason paused. 'You believe that?' he asked finally.

'I dunno,' said Mazz. 'Haven't seen the feller in a long time.'

Jason shrugged then and Mazz could see he was about to be dismissed so he carried on. 'Course you hear stories about people seeing him.'

Jason stared at him. 'Oh yeah? What kind of stories?'

'You know, Emyr playing snooker down on Broadway with a couple of fellers, that kind of thing.'

'Who told you that?' Jason suddenly in Mazz's face, not playing about now.

'Feller I know.' Mazz stayed put, not letting the fear show.

'Yeah, he say anything else, this feller?'

'Said Emyr was carrying a surfboard.'

'A surfboard?'

'Yeah,' said Mazz. 'Mad, innit?'

'Don't suppose he said who else was there, this, uh, feller?'

'Yeah,' said Mazz, 'he said Charlie was there' – Mazz paused, savouring the moment – 'and a big heavy feller in a suit.'

With one movement Jason had Mazz picked up by the jacket and swung him over to an open window. A slight adjustment and he had half Mazz's body sticking out of the window, his face looking fifty foot down at the concrete below.

'Failed rock star commits suicide by jumping out of manager's office – that the story you want to read in the *Echo*?'

Mazz managed to grunt and shake his head.

'Then quit fucking me around,' said Jason, pulling Mazz back into the room and handing him a fresh glass of whisky.

'So what did you think you were going to do? Blackmail me? That the idea? You think I've got Emyr stashed here in the cupboard, is that it?'

Mazz had his head between his knees and was concentrating on taking deep breaths, keep the panic under control. He knew Jason did things like that. Back in the day they used to laugh about Jason and Kenny pulling those kind of stunts. But when it happened to you, fucking hell. Finally the panic rolled back a little and he raised his head. 'Just thought you might know where he is, like.'

Jason stared at Mazz some more, like he couldn't bring himself to believe that Mazz was as dumb as he was playing. Finally he sighed. 'Charlie didn't call you then?'

'Charlie?'

'Yeah, he didn't call you a few weeks back?'

Mazz shook his head. 'I was on a tour.'

Jason poured himself a glass of whisky, then motioned to Mazz to sit down and plonked himself down behind his desk. 'Fair enough,' he said. ''Fraid I may have been reading this situation all wrong. Best thing is I explain what's been going on. I told you Charlie came to see me, right. Well, you could see he was desperate, right, all this crap about security. No way I could have him working for me, the state he was in. But then, like I said. I told him the same thing I told you, you could get the Wurriyas back together again, there'd be a little bit of money in it. Lot of money maybe if you could get Emyr involved. Now I don't think much of it, just something to say, really, get the poor sad old bastard out of my office. But a couple of weeks later he phones me up, out of the blue, like, and asks me to meet him in the snooker club, over on Broadway. Says there'll be someone there be worth my while to meet. Same again, I don't expect much of it really. Be honest, I thought he'd probably dug you up from somewhere. But last minute I decide to head down there, and there's Emyr, large as life and carrying – your mate's right about that – carrying an effing surfboard.'

'Shit,' said Mazz.

'Yeah. Couldn't believe it. Emyr, who I've had bloody private detectives chasing from here to Bali, 'cause the little twerp walked out on contracts worth a bloody fortune, he has the nerve to come up to me in the Broadway snooker club saying he'd like to do a couple of gigs with the Wurriyas. Benefits for Charlie, like.'

Mazz shook his head, bewildered, not sure whether to believe a word of it. 'So?' he said finally.

'So I told him that's fine. He can fit them in between the German tour and recording the new album and giving about five zillion interviews to the media explaining how come he's not dead.'

'Bet he liked that.'

'Yeah, well,' said Jason, sighing and taking a goodish slug of his whisky, 'didn't smack him one, did I?'

Mazz couldn't help laughing. A minute ago he'd been scared out of his wits and now he was amused by the bloke. That was the thing about Jason; he was like a cartoon character – Taz, the Tasmanian Devil from *Bugs Bunny* sprang to mind – that seemed to operate perfectly well in two dimensions while the rest of us tried to struggle along in three. Mazz couldn't image how Jason dealt with all the corporate shit he must be involved in these days; the bloke was still just a football hooligan at heart. Probably that was the secret of his success, though. Those kinds of guys in suits didn't usually mix with people who'd hang you out the window soon as look at you. 'So, then what?' he asked once he'd recovered himself.

'That's what's weird,' said Jason, 'then nothing. We walk out of the snooker club. Fucking Mr Emyr there says he's got somewhere he has to be and he'll be in touch, walks off into the middle of the night carrying this bloody surfboard. Charlie puts the touch on me for some money, so I bung him fifty quid. And that's the last I see of either of them. Apart from poor old Charlie in his coffin there.'

'And that's all?'

'That's all. I sent this wanker of a detective to check out the surfing places. Wanker spends a week in Newquay on expenses, comes up with nothing.' Jason paused, looked at Mazz carefully. 'Why? You want to have a go?'

'What, finding Emyr?'

'No, finding Lord fucking Lucan.' Jason snorted, dug out his wallet, pulled out a big wad of cash, peeled off ten fifties and gave them to Mazz. 'Here, that'll do you for a week. Just go round the surfer beaches till you find him. You don't find him, don't bother showing up here again or next time I will throw you out the window.'

Mazz took the money, stuffed it in his front pocket, then said, 'Surfer beaches, round here, like?'

'No, in fucking Hawaii. How far d'you think five hundred gets you? Course I mean round here. You been away too long, boy. 'S'what people do down here these days. Surfing. There's some shops in town, they'll tell you where to go.'

Mazz stood there for a moment, trying to think what to ask next.

'Didn't I tell you to go?' said Jason. 'Go on. Fuck off. Now.'

7

THE STOWAWAY

1981

Six weeks later things were starting to move fast. It was the beginning of February 1981 and Bobby Sands had announced that the British government had reneged on its promises and he was going back on hunger strike. Christmas had been and gone. The band had recorded a single, played in London, acquired a manager, and a road manager.

The road manager was a feller called Kenny Ibadulla. Round Christmas the band were playing practically every night – parties, pubs, clubs, Cardiff, Newport, Bristol – and had found themselves all of a sudden with a following. Well, two followings really. There were a load of student types would come and see the gigs in town or at the Uni, and then there were the docks boys. They'd played at Mel's, at the Casa, at the Dowlais, and people started coming out – younger kids in little two-tone outfits like they'd seen the Specials wearing on *Top of the Pops* and older ones too, scary skinhead types like Kenny Ibadulla. Mazz never knew you got black skinheads. Mentioned it to Charlie one time, though, and Charlie set him right: 'The whole thing, man – Crombies, braces, Ben Sherman's – pure rude boy.' Way Charlie told it, back in the late sixties all the black boys were dressing like that. Same time the hippy thing was going on so all the mods they either changed into hippies or the hardcore ones – the working-class ones you like to use that kind of a term – they starts dressing like rude boys, right down to getting their hair cut off, pissing the hippies off like hell. 'Yeah, man,' said Charlie, 'skinheads were a black thing first.'

Whatever the history, the reality was Kenny Ibadulla, hulking twenty-year-old light-skinned black guy just out of prison and the scariest person Mazz had ever met. Also his biggest fan. Kenny loved the Wurriyas and any time there was trouble Kenny would sort it out. Least he would if he wasn't starting it himself.

Plot complicated further when they started playing away; Newport, Bristol. Whole bunch of docks boys would follow the band over there, and you'd better believe they didn't take any shit from any local posses. Made for some scary atmospheres from time to time, specially over Bristol where the boys would bring their football colours and the Rovers boys would feel honour-bound to get stuck in – Cardiff City and Bristol Rovers, they fucking hated each other, from time. So the band started getting a little fearful and Kenny noticed this and offered to take over their security. Which was kind of ironic 'cause without Kenny and his mates they probably wouldn't have needed any security, but there you were. So Kenny came on board as road manager. And, be fair, he did a decent job. Had hidden organisational talents did Kenny.

In fact Mazz and Charlie – who had become the kind of ruling duo in the band – were seriously thinking about getting Kenny to be the band's manager full stop. Way Mazz saw it, what they stood to lose in Kenny's lack of knowledge of the business they'd gain in the sheer force he would lend to the role.

But that was before Jason Flaherty came back on the scene.

Mazz hadn't seen Jason since Venomous fell apart. He'd assumed Jason must have gone up to London, started playing in the big leagues. So it was a bit of a surprise to see him looming out of the darkness one night just after a show at the Newport Stowaway, wearing what looked like a bouncer's tuxedo.

Most people Mazz knew he'd seen them dressed like that he'd have taken the piss. Not Jason Flaherty. Come to think of it, when Mazz had rated Kenny Ibadulla the scariest person he'd ever met he couldn't have been thinking. Kenny was scarier first off, in the sense you could feel his capacity for violence right up near the surface. But with Kenny you knew it could come and go in a flash. Jason Flaherty, though, was a man you just knew you didn't want to piss off, not even once. 'Cause he'd never forget.

Still this time it was all silken glove and no iron fist; Jason picked out Charlie from the start, gave him the spiel. The Wurriyas needed management, needed to make a record, needed to play London. They had to move quick; ska wasn't going to be around for ever. So what plans did they have? Charlie ummed and aahed and Jason just nodded, said he figured as much and why didn't Charlie and Mazz come to his office the next day?

The office was in a warehouse on the edge of Splott where Jason was running a van-hire cum security cum property company, and the second Mazz walked in there he knew they'd committed themselves already; you just didn't say no to Jason. And the next few weeks seemed to be showing that they were right not to. Within days Jason had them in the studio, recording 'Lick Her Down'; within weeks he'd had the tape up to London and got a copy to the Specials' own label, Two-Tone. They got a gig in the Rock Garden and a bunch of record-company people came down. Jason told them all to get lost and put out the single with his own money. Two weeks later they sold ten thousand copies independently, Andy Peebles was playing it on daytime Radio One and the record companies were back and begging.

So everyone was happy with Jason. Even Kenny, whose nose could easily have been put out of joint. But instead, after a little bit of pussyfooting around each other, like two rhinos sizing each other up, Kenny seemed to accept that for the moment Jason was the bigger of the two. And in return for Kenny stepping aside, Jason let him into his other business, the security side in particular. Showed Kenny just how close you could go to running an out-and-out protection racket without getting caught. A couple of jobs they worked together. Persuading a car-breaker's over Tremorfa they needed Flaherty security – that was the one involved Jason taking out an Alsatian with a car jack. Collecting payments round Mount Stuart Square – that was the one Kenny held the guy out of the window just like he'd seen them do in the films. Kenny and Jason – came down to it, they were brothers. Brothers you'd cross the road to avoid. Unless, of course, they were your management team.

But still, far as Mazz could see, the thing about guys like Kenny and Jason was to have them on your side and that was just where they were.

And so there they were, February 1981 in the van on the way up to London. A record company waiting to sign them up and take over production of the single, promising to have them on *TOTP* within the fortnight; gig coming up that night supporting the Beat at the Electric Ballroom. Stuff could probably be going better but Mazz couldn't see how.

Well, not until Tyra told him her news. In a little coffee bar just off Bond Street, Tyra told him she was pregnant and Mazz just whooped for joy.

'Christ,' he said, 'Christ,' after he'd calmed down a bit and stopped leaning over the table to kiss her. 'I've got to tell the others. Does your dad know? This is fantastic.'

Mazz was half out of his chair when Tyra pulled him back. 'Mazz, no. Not yet. We've got to talk about it. You don't just say yeah, yeah, everything's cool, let's have a baby. Not you having it, for starters.'

Mazz quieted down quickly. 'You do want to keep it?' he said.

'Oh Christ. Yes. No. I mean, I don't know.'

Mazz didn't reply, just pulled her to him and sat her down on his knee, tall as she was. 'It's just great,' he said softly, 'just great,' and stroked her back and after a little while she twisted round to face him and smiled and kissed him.

'But please,' she said as she disentangled herself and stood up, 'please don't say a word to the others.'

Mazz just buzzed through the rest of the day. The record-company meeting went great. Well, the guy himself was the usual long-haired public schoolboy with a Mick Jagger mockney accent and dodgy bomber jacket, but the point was he was keen and Jason looked to have him pretty well intimidated. He even squeezed him for thirty grand up front to buy the rights to 'Lick Her Down' and then the guy started throwing around telephone-number-type figures for how much the label might invest in the next five albums. All bullshit probably, but nice to hear all the same.

Load of people from the company came down to the gig after, as did a minibus full of docks boys, which made for an interesting combination hanging round the dressing-room afterwards but helped give the band the confidence to tear into the show like they'd never done before.

'Wouldn't like to be the Beat, coming on after that,' said the record-company guy, Simon, afterwards and then he tapped his nose and inclined his head and Mazz smiled and followed him into the bogs expecting a line of speed but instead making his first acquaintance with Mr Cocaine. And maybe it's getting old but cocaine really was cocaine back then. Marvellous stuff. Mazz was buzzing all the more then. Took all his efforts not to blurt out to everyone, 'I'm going to be a daddy.'

The original plan had been to drive back to Cardiff straight after the gig, the way they usually did, and the band were all getting ready to pack up, and Kenny was carrying the gear, when Jason suddenly told them to relax, take their time, he'd booked a hotel in London for the night.

It was shortly after that that Mazz started to lose it a bit. He went out front with Tyra to have a look at the Beat, half wanting to hate them but instead his good mood winning out and he danced with Tyra to 'Mirror in the Bathroom' and 'Stand Down, Margaret' and held her tight during the crappy fast version of 'Tears of a Clown' and everything was fine and then a bunch of kids came up and started telling them how great the Wurriyas had been and that was fine too except suddenly there were loads of kids around them and Tyra had to pull on Mazz's sleeve, shout in his ear that she had to go backstage again, this was freaking her out.

So Mazz led the way backstage and, just as the security guy was waving them through, Jason was coming in the other direction and said why didn't they come to the upstairs bar, the record company was going to be having a little do there after the show. And so of course that's where they ended up and suddenly it was one in the morning and Mazz had had more than a few drinks – 'cause that's the thing with cocaine, of course: you can drink like crazy; in fact you're almost bound to drink like crazy cause of the speediness and it doesn't affect you, not till the cocaine wears off, which is what it did around one – and Tyra was saying she was exhausted and wanted to go back to the hotel and Emyr and Col said they'd had enough of being there too and Jason said he'd get a taxi and Tyra was saying to Mazz you coming then but all he could think about was he'd just spotted Simon again and probably he could get another line of coke off him and keep the buzz going all night 'cause he hadn't even really had a chance to talk to Charlie yet as the old bugger seemed to have at least three girls around him at all times, or to Bobby who was holding court at the bar telling some geezer from the record company stories that looked to have his eyes popping out, and Mazz didn't want the night to end, so he said you go on back, I won't be long.

In fact it was about five when Mazz made it back and he was drunk and Tyra was awake and more miserable than pissed off. But it wasn't as bad as all that, it wasn't like Mazz had got off with someone else or even tried to; he'd just been enjoying his first bit of the limelight and Tyra could see that and didn't blame him. And in fact now he was back she could sleep and so did he and when they woke in the morning they got it on and were the best of a bunch of tired and hungover but very happy bunnies who got in the van back to Cardiff next morning.

The next few weeks were more of the same, magnified, stretched. Now it was happening, it was incredible how fast things came. Different these days, bands have to be marketed with military precision; back then, you were riding something like the ska train you could go from nowhere to the charts in weeks. And that's how it was for the Wurriyas. After London they played Birmingham, Manchester, Glasgow – where Bobby nearly got beaten up by some bunch of Rangers supporting Nazis, before Jason and Kenny waded in and caused some serious damage to the flute-playing boys. Then came the first TV show, some youth thing on BBC2, shot in Cardiff. A couple of days being interviewed, them serious boys from the music papers coming down to Cardiff on the train. Charlie dominating the show every time – boxing stories, gangster stories, drug stories – Mazz doing his best to chip in with some right-on politics – Bobby Sands – the rest of them hardly saying a word. Picture in the *NME* summed it up – Bobby at the front, of course, being the singer; Mazz looking like he's trying to elbow his way into the limelight but failing; Charlie stage left but catching the eye none the less; Emyr and Col barely visible in a cloud of smoke; and Tyra somehow in the picture but alone.

Years after, Mazz would think it all happened too fast. There was a line from a Mott the Hoople song started haunting him – *I wish I'd never wanted then what I want now, twice as much* – like you'd never tasted a bit of success you wouldn't spend the rest of your adult life craving some more.

Instead it had come down hard and fast, hardly a second to savour it or even experience it as much more than a dream. There was a full month without anything approaching a day off as the song charted at thirty-two, went up to seventeen the next week and got them on *Top of the Pops*. That had been pretty horrendous really – Mazz could be sure of that 'cause his mam's brother who had a video had taped the thing and once in a blue moon when Mazz went home they were sure to drag it out. Bobby standing in the middle looking like a frightened rabbit miming hopelessly, the rest of the band looking stiff apart from Charlie, who was caught in a close-up giving this outrageous wink to one of those dancers they used to pay to go among the audience. Only bit of the video Mazz could watch without wincing. That was the only time they did it. Next week the single went up to nine but it needed to go up again for them to get back on the show and instead it dropped down to eleven. Still the momentum carried on for a bit: they did TV in Germany, Sweden, Holland – all of them in and out in a day, pissing off Col and Emyr who'd been pretty keen to check out Amsterdam. And so it went on for another two or three weeks until at last they were dumped back in Cardiff, sick and exhausted, at the end of March.

As for Tyra and the pregnancy and all, Mazz knew the timing was bad. All the stuff they had to do for the record, there'd hardly been any time to talk. Every night there'd been people to meet: record-company people from Germany, journalists from America, distributors from Scotland. Mazz had been pushing himself hard, thanks be to Simon who was always there with a little of the powdered stuff when he really felt he couldn't get up and do it again, but like he kept saying to Tyra, now's the time, got to push now, might not be a second chance – well God knows he was right there. And he did his best to shield Tyra from the worst of it, made sure she got back to the hotel as early as possible each night, held her tight in the mornings when she was feeling queasy. Let her know he was going to be there for her soon. Once they had a little time.

In fact they had two weeks. It would have been less but the studio Jason wanted them to use to record the album was booked up till then, and Charlie, God bless him, had put his foot down when an alternative venue was mooted, told Jason flat out if he wanted this album to have anything going for it at all, he needed to let the band unwind a little. So. Two weeks.

8

THE PLOUGH AND HARROW

1999

The police station was just up the road, so Tyra popped in on her way home. Asked for Jimmy Fairfax on the desk and a minute later there he was, looking like one of the lads this time in jeans and a Tommy Hilfiger sweatshirt.

'Just knocking off now,' he said. 'Anything urgent?'

'Well sort of,' she said.

Jimmy gave her a smile and said, 'Tell you what, let's have a little walk down the road.'

And so next thing she knew she was sat in the White Hart with Jimmy Fairfax buying her a brandy and a pint for himself and she was checking her watch making sure she had time before picking the kids up from school, which she had.

'So what's up?' said Jimmy once they'd sat down at a table, his leg brushing distinctly close to hers.

'My dad's flat,' she said. And then she started sniffling up and he brought out a hanky – clean, believe it or not – and he wiped her face with it which was definitely getting on the intimate side of things and she pulled herself together then sat back and told him about the flat.

Thing was, she sensed as she was telling him all about it that he knew already. He made all the right noises of shock and surprise but there was something off there, she was sure of it.

'It wasn't like that then, when you found him?' she asked finally.

'No,' he said, 'no way. Anything like that, there'd have been an investigation straight off. Nah, he was just lying there on the floor in the front room. Like he'd just keeled over with a heart attack or something. Least that's what the doc reckoned.'

Fair enough, she supposed, but Tyra was still faintly suspicious. 'How about the landlord?' she asked. 'Suppose I should let him know then.'

'Well,' said Jimmy, 'sure, but first thing I'll make sure the scene-of-crime boys get round there and have a proper dig about before the landlord gets stuck into the place. You know who he is then, the landlord?'

'Yeah,' said Tyra, 'Vernon Nichols.'

Jimmy raised his eyebrows like this was news to him, but once again Tyra was not convinced, and it was making her angry. Like, this copper who she was at school with and who this afternoon seemed more interested in staring at her tits than anything she had to say was playing her for a fool.

'All right then,' she said, standing up abruptly, 'let us know if you find anything out. I got to pick my kids up.' Jimmy just smiled at her, gave her a wink and said yeah, sure he'd be in touch. Tyra walked out all angry but on the way to the school suddenly a detailed sexual fantasy involving her and Jimmy brought a flush to her cheeks.

Later that same afternoon Mazz was heading for the seaside, sitting in the passenger seat of the Colonel's VW camper, smoking a joint and trying to find something listenable on the radio.

Mazz was feeling about as mellow as he could remember. Just getting out into the countryside had been like turning a switch. Kind of thing Mazz never realised he missed – fields, peace, fresh air, all that – but right now he felt it restoring him. Even the Colonel was starting to relax, after the blazing bloody row he'd had with his woman, Natalie, when he said he was heading off to the beach with Mazz and wouldn't say when he was coming back.

Turned out, you see, that the Colonel loved to surf. Mazz had schlepped round town, finally finding a place in an arcade with a load of surfing gear where they'd told him a couple of beaches to check out, but he hadn't a clue how he was going to get out to any of them so he called the Colonel on the off-chance and the Colonel had told him to come round and by the time he arrived the colonel was packing wetsuits and boards into the back of the van while conducting a shouting match with Nat.

But that was behind them now and the Colonel was steering the van through country lanes past the go-kart track at Llandow, at which point Mazz picked up the Hollies singing 'Carrie Ann' on Capital Gold and stopped fiddling with the radio momentarily.

'You been surfing before, butt?'

'No,' said Mazz.

'Just a knack. You'll pick it up easy.'

'Hmm,' said Mazz, who couldn't actually swim at all, but didn't feel like mentioning it just now.

Another ten minutes or so and the lane came out on the cliff top at Southerndown, Dunraven Bay spread out below them. The Colonel eased the van down the access road to the car park at the bottom. There were about a dozen other vehicles there – a couple more camper vans, a few rusted-up old hatchbacks – all with surf decals plastered over them. The beach itself was deserted, five o'clock on a coldish Tuesday afternoon in May, but there were figures dotted about in the sea. From the car park the waves didn't look like anything much at all, though.

'Big enough to surf, are they?' asked Mazz as they got out of the van.

The Colonel peered out to sea, his hand shielding his eyes against the sun. 'Yeah,' he shrugged, 'good for learning anyway. Here, put this wetsuit on.'

The Colonel handed Mazz an ancient-looking rubber garment, all black, not like the gaudy efforts he'd seen in the surf shop in town. Mazz looked at it in bemusement for a moment, wondering whether he was really going to encase himself in this thing, then shrugged, pulled his clothes off and started struggling into the suit. Five minutes of wriggling and squirming and the deed was done and Mazz was already sweating profusely from the exertion of it all.

'Right,' said the Colonel, grinning broadly at Mazz's discomfort, 'let's get you a board.' There were two boards in the back of the van: a big heavy-looking one with rounded edges, and a shorter, lighter one with pointed ends and an altogether sportier look. The Colonel handed Mazz the big one.

'Best to start on this one,' he said. 'More stable in the water.'

Mazz nodded and took the big board, feeling obscurely pissed off that he didn't get to have the cool-looking one. Then the Colonel led them down to the sea. They picked their way along a kind of broken concrete causeway, then among the rock pools and finally out on to the sand. The tide was a way out, and seemed to recede even as they approached, but eventually they reached the water and the Colonel stopped. He put his board down flat on the sand and motioned for Mazz to do the same. The Colonel picked up the lead attached to the board and fastened the Velcro strap on the end of it around his ankle. Mazz followed suit and copied the Colonel as he dropped to lie flat next to his board.

'Right,' said the Colonel, 'this is what you got to do when you get on a wave,' and he pushed himself up on to one knee as if about to start a race.

Mazz practised it a couple of times, having no idea really what he was doing, but the Colonel seemed satisfied and led the way into the water.

The second the freezing waves hit his feet Mazz was thanking God for the wetsuit. In fact the thing was fantastic: he was now wading up to his waist in the water and, apart from his feet, not feeling a thing. A little bit of water made its way inside the rubber and started circulating around his body, but that was a good thing apparently; it would be warmed by his body heat, the Colonel said, and almost instantly he could tell it was true – in fact it was a definitely pleasurable feeling. For the first time he had some inkling of why people liked to dress up in rubber at those fetish clubs and that.

Now they were in the water the waves didn't look quite as insubstantial as they had from the car park. Two-or three-foot-high waves were coming at them in nice regular sets, requiring Mazz to jump awkwardly with his surfboard to breast them. The Colonel climbed on to his board and started paddling into the oncoming swell. Mazz swallowed, tried to gauge how deep the water would be up ahead, thought about telling the Colonel he couldn't swim but realised it was too late now – the Colonel couldn't hear him. He either had to head back to the shore and look like a total dick, or paddle after the Colonel and hope to hell that he didn't lose contact with the board which was the only thing likely to stop him sinking.

So Mazz, his pride not for the first time winning out over his sense of self-preservation, started paddling out to where the big boys were. He found if he held the board dead in front of him it was easy enough to ride over the waves on it, and after a couple of minutes he was up to his neck in the water and alongside a good clutch of other surfers. None of them were Emyr, of course, but Mazz figured it would be worth canvassing them once they came out of the water, see if they'd seen the lost boy around. For now, though, the job in hand was to catch a wave. The Colonel came over and told him to get on his board, turn back to face the shore and start paddling, wait for the wave to pick him up, don't bother about trying to stand up this time, just lie on the board and let the wave do the work.

Mazz nodded and did his best. He clambered on to the board, desperately trying, and just about succeeding, not to overbalance it. He'd hardly had time to start paddling, though, when he looked over his shoulder him and saw the biggest wave yet rearing up behind him. Shit, he thought, this one's definitely going to drown me. But it didn't, it picked Mazz and the board up perfectly, breaking just as they came together, and suddenly Mazz was roaring forward on the crest of the wave, riding towards the shore at what felt like an incredible speed. Mazz found himself laughing with delight as he hurtled forwards, his laughter redoubling when he looked left and saw the Colonel next to him standing up on his board and then suddenly losing it, toppling spectacularly into the water.

The wave took Mazz almost all the way to the shore and when he clambered off he found himself in water barely up to his knees. Immediately he turned round and started wading back into the deeper water. He couldn't remember when he'd last had a rush like that without chemical assistance.

He caught another couple of waves, neither quite as good as that first perfect one but pretty good none the less, and was just starting to feel like he knew what he was doing when disaster struck. He was out with the big boys just standing about in the neck-high water waiting for a decent set of waves to come, when he must have walked into some kind of hole. His feet just went down and he was instantly out of his depth. And now he was under, his mouth and nose full of water again. He didn't panic, though, this time, not at once. He was still tethered to the surfboard, and that could float; all he had to do was get back on top of it. Only trouble was he could feel there was a current dragging him and he was still under water and if he didn't come up soon . . . He felt for the bottom of the sea, got his feet on the ground and pushed up. In a moment his head broke the surface and he took a couple of great shuddering breaths. The board, though, was starting to pull out to sea and he couldn't figure out how to pull it back to him. He splashed around frantically trying to keep afloat, but it didn't work. He went back under again and this time he really did start to panic.

He kicked and splashed and opened his mouth to yell while still under water and finally somehow, after what seemed like for ever, came back up to the surface. He yelled for real and flailed some more and a couple of surfers looked across at him and for a moment that Stevie Smith not waving but drowning thing came into his head and then he went down again and felt for sure that this was it until, all of a sudden, he felt someone grabbing him by the shoulder and pulling him up.

Coughing, spluttering and frightened, he came to the surface, his eyes blind from the water in them. He could feel himself being pulled along by whoever was holding him and tried to relax, to go with the flow.

Another small eternity later the movement stopped and a voice said, 'Fucking hell, bra, can't you swim?'

The hands let go of him then and Mazz was about to panic once more when his legs descended and found solid ground beneath them. He stood up, wiped the water out of his eyes and looked at the Colonel.

'No,' he said, once he'd recovered himself, 'no, I can't swim.'

'Jesus,' said the Colonel, looking genuinely alarmed, 'you're crazy. You could have drowned out there.'

Mazz nodded, feeling terribly, terribly tired all of a sudden. He waded into the shallows, bent down and took the Velcro flap off his ankle, untying him from the surfboard, which he carried on to the beach, then doubled over and retched up what felt like a gallon of seawater.

'C'mon,' said the Colonel, putting his hand on Mazz's shoulder, 'let's go back to the van, get you sorted out.'

Tyra had just given the kids their tea and was sitting with her book, the one by an American called Ernest Gaines she'd got on to from the Oprah book club, when the phone rang.

'Hello,' said the voice which she recognised immediately as familiar but couldn't place. 'Is that Tyra?'

'Yeah,' she said guardedly. 'Who's that, then?'

'Jason,' said the voice, 'Jason Flaherty.'

'All right, Jason,' she said, wondering what the hell this was in aid of. First time she'd seen him in years was at her dad's funeral. Which he'd paid for of course. She'd wondered then what the catch was. Oh well, she was probably about to find out now.

'Yeah, good,' he said, then in a sympathetic voice Tyra wouldn't have believed he had, 'So how are you coping? Must have been a terrible shock.'

'Yeah,' she said, 'thanks for paying for the wake and that,' thinking right, here it comes.

'Well,' he said then, 'it was a great shock to me too. Always had a soft spot for your dad, least I could do really. Anyway,' he changed to a businesslike voice, 'I was wondering if we could have a chat. There's a couple of things have come up.'

'Yeah?' she said, now thoroughly mystified.

'Tell you what, why don't we have lunch tomorrow? One o'clock in Woods suit you?'

'Woods?' she said. 'Hang on, is that the one down the docks used to be Scott's?'

'That's it,' he said. 'I'll book a table for one then. OK?'

'OK,' she said, then bye and put the phone down. Hell's that all about she wondered as she got the kids their afters, and then what on earth am I going to wear?

By way of sorting him out the Colonel took Mazz to the van, got him to change into some dry clothes, made him drink a couple of pints of bottled water, then announced it was time to go to the pub. He drove the van back up the side of the cliff then wound through ever smaller lanes for a couple of miles, before arriving outside what looked like just another farmhouse but which turned out, on closer inspection, to be an ancient pub, the Plough and Harrow.

The Colonel led the way inside and into the bar on the right, a dark low-ceilinged room with a bunch of folky-type musical instruments on the walls, and John Martyn playing on the sound system. There was a fire going, which seemed a little unnecessary in May, but fragile as Mazz was feeling it was a comforting thing so he went over and sat by it while the Colonel got in a couple of pints of some dangerously strong real ale straight from the barrel.

'Fuckin' hell, butt, you scared me out there.'

'Yeah,' said Mazz, 'sorry, like.'

'You can't swim then?'

'No,' said Mazz, 'not a stroke.'

'Then what did you think you were doing getting in the water?'

'I dunno. Half of it was, like, showing off or whatever, but the other half was I wanted to do it. I never wanted to swim when I was a kid but today I just thought yeah, I could do that.'

'Yeah, well,' said the Colonel, 'how about tomorrow we just try and get you swimming? Leave the surfing for lesson two, like.'

'Yeah, I dunno. Thing is we're meant to be looking for Emyr, not getting me drowned.'

'Yeah,' said the Colonel, 'but way I see it is you want to find a surfer, you've got to think like a surfer, you've got to know how it feels.'

Now on the one hand Mazz thought this was bullshit – you wanted to catch a surfer you just had to go round all the surfing beaches and hope your boy was on one of them – but on the other hand he had an inkling of what the Colonel meant. Out there in the sea today, riding that one great wave, was some kind of a revelation all right. Wasn't hard to see it as a kind of antidote to the endless night of the rock'n'roll life, wasn't hard to see why Emyr might be following it. Also, one thing about nearly drowning yourself: it didn't half make you feel happy to be alive.

'Nother drink?' he said to the Colonel, picking up the pint glasses they'd both emptied quick time.

'Pope shit in the woods,' said the Colonel and Mazz laughed and walked over to the bar.

Another two or three hours later the landlord was bringing the drinks over to Mazz personally, 'cause Mazz was sat in the corner with an acoustic guitar playing all these songs he hardly even realised he knew, fifties and sixties songs he must have learned when he was a kid. Buddy Holly, Everly Brothers, that kind of thing, even a few Beatles tunes which had the whole place singing along, of course. People were calling out requests now. Just a dozen or so people in the bar now all sitting round listening to Mazz.

Bloke called out for 'Wonderwall' and Mazz told him to twat off. Then a girl asked if he knew any Bob Marley, and Mazz didn't but he had a go anyway, painstakingly picked out the chords to 'No Woman, No Cry'. And all of a sudden in his head he was back in Tyra's bedroom twenty years ago, Bob Marley's picture on the wall, then remembering how it had been the week after Bobby Sands died, the week after the abortion, the last time he'd spoken to Tyra back then, the twelfth of May 1981. It was the third item on the news. Bob Marley had died of cancer aged thirty-something – fuck, younger than Mazz was now – and Tyra he'd never seen her like that, devastated by sadness, and him, Mazz, just sitting there, a ball of confusion, part of him thinking he should be the hurting one – like, you killed our kid – but mostly just feeling this terrible guilt like he hadn't been strong enough to make it all right. And it seemed like he'd been running from that guilt for twenty years now and no woman no cry. Everyone in the pub singing and Mazz not the only one with tears in his eyes.

Probably Mazz was the only person in the house who thought it made sense when he went into 'Lick Her Down' next. In fact most people seemed to think it was an obscure joke when he said here's one of my songs, before launching into it. Still, it transformed the mood in a minute, everyone clapping and hooting along to its relentless rhythm.

And afterwards, once he'd finally been allowed to put the guitar down – inevitably having finished up with the Colonel singing 'Born to Run' with Mazz screwing the chords up manfully – everyone was much impressed to discover that Mazz really had been the main man of the Wurriyas – or that ska band what did 'Lick Her Down', as they were better known.

Weird to realise that some little tune you wrote one day when you were nineteen was now a part of regular thirty-something nostalgia: the record you heard in the youth club, on your first date, on the radio when you worked your first summer in an ice-cream van. Depressing to think that was the only thing you'd ever done that registered on the general radar, meant something to the kind of people who'd never heard of the fat Yank. Didn't half make you feel old. Specially when you looked at this woman was all over you and you're thinking to yourself she looks all right but knocking on a bit and then she tells you she loved your record when she was in school and you realise she's younger than you, and maybe you're just a sad fuck who only likes the kind of little Goth girls who follow the fat Yank around. Or follow Emyr around, come to that.

Follow that train of thought for a little while and Mazz wasn't too upset when drinking-up time came and he had to say goodbye to his new mates.

Later still, crashed out in the camper, drinking from a bottle of single malt the landlord had given them by way of a carry-out once he'd discovered they weren't planning on driving anywhere, Mazz was maundering on to the Colonel about where did all the good times go and shit and the Colonel listened and politely forbore to talk about his own spell in the limelight – his time as Cardiff City's first ever libero, the time that got him his nickname – but just grunted agreement and drank more whisky until finally he said, 'Nat's pregnant, you know.'

'Christ,' said Mazz. 'She . . . is she . . .'

'Gonna keep it? Yeah, she's thirty-eight years old, man, course she's gonna keep it.'

'Great.'

'Yeah,' said the Colonel. 'It is. Last thing I was expecting, mind. Dunno why, really, Nat being the age she is and all. But for me, like, I thought I was past all that. Been there done that.'

'You got a kid already?'

'Two,' said the Colonel, smiling. 'Both grown now. Steve's at college in Swansea, Becca's an artist. That's the funny thing really: it was through Becca I met Nat. She was Becca's tutor at the art college.'

'Oh,' said Mazz, his booze-struck brain becoming ever more addled under this onslaught of new information. 'Great,' he said again.

'Yeah well, great for Nat, really pleased for her, like, but I've got to say I'm worried I'm too old for it. All that getting-up-in-the-night caper. Needs my beauty sleep I do these days. Talking of which, time for a little shut-eye, I think.'

320

And with that the Colonel pulled the sleeping bag tight around him, put his head down on a cushion and virtually instantaneously started to snore.

Mazz meanwhile just lay there in the dark smoking a fag and looking up at the roof of the van, wondering. What it would be like to have had that kid with Tyra, that kid that would have been grown up now. And wondering too what it would be like to have a kid now. Was a thought he seemed to have now and again these last few years. Though one thing about being a bloke, wasn't like you had a deadline or anything. The Colonel was living proof of that, have a kid when you're fifty no trouble. Though there were limits of course; kids didn't want some old geezer for their dad. So, yeah, there it was: he was broody, he guessed. And hearing about the Colonel and Natalie – Natalie, who was his age, Natalie who, assuming he was remembering her right, he'd done it with, that thing that makes babies – well, got to say he felt jealous. How come the Colonel, who did nothing far as Mazz could see except drink and play pool and now surf, how come he had the nice house and the nice girlfriend and the kid on the way? How come Mazz had been working away all these years and he had none of that stuff? Had made a record that all those people in the pub knew and he didn't have shit.

Answer lay in the business he'd got into, of course; rock'n'roll. Pathetic, really, bitching about it not having a pension plan and guaranteed nice little house with a nice little mortgage and nice little wife, but there it was. You might not be able to have your cake and eat it but there was no law saying you couldn't want it, couldn't want it all. Yet it wasn't just the financial insecurity of the life – though that was bad enough – it was also the people you met. The women, he meant. Too fucking young for the most part. Even the ones where it wasn't out and out cradle-snatching – the ones who were like twenty-two or something – they might see you as good for a little walk on the wild side but they didn't want to have your babies. Apart from the stalker anyway.

The stalker had first turned up at a gig in Osaka. Mazz had been flattered at first. This big Japanese girl in a polka-dot mod dress – well, big for a Japanese girl anyway – showed up backstage with all these record sleeves from the Wurriyas on, practically everything Mazz had ever played on. Kind of thing that happened to the fat Yank all the time – fact when you thought about it that was how the fat Yank had met his evil squeeze – but anyway there was this girl giving Mazz the obsessive-fan treatment for once and he couldn't help but be a bit pleased. And she was nice too, far as he could tell, 'cause she didn't speak a lot of English. Not that good-looking though, to be honest; Mazz wasn't exactly aquiver with lust at the sight of her, but yeah she was nice. And so he was happy enough to see her the next three nights of the tour, stretching halfway across Japan, bringing him little presents each time, all wrapped up special and everything – dear God they like their packaging out there – and he'd offer her a drink and stuff though she'd only have a Coke and he'd try and chat to her a bit, and it was fine.

It was only when she turned up a month later in London that he started to worry. In fact not even then – Japs were always coming over to Britain to visit the famous Camden Market and meet all their friends from Tokyo. But when she showed up at Manchester, Liverpool and Newport, Shropshire – a gig at which she was one of only twelve people in the audience – he really started to get uneasy.

And the gifts started getting weirder: packages of very strange-looking sushi, two dolls customised to look like Mazz and the girl, a poem that appeared to be written in blood and, oh God, he still couldn't believe in the midst of all this he'd slept with her. He'd invited her up to his room to tell her, honestly, to tell her to stop, desist and find a more appropriate outlet for her affections and generally leave him alone. But she looked so sad and he'd put his arm round her and let her stay and then they hit the mini-bar . . . OK, look, he knew perfectly well he was crazy, she was crazy, etc. But anyway you can guess where it went from there: the phantom pregnancy, the scenes, the insane, the totally bloody freaky gifts, the awful fucking showdown when he'd told her she wasn't fucking pregnant, she needed fucking help. And then she'd just vanished out of his life. The way women did when Mazz finally managed to hurt them enough. Yeah, well, that was the closest he'd come to having a kid in recent years. Jesus, thought Mazz as he turned over and willed himself to sleep.

Next morning both Mazz and the Colonel were woken by someone banging on the back door. Mazz sat up and peered through the curtain.

Tony, the pub landlord, was standing there looking inordinately cheerful. The Colonel opened the door and shuddered as the sunlight hit him.

'Breakfast, boys,' said Tony.

'Uh,' said the Colonel, and then, after a pause of several seconds in which he appeared to be attempting to remember how to talk, 'OK.'

Tony smiled and shook his head. 'When you're ready, boys,' he said, 'just come in the bar,' and he walked off.

Half an hour later Mazz and the Colonel were sat at the table next to the fire already beginning to feel the hangover-blasting benefits of the full English, black pudding and all.

'Well,' said the Colonel, mopping up the last of his fried bread, 'better get down to work then. You got a picture of our boy Emyr?'

Mazz nodded, dug in his jacket pocket, brought out the picture Jason had given him, a press shot from a couple of years back, and handed it to the Colonel.

'Thanks, butt,' he said, then got up and walked over to the bar where Tony was busy getting things ready for opening time. 'You seen this feller in here at all? Maybe with a bunch of surfers?'

Tony looked at the photo for a while, thought about it.

'He got long hair now, this feller?' he said, tapping the picture.

'Yeah,' said Mazz, 'that's right.'

'Then I'd say yeah, I've seen this feller a few times. Bunch of them come in here, hardcore types you know. Guys who'll come in December and go surfing off the rocks down there.' Tony waved an arm in the direction of the rocky beach a mile or so down the lane. 'Doesn't say much, more of a smoker than a drinker, if you know what I mean. That sound like the guy?'

'Yeah,' said Mazz, 'it most certainly does.'

'So,' said the Colonel, 'any idea where we might find these guys?'

Tony shrugged. 'Usual places, I suppose – 'Gennith, Trecco Bay. Depends on the wind a bit. I were you, I'd head out to Llangennith; that's where you'll find most of the boys sooner or later.'

'Cheers,' said Mazz.

'No worries,' said Tony. 'Why d'you want to find him anyway?'

'Oh,' said Mazz, 'we used to be in a band together, years ago, like.'

'Thinking of a reunion then, is it?'

'Yeah,' said Mazz, 'a reunion.'

'Grand,' said Tony and moved back over to the bar. 'One for the road, lads?'

'Don't mind if I do,' said the Colonel.

9

CONEY BEACH

1999

You came out of Tyra's place, cut through Mount Stuart Square and over James Street, and you were in a different world, and one getting more different every time she walked through it . . . It was funny, the bay development — you'd heard about it for years; since the eighties they'd been knocking stuff down getting ready for it. But for ages that was all it had been, just knocking stuff down and leaving it there. Nice old pubs like the Mount Stuart and the Sea Lock all gone but nothing coming to replace it. Then gradually it started happening. They moved the Norwegian church right on to the bay. Looked nice, to be fair. They built the brand-new Techniquest building and the Harry Ramsden's next to it. Fair enough, kids loved Techniquest. The UCI, of course, suddenly landing like a giant space ship the far side of Bute Street — twelve screens, bowling alley and all. Kids loved that too, and it was packed from the start, all these people never came down the docks in their life piling in, driving there in their cars and driving straight out again. They turned one of the old docks buildings into the Sports Café, which wasn't her cup of tea but her mate Paula had a job behind the bar. And then suddenly there was the new hotel right on the end there and the barrage was meant to be finished soon, and now, looking for this Woods joint, she could see that all of a sudden there was this half-built shopping mall where the Maritime Museum used to be. Pace of it was getting frightening and she could see it was starting to work. Another couple of years and the place would be swarming with tourists and that.

And the old docks, the docks she half remembered herself, and had grown up hearing about in her dad's stories, what about all that? Maybe they'd open a Tiger Bay theme bar to remember it by: cute murals with cute prostitutes and sailors, a little whiff of airbrushed long-ago vice, give the visitors a thrill.

Still, it had to be better than letting it rot, she supposed. It was just a bit unsettling to feel like a stranger in your own patch. Harry Ramsden's, the Sports Café; there were no memories for her there. Only place that looked even vaguely like it used to was the Windsor, all boarded up now but you could still see the big sleazy old pub it used to be and she could still remember the dances there. Her and Tony. Tony and her. All those years – as kids, as grown ups, as grown ups with kids. Tony like a thorn in her heart. A lesson learned: love has its limits. The third time he'd gone to jail, after he'd made all those promises, that had been the limit for her. When he'd come out that last time she'd hardened her heart to him. And now he was gone. Spain they said he'd gone to. Not the only thing they'd said, friends you know, always ready to give you the stuff you really didn't want to know – for your own good, like. Stories about Tony and Mandy. Mandy he'd always said was like a sister to him. Sister!

Yeah, well, like she said there were limits, and Tony was history now, like the Windsor, boarded up and waiting for demolition, redevelopment, she didn't know. Someone had said they were going to open a lap-dancing club there. Hah, chance of a job after all, girl. And right next to the Windsor was Woods, another old building, some shipping office if she remembered right, turned into some posh restaurant. She'd walked past it once or twice, never paid it much mind.

Now, though, walking up to it she felt nervous. Felt shabby, to be honest. It had thrown her into a total panic looking for something to wear. Nothing looked remotely right. Made her realise how long it was since she'd had anything to dress up for. How long it was since she'd been out somewhere nice. She had a couple of dresses she hated and had had for years – things she'd wear for weddings and funerals – and she had the stuff she wore every day: jeans, leggings, T-shirts, sweatshirts – usual mumsy crap. Called up her mate Lisa, who worked in a lawyer's office in town, and was nearly as tall as her, and she brought some things over but it was no good, she just felt like an idiot. Ended up wearing a pair of black jeans that weren't too bad and a velvet blouse she really liked but she'd had for a few years now, and walking in here, seeing all the people all looking if not stylish well rich anyway, she just felt like she should be working in the bloody kitchen. Fact was people like her didn't come to places like this.

Then she glimpsed herself in the big mirror over the bar and thought damn it, girl, don't give into this shit. She looked good, she knew she looked good, she'd always looked good, and she'd never thought she was destined to be bound by her roots, by the docks. She'd proved that when she'd got up and been in the Wurriyas; she could damn well prove it again now.

So she walked straight up to the first waitress she could see, pretty little blonde girl, said she was meeting Mr Flaherty and the girl took her through the bar area into the main bit of the restaurant and there was Jason sitting in the corner looking bigger than life with a bottle of red wine in front of him. He stood up as she approached, nearly tipping the table over, and took her hand then kissed her cheek, and she nearly burst out laughing.

'Jesus, Jason,' she said when they'd sat down, 'you've got a bit smoother over the years.'

Jason laughed, poured her a glass of wine and, not sure how to play or what they were playing come to that, Tyra picked up the menu to give herself something to do. Menu looked nice too – all that stuff you see on the TV food shows and wouldn't dream of cooking yourself. Which always seemed like the point of going to a restaurant to Tyra, getting something you couldn't cook at home. So she ordered a complicated-sounding salad and a confit of duck and Jason smiled and said he'd just have a steak, well done, please, and kept up this solid line of chat. Lot of stuff about the old days, about the Wurriyas, which was nice. It was funny; it was like it was a whole part of her life she'd blocked out 'cause it didn't seem to make a lot of sense alongside the life she was living now, it was like it had happened to someone else really. But there it was and as Jason talked it started coming back.

'You remember that German TV show?' Jason said.

Tyra shook her head then started laughing. 'Yeah, *Club Rock* or something, yeah. The one where the interviewer thought Bobby was a boy?'

'Yeah and Charlie – your dad – pulled the hostess.'

Tyra laughed again. Actually at the time it had been embarrassing as anything, her dad chatting up anything blonde, Teutonic and skirt-wearing, but now she had an aching rush of fondness for how he'd been then, still in the last of his prime. 'Everyone loved Charlie, didn't they?' she said, a choke in her voice.

'Yeah,' said Jason, then paused, 'except for Charlie, I suppose.'

Tyra stopped sniffling and looked at him closely. He was right, of course – you got much sense of self-worth you didn't end up in the gutter – but it wasn't the kind of observation she expected from Jason. Then she hadn't thought about Jason as a person at all really, more a rather scary force of nature you were just glad to have on your side.

'Yeah,' she said, 'I suppose you're right . . .' and tailed off, thankful to see her first course approaching.

As they ate Jason filled her in on what he'd been up to the past eighteen years. He'd stayed in the music business for a few more years, ridden the New Romantic thing for a bit, then saw that the smart money was moving away from bands and into clubs. He'd been a partner in opening a big club in London in the mid-eighties, then spotted that the even smarter money didn't hang around running clubs; it went straight into the property market.

'Late eighties,' he told her, mopping up his steak, 'you had to be a total dickhead not to get rich. Bought any old dump in London, ex-council whatever, converted into flats, flogged them off to yuppies – remember them, funny how people stop using words after a bit, innit – anyway you sold them these shit flats for a fortune then bought up a whole lot more dumps and did it again. Then of course, summer of '88, Chancellor gets it into his thick head to change the tax allowances at the end of July. Any moron can see that it's going to create a feeding frenzy, shoot the prices up and then make them collapse in August.'

Jason paused, picked up the bottle of red wine, drained it off into their glasses then signalled for the waiter to bring another and carried on. 'Least it was obvious to me anyway, so I cleaned my portfolio out that summer then sat around for a year or so waiting for the crash to bottom out, then I started buying again. But this time not so much flats, more office buildings and that. And now construction. Course there isn't that much space for construction in London 'cept for Docklands and the big boys had that all sorted out – no one was going to give Jason Flaherty Canary Wharf to build so I looked around a bit. And you know where I looked?'

'No,' said Tyra automatically, enjoying this, sitting opposite a man who did stuff, didn't just sit about complaining how the world was against him or just doss along in the slow lane for ever. No, she was getting a bit of a buzz off of Jason.

'Course you do,' he said, 'I looked back home. Right here in Cardiff. The docks specially. Loads of land, loads of government incentives to develop the place. Same thing as with the flats in London. You didn't have to be smart to see it, you just had to have a bit of bottle and a friendly bank manager.'

He leaned forward now, giving Tyra a look that was almost soulful if you can imagine a soulful behemoth. 'Difference is of course,' he said, 'difference is that, up in London selling the flats to the yuppies, it didn't matter to me what happened to those places, it was just making money. Situation now it's a little different. First, I've got money now, I don't have to do any of this. Second, I know this place. Not just Cardiff, yeah, but the docks. I've got friends here. Fellers like Kenny. Kenny who I'm not bullshitting is like a brother to me. Ah, bollocks, what I'm trying to say is the developments I'm involved in here all show some respect for the community, bring in jobs, new housing, primary schools, all that good stuff. And what hurts me is when I can see that I'm getting screwed over by some fucker who doesn't care for anything 'cept his own pocket.'

Jason paused finally. Tyra, feeling a little lightheaded now – was that a second bottle of wine they were on? – said, 'Oh yeah, anyone in particular?'

'Yeah,' said Jason. 'Nichols, Vernon Nichols. The bastard who broke into your dad's flat.'

'What?' she said, completely blindsided. 'How d'you know someone broke into Charlie's flat?'

'Like I said, I've got a lot of friends round here. People tell me things.'
'OK, but why d'you say it was Nichols?'

'Well, seems obvious enough.'

'Oh yeah?'

'I heard there was no forced entry and I'm sure the police didn't leave the door open. So must have been someone with a key. And old Vernon's the landlord.'

'Yeah,' said Tyra, 'but why?'

Jason looked at her quizzically. 'You don't know?'

'Course I don't know.'

'Charlie never said anything to you then? 'Bout some information he had, about old Uncle Vern. Evidence, he might have said.'

'No,' said Tyra.

'Well, you know he was having trouble with Vern?'

'No,' said Tyra, 'I don't know anything. He wasn't like that with me. Charlie didn't confide much. Specially not these last few years.'

Jason nodded. 'All right then, let me fill you in a bit. Month or two back Charlie comes to me. It was a bit of a regular event, really. He'd come by, see if I had any little jobs for him or maybe some royalties from the Wurriyas – you know "Lick Her Down" 's out on a compilation? – anyway, be honest with you, he was pretty desperate a lot of the time and I'd see what I could do. But anyway this time he comes and he's in a right state, he's had a letter from Vern saying the council is compulsorily purchasing the property. Well, you can imagine Charlie wasn't too keen on that.

'So I said I'd have a little dig about, 'cause I didn't like the sound of that, sounded to me like old Vern had got the council doing his dirty work for him. But I had to restrain Charlie a bit, he was threatening all sorts about Vern. Said he knew what Vern was up to and he had the evidence to prove it. Wasn't really clear what he was talking about or if he was making the whole thing up. But you can imagine he went round to see Vern and started carrying on like that . . . well . . .'

Tyra sat back in her chair. 'You saying, you saying Vernon Nichols might have killed my dad? Over a bloody flat?'

Jason shook his head. 'I'm not saying anything, I'm just filling you in on some things I thought you most probably already knew. But one thing I should point out: it's not just a flat. If Vernon's got permission to knock that whole block down and build something new there – well, that's lot of money involved.'

He paused, looked at Tyra carefully. 'Look,' he said, leaning forward and putting his hand over hers – a gesture which surprised Tyra – 'tell you what, I'll ask around a bit more, speak to some of my friends in the police force and that, and anything I find out I'll let you know. Meanwhile maybe it'd be a good idea you have a think what Charlie might have done with this evidence – if it exists at all – 'cause it looks like someone believes it's out there. You find anything, you let me know and we'll have a think what to do, how about that?'

Tyra nodded.

Jason sat back, smiled and called over a waiter to ask for the dessert menu.

One for the road turned unsurprisingly into two and a chaser but even so an hour later the VW was rolling out of the car park and along the coast road. They skirted the seaside villages of Southerndown and Ogmore, with their farms and retirement bungalows looking equally grim beneath the day's grey skies and persistent drizzle. Then it was a question of whether to cut inland and take the motorway to the Gower, the prime surfing area in this part of the world, or work their way around to Porthcawl, a faded holiday town that still had a decent surfing beach.

'Worth a try, butt,' said the Colonel and Mazz concurred.

Hardly seemed likely that Emyr would pick a place like Porthcawl, but still he was curious to see how the place had changed from the days when he used to come down with his folks and stay in a caravan there for two weeks every summer. The miners' fortnight. Half the valleys would come down to Porthcawl, whole streets transporting themselves on to a row of caravans. Christ, seemed like another century, another world. The valleys weren't like that any more – you could hold the miners' fortnight in a bloody Portakabin these days – and he didn't suppose Porthcawl was what it was either.

He was right there. Porthcawl on a rainy Wednesday in May was genuinely dismal. The centre of town was the kind of place that would be gentrified if Kwiksave moved in: the beach had a couple of miserable-looking donkeys offering rides to even more miserable-looking kids. The funfair, Coney Beach, which Mazz remembered as the absolute highlight of his childhood, was now tawdry beyond any kind of glamour.

'Tell you what, mate,' said Mazz to the Colonel as they walked past the crooked house and Mazz's eyes scanned the place looking to see what had happened to the boating lake, 'when I was a kid and I used to come here, Coney Island, I used to dream of Coney Island in New York. I figured if Coney Beach here was the best place I'd ever seen and its name was like a rip-off of the one in New York, then the New York one had to be truly fabulous. Anyways. I finally make it over to New York. I'm twenty-two, playing with this fucking eighties haircut band, and first thing I want to do is go to Coney Island. Every New York fucker I meet looks at me like I'm mad, what would I want to go there for? But I'm determined so I get the subway map and spend like bollocking hours taking the Z train all the way through Brooklyn and I finally get there and there's like a giant Ferris wheel, a giant bungee-jump thing and a really, really scary-looking rusted-up old rollercoaster, plus all these Puerto Rican guys fishing off the pier and these old Russian–Jewish guys playing klezmer music on the boardwalk, and basically I had a hot dog and went back again and everyone took the piss out of me for wasting my time.'

'Yeah,' said the Colonel, not really paying attention, watching some sucker trying to lob ping-pong balls into goldfish bowls, 'that's living all right.'

'Uh yeah,' said Mazz, 'but, like, disappointing as it was, yeah, well, compared to this place,' he waved his arm in the general direction of Louis Tussaud's wax museum, 'it was still bloody fucking glamorous.'

The Colonel shrugged and laughed. The further end of the funfair petered out into a kind of half-hearted boot sale, so Mazz and the Colonel turned round and headed back towards the beach. As they passed the water chute a bloke came out of the ticket booth, walked along the side of the big rusty structure, came up to a piece of metal lying adjacent to it and kicked it out of sight under the railings. As he did so he saw Mazz staring at him, gave him a smile and a wink and went back to the ticket booth.

'Fuckin' hell,' said Mazz and the Colonel simultaneously and they headed past the Burger King on to the road winding alongside the beach and up to the caravan park. Mazz was half tempted to follow it and check out the old caravan, see if it was still there, but the Colonel led the way down on to the beach and out towards the rocky headland that separated Sandy Bay from Trecco Bay.

'You see that?' he asked, pointing at the black rocks stretching out from the headland. 'That's the Point.'

'Yeah,' said Mazz vaguely.

'Yeah,' said the Colonel, 'one of the biggest breaks anywhere round Britain, least it used to be.'

'Christ,' said Mazz, looking harder at the rocks. 'People surf by there?'

'Yeah, Well, people who can swim do.'

Coming closer to the sea, Mazz realised once again that he'd been wrong about the waves. From the car park they'd looked like nothing much but up close they were two to three feet and coming in fast sets cracking fiercely against the rocks. But where the previous day's sunshine had brought out the day trippers in relative numbers, today it was just the hardcore few. Or, to be precise, the hardcore one. The only person Mazz could see out in the water was a big bald feller on a board that looked too small for him. Mazz and the Colonel stood there on the headland watching him struggle out through the waves.

'Too choppy,' said the Colonel. 'Miracle if he gets on a wave out there.' Mazz nodded, demonstrating the bloke's inalienable right to become an instant expert on any kind of sporting activity. And for a while the Colonel's verdict seemed to be right; time and again the bloke would try to get on a wave only to be rapidly dumped unceremoniously off it and left with another fierce paddle back out. But then, just as the Colonel was turning to head back, the guy caught one, the biggest smoothest wave they'd seen all afternoon. He got on the wave, got half up on his board, rode it crouching for a while then, with a roar Mazz could hear even above the noise of the sea, stood right up and skimmed along the top of the wave, all the way into the shore.

Once in the guy got off his board, looked back out to sea then shook his head, shouldered his board and headed out of the water, evidently having made his mind up that he'd had the day's one good ride.

Mazz and the Colonel walked slowly along the beach, timing it so they bumped into the surfer just as he was approaching the car park.

'All right, butt,' said the Colonel as the guy came near.

'All right,' said the surfer.

'Nice going,' said the Colonel.

The guy shrugged, his eyes scanning Mazz and the Colonel quickly, assessing them for trouble and then relaxing. 'Been out there a couple of hours and that was the first decent wave I got.'

'What sort of board you got there?'

'Custom,' he said. 'Feller makes them for me.' He turned the board round so the Colonel could see it, an old-school longboard with a logo based around the letters ESP.

'Got your own personal board maker?'

'Yeah,' said the guy. 'I run a surf shop in town here. Point Break Boards.' He carried on past them. 'Come by and have a look. It's just off the high street there.'

Mazz and the Colonel looked at each other and shrugged and half an hour later they were sat in the shop having a cup of tea with the guy whose name turned out to be JT, and who looked even bigger indoors, dressed in baggy surf pants and an oversize fleece, than he had done out in the water.

The Colonel had kicked things off telling JT they were looking for this surfer guy. And brought out the picture of Emyr. This time the guy obviously knew who Emyr was instantly and he immediately narrowed his eyes.

'You taking the piss? This is the rock-star guy went missing innit?'

JT then went from disbelieving to suspicious as the Colonel explained that Emyr was a surfer these days. So Mazz weighed in with the story about wanting to get the band together for a reunion, and the guy looked more sceptical still until Mazz started reeling off names of people JT could call to verify Mazz was who and what he said he was and the guy put his hands up and said, 'OK, fair enough.'

'What's the big deal anyway?' asked the Colonel. 'You seen him or something?'

'Nah,' said JT, 'just don't like people taking the piss.'

'You got any ideas then? Where a bunch of hardcore surfers might hang out?'

JT shrugged. 'Well, the wind keeps on getting up like this there'll be a gang of them out later on, the night surfers.'

'Night surfers?'

'Yeah. Tell you what. You boys meet me in the Hi Tide Amusement Arcade about nine, I'll show you.'

'Appreciate it, man,' said the Colonel, stood up and led the way out of the shop.

The next four hours passed easily enough. Couple of games of table football in the Sportsman's club on the front, then, looking for somewhere to get some food, Mazz spotted a place called the Tribal Coconut attached to some kind of surfer hostel. They went inside, flashed Emyr's picture around to no avail, but decided to stick around anyway and ate a couple of kangaroo steaks and listened to the people on the next table, a bunch of Aussies, lying to each other about how big the waves they used to surf back home were.

After that they walked back round to the funfair which had livened up a little now, acquiring that air of tension and danger which is what distinguishes the old-school carny type funfair from your modern theme park. One option offers you state-of-the-art rides, negative G-force rushes and the finest special effects Hollywood's smartest can throw at you; the other gives you a water chute that offers every prospect of actually dicing with death, a ghost train made of papier mâché, and lots of bad boys with tattoos, G-force hormonal rushes, sex and violence here, there and everywhere. Specially if you were sixteen of course.

At the far end of the amusement park, past the Burger King – the one indication that the last thirty years had impacted on this relic of working-class recreation – they finally came upon the Hi Tide Amusement Arcade.

Inside it was the usual merry hell of strung-out mothers feeding the fruit machines, kids blasting zombies, blokes with prison tats concentrating very, very hard indeed on Tekken 3, and absolutely no sign of JT.

The Colonel wasn't too bothered. He spotted one of those skiing simulators and was on it in a flash, spent the next ten minutes slaloming his way down virtual mountainsides with practised skill. Mazz drifted off, lost a couple of quid on the fruit machines, wandered back and found the Colonel still going, then wandered off again and noticed there was an upstairs, headed up and found JT there finishing off a game of pool.

Mazz lit up a fag, waited for him to finish. Couple of minutes later they'd prised the Colonel off his skis and headed out to the car park between the Hi Tide and the Sandy Bay caravan park. There in the moonlight were half a dozen vehicles; a camper much like the Colonel's, a beat-up Sherpa, a couple of rusty old hatchbacks and, incongruously, a brand-new Suzuki jeep. A couple of teenage boys were standing in the shadows furtively eyeing the jeep.

'Stupid bastards,' said JT and walked over to them. He bent down to say something to the boys, and as he spoke their posture went from hard to defeated, and they slunk off back into the arcade.

'Just told them who the jeep belongs to,' JT said, smiling at Mazz and the Colonel.

'Yeah?' said Mazz.

'Yeah,' said JT, 'Danny Lewis Jones. Father owns half this fucking town. Planning to build a state-of-the-art new theme park here, he can get permission. Danny works for him, runs a couple of clubs for him, looking to expand operations into Cardiff too, from what I hear. Now, got your wetsuits, butts?'

'They're in the camper,' said the Colonel.

'Well, you best go get them. Night surfers aren't going to talk 'less you get in the water with them.'

The Colonel shrugged and said he'd go get the camper and bring it round; JT and Mazz elected to wait. The two of them stood there smoking, looking out towards the black sea below.

'Flaherty says hello,' said JT after a while.

'What?' said Mazz.

'Yeah, you mentioned his name, said he'd vouch for you and the rock-star guy. So I called him.'

'I didn't give you the number, though,' said Mazz, started.

'No need, mate, I knows Jason of old, like.'

'Christ,' said Mazz, 'don't we all? How'd you run into the bastard?'

'Working on doors and that. No, be honest, it was before that. I was going to judo and Flaherty started showing up. Always paired him off with me 'cause we were the two biggest bastards there. Then I found out he had the security business, like, and he started giving me work. Used to do a little bit of business on the doors, like,' he looked at Mazz and winked, 'then when I got a little bit of money together I came here, opened the shop. Anyway Flaherty keeps in touch, called me the other day asking about Danny LJ, as it goes, so, like I say, I called him up and he seemed pretty keen I help you find this guy.' He paused for a moment. 'Fact of the matter is it seems it's more him that's looking for the guy than you, like.'

Mazz shrugged. 'Lot of people looking for Emyr, all right.'

'Uh huh,' said JT, 'Well, probably teaching my grandmother to suck eggs, like, but I were you I'd watch your back on this one. Make sure Flaherty isn't standing right behind you.'

Mazz raised his eyebrows and was about to say something but just then the Colonel pulled up in the camper. Mazz and the Colonel got changed in the back. JT just opened up his kit bag and stripped off right there in the middle of car park, then led the way down a steep path on to Sandy Bay beach, right in front of the funfair. At first there was no sign of any activity at all, apart from a teenage couple staggering across the sand, mouths locked together, evidently in search of a friendly sand dune. Then, as they got closer to the water, the waves started to come into focus and so too did a black shape riding them.

JT strode out towards the waves, his arm raised in greeting. The Colonel deliberately hung back. 'Be careful out there, butt. Don't go deep, don't try to be clever. You get worried, act like you've pulled a hamstring or something, and get out. You got me?'

Mazz nodded the nod of a man who didn't need to be told twice, and shuffled towards the sea with an ever slowing gait. Once in the water, though, it was different. He paddled out a little way, making sure to stay within his depth, then turned and looked back at the funfair, lit up against the night sky, a quarter moon dangling above it. He glanced over his shoulder, saw a respectable-size wave coming at him, started paddling, lying flat on the board, and caught it nicely, and the wave sent him swooping in out of the darkness and towards the bright lights. And once again the exhilaration hit him. He paddled straight out again and repeated the process two or three times. He didn't attempt to stand up on the board the way he could see the Colonel, JT and the others were doing, just worked within his limitations. The fourth time, though, as he paddled out the board got away from under him and Mazz swam after it and caught it then suddenly realised what he'd done: swum. Some kind of a makeshift breaststroke that he'd managed without thinking about it.

Laughing at himself, he got back on the board and paddled further out towards where the other surfers were basking, waiting for the big wave. Took him a little while to get out there and when he did he looked round, his eyes adjusting to the dark now, trying to spot the Colonel. Couldn't see any sign of him; must have just caught a wave, Mazz figured. He saw JT, though, just a few yards over to the right talking to another surfer, bloke with a very flash-looking board indeed, probably the Danny guy, Mazz figured, then he looked to his left and no more than ten yards away he saw, he was sure, Emyr.

Even in a wetsuit in the dark, the white-blond hair was a giveaway. Their eyes locked for a second and Mazz was about to call out when he saw the other surfer's eyes swivel behind his and widen.

Mazz turned too, saw the biggest wave of the night so far bearing down, and with what was now becoming some sort of instinct prepared to get on it. He failed dismally. Timed it all wrong, came off his board, went under and sucked water, came back up, looked around and saw the surfer he took to be Emyr speeding away from him, standing tall on his board and heading for the shore. Mazz spat and choked and swore and tried to ride the next wave and the wave after that, but when he finally got on one under-powered wave he saw the surfer getting out of the water, on to shore and start jogging across the beach.

Mazz gave up trying to surf, just waded through the water as fast as he could. By the time he made it to the shore, though, he could barely see the dark shape of the surfer ahead of him on the beach. Mazz peeled off the Velcro strip holding his board's leash to his ankle, debated for a second whether to carry the board with him, then thought to hell with it, put it carefully down on the sand and ran across the beach, hoping the other surfer's board would slow him down.

The plan seemed to be working at first, Mazz running across the wet sand, the other surfer struggling across the beach heading, Mazz was sure, for the Hi Tide car park. But then as the beach grew drier it became more treacherous and each footstep was sinking inches in the sand. Mazz felt that awful dream sensation of wading hopelessly forward and never moving. By the time he got through on to harder ground again the other surfer was disappearing into the deeper darker shadows closer to the boardwalk. Mazz ran after him, heading blindly towards the Hi Tide, knowing the guy had at least thirty seconds on him. As he came off the beach on to the steps up to the car park, he cursed as something sharp cut into his foot, but didn't slow down. He took the steps three at a time and came running into the half-lit car park.

Nothing. No sign of the surfer at all. Mazz scanned the parked vehicles, frantically trying to work out if there was one less than earlier. He hadn't a clue. He started towards the Hi Tide, opened the door and peered in. No immediate sight of the surfer but three different blokes turned round and laughed at him standing there in his wetsuit. He went back out into the car park and stood there looking around for any sign of movement. Suddenly he heard something from behind him, coming up from the beach. He whirled round and there was the Colonel, carrying both surfboards, a quizzical expression on his face.

'Whassup, butt?'

'Emyr,' said Mazz. 'He was there in the water. He ran off when he saw me. I followed him up this way, but he vanished.'

'In a car?'

'I dunno. Maybe. It didn't seem like there was time. But I dunno where else he'd be.'

'Well, let's have a little look around, shall we?' The Colonel already had his wetsuit half off and was digging around in the van for some towels. He chucked one to Mazz and after a couple of freezing minutes spent extricating himself from the rubber clutches of his suit Mazz was ready.

'So where d'you reckon?'

'Well, let's say he didn't get away in the car 'cause if he did we're buggered. If he didn't he had two ways to go, either through the funfair or the caravan park. He was wearing a wetsuit, yeah?'

'Yeah.'

'Then we can pretty much rule out the funfair. So let's check out the caravan site.'

The Colonel locked the gear in the van and they crossed the road and headed through the gates of the Sandy Bay caravan park. At once Mazz felt it was hopeless. The site looked huge in the dark, caravans and trailers heading off in all directions. They took the main path, heading for the site office. Eventually they came to it, stuck in a little square cum precinct with a boarded-up news agent's and Glynis's Fish Shop; whole place had the vibe of the most depressed council estate you've ever seen, picked up bodily and plonked down next to the sea. The site office was closed, of course, so no chance to find out if any tall blond surfers had recently checked in. There was no one around at all, in fact, except for the inevitable clusters of early-teenage kids doing their best to look hard. They went into the fish shop, Mazz got some chips and the Colonel asked the woman about Emyr. She shook her head automatically.

Out of the fish shop, they hesitated briefly. The Colonel led them away from the main path deeper into the site. Suddenly they came through a row of trailers and found themselves looking at a great sunken oval field, like an abandoned running track set right in the middle of the site, surrounded by caravans. Mazz felt like there were eyes in every caravan staring at him. Christ, if Emyr had chosen this place to hide from the world in, he could hardly have done better. And he was welcome to it.

'C'mon,' he said to the Colonel, 'this is a fucking waste of time.'

Back in the car park, JT, the guy with the flash board and a couple of others were getting changed.

'Any sign of your mate, then?' said JT.

'Yeah,' said Mazz. 'He was out there. I saw him.'

'Yeah?' said JT, apparently surprised. Mazz wasn't sure whether to believe him or not.

'You didn't see him then, blond guy, late thirties? Shit, you know what he looks like.'

JT shrugged. 'No, didn't see him, like I said. Dark out there, y'know, bra. Tell you what, go down the Apollo, over on the front there; the whole crew will be there sooner or later. See if anyone can help you out.'

With that JT went back to changing out of his wetsuit, the guy with the flash board gave them a bit of a look, not hard exactly but suspicious, and Mazz and the Colonel got into the camper, headed round to the town centre.

The Apollo turned out to be a shoebox of a club, stuck between a curry house and a failed theme pub on the front. The DJ was playing oldies when they got there, seventies disco records, which suited Mazz fine – he'd given up attempting to like modern dance music some time in the techno nineties. Apart from reggae, of course; always had a soft spot for anything out of Jamaica. Not much chance of hearing any of that here, though; he knew it was only a matter of time before the housey-house tunes came out.

They found a table over near the bar, got a couple of bottles of Pils in and sat back to wait for the surfers to show up. Didn't take too long; the DJ was only just into his Abba medley when JT and his three mates arrived, got the beers in and parked themselves around the table.

Mazz was sure they must have had a talk beforehand, 'cause it was like they were all on edge.

JT introduced his mates. The guy with the flash board, who was now kitted out like a model for Quicksilver, was indeed Danny the theme-park heir, then there were Steve and Jacko, who looked like regular enough surf bums. Little bit of joshing about, all still feeling a bit artificial, and JT started in.

'Well,' he said, 'I told my brers here about your little problem. And they think they might know the geezer you mean.'

Course they do, thought Mazz, they've been surfing with him an hour ago, but he managed to bite his tongue.

'Thing is they're a little concerned about your motivation, like.'

'Yeah,' cut in Danny. 'The point is it's Emmo's life. He doesn't want to be found, that's his decision, isn't it?'

'Yeah,' said Mazz, thinking *Emmo*, he'd never heard anyone call Emyr Emmo, 'and I respect that. All I want is to have a little talk with him, 'bout a couple of matters, and if he wants to leave it at that – go surfing, let the world think he's dead – that's fine by me.'

Danny nodded, looked like he was taking Mazz's point, so Mazz carried on then immediately wished he hadn't.

'And don't worry about Jason,' he said, looking at JT, 'Emyr doesn't want me to tell Jason, I won't.'

'Jason,' said Danny, glancing curiously at JT. JT shrugged, acting like he didn't have a clue.

Mazz wondered what was going on there, answered anyway. 'Emyr's old manager. He's looking for Emyr too, of course.'

'Oh yeah?' said Danny and went silent for a moment then leaned forward. 'Tell you what,' he said, 'why don't you and your mate go to Llangennith, the camp site there, Hillend. I'll get the word to Emyr, tell him what you said and if he wants to see you he'll find you there in the next day or two. OK?'

'Yeah,' said Mazz, 'that's great. Thanks a lot, man.'

'No worries,' said Danny as he got up, clasped hands with JT, and headed off.

10

THE SALUTATION

1981

First day off from the Wurriyas, Tyra went back to her mum's and Mazz went back to the flat. Got there about five minutes before the landlord, little Polish bloke, always had an unlit roll-up nestling in the corner of his mouth. He was ready to shout blue murder about the rent and nearly had a heart attack when Mazz dug in his pocket, pulled out a wad of money and counted off four tenners. Actually lit the cigarette as he walked off.

Mazz spent the balance of the day reclaiming his territory. He lay in the bath for an hour, took his clothes over to the launderette, bought a couple of samosas from the Indian shop, had a chat with Mr Johnson in the secondhand shop.

'Fucking brilliant what you done for Charlie,' he kept saying, and Mazz shrugged, couldn't see it himself – what Charlie had done for him looked a lot more considerable from Mazz's point of view. Still, someone wanted to see Mazz as a philanthropist, that was a novel enough experience to let it ride. Made him a little uneasy, though, the implication that Charlie was in a state before the band got going. Mazz didn't want Charlie to have troubles; he wanted Charlie to be his rock.

Around six, Mazz walked over to Tyra's. Got his usual reception – giggling girls in the front room, stone-faced mother in the hall. Mazz wondered if Tyra had told her about the baby. Probably not, he reckoned; she wouldn't just be stone-faced, she'd probably have a shotgun ready for him. Instead she just jerked her head towards the upstairs.

'She's up there.' Not a hello, not a how are you doing, not a well done having a hit record making my girl a star. Nothing. Bitch, Mazz thought. Reminded him of the chapel-going types where he came from, never happier than when pursing their lips about someone's transgressions, never a word of praise, things went right. Bitches the lot of them.

Mazz went up the stairs, and found Tyra lying on her bed sobbing, the six o'clock news on in the background.

'What's the matter, love?' he said, walking over and sitting on the bed next to her, stroking her hair for a moment till she slapped his hand away, didn't like anyone touching her hair.

'Bobby,' she said after a while, 'Bobby Sands. I saw him on the news. Hunger strike's going again. He's dying, Mazz. He looked like a bloody skeleton, something out of Auschwitz. They're murdering him, Mazz. Fucking bastards.' She raised her head then sat up. 'But you know what?'

'What?' said Mazz.

'He's standing as an MP. There's a by-election there and he's standing. Think about that. They're saying he's just a common criminal and if he gets elected to Parliament, then what?'

'Christ,' said Mazz.

'Yeah.'

After that she brightened up a bit, stuck a record on, *Scary Monsters*. Tyra loved 'Ashes to Ashes'; Mazz too, something so desperate about it, seemed to chime with the time. Mazz asked if she wanted to go for a drink and she said maybe later but really she just wanted to take it easy. So they sat around, watched *Coronation Street*, listened to some more music, talking about this and that, nothing serious, news again at nine, Bobby Sands all over it. Real edgy stuff, you could see all the TV reporters suddenly waking up to the reality of the situation. All these years they'd been bollocksing on about how the IRA were just a tiny fringe bunch of nutters with no support. Now they were busily preparing the public for the fact that this terrorist might actually win a democratic election. Sad, of course, that the guy had to be killing himself to get any attention but Christ you had to admire the way he was sticking it to them.

Time the news finished, Mazz was starving.

'Fancy coming down the chip shop?' he said, figuring the chances of Tyra's mum coming through with any food for him were on the slim side.

'No,' said Tyra. 'Still feeling a bit sick, you know. You get some.'

'All right,' said Mazz, standing up. 'You sure you don't want anything? Just a plain portion of chips?'

'No thanks,' said Tyra. 'Actually, Mazz, I think I might just go to sleep now, you don't mind?'

'Oh,' said Mazz, 'right. You want me to stay with you?'

Tyra didn't reply, just rolled her eyes theatrically towards the downstairs, her mother's realm, then shook her head.

Then she stood up and kissed Mazz. 'Thanks, love,' she said. 'I'll see you tomorrow, yeah.'

Walking out of the house, the sitting-room door was open and Mazz noticed a big velvet portrait of Elvis Presley on the wall. He shook his head to dispel the illusion and looked again, but there it still was, a portrait of Elvis in his *Jailhouse Rock* period.

Walking back through town, Mazz bumped into Ozzie, one of the social-worker types who ran Grassroots. Ozzie said he was going for a pint, so Mazz followed him into the Salutation, a little Brains pub by the Monument. Ozzie's mates turned out to be a couple of boring-looking lefties, so Mazz went over to the Space Invaders machine, still the mark one model in here, and he spent half an hour or so blasting away, getting a load of dirty looks from the female lefty making loud comments about how nice and quiet it was in the pub – usually.

Mazz sat down for the second pint then, let Ozzie ask him about the band and that, bloke seeming genuinely enthusiastic. Suppose it made him feel like Grassroots was working, bunch of kids who hung about in there getting on to *Top of the Pops*. So Mazz chatted for a little but, be honest, last couple of weeks he'd just about ODed on talking about the band so he drank up and headed out to pick up some chips on Caroline Street and home to crash.

Middle of the night he half woke and turned over to put his arm round Tyra, woke up then with a shock when she wasn't there. Realised how accustomed he'd got to her.

Still, wasn't like he couldn't bear to be without her for a single night so he turned over, went back to sleep and kept on sleeping on and off till two the next afternoon when the phone rang, Tyra asking if he wanted to go into town.

An hour later they met at the Hayes Island Snack Bar. Mazz had a tuna sandwich and a cup of tea, Tyra nothing, said she was still feeling sick. Mazz said she should be eating more not less at a time like this. Tyra told him he knew so much about it he should have the fucking baby. Then she said sorry. Just feeling a bit weird, you know, and Mazz said sure and put his hand on hers and they went for a walk round town.

Walked through the market, Tyra hurrying Mazz past the fish stall, said her sense of smell was going crazy, went up to Kelly's and had a look through the records. Mazz bought Tyra the Susan Cadogan album with 'Hurt So Good' on it; Tyra laughed, asked if he was trying to tell her something. After that they just wandered, looking idly in the shop windows, not saying much, but happy together, and ended up at the Lexington, Tyra suddenly announcing she was hungry after all and proceeding to wolf down half a burger and chips before pushing it aside and saying she had to go home now.

Mazz walked her back and from then on it was the same deal as the night before. Past the gauntlet of Tyra's mum's disapproval into the bedroom. News on. Government obviously waking up to the possibility that Bobby Sands would win, starting the damage limitation. Record on after that, the Susan Cadogan. How about doing a cover said Tyra after they listened to it the third time. You reckon Bobby would sing a thing like that said Mazz and Tyra laughed.

'You told your mum yet?' asked Mazz later on, lying jammed up on the single bed together, Mazz spooning Tyra, his hand stroking her belly.

'Christ no,' said Tyra. 'She'll bloody kill me.'

'Bloody kill me, more like.'

'Yeah.'

'Seriously, though, you got to tell her.'

Tyra sat up, suddenly angry. 'She's my mother, right. Just leave it to me.'

Mazz put his hands up in surrender but something went out of the evening then and it wasn't long before Tyra said she was tired again, and Mazz said there's no way he could stay was there and Tyra shook her head and said sorry, babe, no way, and see you tomorrow, and kissed him and there he was back on the street again at nine o'clock.

This time he didn't even pretend to head straight home; he went round the Philharmonic and found a handful of student girls he knew, friends of Kate's, who all went ooh Kate's so pissed off with you and pretended to give him a hard time but really he could see two out of the three at least would be seriously interested in taking Kate's place.

So he stayed about and even though he didn't do anything he shouldn't have, just flirted a little bit and stayed there till the late licence expired downstairs some time after midnight, he couldn't help feeling a little disloyal as he walked back over the river to the flat, still feeling the place where one of the girls, Miranda, had put her arm round his neck for a slightly too long moment, making a joke about something or other, letting him know she was interested.

Christ, he thought, must be growing up, turning a sure thing like that down.

Again he woke up in the night expecting Tyra to be there and again soon forgot and went back to sleep. It was only when the same sequence was repeated for a third day and night – the meeting, the cup of coffee in the Sarsparilla Bar, the heading back to Tyra's place, the sitting around, the I'm feeling a bit sick now you'd better go, the walk home that this time somehow took in the Student Union disco – that Mazz started to wonder if things were OK.

'Next day he came out with it point blank.

'Listen,' he said, sitting in the big Astey's café, 'why don't you come over to mine tonight?'

It was like he'd slapped her.

'Look,' she said, 'I don't need this.' And started crying.

'Christ,' said Mazz, 'I'm sorry. I didn't mean to . . .'

'Didn't mean what?' she said, suddenly raising her head up from the table. 'Didn't mean to get me pregnant?' Put her head down again, resumed crying.

'Look,' he said. 'Look, it's great you're pregnant. It's like everything's going right.' And he put his hand on hers and stroked it.

'Mazz,' she said after a while. 'Think about it. How are we going to look after a baby? You're living in a rented room, I'm living with my mum. We're in this band, the last few months we've been on the road. We still haven't got any money . . . It's just not going to work.'

Then Mazz let himself think, and then say, the a-word for the first time. 'You want to have an abortion, that what you're saying?'

'Yes. No. Oh Christ, Mazz, I don't know what to think. I'm sorry, that's why I just have to be by myself at the moment. It's not you. I just feel so confused.'

They left then. Mazz offered to walk Tyra home but she shook her head, kissed him on the lips, said she was sorry again and she'd see him tomorrow. Mazz walked home feeling like shit, went over the Four Ways later on for a couple but didn't even feel much like drinking. Back at the flat he watched the football highlights and was asleep by midnight.

A banging on the door woke him up an hour later. Mazz stumbled downstairs and opened up. There was Tyra standing there on the doorstep, looking half-drowned. She threw her arms round him at once and practically dragged him up the stairs and into his bedroom. Neither of them said a word and in just a few more seconds they were both naked on top of the bed and fucking like, well, like there was no tomorrow, like tomorrow was something that had to be denied. The first time it was hard, fast and tumultuous, neither of them holding back, just sucking, biting, scratching, grinding their way to what felt like an explosion of pent-up emotion. As Tyra came she was hammering Mazz on his back with her fists, screaming obscenities in his ear.

Mazz would probably have called it a night at this point but Tyra barely relaxed for a moment before she was stroking his dick again, getting down and sucking him, getting him hard even though it was almost painful. Soon as he was ready she was on top of him, sitting up riding him and so it went on. Afterwards it seemed dreamlike; how often had they done it? Three or four times? The memory that always came back to him of that night was somewhere lost in the pre-dawn, fucking Tyra from behind, his hand curved around her belly, feeling for signs of life.

II

THE KING'S HEAD

1999

Next morning Mazz woke up early with a crashing headache and an urgent need to take a piss. He staggered out the back of the camper, found himself being stared at by an old man and a dog, smiled feebly, then hopped over the sea wall and clambered down on to the beach looking for a secluded spot. Unable to find one, he just turned his back to the town and pissed on the rocks, looking out to sea as he did so. There was a lone surfer out there. Not much of a swell, a couple of feet maybe, but enough for this die-hard to ride easily. Mazz wondered for a moment if it might be Emyr, but couldn't muster up the enthusiasm at this time of the morning to care very much either way. So he climbed back up over the rocks and the wall, endured the glare of the old man and the dog, who didn't seem to have budged an inch, and got back into the relative warmth of the van.

It had been three or so before they'd crashed the night before. After Danny'd left the club the atmosphere seemed to lighten up and JT and the Colonel, in particular, seemed to get on pretty well. Specially when JT figured out who the Colonel was – bad boy of Welsh football 1973, the first sweeper Cardiff City ever had, and near on the last when the manager sacked him for smoking dope in the changing rooms at half time. Long time ago and a lot of water under the bridge and for the most part the Colonel didn't seem to like to talk about it, even though he'd kept the nickname the fans gave him back then – 'the Colonel', like Beckenbauer was 'the Kaiser' – but last night he'd been up for it. Lot of stories, lot of drinks.

Mazz had got a bit fed up with it, to be honest. Kept trying to get the conversation round to the Wurriyas. Sad, really, like my one top-ten hit's better than your two seasons at the City. Anyway no one seemed much interested in Mazz's on-the-road stories, just wanted to know what Robin Friday'd really been like, and Mazz had ended up spending the last hour or so pumping money into the fruit machine. Then when he'd gone to sleep he'd dreamed of Tyra. Simplest dream he'd ever had: no weird plot, no complicated business with people changing into other people, just Tyra getting into bed with him, him reaching out to her, touching her, holding her, bringing her close to him, kissing her, letting his hands wander over her body. And waking up to find himself thirty-nine years old and stuck in a camper van in Porthcawl with the Colonel snoring across the way.

He lay back on his bunk convinced that he was doomed to stay like that for hours waiting for the Colonel to wake up. Next thing he knew was the Colonel standing over him with a cup of tea saying, 'Rise and shine, mate, time we were moving on.'

Mazz couldn't believe it. He knew he was going to be feeling like shit the whole day after last night's excesses, and yet the Colonel, who was a good ten years older than him, didn't seem to feel the pace at all. Be honest, it was starting to get on Mazz's nerves. Far as he could see, the Colonel had it all. Money, house, woman, kids grown up, kid on the way. And he didn't even get hangovers.

Mazz was still in a foul mood as they drove out of Porthcawl, heading west towards the Gower.

'You think he's going to show, your mate?' asked the Colonel.

'Probably not,' said Mazz. 'Still, may as well go and have a look. I got fuck all else to do.'

'Hey,' said the Colonel, 'what's the problem? We got the weather' – he waved his arm in the direction of the blue sky that had replaced the early-morning mist – 'we got the music' – he stuck a tape in the stereo and turned it on – Southside Johnny doing his soul revue thing – 'and out there we got the waves.' The Colonel gestured towards the sea, just visible beyond the miles of belching gasworks that welcomed you to Port Talbot, the heavy industrial sprawl town that stretched for most of the way from Porthcawl to Swansea Bay.

Mazz just hitched himself back into his seat, didn't say a word. Though to be fair he did restrain himself from telling the Colonel to shut the fucking plastic soul off.

The Colonel looked over at him. 'Fancy a smoke then, butt?' With one hand he pulled a cigarette case out of his pocket and flicked it open, took out a ready-rolled joint and snapped the case shut again. Picked up a lighter from the dashboard and lit up, inhaled deeply then passed it over to Mazz. Mazz raised his hand to refuse the spliff.

'Christ, butt,' said the Colonel, 'got out the wrong side of the bunk this morning, didn't we? Tell you what, though, this'll give you a laugh.' He suddenly braked, pulled over a couple of lanes of motorway traffic and took the next exit, for Port Talbot.

Then, instead of following signs to the middle of the town, he headed straight for the giant gasworks. A couple more turns and they were on a company road almost through the gasworks and out the other side. Finally they came to a wire-frame gate that blocked the road off. There was a sign on the gate warning people to keep out – British Gas property – but it didn't look like anyone had been down here in years. The Colonel parked the van and Mazz sighed theatrically, uncomfortably aware that he was starting to behave like a moody adolescent, and followed the Colonel out.

The Colonel clambered over the gate, then down the track in between a couple of deserted storage areas. The track took a sudden right turn and promptly petered out in the middle of a sand dune. Mazz and the Colonel scrambled over the dune and then there they were, looking out at a completely deserted beach.

'Christ,' said Mazz, unable to stop himself from smiling.

'Yeah,' said the Colonel, 'good, eh?' He surveyed the area carefully. 'Actually, I just had an idea your mate might be here. JT told me about this place last night, said it was a real hardcore spot. Figured it had to be worth a go.'

'Worth it anyway,' said Mazz and led the way back to the van, then sat there in a more companionable silence as the Colonel drove back on to the motorway, through Swansea, up on to the moor that took up the central part of the Gower Peninsula, through the little town of Llanrhidian, and along the winding lanes that ended up in the village of Llangennith, where the Colonel got the van parked in the campsite another half mile down the windiest lane yet. It was a different ballgame from Porthcawl this place, though: nice cars parked up by the trailers, whole place neat and tidy, hippy takeaway place set up in a van down the hill. Big scene all night when the summer gets going said the Colonel.

Wetsuits on then and a short walk through the dunes and out on to one of the longest, finest beaches Mazz had ever seen. Which wasn't saying that much as, not being able to swim and all, he'd never been a great one for the beach. But still, by any standards, a good beach and today with the sun out it looked idyllic. There was a fair bit of wind up and the temperature wasn't really sunbathing-hot yet so there weren't too many people out on the beach, but there was a steady stream of folk with wetsuits and boards heading for the water and Mazz followed the Colonel along the beach away to the right and then into the water near a line-up of older-looking guys with real anticipation.

Somehow, though, he couldn't get into it. The waves were a little bigger than anything he'd dealt with before, and he still hardly felt confident in his ability to swim. Plus he felt intimidated seeing the Colonel with these older surfer guys who he seemed to know from time, though with the Colonel you could never be sure: people seemed to gravitate to him so naturally that for all Mazz knew he'd never met any of them before in his life. Anyway they were all doing the business, riding the waves, standing tall, and Mazz was feeling like more and more of a dickhead as he lay flat on his board doing his best not to get drowned and occasionally picking up a little bit of a ride through the shallows. Then, after an hour or so, he was just paddling out as a surfer picked up a wave and came arrowing towards him. Mazz thought he was going to get his head taken off but then the surfer swerved out of his way at the last moment, and then when the guy came back out he swore at Mazz and Mazz thought fuck this for a game of soldiers, waved to the Colonel indicating he'd had enough and trudged back to the van.

Which was where he found Natalie. She was sitting next to the van in a deckchair reading a book, wearing a fifties-style sundress with a cardie over the top and a pair of Catwoman sunglasses. The baby wasn't showing and she looked, Mazz reckoned, as cool as fuck.

'Hi,' she said, stretching and putting the book down. Mazz glanced at it quickly, just to make sure it wasn't *Captain Corelli's Mandolin*, like every other sorry girlie on the beach was reading waiting for their surfer boys to return. It wasn't, it was some Ted Hughes thing.

'Hi,' he said back, and wondered why she was smiling quite so broadly at him, then became conscious he was standing there wearing an elderly wetsuit. He reached round trying to undo the zip.

'Want a hand?' said Natalie. She stood up, walked round behind him and pulled down the zip with one easy movement.

'Ta,' said Mazz, then went round the far side of the van to get changed in relative privacy.

'Wasn't expecting to see you here,' he shouted as he towelled himself.

'Oh,' she said, 'Ronnie called me this morning and said you were heading this way so I thought I'd surprise you boys. Make sure you're not having too much fun.'

Mazz pulled on his jeans and a new shirt and walked round to where Natalie was sitting. She stood up, stretched.

'Fancy a walk?' she said. 'Ronnie will be in the water for hours yet, I know him.'

''Spect you're right,' said Mazz. 'Let's go.'

Natalie led the way, walking north from the campsite through the dunes parallel to the beach, heading towards somewhere called the Blue Pool – a special place she said. As they walked Mazz filled her in on the doings of the previous few days and Natalie nodded and laughed as appropriate but didn't say much. Then Mazz asked her about her book and she started telling him about how it was these poems Ted Hughes had written about his wife who'd killed herself – 'a wonderful poet called Sylvia Plath,' she said, like Mazz wouldn't have heard of her which pissed him off a bit – and how interesting it was because, like, she'd always thought that Hughes was a right bastard but now, reading his side of the story, you could really relate to him and actually she thought it was kind of noble that he had waited all this time and let people write all this stuff about how evil and macho he was, and didn't it make a change from all these people these days who the minute anything even vaguely interesting happens to them they go and write about it in the papers.

And then they were at the Blue Pool, which is this big rock pool up in the hills above the next bay round the corner from Llangennith, and it was lovely and mysterious and deserted and the sun was shining so of course Natalie stripped off and jumped into the pool and laughed at Mazz when he said he'd had enough wet for one day and he got in anyway 'cause he didn't want to feel like a voyeur sitting there on the side watching Natalie bounce around. So they splashed around a bit and Mazz was trying to keep near the edge 'cause the pool shelved steeply and God knows how deep it was in the middle. He asked Natalie and she said like way, way deep and then, playing around, she dived underwater and pulled his feet from under him, dragging him down like a mermaid. And Mazz kicked out in panic to get her hands off him and she reared away, and came up looking hurt. Then, when she saw Mazz gasping frantically for air, she started laughing and couldn't stop even as he scrambled to the side and got out, and kept laughing as he tried to get dry, and Mazz was sure she was looking at his dick which was about as big as you'd expect it to be when you've just jumped in a freezing rock pool, then been roundly terrified and half drowned.

'Oh God, I'm sorry for laughing,' she said a little later when they'd got their clothes on and were walking back towards the campsite, 'you should have told me you weren't much of a swimmer.'

Mazz laughed too and they kept on walking up dune and down dune and after a while, standing at the top of yet another smooth bracken-covered incline, Natalie said, 'D'you get the feeling we're going round in circles? We don't seem to be getting anywhere at all.'

Mazz just laughed once more and then suddenly tripped Natalie and sent her rolling down the dune and then he dropped down and rolled himself after her, rolling over and over and falling on top of her. And suddenly her arms were round his neck and his around her waist and then they were kissing and then Natalie broke off and looked Mazz in the eye and said, 'You don't remember me at all, do you?'

Mazz took this in in the space of a single blink. She was the same Natalie he'd had the one-nighter with all those years back. It stood to reason really. But the funny thing was that the more time he'd spent with her this time around the less he seemed to remember the art student he'd picked up in 1981. He realised there was only one thing to say that wouldn't get him into trouble. Nothing. He didn't say a word, just smiled and rolled his eyes at her in a way she could interpret how she liked.

'You were a fucking bastard,' she said, 'only time that's ever happened to me. I let someone pick me up, shag me and kick me out the next morning, didn't even give your phone number.' As she spoke she was methodically undoing the buttons of Mazz's shirt and pulling it off. 'I thought about you for months. Waited for you to call, went to your poxy gigs.' She had his zip down now and with his active co-operation was pulling his jeans off.

She pushed him back on to the bracken then, didn't undress, just pulled her dress up. Nothing underneath, climbed on top of Mazz and took him inside her. He almost asked her if she was using anything, you know. Then he remembered, she was pregnant. Then she started moving on top of him and, well, if it was a bloke you'd have called what happened next premature ejaculation. She can't have lasted more than a minute before she was shuddering and biting his neck, her whole body in orgasmic spasm. Mazz was just lying there, bewildered as much as anything.

'Well,' she said after a moment, 'you going to fuck me then?'

'Yeah,' he said, 'not this way, though,' and he pushed her up and off him, then clambered round behind her.

'Mmm,' she grunted, on her hands and knees now, sticking her face in the ground and her bum up in the air. He started fucking her then, fast and hard, only one goal in sight. As he did his hand curved around her to feel her tits under the dress, but ended up resting on her belly instead. And suddenly he was plunged back into memory, fucking Tyra this way when she was pregnant. He came in an instant. And as he pulled out and sank to the ground next to Natalie it was all he could do to stop from crying – how had it all come down to this?

They rearranged their clothing in silence and started heading back to the campsite. Mazz led the way, stomping up dune and down dune, his mind in turmoil. Now and again he'd look back and Natalie would be there calmly following in his wake, a small smile playing on her lips from time to time. Mazz had an urge to hit her to wipe the smile off, or maybe to grab her, throw her down on the ground and do her again, keep on doing her till everything else went out of his mind. He kept on going on his hands and knees now, struggling straight up an almost sheer dune rather than go round it. What the hell had he been thinking of? The Colonel was his mate. As good a mate as he had right at the moment. Was Natalie going to tell him? Was that how it worked, a little power game between the two of them – 'Ooh, guess what, Ronnie, I've just fucked your mate'? Sit there and watch the Colonel beat shit out of Mazz, as he no doubt would? Maybe that was it, all an elaborate plan to get back at Mazz for that one-nighter. Probably no more than he deserved anyway.

'Cause more than that, the thing that was in the front of his mind was how he'd felt with this pregnant woman. What he'd remembered: Tyra, Tyra, Tyra. How she'd had the abortion, then. How he'd thought after that she was probably right and it was all for the good, they were too young, there was plenty of time. Well, he was thirty-nine now and genuinely felt older like they don't say in the personal ads. And he felt empty.

The Colonel was lying on a rug next to the van smoking a fat joint and staring up at the clouds. Mazz walked towards him with a sense of utter dread, sure he had the world's cheesiest smile plastered over his face. But he needn't have worried. Natalie just went towards the Colonel, bent down and putted her arms round him, kissed him, natural as anything. The Colonel patted her belly then sat up and made room for her next to him on the rug. Mazz stood there feeling like an idiot and when the Colonel passed him the joint he accepted it gratefully, Tried to drag the whole thing into his lungs with one great intake of breath.

'I still don't believe it,' laughed Tyra, talking to Bobby that night, the day after her lunch with Jason Flaherty, Bobby there to tell Tyra what she'd found out about the ransacking of Charlie's flat.

'Me either, girl,' said Bobby. 'So what happened next?'

'Well,' said Tyra, 'like I said. 'He ordered up another bottle of wine and talked me into having a dessert, twisted my arm right, and then I saw the time and said I had to go get the kids. But he says can't anyone else pick them up, and I say well I'll call my mum so he passes me his mobile and I get that sorted and we have the dessert and that and it's about half three and he says why don't I come back to the office with him.'

'Oh yeah?' said Bobby.

'Yeah, well I was interested, wasn't I? Not every day I get to spend time with someone actually has an influence on things, like. So anyway I says OK and he calls a cab and we go into town and we're just going round by the city hall when he tells the cab to stop and we get out and he says you been in the Hilton yet? And I nearly say what Hilton but I look over the road and the old Prudential building there it's got a sign on it saying Hilton and they've gone and converted it and I hadn't even noticed, so I says no, and he says oh let's go up to the bar, it's got a marvellous view.'

'C'mon, girl,' said Bobby, 'you must have figured he was chatting you up by now.'

'Yeah, well,' said Tyra, smiling, 'doesn't happen to me that often these days I'm going to walk away from it. So we take the lift up to the top floor and we walk in and the guy there he takes one look at Jason and it's all Mr Flaherty this and can I help madam off with her coat and then we're sat by the window looking out at the city and it's a beautiful day and he's right, the view's marvellous, you can see the stadium being built – really looks like they're getting it finished now and all – you can see the new hotel down there and everything – and he orders up a couple of cocktails and . . .'

Tyra broke off halfway between blushing and laughing. Bobby hooted. 'Yeah!' she said. 'Go on, girl, then what?'

'Then what yourself. Then what d'you think?'

'Wouldn't know, girl, wouldn't know. Probably you just had the drink, went out and got the bus back.'

'Not exactly,' said Tyra. 'Then I lean over and snog him – even as I'm doing it, I can't believe myself. Like, is that all it takes to get me going? Let alone what the waiters and that must have thought. Anyway one thing leads to a bit of the other, like, and then he tells me he's got a suite on permanent standby any time he wants it, like. Did someone a favour sorting out the planning apparently. So . . . Well, I'll spare you the details, like . . .'

'Too right,' said Bobby, making a face. Then she added, 'Just as long as you didn't let him get on top of you, girl!' and started laughing. Tyra joined in and soon the two women were in near hysterics sitting there on the sofa, Robson Green smarming away on the TV in the background.

'You going to see him again then?' asked Bobby once they'd both calmed down.

'Dunno,' said Tyra, suddenly serious. 'It didn't really seem like that. More a spur-of-the-moment sort of thing, you know what I mean. Nice, though,' she said, her eyes lighting up, 'nice.'

In fact it had been great. One thing about getting older, all that stuff you read in the women's magazines about women hitting their sexual prime in their thirties, it was true enough. It was like she could really enjoy it these days for what it was. Thing that pissed you off was thinking about all that sex you had when you were young and men were all over you and most of the time you didn't get much out of it. Now she was well ready for it but hardly anyone seemed to want to give her the chance. And Christ had she needed it. She'd felt so much better after. Got home, picked the kids up from her mum and her mood was just so up. So no, it was hardly love, her and Jason, but he wanted to do it again she wouldn't say no, Nice meal, nice hotel room, no commitments, no bullshit, why not?

'So,' said Bobby, 'get that grin off your face and tell me what he said about Charlie.'

Tyra ran through what Jason had said about Vernon Nichols.

Bobby listened intently then frowned. 'So how did Jason know about the break-in?'

'That's what I was wondering. He said something about friends in the police . . .'

'Yeah,' said Bobby, 'that'll be it. Who was the copper you saw?'

'Fairfax. Jimmy Fairfax.'

Bobby burst out laughing. 'Jimmy Fairfax. Course it would be. City boys together they were. When I first used to go down the City back in the day, seventy-seven, seventy-eight, Jason and Jimmy they were two of the top faces. Any trouble kicked off, you just got in behind one of them you'd be all right. Specially Jason, you remember how big he was even then?'

Tyra nodded.

'Yeah, well, you lined up with Jason nine times out of ten the other lot would just run for it. That'll be the connection all right. Jason and Jimmy. So – you believe him, this stuff about Vernon Nichols?'

'Yeah, I suppose. Why, you heard anything?'

'This and that,' said Bobby. 'No dirt on Nichols in particular. But one of the girls was talking about how she'd heard they were planning to build a casino down the docks.'

'A casino?'

'Yeah, a big casino hotel like in Las Vegas. Probably just pie-in-the-sky stuff, but the girls were getting quite excited by the idea, bound to pull in the punters a place like that. Most of what's happening in the bay so far is all family stuff – not much good for the girls hanging round Techniquest or Harry Ramsden's, is there?' Bobby paused, 'Though we got hopes for the Assembly,' and gave a big dirty laugh.

'Oh yeah, that's the other thing,' said Tyra then, 'Jason was talking about how Nichols has some MP in his pocket, like he was blackmailing the guy or something. You hear anything about any MPs from the girls?'

Bobby shrugged. 'Not off-hand, like – well apart from Ron Davies of course but everyone's talking about him – but I'll check it out. Any MP in particular?'

Tyra's turn to shrug. 'The local guy, I suppose, Derek what's-his-face?'

'Christ,' said Bobby, 'doesn't look like he'd have the bottle to get up to any trouble, but you never can tell, like, so I'll ask about.'

Bobby fell silent for a bit, then spoke up again in a quieter voice. 'Talking of asking about, I've been thinking of trying to trace my dad.'

'Yeah?' said Tyra.

'Yeah, well, be honest with you, it's your dad dying that did it. Look, I know this sounds pathetic but I always had a little idea that maybe he was my real dad. Sorry, it's like I'm trying to muscle in on your . . .'

'No, I understand,' said Tyra, thinking about how urgently Bobby had been looking through Charlie's papers the day they went round to the flat, and a wave of sympathy went through her.

'Yeah, stupid I know, but anyway, I thought it was about time I made an effort to find out . . . Before he dies too.'

Bobby stopped talking and choked back a sob. 'Shit,' she said, 'I'm sorry. Just talking shit.' She stood up. 'I'll see you,' she said and made for the door but before she could get there Tyra was cutting her off and folding her in her arms, holding Bobby the way she'd hold Jermaine. Bobby stiffened then relaxed in the hug, stayed there for a full minute, then pulled apart, whispered the word thanks and headed out the door into her car and round to the Custom House to meet her girlfriend Maria at the end of another hard night's hustling.

Later that night Mazz, the Colonel and Natalie were in the King's Head in Llangennith itself. It was the first really warm evening of what now seemed like summer and the place was rammed. They were sitting at a table in the garden out in front of the pub and all the time more people were piling in, more and more cars and vans were streaming down the lane towards the campsite. Most of them seemed to be Cardiff people who all appeared to know each other, all talking about this club they'd been to or that docco they were making.

Mazz had calmed down now. Calmed down pretty quickly in fact soon as he realised Natalie wasn't going to say anything. Colonel didn't seem to suspect a thing, thought it was nice of Mazz to take Nat walking. Made you feel a bit shit that, but to be honest it wasn't exactly the first time Mazz had been in that sort of situation. Story of his life, really, knocking off his mate's women. Most awkward one had been when he'd done it with the fat Yank's wife the evil Jap – that was before he'd realised how evil she was, mind. Done it a couple of times, on an American tour. It wasn't that Mazz had been worried about the fat Yank finding out – the amount of smack he was taking that tour he was hardly doing his bit in the marital-duties front – but more that if he pissed Kizumi off he could end up getting kicked out of the band, which would not have been cool, the money he was earning already owed. Made him feel like a bit of a dick that, though, Mandingo servicing milady.

So, anyway, there they were sitting in front of the King's Head, Mazz and the Colonel getting drunk, Natalie watching them. They went inside for a bit, had a game of pool. Natalie said she was tired, she'd head back to the campsite; Mazz and the Colonel could come with her now in the car or walk back later. The Colonel said they'd walk. Natalie gave him a bit of a look but then smiled and kissed him and said she'd see him later.

Thought hit Mazz then, where's he going to sleep? In the van with the Colonel and Natalie had to be a bridge too far, even by Mazz's standards.

'No worries,' said the Colonel, 'got a tent in the van. Put it up when we get back. 'Nother drink?'

Another drink it was, and then a couple more. At one point Mazz was coming out of the bar into the garden carrying a couple of pints and he nearly walked into the Asian girl he'd seen in Le Pub. Didn't recognise her at first, which wasn't too surprising, state he'd got into that night, state he was getting into this night. But she remembered him all right, gave him a big smile, said why didn't he come and join her and her mates; she waved at two girls perched on the wall, they'd just got here. Mazz just said yeah sure and walked through the crowd to where the Colonel was sitting slumped over the table showing every sign of being asleep.

Mazz whacked down the pint in front of the Colonel and he raised his head and said, 'Oh God, am I still here?' and promptly put his head back down again.

Later still Mazz and the three girls, with a couple of blokes from Swansea and a partially revived Colonel, were walking down the lane towards the campsite passing round an assortment of bottles.

At the campsite the Colonel pulled himself together remarkably to put up Mazz's tent in no time flat then crawled into the van. Mazz wandered off to where the girls were, sitting round a campfire with the Swansea boys and a bunch of German hippies. Mazz had a bottle of red wine in his hand. He reckoned the girl from Newport, Anita, might be up for something, but he was too drunk and too confused by what had happened with Natalie to reciprocate.

Next morning Mazz had a vague memory of passing a joint back and forth with her and snogging in between puffs. But that was all. There was another memory too. Sometime deep into the night a couple of the surfers from Porthcawl showed up and, somewhere round the bottom of the bottle of red wine or maybe the bottom of another bottle, who knew, one of the guys said to Mazz, 'You won't find your mate here, butt.'

Mazz nodded. Actually he'd all but forgotten that was why he was here at all, looking for Emyr.

'You want to find him, try the Severn Bore. It's a five-star on Tuesday.'

The bloke probably said more than that but that was all Mazz could remember when he woke up the next morning, the tent half collapsed around his lower body, his head full of the unbearable heaviness of living. Severn Bore. Five-star. Tuesday. What did that all mean?

12

THE SEVERN BORE

1999

Next morning Tyra realised there was one person could probably fill her in as to what the story was with Charlie and Vernon Nichols.

'Hiya, Mum,' she said, 'all right if I come round after I drop the kids off to school?'

Her mum, Celeste, sounded a little surprised which made Tyra feel guilty, like she never went round there to see the old lady apart from to drop the kids off or pick them up. Still, just 'cause you were family didn't mean you had to live in each other's pockets. Least that's what she'd always thought, but with her dad dying alone like that maybe she was just being a selfish bitch. Trouble was, she spent too much time with her mum she'd probably end up killing her and all.

Anyway, quarter past nine there she was round at Angelina Street at her mum's place, the house she, Tyra, mostly grew up in. When she'd been little – though she didn't really remember this much, only half remembered it the way you do from looking at old photos and people telling you this is where you used to play – they lived in Sophia Street. That was in the old Butetown – the crumbling overcrowded Victorian terraces they used to call Tiger Bay. Then the sixties redevelopment had come when she was three or so and they'd been moved out to Ely for a year or two – a time her mum used to talk about with great bitterness.

Then they'd moved back to Butetown to the brand-new house in

Angelina Street. And Tyra grew up hearing the mantra that the house was lovely but it wasn't the same. Course people always go on like that . . . When did you last hear anyone say how much better things are these days? But still it was true, though, her mum's mantra. The houses were nicer; even the big blocks of flats in Loudoun Square were a hell of a lot nicer than the – no other word for it – slums that had been there before. No one's nostalgic for TB and outside toilets. But the life thing, that was true too. It wasn't just the redevelopment. Butetown had been declining since the war; coal and steel weren't what they were, the shipping dropped off, the population declined. March-of-history time. But still again she had a powerful nostalgia for the docks life her dad used to tell her about, a nostalgia all the more powerful for being on the very fringes of her memory. Scattered images: her dad standing outside a club on Bute Street – was she there herself, a little girl, or was she remembering a photo? She couldn't say. But she missed all these places she couldn't really remember – the Cairo, the Ghana, the seamen's missions, the opium dens, the whole Tiger Bay business.

And her dad, of course, had missed it more than anyone. It had been his kingdom for a while back in the late fifties when he had his Lonsdale belt, when he was the quickest lightweight in the world according to the best judges. When he'd fight in London or New York and come home to a club full of people all waiting to shake his hand and buy him a drink. Then it had all gone at once. He'd started losing, the way all boxers do when the reflexes slow, and Tiger Bay got knocked down too, right from under him.

When Celeste and Tyra had been moved up to Ely, Charlie had simply refused to follow. He'd hung around Butetown then signed on for a while as part of a band touring the Northern clubs impersonating the Drifters – apparently there were three different sets of Drifters all out there simultaneously. By the time Celeste and Tyra were back in Butetown he was established as the semi-detached daddy she knew and loved.

Drove her mum mad when she was a kid, how she would idealise her dad. All the while she was growing up, her mum never seemed to have a good word to say about the man. Even when she'd had another kid by him, her little sister Corinne, there'd been no let-up, like the baby was just another wrong he'd done her.

Result was over the years Tyra had pretty much stopped talking to her mum about Charlie. Specially as Charlie had gone downhill these last years. She couldn't face her mum going I told you so – her dad nothing more than a shiftless drunk, boring people in the pub about what he used to be. That's what had made her furious at the funeral, seeing her mum giving it the grieving widow. She shivered at the door, not looking forward to broaching the subject now.

Inside, her mum made the tea and looked at her, obviously waiting for Tyra to reveal the reason for her visit, so she jumped straight in.

'Mum,' she said, 'what d'you know about my dad and Vernon Nichols?'

'Vernon Nichols,' said Celeste heavily, 'Vernon Nichols. I just don't know, girl. Long time ago I would have told you Vernon Nichols was a good man. He was Charlie's backer, like a boxing manager, you know. Big Vern they used to call him, which was a joke 'cause he was a sawn-off little man. Well, Big Vern help your father a lot in those early days, that's what he used to tell me. Any time he needed a loan or something, Big Vern was always there. Use to have big parties too, all sorts of people would come, boxers from London and all over, singers, Shirley Bassey, Lorne Lesley, American singers too like the Platters, they all used to come down to Butetown back then. Of course those were different times, dear. Lot of water under the bridge since then.'

'Yes, Mum,' said Tyra. 'But he kept in touch did he, Vernon?'

'Not for a long time, girl, least not as far as I know. Though what your father got up to, who he saw, I can't tell you. Next time I remember hearing that name was in the seventies, I think, when your father told me that Big Vern had offered him a job.'

'A job?'

'Well, not what I would call a job, girl. He said he'd pay your father to be at the new casino he opened up in town, Caligula's. All your father had to do was hang around the bar, greeting people who came in and have a drink with anyone old enough to remember when Charlie was the champion. Like a mascot. You ask me, that's when your father's drinking started to get bad. Every night sitting there telling the same old stories, people buying him drinks. Now I told him he shouldn't do it, he should have more dignity. But he wouldn't have it – nothing but thanks for Vern Nichols for giving him the job. You ask me, girl, I think Vern was enjoying it, watching your father humiliate himself for a few drinks. Like he was getting his own back. He was always jealous of your father, of course.'

'Jealous?' said Tyra. 'Why was that?'

'Oh, the usual thing with men. You know, women.' And then to Tyra's great surprise she saw her mother start to crease with embarrassment.

'Mum,' said Tyra, laughing, 'not jealous over you, was he? Is that it?'

'Was a long time ago now, girl, I don't remember too well,' said Celeste feebly.

'C'mon, Mum,' urged Tyra, delighted to have found some sign that her mother wasn't always the stern disapproving figure she remembered.

'All right, it was nothing really. There I was, just fresh off the boat, living with my neighbour auntie's cousin Pearl and her family in Loudoun Square, and just starting work in the infirmary. So a few of the girls we go out to the Ocean Club every Friday, dance to the rhythm and blues, and there's all sorts down there and one day this little white guy, smart-looking feller in a nice suit, comes up to me, asks if I ever did any singing, said he could put me in a talent show . . .' Celeste broke off, looking more embarrassed than ever.

'Mum,' said Tyra, laughing hard now. 'You fell for that old line?'

'Course I knew it was a line, girl, I wasn't born yesterday, but like I say he was a smart feller and, well, you know things were different to what they were back home, so I went out with him a couple of times, let him think I was swallowing his line about the talent contest and . . .'

'And what?' said Tyra eagerly.

'And nothing. Just round then Pearl's cousin friend Charlie, the famous boxer she was always talking about, came to visit and that was that for me. Bye bye, Vern. And Vern couldn't say nothing of course 'cause Charlie was his great black hope.'

Tyra fell silent. She wanted to know just how far her mum went with Vern, but she couldn't quite bring herself to ask. And at the same time she was assailed by a memory of her and Jason in his hotel suite two days ago. What was she to him? Another notch on the bedpost? She didn't think so. He'd been kind of shy, Jason, when it came down to it, vulnerable with his clothes off. But maybe it was worse than just point-scoring, maybe there was revenge there too, revenge on Mazz. Mazz who'd been the golden boy when Jason was the big fat manager. A cold wind suddenly seemed to blow right through her. Time to get back on track.

'So what then, Mum? He didn't stay at the casino for long, did he?' She had a distant memory of this casino period, must have been when she was nine or ten, Charlie bringing her a toy roulette wheel.

'No, six months, a year maybe, then him and Vernon have a big row. Your father getting a little fresh with this young lady croupier. Probably Vern had his eye on her as well . . .'

'And after that did Dad have much more to do with Vernon?'

'Not that I heard of.'

'You know he was Dad's landlord, the place on James Street?'

'No,' said Celeste, her brow furrowing, 'I never heard that.'

Mazz figured the Colonel would know. The Colonel near enough knew everything. Mazz had seen him in action on Quiz Night in his local in Penarth; they had to handicap him to give the other teams a chance. State capital of Iowa, first man to score a century and double century on test-match debut, number of comets to enter the earth's atmosphere in the past century, number of top-ten hits Bananarama had . . . all well within the Colonel's purlieu. So the significance of Severn Bore and five-star should be no problem. Tuesday Mazz guessed he could work out for himself. He clambered out of his tent and walked towards the van. Even from a little distance he could see it moving, rocking. A couple of involuntary steps closer and he could hear Natalie crying out. Mazz shook his head, walked on past the van over the dunes and on to the beach, saw the water as flat as anything, stripped down to his boxers and taught himself to swim.

Couple of hours later he'd managed to swim twenty yards or so in a kind of makeshift breaststroke, his hangover had dissipated somewhat and he was feeling a whole lot better. Back at the van Natalie and the Colonel were sitting out on deckchairs drinking cups of coffee and looking like an ad for bohemian holiday-making.

'Bloke comes up to me last night,' Mazz said, once he'd sat down, 'says,

"You're looking for Emyr, there's a Severn Bore, five-star, Tuesday" — any of that mean anything to you?'

'You know the bore's a wave, yeah?' the Colonel said.

Mazz nodded. He had some vague memory that there was this, like, tidal wave that went up the River Severn, but he thought it was every seven years or something.

'Yeah,' he said, 'goes every seven years or something.'

'Nah,' said the Colonel, 'there's a few every month, more in spring and autumn.'

'All right,' Mazz said, 'how about five-star?'

'Well, I'm guessing now, butt, but I reckon that's how big the wave is. They have like a timetable and stuff for it. So that's got to be it, yeah, and like, a five-star wave's got to be a big one.'

'OK,' said Mazz, 'and I can work the Tuesday bit out myself. So there's going to be a big Severn Bore on Tuesday. What's that to do with Emyr?'

'S'obvious,' said the Colonel.

'Yeah?' said Mazz.

'Yeah. It's a wave, innit? People surf waves. Your mate's going to be surfing the Severn Bore on Tuesday. Least that's what this bloke thinks.'

The Colonel was right of course. Mazz got a lift back to Cardiff that afternoon with the Anita girl and her mates, all pissed off because of the lack of waves — everybody was a surfer these days, far as Mazz could see. He'd gone with them as being around the Colonel and Natalie was just too weird really, after a while.

Back in Cardiff he went into this surf shop, asked about the bore. Guy there scratched his head, said yeah he'd heard people did that. Fuckin' hardcore thing to do, you asked him. Mazz thought that sounded like Emyr and went round the cyber-café where a little bit of work on the Internet got him the timetable and said that yeah sure enough there would be a five-star wave passing a place called Newnham, ten o'clock Tuesday morning. Tomorrow morning.

He called the Colonel on his mobile. The Colonel was well up for it. Said him and Nat would be back in Penarth that night. He'd pick Mazz up at eight in the morning from outside the castle.

Mazz was there on time, clutching a cup of coffee and an Egg McMuffin. The Colonel rolled up a couple of minutes later and Mazz got in the van, still eating the muffin.

'Breakfast of champions,' he said, expecting a laugh, but the Colonel just grunted. Early-morning ill-temper, thought Mazz, and sat back quietly in his seat, finishing off the food while the Colonel drove out down Newport Road.

Forty-five minutes later they'd turned off the M4 at Chepstow and headed up the A48, the road that follows the Severn up to the bridge at Gloucester, and the Colonel still hadn't said a word. Mazz started to figure that maybe this was down to more than the earliness of the hour. Bastard Natalie must have told him last night. Bastard women can't just do a thing, they've got to talk about it too, make sure everybody gets to hear about it. Bollocks. Nah, that was pathetic. Like fuck it was her fault. What the hell had he thought he was doing? Didn't even fancy her that much or anything; when he'd come he'd been thinking about Tyra. Maybe that'd make it all right. Don't worry, mate, I wasn't really shagging your woman 'cause I was thinking of someone else while I was doing it.

Trouble was till the Colonel said something there wasn't much Mazz could do. Otherwise he'd be starting off saying, 'Colonel, look I'm sorry I shagged Natalie, right, it's just we had a bit of history and I wasn't feeling myself, like,' and then the Colonel could just look at him like what the hell did you just say. So they just sat there in this festering kind of silence till they got to Newnham which is some Heart of England-looking place, an olde worlde rivertown. They carried on through to the end of town then the Colonel pulled over into a little car park on the right. There were a couple of cars parked, and on a small embankment a regulation middle-aged anorak stood there consulting some kind of timetable.

'Christ,' says Mazz, 'a wavespotter,' and the Colonel actually started to grin for an instant.

Mazz climbed up on to the embankment and had a look around. The river was higher at this point, looked a good couple of hundred yards across. As wide, he reckoned, as the Mississippi in Memphis and about as viscous and muddy and generally unappealing to get into.

'Fucking hell,' said the Colonel, the first words he'd uttered all morning.

'Yeah,' said Mazz, grateful for any kind of an opening. 'You see anyone out there?' and he scanned the mudflats and sandbars downriver.

'Yeah,' said the Colonel, 'I think. Over there.' He pointed towards a sandbank over on the far side of the river. There was a small black figure just visible.

'So,' said Mazz. 'What d'you reckon?'

'Well,' said the Colonel, an expression of grim resignation on his face, 'it's what we came to do so let's do it.' He led the way back to the van and they changed into their wetsuits. They clambered back on to the platform and the anorak turned to look at them.

'Have to be quick, lads,' he said, tapping his timetable, 'bore's coming through in five minutes. Best thing you can do is get in just by here,' he pointed to the edge of the raised platform area they were standing on, 'drift downstream and paddle across to the far side, I think you'll find.'

Mazz nodded his thanks but the bloke carried on, 'Course, you ask me it would be better if they banned all you surfers and canoeists from riding the wave. Then maybe we'd have a proper one, 'stead of it getting all broken up.'

Mazz smiled again, this time rather fixedly, and started gingerly lowering himself off the platform and on to the riverbank itself. A moment later the Colonel was there next to him.

'You sure you want to do this?' said the Colonel.

'Yeah,' said Mazz, smiling unconvincingly.

'Your funeral, bra,' said the Colonel and walked into the water, his board held in front of him.

Mazz put a foot in the water, thanking Christ the Colonel had brought along flippers for them both, took another step, then another, then lost his footing completely and bellyflopped in on top of his board. His face plunged into the murky river and he frantically tried to pull it back out without swallowing any of the water. Ahead of him the Colonel was lying prone on his board and paddling across the river while letting the current pull him downstream.

Mazz did his best to do likewise, which turned out not to be too difficult, the current doing most of the work. No, the difficult bit was not being put off by all the shit being carried down the river. The usual plastic detritus was bad enough; worse was the animal refuse. Mazz saw two dead rats, then another one which, Christ, didn't seem to be dead at all. Then, shit, he didn't believe it, a dead dog, a big dog all puffed up. He turned his head away, concentrated on paddling like hell to get away from this nightmare.

As they got closer to the sandbank on the far side, the figure there started to come into focus. It was a surfer, all right, one wearing a natty Billabong suit and carrying a shortish gun of a board, which surprised Mazz as the night before the Colonel had assured him this would be a longboard job. Closer still and Mazz could begin to make out the surfer's features. Emyr, he was sure of it. At the same time he could hear this faint roaring noise, something like a big plane in the distance, but he looked up at the sky and there was no plane. Christ, it had to be the bore, coming their way.

Closer still now, and the waiting surfer was Emyr all right. But just as they approached the sandbank, Emyr started wading into the water then climbing on his board and paddling out into the river.

The Colonel changed direction to follow him and for a moment Mazz wasn't sure what to do; most of him just wanted to get to the sandbank and forget about the whole thing. Really there was no choice but to go after the others, unless he wanted to walk to Gloucester, cross over the bridge there and walk back again along the other side.

The noise was building up now, a great roar coming from downriver. He looked to his left and could see it, a great wave spanning the whole width of the river, still a couple of hundred yards away but moving at a stately pace towards him. There was nothing else for it. He started paddling upstream.

Emyr was twenty yards ahead of him, the Colonel maybe ten yards, both of them paddling hard, going against the current, trying to get up a bit of momentum ready for when the wave picked them up. Mazz had a go but he had no rhythm and the current was dragging him downstream. He hoped to hell the wave would pick him up. If it somehow passed him by, he suddenly realised the current would like as not take him all the way downstream, past the Severn Bridges and out into the Bristol Channel. That happened and he would be, not to put too fine a point on it, dead.

He was just about ready to panic when he looked back over his shoulder, the noise now amazing, near deafening, and he saw the river gone mad, the placid inevitable downstream current replaced by a four-foot-high wall of water coming straight towards him.

And then – woooff – it picked him up and, once again, despite everything, the exhilaration hit him. He was flying down the middle of a river. Well, not flying exactly – there wasn't the pace of a sea wave – gliding was nearer the mark; he was gliding down the middle of this enormous river. The wave picked up the Colonel next and he got on easily and after a moment or two stood up, looking as relaxed and unconcerned as a man on one of those long horizontal conveyer-belt escalators you get at airports.

Next up was Emyr. Emyr's style was completely different. The moment he got on the wave he was up on the board and not content to ride it peacefully forwards like Mazz, lying prone, or the Colonel, standing up, but fighting the wave, gunning himself to left and right across the wave, heading for the edges of the wave nearer the bank where it was bigger and looked, though Mazz couldn't figure how it could be, faster.

They were carried along this way for what seemed like miles but was probably only a few hundred yards, past the platform where they'd got on and into a long straight passage running parallel to the road, when suddenly Mazz noticed that up ahead the wave seemed to break into three. Emyr seemed to be heading for the right-hand part of the wave, the one that looked to be heading dangerously close to the far bank. Mazz was still in the middle and the Colonel had somehow drifted over to the left and his wave was suddenly building in size and destined, as far as Mazz could see, for a spectacular wipeout in a clump of trees dead ahead of him.

Mazz wasn't sure what to do. Try and keep on the wave and follow Emyr or try to get over to the side and help the Colonel out. His instinct was to go after the Colonel; only problem was he wasn't sure how to move sideways along the wave. The one thing he wanted to avoid was losing the wave himself and getting swept downstream. He was just cautiously trying to shift his weight to the left when he looked down and realised that he was not the only creature to have been picked up by the bore. Right next to him was one definitely live rat, surfing like a pro, and there – oh shit – swept in front of him was the dead dog. Mazz had a sudden nightmare vision of the pointed fins underneath his board catching the dog's carcass and ripping its putrid stomach open. He yanked the board over to his left, suddenly gained momentum and started shooting along the wave just as the Colonel was trying to edge his board to the right and away from the clump of trees. Mazz caught the Colonel full amid boards, they both came off, and the wave suddenly building to six foot of foaming water flung them both, boards and all, into the trees.

They came to rest on a mud bank tangled up in brambles and tree roots. Mazz opened his eyes and looked left and saw the Colonel sprawled upside down on the bank. He couldn't help laughing and all at once the Colonel started laughing too.

This was the moment, Mazz thought. Tell him now, get it out in the open and deal with it. But he didn't. He hesitated, thought he'd wait till they were on dry land. And then, once they'd pulled themselves, muddy and stinking, up on to the bank, the Colonel got in there first.

'Sorry, man,' he said, 'I'm a bear with a sore head today and I know it. Just had this total stand-up shouting row with Nat before I came out. I'll swear this baby thing is driving her crazy.'

There it was, the moment gone. No way was Mazz going to launch into his spiel now. 'Yeah?' he said non-committally. 'Best to give her some space then.'

The Colonel nodded. 'Yeah, that's what I reckon, butt. So let's go catch up with your mate.'

'How we going to do that?' said Mazz. 'You got a motor boat? The wave's gone.'

'Yeah,' said the Colonel, 'the wave's gone, all right. It's gone at about ten miles an hour up the river. We get in the car and drive at fifty miles an hour up the river. Find somewhere to park, then we spend half an hour freezing to bastard death waiting for him.'

'D'oh,' said Mazz and he followed the Colonel's lead, clambering back on to the bank then squishing his way along the towpath back to the car park. They got into the van still wearing their muddy soaking wetsuits, the Colonel just discarding his flippers so as to drive in bare feet, and headed back on to the A48, both aware by now that this quest had long since ceased to have any rational purpose, just its own increasingly insane momentum.

The road carried on straight along the riverbank for a half mile or so till it reached the White Hart at Broadoak but the bore had already passed by this section and now the road headed a little way inland. They kept on going for a few more miles and the road resolutely refused to get back to the river; instead they were cresting a rise well above the river. They came to a place called Westbury-on-Severn that nevertheless seemed to be a good mile or two from the water. Finally, in impatience, the Colonel swung the van right into the next lane he saw, signposted to somewhere called Epney.

The road dead-ended with a house and a stile. The Colonel parked the van as close to the verge as possible, then the two of them jumped out and climbed the stile. Ahead was a small field and the river embarkment. The field turned out to be a bog, though and they had to skirt it gingerly. Eventually they came to the riverbank.

'Listen,' said the Colonel, and there was the roar of the bore.

'Shit,' said Mazz, 'cause there it was no more than twenty yards away. No chance of getting through a thicket of brambles and down into the river in time to catch it. And there was Emyr, lying prone now but still riding the bore, as easy as you like.

'Hey,' shouted Mazz, and Emyr turned and waved. Then he climbed up on to his board and slalomed his way out of sight.

Mazz turned to see the Colonel already running round the edge of the field back towards the van. Mazz pelted after him and the two of them, now wet and muddy and stinking, got back in the vehicle. The Colonel pushed it through the lanes, driving like a madman now, and in two or three minutes they burst back on to the A48. The Colonel turned right, shot straight in front of an infuriated artic and floored the accelerator. No more than a couple of miles further on they crested a hill and saw the river coming back towards the road below them. At the bottom of the hill was a pub, imaginatively named the Severn Bore. The Colonel swung the van into the car park, once more paying no heed to the oncoming traffic, and the two of them jumped out once again. There was no easy access to the river from this side of the pub, so they walked around to the far side, climbed over a stile and found themselves on the towpath, along with a half dozen or so spectators: a family group, a couple, and an intent-looking bloke with a beard and serious camera, who was busy fiddling about with his light meter.

There was no obvious way into the water from here, apart from a strange rusted-up piece of machinery in the pub garden itself, looking like it was some kind of loading bay and including a ladder leading directly down on to a mudflat. Mazz and the Colonel looked at each other.

'Try down the footpath,' said Mazz and the Colonel nodded.

They walked on for another fifty yards or so, then found a spot which had evidently been used before and lowered themselves into the water. The Colonel forged ahead as usual; Mazz had to battle with himself before getting back in the river, but eventually he pushed off too.

They paddled over to the far side and just concentrated on keeping their position for a minute or two until the now familiar bore roar started resonating in the distance.

Five freezing minutes later and the bore was upon them. Emyr was still there, still prone on his board. He must have done this dozens of times before, Mazz figured, otherwise it was a miracle he'd managed to negotiate the changing currents without losing the wave. Anyway, he was here and so was the bore. The Colonel was just ahead of Mazz and got on the wave, which was now a pretty ferocious four-footer, with ease. Mazz started paddling hard, half caught the wave then lost it, spun off his board and went under. Came up to find himself in the backwash with the Colonel and Emyr disappearing into the distance.

Mazz flailed about till he reunited himself with his board then paddled hard to the shore. More by luck than judgement, he'd ended up right by the spot where he'd climbed in. So he pulled himself out and walked back along the footpath.

'Hard luck, mate,' said the male half of the couple waiting on the embankment.

'Fuck off,' said Mazz without even looking at the bloke and climbed over the stile while the bloke's girlfriend restrained him.

Mazz walked round to the van. Blessedly, it was open with the key still in the ignition. He pulled off his flippers and sat down on the already soaking seat. He took a couple of minutes to get acquainted with the controls then nearly reversed straight up on to the embankment. Eventually he got the thing going forward and got back on the road.

Three or four miles further on he finally got close to the river again. There was a big junction with the A40 and the first bridge over the river since the Severn Bridges twenty miles back. Mazz pulled the van over into a layby just off the roundabout, right next to a Suzuki jeep, shouldered his surfboard one more time and, ignoring the stares of the passing motorists, followed a path down towards the riverbank. He climbed over a fence with a No Entry sign and made it to the embankment. Looked up and he could see there were not one but two bridges, the other being a railway bridge just downriver of the road bridge. Up on the road bridge Mazz could see another gaggle of spectators, the glint of more cameras. Mazz wondered if they would realise just what a picture they'd be getting. Missing rock star surfs the bore. Nah, course they wouldn't.

Mazz sat there by the river for ten minutes or so, as cold and uncomfortable as he'd ever been. It was actually a relief when he finally heard the bore coming and jumped in. This had to be something close to the end of the line, he was sure. Soon enough the wave came and there were Emyr and the Colonel both rising from prone to greet the watchers on the bridge and moving from left to right as you looked at them, to pick up the dominant wave barrelling along the west side of the river. The Colonel raised his hand to the watchers and Emyr did the same. They raised their hands again as they saw Mazz peel off the back and join them.

This time he too caught the wave fine. And felt the rush as the three of them entered a long fast straight section.

In fact Mazz was so thoroughly wrapped up in it that it was only Emyr yelling in his ear that saved him from disaster.

'Mazz, man,' called Emyr, 'time to bail out.'

Mazz just grinned vacantly and pointed up ahead, determined now he was finally on the wave to enjoy it. But then Emyr peeled off left towards the bank and the Colonel did the same and reluctantly Mazz followed suit, pushing his board left until the wave deposited him none too gently on the side.

'Christ,' said Emyr when Mazz rejoined the others on the towpath, 'I thought you were heading straight for the damn weir.'

'Weir?' said Mazz.

Emyr laughed. 'Yeah. Rips there could cause you some serious trouble, bra. Anyway, man,' he went on, putting his wet rubber arm round Mazz's wet rubber shoulder, 'you've been looking for me, I hear?'

13

TK MAXX

1999

Tuesday morning, Tyra thought she'd go into town, have a little look round, maybe buy a new dress, about time she had something decent and next time she saw Jason — next time, she chided herself, thought you said there wasn't going to be no next time.

She walked over on to Bute Street and was just passing the Custom House when a car pulled up, and Maria and Bobby got out. Tyra nodded at Maria; she'd had the kid for Col and Tyra wasn't going to blank her like a lot of people did just 'cause she was hustling. Maria nodded back, gave her a quick smile then darted into the pub. Bobby came round the car, smiled at Tyra.

'Fancy popping in for a quick one?' she said.

Tyra shook her head. No way was she going to be seen drinking in the Custom House. 'No,' she said, 'just going into town. You fancy a little walk?'

'Yeah,' said Bobby, 'why not? I'll just park the car.'

Tyra watched as Bobby drove the car into a private lot over the road, winked at the attendant and came back over.

'Let's go,' she said, linking arms with Tyra.

In town they had a bit of a laugh finding Tyra a dress. Bobby kept trying to squeeze her into the skimpiest, most figure-hugging thing you could imagine, kind of thing Tyra reckoned you had to be about sixteen to wear. Anyway that's the way it went, Tyra trying to find things looked as much like a chador as possible and Bobby digging out things Scary Spice might have found a bit too revealing.

Eventually, after what seemed like days trawling through the jumble-sale racks of allegedly designer clothes in TK Maxx, Tyra managed to find something she could live with: a grey dress not too sexy but didn't make her look like an off-duty nun either.

Desperate to sit down now, Tyra led the way over to the Queen's Arcade and the café there.

'Well, girl,' said Bobby once they'd sat down with a couple of coffees, 'I been asking around a bit, about what you said, the MP guy Derek whatsit.'

'Yeah?' said Tyra expectantly.

'Not a thing,' said Bobby. 'Well,' she carried on, seeing the look of disappointment on Tyra's face, 'that doesn't mean much. Most of the girls wouldn't notice if Tony bloody Blair showed up, long as he paid. But I put the word out there, like, so . . .'

'Yeah,' said Tyra, 'thanks.'

'Told Maria too,' continued Bobby, 'well, I tells her anyway to keep a look-out for anything strange, anyone wants a bit of strange.' She paused for a moment, her face darkening. 'Lot of strange fellers out there, you know. I worries about her.'

'Yeah,' said Tyra feelingly, her sympathy right out there on the street with Maria. She'd been there once or twice in her life. That terrible couple of weeks in Bristol after the abortion and the band splitting up. She'd been in strange men's cars. She knew worried all right. And she knew not caring what happens to you. She'd felt it again year or so back, when Tony was inside and everything had gone to hell, Kenny coming round asking for his money. She'd tried to but she couldn't go through with it. It was her kids made the difference. You might not care what happens to you, but what happens to them that's something else . . . Course Maria had a kid too. She'd know worried.

'You ever get tired of it all, Bob?' she asked finally.

'Yeah,' said Bobby eventually. 'Seriously tired. You look at me. C'mon, look at me like you've never seen me before.'

Tyra looked at her, saw a short stocky mixed-race girl with short dreads, wearing a pair of Calvin Klein jeans and a brown leather jacket, gold chain round her neck and a couple of gold teeth in her smile. She knew everyone mistook Bobby for a boy, a teenage boy at that, but she couldn't see it any more. All she could see was the woman.

'Right,' says Bobby, 'you knows me, you knows I'm the same age as you. I'm thirty-six years old, I had a hysterectomy last year, you know that?'

Tyra shook her head.

Bobby ground out a half laugh devoid of humour. 'Had a cyst in my womb, size of a bloody orange. Course everyone said it was luck really, what did I need a womb for? Wasn't like I was going to have kids. True enough. But I'm a woman, Tyra, you know what I'm saying?'

Tyra nodded, put her hand on Bobby's.

'And now I'm empty. Thirty-six years old and empty.'

They sat there for a moment, Tyra's hand on Bobby's, not speaking. Then suddenly, and with an obvious effort, Bobby pulled her hand away, drank up her coffee and gave Tyra a smile.

'Tell you what, though,' she said, 'you do have to laugh sometimes. I was out talking to Maria on the beat the other day when this car pulls up. I'm about to fade out, leave Maria to do her business, when the window rolls down and there's a woman in there. And she calls out excuse me and waves at me. At first I think it's a mistake but then she waves to me again and says excuse me, young man, and Maria's cracking up right next to me and then I get up close to the car and you can see it's not a woman at all but a man in drag, and he asks me if I'd like to take a ride with him. Can you believe it?'

'What d'you do?'

'Told him to fuck off of course. I think he realised and all when he got up close I wasn't going to be doing him much good. Nice motor he had and all, one of them Audis.' Bobby shook her head in bewilderment at the ways of people, then sat forward with a start. 'Christ,' she said, 'I knows what I wanted to talk to you about, sister. You give Big Jason my mobile number?'

'No,' said Tyra, looking surprised. 'Haven't got it myself.'

'That's weird then,' said Bobby, ''cause he called me.'

'Yeah?'

'Yeah, yesterday afternoon. Asked if I wanted to come by his office, talk about some Wurriyas business. He say anything about that to you?'

'Not really,' said Tyra, trying to recall anything about that lunch rather than what followed it. 'No, he said something about some people wanting the band to get back together to tour America.'

'Damn,' said Bobby.

'Yeah, mad. He was talking to Charlie about it before . . . First I'd heard of it, though. Apparently "Lick Her Down"'s been reissued on some compilation album too. Maybe that's what it's about, p'raps he's got some money for you.'

'P'raps,' said Bobby. 'Doesn't sound like Jason, though, calling you up 'cause he's got money for you.'

Tyra shrugged. 'You going to see him then?'

'Might as well,' said Bobby. 'Tell you what, girl, seeing as we're in town, why don't we go round there now?'

Mazz, the Colonel, Emyr and Danny Lewis Jones were sat round a table in the White Hart, right on the river. Lewis Jones, who was evidently an old mate of Emyr's, hadn't been in the water; he'd been following Emyr along in his jeep, shooting a bit of film with a top-of-the-range digital camera the Colonel was examining appreciatively in the pub.

All three of them who'd been in the water were still shivering and damp under big jumpers but starting to warm up under the influence of a second round of pints of Guinness. The introductions and the haven't-seen-you-for-years bullshit had been done and it was time to get down to business.

Mazz had been studying Emyr looking for signs of the feller he used to know. The physical changes were obvious – even under a big baggy surfer sweatshirt it was clear that he was thinner, almost gaunt, his face nothing but cheekbones and sharp blue eyes.

The person inside, though, was harder to read. To be honest, when he thought about it Mazz had never been that close to Emyr all those years back in the band. For one thing Emyr had always been stoned; for a second thing he was a drummer. Yeah, yeah, all that what d'you call a bloke who hangs around with musicians stuff, but it was true, you couldn't help stereotyping people. Or maybe people couldn't help stereotyping themselves. Mazz knew he was pretty much of a typical guitarist, but which came first, chicken or egg, he wouldn't like to say. But a musician changing identity the way Emyr had done, going from drummer to singer and piano player, that was frankly weird. So Mazz was studying him hard now trying to fathom what he'd missed all those years back. All he could see, though, was what looked like just another skinny surfer bum, easy and jokey in the company of his old mate Danny. No sign at all of the tortured poet he was on record. Curious.

Mazz was just about to turn the conversation to the business at hand when Emyr pre-empted him.

'So, how's old Jason then?' he said, fixing Mazz with a grin that didn't reach his eyes.

'Jason?' said Mazz, returning the grin.

'Yeah,' said Emyr, 'he sent you, didn't he?' Emyr's eyes were slipping right to look at Danny.

'No,' said Mazz and paused, giving Emyr time to give him a disbelieving look before carrying on. 'He's looking for you, all right. And I dare say he'd appreciate it if I got you to give him a call. But Jason's not why I'm looking for you. It's for Charlie.'

'Charlie,' said Emyr, his face breaking into a genuine smile this time. 'He been on to you about re-forming the Wurriyas, has he?'

'No,' said Mazz, puzzled for a moment. Then he caught on. 'You know he's dead?'

'What?' said Emyr, the little colour there was in his face draining away. 'Charlie's dead?'

'Yeah.'

'How?' said Emyr, an urgency in his voice now.

'Natural causes, they say.' Mazz shrugged. 'Heart attack maybe, though God knows how they can tell. He'd been lying in his flat for a week before they found him.'

'A week,' said Emyr, 'I only saw the old bastard a couple of weeks ago.'

'Yeah, well,' said Mazz, 'sound of it, you may have been the last person to see him. You and Charlie went to see Jason, yeah?'

'Yeah. Jason tell you why?'

'Like you said, Charlie wanted to get the Wurriyas back together again.

And he pulled you out of the hat. Never mentioned it to me, mind. So was that right? Were you really going to do it?'

Emyr looked awkward then, stared down at his hands. 'I dunno really. Thought I might get something out of Jason for him anyway.' He smiled up at Mazz then. 'Actually I thought it might be a laugh, you know. Make a change from the old doom and gloom.'

Mazz grinned back. 'Yeah, I can imagine. But how'd Charlie get hold of you? Thought half the world was looking for you.'

'It was the other way round really. We were on a little run into town to pick up some windsurfing gear. And I just saw him. We're at the lights and I'm looking at this old alky stood outside the bookie's drinking a can of Special and suddenly I realise who it is. So we ended up going for a drink with him and he told me about Jason looking to get the Wurriyas back together again, go to the States. Well I wasn't up for that, of course, but a one-off sounded OK. Well, it did in the pub, you know what I mean. Anyway I gave him Danny's number and really the state he was in I wasn't expecting to hear any more about it. But a few days later he calls me, tells me he wants a meet with Jason, and I thought what the hell.

'But this time Charlie was a bit different. Seemed to think people were out to get him. I thought he was being paranoid really, didn't really take it too seriously. In fact it put me off the whole thing. That and seeing Jason. Me and my brers been on a little surfing trip and Charlie never called, so I was kind of thinking that was the end of it.'

'So did he say anything in particular to you?' asked Mazz. 'Anything in particular he was worried about?'

'I dunno,' said Emyr. 'Just ranting and raving about how they couldn't take his home away. And then he kept going on about this treasure he had stashed away. Just raving, man.'

Mazz shrugged, couldn't think what else to say.

'So where've you been hiding out, bra?' asked the Colonel, filling the lull in the conversation.

Emyr laughed. 'This trailer out in Porthcawl. Danny's people own a whole bunch of them. Got a few specially done-up ones for his mates. And no one stays there would have a clue who I was.'

The Colonel got up then to get some more drinks in and Emyr leaned over to Mazz. 'Bad news about Charlie, man. They have a funeral and everything?'

'Yeah,' said Mazz, 'big do down the docks, Jason and Kenny Ibadulla all over it.'

'Kenny,' said Emyr. 'Christ, is he still around? Thought someone would have shot him years ago.'

'Hey,' said Danny then, chipping in for the first time, 'Emmo, I just remembered something else your mate Charlie told us, you know that last time we saw him. Kept going on about how people were out to get him. Said it was a bloke called Vernon Nichols. You remember?'

'I dunno,' said Emyr, puzzled. 'Vernon Nichols? I don't remember.'

'Vernon Nichols?' said the Colonel. 'What's Big Vern got to do with anything?'

'You know who that is?' asked Mazz.

'Yeah,' said the Colonel. 'Big Vern, construction business, used to be a boxing manager. Big interests down the bay.'

Tyra was sat in the corner of Jason's office drinking a cup of coffee and watching Jason and Bobby play pool. Bobby and Jason were obviously locked in competition but Tyra wasn't really paying attention. Instead she was locked in a deeply sad little fantasy involving her being Jason's secretary and him making her do all these sexual things for him so she could keep her job. Sad, you see. God knows where you had these ideas stashed away in your brain; she wasn't careful she'd be dressing up in French maids' outfits next. That was the thing about fantasies, she supposed: they were clichés 'cause they worked. Kept Ann Summers in business anyway. That was another thing she couldn't believe about the way things were today: Ann Summers shop right in the middle of town you'd see mums and daughters walking in there together, couples, teenagers. Didn't anyone have any modesty any more? Not that she could talk just at the moment. She uncrossed her thighs then and made a conscious effort to follow Jason and Bobby's game.

Bobby wound the game up a couple of shots later, doubling the black the full length of the table, and both players turned to face Tyra.

'What d'you think then?' said Bobby.

Tyra shrugged; she didn't know what to think really. Jason had told them he'd been contacted by an American promoter wanted the Wurriyas to play a thirty-date tour across America. The money was not great but OK – oh and by the way here are some royalties from the reissue of 'Lick Her Down'. Three hundred pounds each which had them both buzzing. Wasn't every day three hundred quid came to you out of thin air.

Touring America, though, that was something else. She could see it appealed to Bobby – big smile came over her face when Jason said the word America – but for her with the kids and all she couldn't really see it.

'How about the others?' she said. 'You asked them yet?'

'Mentioned it to Mazz and Col,' said Jason. 'Emyr, as I expect you know, has gone walkabout and your father of course is sadly out of the picture. But, to be honest with you, as long as one or two of the originals are there – specially you, Bob, you don't want to do it then we do have a problem – we can always bring in a couple of new guys.'

'I dunno,' said Bobby, 'dunno if it would feel right with new people. Bad enough without Charlie.'

Jason's turn to shrug now. 'Up to you, Bob. No skin off my nose you do it or not. I'm just passing on the information really and I'll help out with it if you want me to. Normal fees apply of course.' He winked at Tyra then and Tyra couldn't help blushing, was relieved when Jason's phone buzzed and he walked over to his desk to answer it.

Put the phone down then and came back over to Bobby and Tyra. 'Well,' he said, 'guess what? Looks like we're having a little reunion . . .'

'Yeah?' said Bobby.

'Yeah. Mazz is downstairs. And not just him, the man of mystery and all.'

'Emyr?'

'That's the feller.'

'Christ,' said Bobby and all three of them lapsed into silence for a moment until there was a knock on the door and Jason's secretary ushered in four blokes. Two of them were Mazz and Emyr, who neither Bobby nor Tyra would have recognised if they hadn't known he had to be one of the four fellers walking into the room. The other two were a tall grey-haired hippy, who Bobby recognised as the Colonel, and a sharp-looking bloke who was a stranger to them all.

The sharp feller introduced himself to Jason straight off. 'Danny Lewis Jones,' he said, sticking his hand out.

Jason paused, his eyes narrowing, then he stuck his hand out too. 'Porthcawl?' he said.

'Yeah,' said Danny, 'that's right.'

Jason stared at Lewis Jones for a moment longer then turned to Emyr. 'No surfboard today, then?'

'Nah,' said Emyr, deadpan. 'It's in the van.'

Jason smiled and shook his head, but Emyr ignored him, walked over to Tyra and hugged her. 'Just heard about Charlie,' he said. 'Really, really sorry to hear it.'

'Thanks,' said Tyra, pulling back from him, confused. Then she caught Mazz's eye looking at her over Emyr's shoulders and the confusion suddenly turned into something deeper and she felt her legs start to go and next thing she knew she was in a chair with Bobby bending over her handing her a glass of water.

Whoa, thought Tyra, I must have fainted. Suddenly she just felt like she had to get away from these people. She looked at her watch, not even registering the time, stood up and said, 'Look, I've got to go, pick my kids up from school,' and before anyone could say anything she was out of the room and down the stairs.

Tyra was fifty yards down the road and just going into Queen Street when Mazz caught up with her.

'You all right?' he asked.

'Yeah,' she said, not even turning her head, crossing the road towards Burger King. 'Fine.'

Mazz didn't say anything more for a bit, just walked alongside Tyra as she went left by Marks & Spencer's into the quieter surrounds of Charles Street. He was just wondering what if anything to say next, when he realised they were walking past Grassroots, the coffee bar for unemployed teenage punk rockers where the whole Wurriyas thing had started, the place Mazz had first met Tyra when Charlie brought her down to rehearsal, said here's your new bass player. Scared-looking tall girl with a bad-tempered boyfriend. Wonder whatever happened to him.

'Hey,' he said, 'Grassroots still going, is it?'

Tyra stopped for a moment and looked at him. Mazz thought she might be going to faint again but she didn't, she just said, 'I've got no idea,' then turned on her heel and walked on.

'Hey,' he said again, 'c'mon, let's have a look,' and he walked up the four steps to the front door of Grassroots. Tyra didn't follow him, but he opened the door anyway, went in and saw nothing but a brightly lit, leaflet-strewn government-initiative zone. He backed out of the door, saw Tyra still stood where she was, grimaced extravagantly and detected this time, he was sure of it, the glimmer of a smile.

He looked to his right, then saw that the building next door was some kind of coffee house. 'C'mon,' he said, 'have a coffee with me.'

Tyra shook her head. 'Got to pick the kids up.' She looked at her watch. 'They'll be out in twenty minutes.'

'Mind if I walk up with you then?'

She raised her eyebrows. 'If you want.'

Mazz fell in beside her and they walked on round the corner, past the library and Toys 'R' Us, still in silence but a more companionable silence this time. They crossed the road by the Golden Cross and headed down under the railway bridge.

'So where d'you find him then?' said Tyra suddenly, shocking Mazz out of a reverie in which he was picturing himself riding the Severn Bore effortlessly for mile upon mile.

'Emyr?' he said. 'Oh, surfing.'

'Surfing?' said Tyra, smiling broadly now. 'I thought Jason was joking about that.'

'Nah. Deadly serious. That's all he's been doing, all this time he's been missing. Living in some trailer in Porthcawl and surfing all the time.'

'Yeah? Thought he was meant to be some sort of sensitive poet type these days.'

'Yeah, well, be honest, I think that's why he disappeared. He's got this image, like, of being this doomy, dressed-in-black Goth type, but basically he's just a bit of a lad, as far as I can see. Wants to hang out with his old mates, have a bit of a laugh.'

'It's funny really, I hardly recognised him. All that time we spent together stuck in the back of vans and that, and I'd probably have walked past him in the street. Only 'cause he was with you I knew who he was.'

'Lot skinnier than he used to be, that's for sure.'

'True, but I think maybe it's me. All that stuff – the Wurriyas – seems like it was another lifetime it happened in, someone else's lifetime.'

Mazz paused. He knew what she meant of course. Playing in bands the way he'd done for twenty-odd years was like continually being reincarnated: the punk Mazz, the ska Mazz – must have fucked up badly there 'cause next time he came back it was as the New Romantic Mazz – then the indie Mazz, the baggy Mazz, last few years it had been the junkie's sidekick Mazz. What was next, he wondered, the industrial Mazz, the lounge Mazz? But still, something in what Tyra said stung. He turned to face her and blurted it out. 'Does the same go for us?' he asked. 'That happen in another life too?'

'Come on,' she said, her voice flat, picking up her pace and walking down Bute Street now, 'you know it did.'

Mazz didn't say anything. What was there to say? It was true. Leastways, you'd asked him a couple of weeks back about Tyra he'd have said it was true. A memory buried away as much painful as sweet, a part of what happened to ska Mazz, nowt to do with fat Yank cohort Mazz. Now, though, just standing near her was giving him an ache. Not a heartache so much as a physical ache that seemed to encompass his entire body, a yearning. A yearning for the child they didn't have, the love that went wasted, the things he'd never settled down for long enough to enjoy. Things? Kids, he supposed. Suddenly he wanted to see Tyra's kids, see how she was with them. Pretend they were his? Well, maybe. He quickened his step, accelerating towards the school.

And was taken from his line of thought again when Tyra changed the subject on him.

'And what about my dad, then, you dig out anything there?'

'Nothing really. Emyr said he saw him all right,' he said. 'They were talking about getting the band together again. Sounds like Emyr was just humouring Charlie really.'

'That's all?'

'Well, he said your dad was going on about some treasure.'

'Treasure?' Tyra frowned. 'You think that's why his flat got turned over?'

'Maybe, but I wouldn't get too excited. Doesn't sound like Charlie was making a whole lot of sense, going on about how people were out to get him.'

'Anyone in particular?'

'Someone called Vernon Nichols, apparently, he kept going on about.'

'Vernon Nichols,' said Tyra. 'Fucking hell.'

Mazz stood silent, wasn't like Tyra to swear, but he still couldn't see what the fuss was about.

'Vernon Nichols? You're sure?'

'Yeah, construction game, isn't he?'

'Not just that, he was Charlie's landlord,' said Tyra, then paused. Mazz could see she was deliberating as to whether to tell him more. He stayed silent and eventually she carried on.

'It was just here, he was living.' They were turning into James Street now and Tyra gestured towards the flats above the newsagent on the other side of the road. 'He was trying to move Charlie too. Apparently he wants to build a casino or something down the docks and he needs to knock down these houses to do it.'

'Jesus, you think he killed Charlie because of that?'

Tyra shook her head. 'Seems a bit extreme, doesn't it? But I thought it might be something to do with this so-called treasure. Someone had searched Charlie's flat after he died looking for something.'

Mazz whistled. 'Maybe you should have a word with Emyr, see if there's anything else he remembers.'

'Yeah,' said Tyra. They were approaching the school now. And Tyra stopped. 'Look, thanks for walking me down, but, you don't mind, I'll pick the kids up by myself. Give me a call about Emyr, though, yeah?'

'Yeah,' said Mazz, 'I'll call you tomorrow.' Then he hurried on, 'And I dunno, p'raps I could bring him over and then we could go and have a drink or something. Or a film. You seen *Human Traffic* yet?'

'No,' said Tyra, frowning slightly.

'Well, come on then, let's do it. Friday night, I'll give you a bell.'

'I dunno,' said Tyra but Mazz had already turned and walked off, left her with it. She didn't want to really, but she couldn't help smiling a little. Got another date.

Tyra hadn't been back home more than an hour, just got the kids' tea and halfway through the washing up when the doorbell rang. Not much good ever came through the front door; mostly anyone she knew would come round the back. She took her gloves off and went to answer it scowling, half expecting to see Mazz there, which would be pushing his luck. She was just planning how she was going to tell him to leave her alone when she opened the door and found herself looking at a skinny old white bloke in an expensive suit.

'Vernon Nichols,' he said, sticking his hand out, 'and you're Tyra Unger, and you know what, you haven't half grown since I saw you last.' He chuckled. 'Bet it's a while since someone used that line, eh?'

Tyra just stood there motionless.

'You mind if I come in then?' Nichols said, still smiling.

Dazed, Tyra nodded and led the way into the front room.

'Nice room,' he said, looking appreciatively round at the freshly painted walls, the books and the African ornaments, the big picture of Robert Nesta in the centre. Then he sat on the nice rust-coloured sofa Tyra had picked up in this place over Grangetown, sold off stuff that got returned to catalogues and that, Habitat-style they said, well near enough for the money anyway.

Tyra couldn't help smiling back; she was pleased with the room. The bit of money she'd come into when Tony had left town, the first thing she'd done was redecorate, make it her place, good and proper, every sign of Tony and his taste dumped in a mini-skip.

'Yes,' said Nichols. 'Celi told me you kept a nice place.'

Tyra's smile turned to surprise. Celi? No one but family called her mum Celi.

'You knows my mum?' She winced. Dead giveaway she was nervous; her accent started getting all Cardiff on her.

'Of course I do. Old friends, Celi and me. Right back from before you were born, dear,' he sighed, 'back when the world was simple and all this was Tiger Bay,' he waved his arm towards the window.

He coughed. 'No time for nostalgia now, though. I expect you know who I am and what I do?'

Tyra nodded. 'I've heard a few things.'

'Yes, I bet you have. Little Jason Flaherty been running round telling tales, has he?'

Tyra almost burst out laughing; first time she'd ever heard anyone call Jason little. But she held it back, just sat there and waited.

'Well, no matter. He's a businessman, I'm a businessman. One thing I should say, though, is that no matter what anyone else tells you, your father was a good friend of mine and I did what little I could to help him. To put it bluntly, it wasn't Jason Flaherty gave your father a flat to live in when he didn't have a bean to pay for it with, was it?'

Tyra felt like chipping in with 'And it wasn't Jason tried to evict him the second he realised the place was worth money', but she didn't, she held her counsel, waited for this Vernon Nichols to reveal himself.

'Now,' he went on, 'if you're anything like Celi, you'd prefer it if I didn't beat around the bush any more and told you why I'm here.' He paused and looked at her carefully. 'Has anyone mentioned allegations Charlie was making before he died?'

Tyra nodded.

'Allegations about me?'

Tyra nodded again.

'Specific allegations?'

'No,' said Tyra.

Nichols sighed. 'This is embarrassing. You see, in his last days your dad took a bit of a grudge against me. The thing is I wanted to move him out of the flat he was living in, that frankly rather squalid place over in James Street, and he wasn't having it. Set in his ways, Charlie was.'

'Not surprising,' cut in Tyra, 'you turf a man out in the street when he's in Charlie's state.'

'Hold on, young lady,' said Nichols. 'No question of that happening, no question at all. I offered Charlie his choice of flats in a new development of mine over on Atlantic Wharf. He just wouldn't listen.'

'Girls upstairs didn't say nothing about being offered an alternative.'

'The girls upstairs are, if you'll pardon my language, a pair of common whores who can quite frankly fend for themselves. Charlie was different. I put Charlie in the flat and I wasn't going to dump him on the street, what d'you take me for? Anyway sadly that's all water under the bridge now. The point is Charlie was making allegations that could do quite a lot of damage.'

'Yeah, well,' said Tyra, 'like you said, all that's water under the bridge now, isn't it?'

'Hmm,' said Nichols, 'let's hope so.' Then he paused. 'Charlie never mentioned any treasure to you, did he?'

Tyra forced out a laugh. 'Treasure? Hardly.'

'Or evidence,' said Nichols, 'he might have used the word evidence.'

Tyra shook her head.

'Ah well then,' said Nichols, 'that's grand. Anything shows up, though. Any of Charlie's property. Maybe papers or something – photos even – who knows, perhaps you could let me know before you go showing it to the world.'

Before Tyra could respond to this curious request, Nichols was standing up again and thanking her for her hospitality, of which there hadn't been any really, and saying he'd be in touch and how nice it was to have had this chat – the first bit of which sounded ominous and the second pure bollocks. Tyra was still frowning as he showed himself out the door.

14

ATLANTIC WHARF

1999

Mazz woke up early the next morning, partly because it was damn uncomfortable on Lawrence's sofa, and partly because he had things to think about. Afternoon before, after he'd left Tyra by the school, he'd drifted back into town and tried two or three bars before he found the Colonel, Emyr and Danny sat in some half-hearted designer joint converted from one of the brownstone offices up the road from Jason's HQ. Apparently Jason had been all over Emyr for information on Charlie's last days, but Emyr had blanked him completely. Danny said he figured a bit of background research would be in order before they filled him in on Vernon Nichols.

Sounded like sense to Mazz, though he was wondering why Emyr seemed to be letting Danny do his thinking for him. Well, apart from the fact that Emyr seemed to be as stoned as ever, popping out back into the deserted yard area, trying to pass itself off as a beer garden, to share a fat one with the Colonel. Little while after that Danny and Emyr had split for Porthcawl, but Danny had given Mazz his mobile number and Emyr promised to come by in a day or two, talk to Tyra – 'Not that I've got much to say, bra. Be honest, I'd never have remembered this Nichols guy's name if Danny hadn't been there.'

Anyway, Emyr and Danny had gone off about seven or so and the Colonel suggested they find somewhere a bit less poncy to drink so they'd walked over the Old Arcade which had been all right for the first three pints but then the karaoke got going and Mazz suddenly couldn't face watching the Colonel do 'Born to Run' one more time and then going back to Penarth and staying there under the same roof as Natalie. So he'd begged off and, unable to think of anywhere else to go, ended up round at Lawrence's which was just as depressing as he'd expected.

And now here he was taking stock. Charlie was dead. He'd been in fear of his life before he died. He'd talked to Emyr about a man called Vernon Nichols who was Charlie's landlord and, by the sound of it, had searched Charlie's flat. You didn't have to be Jim Rockford to figure out that Nichols might just hold the key.

OK then, Mazz resolved to spend the next couple of days finding out what he could about Nichols, have something to surprise Tyra with when they went out. And that was the other thing he needed to take stock of. What was he thinking of there? Let's twist again like we did last summer, rock me tonight for old times' sake, or something more? Did he want to be a stepdad to a couple of kids down the docks? How plausible was that? Best thing he kept himself in line. This was one woman didn't deserve to experience the full Mazz more than once in her life.

On the other hand, when, around nine, he was doing his best to brush his teeth in Lawrence's sink, he noticed he was whistling 'Que Sera Sera'.

Friday evening Tyra was lying in the bath. She'd taken the kids round her mum's, she had a glass of wine next to her, little bit of Grover Washington playing on the radio-cassette. Tacky, she knew, but why fight it? It wasn't about Mazz, she was pretty sure; it was just nice to be going out. Last few years she felt like she'd been cutting off her nose to spite her face. So caught up in her anger with Tony and – to be honest – her love for him, that she'd been staying in acting like a nun, just showing him what a good strong woman she was. Well, he was gone now, Tony, once and for all, and it was time she enjoyed herself. So there she was chilling nicely, letting the warmth of the bath soak into her, when the doorbell rang.

She ignored it, put her head under the water and kept it there for half a minute or so. Sat back up and the bell rang again. She put her head back under again, brought it back up and – fuck – there went the bell again. She checked her watch lying next to the bath. Six o'clock. Mazz wasn't due till half past, so who the hell was it? The doorbell rang once more. She swore, her mood switching instantly to black, got out of the bath, put on her dressing gown and went down to the door.

She opened it, ready to give whoever was there a piece of her mind, and there was Mazz. She was minded to slam the door straight in his face, but before she could do anything he was up to her, pecking her on the cheek, and walking into her front room. She could smell the pub on him as he went past her and hear the clank of bottles in the carrier bag he was plonking down on her table.

'You're early,' she said, cold as you like, tone she'd practised on Tony for, oh, too long.

'Yeah, sorry,' he said, then opened up the carrier, pulled out a bottle of wine and said, 'Bought you some wine,' a big grin on his face like the fact he'd brought a bottle of wine – purely so he could get even drunker than he already was – was meant to make her go into spasms of gratitude. Men. She didn't like to generalise; far as she was concerned people were people and God knew women could treat you badly enough. But this was pure male foolishness, what she was witnessing here. And she'd had enough of it for a lifetime.

'I said you're early. And where's Emyr? I thought you were bringing him.'

'Yeah,' said Mazz, finally seeming to take in the coldness of her tone, 'yeah, look, I'm sorry Emyr can't make it today but, listen, I've found some stuff out you've got to hear.'

Tyra sighed. It was probably nonsense but perhaps she should hear him out before she kicked him out. 'Look,' she said, 'I'm going to go up and get changed. And why don't you make a cup of tea?' she chucked in, pointedly giving the bottle of wine an evil look. Sure enough, like a shamefaced schoolboy, Mazz moved over to the sink, filled up the kettle. Men.

She took her time upstairs, drying her hair, changing her outfit a couple of times, trying to find something she felt nice in but didn't give the wrong signals out to Mazz. A good half hour, spot on half past six, when she finally came back downstairs wearing a cotton skirt and her velvet blouse, a blue denim jacket over the top, to show she wasn't trying to impress him.

Mazz was sat in front of the TV, cup of tea in his lap, snoring. She laughed, she couldn't help it. Then she was suddenly attacked by a pang of tenderness, remembering Charlie there when he'd come to visit those afternoons he'd already lost his stake down the bookie's. And always he'd fall asleep.

'Hey,' she said, standing behind him and shaking him quickly by the shoulders. Mazz came to in a fog of bewilderment closely followed by guilt.

'Christ,' he said, 'was I asleep?'

Tyra nodded and Mazz quickly gulped down his tea and shook his head in an effort to restore some clarity.

'So,' said Tyra, 'what's this you've found out?'

Mazz dug in his bag, pulled out a bunch of photocopied sheets. 'Spent the day in the library going through the old newspapers. Found out this Vernon Nichols is planning to build a casino hotel. And guess where?'

Tyra looked at Mazz smiling up at her and for a moment was tempted to pretend she didn't know the answer, but the moment passed. 'Right on top of Charlie's flat,' she said.

'Oh,' said Mazz, sounding like Jermaine when Tyra failed to be sufficiently impressed by one of his paintings in school, 'you know already.'

'Yeah,' she said. 'But thanks.'

'Oh well,' said Mazz, 'so much for my career as a private detective.' He checked his watch. 'Better get going to the film, yeah?'

Walking to the UCI, down James Street, both averting their eyes from the flat Charlie had died in and hurrying on through the wasteland of building sites that separated the old Butetown from the UCI, Mazz agreed to try and find out some more about Nichols and the planning application before they took Charlie's allegations to the police. To be honest, Mazz would have agreed to anything, he thought it would keep him close to Tyra. When she opened the door to him wrapped in her dressing gown wet from the bath, he damn nearly fainted with desire.

She was so lovely and still had that thing he remembered from back when, she didn't seem to know it. Didn't give herself the airs and graces most pretty girls did. And now she was getting older it was still working for her. Lot of girls, women, Mazz's age, late thirties and that, they started trying a bit hard;

you could see a desperation in them, a disbelief that a prime asset, your looks, could go like that.

Queuing up for the tickets, Mazz realised it wasn't just women worried about getting old. There they were surrounded by hundreds of spotty student types, half of them with long hair and scruffy hippy gear, just like students were when he was growing up. It was like the whole world had come full circle, and the unmistakable fact was he'd moved up a generation. He leaned over to Tyra, whispered in her ear, 'I feel like their bloody parents,' and she gave him the nearest thing she'd offered to a smile all evening. Her frown came back full force, though, when he insisted on going up to the bar beforehand and she stood there pointedly drinking nothing while he choked down a Bud, that great Satan of beers.

Inside the cinema Tyra sat as far away from Mazz as it's possible to sit when you are in adjoining seats, and as the nasty techno music and spotty young cast, who looked unnervingly like the spotty young cinema audience, showed up on screen Mazz started to wish he was anywhere else but there. He didn't much like going to the cinema anyway any more, got out of the habit, hardly seen a film in years, apart from the odd video on the tour bus any time he was in a band doing well enough to afford a tour bus with a video, and nine times out of ten that meant watching *Spinal Tap* all over again. Strange thing was, the more the band resembled Spinal Tap the funnier they found the film. Weird really, like nurses all sitting round watching *Carry On Matron* or priests watching *Father Ted* or Woody Allen watching Woody Allen films. Yeah, yeah, calm down, Mazz, maybe that little line of coke in the toilets to perk yourself up wasn't such a good idea.

Anyway, here he was sat in a cinema in Cardiff watching a film about people young enough to be his kids sitting next to the woman who might have been the mother of one of those kids but who was now making it evident that she too would sooner be any place other than here and he wondered who he was kidding. No way he was hanging around here for long. Chasing old memories. Time to make a few calls, get back on the road.

There it was; he'd said it. Every time it was the same: you came off the road, particularly after a nightmare like the last trip with the fat Yank, and you swore never again. You'd play sessions, you'd play weddings and restaurants, you'd build your own studio. And then a month later you'd wake up one morning, no money left and a sudden hankering to see the Days Inn in Milwaukee, or the Ibis in Lyon, one more time.

His attention drifted back to the screen. Wasn't like it was too hard to keep up with the plot. Bunch of kids with crap McJobs getting ready for the big night out. Main bloke's got a problem getting it up 'cause he's taking so many Es. He's best mates with this blonde girl who's fed up about something or other. You can see it a mile off they'll get together by the end of the movie. In spite of himself, though, he starts getting into it, stops noticing the soundtrack for starters, and laughs out loud at this one guy, this teenage dope dealer who's doing the best impression of someone completely out of their gourd that Mazz has ever seen on film. Reminds him of someone. Emyr, that's who it reminds him of, the way he used to be, back in the day. In fact the whole story, the whole big night out in Cardiff, takes him back to the Wurriyas, the great months when it first clicked and before it turned into a business.

The Wurriyas. Christ, he'd almost forgotten: Jason and the American tour. He'd do it, why the hell not? Got to be better than the fat Yank. Would the others do it? Emyr, he doubted it. Col would, he'd have thought. Bobby might: God knows whether the pimping game was something you could take a sabbatical from. And Tyra. Wouldn't be easy with the kids. He looked sideways at her and saw her leaning forward, obviously wrapped up in the film, and he dragged his attention back to the screen, getting a buzz off it now.

Course the main bloke and the girl do get it together towards the end, and the erstwhile Mr Floppy did the business and Mazz smiled and then almost jumped in amazement as Tyra's hand reached over and clasped his.

Neither of them said anything, just sat there holding hands watching the last scene till they came to the finale with the bloke and the girl walking through the deserted city centre, all young and in love, and just then Tyra pulled him to her, put her lips on his and he didn't know about her but he was nineteen again in an instant.

A little bit of maturity came back with the house lights, however, and Mazz remembered to nip into the Gents before they left and get a packet of condoms.

'You coming back then?' said Tyra when he rejoined her in the foyer, her tone almost aggressive.

Mazz didn't say anything, just gave her his best smile, took her arm in his and they headed out into the night.

'Let's walk this way,' Tyra said, turning to the right as they reached the car park, 'take a little walk round the bay.'

'OK,' said Mazz and let her lead him past the projected site of the Assembly and through to the sea wall by the Norwegian church where they stopped and gazed out at the water. The barrage that would shortly turn the muddy estuary into an elegant marina – at least it would do if you believed what you read in the brochure – was over to the left blocking off the mouth of the bay between the Cardiff Docks and the Penarth headland. Straight in front of them was the new St David's Hotel and above them the stars.

'So what did you think?' asked Mazz after a while.

'About the film?'

'Nah, the football.'

'It was good.' She laughed. 'God, I sound stupid. Made me sad a bit too.'

'Yeah?'

'The old man, the black guy's dad. Reminded me . . .'

'Your dad.'

'Yeah.'

They fell silent for a moment, both thinking of Charlie, then Mazz decided to lighten things up a bit.

'Did we take that many drugs when we were that age?'

Tyra laughed again. 'I certainly didn't. Dunno 'bout you though.' Then she paused again. 'Did I tell you Charlie had taken a load of cocaine before he died?'

'No.'

'Weird, isn't it? Christ knows where he'd have got the money for that from. Wasn't really his thing anyway.'

'No,' said Mazz, 'you're right. Wonder what that was all about.'

He frowned out to sea, puzzling it over, then turned to see Tyra smiling at him. He smiled back, pulled her to him, banished all thoughts of Charlie from his mind as Charlie's daughter put her tongue in his mouth, pulled his hand to her breast with one hand while the other moved down to his crotch. Mazz groaned as she found his dick and squeezed it through the fabric of his jeans. He slid his right hand under her blouse, pulled her bra down till the nipple sprang free then squeezed it, bringing an answering groan from deep in Tyra's throat. She let go of his dick then, guided his free hand under her skirt. He pushed his hand inside her knickers, could feel the heat and moisture from outside, and one, then two fingers slid inside her easily. They stayed like that for how long he couldn't say – maybe five minutes, maybe ten – up against the sea wall, then he breathed into her ear, 'Let's go to yours.'

'No,' she said, 'let's do it here.'

'Here?' He looked around. They were in full view of any passers by but he hardly cared. He was about to lower her to the ground when she said, 'No, follow me,' and pulling herself away, his fingers sliding out of her with an audible squelch, she led him past the Norwegian church and the ice-cream stand to the old lighthouse ship moored in the dock.

By day it served teas but now it was deserted. A couple of chains barred the way to the gangplank but Tyra and Mazz easily climbed over them. Once on deck, Tyra led the way to the far side and then, standing there in the light of the moon, the dark water of the dock behind her, she pulled off her jacket, then her skirt, her blouse, her knickers and finally her bra while Mazz stood there pole-axed by beauty and desire.

'Come on,' she said then, 'what are you waiting for?' and he was out of his clothes as quickly as he'd ever been and no sooner was he naked than she was on him and he was tearing the wrapping off the condom packet with his teeth, and then he was in her and they were fucking so hard Mazz would swear he could feel the big boat rocking in time with them. It didn't last long, couldn't last long before Mazz felt himself losing it, shouted out 'No' into the night, and then Tyra was digging her nails hard into his back, pushing up and grinding herself against him as he came, and then she was coming too and all too soon consciousness rushed back and they were suddenly aware of lying there naked and freezing on the side of a boat that hadn't left harbour in years.

They dressed then in silence, suddenly awkward and unsure. Once they reached dry land again, Mazz moved to kiss Tyra but she turned her cheek away, and he thought he saw her brush away a tear and was taken back twenty years to the first time they'd done it when she'd cried and cried afterwards for what he never knew.

'Shall I come back?' he said nervously.

'No,' she said, 'the kids,' and he nodded and walked along with her in silence to the corner of Bute Street and James Street where she stopped and kissed him quickly and said she'd be fine by herself the rest of the way back and why didn't he call tomorrow and it was only as he was walking away he remembered that the kids hadn't been there when he called.

15

XANADU

1981

Next day was a Friday. Charlie had called a band meeting for that evening. Told everyone to turn up at the Royal Oak at six and bring their sports gear. Mazz was knackered before he even got there. Managed a couple of hours' sleep after Tyra left but it had barely made a difference. His limbs were tired and his head was spinning.

Still he got to the pub early and had a quick pint of SA which perked him up a bit and he was just about to have another when Charlie showed up, told him drinking was for after you did your work, not before, and led the way upstairs. Bobby was there already, looking more like a boy than ever in singlet and shorts, jumping around the heavy bag and jabbing it with much enthusiasm and practically no discernible effect. Col and Emyr turned up pretty soon after, and Charlie had them all well lathered with sweat when Tyra arrived around half past.

Mazz shot her a look like you sure you should be doing this but she just blanked him, found a skipping rope like she'd been here often enough to know where everything was and started working away.

Bobby evidently loved it in the gym. She was buzzing around Charlie asking questions, most of which boiled down to when can I start fighting? Charlie started out laughing her off but Bobby kept on pushing and eventually he caved in and said no reason she couldn't do a bit of sparring.

'Great,' said Bobby, 'ace.'

'Course,' said Charlie, 'you'll have to find someone your own weight.'

Bobby's face fell. 'I don't want to fight some little kid. She whirled round at Col who was openly snickering behind her. 'Shut up, I'd fucking have you. No fucking trouble.'

Col laughed, patted her on the head and Mazz thought Bobby was going to smack him one right then but Charlie was in there in a flash.

'Hey,' he said, 'children, cool it. You want to show someone what you got, show Charlie.' And with that he put on a pair of the big training gloves, climbed into the ring and invited Bobby up there after him.

He held the big gloves out in front of him and looked at Bobby. 'C'mon then, sister, give it what you've got.'

Be honest, it was hard not to laugh. Bobby gave it her best shot, all right; you could see her winding up her frame to put all of her weight behind a series of roundhouse punches. But Charlie just absorbed them on the pads like they were nothing, just smiled and told Bobby to move more, try and jab a bit, not just swing like a fucking farmer, and all the while Bobby was getting madder and madder till she was almost crying with rage by the time Charlie called a halt.

Col was next and, be honest, he wasn't that much better. Used to chops on a lot about how he did karate but when it came to boxing he was just like a stronger version of Bobby, all wild swings and nothing that caused Charlie the slightest discomfort. Emyr and Mazz were no better either. At least Mazz wasn't; be honest, he hardly felt like he had the energy to lift the gloves, let alone swing at Charlie, so he concentrated on trying to get a bit of rhythm going, started moving to the beat in his head till Charlie started laughing at him, told him he should be on fucking *Come Dancing* not in a boxing ring. Emyr was different; he was like a whirlwind. Didn't even aspire to any technique, just flailed around, arms and legs and elbows everywhere, and he actually had Charlie down on the floor, not through a punch but 'cause he tripped over Emyr's legs. Charlie hooted with laughter then and put his hands up in surrender.

'Never fight a drummer, man,' he said, 'they're all crazy.'

Then it was Tyra's turn. She stepped up into the ring and Mazz couldn't help it, he just called out to her.

'You sure this is a good idea?'

Charlie caught it, glanced at Tyra then Mazz, then shook his head and looked away. Tyra came forward then, but you could see she was just going through the feeblest of motions and after a minute or two Charlie put his arm round her and called a halt. 'Don't want to hurt your old man, eh, good girl?' he said, and as they climbed out of the ring his eyes sought out Mazz again.

Down in the bar after, the band for the most part were in good spirits, Bobby taking the piss out of Emyr and Col for their lack of boxing skills, happily oblivious to her own shortcomings. In her head Bobby was the toughest girl on the block and that was all that counted. The other end of the table, the Mazz, Tyra and Charlie end, things were a little more strained. From a distance Charlie was the same as ever – getting the SAs in, joking with his mates at the bar about his new career as a pop star, the landlady threatening to take his picture off the wall, the one with the Lonsdale belt, replace it with the one from the *NME* – but close up you could spot the sidelong looks he kept giving his daughter. Mazz was edgy too, tried to get the whole table engaged in a serious conversation about where the band was going, what they were going to put on the album etc., but that soon dissolved in a barrage of stupid jokes from Emyr and Bobby, and Mazz just slumped back in his seat concentrating hard on his pint.

Little while later he went to the toilet, stood outside for a moment in the cool night air listening to the trains roll by in the distance and wondering why life was going so fast all of a sudden. Back in the pub Tyra and Charlie were on their feet.

'Little girl's decided to come and stay round her old dad's tonight, that's OK with you, boss,' said Charlie. Mazz nodded like he had some say over where Tyra spent the night, and Tyra smiled, kissed Mazz quickly on the cheek and followed her father out on to the street.

Mazz sat down wondering what the hell was going on and fully intending to leave himself soon as he'd finished his pint. Instead he ended up piling into the back room with the rest of the band to see some pop punk group with three girl singers, who were crap but quite a laugh, and Emyr knew one of the girls and she said they were all going to a new club in town, some place called Xanadu near the station, and so they all ended up there in the midst of a bunch of hairdressers listening to David Bowie's 'Fashion' every third record which was OK with Mazz. There was something about that drum sound you couldn't resist; he wondered if they could get anything similar in the studio.

By now he'd really got the taste for drinking and then, digging into his wallet to pay for another round, he noticed a little paper wrap which felt like it still had something in it. A quick tasting session in the toilet revealed the contents to be Simon's best-quality record-company coke, and Mazz not being one to bogart his drugs he passed the wrap round to a couple of acquaintances and so one thing led to another and at four a.m. that morning he was in the Patrice Grill on Clifton Street with two girls from the art college and a bloke called Dave who was Kate's ex and they had one plate of spaghetti between the four of them and a pint of bitter each for Mazz and Dave plus a couple of glasses of liebfrau for the girls.

Later still he was snogging one of the girls – Nicky he thought her name was – all the way through town as he walked back home, got as far as the castle and they'd just pulled into the beginning of the arcade to give it some serious action, when suddenly – it was like in a dream when you're happily flying along and then you remember you can't fly after all and you plunge down to earth – the reality hit him like a sledgehammer – my girlfriend's pregnant, what the fuck am I doing? So he disengaged himself from Nicky, if that's what her name was, and at first she thought he was joking and then when she realised he was seriously going to walk off home and leave her there, lipstick all over her face, her left tit already out of her bra under her sweater, her motor revved up and running, she cursed him out in language that genuinely surprised him.

Tyra came round at seven the next morning, Mazz having had an hour and a half's sleep maximum and not so much hungover as still drunk. Which was lucky really as Tyra just threw herself on him again. At first part of him resisted, like he was being used as some kind of life-size sex toy, but then his libido kicked in and his heart followed, melted by the real need he could feel beneath the hunger.

After the second time Mazz was about ready to cry uncle if she wanted to carry on – in fact every particle of him was screaming the message 'Sleep now' – but instead she turned to him and said, 'I've told my dad.'

'Yeah?' said Mazz. 'What did he say?'

'Nothing really. I thought he was going to go mad, but he didn't, he just said yeah, thought so. Said he just wanted to know if I was all right.'

'What did you say?'

'Said I dunno. I think so. Said I needed any help I knew where to go. Which is a joke, really, never gave my mum much help. Oh God, Mazz, he looked old, you know.'

'He's not old. Never be old, not in his head, Charlie.'

Tyra didn't say anything, just put her clothes on, said she'd call him later, better go back before her mum started worrying.

Mazz was asleep before the door closed behind her.

It went on like that for the next week. Tyra remote and distracted one minute, worried obviously about the baby; the showing up all hours of day and night, acting like she'd just been told this was the last time she'd ever get to have sex. For his part Mazz was doing his best to reassure her. Course he could understand her worries and that about being a mum, but it wasn't like they would be the first twenty-year-olds to have a kid, far as he could see. Christ, his cousin Bethan had had one when she was fifteen, though that was a bit different, like, but his brother Bryn had two already and he was only twenty-four now. Course Bryn was in the army so it wasn't like he did too much of the childcare or anything, but Donna seemed to be fine. In fact Bryn was on leave at the moment, whole lot of them should be in Newbridge.

So Mazz thought it might be an idea to take Tyra back, let her meet the family, and it might reassure her a bit at the same time, see how Donna managed.

The idea came to Mazz on the Saturday afternoon, the weekend before they were due in the studio. He called his mam, said he might bring his girlfriend over for Sunday lunch, like, and when his mam had picked herself off the floor she said that'll be lovely and you know our Bryn's home and Mazz said yeah and his mam said tomorrow then, and Mazz said yeah and put the phone down, and realised he'd done it now, his mother would go spare if he didn't turn up. So he decided to tell Tyra the plan in person.

Walking towards town, he realised how wrapped up in himself he'd been lately. The roars coming out of the Arms Park were hitting him in waves as he headed towards the river. Crossing the Taff there was one almighty bellow which could only mean that Wales had won and Mazz couldn't believe he didn't even know who they were playing.

Didn't take long to find out, of course. The crowd started pouring out of the ground as Mazz got to Westgate Street and as he spotted the England hats and scarves he felt a little burst of exultation. Things were surely going the right way.

Mazz fell in with a bunch of lads from Pontypool as he was walking up St Mary Street and started to get a contact high from their elation. Lads asked if he was coming for a drink. Mazz nodded and said, 'Fuck, aye,' and that's how they ended up in – where else – the Custom House. Wall-to-wall hookers and valleys boys, carousing for the first couple of hours then a steady stream of boys heading for the car park, show that they could score and all in Cardiff on a spring Saturday.

Mazz escaped around half seven – five quick cans of Breaker to the wind – and headed for Tyra's place.

Probably would have been OK if Tyra had opened the door herself, but instead it was her mum as per usual. As Mazz approached her she sniffed theatrically.

'You been drinking?' she said.

'Yeah,' said Mazz, 'there a law against it, is there? Round here?'

Was the most he'd ever said to Tyra's mum and though there wasn't much in the words he supposed the tone made them sound ruder. Either way, Tyra's mum – Celeste, her name was, not that Mazz ever called her that – just went right into one.

Out of my house, leave my daughter alone, you drunken hooligan – all of that. Mazz thought she was going to swing at him for a moment, and he wasn't sure what the appropriate action would be in those circs, seeing as Celeste wasn't maybe quite as tall as Tyra but had serious hard-work forearms looked like she could deck the average bullock with a single punch. Anyway, things were going from bad to ugly when Tyra came down to see what the aggro was all about.

Absurdly, both Mazz and Celeste turned to Tyra to justify themselves.

'Your boyfriend' – she said it like she was saying leper or something – 'comes in here drunk, girl. You know we don't have no drinking in this household.'

'Christ,' said Mazz. 'Had a couple of drinks after the rugby. We won, you know. I've not got any drink with me.'

'And back-talking me, girl, in my own house. You get him out of here.'

'Fine,' said Mazz, 'I'm gone,' and walked out of the house. He got to the end of the street when he remembered he was supposed to be asking Tyra to come to Newbridge with him the next day. He stood still for a moment, decided there was no way he was going back, he'd phone instead, when Tyra came bursting out of the house and ran up the road towards him.

'You bastard,' she said. 'Why d'you have to be like that?'

'Christ,' said Mazz, 'she just went for me. All I did was stand there. She hates me, your mum.' He paused. 'Have you told her or something?'

'No,' said Tyra, and started crying, no preamble just tears coming straight out of her eyes. Mazz pulled her to him then and a couple of kids standing over the road wolf-whistled. Mazz flicked a V-sign at them from behind Tyra's back and they scarpered laughing.

'You want to see my folks?' he said once the tears began to subside.

'What?'

'Meet my family. Come up to Newbridge with me?'

'Yeah . . . I dunno . . . When?'

'Thought we might go up tomorrow, have Sunday lunch, like.'

'Jesus, Mazz, you haven't told them, have you?'

'No. Not yet.'

Tyra didn't say anything for a moment, just kept her head buried in Mazz's neck. Mazz was uncomfortably aware that there were several curtains twitching and passers-by clocking them. Then Tyra raised her head and smiled.

'Yeah,' she said, 'OK. Just don't say anything, OK?'

Mazz shrugged and nodded.

16

CAROLINE STREET

1999

Tyra felt better the second she was on her own. She didn't know what it was with sex: she always felt so guilty after it, specially if it was good sex the way that had been. Good and dirty was what she really meant. 'Cause it hadn't been like that with Tony, least not once they were married and everything – she'd been all right with it. Then again it wasn't that dirty was it, doing it with your husband? Funny thing, though, she hadn't felt that guilty with Jason either and she certainly wasn't married to him. Her thoughts drifted away as, overcome by tiredness, she unlocked her front door, then climbed into bed secure in the blissful knowledge that she was going to be asleep the moment her head hit the pillow.

Six hours later she woke up screaming, fighting her way out of a nightmare where her mother was a man and Charlie was in drag and some kind of a zombie and she put her hand up to his face to touch him and there'd been nothing but worms there and aaaagghhhh she'd woken up. Woken wide awake too, no chance of going back to sleep, nothing to do but think about the night before and ponder what the hell had happened there.

So much for not fancying Mazz any more, eh? Amazing how you can lie more effectively to yourself than to anyone else. She'd told Bobby she didn't fancy Mazz no more, Bob'd probably have laughed in her face. As it was, she'd taken herself in completely. And hadn't prepared herself. And now?

What was the thing they said about buses – they don't come for hours then three come along at once. Well, looked like the same thing was happening to her. No sex for what seemed like decades then two men in a week. And one of them Mazz. Mazz who had caused her more pain than anyone, even Tony. Mazz had broken her heart; all Tony had done was to just about break her spirit. It was Mazz who'd taken her down the first time.

And why'd she done it? 'Cause she was lonely, 'cause her daddy was dead, 'cause she wished she was nineteen again. 'Cause she still fancied him, goddamnit. Maybe you always fancied the first one to catch your heart. Who knew? Maybe if he'd been fat and bald and worked in a bank she'd have felt nothing for him. But he wasn't, he didn't, he was the same old Mazz. Still the guitar player with the cheekbones and those eyes. Battered and lined by the years, maybe, but that only made him better looking, really. Still remembered how she'd felt about him back then, skinny white boy from the valleys burning with ambition; his skin had always felt hot back then, like he was running a permanent temperature. He'd seemed like he was from another planet. And she'd loved him. Which was her big mistake. Didn't do to love a being from another planet.

And the same went double for now. What could Mazz offer her now? Would he be a daddy for her kids? She couldn't see that. Would he live with her and support her? She couldn't begin to imagine it. Would he come and go without warning, leave her lonelier than before? She could see that all right. Bastard couldn't offer her anything but love.

Love? Her mind didn't want to even entertain the idea. You think he loves you, girl? You're nothing but a nostalgia ride for him. Her body said different; her body remembered last night in every pore, and it ached for him.

She sighed from deep down inside and got up, got dressed, got the kids back from her mum's, got herself some coffee and there was Bobby knocking at her back door, well early for a Saturday morning.

'Hey, girl,' she said, flopping down on Tyra's sofa, 'give us a cup of coffee. I'm bloody dying I am.'

Looking at the state of her, Tyra thought she was barely exaggerating. Red eyes practically out on stalks, shaking visibly and her face more grey than brown, it looked like she hadn't slept since Tyra saw her last the day before yesterday in Jason's office. Of course that had to be it: the money Jason had given each of them. Tyra's had gone straight in the Abbey National; Bobby's was evidently circulating around her bloodstream. She made Bobby's coffee then sat down on the sofa next to her.

'So what d'you reckon, girl?' asked Bobby.

''Bout what?'

''Bout what. 'Bout this tour of America, that's what.'

Tyra shrugged; she'd hardly given it a moment's thought. Seemed about as real as those envelopes come through the door telling you you've just won a hundred thousand pounds or a new car. Just some bullshit people dangled in front of you and you learned to ignore. 'I dunno,' she said. 'Just talk, isn't it?' Then she instantly regretted her words as she saw the look of disappointment come over Bobby's face.

'You reckon?' she said, frowning. 'Didn't seem to me like Jason was joking. Never seemed like the joking kind really. Course you'll know him a lot better than me, like.' Bobby was rallying now, giving Tyra a wicked grin.

'No,' said Tyra, 's'pose you're right. Thing is it just doesn't seem real. The Wurriyas – all of that – it seems like another lifetime.'

'Yeah,' said Bobby, 'seems like that all right. Different life anyway.'

Tyra took another sip of her coffee and waited for Bobby to carry on.

'America,' she said then, in some kind of reverie. 'Sounds all right to me, like. So you up for it or not?'

'I dunno,' said Tyra, forcing herself to take it seriously. 'The kids and that . . . Thing is you don't really need me anyway. Who cares who the bass player is? Only person anyone'll remember is you.'

'Yeah?' said Bobby, her face lighting up. 'You reckon?'

'Yeah,' said Tyra, 'course. You're the singer, aren't you?'

'Yeah,' said Bobby, 'that's me,' her gold teeth glinting in the middle of her gap-toothed grin.

Mazz had ended up back at the Colonel's. He'd gone into town after leaving Tyra, still pretty much walking on air. He couldn't believe what it was like once he got there. Friday nights in town he remembered there was hardly a place open, just a couple of night clubs and the casino, and the streets were deserted by midnight. Now it looked like a Hieronymus Bosch made over by Tommy Hilfiger. There were gangs of pissed-up boys and girls all over the place: gangs queuing up to get in and out of the dozen or so theme pubs and clubs in St Mary's Street, gangs roaming Caroline Street in search of dangerous-looking food – that much hadn't changed at least – and gangs just throwing up in every alley and doorway. The benefits of the two bottles of Hooch for the price of one before eleven p.m., no doubt. And from every doorway the sounds of house music. Sometimes, it had to be said, you wondered why you bothered making music. All people wanted in life was to hear a four-square bass drum and Casio tune on the top – the perfect soundtrack to a dozen Red Bull and vodkas.

Time to get out of there before his elation turned to bitterness. A classic foursome were right in front of him flagging down a taxi, two blokes in Helly Hansen jackets, two girls in next to nothing; one of the girls turned to one side and threw up right there on the pavement. The cabbie looked disgusted, wound his window back up and was just about to accelerate forward when Mazz jumped in the front seat next to him.

'Constellation Street, mate,' he said and the cabbie shrugged and put his foot down.

There was no sign of life at all, though, round at Lawrence's place. Mazz banged on the door for a good five minutes then gave up, got back in the cab and told him to drive to Penarth. It was nearly two by the time they got to the karaoke club but thankfully the Colonel was still there, stood by the bar talking to a feller in a big leather jacket looked like an ex-football player. Which turned out to be just what he was.

Couple more drinks then and a nightcap back at the Colonel's and Mazz had woken up on the Colonel's very comfortable spare bed feeling better than he had done in far too long. The memories of what he'd done with Tyra ran through his mind and he could hardly stop smiling. Sure, she'd gone a bit funny afterwards but she'd always been like that. Best thing to do, far as he could see, was give her some space, do some checking up on this Nichols guy then give her a call later on.

So ten o'clock Mazz was sat in the kitchen with a cup of tea all ready to go out and sleuth when the Colonel came in looking as uncannily chipper as ever and started making a cup of tea to take up to Natalie. Mazz told the Colonel what he was planning and the Colonel pointed out that Saturday wasn't likely to be too good a day for checking up on anyone. Plus it was a lovely day out there.

'So why don't we go surfing, butt? Llangennith'll be perfect today.'

'Well, count me out,' said a voice from the doorway. Natalie was standing there in a pair of oversize men's pyjamas, looking pissed off.

'No worries,' said the Colonel, affecting not to notice. 'You stay here and work, that's what you want.' He turned to Mazz. 'So you up for it, butt?'

Mazz was about to say no when he had an idea. 'All right if I make a call?' he said. 'Friend of mine might like to come along.'

'Go ahead,' said the Colonel while behind him Natalie rolled her eyes and gave Mazz a nasty little knowing smile.

Mazz dug in his wallet, found the piece of paper he'd written Tyra's number on, called her.

'You busy today?' he said.

'Mazz,' she said, exasperated, 'I got kids, you know.'

'Yeah, that's why I'm calling. You fancy going to the beach?'

'Beach?'

'Yeah, we can go to the Gower, go surfing.'

'Surfing, Mazz? What the hell are you talking about?' Then a pause at the end of the line. 'You serious?'

'Yeah, my mate's got a camper van. We can all go.'

Another pause. 'OK then,' she said finally. 'That'd be nice.'

And it was nice. Ended up taking for ever to get everyone ready to go, so they had to stop to feed the kids – eight-year-old Jermaine and four-year-old Emily – on the way and the Colonel was getting visibly antsy about missing valuable surfing time, but once they were finally there, walking through the dunes carrying a motley assortment of surfboards and body-boards the Colonel had dug out for the kids, and then looking out on the great expanse of beach, a clear blue sky and nice inviting two- or three-footers rolling steadily in, everyone's spirits soared.

The Colonel spent the whole afternoon out in the deep water with his long-time surfer mates, while Mazz and Tyra just messed around with the kids in the shallows, Tyra trying to stop the fearless Emily from venturing in too deep, and Mazz trying to persuade the fearful Jermaine that lying down on a board in the water and letting the waves whoosh him into the shore might be fun.

Only problem Mazz had all afternoon was keeping his hands off Tyra. She took to body-boarding easily – always had been a sporty girl, he remembered, and having her right next to him in a swimsuit, well it wasn't easy. But she made it clear from the get go that there should be no fooling around in front of the kids and Mazz respected that.

Later on, though, when they were dropping Tyra and her exhausted but happy kids off back at her place, she leaned over to Mazz and whispered in his ear for him to come over after eleven.

So he did and what followed was like an indoor re-run of the night before. Again the sex was almost ferocious in its intensity and again Tyra went moody afterwards, wouldn't countenance him staying the night. So again he ended up on the Colonel's spare bed.

Tyra couldn't stop laughing. She was sat in her front room, a bass guitar perched in her lap. First time she'd played it in at least ten years, been half surprised to find it was still there stuck under the stairs. Col was sat on the edge of the sofa, playing an electric keyboard, and Bobby was prancing up and down in the middle of the room singing through some little karaoke set-up Tyra had borrowed off Linz next door. It was Bobby who was cracking her up. They were trying to run through some of the old Wurriyas songs and Bobby had forgotten most of the words outside the choruses and she was singing the first thing that came into her head instead and it was just so funny, all these lines she was coming out with. Even Col, who never laughed much at anything, too cool for that, was cracked up, had to start rolling an extra large one to get himself back under control.

The more she thought about it, the more Tyra realised she was up for getting the Wurriyas back together. It's a weird thing growing up, it's like an attitude of mind really, she reckoned. Of course you have kids and stuff and you have to get more responsible, get up in the morning, feed them and clothe them and beg, steal or borrow the money to keep a roof over their head – all that was grown up, fair enough. But lot of people – specially women, she had to say – acted like that wasn't enough just doing the grown-up business. No, you had to get all mature. And being mature, what was that all about? Mostly it seemed to be about not going out any more, not listening to music, not going to films unless you were taking the kids – not doing anything much apart from sitting around and moaning about what losers your men were. Well, she knew she'd done plenty of all that herself. But just this now, sitting down and playing with Col and Bobby, made her feel like she was connected to the world. So, yeah, why not give it a go and see what happened?

'What d'you reckon, Bob?' she said as they came to the end of an utterly dissonant run-through of 'Lick Her Down'.

'Sounds like shit,' said Bobby, laughing.

'Nah, about doing it again. Out on tour.'

'Like I tells you, sister, sounds good to me. How 'bout you, brer?' She turned to Col.

Col shrugged and said, 'Dunno, man, depends how the little money things work out, y'know what I mean,' sounding bored but really pretty excited Tyra could tell; he just wasn't going to show it to Bobby. Lot of history there.

'Mazz up for it?' Bobby turned to Tyra.

Tyra shrugged. 'Don't know why you're asking me, girl,' she said, fighting the urge to smile. She didn't want people knowing about her and Mazz yet. Not till she'd thought about it long and hard, what she was getting into there.

'And old Emyr?'

Tyra shrugged again. 'Don't sound too likely but I suppose we can find another drummer easy enough.'

'Yeah,' said Col, 'couple of brers I can think of could play this shit easy enough.'

'All right,' said Bobby, all but clapping her hands together with enthusiasm. 'So how about you and me go see Jason tell him we'll do it?'

Tyra frowned for a moment. Was she really going to go for it then? She couldn't help herself; she burst out in a big smile. 'Yeah,' she said. 'I'll call him in the morning.'

'Bet you will, sister, bet you will,' said Bobby, making little kissing movements with her lips.

Col looked at her in puzzlement then looked at Tyra, who blushed furiously.

'You didn't,' said Col, 'you didn't,' and then, for the second time that evening – possibly a record – Col cracked up laughing.

Monday morning Mazz was just getting a late breakfast together at the Colonel's place when the phone rang. Mazz picked up, said, 'Yeah?' in a neutral tone then was startled as the voice on the other end of the line said, 'Is Mazz there?'

'Yeah, speaking,' said Mazz.

'Mazz, man,' said the voice, sounding so high-pitched and anxious it took Mazz a moment to recognise it.

'Emyr. What the hell happened to you, man?'

'Long story,' said Emyr. 'Listen, man, I'm in Cardiff now. We've got to meet, something I've got to tell you.'

'Where?'

'David Morgan's. Roof-garden café. An hour's time – that long enough for you?'

'Sure,' said Mazz.

'Good,' said Emyr, then he paused. 'Could you get Tyra to come?' he said eventually. 'She ought to hear this as well . . .'

'Do my best,' said Mazz.

'Great,' said Emyr, sounding more anxious than ever. 'I'll see you,' and the line went dead.

17

PENARTH PIER

1999

Tyra led the way into David Morgan's. She liked David Morgan's, old-school department store, reminded her of being a kid watching her mum choose fabric. Mazz followed her through haberdashery and glassware, curtains and gifts till they reached the top floor, then through the toy department and into the café. Tyra ordered them a couple of coffees and Mazz opened the door, walked on to the little roof terrace itself. And there was Emyr in the corner, trying to look inconspicuous, wearing a big sweater and a Quiksilver cap jammed down low over his eyes.

When Tyra got close to him she could see he was shaking, wearing a sweater on a summer's day and shaking. Not too hard to jump to conclusions there. Second he started talking, though, she could tell she'd jumped to the wrong one.

'I'm sorry,' he said, clasping her hand as she sat down, his voice shaking as much as the rest of him.

'Sorry?' she said. 'What for?'

'Charlie. Your dad.'

Tyra's brow furrowed. 'What d'you mean?'

'It's my fault. Me and Danny. You know after I met up with Charlie and Jason talking about getting the Wurriyas together, little benefit for Charlie? Well, I'm walking back with Charlie down towards the Oak. Got the van parked there, and you know how he was, he asks if I've got a few quid to help him out. Course I would have given him some but I literally don't have a penny on me, so I turn to Danny, ask him if he's got anything and he doesn't either and Charlie's cool about it, starts going back on about how his landlord was persecuting him and how he'd got the evidence all stashed away, whatever that meant, and we just stand there for a bit, listening to all this, humouring him, I suppose. And then we were just heading back to the van when Danny says to hang on, he's got an idea, maybe Charlie would appreciate a gram of this coke he had, this super-pure gear. So I said nice one Dan and I ran back after Charlie and gave him it, thought he could probably sell it on to someone, didn't think he'd take it himself. Christ.'

Tyra sat back in her chair. So there was the big mystery solved, it looked like. Pure bloody stupidity all round. Wasn't really Emyr's fault; way she saw it, no one made Charlie stick it up his nose. His age and health, he should have figured his heart wouldn't stand for it.

'Not your fault,' she said coolly, 'just pure stupidness all round.'

'Thanks,' said Emyr quietly, seeming to calm down almost immediately, like she'd said the magic words – 'not your fault'. Tyra shook her head. Christ, weren't men all little kids waiting for Mummy to tell them off. Then she thought of something.

'So you still up for a Wurriyas reunion?'

Emyr frowned. 'Well I'd like to be involved, you know, but strange thing is, Charlie dying and that, well I've started writing some new songs and I've been figuring it's time I got back on the horse, got back to my line. You want to hear the song I've written for Charlie?' He pulled a mini-disc recorder out of his pocket.

'No,' said Tyra, 'I don't,' and she turned and walked back off the terrace into the store, not looking back, but sensing Mazz a few paces behind her.

'Christ,' she said, suddenly coming to a stop in the carpet department, 'the total creep.'

Then she started crying and Mazz held her and when she stopped crying he still held her and they walked back to her place and had sex and afterwards she cried and he held her some more and she cried some more, just because she could, just because there was someone holding her.

★   ★   ★

Later, Mazz met the Colonel in the Oak. The mystery of Charlie's death apparently resolved, Mazz relaxed and he and the Colonel, not for the first time in their lives, had a few drinks.

Mazz woke up on the Colonel's spare bed not feeling any better than he expected to and lurched out into the kitchen to find the Colonel studying the *Western Mail*.

There it was on page three. Casino corruption probe.

'Christ,' said Mazz, peering over his shoulder to read the accompanying story.

Apparently a tip-off had alerted the newspaper to questionable links between Nichols and the council's chief planning officer, one Trefor Howells. Hospitality had been accepted, blah blah blah. And to make the story look rather more sensational Charlie's death had been thrown into the mix. Well-loved Cardiff boxer Charlie Unger had been found dead in a flat belonging to Nichols, a flat the planning officer had just agreed to recommend for demolition. Wheel in a couple of churchmen to vehemently oppose the building of a casino and there you had it, a nice little scandal. Both Nichols and Howells were described as unavailable for comment, though Vernon's office had put out a bland little statement describing the casino plan as a prestige development that would help build tourism in the bay.

'Doesn't look good for Big Vern,' said the Colonel.

'Hmm,' Mazz grunted. 'Thing I don't understand, though, is who gave them the info.'

The Colonel shrugged. 'Your man Jason,' he said, 'Jason Flaherty.'

'Yeah?'

'Makes sense,' said the Colonel. 'Screws Vernon Nichols over good and proper, then Jason moves in.'

'Yeah?' said Mazz. 'What d'you think he'll do?'

'Vernon? Not much he can do, is there?'

'It'll be Tyra he blames, though, all this stuff about Charlie getting out.'

The Colonel thought for a moment. 'Maybe,' he said, 'maybe not. You could always give him a call, tell him you reckon it was Jason. But if you're worried about it, why don't you borrow the van, take your girl Tyra and her kids off on a little camping trip for a week or two, wait till the fuss dies down?

School holidays must be starting now. Go down to Cornwall, get ready for the eclipse. No fucker'll find you there.'

Tyra was just getting the kids ready for school, trying to get them to stop watching *Nickelodeon* and get their trainers on, when there was a banging on the door. She peered out the window to find out who it was and saw Mazz, standing there holding a newspaper.

She opened the door to him and he unfolded the paper, showed her the story.

'Who's behind that then?' she asked.

'Jason,' said Mazz, 'far as we can tell.'

'Jason!' Tyra was outraged, angry, hurt that Flaherty would use her dad's death like that, just as a weapon to screw over a business rival. Using him just like he always had. 'You sure?'

Mazz shrugged. 'Like I say, just seems the most likely person. The only one had much to gain from this. But anyway I'm thinking we should get away from here for a bit, in case Vernon freaks out, blames you for all this. The Colonel said we could borrow his camper, go off on a bit of a trip.'

Tyra felt dizzy, walked back into the kitchen and sat down. She felt betrayed. Jason, she'd thought he was all right. For Christ's sake, she'd slept with him, and now this. She wasn't sure why she cared but she did; somehow it seemed like one more betrayal of her dad. If Charlie had wanted Jason to get involved he'd have asked him.

'All right,' she said to Mazz finally. 'Let's go.'

They were gone a week. A strange week spent in Devon, in a broken-down old mill belonged to a producer Mazz had worked with a few times. Place had no hot water and a stream ran through the living-room, but it was set in some nice countryside and the sun shone and the kids actually seemed to enjoy themselves which surprised Tyra a bit.

The strange thing, the difficult thing, was how to handle Mazz. The kids weren't a problem – they liked him from the start, already liked him from the day they'd spent at the beach, and he was good with them, she was happy to admit that. Trouble was it was pushing things too fast. They were just back in

Cardiff, she could have been taking things at her own pace. Seeing him every few days or whatever. Give it time to sort out the nostalgia and the sheer bloody randiness, and see what lay underneath. Something real or not. And she would have kept him away from the kids as much as possible, didn't want them thinking here was Mum's new boyfriend till she knew what she wanted.

But now, thanks to Jason Flaherty, they were stuck together all week and the kids couldn't help but know he was Mum's new boyfriend. Well, she'd thought about having him sleep out in the van or something but then the first night one thing had led to another and before they'd made any proper plans they were waking up together in the morning, the kids looking at them, and it was too late. And the thing that broke her heart was just how pleased the kids were, specially Jermaine. She'd thought he might be jealous, and maybe that would come, but for the moment he just seemed to be thrilled to have a man around the place.

Thing was, though, the more the kids liked Mazz and the more they went out and did stuff – went to the beach, went walking on Dartmoor – the more they did family stuff, the more uncomfortable she felt. By the end of the week she felt like she was withdrawing from the whole lot of them, Mazz especially. Except in the night times, of course, in the night times. In the night times she felt like she was nineteen again, so full of need beforehand, so inconsolable afterwards. What had she lost? How much had she lost, all those years since then? Since she lost him. Since he lost her.

In the night times, in the aftermath, after she'd cried and he'd held her and finally he'd gone to sleep, she would get up and go to the room her kids were sleeping in, just stand there and look at them. Wondering how you could love people so much and yet they could sometimes seem so strange to you.

Mazz and the kids would probably have been happy to stay for another week, to wait for the eclipse. Tyra wasn't having it; she said it was because of all the traffic, all the millions of people they were saying were coming down for the eclipse, which sounded like rubbish really – what you heard in the shops was everyone was staying away – but still she said she was worried about the overcrowding and she wanted to get back. Really what it was was she couldn't stand it any more. She had to get back to her life, try and get some distance between her and Mazz before the kids elected him their de facto daddy.

They went to the Colonel's place first on their return to South Wales, to find out how the land lay. Turned out the land looked OK. Vernon Nichols had clearly come to the same conclusion as Mazz and Tyra as to who had the most to gain from giving the story to the press. An arson attack had been launched on Jason's office building the night after they'd left town. The next day there was another story in the press, this time linking the arson attack to Vernon and once again mentioning Charlie's death – which was now described as 'suspicious'. Suddenly Vernon Nichols looked dirtier than dirty.

The following day, in a fit of apparent piety, the council had decided to reject Vernon Nichols's planning application. No wrongdoing had been seen to be done, a pompous statement said, but the council could not afford for even the appearance of wrongdoing to occur. An inquiry would be launched into the full history of Vernon Nichols's dealings with the council. However, they were going to go ahead with the compulsory purchase of the houses on James Street and they were inviting new planning applications for the site. Vernon Nichols had been unavailable for comment, doubtless busy consulting his learned friends and/or hired leg-breakers to plan his next move.

'Looks like that's the end of it,' said the Colonel, and the others agreed. Wasn't exactly satisfying to learn that Charlie had most probably died of a cocaine-inspired heart attack, while all the rest of it was basically no more than sharp-end business as usual.

That night Mazz and Tyra went out. It was his idea. He'd said, 'Why don't you get your mum to look after the kids?' She'd said, 'All right, you want to go over the UCI again?' and he'd said, 'No, it'd be good to go out in the neighbourhood, like,' and she'd given him a bit of a funny look but then shrugged and said all right and now there they were sat downstairs in the Baltimore and suddenly there was that married-couple thing going on, where you've spent, like, all week with someone doing the family stuff, and then when you're out together and you're meant to be having a good time, you haven't got a thing to say and you're looking round desperately for someone else to talk to.

In fact Mazz was about to suggest they went over to the UCI after all when this feller walked in, little guy their age with a flat-top growing out into short locks, and his eye positively twinkled when he saw Tyra.

'How's it going, sweetheart?' he said and came over and kissed her and stuck his hand out at Mazz.

'Mikey,' he said. And Mazz clocked the name, a friend of Col's he was sure.

'Mazz,' he said and then, glad of the company, 'get you a drink?'

'Yeah,' said Mikey. 'Diamond White would be sweet.'

So Mazz went up to the bar and got them in. When he got back Mikey had drawn up a stool a little closer to Tyra, to be honest, than Mazz really appreciated but then they were all sat down and this Mikey it had to be said was a good laugh and after a bit he asked Mazz what he did and Mazz explained about the band and Mikey remembered and told a couple of good stories about Charlie in the old days and Mazz was a bit apprehensive but Tyra laughed harder than any of them and Mikey said well seeing as you're a musician let's go up the karaoke and Mazz groaned and said all right but was really not too disappointed at all when it turned out to be the wrong night.

So then Mikey said, 'Let's go round to Kenny's place. You knows Kenny, Mazz? Course you does, used to be your manager, didn't he?'

'I dunno,' said Tyra, and this Mikey gave her a bit of a funny look but Mazz fancied a drink now so he stood up and said, 'Sounds good to me,' and they headed round the corner to Black Caesar's, smoking Mikey's spliff as they walked.

Going up the stairs that led up to the club a feller passed them on his way down wearing a sharp suit and a frown. Mazz didn't figure out who he was till he'd gone. 'Hey,' he said to Tyra then, 'that was Emyr's mate, Danny Lewis-thing, wonder what he was doing here?'

'Free country,' said Tyra, uncharacteristically short, and Mazz shrugged in return and they headed inside.

Through the door, Mazz got a couple more bottles for him and Mikey, a glass of water for Tyra who hissed in his ear that she was tired and didn't want to stay long. Mazz said sure and leaned back against the bar, took the place in. When he'd been here before for Charlie's wake it had been rammed; now the place was a quarter full at best but dark enough that it didn't feel empty. One thing Mazz did like about it, for once in a club he didn't feel old; most of the punters looked to be locals around his own age and the music was reggae and old-school funk, comfortingly familiar tunes in an atmosphere that otherwise bordered on the heavy.

Mazz walked over to the DJ, one of the few other white guys in the room, to compliment him on the music, when he realised he knew the guy. Old hippy called Ozzie, used to work at Grassroots.

Ozzie was well pleased to see him, passed over the spliff and they had a bit of a chat, then Mazz headed back to check Tyra was OK and found her talking to Col.

'How's it going, man?' said Mazz, putting out his hand to shake.

'All right,' said Col, and maybe hesitated a second before shaking Mazz's hand.

'So you two got it back together then?' said Col after a pause.

'Yeah,' said Mazz, leaning over to kiss Tyra on the cheek.

'Yeah, well,' said Col, 'you try and treat her better than last time, man,' and walked off.

Mazz turned to Tyra. 'What's got into him?'

She shrugged and said, 'He looks out for me, you know.'

'Oh,' said Mazz and fell silent, suddenly worrying that people – black guys – were staring at him, like he was coming down there and stealing their women, that kind of vibe. Then, all at once, the biggest, meanest-looking guy in the place was walking towards him and Mazz tensed, felt his hand instinctively tighten around the neck of his bottle, ready to do what he had to do if attacked. Then, as the guy got closer, he looked hard at him and relaxed.

'Kenny,' he said then. 'Long time no see, man.'

'Yeah,' said Kenny, 'long time. You bring that guy down here?'

'What guy?' said Mazz, confused.

'Guy was just here, Danny Lewis Jones. Feller asking if I wanted to sell him my club. Talking about how the area's changing and he could do a real job on this place, redevelop it for the tourist crowd. Pay me top dollar. All that kind of shit. Friend of yours, is he?'

'No,' said Mazz and turned round to look at Tyra, see if this meant anything to her, but she had her back to him already, was talking to a couple of mates Mazz had never seen before. Suddenly he started to feel a long way out of his element.

'No,' he repeated, 'I've seen the guy around. He's a friend of Emyr's – you remember him? – but I don't know anything about him.'

'I'll tell you what he is,' said Kenny, 'that feller he's got it written all over him. He's bad fucking news is what he is.'

With that Kenny walked off and Mazz stood there for a while in a little bubble of his own, next to the bar, wondering if this was somewhere he could ever belong.

Tyra spent the next few days getting the kids back into their usual holiday routines, going round her sister's and her mum's. 'Where's Mazz?' Jermaine kept asking and Tyra was able to tell the truth and say he was up in London, sorting some business out. Plus his ex was threatening to dump his stuff on the street, he didn't come and move it. Tyra hadn't offered to let him bring it round to hers, though he'd hinted pretty hard, so he'd huffed and puffed a bit and finally decided to take it round his mum's, up in Newbridge, get a mate of his to drive it down.

Mazz got back to Cardiff the morning of the eclipse. His mate Mac was driving and they were talking about getting a band together. Didn't mean much; they must have had half a dozen conversations like that over the years. Mac had been around even longer than Mazz, been the singer in one of the real hardcore early punk bands, bunch of Manchester headcases who'd have done a lot better if one or other of then hadn't been in jail most of the time. Anyway Mac had had his difficulties over the years, usual rock'n'roll problems, but he was pretty much clean these days, spent most of his time road-managing for other bands. That was how Mazz met him and mutual loathing of the fat Yank had turned into something more positive.

'So where are we going to watch this thing?' asked Mac as they came down the A470 into Cardiff.

Mazz looked up at the sky. It had been so completely clouded over when he woke up that morning he'd more or less given up on seeing anything, but now the clouds were clearing fast and Mazz couldn't help seeing an omen there.

'Give us your phone,' he said and Mac passed him the mobile. Two calls later he had it set up. They'd pick up Tyra and the kids then meet the Colonel on the pier in Penarth at quarter to eleven.

'Your girlfriend?' said Mac when Mazz got off the phone.

'Yeah,' said Mazz. 'I hope so.'

By the time Mazz had finished giving Mac a little background on him and Tyra, they were pulling up outside her house. Tyra and the kids piled in the back, the kids putting their special eclipse glasses on and then laughing when they couldn't see anything through them.

The Colonel and Natalie were already waiting at the pier when they arrived. The sky was now miraculously blue and a steady stream of people were making for the seafront. Mac endeared himself immediately to the kids by getting them cones of Thayers ice-cream and the party wandered on to the Edwardian pier.

'How was London, butt?' asked the Colonel and Mazz told him while watching Mac play with the kids and Natalie walk over to Tyra and start talking to her with what looked to Mazz like a too-friendly smile on her face.

'Hey,' said Mac then, staring up at the sun, a pair of eclipse wraparounds over his eyes. 'It's starting.'

And so it was. Everyone took turns with the four pairs of glasses Tyra and the Colonel had brought along between them and watched the moon inch its way across the face of the sun. The sky, though, stayed resolutely light. All that seemed to be changing was the temperature; there was a noticeable chill in the air and Tyra had the kids put on their coats.

'Ninety-seven degrees,' said Mazz. 'You'd think it would get darker than this.'

'Makes you think, though,' said Natalie, coming up close to him. 'Three per cent of the sun can still light up the world. Wonder how much good three per cent of a person would be for anything.'

Mazz didn't say a word, just smiled blankly back at her.

Natalie moved closer still, put her arm through Mazz's, smiling at Tyra then at the Colonel to show she didn't mean anything by it. 'I was telling Tyra here how I remembered her from your band.'

'Oh,' said Mazz, suddenly gripped by dread at the thought of what Natalie might say next.

'Hmm,' she said, 'I only saw you all once of course. At the Casablanca. It was a party or something . . .'

Mazz was struggling to stop from shaking; the temperature seemed to be icy all of a sudden.

'Yeah. I was just saying how sexy you used to be. Back then.' She gave a little no-offence giggle.

Mazz swivelled his eyes to look at Tyra then, hoping she wasn't paying attention, but she was. The Casablanca gig, the last gig.

18

NEWBRIDGE

1981

Sitting on the bus winding its way through Risca, at the start of the valley, Mazz was wondering whether this was a good idea. Him and Tyra were sat at the back, but they were getting some looks from the old dears on their way back from chapel. He hadn't really thought about what his mam and dad might think. About Tyra. Didn't think about it much himself – that was why, he supposed. Wasn't like there was any big difference between Tyra and any of the other girls he knew: listened to the same records, watched the same TV shows, wore the same kinds of clothes. Actually there was a bit of difference; he could see it in Bobby too. Thing about black girls, Mazz reckoned, least black girls his age, they weren't quite so fucking up themselves as most of the girls you met. Most girls, pretty ones anyway, nineteen, twenty, you could just tell they thought they were the best thing ever, never had any idea the world was there to do anything except kiss your arse. Girls like Tyra, or Bobby come to that, you could see they knew it wasn't like that; world was waiting there with a baseball bat behind its back ready to lick you down any time it felt like it.

He could tell Tyra was edgy too. She stopped talking as they got to Cross Keys, just looked out the window at the closed-up Sunday streets, the pubs and schools looking greyer than ever in the spring sunshine. She was so wrapped up in whatever she was thinking that it took Mazz two goes to attract her attention when they finally got to Newbridge.

Mazz put his hand in hers as they walked up the hill to his home. A kid on a brand-new BMX made a lewd noise as he passed them and Mazz thought it was pretty much the same deal as him going down to Butetown to her place. Holding Tyra's hand, though, he could feel just how tensed up she was.

Worst moment was when they walked round to the back door and ran straight into Bryn standing in the back garden having a fag while the two little kids mucked about with a plastic ride-on tractor used to be Mazz's when he was little. You could see Bryn was a squaddie from a mile off. Tyra stiffened even more as she saw him and Mazz caught the flicker of sheer surprise that crossed his face when he clocked Tyra and for a moment Mazz thought oh fuck. But then Bryn beamed and stuck his hand out.

'Bryn,' he said, 'and who are you?'

'Tyra,' said Tyra and stuck her hand out in return.

'Christ,' said Bryn, 'and what possessed a lovely girl like you to go out with this little toerag?'

Same kind of thing went on with Mazz's mum; you could see the surprise but what followed it was pure hospitality. As for Mazz's dad, he was at the stage of his drinking by this time of day that the whole world had a rose-tinted glow for a bit. Be different later on, but three or four drinks into the day Mazz's dad loved everybody. Mazz practically had to pull him off Tyra before he could make a complete fool of himself trying to kiss her hand.

Only person who was a bit reserved was Bryn's missus, Donna, but then when she wasn't chasing around after the two little kids she was just sitting there, knocking back the cider, looking completely out of it. Actually after a little while she wasn't the only one who was knocking back the drinks, just the only one who wasn't saying much.

Mazz was enjoying being back, bullshitting around with Bryn who was telling him improbable stories of life in Germany with the Welsh Guards, their dad chipping in with even more unlikely tales about what he got up to in Cyprus during his National Service. Meanwhile Tyra and Mazz's mum seemed to be hitting it off like anything. Tyra went into the kitchen after a bit to help Lena, Mazz's mum, get the roast together and there were peals of laughter coming from that direction. Later on, while the blokes were doing the washing up, Lena took Tyra upstairs to show her the bedrooms and that.

Mazz didn't think anything of it till they were on the bus back about half five, both stuffed to the gills and half pissed and, far as Mazz was concerned, having had a good time. A family time.

'I told her, you know,' said Tyra.

'Who, your mum?' said Mazz in alarm.

'No, your mum.'

'Shit,' said Mazz.

'Well, she guessed really. She asked me if I was and what could I say . . .?'

'Oh,' said Mazz, 'great.'

'Yeah,' said Tyra vaguely, like she hadn't been listening, didn't know what she was agreeing with.

Monday morning Jason rounded the band up in his blue transit, drove them to the studio, a converted chapel in Pontypridd. Smartest studio Mazz had been in yet: twenty-four tracks, separate drum and vocal booths, games room for the band to hang out in with a pool table and drinks and chocolate dispensers.

The producer was there already. Fella called John the record company had decided on. Mazz knew the name; he'd done some power-pop stuff, kind of thing you heard on the radio without noticing much. Anyway seemed like a nice enough bloke.

First day was unutterably tedious once the initial excitement of being there had worn off. John the producer had Emyr in the drum booth all day long just getting the sounds right. Said the drums were the key to the whole thing, you wanted your record to come over on the radio. Mazz took his word for it, though he couldn't help thinking that they recorded 'Lick Her Down', the whole thing, in the time it took this guy to get a snare sound he was happy with, and that had sounded all right on the radio.

Anyway the rest of them just goofed around the games room all day. Bobby ran through the entire supply of Toffee Crisps in the vending machine and won the pool tournament they had so easily that they had to have another one where she had a three-ball handicap. She won that too and the three blokes, Mazz, Col and Charlie, all sulked like mad.

Tyra just sat in the corner most of the time, reading her book. When the rest of them nipped out to the chippy, around lunchtime, she stayed put, said she didn't feel hungry. When they got back she was talking on the payphone.

Next day they finally got down to doing some recording. First the drums, which took up all the morning and was starting to thoroughly piss Emyr off. Why don't we just record it all live? he kept asking and John the producer kept saying something about how that would never work on American radio. Mazz worried a little that maybe they should be thinking about British radio at this stage of the game but he kept his mouth shut. And after lunch John was finally happy with Emyr's drums and started on Charlie's percussion. This time John seemed happy with the sound right away and Charlie got his part down first take.

Tyra was up next. She was nervous, you could see, or at least Mazz could see. John didn't seem too notice, though, just gave her a hard time when she had trouble tuning up. Brought out an electronic tuner, first time Mazz had seen one of them, and did it himself in the end.

After that Mazz was expecting the worst. These days he'd have just told the cunt to fuck off and leave her alone but back then he was impressed, he supposed, and left him to it. As it happened, though, Tyra played perfectly, got a take that John was happy with fifth time through and, be fair to him, he was nice enough to her then.

Mazz was playing pool with Bobby at the time, just lining up a tricky red, so he didn't say anything immediately to Tyra as she came out of the studio. She just looked at him for a second then walked over to the payphone. Started talking quietly into it.

Two more days and they had three tracks more or less down: covers of '007' and 'Skinhead Moonstomp' plus an instrumental of Col's, a kind of speeded-up Augustus Pablo thing called 'East of the River Taff'. Simon from the record company had been down on the Thursday afternoon, said he reckoned '007' should be the next single. Mazz thought that was a bit obvious, better to go with one of their own tunes – he had hopes for a tune he and Bobby had written called 'Night Time', a moody thing sounded a bit heavier than the rest of the stuff. Anyway, point was Simon was happy and took them all out on the town after. Pub, Taurus steakhouse, Monty's, the full works. Bloke was even up for a trip down Kenny's blues at the end of the night. Paid for everything and a constant supply of coke on tap any time anyone fancied nipping to the bogs for a livener. A couple of years later, of course, they'd find out that Simon had done everything, right down to the coke (billed as flowers and champagne), on expenses, the band's expenses, taken straight out of royalties, but that's by the by.

Mazz fell into bed about five and it took Jason practically breaking his door down to get him up the next morning.

First thing Jason said, when Mazz finally lurched out of the front door, 'Tyra there too?'

Mazz shook his head. 'Course not, she went home after the meal, didn't she?'

'Well she's not there now. Nobody there at all.'

The rest of the band were slumped around the back of the van, looking like Mazz felt. Mazz looked at Charlie questioningly. Charlie just shrugged.

'You get in, Mazz,' said Jason. 'Let's go. She'll turn up sooner or later.'

Driving to the studio, Jason had the radio on. Mazz wasn't paying attention, wondering what the hell had happened to Tyra – maybe she'd had to go to the doctor, been feeling pretty sick lately – when suddenly the news came on. Bobby Sands had been elected MP for Fermanagh and South Tyrone, with 30,492 votes. Christ. A government spokesman was quickly wheeled on to explain that this meant nothing at all but Mazz couldn't believe it. Maybe it was the hangover but he found himself actually shaking from excitement at the news. Like all at once a hole had been ripped in the fabric of the lies the establishment told you. The IRA have no popular support, all that shit. Just lies.

Mazz was buzzing by the time they got to the studio.

'Let's do "Night Time" next,' he said.

John the producer pointed feebly at the schedule he'd drawn up that said they were meant to be doing 'Downtown' next, but he looked to have the worst hangover of the lot of them and was no match for Mazz's enthusiasm.

'What about Tyra?' said Charlie as Emyr got behind his drums.

'S'all right,' said Mazz, 'I'll play the bass on this one.' It was easy enough as Mazz had written most of the bass lines himself then taught them to Tyra. In fact Mazz's energy level was such that he managed to override John's protests and get him to record bass and drums together.

'Groove's got to be right on this one.'

In fact the groove was terrific. Mazz and Emyr laid down this dark, sinister back-beat, Charlie added some slow menacing percussion, Col put on a ghost-train keyboard line and when Bobby put down the vocal, as far as everyone in the room was concerned it was there, the track that proved the Wurriyas weren't just one more novelty ska band but serious contenders.

It was late afternoon by the time John had a vocal take he was completely happy with and he was just fiddling about with different reverb sounds when the studio doorbell rang. Charlie went to get it and came back a minute or so later with Tyra plus her friend Maggie.

The second Mazz saw her he knew something was wrong. He walked over to her and was just about to say 'Where the fuck have you been?', pretend to give her a hard time about her no-show, when something in her face stopped him.

'Mazz,' she said quietly, 'you want to come for a walk?'

'Now?' he said, looking round at the band.

'Yeah,' she said, 'now.'

'Shit,' said Mazz. 'OK.'

Mazz turned to Charlie and Col, raised his palms towards them in a gesture of helplessness, said, 'Back in five, yeah,' and followed Tyra towards the door. Maggie started to follow them, but Tyra put her arm out and said, 'D'you mind waiting for me here, Mags.'

Maggie looked at her. 'You sure?'

'Yeah,' said Tyra, 'I'm sure,' so Maggie dropped back, not before giving Mazz a distinctly evil look.

Outside they walked along in silence for a while till they came to a little municipal park, deserted in the drizzle. Tyra led the way to a bench and sat down. Mazz sat down too, and Tyra clung to him. Not saying anything, just holding on to him for a while, then crying. Just crying and crying and crying like she wasn't going to stop.

'I'm sorry,' she said at last, 'I'm sorry, I'm sorry, I'm sorry,' over and over again. For a single moment Mazz had been about to ask what she was sorry for but then he knew, knew where she'd been, knew what she'd done, knew she hadn't believed it could work, and then he was crying too. The two of them sat on the bench together in the rain crying and holding each other, Tyra mouthing 'I'm sorry' over and over in his ear, a mantra of loss and disillusion, on the ninth of April 1981.

Later on Mazz would think maybe he read it wrong, maybe things could have worked out. At the time he figured it was all simple enough; Tyra had made a choice. She'd rejected his baby, she'd rejected him. The next few days in the studio Tyra insisted on coming down, said there was nothing wrong with her physically. Mags was there all the time. Mazz couldn't help it, felt like she was cutting his balls off and laughing at him. Except he could see she wasn't laughing. Her pain was obvious but any time he came near her she just retreated more and more into herself, got to the point where Maggie seemed to be doing all the talking for her, and time and again Mazz's sympathy would turn to anger at being frozen out. God knows how they came out of this time with a record, but they did. 'Night Time' was the standout but there were a couple of other tracks didn't come out too bad at all and Simon was over the moon.

Took another couple of weeks to muck around with the mixing and then they were done. The night after they finished they decided to celebrate with an impromptu gig down the Casablanca. Kenny organised the runnings and it seemed like half Cardiff turned up – docks boys, art students, looked like the Royal Oak had sent a coach party.

On stage it was great, one of their best. Afterwards everyone was elated, all headed straight round to the front of house after the show, all except Mazz and Tyra who sat there backstage looking at each other.

'You OK?' said Mazz, nervous now, the first time he'd been alone with her since she told him.

'Yeah,' she said, 'fine . . .' and then paused. Looked like she was about to say something else when Mags came in. She gave Mazz a baleful look then turned to Tyra. 'Christ,' she said, 'it's a zoo out there. You want me to take you home? I've got the car, we can go straight out the back.'

Tyra nodded wearily, then stood and picked up her bass.

'Right,' she said to Mazz, 'see you,' and followed Mags out the back door.

Mazz just stood there for a moment watching the door shut behind them. Then he shook his head, walked into the club, straight to the bar and ordered himself a pint with a whisky chaser.

A couple of hours later, he was steaming drunk and climbing into a cab with an equally drunk art student called Natasha or something. They ended up back at his place and managed to have brief but surprisingly enjoyable sex before both of them took turns to throw up in the bathroom.

Mazz had woken up dying of thirst with a whisky headache around five in the morning and was lying there trying to summon the willpower to get up and fetch a glass of water when the doorbell rang.

Tyra.

He hadn't realised how angry he was with her till he saw her then. Or maybe he was still whisky-drunk, maybe that would be a kinder explanation. Either way, he lost it as she stood there at his door.

'What the fuck d'you want now?' he roared at her. 'You already killed my fucking baby,' loud enough to wake the dead or at least the couple downstairs – which didn't bother him too much, the number of times they'd rowed, the bloke had stormed out and the woman had played bloody Janis Joplin's 'Piece of My Heart' over and over, four in the morning.

He said other things too, ugly things, and Tyra just stood there in the early-morning cold, her head bowed, till Mazz finished and slammed the door in her face.

Less than a month later Bobby Sands was dead and so was the Wurriyas' career. Things had come to a head when they took the tapes up to London, played them to Simon's boss, Ric. You could see the last drop of Mazz's optimism leak out of him the moment Ric listened to 'Night Time' and pronounced it total fucking crap. The record company, in their wisdom, put out the Prince Buster cover, '007', instead. It flopped, Mazz didn't show for a TV appearance – *Tiswas*, Saturday morning – end of story.

The Wurriyas returned to Cardiff to lick their wounds, to meet up in odd combinations and discuss what should happen next. Emyr was headed for London; he had a new girlfriend up there and was getting bored of banging out the same old beat he said. Meanwhile if Emyr was thinking big, Charlie was thinking small, had a bunch of pub and club gigs lined up if anyone wanted to do them. Col went along with him, as did Bobby, neither of them finally able to countenance the move up to London. Mazz hung between the two camps for a while, not wanting to let Charlie down but knowing in his heart he'd rather be off with Emyr, get another taste of the bright lights. Tyra? No one saw Tyra for a while. Then Bobby Sands died, starved, skeletal and insane, and there was a march on the day of his funeral and Mazz was there on his own in a big black Crombie, and Tyra and Maggie were there too, and maybe they crossed eyes once or twice but they didn't speak.

Mazz spent a lot of the next week drinking, plucking up the courage to tell Charlie he was off, and then on a Tuesday morning, May the twelfth, just as he was packing up his records and his clothes, getting ready to move, the bell rang and he went down and there was Tyra.

He didn't shout at her this time, didn't say a word, just walked upstairs and let her follow. They sat at a table in the empty front room, surrounded by boxes, looking out on the grimness of Neville Street, and neither of them spoke for a while.

'You heard he died?' said Tyra eventually.

'Yeah,' said Mazz. 'I saw you at the funeral.'

'No,' she said, 'not Bobby Sands. Bob Marley, he died yesterday.'

Mazz just looked at her, hardly able to compute what she'd just said.

At the time all he could say was, 'Shit, it's all turned to shit, hasn't it?'

Later he would realise it was one of those pivotal moments, the end of innocence if you like. It was the moment he saw the world wasn't going to change, and with that knowledge came a kind of release. All of a sudden Mazz had the strength to do what he knew he had to do.

'I'm going to London,' he said to Tyra.

'Good luck,' she said.

'You want to come?' he asked.

She shook her head then and reached for him and pulled him down so his head was in her lap, nestled against her empty belly, and they stayed there in silence for a long time, waiting for the dark to let them leave.

19

THE MILLENNIUM STADIUM

1999

Nearly three months after the eclipse, on a Thursday afternoon in late October, Tyra's walking through town, caught up in the atmosphere generated by the Rugby World Cup, forgetting her troubles.

Wales are about to play Western Samoa in the Millennium Stadium which has somehow opened on time and forever changed the way Tyra saw the city she'd spent her life in.

The old stadium, the Arms Park, was almost invisible from the centre of town. You were only really aware of it when you looked at it from over the river in Riverside. The new stadium dominated the centre and you could see it from almost anywhere in Cardiff. And, like pretty much everyone else, Tyra found it surprisingly inspiring. It suddenly made you aware that Cardiff was changing, that all the bollocks you heard people spit on the TV about being a European capital for the new century was really true. Even made you believe that all the bay development could come to something.

And this Rugby World Cup too – another thing you'd been hearing about for years but never seemed to materialise. Well, it was here now and you never saw so many people out on the streets having a good time. So each of the match days Tyra's made a point of being there for a while. Just wandering around soaking up the atmosphere, taking her mind off things.

'Cause things were bothering her. Her and Mazz. Mazz, who was in the Royal Oak now with the Colonel and his mates, born-again rugby fans one and all. Mazz, who she'd been living with more or less since the eclipse.

The eclipse. It was funny that girl, Natalie, trying to upset her then – had the opposite effect really. Course it brought up all that old shit. The abortion, and what happened after. But it wasn't like she'd forgotten any of that. More the opposite, really; it was the memory of it all that was making her keep Mazz at bay. Natalie chucking it in her face like that made her think about it properly. Made her realise maybe she hadn't been that perfect either, you think about it. Freezing him out of the whole thing the way she'd done. Hardly surprising he'd gone off on one. Not like she forgave him or anything, not like she'd put up with anyone screwing around on her now. But you got older you understood stuff, you weren't so self-righteous about life. Couldn't afford to be.

And the sad thing was he still had it, Mazz, that thing he'd had back then which made you dread going out in public with him, knowing half the girls there would have him if they got the chance. Only reason Natalie had behaved the way she had – jealousy, Tyra figured. Yeah, Mazz could still do it to her, still made her feel stuff no one else made her feel.

Trouble wasn't that. Trouble was the things he didn't make her feel. Like safe. Or supported.

'Cause that he hadn't changed was what made him still sexy but it was also what made him impossible. He hadn't changed – he was still a guitar player. Couldn't do anything else, could barely feed himself. And far as she could see, the only way he could make any money doing it was to tour all the time, which she didn't want, but the alternative was to have him there all the time doing nothing, which she didn't want either. She could see him wilting in Cardiff, playing gigs for beer money down the Oak – first time was a laugh, second time was a wake – auditioning for fucking hotel cabaret bands which in the end she wouldn't let him do, couldn't bear to see him humiliate himself that much. Reminded her too much of her dad greeting people at the casino.

So he was just there. Well, except when he'd spend a few days at his brother's up in the valleys when it all got a bit much. But basically he was just there and he was doing his best. He was good with the kids and all but really he was going mad and she was going mad and after a bit all that passion stuff just feels a bit pointless and what was she going to do?

She was just heading up Bute Street, passing the Custom House, leaving the noise of town behind for the quiet of Butetown, when she heard a car pulling up behind her. Her first thought was a kerb crawler, some salesman thinking she was a Custom House girl, and she spun round ready to give the bastard what for when through the car window she could see it was a bastard all right but a bastard she knew.

Jason Flaherty.

'What d'you want?' Just the sight of him enraged her. 'Coming to see where you're going to build your casino?' It had been in the papers, a few weeks back. Council were planning to give the go-ahead for a consortium headed by Cardiff property developer Jason Flaherty to build a casino hotel in the bay. Surprise, surprise.

'No,' said Jason, his big head sweating in the autumn sun.

'Not going to see it?'

'Not my casino, for starters,' said Jason, 'and that's not why I'm here anyway. I wanted to see you.'

'Me?' said Tyra. 'What d'you want to see me for? So you can stick my story all over the newspaper like you did Vernon?'

'What?' said Jason. 'Listen, why don't you get in the car and I'll explain.'

Tyra looked up and down the road. She didn't want her business becoming public property, she'd better get in the car. She opened the passenger door and sat there on the nice leather seat as far from Jason as she could manage.

'Where d'you want to go?'

'Just take me down to James Street, that'll do.'

They drove on in silence for a hundred yards or so, then Jason, who seemed unusually nervous, coughed and said, 'Vernon tell you I gave that picture to the paper, did he?'

'No,' said Tyra, 'Didn't have to. It was obvious.'

Jason didn't say anything for a bit, just drove on round the one-way system and into James Street, then pulled up on the left by Charlie's old flat, now all boarded up and waiting for demolition.

'Wasn't me,' he said flatly.

Tyra laughed sarcastically.

Jason took no notice, carried on talking. 'People in glass houses and all that. I'm hardly going to start bleating to the papers about planning corruption. And I'd have thought you'd have figured out by now who really did give them the info.'

'Who?' said Tyra, curious despite herself.

'Same feller who's going to make a killing out of this casino,' said Jason, waving towards the buildings waiting to be demolished.

'Thought that was you,' said Tyra. 'What it said in the paper.'

Jason's turn to laugh sarcastically. 'Aye, and they never get anything wrong in the *Western Mail*. But you're right, I was in there quick as soon as old Vernon got shafted. Only then I got shafted myself. Same little bastard did Vernon over went and told the council that, as a convicted felon, I was hardly suitable to be running a casino. And next thing I knew the little bastard had blindsided the lot of us, got the contract for himself.'

'Who?' said Tyra again.

'Your mate, the Porthcawl golden boy,' said Jason heavily. 'Danny Lewis fucking Jones.'

'Danny Lewis Jones,' said Tyra, now really confused.

'Yeah,' said Jason, 'Danny. Listen, you got time for a drink before you pick your kids up?'

Tyra frowned, then checked her watch, nodded.

'Good,' said Jason and he started the car up again and took the next left, left again past Techniquest and into the car park for the St David's Hotel, there right on the bay.

Jason led the way into the bar which was deserted thanks to its lack of a TV.

'How come you're not watching the rugby then?' asked Tyra, unbending a little.

'Can't stand the game,' said Jason, pulling back a seat for Tyra.

'No?' said Tyra, eyeing his bulk. 'Thought you'd have been a natural for it.'

'Yeah,' said Jason, bleakly. 'That's what everybody thought. But I never had any skill, I was just big. And after a bit that's not enough.'

Jason sat down opposite Tyra, picked up a drinks list and then, so quickly she wasn't sure if she'd imagined it, brushed away a tear from his eye.

'Look,' she said then, 'this the truth what you're telling me? Danny Lewis Jones got the contract for the casino?'

'Yeah,' said Jason, 'it's the truth all right. Phone the council and ask, you don't believe me.'

'OK,' said Tyra slowly. 'And you say it was Danny gave the picture to the paper.'

'Had to be,' said Jason. 'Only people stood to gain anything from screwing Vernon were fellow developers. Developers who knew about Charlie's death. And I must admit that seemed to narrow the field down to me. That's definitely what Big Vern thought, 'cause he went and attacked my office. But I was forgetting about young Danny. He's making a play to impress his dad, show he's not just the little waster everyone's taken him for up to now. His dad's had plans for years to knock down Coney Beach completely, redevelop the site as a state-of-the-art theme park. That's run into planning problems, though, so old man Lewis Jones has been looking for something else to put his money into, and young Danny's come along saying here you go, Pop, I've got just the project for you. All we've got to do is play old Jason Flaherty for an idiot.

'Which he did very nicely, to be fair, blindsided me completely. In fact it was even me who actually asked him to come in one the deal. He made a few subtle hints when we had that meeting and I bought his line. Didn't see what was coming till he stabbed me in the back.'

Tyra stayed quiet for a moment thinking on that, then something struck her forcefully. 'Christ,' she said, 'he bloody killed him.'

'Who?' said Jason. 'Who killed who?'

'Danny,' said Tyra. 'He killed Charlie.'

'What?'

'Emyr said he gave Charlie a gram of Danny's cocaine. Extra pure or something. Might have been what caused Charlie's heart attack. Emyr said it was an accident. He hadn't thought Charlie would take it himself. But now I'm wondering . . .'

Jason's turn to ponder. 'Yeah,' he said finally. 'That must have been the start of it when they bumped into Charlie – Danny and Emyr – and Charlie started ranting on about Vernon. Danny must have figured it out straight away. Say he did kill Charlie. Deliberately overdosed him. He probably thought that might have been enough to do Vernon by itself. Having Charlie die there just when Vernon was trying to evict him. But it didn't matter when nothing happened 'cause he knew he could just give the newspaper a little tip-off. And being a smart lad he waited till I blundered into the frame. Made everyone think it was me getting even with Vernon and him and his dad stroll through the middle and pick up the prize. Leave me and Vernon standing round scratching our balls looking like prize twats.'

'And my dad dead.'

'Yeah, and your dad dead.'

'Think we can prove it?'

'Prove what?'

'He killed my dad.'

Jason shrugged. 'Like to say yes but I can't see it. He's been cremated, yeah?'

'Yeah,' said Tyra despondently.

'Well,' said Jason carefully, 'in that case I definitely can't see it.'

'So what do I do?' said Tyra. 'Just let him get away with it, that what you're saying?'

'No,' said Jason, 'I'm not saying that. What I'm saying is it doesn't sound to me like you're going to get the police to charge him with anything. Not unless he left some bloody great piece of evidence round Charlie's flat that no one's noticed so far, which doesn't sound too likely. But what I can say is if that's what he did – and it's still not much more than a guess – well, I don't know if it helps but there's something I read I think is true, goes something like this: people pay for what they do, and they pay for it simply, by the lives they lead.'

'James Baldwin,' said Tyra, and they looked at each other, surprised.

Mazz couldn't concentrate on the game. He wasn't the only one, he reckoned; it didn't look like the Welsh team were concentrating on it any too well either. Game they ought to be running away with and they were making stupid mistake after stupid mistake. They didn't pull themselves together, he could see them losing it.

But that wasn't why he couldn't concentrate. Emyr had called up just before kick off. Rang the Colonel on his mobile trying to get hold of Mazz, and the Colonel had just passed the phone over. Emyr said he had a tour lined up. Australia followed by the States. Did Mazz want to play guitar? His regular guy was too fucked up to do it. Well, Emyr didn't say that exactly but Mazz knew the guy in question and he could put two and two together. Be away for two months, decent money – not fantastic but decent – make his mind up by tomorrow.

So was he going to do it? He knew Tyra wouldn't want him to. Made it plain she'd had enough of absentee men. But still, surely being on tour was a bit different to being in prison. Colonel said he should do it. 'Never do anything just to please a woman,' he'd said, 'never works out.'

Mazz had laughed but the Colonel said no, he was serious. 'Thing you've got to learn about women – thought you'd have known it by now – they never want what they think they want.'

Mazz hadn't laughed at that because he knew it was true, and not just of women. Him too. He looked around the Oak – the pictures of the boxers on the walls, Charlie over there behind the bar – and felt an awful sense of kinship. Fellers like him and Charlie, they thought they wanted a family and that, thought they wanted to do the right thing. But, it came down to it, it just took one phone call to remind him where his heart truly was. Always out to sea and looking for the next port of call.

Just then the Colonel's phone went off. He listened for a moment then passed it to Mazz.

'Tyra for you, butt. Says there's something you've got to see.'

Jason had said he'd drive Tyra to the school.

'Only two hundred yards,' she said, 'not worth it,' but then they came back to the car and he unlocked the door for her and she got in, inhaled the rich-man smell of it.

As Jason sat down she turned to him and said, 'You know when you stopped the car by me this afternoon? I asked what you were doing, you said you were looking for me. You never said what you wanted.'

Jason blushed. His whole face went bright red. 'I missed you. I had hoped . . .'

'Hoped what?' said Tyra, suddenly breathless.

'Hoped we'd see each other again. I'd hoped maybe you and me?'

'You serious?' said Tyra, and watched Jason's face fall like he'd had a lifetime of girls laughing at his big self. And remembered how he'd been in that hotel room, how nervous. And she leaned over without thinking what she was doing and kissed him quickly, not knowing herself what if anything it meant, then pulled back before he could react.

'Jason,' she said, 'better get moving. Kids are coming out now.'

Jason looked dazed but still managed to put the car into drive and head for the school. Less than a minute, they were there and Tyra jumped out, 'You mind giving me and the kids a lift back? Be a treat for them,' and shut the door before he had time to say anything.

She went in through the school gates and had both kids out of there in record time, barely exchanging a word with the other mums. Jermaine had hardly time to cry out in delighted surprise before she had him and his little sister bundled into the back of the car. Two more minutes and they were outside Tyra's house.

'You want to come in, have a cup of tea?' she said to Jason, who, still looking like a disorientated bear, nodded and followed her and the kids in. Where they walked slap into the arms of a reception committee.

Tyra's mum and Vernon Nichols were stood together in the middle of Tyra's front room.

Vernon smiled and walked towards Tyra with his hand stretched out to shake, then literally jumped backwards when he saw Jason Flaherty follow her into the room.

'What's going on, Mum?' said Tyra, trying to take control of the situation.

'Vern here, Mr Nichols,' said Celeste, 'was looking for you. He's got something he wants to show you. So I brought him round here to wait for you to bring the kids back.'

Tyra turned her attention to Nichols, who, keeping a wary eye on Jason, started to speak.

'I was just cleaning out the house in James Street, before the demolition boys get to it,' he said, 'when I opened the storeroom at the ground-floor back. Far as I knew, no one had used it in years, bookies had no use for it. Nor did anyone else. Least that's what I thought. Turns out your dad had a use for it.'

'Yeah?' said Tyra. 'What did he keep there?'

'Well,' said Nichols, an odd smile on his face, 'I think maybe it's best if you see for yourself.'

'OK,' said Tyra, 'just give me a minute.' She walked upstairs and into the bedroom, her head spinning, wondering what she was going to find. Evidence of what Danny Lewis Jones had done, perhaps? She couldn't imagine what, but still. Or maybe this was the so-called treasure, the treasure Charlie used to talk about. Though what kind of treasure Charlie might have accumulated she still found it hard to imagine. Or what was the other word Nichols had used? Evidence he said Charlie had called it. What could that mean? Was some new light going to be shone on Charlie's death? And if so why would Vernon Nichols be leading them to it?

Whatever it was waiting for them in James Street, she figured Mazz should see it too. She picked up the phone and called the Colonel's mobile. Mazz sounded pissed off at first, a woman interrupting his rugby bonding session, but when she told him what was going on he sounded eager enough, said he'd be there in five. Just to make sure he'd have time to get there, Tyra spent a couple of minutes freshening up then rejoined the awkward-looking posse downstairs.

And so a motley procession comprising Tyra, Celeste, Emily, Jermaine, Vernon Nichols and Jason Flaherty made their way from Tyra's house to the boarded-up property on James Street. As they reached the doorway a taxi pulled up and out got Mazz and the Colonel.

Vernon Nichols unlocked the front door and led the way down the dark corridor till they reached a locked door at the back of the building. He found another key and opened the door, reached inside to switch on a light then stepped aside.

Tyra walked in and for a moment she thought there was nothing there. Then she looked more carefully and gasped in surprise. There, nailed to the walls, were maybe fifty, maybe a hundred, signs: street signs, a couple of pub signs, a few shop signs. Some of the street names she knew well: Maria Street, Angelina Street, West Bute Street, Sophia Street. Others, though, barely tugged at the edges of her memory: Nelson Street, Gladstone Street, Canal Parade. The pub names too – the Freemasons Arms, the Marchioness of Bute – were just memories. She knew what they all were, though. Her birthright. Her treasure. And evidence too. Evidence of what had once been here and was now gone, past, lost.

'Tiger Bay,' said a voice next to her, her mother. 'These are the old street signs.'

'Yeah,' she said, then she turned and buried herself in her mum's chest, started bawling her heart out, crying for Charlie, crying for herself, crying for Tiger Bay, crying for all the places and people who were lost and gone. Crying for Mazz and her who could never work out, and crying for the baby they never had, crying for her kids standing next to her looking at her with worried eyes, kids growing up in a world she didn't know if she understood any more.

Mazz didn't know where to look, where to put himself. Tyra there bawling her eyes out, him there with leaving on his mind. All these other people – Jason, Celeste, the old guy – just confusing him. He looked at the kids, saw them clinging on to Tyra, could see when it came down to it he was just a nice uncle. Stayed around longer, maybe that would change but for now that's all he was – their mum's new friend.

Unable to look anywhere else, he looked at the signs. Charlie's signs. Charlie's relics of a long-gone life. He looked at one of the pub signs, the Freemasons Arms. He remembered a picture – Charlie standing in front of the Freemasons, wearing a cashmere coat and the coolest hat Mazz had ever seen, smoking. Charlie at twenty-two – king of the world.

And then Jason was standing next to him starting to take the signs off the walls, and Mazz began to help and that's what they did the next half hour or so, carefully removed the signs, piled them up, and took them round to

Tyra's house. And gradually then they all left, Jason first, Jason looking on the verge of tears too, which Mazz could scarcely credit, then the old guy and Tyra's mum, and then the kids went to bed and finally it was just the two of them left, sitting on the sofa, *Friends* on the TV, and they looked at each other and both of them knew without saying that that was it, and neither of them wanting to say it, not just yet, not in the night time.

So they went upstairs and held each other for a while and then holding turned to something else and after a while they were fucking, not love-making, nothing deep or sad, but straight-ahead friendly fucking, the kind that made Mazz at least think that maybe this wasn't over for ever, that maybe there'd be a somewhere down the line, and at least it gave him the strength to say when they'd finished, 'You know I've got to go?' and Tyra just nodded and put her finger to her lips and looked about to cry for a moment but then suddenly smiled and they both knew, he was sure, that in this end there was a new beginning.

And in the morning Mazz was riding the ghost train, Cardiff to London Paddington.

THE PRINCE OF WALES

ACKNOWLEDGEMENTS

Thanks to my agent, Abner Stein, my editor, Mike Jones, and copy-editor, Sarah-Jane Forder. Thanks also to Phil John, Des Barry, Jim Hawes, Anna Davis, Niall Griffiths, Boro Radakovic, Colin Midson, Rosemarie Buckman, Sean Burke, Peter Finch, Richard Thomas, Jon Gower and Pete Ayrton. Thanks always to Charlotte. Special thanks to Mike Hart, without whose guidance and encouragement I would not be writing the books I am, and who will be greatly missed.

For Abner

1

Bobby Ranger was sat in the back of the cab waiting for her girl, Maria, to get the chicken and chips from the Red Onion. She looked out at Caroline Street, a sixty-yard stretch of chippies and shops selling army surplus or dirty mags, populated this time of night by very drunk people trying to get a little ballast into their stomachs and even drunker people busy unloading their stomachs into the gutter. Still and all, Bobby felt at home on Caroline Street. It was a single defiant blast of seediness in a city that was getting slicker by the month.

What was happening to the city was rubbing out Bobby Ranger's life. Five years back she had a routine. It was simple. Get up in the morning, sort out your domestic business: shopping, whatever. Midday you'd hit the Custom House, get your girl out there on the street, working the lunchtime beat, while you sat inside having a laugh, game of pool. Back to the pub again in the evening. Then, soon as your girl had made her corn, you'd head off, get something to eat – Red Onion, Taurus Steak House – then down the docks to the North Star, little club full of ship guys, lesbians, prostitutes and queers. Stay there chilling out, dance, fight, whatever. Maybe your girl'd do a couple of the ship guys, she was still sober enough. Chuck you out at three thirty and then it was home to bed or down the Cabbies Club if you was in the mood.

It wasn't much of a life, Bobby knew that. It was a bunch of places any respectable person would have run a mile from, fair enough, but they didn't need to go there. It was Bobby's world, one that had accepted her, one she'd been at home in, one where people let her be.

But step by step all the nice respectable people were taking it away from her. First they took the North Star, knocked it down so they could build a shopping mall. Right down there in the docks. She couldn't believe it when she'd first heard about it, thought they were taking the piss, but now there it was – Mermaid Quay – and all of a sudden it wasn't the docks, it was somewhere called 'the Bay' – rebranding was the word – like Opal Fruits changing to Starburst.

And now they were going to demolish the Custom House. Three more days and it was closing its doors for good. Jesus, how much of her life had been spent in there, listening to the jukebox, playing pool, drinking cans of Breaker cause everybody knew you didn't want to drink anything on draught, watching the girls and the punters, watching your back when the other pimps were about. It had been her workplace for nearly twenty years and now they were tearing it down to build something called Bute Square, a nice big roundabout with a bunch of bloody office blocks around it.

All her life the city had left the docks alone. Whatever went on down under the bridge, people turned a blind eye. Then all of a sudden someone somewhere decided there was money to be made out of tarting up the docks and they were just going to flush the Custom House out of existence.

So what was she going to do? To be honest, she hadn't a clue. One thing you didn't find a lot of in the pimping and prostitution business was career planning. You lived for the night. Never saved, never thought about tomorrow if you could avoid it. Once or twice it struck her that she was making a fair bit of money by anybody's standards: hundred quid a night, two hundred even. What was that a year? Plenty. Tax free and all, but where had it gone? Up her nose, up her girl's nose, cabs and drinks and takeaways. Any time there was anything left over there would always be fines and payoffs to take care of that.

So what now? Most probably she'd do what she always did — wait till the worst happened and take it from there. For tonight, though, she knew what she was going to do. Forget about it. Have a good time.

Maria got back in the cab, one hand already raising the chicken to her lips.

'You want some chips, Bob?'

Bobby shook her head. 'Where you fancy going then?'

Maria shrugged, kept on stuffing the chicken into her mouth.

'Hippo?' said Bobby.

Maria nodded, kept on eating. Two minutes later the driver, Len, dropped them off outside the club. Maria dumped the remains of her takeaway in the bin and Bobby led the way inside. Karl was on the door as usual so he didn't charge them and they headed upstairs towards the rhythm. Half two in the morning and the place was rammed. Big black room full of all sorts; plenty of students and kids, of course, but a lot of older faces too, people Bobby had known for ever: docks boys, city boys. Didn't take a moment to get sorted; everyone knew the Hippo was the place to go for that. Maria was off on to the middle of the dance floor straight away. Bobby stood by the bar letting the music wash over her, letting the E take the edge off, gazed around her, saw Mikey Thompson all over some girl looked like she'd come out in her underwear, smiled to herself and wondered why the night ever had to end.

2

Pete Duke was trying hard to have a good time. After all, that's why he'd done it, wasn't it? That's why he'd walked out on his whole life, so he could have a good time. Well, here was his chance.

Pete was stood at the bar on the second floor of Clwb Ifor Bach listening to what might or might not have been deep house, he wasn't sure. House was about where Pete had lost track of dance music, somewhere in the mid-Eighties. Back then house seemed to be fast gay disco music from Chicago; now it seemed to be more a lifestyle choice than a kind of music and there were about three hundred different varieties of it. Still, he was pretty sure that this was deep house, that's what it had said on the poster outside, and it had a lot of bass and nothing whatsoever that approached a song so he figured he was probably right. Deep house. Fine. Cool even.

The people he'd come with were having a good time. Dan, Guto, Liz, Angie and Angie's friend who he supposed he was probably meant to be checking out but so far he hadn't said a word to and couldn't even remember her name. They were all dancing and laughing and generally acting like this was the finest time you could possibly have. Course that almost certainly had something to do with the pills they'd all taken in the pub beforehand. He was starting to regret not joining in now, standing there drinking a bottle of Budvar watching all the young people having a good time. Not that they were that young really, you looked closely. Lot of them past thirty. It was just he couldn't help feeling like sad dad at the disco. Hardly surprising really, seeing as he had two teenage kids. Actually that had been his big dread, running into Becky and her boyfriend – whatever he was called. Like 'Hi, Dad, what on earth are you doing here?'

'You all right?'

It was the girl, Angie's friend, yelling in his ear. Obviously he wasn't doing much of a job of looking like he was having fun.

'Yeah,' he said and then, for want of anything else to say, 'you want a drink?'

'Thanks. Bottle of mineral water.'

Pete ordered it along with another beer for himself, staring at his reflection in the mirror behind the bar, seeing a tall fresh-faced bloke with short wavy brown hair, good-looking he supposed, though he'd never really made much of it. The drinks came and he turned round, aware that he was getting drunk in a decidedly unpleasurable, already-feeling-the-headache-and-anticipating-the-hangover kind of way.

'Ta,' she said, then, 'I'm boiling, let's go out by the stairs.'

Pete shrugged and followed the girl out to the relative quiet of the stairwell, still racking his brains for her name. She was nice enough looking: late twenties, mid-length black hair looked like she was growing out a short haircut heading for long, little bit on the heavy side maybe but better than being a stick insect, a strong face, looked like the kind of girl knew what she wanted and mostly got it, and what the hell was her name? Angie came into the pub with her, said hello to Pete and then, 'This is my friend . . . Kim.' That was it.

'So, Kim,' he says, standing at the top of the stairs watching a couple on the next landing down get seriously intimate with each other, 'how d'you know Angie then?' Christ, smooth line or what.

'Ange?' she says, flicking her hair back out of her eyes. 'We were in college together, though I didn't really know her then, but her boyfriend used to go out with my flatmate and then when I started at the BBC I saw her about a bit cause she was working for the Assembly before she started with you lot,' she paused briefly to take a breath, 'but anyway really I know her cause we both joined the same gym on the same day and it was like oh God it's you, yeah?'

'Yeah,' said Pete, wondering if it was just the E or she always talked like that.

'So how about you?'

'Well,' said Pete, 'I work at the *Post*, you know, with Angie.'

'Yeah,' said Kim, 'Ange said. Are you new?'

'No,' said Pete, 'I've been there fifteen years.'

'Christ,' said Kim, 'so how come I haven't seen you before?'

'Well,' said Pete, 'I was married.'

'Yeah,' said Kim, 'so?'

So indeed. How to explain it? Seventeen years of marriage, and after the first year, once Becky was born, he'd been out at night on his own maybe twice, and both times there'd been hell to pay. Viv, his ex-wife, had done her nut. And he had decided that it wasn't worth it, seeing his old mates, if it pissed Viv off that much, plus none of them had kids, they didn't know what it was like. So sixteen years and the only times they went out was to see Viv's parents, Viv's sister, Pete's parents, Pete's sister. And it wasn't like they were unusual. None of the people in the close did anything much different. Julie and Duncan next door, they literally never went out. Sixteen years.

'So,' said Pete, aiming for light, 'so I've stopped being married.'

Which was about as good a way of putting it as any. That was all it was really; it wasn't like he and Viv had had a big bust-up or anything, it was just he woke up one morning and thought there's no need for this any more, this marriage thing. The kids are fine, not even kids any more, Viv's fine, the house is paid for, more or less, and I'm bored out of my mind and if I don't want to become a complete bloody vegetable I am going to have to stop being married.

'Oh yeah,' she said, 'well, good for you . . . Sorry, I can't remember your name.'

'Pete.'

'Yeah, good for you, Pete,' she said and tipped the remains of her water over her head. 'You going back in?'

'No,' said Pete, 'I think I'd better get going.'

'Oh for Christ's sake, mun,' said Kim, 'I thought you said you stopped being married,' and with that she grabbed him by the arm and practically dragged him on to the dance floor. And once he was there and stopped thinking about how much he hated this music, it was actually kind of OK, you just had to surrender to it. So he did and after a while even loosened up enough to try a few little moves, things his feet remembered from twenty years ago. Probably he looked like an idiot but no one seemed to mind, and then it was later and he was back at the bar ordering another beer and a water and he was telling Kim about his job, how he was the features editor, oh and motoring editor every Thursday afternoon, and then all of a sudden Kim was saying c'mon, this place is closing now, you want to come to the next club and Pete just laughed, no way was he going anywhere else, he was suddenly somewhere beyond tired, and told Kim he really really did have to go this time and she said good to meet you like she really meant it and told him to give her a ring at the BBC and Pete smiled and said sure and walked down the stairs on a bit of a high.

Which lasted all the way out the door and on to Womanby Street before the night air seemed to chill not just his bones but his soul and a wave of sadness swept over him. What the hell had he done? Where was the excitement in being alone at night in the city heading back to nothing but an empty bed?

Pete was woken up at six by the sound of Randall coughing in the next room. Not just any old coughing, mind, but the kind of coughing fit that sounded terminal. Par for the course if you'd been smoking God knows how many fags a day for the past fifty years. But still, Jesus, the sound of it. Not that Pete could complain. Robert Randall, the *Post*'s senior reporter, had done Pete one substantial favour, letting him stay here.

He'd certainly landed on his feet. Westgate Mansions was a grand old Thirties mansion block made you feel like you were in some pre-war movie every time you walked in there. Great views of the city and not the sort of place Pete would ever have imagined living in if Robert Randall hadn't extended the hand of friendship those first couple of days after Pete moved out and was staying in a guest house on Newport Road.

So, yeah, if Randall's coughing woke him up Pete was hardly going to complain. Instead he buried his face in the pillow, tried to get back to sleep. Wasn't easy; this was always the time he missed Viv, waking up next to her in the morning, a warm sleeping body next to you, it was just an inexpressible comfort. Just another heart beating close to yours. He missed that. That and the sex of course. Funny, really: the sex had carried on regardless. God knows who she was thinking of when they were doing it but it had never been a problem and now he missed it.

Been a month now and he hadn't had the glimmer of any action. His mates on the paper had all been joking about how he was going to have the time of his life now he was single again, girls all like older fellers, blah blah. Well, maybe it was just he was out of practice. Truth of it was he'd never been much in practice. He'd hardly been Mr Loverman before he'd got together with Viv. Like she always said, if she hadn't come up to him and asked him out the first time he'd still be living with his mam. Jesus.

Still, there was that girl last night. Kim. He had her number and he would ring her, definitely. Just a question of when, really. Was it too keen if he rang her today? Almost certainly. Anyway she'd probably be in a right old state today. Probably hadn't even got to bed yet. Just the thought made Pete groan involuntarily and wrap himself tighter in the duvet, glad to have had at least some sleep and a hangover that already felt manageable.

That was another thing he'd had to get used to all over again – drinking. After years of a bottle of wine lasting a week and having a headache after a couple of beers with Viv's dad, all of a sudden he was hanging out with Robert Randall who was firmly established in the pro drinking leagues. But unlike womanising, he'd managed to adjust to the drinking easily enough; rather ominously so, in fact. Sitting in the Old Arcade with Randall at lunchtime or in the Cottage of an evening, he could see a rather scary vision of his future – a geriatric hack with an Irish tan and an outsize beer gut whose only sexual encounters were strictly commercial.

Not that Randall was like that. Randall at sixty-two was a cove with sparkling blue eyes, a shock of white hair and lines that looked mysteriously distinguished, given that he'd spent the last twenty-odd years doing nothing more arduous than the occasional vox-pop interview on international days. He also had twice the stamina of most people half his age, let alone someone two-thirds his age like Pete. He never went to sleep before four. He'd roll in from the pub around midnight then closet himself with his ancient typewriter and a bottle of Bell's and Pete would hear him furiously banging away. He never told Pete what he was working on and Pete didn't like to ask; it certainly wasn't his journalism as that was always knocked off in a couple of hours in the morning before the pubs opened. Maybe it was a novel; it was amazing how many journalists had a secret novel in them. All the girls at the *Post* were busy attempting to do *Bridget Jones Comes to Cardiff*, and the younger blokes would always brag on about how they were going to do *Trainspotting Comes to Cardiff*, except right now they were like living the life, man. Pete had even had a go himself – not a *Trainspotting* clone of course, he was hardly qualified to write one of those, but a thriller set in the world of rally driving. He'd really enjoyed working on it for a bit, but Viv would always go on at him to do stuff around the house and he ended up shelving it.

Looking back now, he could see she was jealous of anything took up his time, but then he'd just thought it was normal. But enough of that it-was-all-Viv's-fault crap. Pete knew it had suited him, all that domesticity, all that predictability. The strange thing, and the thing Viv would never forgive him for, was the way it had suddenly stopped suiting him. Strange . . . he thought, then early-morning tiredness swept over him and he gratefully submitted to it.

When he woke up again, just before eight, he could hear Randall coughing once more but this time from further away and the smell of bacon was in the air. Soon he was sat at the table across from Randall, a mound of newspapers between them. Randall was smoking, of course, and drinking coffee, of course. Pete was finishing off two eggs and two rashers of bacon, mopping up the egg with a chunk of stale baguette. Randall had obviously been much impressed by France some time in his youth, as its products seemed to make up most of his staple diet: French cigarettes, bread, cheese, coffee, red wine.

Randall waited till Pete had finished eating, then looked over the top of the *Telegraph*. 'How was your night out?'

'All right,' said Pete, never a great one for breakfast conversation. But Randall wasn't going to leave it there.

'Welsh club, was it?'

'Yeah,' said Pete, 'you know.'

'Bunch of you go, did you?'

'Yeah,' said Pete, 'Dan, Guto, Liz, Ange and a mate of hers.'

'Oh yes, she's a nice girl, Ange.'

'Leave me alone,' said Pete, 'you're sounding like my mother. Anyway, she's going out with Guto.'

Randall shook his head. 'Not yet she isn't.'

Pete's turn to shake his head. 'Oh. Right.'

'Oh right indeed. You could do a hell of a lot worse, I can tell you, Pete boy.'

Pete laughed, looked down at his copy of the *Post*. Here he was being told how the land lies by a bloke who was only a year or two younger than his dad. But then again, when it came to romantic entanglements Robert Randall reputedly wrote the book. How many times had he been married? Five? Six? Whatever, the trouble Pete was finding at the moment was that in a lot of ways he felt like this old pipe-and-slipper geezer – kids practically grown up, about as wild and crazy as a cagoule – and that was the way most people related to him, reliable old Pete. But then there was another side to him coming out now which felt like he was still twenty-three and had been in cryogenic suspension for years.

He leafed through the paper, checked his pages were in order. It all looked OK, the photos had the right names under them, his interview with the ex-rugby player turned TV presenter was present and correct. Fashion page, recipe, token book review, check check check. Sometimes he looked at this stuff of a morning and couldn't remember ever having written or commissioned any of it. It was as though he actually was doing it in his sleep. Maybe his job wasn't challenging enough. He smiled. Of course it wasn't challenging; that was the whole point, the whole way he'd run his life. You could put it on his tombstone –

Pete Duke: he ducked life's challenges. He put the paper down. Time to start another day of it.

'You ready to go?' he asked Randall. Like he always did. And Randall shook his head like he always did. 'Be along a little bit later,' he said.

3

Bobby Ranger was in Asda's thinking bad thoughts about Maria. Like how come it was always Bobby got up in the morning, got Jamal his breakfast, took him to school? How come Lady Muck got to lie in bed snoring like a bloody heifer cause she's drunk God knows how many Moscow Mules the night before? Come to that, how come it was Bobby in Asda's checking out the two-for-one offers on oven chips and remembering to get some more bubble bath?

It was a joke was what it was. There was her, meant to be this evil mean bloody pimp, and yet she spent all her bloody time running round for a lazy cow, only ended up being a hustler cause she was too bone bloody idle to do a proper job. It was time Bobby got a few things sorted out.

She left the trolley where it was, next to the frozen-foods aisle, and wandered over to have a look at the clothes. Clothes in Asda weren't too bad. Coming to a bit of a pass, mind, when you started looking at the clothes in supermarkets thinking they're not too bad, but that was getting older for you. Anyway mostly she just ended up buying stuff for Jamal. But Bobby didn't begrudge that; she loved Jamal, loved buying him things, liked to see him look smart when she took him into school.

So there she is looking at these kids' jean jackets and thinking they're actually pretty nice and they've got them right up to teenager's sizes, so she tries one on herself, then looks in the mirror and sees herself there – a short but stocky 38-year-old woman, light brown skin and freckles, her hair still in the same short locks she's been wearing since the dawn of time, and she knows she really does still look like a teenage boy, but today she kind of wished she didn't, wished she looked her age. So she takes the jacket off and hunts for one in a little-kid's size, thinking Jamal'd look nice in one of them even if wasn't that practical if it rained or whatever, when someone taps her on the shoulder and she turns round and there's Mikey Thompson.

'Mikey,' she says, 'hell are you doing here?'

'Easy, Bob. You like that jacket?'

Bobby shrugged.

Mikey looked at the price tag. £19.99.

'Tenner, Bob?'

Bobby did her best to suppress a smile. 'Nah,' she said, 's'not that nice. Fiver maybe.'

'Fiver? What are you talking about, girl? You think it's worth risking getting nicked for a bloody fiver? Fuck off.'

Bobby paused; she still had a hundred quid left over from last night. What the hell. 'All right,' she said, 'tenner.'

'Sweet,' said Mikey. 'So how's your girl Maria?'

'Same as,' said Bobby, 'and you keep your hands off, right.' Mikey'd had a go at pimping once or twice over the years, always ended up with some girl giving him a good slap.

'Christ, Bob,' said Mikey, acting all injured, 'what d'you take me for?'

Bobby was just about to reply when she noticed that sometime in the last thirty seconds Mikey had made the jacket vanish. Calmly he led the way over towards the lingerie. 'Anything else you fancy, Bob?'

Bobby laughed; she wasn't a lingerie kind of girl. 'Later, Mikey,' she said, 'got to finish my shopping.'

'Sure,' said Mikey, 'you catch me in the Custom House later on, yeah, I've just got a couple more orders to fill.' He paused.

'Yeah, Bob,' he said, 'last day this week, isn't it? Where you going to go?'

'Search me, Mikey,' said Bobby, 'search me.'

'Yeah well,' said Mikey, 'long as they don't search me.'

Bobby laughed and walked back over to the food section shaking her head. Mikey Thompson was one of those people, no matter what they did – and he was always trying to pull shit – you just had to laugh. Partly it was his size, hardly any bigger than her five two, partly it was just the way any time you saw him didn't matter how pissed off with life you were you couldn't help smiling. Anyway, that was Mikey. And he was a damn good shoplifter, no question about that.

She was looking forward to giving Jamal the jacket. He was just at the age now, five, that he'd started to notice what he was wearing. She loved buying him stuff, seeing his face light up, all that. Suddenly, as she was reaching around in a giant box of potatoes, trying to find some weren't already going green, there were tears rolling down her face. What was the matter with her? Ever since she'd had the hysterectomy, two years ago now, she'd been like this, crying over nothing. Crying over milk that was so long spilt, it was practically fossilised.

Yeah, sure it was hard when your mum doesn't want you, dumps you in a home. Yeah, it was hard not even knowing who your dad was. Well roll over Beethoven, tell him the fucking news.

Bobby wiped her face. Bobby Ranger was damned if anyone was going to see her crying. But what dried her tears from the inside was letting herself say it. Something she'd been brooding on for months now. She was going to look for him. She was going to find her bastard dad. Living or dead, Bobby Ranger was going to find him.

4

Pete was sat at his desk, ten to eleven, just waiting to go in for his regular eleven o'clock with Graham the editor. In front of him he had a shortlist of today's features plus a longer list of possible stories for the future. Central to this was an ever-present wish list of the three or four A-list Welsh celebs that the *Welsh Post* would gladly interview any time they hoved into view. Catherine Zeta-Jones, Sir Anthony Hopkins, Tom Jones. Charlotte Church. Below that was the list of names you actually landed on a good day: Ioan Gruffudd and/or Matthew Rhys, Cerys from Catatonia, Julien MacDonald. Underneath that was the list of people you'd settle for on a quiet news day and to be honest most days on the *Welsh Post* were quiet news days – soap stars, weather girls, sportsmen, TV chefs and all the rest of them. Pete hardly ever did these. He hated doing interviews and Graham was convinced that women made the best interviewers anyway. So he had a couple of girls took care of those, while Pete himself would do most of the think pieces – should the Assembly building go ahead, where to now for Welsh rugby, that kind of stuff. Which more often than not meant simply dusting off last year's article and sticking in a couple of references to something that had been on the TV in the past week.

Was that cynical? Pete didn't think he was a cynical kind of person, just a realist really. The point was that he wasn't dissatisfied; he didn't think he ought to be writing leaders for *The Times*. Far as Pete was concerned he'd done pretty well to get where he was and, if he could do the job in his sleep these days, well so what, better than not being up to it. Plus there were some decent perks; just now, for instance, he was on the phone to the Audi people trying to get them to let him review the new TT over the weekend. That was a little gig he'd secured for himself, motoring correspondent, and he really enjoyed it — every weekend another new motor to try out. It was the one part of the job Viv had been impressed by and all. She liked to see a flash motor parked in their drive, liked to wave at Julie and Duncan next door when they'd head up to the Brecon Beacons for a tryout of a Sunday. Damn, he didn't want to think about that. It was amazing how it was the little things that made you miss being married, just those bloody boring familiar little rituals you never thought twice about at the time.

The Audi PR came back to his left ear, said the car would be fine. Pete said thanks, put his phone down, wondered if he'd be driving it alone.

'Pete.'

Graham calling him in. Pete gathered up his papers, walked into Graham's office overlooking St Mary Street, sat himself down.

'So what've you got for me today?'

Pete handed Graham the piece of paper. Graham scanned it quickly, said, 'Who's Owain Meredudd?'

'Young Welsh artist, Catherine Zeta-Jones bought one of his paintings.'

'Got a picture of them together?'

'Yeah.'

'Good man.'

Graham put the piece of paper down. Editorial discussions didn't take long. They'd both been doing their jobs for what seemed like for ever and Pete knew exactly what Graham was looking for. Pictures of CZJ mostly.

'Anything good in the pipeline?'

Pete shrugged, ran through the list of usual suspects.

Graham sat back, rubbed his chin a bit and generally acted like the great thinker rather than the efficient sub-editor and good man with a budget that he was. Pete braced himself for a suggestion.

'How about a feature on Leslie St Clair?'

Pete raised his eyebrows. This was actually a perfectly solid idea. Leslie St Clair was an interesting man, from what Pete knew about him. Came from the Cardiff docks, been a pop singer in the early Sixties, now he was a publisher and entrepreneur – computer mags and dirty mags. There was repeated talk about him being in the market to buy Cardiff City football club. He was based in London, though, which was why Pete had never got round to covering him before.

'Sure,' he said, 'good idea. I'll put Cherri on to it.' Cherri was Pete's star interviewer; he was sure he was going to lose her to one of the London tabloids before long.

'Great,' said Graham, 'I was thinking for Saturday week, yes?'

'Fine,' said Pete, 'I'll get her on it right away.'

He called St Clair's company, Rival Publications, got on to St Clair's PA and in no time was passed on to the man himself, who seemed bizarrely pleased to be talking to Pete, and would you believe it he was going to be in Cardiff tomorrow so why didn't they meet for lunch, and before he knew it Pete had said yes. Oh well, looked like he'd be doing the story himself. Never mind, he'd been thinking he should get out of the office more. Time to live a little, you know. He laughed at himself but even as he did so he was digging into his wallet till he found Kim, the girl from last night's number. Was it a bit pushy calling her next day? Maybe, but then again Pete figured he wasn't that interesting a guy that you'd remember him for weeks, might as well strike while the iron was warm. He picked up the phone.

5

Half six Bobby and Maria were ready to go to work. At least Bobby was; Maria was still pissing about with her make-up. Little Jamal was running round in circles shouting while *The Flintstones* was on full volume on the Cartoon Network and Maria had some garage nonsense blasting out in the bedroom and Donna the babysitter was chopsing on about her new boyfriend and what a fucking great car he had and if he didn't she'd dump him cause he didn't show her half enough respect, like, and Bobby was thinking she didn't shut up she'd show some real disrespect, right in the gob, and the same went for Maria she didn't get her arse in gear, and oh fucking hell Jamal love could you stop doing that.

'Fuck!' she shouted at no one in particular and stomped into the bathroom where she dug out a couple of Ibuprofens and chased them down with a swig of mouthwash, half of which spilt on the floor, her hands were shaking so much. She sat on the edge of the bath, amazed. She was nervous. Just cause she'd got a little date lined up for this evening, soon as she'd got Maria safely on the beat. She was shaking like a bloody teenager. Actually, cancel that: when Bobby was a teenager she'd had no nerves at all. Balls of bloody steel she'd had back then, little sixteen-year-old black girl going down those hardcore lesbian clubs, Barrells and that, walk straight up to the sharpest girl in the room, ask her how's about it. No, it was getting old fucks you up. Here she was, thirty-eight and shaking cause some pissy little piece worked for the TV had asked her for a drink. Hell was wrong with her? Next thing she'd be feeling guilty. Like she should be sitting at home with her legs crossed while Maria did it with half Cardiff. Bollocks. Still, it had been a while. Four, five years they'd been seeing each other now. On-off, like, at first, but most of the time it had been good. Not so much lately, though. Maria was letting herself go a bit, truth be told. Couldn't blame her, really, what she had to do, but still you didn't keep your standards up in this game you went downhill fast. Bobby knew that all right, seen it happen enough times with other girls.

'Christ,' she said, back out in the living room, 'get your arse in gear, girl. We got a job to do.'

Maria sighed extravagantly but then caught one of Bobby's coldest looks and swiftly got to her feet, went over to Jamal and gave him a big hug and kiss. Bobby followed suit while Maria gave Donna instructions as to what programmes Jamal was allowed to watch before bed, like Donna didn't know from the five nights a week she was usually here, but still Maria liked to feel she was doing the proper mum business.

They parked up round the back of the Custom House, had a quick spliff and Bobby came in with Maria. They had a drink together then Maria went out on the beat and before Bobby had got back to her car she saw a newish Escort pull over and the window wound down next to Maria.

Five minutes later Bobby was at the bar of the Dome in the Atlantic Wharf UCI. Bobby loved the UCI – twelve-screen cinema, bowling alley, restaurants, bars, the worst nightclub she'd ever been in – of course she did. Cardiff loved the UCI; you went there any time day or night it was packed. There it was parked in a bit of old docks wasteland no one had bothered with for decades, like a giant spaceship come to land, and from the start Cardiff loved it. Course Bobby and Maria were some of the few people who could walk there and they'd do that a lot in the afternoon, take Jamal over there after school, let him have a look at the video-game machines and take him to a film there was anything on. Bobby'd buy him loads of sweets from the pick-'n'-mix – most expensive pick-'n'-mix in the known world by the way, don't say she didn't warn you – and it was nice. You know, an improvement of the area, like.

But Bobby wasn't stupid and she could see what it was as well. Another death-knell for the kind of life she knew down there. The street prostitution – how long were they going to let that last down here? And now they had the Assembly. No way all the politicians were going to want to see all that. Not that they weren't regular customers, a few of them, but they liked it all out of sight and out of mind the way the docks used to be. Now, well Christ only knew.

'Hiya,' said a voice beyond Bobby. It was Kim, the girl from the BBC, standing there in all black; trousers and shirt buttoned up to the neck.

'Hiya, darlin',' said Bobby, smiling. 'What're you drinking?'

'Gin and tonic,' said Kim and Bobby waved to Roger the French guy behind the bar and ordered the drink along with another bottle of cider for herself. She didn't usually drink much these days, but she'd got the feeling tonight might be a bit of an exception.

'So,' said Kim, once they'd got their drinks and found a little table right at the back of the bar, 'you want to go and see a film then?'

'No,' said Bobby. 'It's you I was wanting to see.'

Kim giggled and blushed a bit and said, 'Oh yeah, I just thought meeting here . . .'

'No,' said Bobby. 'This is where I live down here, innit.'

'Oh yeah, of course,' said Kim, blushing again.

Bobby could see she was on a winner here already so she didn't say anything, just moved her chair round so she was right next to Kim and put her hand on Kim's thigh.

Kim didn't bat an eyelid, just smiled and waved her hand towards the waiter to order up another gin and tonic – more, Bobby suspected, so she would have an excuse for what she was about to do than because she needed it.

'So,' said Kim once her drink showed up, 'I suppose you'd like to know a bit more about the documentary.'

'Um, yeah,' said Bobby, who to tell the truth had completely forgotten that that was Kim's pretext for setting up this drink. Kim was this girl from the BBC, a researcher. She'd done some story before down the docks, and got to know a few of the people. Anyway Bobby had met her down the Hippo the night before, and Kim was chatting to Maria who she knew from God knows where and Bobby barged in thinking the snotty bitch wasn't stealing her girlfriend and then Maria told her not to be stupid, which normally she'd have given her a slap for but this once she could see she had a point, so Bobby'd got to motor-mouthing away about this and that and the life and Maria'd got bored and gone off for a dance and Bobby got into one about what a great pimp she was and this Kim had got horny for it you could see but she, like, covered it up with all this horse-shit about what a great subject for a documentary – the secret world of the lesbian pimps or something. Course Bobby knew a chat-up when she heard one but now here they were and this Kim wanted to carry on pretending – well, fine. So 'Yeah,' she said, 'what about it?'

'Well,' said Kim, 'are you up for it?'

She was leaning into Bobby now, their cheeks almost touching, and Bobby could feel her squeezing her thighs closer together. Christ, she thought, time to get on out of here and into some private place soonest.

'Yeah,' she said again, 'well maybe. Tell you what, this isn't the best place to discuss that kind of business, you know. How about we go back to mine?'

'Your place?' Kim looked almost shocked for a moment. Bobby wondered what she'd been expecting. A quick one in the Ladies'?

'Or yours, darlin', I don't mind.'

Kim looked suddenly relieved. 'Yeah,' she said, 'that's fine. You want a lift?'

'No,' said Bobby, 'got my car out the front too. I'll follow you like.'

They had just made it out to the car park and Kim had half turned to Bobby, ready to snog her Bobby was sure, when a mobile went off. Bobby and Kim both reached into their pockets but it was Bobby's that was ringing. Maria.

'Quick,' she said, 'I got trouble. Back of Aspro's.'

It took Bobby three and a half minutes to make it down Bute Street to the front of Aspro's Travel Agency – three minutes' driving and half a minute to put Kim off – 'Sorry, love, emergency come up, call me, yeah?' Kim had nodded quickly and Bobby was sure she was in there. Driving down Bute Street, though, she couldn't help feeling like a total bitch.

As she got out of the car she pulled her lock knife out from where she kept it hidden, taped in place under the gear-stick cover. She walked round the back of the boarded-up old travel agency till she came to the alley.

'Ri,' she called. No answer. Bobby kept on walking down the alley. It was pitch dark; there was a street lamp at one end but someone had smashed the bulb out of it ages back. Mostly the girls liked it dark; kept you from having to focus too much on the punter. Personally Bobby liked to keep as far away as possible from the business end of things. You went out with a hustler, you didn't want to know all the details and you sure as hell didn't actually want to see them on the job.

There was still no sign of life in the alley. She came to the point where it dog-legged round to the right and dead-ended in a warehouse. Christ, she was scared now, she had to admit. She turned the corner and called out 'Ri' again. Still nothing. She waited for a moment, letting her eyes adjust to what little moonlight there was. Still nothing, just a few horrible little noises she was sure were rats. Christ, she didn't know how the girls did it, coming down here with some bloke they'd met thirty seconds previous, opening themselves up to the bloke up against the wall. She was almost at the end of the alley now and there was definitely nothing and nobody there. No crazed punter, no Maria lying bloody on the ground. Nothing. Just a door flapping open on the side of the warehouse.

Bobby freaked when she saw that door swing open and she just ran back out the alley, almost falling as she skidded round the corner. As she made it back on to the street she was at the point of hyperventilating. No way was she going in the warehouse. No way no way no way. She'd seen enough movies, shouted enough times at the screen telling the stupid girl not to go in the haunted house on Friday the thirteenth to meet Freddie. She was going to do the sensible thing, get help, ring the police. No way was she a coward, no way no way. She was doing the right thing.

She got out her mobile, cursed One 2 One to hell and back when she couldn't get a signal, then crossed over the road to the Custom House, knowing the payphone wouldn't work but it was an emergency, like, and Peter the landlord would let her use the phone behind the bar.

First person she saw when she walked in the door was Maria standing with a can of Breaker in her hand, arm round Big Lesley.

Bobby walked straight up to her and smacked her one full in the face.

6

Pete was sat at a table in a place called the Cambrian Club along with Robert Randall and a bloke called Gary or possibly Geraint who was a playwright and a girl called Natalie who worked for a film company.

The Cambrian was the place you ran into these kinds of people. Up till three weeks ago Pete had never been there in his life; since he'd been staying with Randall he'd practically become a regular. Not that Randall was particularly bothered about drinking with micro celebs from the Welsh media, but he was certainly fond of somewhere you could get a late drink.

So, round about eleven, they'd decamp from whichever pub Randall had chosen for the evening and walk down leafy Cathedral Road away from the city centre till they got to the short strip of shops that made up the heart of Pontcanna – or 'Cardiff's media village' as it was obligatory to refer to it in the *Post*. Past the shops and you came to the Cambrian which looked like your average wine bar but being a members' club could stay open till all-hours.

Randall wasn't a member, of course, he was just one of those blokes that everyone knew and no one could say no to, so they'd be waved in and Pete would get the drinks in while Randall glad-handed and then they'd end up at a table talking to techies or directors, writers or editors or, as in tonight's case, dodgy playwrights.

Pete had drifted away from the conversation, some typically bloody Welsh argument about Arts Council funding – you took the subsidy out of the arts in Wales you'd have a big fat zero far as Pete could see – but, hey, meanwhile good luck to them. Pete wasn't in the mood for an argument. He was feeling pleased with himself. He'd called up Kim at the BBC, nervous as all get out, and she'd sounded pleased to hear from him and didn't even wait for him to ask, just went, 'You fancy meeting up, then?' and just about gave him time to grunt a yes before telling him she couldn't do tonight as she was on a top story but how about Friday, meet in Ha Ha's about eight, see you, and put the phone down, leaving Pete gazing out the window thinking how simple was that? How different to when he was twenty or so, last time he'd been in this position, when he'd spend for ever faffing about chasing after some girl who most likely didn't want to know. Which sort of explained why he'd ended up with Viv, who clearly hadn't cared what the rules were and had just walked up to him at a barbecue on a Sunday afternoon in 1980 something and kissed him and taken the whole thing out of his hands for which he had clearly been so bloody grateful that he'd married her and spent umpteen years with her.

And then, just to prove that Pete Duke was now the kind of guy made things happen, didn't hang around scratching his arse while the world whistled by, Kim walked into the Cambrian Club.

She didn't see him at first, just walked in by herself, frowning a bit till someone waved at her and she plastered on a smile. She didn't notice Pete till she'd gone up to the bar, ordered a drink then turned round to survey the room. As soon as she spotted him, though, she waved, and moments later she was pecking him on the cheek and squeezing in next to him.

'All right, darlin'?'

'Yeah,' said Pete, 'you know,' and smiled at her and she smiled back and hey, just like that, he thought of something else to say. 'How did your interview go?' Easy.

Kim made a face. 'Started off all right, but went a bit pear-shaped after that.' She picked up her drink that looked like a vodka tonic, took a big gulp. 'Christ, needed that.'

'Yeah,' said Pete, 'so who was it with, what's the story?'

'Christ,' said Kim, laughing, 'I've only known you ten minutes and you're already trying to nick my stories.'

'No, no,' said Pete, immediately embarrassed, 'I didn't mean . . .'

Kim nudged him in the ribs. 'No, only teasing. I don't mind telling you what it is, just don't tell anyone else, specially not anyone in here. Anyway, right, the story is, well basically I met this amazing woman the other night. She's this really tough black woman, right, and I asked what she did and you know what she said?'

Pete shook his head.

'She goes, "I'm a pimp. Top pimp." You believe that? People think of pimps, it's always some big guy with gold teeth and a Rottweiler, not a girl. So I can see it straight away, the documentary title *The Secret World of the Lesbian Pimps* – great, yeah? – and I ask her right out if she'll do it and she just says yeah, sure, and I'm like I don't believe it, what a great story.'

'Christ,' said Pete. 'So was that who you just went to see? Did she do the interview?'

'No,' said Kim, 'that's why I'm in here drinking vodka. I met up with her at the UCI, had a good chat. We were all just ready to go back and do the interview when her bloody mobile goes and she has to charge off somewhere, so I don't know if I pushed too hard and pissed her off or what.'

'Doubt it,' said Pete. 'Probably just had to get back to work.'

Kim frowned. 'Yeah, I guess.'

'So who else are you going to talk to?' asked Pete, getting into this now, thinking how he'd handle a story like this, not that the

Post would be seen dead with something this seedy. 'Are you going to talk to the hookers?'

'Hustlers,' said Kim.

'Oh, right. Anyway, d'you think this woman will let you talk to her girls?'

'I dunno,' said Kim, looking worried, 'it's early days.'

'What about the punters?' said Pete. 'It might be interesting to talk to the punters if you can.'

'Who cares about the bloody punters? This is about women, it's not about some sad old perves.'

'Hmm,' said Pete, not wanting to say that it was the punters that interested him, that he had often wondered what depths of loneliness, what desperate need for human comfort, sent men down to the Custom House, not wanting to say there were four-a.m. times lately when he'd seen this vision of himself in years to come, a grey man in a grey car paying some lost young girl to make him feel joined to humanity for half an hour. Not thoughts you wanted to share with a girl you'd just met, really, and anyway it probably wasn't like that, probably all the punters were married blokes with Vauxhall Vectras and nasty little desires. Except he knew they weren't all like that. Hadn't he been driving past the Custom House years ago, seen a familiar car pull up, seen a girl get in, checked the car's number plate to be double sure it was his cousin Carl, lived with his mam in upper Bargoed, went to chapel every single bastard day of the year. Cousin Carl with his stupid moon face and clothes his mam put out for him. Hadn't he seen cousin Carl take a girl in his car and hadn't he driven round the corner, pulled up his own car to the kerb and put his head in his hands and cried, overcome by the sadness of the world? Of course he had, but it still wasn't anything you wanted to say to this girl you'd just met, so he just smiled and shrugged, and said, 'Still, might be an interesting angle, though.'

'Yeah, maybe,' said Kim, but he could see she'd lost focus on him now; her gaze was wandering past him, checking out who else was in the club. 'Shit,' she said then, her eyes finally resettling on Pete's face, 'you know what I could do with right now?'

'No,' said Pete, his heart suddenly beating faster.

'A nice fat line of Charlie. You don't have any on you, do you?'

'No,' said Pete, feeling an involuntary wave of repulsion, telling himself not to be such a bloody puritan, didn't he read his own bloody newspaper, didn't he know that the young, free and single used drugs with casual ease? 'Sorry.'

'Oh God, your face,' said Kim, and laughed and grabbed his cheek, gave it a quick squeeze. 'Course you don't. Ange told me you were Mr Straight and Narrow.'

Pete started to protest, 'I'm not . . .' but Kim cut him off.

'Course you are. But don't worry, it's all right, makes a change from most of the people you get in here, all – what's the opposite of straight and narrow?'

'Bent and wide?' offered Pete.

Kim laughed. 'Yeah, bent and wide, that's about right. Thing is, though, I'm feeling like getting a bit bent and wide myself tonight, so if you'll excuse me . . .' She stood up then, picked up her drink. And started to move off then thought of something and turned and bent down to Pete. 'I tell you what, though. Friday night, how about instead of Ha Ha's you come down to the Custom House with me? It's the last night before they close it down, be good for my story and should be interesting.'

'All right,' said Pete, thinking that was one weird place for a date but what the hell.

'Cool,' said Kim and pecked him on the cheek, 'see you Friday,' and walked off towards the bar and started chatting animatedly to a tall bloke in a leather jacket, goatee and an earring. Pete saw her whisper conspiratorially in his ear, saw them head off, one a few seconds after the other, up the stairs towards the toilets, then felt an acrid mix of jealousy and disgust – or was it desire? – knot up his stomach.

7

Bobby was thinking. Jamal had woken them up at six and Bobby couldn't get back to sleep, still pissed off with Maria, and she'd got up and made a cup of coffee and was sitting in the living room watching the sun come up from behind the UCI and thinking through her options.

Something had to change. She just couldn't handle things like last night any more. Thinking your girl's been killed in some alleyway. And now with the Custom House on its way out the girls were already looking around, finding a patch here or a patch there, but without the pub as a base it was going to be hopeless.

So what were the options? Well, a lot of girls worked in the massage parlours now, three or four of them around town. And from the girls' point of view it had its advantages. You were inside, for one thing, and you had a bit of back-up any punters started getting funny. On the other hand, though, a lot of the girls didn't like it cause it was a bit too much like having a job, clocking in clocking out, and they'd always be complaining about how the management wouldn't let them have a little smoke on the job, or a little drink, wasn't the laugh you could have in the Custom House.

Other problem, from Bobby's point of view, was Maria went to work in one of them places, what would Bobby's role be? Maria's handing over half her earnings to the management in Dawn's Sauna or wherever, she's not going to be wanting to cut Bobby in after. Unless . . . unless Bobby was the management.

Why didn't she open up her own place? Bobby shook her head. Could she take a step up?

Maria came out of the bedroom then, rubbing her eyes, looking rougher than rough, heading straight for the bathroom. Bobby waited for her to come out then grabbed her.

'Sit down, girl, I got an idea.'

'Not now, Bob, I'm sleeping.'

Bobby grabbed her by the wrist. 'No, you're not. Sit here and listen.'

Maria shook Bobby's hand off. 'Give us a cup of coffee at least.'

Bobby sighed and turned round to the kettle, busied herself making a couple of mugs of coffee while Maria slumped down at the table and lit a fag.

'I've been thinking,' said Bobby, once she'd put the coffee down on the table, her voice a little nervous, 'maybe I could open us up a little sauna-massage place.'

'Where's the money?' said Maria.

'What?'

'Where's the money, you going to buy a place, put the saunas and shit in it. Where's the money?'

Bobby frowned. 'You got to have all that stuff?'

'Course you have,' said Maria. 'You don't have the sauna, the massage tables and that, you think they're going to let you stay open? You don't have that stuff, you might as well hang a red light outside, call it Bobby's Knocking Shop.'

'Yeah,' said Bobby, frowning, 'I suppose.'

Maria sipped her coffee, then brightened. 'Tell you what I've been thinking.'

'What?'

'Lap-dancing. You know up town they got a couple of nights. Was talking to one of the girls in the Cross the other night, said she's making a packet doing it.'

'She shag the blokes afterwards or what?'

Maria shrugged. 'Just dancing. Least that's what she said she did. Said some of the other girls do some extras, like. But they kick you out, they catch you setting something up.'

Maria jumped up, pulled a dancing pose, then bent herself right over and looked back at Bobby from between her legs. 'What d'you reckon? Think I'd be good at it?'

Bobby looked at her, trying to imagine, if she'd never seen Maria before, what she'd reckon. She saw a tallish girl – five seven or so – dark brown hair with a dodgy henna job scraped back in a ponytail, good body, tits a bit small maybe, dunno if the blokes expected the girls to have boob jobs. Still, she had a nice rose tattoo on her left one. Had a couple of piercings too – nothing kinky, just nose and navel. Worst thing was her skin; dead pasty, though what d'you expect you live on chips and Red Bull and vodka and speed? Hurt Bob to acknowledge it but there it was: two years of street prostitution were starting to leave their mark on Maria. She didn't make some changes soon she'd be on the fast track down. And try as Bobby might to tell herself it was none of her business, she knew it was crap. She wanted Maria to come off the streets, it was up to her to make it happen.

'Dunno, girl,' she said eventually. 'Clean yourself up a bit you might have a chance.'

Maria flicked a V-sign at her from between her legs then stood back up and walked huffily into the bedroom. But ten minutes later, much to Bobby's amazement, she was running a bath. Stayed in there for hours too and by the time she came out – after Bobby'd given Jamal his breakfast and was just about to walk him to school – she was really looking dead good – something like the way Bobby remembered her, first time she ever saw her come in the Custom House, back when doing the odd punter was still a bit of a laugh, little top-up for the giro, and not the life.

'What d'you reckon then?' said Maria. 'Think I should give it a go?'

Bobby patted her on the bum, a for-real smile coming unbidden to her lips. 'I'd pay you, girl, I'll tell you that much.'

Bobby headed into town around lunchtime, drove in even though it was less than a mile and probably quicker to walk by the time you'd parked and all, but she couldn't face all the dumb conversations she'd have to have on the way if she walked down Bute Street. She left the motor in the car park next to Toys 'R' Us and started walking up through the Hayes, her head still crowded with thoughts.

One moment she had her mind on business, checking out the new lap-dancing club in town, finding out what the deal was for the girls, next minute she was lost in the past, walking past Halfords looking down the Oxford Arcade and remembering the club they used to have down there – Hunters. First nice-looking gay club they'd had in Cardiff. Before that all the girls used to go to Barrells, just over by the bridge, but they knocked that down and opened up Hunters. Nineteen years old she was then and already queen of the scene. Old before her time, she thought about it now. Nineteen: she'd been running with the City Boys for years, only girl in the soul crew. She'd been in the band too, had the hit record. Thought she was ace. And she was. Had she felt higher than that – nineteen years old in Hunters, Evelyn King singing 'Love Come Down' on the sound system, any new girl walked in the room Bobby knew she could have her.

Eighteen more years past and gone and where was she now? A bastard pimp. Top pimp, though, she'd say that for herself and all the girls would agree. Top pimp with the gold teeth to prove it. Top pimp with two hundred and fifty quid in the building society, a girlfriend who was right on the edge of the skids, right on the edge of a decline Bobby had seen too many times with too many other girls. Top pimp with a hysterectomy two years ago. Top pimp who was tired of the life. Top pimp who felt like sitting down in the Hayes Island Café with a cup of tea and never moving again, letting them roll her into the gutter when the night came down. Let her be, leave her in peace.

Christ, snap out of it. She was Bobby Ranger and she was going to get it together.

Her mobile went off. Disorientated, it took Bobby a moment to remember which pocket she had it in. Finally she snapped it open just before the call got redirected to her voicemail.

'Whassup?' she said.

'Is that Bobby?' said a voice. Female, Cardiff but educated. Kim.

'How you doing, darlin'?'

'I'm fine,' Kim giggled. 'You sort out your problem last night? I was sorry you had to go.'

'Me too,' said Bobby, 'me too.'

'Where are you now?'

'In town, going round Cupid's Lounge.'

'The lap-dancing club? Really? I was thinking of doing a story about that place.'

'Yeah?' said Bobby. 'Why don't you come down, meet me there?'

'Now?'

'No, next week.'

'Well, I don't know . . . yeah, why not? Will there be anyone there?'

'Manager should be there. I knows him a bit.'

'Yeah?' Kim sounded really interested now. 'D'you think he'd mind me coming along?'

'Don't see why, pretty girl like you.'

Kim giggled again. 'No, you know, me being from the TV.'

'Don't tell him,' said Bobby. 'Say you're looking for a job there. Go undercover, like.'

'Oh,' said Kim, and paused. 'Well I'm hardly dressed for it.'

'It's not exactly about what clothes you're wearing, darlin', is it?'

Kim laughed. 'I suppose not. OK, you're on. I'll see you in Ha Ha's in fifteen minutes, all right?'

'Fine,' said Bobby, and smiled to herself. This ought to be a laugh, she reckoned.

Half an hour later and Kim was taking Bobby's arm as they came out of Ha Ha's, Kim's face flushed by the two gin and tonics she'd downed in the fifteen minutes they'd been in there.

Bobby squeezed her arm briefly then removed it. Bobby wasn't one for public displays of affection. Girls from the beat saw her walking arm in arm with an up-herself piece like Kim they'd piss themselves. Any suggestion she wasn't tougher than the rest, she'd have a mutiny on her hands.

The club was in Crockherbtown Lane down the side of the New Theatre. One of those buildings must have been there for ever but you never noticed it before. There was a lorry pulled up outside and a feller lugging beer kegs over the pavement. Bobby and Kim stepped round him and walked into Cupid's Lounge.

Inside it was a typical nightclub by day; all rips in the velvet banquettes and a pervasive stink of beer, fags and cleaning solvents. Marco was stood behind the bar reading the racing page of the *Mirror*.

'All right, bra?' said Bobby.

Marco looked up, then did a comedy double-take. 'Looking for a job then, Bob? Bob a job?' He started laughing at his own joke.

'No,' said Bobby, rolling her eyes, 'but my friend here is. Marco, this is K . . . Kelly.'

'Hi, Kelly,' said Marco, looking Kim up and down. 'You a dancer then?'

'Not really,' said Kim, then paused for a moment before carrying on, 'but I'm good at taking my clothes off.' She burst out in a peal of laughter.

Marco looked at Bobby and raised his eyebrows. Bobby shrugged.

'You done it before then?' asked Marco.

Kim shook her head, said, 'Well, not in public,' and laughed again.

'So you haven't got an agent then?'

Kim frowned. 'What, you need an agent to take your clothes off, do you?'

Marco nodded.

'All right then, Bobby here's my agent, how about that?'

Marco shook his head. 'Sorry, love. Thing is, all the professional dancers we use come from one agency; it's like a contractual thing. Tell you what, though, we're running an amateur night Tuesdays, hundred-quid prize for the best dancer. Why don't you come along to that, love? Feller from the agency'll be along too. You want to do some more, maybe he'll sign you up.'

Kim pouted. 'Don't you think I look good? Why don't I do a dance here for you now?'

Marco put his hands up in fake horror. 'Save it for Tuesday, darling. It's not what I think, it's what Bernie thinks that counts.'

Kim looked all hurt, like she couldn't believe the whole world wasn't dying to see her take her clothes off, but Bobby didn't have time for that.

'Bernie?' she said.

'Yeah, Bernie Walters,' said Marco. 'He's the agent books all my dancers.'

'Fuck,' said Bobby.

'Don't tell me you got a problem with Bernie,' said Marco, grinning. 'Everybody loves old Bernie.'

'Yeah,' said Bobby. 'They don't all love Kenny Ibadulla, though, do they?'

'Bobby,' said Kim, 'what are you talking about?'

'Nothing,' said Bobby, grimacing. 'C'mon, girl, let's get out of here.'

Marco smiled, went back to his paper. 'Tuesday night, Kelly, if you fancy it.'

'Yeah, maybe,' said Kim, then saw that Bobby was already out the door, gave Marco a quick wave and followed after her.

'What was that all about?' asked Kim, catching up with Bobby as she turned down towards Queen Street.

'Old business, old bullshit.'

'Anything I can help with?'

Bobby looked at her, started to scowl then managed a weary smile. How to explain it? Kenny Ibadulla, Bernie Walters – all these fellers had her world wrapped up, left her to feed on the crumbs. Christ, was she tired of it.

'No,' she said eventually, 'I don't think so, doll. Listen, I better go, got business to attend to. You give me a ring, yeah?'

'Yeah, sure,' said Kim, looking a little crestfallen, then brightening. 'Oh, and I'll see you tomorrow, won't I?'

'You what?'

'Last night of the Custom House, remember? I'm going to be doing some filming.'

'Oh right,' said Bobby, 'later then,' and walked off fast before she could say any of the things she felt like saying, like sod your film. Is that all my life adds up to? A couple of minutes' lowlife entertainment for Mr and Mrs Normal at home in front of their TV? Look, love, there's a lesbian pimp, last one left in the wild.

8

Leslie St Clair was a laugh.

Randall had said he would be. Pete had asked him about St Clair the night before, while Randall's memory was still more or less functioning.

'I remember him when he was plain Les Sinclair, before they canonised him!' Randall had said, laughing at his own joke then carrying on. 'Started out as a boxer, mean little lightweight. Didn't like getting his pretty face messed up, though, so he moved into singing. Followed in Shirl's footsteps up to London. Used to do a lot of calypso stuff – watered-down Harry Belafonte, if you can imagine anything more horrible. Your parents probably inflicted it on you as a baby. They'd have the social services round in an instant, you tried anything like that these days. But he was a smart one, all right, old Les, always knew just when to change horses.

'I remember interviewing him years ago when I first started on the paper, must have been 1961, and he'd just done the Royal Variety Performance. And I just asked him so how long d'you think the calypso craze will carry on, just a standard little pat-ball question and I'm expecting him to say the usual shit, I'll be singing calypso till I die, and he just looks at me and says, casual as anything, "Six months, maybe nine. I'm getting out at six, though." And he did.'

'Yeah?' Pete had said. 'So what did he do next?'

'Sort of a Sammy Davis Junior thing, 'cept Les couldn't dance for toffee. Then the Beatles came along and he was at a bit of a loss for a while. Came back a bit with *The Leslie St Clair Rock and Soul Revue* but I don't know many people took him seriously. Course by then he was already diversifying, had his own theatre and everything. Lost touch with him after that. But he's still a good laugh, by all accounts, so you make sure and send him my best.'

It was fast becoming clear why Randall had liked St Clair. For starters, they weren't doing the interview in the Hilton or the St David's or any of the shiny new Cardiff landmarks the celebs usually confined themselves to, but in the Red House, a pub stuck out on the spur between the Rivers Ely and Taff, the last unmanicured bit of the bay, home to a bunch of scrapyards, a down-at-heel yacht club and a boozer that looked a bit posh about thirty years ago but had roughened up considerably in the interim while the rest of the world got smooth.

St Clair was a funny mixture of the two. He was smooth, all right, glad-handed everyone in the pub, but he was rough too in a you-can-take-the-boy-out-of-the-docks-but-you-can't-take-the-docks-out-of-the-boy kind of way.

Anyway, Pete had got there at two, expecting he'd have half an hour tops, and he'd been there for two hours now, on their third round – Pete buying them all, of course; one thing Pete had noticed about the rich was they didn't get that way by putting their hands in their pockets to buy the drinks – and Pete had had to phone Graham twice to say he was going to be late back to the office but not to worry cause he was getting some great stuff. And he was.

God knows how much of it the lawyers would let him use, of course. The stories about Dame Shirley back in the day were definitely not going to be running. Nor the stuff about Tom Jones. Wales didn't have so many cultural heroes that it was ready to see their reputations besmirched. Plus of course Pete was far from sure St Clair was telling the truth. He was the kind of feller liked a bit of mischief-making for its own sake.

Finally St Clair switched the subject to the present. He moved quickly past his computer-magazine business ('Doing fine, course it's a difficult market at the moment, but it's a lean, mean operation') and his often-stated ambition to buy Cardiff City ('Still interested, obviously, but of course Sam's doing a great job') before getting on to what was evidently his current passion.

'The Castle Market,' he said to Pete, 'that's what I'm going to call it. You know where the old Sophia Gardens exhibition centre was? Well, that's where we're going to build it. Assuming our bid's accepted, of course.'

'So what's it going to be?' asked Pete. 'Another shopping mall?'

'No,' said St Clair, 'what it is, and don't laugh, cause in my old age I've acquired a bit of a philosophy – what I call community capitalism.'

'Oh yes?' said Pete, wondering if St Clair was putting him on. 'So what's that then?'

'Let's just step outside a minute,' said St Clair, 'and I'll show you what I mean.'

'OK,' said Pete and they walked out of the pub, leaving their drinks on the table. Outside St Clair led the way to a vantage point where they could look across the bay. He pointed over towards the new development.

'What d'you reckon?' he asked.

Pete looked across the water. He could see the St David's Hotel, Techniquest and the Sports Café, hidden behind which he knew there was Mermaid Quay, with its half-dozen restaurants, bank and comedy club and so-called designer clothes shop. He didn't think anything much about it. He used to go down there with Viv and the kids now and again, for a walk on dead

Sunday afternoons, the girls complaining at being dragged away from the TV, or occasionally a family dinner at Harry Ramsden's or the Sports Café. It was OK.

'It's OK,' he said.

'Yeah,' said St Clair, 'that's exactly what it is. Nice. Nice like OK. Nice like it'll do for a place to go and eat in the evening if you can't face going into town. Yeah, it's nice. How about individual, though? Would you say it was individual?'

Pete thought about it, visualised the Mermaid Quay restaurants, the Bar 38 and the Via Fossa, the flash Italian and the flash Chinese.

'No,' he said, 'I suppose not.'

'No,' said St Clair, 'you're dead right it's not. What it is is off-the-peg bloody global capitalism. It's the kit version of a waterfront development. Half the restaurants here you could find the same place in any decent-size city in the UK: same menu, same gormless eighteen-year-olds pretending to be waiters on four quid an hour. You know what I mean?'

Pete nodded.

'Well, is that what you want for Cardiff, you want to see a whole identikit city? Cause that's what'll happen if people like you and me don't make a stand. You take the young politicians over there in the Assembly – ' St Clair gestured in the direction of the office block that still housed the Welsh Assembly while they argued about whether to build a proper one. 'That's what they think is progress – inward investment, new leisure-themed industrial park, McDonald's and Starbucks opening ten new branches a month, more jobs – bet it's the same with the young journalists on your paper.'

'Not just the young ones,' said Pete, involuntarily going along with St Clair's line of argument.

'No,' said St Clair, 'you're right there. I'm just showing what an old fart I am; it isn't just the young ones over at the Assembly or City Hall either. But what I think a city needs is a bit of soul and with this little plan I've put together – well, we might just preserve a little bit of that.'

'Oh, come on,' said Pete. 'You build a shopping mall, that's what happens, isn't it? You end up with a Starbucks in there and all?'

'Over my dead bastard body we will, son. No, what we're planning is something different – affordable units for real people to open bars, shops, restaurants – no chains, no franchises, just a place where people like you and me can be at home and a place that'll still be there when your kids grow up and they'll say oh yeah that's Cardiff that is. You see what I'm getting at?'

'Mmm,' said Pete, 'I guess.'

'Course you do, son,' said St Clair. 'So you want to mention that in your piece, I'd be very grateful. The Welsh Development Authority are making their minds up at the moment which bid to accept; won't be announced for another month but meanwhile any little nudges they get from your paper, be much appreciated.'

'Well,' said Pete, a little stiffly, 'we're not in the business of taking sides in these kinds of matters.'

'Course you're not, son, course you're not. All I'm asking is you report what I have to say. Give me a fair hearing, like. Now,' he checked his watch, 'time we were all getting back to work, I suppose. Good to meet you, Pete.' He stuck his hand out and Pete shook. 'Anything else you need to know, call any time; I'll give you my personal mobile number. And anything else I can do – you want tickets for Big Tom, private box, the works – you just give me a call. Leslie St Clair looks after his friends.'

'Great,' said Pete, 'thanks,' and shook St Clair's hand again and walked back through the pub to his car, unable to repress a smile. He liked guys like St Clair, old-school hustlers. Be a nice story too, they dug around in the archives and got some photos of the Fifties and that. He was just working on composing the opening paragraph in his head when his phone rang, told him he'd got a message.

He picked it up expecting some voicemail from Graham yelling at him to get back to the office but instead it was a text message. 'Custom Hse 9pm Fri OK? xx Kim.'

Pete paused, thought keep it simple, texted back with OK x. Then he headed back to the office with a smile on his face.

9

Bobby Ranger couldn't sleep, was getting to be a habit. The day the Custom House was due to close she woke up around six. She was wondering where her future was headed. Lap-dancing was out. She should have known the whole lap-dancing thing would be sewn up by that old cunt Bernie Walters. Him and Kenny, chances of them giving Maria work were slight, and chances of there being anything left over for Bobby were less than zero. Back-to-the-drawing-board time.

Then there was the massage-parlour plan. Thing was you had to have some premises. No way was Bobby conducting the business round her flat, have Maria fucking God knows who on her nice bed. Neither was Maria's place a possibility, not with Jamal running around asking for his tea. No, somewhere else.

Well, there were always the kind of horrible bloody rooms the girls used, places with no leccy and no light, just one step up from doing it in the car park, but that wasn't what Bobby was after; she was looking for something classier. A place you could treat the punters properly and charge them properly too. Question was where could she find a place where the neighbours and/or landlord wouldn't freak out they saw a procession of men turning up at all hours? She was standing in the kitchen making herself a coffee when a possible answer came to her. Something one of the girls, a part-timer from Llantrisant way, had said, how she'd been using a nice pad over Atlantic Wharf, the new flats there.

Perfect, that would be. They'd built them about ten years ago, before the whole bay-development thing got going, a whole load of new flats along this big old disused wharf, half a mile or so east of Butetown. Ahead of its time, probably, but when it was built it just seemed stupid; no way were lawyers and that going to live down the docks and there was no need for anyone from Butetown to move over there – one thing Butetown didn't have was a housing shortage: the council was forever moving people out of Butetown, never moved anyone in except the odd Somali refugee. Bobby reckoned it was a deliberate policy: another twenty years or so there'd be hardly anyone left in Butetown at all and the council would be able to knock the whole place down, build a whole lot more posh flats and Tiger Bay would have vanished from history, replaced once and for all by Cardiff Bay.

Anyway, thing was, no one rich wanted to live by the side of a derelict canal in the docks so most of the flats were just sitting there empty. All of which was why it was the perfect place for a girl to do some business. Bobby didn't know why she hadn't thought of it before. Plenty of parking space, hardly any nosy neighbours, nice and private for the punters too, no chance of being spotted. Yeah, perfect.

Nine o'clock she'd got on the phone, checking out who rented out flats in Atlantic Wharf. Now she was going to see a man named Malcolm Hopkin and she was nervous. He'd told her to come to the Wharf pub; just ask behind the bar, love, he'd said, they'll point me out.

In fact there was no need for that as he was practically the only person in there and even if he hadn't been she'd have known him at once: one of those times when the voice on the phone and the real-life feller go right together. Funny thing – don't know why she thought of this – was that seemed to happen more often with blokes; with women quite often the ones with the sexy voice on the phone were some fat old sort with glasses in real life, and the pretty ones sounded like Kate Moss does in that advert – Obsession – dumb plain little voices.

But anyway, like she said, Malcolm Hopkin matched his voice. Dodgy. Well dodgy. Fiftyish feller with bit of a bouffant and a drinker's face sat over a pint at a little table by the window, bunch of newspapers on the table in front of him, talking on his mobile.

As she walked over he snapped the phone off, looked up at her and asked, 'You the young lady interested in the flat?' Little bit of a Valleys accent in there.

'Yeah,' she said, sitting down opposite him, 'that's me.'

'Hmm,' he said, looking her up and down and frowning a little, 'well, I'll just finish my drink and we'll walk round to the flats. You care for one yourself?'

'Coke, ta,' said Bobby.

Hopkin came back with Bobby's coke and a whisky for himself.

'I've seen you before,' he said after taking a swallow of his pint.

Bobby shrugged. 'Probably, I've lived here all my life,' she said, wondering too if she'd seen him before. Only place she mostly saw blokes like that was out on the beat pulling up next to Maria and winding their windows down. Was he a punter?

'Definitely seen you around,' said Hopkin again, nodding to himself. Then he fixed her with a look. 'Now, would you be planning on actually living in the flat yourself?'

'Yeah, well,' started Bobby but Hopkin cut her short.

'Or would you be thinking of using it as a business base? A lot of entrepreneurial types favour these flats.'

Bobby's turn to look at the bloke closely. Was he saying what she thought he was saying?

'Well, perhaps,' she began tentatively but he cut her off again, big smile on his face this time.

'No, no, no need to go into the detail of your business, up to you entirely. It's just that were there to be business use then of course a special business rate will apply. You understand, I'm sure.'

Bobby understood all right: this Malcolm Hopkin was a pimp just like her, only a layer further up, kept his hands nice and clean.

'Course,' she said. 'I understand but it depends what it is, this special business rate, doesn't it?'

'Does indeed,' said Hopkin, draining off his pint and chasing it with the last of his whisky. 'Tell you what, let's go round to the flat and if you like it then we can talk about the financial side.'

Bobby did like the flat. You could see why it hadn't appealed to any regular person. The only reason you might want to live in these flats was to get the view over the water and this one looked straight out on to the car park. But that suited Bobby fine; meant you could get a good look at the punters before they came in the front door. Then you had an entryphone system, so if you didn't like the look of them close up, you could just tell them to fuck off over the intercom. Otherwise the place was just what you'd expect: boxy little rooms halfway between a hotel and a home. Soulless as anything. The layout was fine, though. You walked into the living room – that's where Bobby could base herself and the girls could sit around – then there were two bedrooms opening off, neither of them much bigger than a cupboard but big enough for them to do the business. Nice kitchen, which would come in handy, and a decent-size bathroom, which would be a definite plus. Yeah, Bobby liked it a lot; big step up from the Custom House beat this would be for all concerned.

'Bit bloody small,' she said to Hopkin after he'd finished showing her round.'

He shrugged. 'Compact, love, that's the word they like to use – the developers,' and he laughed.

'Can't even see the water,' said Bobby.

Hopkin laughed again. 'Good view of the car park, though,' he said. 'Some of the other . . . entrepreneurs appreciate that.' Then he smiled and waited.

Bobby's turn to shrug; no point in carrying the charade on any longer. 'Yeah, suppose it's OK,' she said. 'How much?'

'Five hundred.'

'What?' said Bobby. 'A month?'

Hopkin chuckled, no mirth in it at all. 'No, love, a week. Payable Friday morning. On the dot. Two late payments and you're out.'

Bobby walked over to the window, looked at the car park, thought about it. Five hundred a week. Bloody hell. Any way you looked at it, that was a lot of money for a flat. Specially one you weren't even going to live in. Five hundred quid: what was that? Seventy-odd quid a day. Meant Maria doing three guys a day just to pay the rent. Except those were street rates. Working inside like this she could charge more. Fifty a time, say, basic. And then it didn't have to be just Maria working here; say she had three or four girls working, all charging fifty a go, well it was nothing really. If if if. Thing was she barely had five hundred quid to put down for the first week. Nah, this was crazy, out of her league. And a rip-off too.

It was like Hopkin was reading her mind.

'You get more than the flat for five hundred, mind, love, you also get a bit of protection. Say, for instance, your business might be the kind of thing gets the law interested, gets coppers coming round with their hands out asking for little contributions to keep it all running smoothly, you know what I'm talking about? Well, all that's covered, I guarantee you. Any copper comes round with their hands out, you send them straight to me.'

'Hmm,' said Bobby, thinking that made a difference.

'All right,' said Hopkin then, 'don't know why I'm offering

you this, but I like you. First two weeks you can buy one get one free, just till you get settled in, like. Give us five hundred now and that's the first fortnight taken care of.'

Sod it, thought Bobby, why not, so she smiled and stuck her hand out. 'Deal,' she said.

10

Five o'clock Pete went to pick up the Audi TT from the dealership. Couldn't deny it was a lovely-looking motor; even just driving it back to the office you could see the envy radiating off every bloke you passed. Three hours left before it was time to meet Kim and rather than go back to the flat Pete carried on working, transcribed his St Clair interview, impressed again by the sheer chutzpah of the man. Chutzpah: could you use that in the *Post*? Pete wondered, and decided you probably could, though he still remembered the piss-taking he'd received from Graham when he tried to use schadenfreude in a piece about Anglo-Welsh rugby rivalry. It was funny it was only the Germans had a word for it; you'd have thought the Welsh would have half a dozen, like the Eskimos have a hundred different names for snow, cause if there was one thing the Welsh were good at, it was schadenfreude.

Anyway the time passed by easy enough; the quiet of the evening was always the best time for getting some serious work done in the office. And suddenly it was quarter to nine and Pete was closing down his terminal and heading out. He debated for a moment whether to take the car, weighing the practical – the fact that it would be quicker to walk – against the desire to show off. To his surprise he found himself opting for being a flash git. He walked down to the office car park, gunned the motor out of there, couldn't resist taking it for a quick spin on the feeder road from the town centre to the bay before pulling up in the Welsh National Opera car park, across the road from the Custom House.

You could hear the noise from outside the pub, Tom Jones's 'Sex Bomb' – what else? – blaring out at hideous volume accompanied by the sound of a lot of very drunk people singing along. Pete paused for a moment, wondering whether he was really up for this.

Just then there was a yell of rage from inside and the window to the lounge bulged out momentarily before giving way altogether in a shower of glass as a body smashed through it. Pete stopped moving, watched open-mouthed as the victim stood up apparently unscathed, made a vague effort at brushing some of the glass off his clothes, ignored a bloody cut on his forehead and headed back into the pub.

Looking through the hole in the window, Pete could see a bloke with a hefty, professional-looking video camera looking out at him. Then in a kind of slow motion Pete saw someone approach the cameraman, shout something in his face, snatch the camera, throw it through the broken window and rapidly follow it up with the cameraman himself.

'Fuck,' said the cameraman, 'fuck, fuck, fuck.' He was a tall bloke with a straggly beard wearing heavily padded clothing that looked to have protected him from much physical damage. The bloke didn't seem too bothered about his own welfare, though; he was much more concerned about his camera.

He picked it up tenderly as a child. 'You see that?' said the bloke. 'You see what happened?'

'Yeah,' said Pete, 'I saw it. You all right?'

Before the cameraman could answer, the pub door opened and a woman in flared jeans and a tight top emblazoned with the word Pornstar emerged. Kim.

'Christ, Dan,' she said, 'is the camera all right?'

Pete couldn't help it; he burst out laughing. Kim spun round.

'What the fuck are you laughing at?' Then she saw it was Pete. 'Oh,' she said. 'Hiya.'

'Hiya,' said Pete. 'You need some help?'

'No,' she said, 's'all right. Let me just sort this out. If it's broken it could cost me my bloody job. Dan, tell me it's all right.'

Dan was busy fiddling with the camera, still swearing under his breath. Finally he turned round, looked at Kim. 'It's OK, I think.'

'Thank Christ for that,' said Kim. 'Right, let's go back in.'

Pete laughed again. The cameraman just stared at her. 'You serious?'

'Yeah,' she said, 'we're getting some great footage in there.'

'You're out of your mind,' said the cameraman, picked up his camera and walked across the road to an MPV. He unlocked the back, put the camera in, walked round to the front and got in the driver's seat. 'You coming?'

'No,' shouted Kim, 'I'm bloody not. I'm staying here. I'll record some more stuff.'

'Fine,' said Dan the cameraman, 'your funeral,' and drove off.

'Gutless fucking hippie twat,' said Kim, obviously not impressed by this turn of events. 'So what are we waiting for, let's go in.'

This time it was Pete's turn to say, 'You serious?'

'Yeah,' said Kim, 'course. C'mon in, it's a laugh in there.' And with that she took Pete's hand and practically pulled him into the pub, Pete thinking to himself, well you wanted a bit of excitement in life, no point in complaining when some's on offer.

Inside the place was riotous but not, as far as Pete could see, especially menacing. The bloke who'd been chucked through the window in the first place was stood at the bar with his mates, all of them clearly under the impression it had been a great laugh. The overall vibe was of the party at the end of the world. One and all off their faces, looking like they'd been drinking since eleven o'clock opening time. Young hustlers, old hustlers, lesbian pimps, middle-aged black pimps, even the young hard boys cruising around the scene dealing a little bit of this, little bit of that; they were all pissed. Pete pushed towards the bar, got a couple of cans of Breaker, made his way back to Kim and they perched themselves on top of an upended fruit machine and watched the show.

They got a few looks at first. Couple of pissed-up old girls made some remarks; a bunch of hard, shaven-headed black boys swaggered into the pub, looked them over then decided whoever they were they weren't the law. At least that's what Pete assumed they figured when one of the fellers offered to sell him a couple of rocks. 'How did he know I wasn't a copper?' Pete asked Kim, outraged.

'If he'd thought you were a copper, he would have given you them,' said Kim, laughing, and Pete shook his head and wondered if she was joking. Only copper he'd had much to do with was a bloke called Simon lived four doors down in the close, and he couldn't really imagine Simon having much of an interest in crack. But then sometimes he thought he was simply naïve; maybe he really knew nothing of the life of this city he'd been chronicling for the past decade and a half.

By now talking was almost impossible; the jukebox had been turned up to total distortion level, blasting out the usual unlikely mixture of chart hits through the ages. Pete remembered coming into the Custom House years ago, in search of an errant journalist, and finding the whole place singing along to Salt'n'Pepa's 'Let's Talk about Sex' – which you might have thought would be the last thing anyone in here would want to listen to. Tonight it was anthems all the way: Rod's 'Sailing', Kool and the Gang's 'Celebration' three times in a row, TLC's 'No Scrubs' and now 'Dancing in the Streets', the grisly Jagger and Bowie version.

Pete was enjoying himself, sucking on his beer, soaking up the atmosphere of this wake for a vanishing era, wondering how he'd write it up: 'Old-time street prostitution — another great British industry goes under the cosh.' Maybe it would work on the financial pages. He looked over at Kim to see her gazing at a couple who'd just emerged from the toilets, a stocky boyish-looking black woman with short locks and a tall white girl with hennaed hair scraped back from her forehead.

'Hiya, Bobby,' shouted Kim, 'over here,' and the black woman rolled her eyes in mock amazement and headed over towards Pete and Kim.

Pete felt a momentary tinge of alarm at the prospect of actually having to engage with this world rather than simply look at it, but also an undeniable excitement.

'Hiya, darlin',' said the woman, Bobby, 'brought your boy-friend have you?'

Kim ignored the suggestion, just said, 'Pete, this is Bobby and this is . . .' Kim looked towards the hennaed girl.

'Maria,' said the girl. 'You don't remember me, do you?'

Kim stared at her and then her hand flew up to her mouth. 'Maria, Christ. How are you, girl?'

'You two know each other?' said Bobby.

'Yeah,' said Kim, 'I met Maria when I was doing a doc down here before about the drugs trade, yeah?' and with that first Kim and then Maria burst into a fit of giggles.

Bobby stared at them, shook her head wearily then turned her attention to Pete. 'Who are you, then?'

'I'm Pete,' said Pete and got halfway through sticking his hand out to shake when he decided that the Custom House wasn't a shake-hands kind of place and let the motion abort in mid-air.

'That right, you her boyfriend?'

Pete shook his head, managed a smile. 'Just friends, you know.'

Bobby rolled her eyes, seemed to find him of no further interest. Before she could move away, though, another bloke came up to them, short black guy in a big jacket, looked to be about Pete's age, big smile on his face and what Pete couldn't help thinking of as a joint in his hand, though he was sure people didn't call them joints any more.

'All right, Bob,' said the guy.

'Later, Mikey,' said Bobby and immediately moved away. Pete watched her go; maybe it was the whole world she was pissed off with.

'All right, man, what's happening?' the feller, Mikey, said to him.

'Nothing much,' said Pete, raising his can in what he hoped was an appropriate gesture of matiness.

'Yeah, man, that's the truth,' said Mikey and laughed like Pete had said something profound yet funny. Then he took a long draw on the — what the hell was the right word — spliff? Spliff would do, it was better than joint; anyway he handed the herbal cigarette to Pete, who was so busy wondering what to call it, if asked, that he took a long toke without even considering that this was the first dope he'd smoked since 1984 and he'd never smoked much even back then cause most of the time it made him paranoid.

It was only when he let the smoke out and felt the dimly familiar spread of intoxication in his brain that he had a moment of panic but it subsided at once. Maybe it was getting older, but the pleasure centres were winning over from the paranoia nodes. He took a second long drag, then handed the spliff back to Mikey. 'Thanks, man,' he said, 'nice one.' Man? Nice one? What was going on? His whole vocabulary was reverting to the early Eighties.

'Nice,' agreed Mikey and Pete was just thinking what a cool guy he must be, just making friends, hanging out like this, when the Mikey feller leant up close and shouted in his ear, 'You looking for a girl?'

For a moment Pete thought he meant had Pete lost someone then the penny dropped and it was all he could do to stop from blushing. 'No,' he shouted back and then, feeling the need to justify himself, added, 'I'm with her.' He turned to point at Kim who was out in the middle of the ad hoc dance floor, dancing suspiciously closely with Maria.

'Oh right,' said Mikey, looking genuinely contrite, 'sorry, man.'

Pete waited for Mikey to walk on, find another lonely-looking bloke who might be interested in a little commercial intimacy. But he didn't, he just passed the spliff back to Pete, waited till Pete had taken another couple of tokes, then said, 'So what sort of business you in, Pete?'

'Newspaper,' said Pete, before breaking off into a coughing fit. When he'd pulled himself together he elaborated, 'I work for the *Welsh Post*.'

'Oh yeah?' said Mikey. 'You're a journalist?'

'Yeah,' said Pete, thinking that was one of the few questions he could manage a categorical answer to right at the moment. Christ, he felt out of it. And he had the car outside; what was he thinking of?

'Oh yeah? A news reporter, is it? You doing a story on this place?'

'No,' said Pete, 'just. . .' He paused, trying to remember why he was here. 'I just came with her, Kim. I do, like, features and stuff.'

'Cool,' said Mikey, looking bored now.

'I do the motoring, though,' Pete blurted out, thinking where did that come from, and, before he can stop himself, he says, 'You want to see the motor I'm trying out?' and Mikey nods and suddenly they're draining their pints and heading over the road to pay homage to the Audi TT.

'Sweet,' said Mikey reverently as he got up close. 'They let you drive it?'

'Yeah,' said Pete, aware he was showing off but powerless to stop himself. 'Yeah, I've got it for the weekend.'

'Nice, man,' said Mikey. 'Can I have a look inside?'

'Sure,' said Pete and then they're both sat inside the car playing around with the controls like a pair of kids when Kim, Bobby and Maria emerge from the pub, Kim looking around like she's wondering where Pete has got to.

Pete leaned out of the car, shouted at Kim and waved them over. This time Bobby's first to come out with 'Nice car' and Pete can't help but reflect that there is a reason why blokes buy these kind of motors. You want to impress the girls, spend thirty grand on one of these babies. You'll see.

'So,' said Kim when she got up close, 'you going to take us for a ride then?'

Pete shook his head. 'No way. I've got a lot of sobering up to do before I'm going anywhere.'

'Aw, c'mon,' says Kim, who was obviously some way out of the vicinity of soberhood herself. 'Be a laugh, wouldn't it, Maria?'

Kim turns round to Maria who, now Pete sees her in the outdoors, is not looking well at all. She's swaying and glassy-eyed and suddenly she just turns her head to one side and throws up.

'Fucking hell, Ri,' says Bobby, 'state of you.'

Maria doesn't say anything, just finishes retching then stands up, wipes her hand across her face and says, 'I'm going back in.'

Pete, Kim, Bobby and Mikey stand there watching her.

'Kin'ell, Bob, aren't you going to see she's OK?' says Mikey.

Bobby shrugs. 'What's the point? She's like that every other bastard night. Let's have a look inside.'

Bobby's turn to admire the inside of the Audi. 'How fast does it go?' she asks.

Pete tries to remember. 'Hundred and seventy miles an hour, I think's what they said.'

'Shit,' says Bobby, 'not bad. You sure you don't want to take us for a ride?'

'I'll drive it,' says Mikey. 'I haven't been drinking and I'm a hell of a driver, aren't I, Bob?'

And then Bobby starts telling Pete some long story about Mikey being chased by the police and losing them after twenty minutes of leading them through every alley in Butetown and Pete's thinking sure you may not have been drinking but how much have you been smoking but Kim's got her mind absolutely fixed on going for a drive and her hand's on his back and clearly he isn't sober or unstoned or in his right mind but eventually he finds himself giving in – just a short ride, right – and then Mikey's at the wheel and Pete's next to him and Bobby and Kim are squeezed into the tiny back seat both giggling and suddenly they're off, and fair play Mikey takes it nice and slow out of the car park and round the roundabout but when he hits the arterial road fucking hell the acceleration's like something else and they're all laughing and Pete's caught between terror and exhilaration, feeling like he did on the back of his cousin Rog's bike up on Cwmcarn Scenic Drive when he was sixteen.

Mikey slows round the roundabout then turns right down into the underpass and floors it once again. Now he has a ten-mile straight run, dual carriageway all the way, to the motorway, and within seconds he's up to a hundred miles an hour; they fairly flash past the few other cars on the road. Mikey is indeed a good driver, not over-steering, easing the car round the bends, and Pete allows himself to relax a little; he swivels round to look at Kim, her eyes are shining, her face flushed, thrilled. Bobby next to her is casually lighting up a spliff. Pete blinks, imagining what would happen if the police stopped them now, how completely screwed he'd be, but then Kim grabs him from behind and leans over into the front and kisses him hard on the mouth and says, 'This is fucking brilliant,' and he lets go of his worries.

Three minutes later, give or take, they arrive at the motorway junction.

'You want to go to Bristol?' says Mikey and Kim goes yeah but Pete gathers his strength sufficiently to say no. So they head back to Cardiff, possibly just a tad faster than they left it, the needle touching a hundred and forty on a straight section. They're almost back, within sight of the Millennium Stadium, illuminated to their left, and Pete's just thinking that they've got away with it when he sees the police car parked up by the side of the road. They're past it in a blur of speed but behind them Pete can hear the siren start up.

Mikey just laughs, guns the car forward towards Butetown and at the last minute just before the underpass he brakes hard and swings the car up and left. The brakes do their job miraculously well and suddenly they're up by Techniquest and the siren's still off in the distance. Mikey turns and clashes fists with Pete who responds awkwardly.

They're just motoring back down Bute Street, more sedately now, Kim telling Mikey what a great driver he is, when they hear another siren and this time it's right on top of them. Just a quick blast and the cop car cuts in front of them and Mikey's got no alternative but to stop, pulling up just by the Loudoun Square shops.

Pete has his head in his hands as the copper gets out of his car and walks round to the driver's side. Mikey winds his window down and says, casual as anything, 'All right, Jimmy?'

The copper laughs. 'For Chrissakes, Mikey, who did you rob that off?'

Mikey shrugs. 'No one, Jim, it's my mate's car here.' He points at Pete.

Pete's still waiting for the breathalysers to come out or the cop to ask what the herbal–cigarette smell is, but there's none of that. Instead the feller just waves at Pete and says, 'Nice car, boss. Time you took it home, though, you know what I mean,' and Pete just nods, unable to speak, relief flooding over him.

The copper gets back in his car, drives off. Mikey claps Pete on the back. 'Welcome to Butetown, bra.' And all of them are laughing.

For the rest of the night Pete feels bulletproof. It's a blur of returning to the Custom House, drinking, dancing, snogging Kim sat together astride the fruit machine, seeing Kim snogging Bobby when he walks outside for fresh air, snogging Kim again as they all stagger out to the car when time is once and forever called.

Outside, Bobby's going, leading a comatose Maria away. Kim, Mikey and Pete are stood together, wondering what now? The car's still sat there and Pete is now not remotely in any condition to drive, but suddenly paranoid about leaving such a car in such a place. Mikey, still sober, if seriously stoned, says he'll be the taxi man and Pete's new bulletproof brain can't think of a problem with that so he gives Mikey the keys once more and sits in the front and drifts in and out of sleep and Mikey drops off Kim then delivers Pete to his door and Pete staggers out of the car and when Mikey says you mind if I bring the car back tomorrow he just nods and says sure and it's only when he wakes in the very early morning, aching and sweating, that he realises he's en-trusted a thirty-grand car that he doesn't own to a Butetown lowlife he's never met before and he can't sleep for worrying, just lies there wishing he could die.

II

The morning after the Custom House closed Bobby began trying to explain her new plan to Maria who didn't seem to get it at all, probably cause she had the hangover to end them all and was gazing fixedly at Ant and Dec while Jamal bounced around the room.

Wasn't till six in the evening, by which time Maria'd had a couple of reviving bottles of Hooch, that Bobby was able to get any sense at all out of her.

'Might as well just use this place, innit?' she said finally. 'That's what Nikki does: just gets them to bell her on the mobile and round they come.'

'Fuck's sake,' said Bobby. 'You really want that? You want him – ' she pointed at Jamal concentrating furiously on his N64 '– seeing you bring back Christ knows who? You think I'm going to sleep with you in the same bed you does it with the punters?'

Maria pouted. 'Yeah, OK, but couldn't you have found somewhere closer?'

Bobby felt like strangling her. Atlantic Wharf was all of five minutes' walk away. 'It's closer than the Custom House,' she said, doing her best to keep her temper in check.

'Yeah, but it's not going to be the same laugh, is it, not going to have our mates there?'

Bobby shrugged. 'Well, I was thinking of asking a couple of the other girls they wanted to work there too.'

'Oh yeah?' said Maria suspiciously. 'Who?'

'I dunno,' said Bobby. 'Tanya, I was thinking. Maybe Lorraine.'

'Nikki'd be good.'

Bobby frowned. Great, the two laziest cows in Cardiff together under one roof, but what the hell, she was Maria's mate, might stop her moaning. 'All right,' she said, 'Nikki.'

'Great,' said Maria, 'I'll tell her. So when do we start?'

'Feller said we could move in Monday, then we'll have to put an ad in the paper and stuff, see what happens.'

'That'll be cool,' said Maria, digging in the fridge for another Hooch. 'You want one?'

'No, ta,' said Bobby.

'So, you want me to work tonight or what?'

'No,' said Bobby, 'nowhere to work is there?' That wasn't strictly true — they could have gone over by the Embankment and tried their luck, Bobby sitting in the car, Maria out on the street — but now Bobby had got it in her head that they were taking a step up in the world and that would be a definite step down. Plus she felt like a day off. Walking past the Custom House this afternoon, seeing the boards up already, the demolition notices plastered on the walls, she felt like she'd been to a funeral or something. Needed a bit of time to mourn, like.

'Cool,' said Maria, 'cause I was thinking of going out with Nikki, have a few drinks, tell her about your idea, like, so if you don't mind looking after Jam?'

'Nah,' said Bobby, 'that'll be all right.'

In fact it sounded like an excellent idea. She couldn't face having Maria getting sloppy drunk around her, and now she could spend an hour or two playing games with Jamal, then settle down to sorting out a few things for herself.

And so by nine o'clock Maria was safely out of the way, getting pissed with Nikki in some hellhole in town, Jamal was tucked up in bed and Bobby was sat in the bedroom playing with her new computer. Neville, feller she'd known for years, sold it her, fell out the back of a warehouse no doubt. Anyway, seventy-five quid for a brand-new computer still in the box; Bobby was well pleased.

So far she hadn't done much more than play games on it, but now she'd got the flat sorted she was starting to feel a bit inspired. She'd been thinking about how to advertise for business. First thought was the obvious one: stick an ad in the evening paper like all the massage parlours had been doing for years. Well of course she'd do that, but then she thought what about the Internet? The Internet had to be the future in the sex-for-money business, everybody knew that. So Bobby decided to have a nose around, see how it all worked.

First off she checked out whether her competition was up to anything on the Net. There were half a dozen 'massage parlours' in Cardiff that Bobby knew of, either through girls who worked in them or because they advertised in the *Echo*. A couple of them had been going for ever; the rest were pretty much fly-by-night operations, waiting till the police or their rivals put them out of business.

The Internet, though, none of her rivals seemed to have got hip to it at all. All she could find was something called the Good Sex Guide where the punters actually wrote up what they thought of the services on offer and none of them were too impressed. That didn't surprise Bobby much; pride in their work wasn't something you associated with the girls of the Cardiff sauna–massage industry.

Not one of the outfits had its own website either and Bobby was getting excited at the prospect of being the first. You're a punter, what did you want to do? Take a pig in a poke out the *Echo* classifieds or d'you want to browse through a selection of beautiful girls and phone up and book the one of your choice? It was obvious really.

The main problem, of course, was the beautiful-girls bit. Maria really was pretty damn fit, Bobby said so herself. The other three girls Bobby was using, though, were a bit more a mixed bag. Tanya the half-caste wasn't too bad, nice body specially; Lorraine was frankly getting on a bit and well on the fat side, but then again she was a genuine blonde and with a lot of slap and her tits sticking out she worked all right for the punters liked a mature woman; and as for Nikki, well she'd maybe appeal to the market liked a sulky cow.

Anyway, Bobby started to get positively inspired. She was definitely going to get a website. Question was did she get someone to design it for her – and if she did find someone they might have a bit of an attitude about setting up a cyber brothel. Option two: she could have a go herself. How hard could it be? She'd seen all these magazines in the newsagent with free cover disks all said they could help you build your own site. Got to be worth a go.

Lying in bed later on, half asleep, waiting for Maria to come back pissed and aggressive, she had a vision of herself in a white room programming a computer and felt an unfamiliar calmness replace the usual jangle of her nerves. She'd always seen the future as the same but worse, the same but ageing and violent and unloved or wanted, the same plus addiction or madness or both. But now, just maybe, she thought that the closing of the Custom House might not be a death but a rebirth.

12

Pete had spent most of the morning pacing about. He'd racked his brains to work out how to find this Mikey. He'd been into work for a bit but there was hardly anyone in as it was Sunday tomorrow. He'd gone back to the flat and aggravated Randall obsessing about what to do. Randall buried himself in the papers, clock-watching for twelve when he would stroll over to the City Arms and have the first eye-opener of the day.

Half twelve and Pete was actually looking through the phone book for the police-station number wondering what on earth he was going to say when the doorbell rang. Pete answered the intercom. A voice he didn't recognise for a second, then identified with a surge of relief. Mikey.

'Got your car here for you, boss,' he said.

Pete walked downstairs and there was Mikey standing next to the car. Pete felt like kissing him, felt a wave of shame and guilt. What a bastard he was stereotyping a feller like Mikey who'd been nothing but helpful and had even – bloody hell – sprayed the car with some kind of air-freshener stuff made it smell like new and removed all traces of the dope and drink that had been consumed in it the night before. He stuck his hand out. 'Thanks, man, I owe you.'

'No problem, boss,' said Mikey. 'Pleasure to drive it, like. How long you got it for?'

'Till Monday,' said Pete.

'Oh yeah. Going to take your girlfriend out for a Sunday drive then?'

Pete just smiled and said, 'We'll see,' then dug in his wallet and found a business card, handed it to Mikey.

'And like I said, you need a favour, there's anything I can do –' even as he was talking, he couldn't imagine what kind of favour he could do for a feller like Mikey, but still '– just give me a buzz, yeah, cause you saved my life last night.'

Mikey laughed. 'C'mon, man, it was a laugh, don't take it so serious,' he said and with that he was off towards town. 'Got a little business to do, boss.' And Pete was left leaning on the Audi wondering when the last time was anyone did him a favour without expecting something back.

He thought about taking the Audi out for a test run but he was still feeling the effects of the night before and anyway what Mikey had said about taking Kim out sounded like a good idea, so he drove the car round to the *Post*, stuck it in the protected parking lot, and spent the rest of the day quietly working on the Leslie St Clair piece.

Took him till six o'clock to finish it but when he did he was well pleased. Definitely the best thing he'd written in years, made him realise how much he'd become a kind of journalistic automaton, always doing exactly what was right for the *Post*, never even letting himself think that you could try to do more than what was expected.

He'd got all the regular stuff in, the background, all the showbiz stories, even mentioned community capitalism, but he'd put his own stamp on it too. And it was a nice story. This smart kid from the docks, got nothing more than quick hands in the boxing ring and an OK singing voice, manages to make himself a name as a boxer then smoothly glides into showbiz and then, when that starts going down, moves into business. And all the time without losing touch with his roots. Just writing it down made Pete think about what a safe little life he'd had by comparison. No, it was a cracking piece by any standards and for the first time in years he was buzzing at work.

Just to prove it, he picked up the phone and, without even thinking about what he was going to say beforehand, called up Kim. She was on good form too, said she'd been working all day and all, cutting together the footage she'd got from the Custom House the night before. And yeah, she said, she'd love to go for a drive tomorrow. He knew where she lived, why didn't he pick her up about twelve? Pete put the phone down. Sorted, he thought, and grinned, realising his vocabulary was being hijacked. Better be careful before he turned into one of those forty-year-olds Cardiff seemed to be full of, all piercings, dodgy facial hair and clothes nicked off a passing teenager.

Twelve o'clock Sunday Pete had rung on Kim's bell standing outside the house on Romilly Road where she had her flat. After a couple of minutes he rang again and a couple of minutes after that the door opened and a decidedly bleary-looking, dressing-gowned Kim half opened the door, looked out at Pete in evident bewilderment, then slowly nodded and said, 'You want to come in? I'm not quite up yet.'

'Yeah,' said Pete, 'I kind of gathered that,' and laughed, and Kim half laughed back and led the way up the stairs and into her flat.

'You mind waiting in here,' she said, pointing to the living room, 'I'll just be a minute,' and disappeared into her bedroom.

Pete walked into the living room, looked out the window to check no one was taking an unhealthy interest in the car, then scanned the room. Stripped floorboards, Ikea rug, Ikea sofa, couple of Sixties-looking chairs, Matisse print, Modigliani print, framed arty photo of Kim herself, TV, video with a bunch of videos lying around it, midi system, bunch of CDs, no vinyl, and a bookcase.

He went over to the bookcase; generally it was the most reliable window to the soul. CD collections didn't tell you much, people had CDs they didn't care about, ones old boyfriends had given them, ones everybody else had – he was willing to bet he'd find Travis, Chilled Ibiza and at least one Sixties soul compilation amongst Kim's CD collection – but nobody bought books quite so casually.

Scanning the shelves, he was relieved not to be assailed by rows of self-help titles, no sign of *The Road Less Travelled* or *Men Are from Mars*; there was a copy of *The Rules* but that was probably a joke. Instead there was a surprising amount of serious fiction and poetry. She must have done English at university, he figured – hard to imagine anyone actually read George Eliot or Ezra Pound for pleasure – but the new stuff all looked pretty heavyweight too, all that Booker-prize stuff that Pete felt like he ought to have read. Well, well, and there was him expecting to find wall-to-wall primary-coloured books about girls called Jemima and their topsy-turvy love lives. Just went to show you never could tell.

Meanwhile there was a copy of yesterday's *Guardian* under the sofa so he picked that up and settled down to reading the magazine.

He was aimlessly scanning the wine column by the time Kim emerged. She was wearing jeans and a very tight T-shirt that Pete had to stop himself from staring at. She flopped down on the sofa next to him.

'Christ,' she said, 'I am absolutely fucked. I must have coffee. You want some?'

She sprang up and Pete felt a flash of irritation. If they didn't get going soon he was sure they wouldn't reach anywhere in time for Sunday lunch, but he kept it back, reminded himself that the point of the day was to see Kim, not to have roast beef and all the trimmings, though just the thought of Yorkshire pudding had him salivating. Swallowing hard, he said, 'Yeah, sure, if you're making one.'

Kim led the way into the kitchen, where she fiddled about with a flashy Italian coffee-maker and Pete propped himself up against the fridge, enjoying the domesticity.

'So, what did you do last night?'

'Oh,' she said, 'same old same old, you know. Went to the comedy club down the bay first, then we ended up in the Emporium cause Guto's mate was deejaying. How about you?'

'Oh,' said Pete, not wanting to say that he'd had a quiet night in, had begged off drinking with Randall in favour of *Match of the Day* and a takeaway, wanting to be in good shape for Sunday, 'nothing much'.

'Listen,' he said then, looking at his watch, 'maybe we should get moving if we're going to get something to eat.'

'Yeah, yeah, sure,' said Kim, 'let's just drink this,' she poured out the coffee, 'and we'll get going.'

In fact it was another half hour before they actually made it out and Pete was finding it hard to conceal his annoyance but at last they were on the move.

There wasn't the heady excitement of the Friday-night drive. In the cooler light of lunchtime the car was ultimately just a car, but even so once they got on to the motorway, and then on to the Ross Spur heading up to Monmouth, a fine empty road with sweeping scenery, there was a simple pleasure in navigating this fairly supreme product of human ingenuity through a slice of nature's finest landscaping.

Just before Monmouth Pete headed south, wound his way down Wye Valley lanes till he came to a pub called the Trekkers, which – glory be – was still serving Sunday lunch, and the sun made an appearance and they were sat in the garden and all would have been well with Pete's world if he could have shaken off the memories of coming to this same pub years ago with Viv and the kids.

Suddenly, sat there across the table from Kim, a vodka tonic in front of her, a pint of randomly selected real ale in front of him, he felt like an adulterer, a middle-ageing bloke furtively off with his cute young secretary.

Of course he knew that was unfair on him – he wasn't that old, for Christ's sake, and he was fully separated from Viv – and unfair on Kim, who wasn't that young and wasn't his secretary either and probably earned easily as much as he did.

And anyway, far as he could see, him and Kim were still some way from adultery. All he'd done was snog her once on a very drunken late night. Maybe he should have made a move when he was round her flat. Maybe that's why she was in her dressing gown when he showed up, maybe she was expecting him to . . . Maybe he was just as hopeless at reading women and their signals after seventeen years of marriage as he had been before.

'Christ, Pete, d'you always talk this much?' Kim was looking at him, shaking her head in mock despair.

'Oh God, sorry,' Pete said, 'I was miles away,' then, before he could stop himself, he added, 'Viv always goes on at me about that.' Christ, like he was still married to her.

Kim grinned, shook her head. 'She really did a number on you, didn't she? How long were you together?'

'Seventeen years.'

'Seventeen years – how old would I have been then . . . fourteen. Think you'd have liked me then? Second thoughts, don't answer that question.' She laughed.

Pete laughed too, thinking she knows I like her, thinking c'mon, man, the whole thing about this man–woman stuff, the whole thing you never managed to get into your thick head back in the day, is it's simple. You like her, she likes you – just do something about it. A flash of a half-remembered Captain

534

Beefheart song went through his head: 'Nowadays a woman's gotta hit a man just to let him know she's there.' And before he knew it he was sliding his hand over her hand on the table and leaning forward to kiss her hoping like hell she was going to respond.

And when she did, when clear and sober on a Sunday lunchtime, she opened her mouth to his, let her tongue flick against his teeth, Pete felt a lightness in himself that he didn't recognise.

13

Two weeks later Bobby was looking out the window, trying not to think about what was going on in the bedroom next door. This was one part of the new arrangement she hadn't really planned on. How close she was going to be to Maria when she was working, specially in these new flats where they made the walls out of papier mâché. You could hear everything if you wanted to. Or if you didn't want to.

Wasn't like she was squeamish about it. There'd been plenty of times she'd had to sort out problems with punters on the street. Some punter with his dick hanging out having a go at Maria round the back of Aspro's. Been plenty of times when Maria had had punters round her own flat, till Bobby put her foot down. But this was different. Every bloody time. You couldn't help thinking about it, what your girlfriend was doing in there. She could have put a Walkman on, of course, but then the whole point was that she could hear what was going on in case a punter turned nasty. So there she was, sitting at the table, trying to distract herself with last week's *Post* magazine, when something caught her eye. Just idly flicking through the pages, his face leapt out at her. Leslie St Clair. Just as vivid on the page of a magazine as the first time she'd seen him.

That was in Barrells seventy eight, seventy nine; she would have been sixteen or so trying hard to look older. Anyway, there she was dancing away in this little dyke club on the edge of town and the handsomest man in the world walks in. That was the first thing she registered, how good-looking he was. Maybe she was wrong but there weren't so many handsome people around back then. Men in particular used to look terrible. Bobby thought of the Seventies – the Sixties and the Seventies, all the time she was growing up – and she thought ugly ugly ugly ugly. And seeing this guy who looked like he'd come straight off the TV walking into your club, well it was a shock.

And of course he really had walked in off the TV, more or less, cause when she'd stopped gawping at how pretty he was – yeah, yeah, just cause you're a dyke doesn't mean you can't have opinions – she recognised him. Leslie St Clair. It was one of the sad things about living somewhere like Cardiff; anybody from the city ever did anything, the whole place knew about it. Back then it was Shirley Bassey, John Toshack, Andy Fairweather Lowe, Dave Edmunds and Leslie St Clair. Didn't have anything to do with liking their music or whatever. Leslie St Clair's music was horrible, real lounge-bar-smoothie shit like the 'Music to Watch Girls By' thing they have on the advert now, but he was on TV a lot, the sort of feller would show up doing the song on *Morecambe and Wise*. Regular housewives' favourite, really, light brown skin; you could take him for whatever you wanted. Though everyone in Cardiff knew he was a docks boy. Him and Shirley – the ones that made good.

Anyway, there he'd been, Leslie St Clair, large as life, walking through Barrells like it was the most natural thing in the world that this TV celebrity should be in a dyke bar, and he goes over to the DJ booth where Big Norma is playing the records and he nods his head and Norma gets someone else to take over playing the records and leads the way into the office and Bobby leans over to Roz who she's dancing with and says, 'Did you see that?' and Roz is like Leslie St Clair, oh yeah big deal, he's in here all the time. Then Roz paused and put her mouth closer to Bobby's ear and whispered, 'Talent spotting,' then burst out laughing.

At the time Bobby just laughed without knowing what Roz

was talking about. It wasn't long, though, before she got to know very well what kind of talent spotting Leslie St Clair was engaged in. Took a whole lot longer to forget it, though, all the things she'd seen and done with Leslie St Clair. But she'd managed in the end, hadn't thought about him in years. Even when she'd hear his name on the news, the way you did from time to time, she'd let it brush past her, no more than an echo of an echo.

She leafed back to the start of the article, started reading the story of this poor kid from the docks who'd worked his way up from boxing to showbiz to business and as she read and noted all the gaps, all the things not said, all the things swept under the carpet, she laughed, laughed the laugh that says don't go pulling the wool over my eyes, the laugh that says don't try telling me this whole world isn't full of shit cause I know better.

It was only when she put the magazine down and started to light up a fag that she saw her hands were shaking, realised that under the cynical 'well what d'you expect him to tell the papers, what do you expect the papers to print?' response, she was raging. Something about seeing him there, smug and rich and hardly looking a day older than twenty years ago, and talking about something called community capitalism, that made her want to rip that smile from his face, tell the world what Leslie St Clair was really about.

She put the paper down and went over to the computer. Working on her website had become a way of banishing all troublesome thoughts.

Today, though, she couldn't settle to it. Copy of *Web Design for Dummies* in her hand, she was trying to figure out how to connect up video files to the site, but then Maria's four o'clock turned up, classic married bloke on a business trip, and Bobby found her mind couldn't keep track of the complexities; thoughts of St Clair first kept returning. What was she going to do – tell her story twenty years too late to that newspaper guy Kim was seeing? Couldn't really see how that was going to do her any good. But maybe it would, maybe it would make the memories go away. Christ, the memories.

In another effort to distract herself, she logged on to the Internet and started aimlessly surfing around. She checked out Friends Reunited, laughed at the pictures of Donna and Jane trying to look slim, then started to wonder if the Net might help her find her dad.

Now here was something strong enough to drive St Clair out of her head. Busy rooting around for something, anything, that might help her find her dad, she barely registered the door slamming as Maria's punter left. Maria walked round behind Bobby, started massaging her shoulders and looking at the screen.

'What you doing, Bob?'

'Nothing,' said Bobby. Maria didn't say anything, but Bobby knew she knew what was going on. Knew all about Bobby's dad. How she'd never known him. How her mum had hardly known him either. How he'd fucked off well before Bobby was born. How her mum had waited till about three weeks afterwards before getting shot of Bobby herself.

Bobby knew where her mum was, though; they told her that when she came out of the home. Pam Ranger, now living in Essex. Bobby spoke to her once in a while, generally after a couple of Diamond Whites. Always asked what her dad's name was, but her mum wouldn't give it up, pretended like she couldn't remember. Bobby knew Maria was kind of hoping she'd just let it lie. After all, she kept saying to Bobby, she didn't know when she was lucky, not having her dad around. Maria's dad had been around all right.

But sod that, it had to be better to know than not know, and if she could just get a name out of her so-called natural mother then she was sure with the Internet she'd have a chance of running the bastard down.

'Not now, Ri,' she said, loosing herself from Maria's grip. 'I've got to make a phone call.'

'C'mon, Bob. Let's get moving. I want to go out.'

Finally. Bobby sighed with relief. She'd been on edge ever since she'd spoken to her mum, waiting to get back on the Internet, see what she could find out. The night had just crawled by, but now at last Maria was finished. What time was it? Quarter past midnight. The other girls were still off doing hotel visits. Bobby'd got a mate to slip a few business cards in the toilets in the Hilton, paid off nicely. Maria'd been looking after the punters wanted to come out. Last one was some Jap business feller staying at the St David's where they were really fucking hot on keeping the girls out. Now that was the kind of punter you wanted – loaded, no trouble – not like the kind of lowlife you got out on the streets.

And now he was out the door and Maria wanted to go out, which was fair enough, Friday night and all that. But all Bobby wanted was for Maria to go out, leave her in peace, check out this name her mother had finally given up.

'Give us half an hour, love, and I'll be ready.'

'Fuck that, Bob. I'm the one been fucking working all night. Six fucking punters, five hundred quid, and now I wants to go out.'

'Fine,' said Bobby, 'you go out. I'll see you down there.'

'Jesus, Bob, it's past bloody midnight already.'

Bobby hesitated for a moment. She knew she was being selfish, but right now she just felt like getting on with her search.

'I said half an hour, didn't I? You wants to go out, fine. Like I says, I'll see you down there.'

'Christ, you're getting to be a boring cunt these days, Bob.' Maria grabbed her bag and her coat and moved towards the door.

'Aren't you going to call a cab?' Bobby asked as she turned on her computer.

'Fuck do you care, Bob, I get raped walking into town? You just carry on playing with your bastard computer.'

Bobby turned round, angry now. 'Look, I said you wait a half hour I'll fucking drive us into town, all right? Just box up a fucking draw and watch the TV and I'll be done in a minute.'

Maria shook her head. 'I'm going out, Bobby. Going down the Hippo, see my mates, have a bit of a laugh. You do what the fuck you want.'

'The Hippo, you sure?' said Bobby, thinking maybe she'd feel like it in a bit. But the door had already slammed behind her. Bobby frowned for a moment, aware that she was in danger of cocking up the golden rule of pimping – you've got to have the carrot as well as the stick, a little dollop of sweet to set against the sour. But then who was she kidding? Her and Maria, it was long gone beyond pimp and hustler. They were like an old married couple these days, bickering all the bloody time. Christ, she was feeling her age; that was another part of it. Maria's idea of a big night out – couple of Es, few lines of coke, up till dawn at the Hippo or the Emporium or whatever they called the Top Rank these days – well, once in a while Bobby could handle it but mostly, to be honest, she'd rather stay in, takeaway and a couple of videos. Getting old, for sure. She was in the car these days, she found herself tuning into Radio 2 just cause there were some songs she remembered.

Bobby shook her head, banished these thoughts, then clicked on the Internet Explorer icon. Her mum had been drunk when she phoned her, as per usual for a Friday night, far as Bobby could tell, and she'd whined and cried but finally given up a name for her dad. Only trouble was it didn't sound like his real name. 'Troy Thursday,' she'd said he was called. Well, you had to laugh really, didn't you? What kind of stupid slapper would get herself up the duff with a bloke called Troy Thursday, think it was his real name? Her mum, that's what kind. But still it was something, Bobby supposed.

She typed in Troy Thursday, waited, and the screen came back with 126,000 answers. That couldn't be right. Bollocks, she'd forgotten to put it in inverted commas. She put the commas in, clicked on Go again and waited, suddenly aware she was holding her breath. Two seconds later the screen came up and fucking hell – eighty-five matches found.

Her excitement quickly faded when she realised that they all seemed to relate to some place called Troy somewhere in the States and things that happened there on a Thursday – you know, girls' softball team play next match in Troy, Thursday 10 April. But she kept on going and on page six of the results there it was. Some kind of Tom Jones fan page offering a list of all the gigs Big Tom had played. She clicked on the link and a huge list of venues and dates came up, starting in the year 1960. She scrolled down and almost immediately she saw it: 13 January 1961, Ocean Club, Caerphilly. Tom was fourth on the bill alongside Lorne Lesley, the Bombardiers and Troy Thursday.

Bobby felt her hair stand on end. Her dad. Shit.

14

Pete was starting to wonder if he was entirely in control of his life. He was sat in his latest weekend motor – this time a rather more subdued new Toyota – sharing a spliff with Kim – who he was starting to think of less as Kim and more as my girlfriend though he had to be careful about that, he could tell you didn't want to put too many fences round Kim – and Mikey – who seemed to have appointed himself as Pete's best mate.

They were parked on the edge of Mermaid Quay outside what had been the Tiger Bay Café, about the only locally owned and run place in the whole neighbourhood and would you believe it the first to close down. People didn't come down here after authenticity; far as Pete could see, what they wanted was chain bars and restaurants offering new concepts in Italian dining, the same ones being rolled out in waterfront develop-ments and shopping malls from here to Bluewater. Anyway, they were sat in this car, the three of them, and it was coming up to midnight and they'd had a few drinks and Pete was now getting thoroughly stoned and they were trying to decide where to go next.

'We could go to the karaoke, over the Balti,' said Mikey.

Pete was about to say he'd rather listen to house music or nu-metal or absolutely bastard anything than go to a karaoke night, which was the kind of thing he just plain dreaded, but before he could get a word out Kim had chipped in with, 'Yeah, cool,' and dug Pete in the ribs and said, 'Be a laugh, eh?' and before he knew it Pete was trailing off after Kim and Mikey round the makeshift car park, across James Street, and a little way up Bute Street to the Baltimore Arms.

Once they were inside and upstairs Mikey peeled off to chat to the guy on the door and Pete headed to the bar with Kim.

'Now, let's get one thing straight,' he said. 'I am not singing. You can beg, you can plead, you can make me feel like a total wimp, I'm still not singing.'

Kim looked at him and shook her head in mock disapproval. 'You really are determined to be one boring bastard, aren't you?'

Pete shrugged, 'I told you.'

'Yeah,' said Kim, then, in an exaggerated Cardiff accent, she added, 'That's why I loves you, see,' and kissed him on the lips and Pete felt better and got the drinks in and was pleased he had made his stand, but then as the drinks got drunk and Kim went up and sang and Mikey went up and sang and Kim went up and sang again with a couple of other girls she seemed to know, and Pete sat there with his first pint still hardly touched and less and less to say, he couldn't help feeling like really he was a boring bastard and while he might be a bit of a novelty to a girl like Kim it wouldn't last, she'd have to find someone who was more of a laugh.

Watching her up on the little stage belting out 'Angels' with her mates, Pete couldn't help wondering what he was doing with a woman like this.

He'd slept with Kim three times now. First time had been the day they went out driving. They'd driven back to Kim's from the pub at warp speed. The excitement had carried Pete through the potentially awkward moments back at the flat, no shilly-shallying around making cups of coffee and stuff, but straight into the bedroom and unwrapping her clothes and his own clothes falling off and hands everywhere and just thrilled by the sight and the feel of an unfamiliar body after twenty years; a younger thicker body, not specially a better body than Viv's, it wasn't that, but a body that was responding with an eager lust not an easy familiarity.

It was only when things got down to the nitty-gritty that some weirdness crept in. The foreplay was fine; the foreplay was more than fine; it was – Pete couldn't help saying to himself – bloody great. It was what followed that was harder. When it came to the actual act Pete couldn't help but think of Viv, think of how Viv responded if he did *a*, wondered if Kim would like it if he did *b* because that's what Viv liked. Suddenly everything he wanted to do, every thrust or lick or bite, he realised he was doing because that's what he did with Viv, that's what Viv liked, and his head wasn't with Kim any more, it was thinking what would Viv think about this, and then wondering whether Viv had done this with someone else – a thought that hadn't crossed his mind before. He wasn't sure whether Kim had noticed or not – maybe she too was thinking of her ex – but suddenly, in the final stages, something was lost, some spark of intimacy and excitement was replaced by a sweaty ordinariness, and he was hit by a wave of utter misery.

It went after a while, of course, though if ever there had been a moment he wished he smoked that was it. And it wasn't long – in fact it was only a couple of hours – before they did it again. And it was good – less excited maybe but better controlled – and Christ knows it wasn't like there was any place in the world he'd have sooner been, but again there was that nagging sense of three of them in the bed and Pete knew that it would be a while before seventeen years of marriage worked their way out of his system.

Kim, to be fair, had been great about it. 'I bet you think of her, don't you?' she said after they'd done it that second time and Pete had squirmed and evaded and she'd laughed and said, 'Don't worry, I'm not asking you to do a comparison report, I was just thinking it must be weird for you, you know,' and Pete had managed a laugh too, and said yeah, weird was the word and that little moment had really helped to break down whatever barrier he'd been building up and suddenly he felt that much easier being around Kim, felt like she understood him.

Only trouble was, she might understand him but the way things were developing he was damned if he understood her.

Day after they'd been together he'd been thinking about her all the time. He'd phoned her up at work in the afternoon. God knows what the etiquette of these things was these days. Were you meant to wait weeks before you called someone just so they didn't think you were too keen, or was it only girls who were meant to do that? Anyway, he figured that he'd be pleased if she rang him so why shouldn't she be pleased if he rang her? So he did and it was a bit weird. It wasn't like she was unfriendly; she was perfectly friendly as ever. That was the thing. As ever. Friendly like she'd been the week before, not friendly like hey baby that was so gooood. But then maybe her boss was standing next to her when she took the call, maybe that was just her phone manner. Maybe, maybe, maybe.

He was plunged back into the thing he'd really hated about being single, never bloody knowing what was going on. Trying to figure out women like they were some alien species.

Shouldn't complain really, cause it made a change from trying to figure out Viv, as he had over the years, only to discover eventually that here was a woman who really was happy with her life – liked her job, liked her house, liked her kids, liked her washing machine, liked her husband, in about that order. Seventeen years figuring out someone who did exactly what it said on the packet. One thing about Kim, he was pretty sure there was more to her than met the eye.

Certainly, two weeks in, he wasn't getting much closer to figuring her out. Next time he'd seen her, the Thursday, she'd been fine; they'd gone out for a meal, Italian in town, gone back to hers again – and the sex had been good, definitely starting to get used to her, but then when he phoned her the next day to see what she was doing over the weekend she'd said she was busy the whole time which was a bit of a 'what the hell's that about', but had a kind of upside as it meant he did his duty and went to see Viv and the kids. They probably thought he was going completely mad cause he hardly said a word the whole time he was there, so weird had it all become now that he'd slept with Kim; it had somehow made the whole thing real, made him realise he really wasn't going back, this wasn't just a fantasy, this was his new life. And then he'd seen Kim again on the Monday and it had been fine, great even, and he could see that there was some kind of pattern emerging, some kind of dance, and one thing for sure, he wasn't the one leading it.

And now it was Friday night and Kim had come off the stage and people were buzzing around her and Mikey was sitting down at the table and introducing someone called Darren who was a moderately scary-looking white guy with prison tattoos on his forearm and a Cardiff accent so thick that even Pete who was born and bred had trouble with it, and then Kim was sat down too and had her arm around Pete and all the time the conversation seemed to be floating over or around him and then suddenly it was time to go and Pete was stood outside in the street and Kim's there saying that they could go back to her mate's place and Pete doesn't want to, all he wants to do is go back to Kim's place because when he's alone with her he feels fine and he can talk and be funny and alive but in a crowd like this he feels nothing but old and tired, so he says you mind if we go home, I'm really tired and Kim looks grumpy but says OK, but then when they get back to Kim's flat she turns to Pete and says, 'D'you mind not staying tonight? It's just I've got an early start in the morning' – first Pete had heard of this – 'and I've got my period and I just kind of need to be on my own. Is that OK?'

'Yeah,' said Pete, in that sense of 'yeah' that means 'not really but what can I do?'

'Oh God,' said Kim, 'you are sweet,' and leaned over and kissed him hard, let her tongue slide into his mouth, and then she pulled away and quickly got out of the car and waved goodbye, leaving Pete to drive off, the taste of her on his lips, completely unsure of where he stood.

15

Maria was late and Bobby was fed up. Maria hadn't come back from the Hippo till God knows what time the night before. Bobby hadn't minded too much about that cause she was still buzzing from finding her dad's name on the Net. Maria had blown out her two morning punters cause she was too hung over, and Bobby hadn't minded that either cause Tanya had filled in and Bobby spent the day making calls trying to trace her dad. But now it was well into the evening and Maria still hadn't shown up and Bobby was getting angrier by the minute. Tanya was off, Nikki was God knows where, there was a punter due any minute and Bobby's sweet high at finding a mention of Troy Thursday on the Internet had, with a complete lack of any further leads, steadily turned sour.

First she'd tried the Ocean Club where he'd played that gig long ago, but the Ocean Club wasn't there any more or at least it had changed its name half a dozen times and of course the manager now didn't have a clue what had happened in the Sixties. She kept on persevering, though, and eventually got hold of some old geezer who had been the manager sometime in the Sixties but he was worse than useless, he was one of those helpful bastards.

'You remember a singer called Troy Thursday, used to sing there back in the Sixties?' she'd asked.

'Yeah,' he'd said and her heart had leapt.

'Really?' she'd said.

'Yeah,' he'd said again.

'Well, d'you remember anything about him?'

'Yeah, he was a singer.'

'Well, what did he look like?' She could feel herself getting impatient now.

'Look like? I've no idea.'

'I thought you said you remembered him.'

'No, love, I said I remembered the name. Why, what d'you want to know?'

Bobby had felt like beating her brains out with the telephone; instead she pressed on, trying to get some sense out of him and getting precisely nowhere. He ended up giving her the names of a few other old-timers been on the club scene in the Sixties but they were useless and all. She was doing her best to face it. Her dad was a nobody who no one remembered. There you go. End of story.

The buzzer went. Bobby looked out the window. It was Nikki checking in for work, about eight bastard hours late. She sighed and got up from her computer, walked over to the intercom and buzzed her in. Time for a little chat.

Bobby waited till Nikki had plonked her bag down in the middle of the floor, sighing like she was exhausted from all the hard work of walking half a mile round to Bobby's place, then climbing a flight of stairs, even though she was still in her mid twenties and skinny as anything thanks to the fact that she lived on fags and tuna fish. She lit up a Marlboro Light the second she let go her bag, and Bobby walked over to the kitchen area, grabbed an ashtray and stuck it down in front of her.

'So,' she said once they were sat down nice and cosy across the coffee table, 'you like working inside then, Nikki?'

Nikki shrugged, flicked her ash just to one side of the ashtray. 'S'all right.'

'S'all right. That all you reckon it is? What d'you think walking up and down Penarth Road in the freezing fucking cold waiting for some punter to flag you down is then? That all right too?'

Nikki stared at Bobby. 'Same fucking thing, innit, Bob? Inside, outside. Still the same thing, innit?'

'No it fucking isn't. Out there, right; out there you're a slag. That's it. You're five minutes in the back of the car.'

'Two minutes.'

'Two minutes – that's your fucking attitude all over, right. Well, fine out there on the streets two minutes, yeah, fine. Get the money, get it done, get out of there. But this is different, right. In here, right, you're not a slag. You're like an escort, you're just a girl likes to show a bloke a good time.'

Nikki snorted with derision at this and Bobby barely resisted the temptation to grab her by the hair and smack her face.

'Come on,' she said instead, 'have a look at this.'

Bobby led the way over to the computer and opened up the Good Sex Guide website, clicked on Cardiff then showed Nikki the list of girls there.

'You see that? That's where all the blokes write down about all the different girls what they been with. Like reviews, right.'

Nikki wrinkled her face in a mixture of horror and disbelief. 'Reviews?'

'Yeah,' said Bobby. 'And this here, right, where it says Nikki, right, that's where this bloke writes about you. Now, let's see what he has to say, shall we?'

Course what the bloke says is none too complimentary. He doesn't say his name or anything but Bobby reckons she knows who it is. Feller looks like a teacher but drives a white van. Probably an electrician or something. Anyway, bloke's a semi-regular and he starts off saying he's been round to Bobby's place a few times and he's always had a good time; Tanya obviously got him off big-time and Lorraine was fine too. But Nikki – well, the feller was not impressed. Snotty, lifeless, looked at her watch after about ten seconds, wouldn't get on top, wouldn't let him touch her tits, would just lie there chewing gum and lit up a fag the second the bloke came. Ends up saying he was thoroughly disappointed, didn't know if he'd be going back there again.

Bobby waited till Nikki finished reading. 'Well?' she said.

'Well what? Who gives a fuck what some punter thinks? I'm not his fucking girlfriend, am I? I'm a fucking hustler. He wants a fuck, fair enough. But I'm not doing any of that other shit.'

Bobby looked at Nikki and her anger suddenly subsided. She could see the girl was actually upset at the thought of giving the punters any kind of intimacy. She sighed; she knew the story. Same old same old. Most of the girls she'd ever been with, the working girls, there was usually abuse one sort or another. Just because it was a cliché didn't mean it wasn't true. Lot of girls – not all the girls, definitely not – but a lot of the girls out there, they'd have some pretty fucking bad stuff to contend with. And Nikki was one of them, all right.

Bobby was on the point of saying something, probably something she would regret, like don't worry about it, girl, we'll keep on carrying you, when Nikki pulled herself together and spoke first.

'Anyway, Bob,' she said, 'I was talking to Maria last night . . .'

'Oh yeah?' said Bob, a note of menace in her voice, waiting to see if this was going where she suspected it was going.

'Yeah,' said Nikki, 'and she reckons you're not paying us enough.'

'She what?' Bobby stared at her. The deal Bobby gave her girls had to be the best in town. 'Fine,' she said. 'You don't like it, why don't you just fuck off out on the street, and the same goes for Maria and all. See how much fucking Scott or Chrissy Boy taxes you. Fact, fuck it, you just go and do that anyway. Had enough of you sitting round here looking like a miserable cow doesn't know a good thing when it's staring her in the face. Just fuck off.'

Nikki looked at Bobby in horror, her mouth dropping open, her eyes flicking from left to right as her brain struggled to find the words to make Bobby back down. Then the intercom went again. A regular punter. Bobby looked at Nikki. 'You're one lucky fucking cow, you knows that? Now, this feller comes round, you try and be nice, you got that?'

Nikki looked down, bit her lip and nodded.

Bobby shook her head. She'd believe it when she saw it. And as for Maria – she wasn't going to stand for that, no way. She was just about to put her headphones on, get back to her computer, blot out the sound of Nikki and the punter, when the phone rang. She picked up. It was the TV girl Kim, sounding all excited – her documentary was definitely happening. When could Bobby do an interview? Bobby thought about it. First reaction was it was asking for trouble publicising what she was doing. But maybe that was old-world thinking, Custom House thinking. Maybe now it would be cool to go on TV, tell the world you're a cyber pimp, free advertising basically. Plus right now she just felt like getting out of the flat and away from Nikki and Maria and the rest of them for a bit.

'Sure, darlin',' she said eventually. 'You just tells me the when and where, I'll be there.' And Kim says how about tonight and Bobby says OK and puts the phone down and then curses herself for not asking if there was any money in it.

It was late going on very late at night. The filming which had seemed to take for ever had finished hours ago and now Bobby was sat at a table in Floyd's bar right at the back by the window. She was right next to Kim who seemed to be somewhere on the cusp between drunk and very drunk or maybe she was putting it on a bit the way straight girls did when they put their hand on your leg.

It was surely up to Bobby now, how far she wanted to take it.

A week or two back, whenever it was she'd gone to meet her at the UCI, there wouldn't have been no question about it. She'd have had a bit of fun and forgotten her; she was a nice-enough-looking girl, no question, and you could just tell she'd be up for it in bed, wouldn't be one of those girls just lay there like they were doing you a favour just turning up. Now, though, Bobby didn't know. She wanted to take it light, but she had this scary feeling like maybe she couldn't do light any more, maybe light wasn't what she needed.

But then what she had with Maria was pretty heavy and that sure as hell didn't feel like what she needed either, so what the fuck. She leaned into Kim, found her mouth with her own, waited till Kim's tongue slid inside then bit down on it, not hard but firmly. She could feel Kim's whole body wriggle with anticipation. Oh well, maybe a bit of fun wouldn't be too terrible, thought Bobby.

And it wasn't either. They went back to Kim's place and it was like Bobby had expected, kind of grown-up student, loads of books and videos and CDs, stripped wooden floors. Bobby liked it too. In fact she almost felt like she was as horny for Kim's flat, Kim's nice safe life, as she was for Kim's nice round safe body. Whatever, it was a good time and Bobby slept better than she had for ages, which made it all the more surprising that when she woke up, Kim lying next to her snoring faintly, it was like someone had tipped a bucket of cold water over her, pure dread coming down.

It took her a moment to locate this dread. First thing she thought of was her father. Drawing a blank in her research for him. Nah, too old a wound. Maria? Not hardly; difficult to place too much value on sexual fidelity when your girlfriend's a hustler. So what was it? Getting older? Her uncertain future? Yeah, well all those things were worrying, all right, but none of them had the sharpness of this fear. Then she got it. Leslie St

Clair. Just saying his name to herself triggered deep and ancient pain. Leslie St Clair under her skin.

And lying there in the early-morning light, lying there in this nice safe flat with this nice safe girl, she realised she had no choice but to let herself remember. Remember it all.

End of the Seventies. Summer nights Bobby used to scrounge a bus fare off this social worker took a bit of a shine to her and head into town. She'd get off at the bus station and have a look in the Big Asteys café, see if anyone was about. Most times her friend Lee would be there, another half-caste kid – home used to be full of them back then, not like today when every other girl on the estate's got a little brown baby and nobody gives a toss.

If Lee was there, she'd go get a cup of tea and a Club biscuit, then sit at the corner table and take the piss out of all the old grannies down from the Valleys. That or talk about the football, who was coming up next, who was supposed to have a good firm. Living for Saturday afternoons the pair of them then.

It was obvious now, of course, became obvious pretty quickly even then, that they were both bent but neither of them was exactly broadcasting it. Lee specially. She supposed she'd known all the time what was driving him, what made him the vicious little fucker he was if it came to a fight. If you live in a home you hear all the stories, stuff Lee and a couple of other kids got up to, stuff they got up to with Mr Allen and all. But you ignored it, treated it like it was all a joke. And anyone called him a queer to his face – well, they didn't do it twice, not unless they wanted a taste of Lee's trusty Stanley knife.

Been a bit different for her, of course. For a start she never looked like the other girls, always looked like a boy, partly cause no one ever had a clue what to do with her hair and you never saw any girls in the magazines or anything weren't white, so she ended up having her hair short and she had this stocky kind of build and she liked sports – course that was the one thing they thought you might be good at – and she wasn't what you might call happy with her body shape, so she used to end up wearing tracksuits a lot, and so, basically, she looked like a boy and acted like a boy and in a funny sort of way it seemed only natural that she'd fancy girls like a boy – not just natural to her, seemed like everyone was expecting her to be a les. But all that said and done, it wasn't exactly an easy option – for one thing lesbians were like practically unknown back then. Least if you were a gay boy you could hang around the bus-station toilets and someone would soon show you what went where. Taken Bobby bloody ages to find out about Barrells.

That was where she'd go later on on Saturday night, nine, ten o'clock. But before that they'd just hang around, Lee and her. Asteys would turf them out after a bit. Sometimes they'd just stick around the bus station. Lee would stand around near the toilets, try and get money off of the old queers – give me a quid and I'll be in in a minute – now and again they'd fall for it if they were from out of town. Once or twice, and Bobby didn't feel good about it, they'd followed an old feller away from the station, waited till he crossed over the bridge then dragged him down on the towpath and robbed him. Never done any real harm, like, though the last time Bobby'd been a bit frightened by the expression she'd seen on Lee's face. So she hadn't wanted to do that again. And of course she'd found a new plan for them. Go round the Prince of Wales.

Tonight would be the fourth time they'd been there. First time had been funny. They'd hardly got in the door before the old bat in the ticket office was yelling at them to get the hell out of there, you dirty little bastards. Should have seen her face when Bobby said Mr St Clair asked her to come round. Woman kept shaking her head, looked like she was going to start crying or something. Anyway, in the end she showed them the way through the main doors into the foyer, pointed out the door that led upstairs, then left them to it. They'd made their way up this winding staircase till they came out on the top-floor landing, through another door and into a big room like a ballroom or something, all this old decoration on the walls and ceiling and that, and a bar at the back and a few tables spread around. St Clair was sat at the middle table, bottle of wine in front of him, people buzzing all around him, most of them not much older than Bobby or Lee. Made Bobby think of Fagin in *Oliver* – not that the kids were like pickpockets or anything. Well, some of them probably were but that wasn't the point – just that feeling of dodginess.

So, yeah, since then she'd been there twice and it was cool. Nothing much happened; St Clair was dead friendly, gave them Cokes and that, and it was just nice to be somewhere you didn't get any hassle. And of course Bobby knew there was going to be something St Clair wanted from her – or more likely Lee, she figured – she wasn't born yesterday.

Anyway, the fourth time they just gave the old bag a nod and headed straight up to the top floor. Moment they entered the big room Bobby could see something was going on. The tables had all been moved to one side and there was a guy Bobby hadn't seen before fixing up a couple of big lights.

St Clair spotted them immediately, came over and led them to the bar.

'Well,' he says, opening a Coke for Bobby and a barley wine for Lee, 'fancy you two dropping in. You like films?' He was looking at Lee not Bobby.

'Yeah,' says Lee and Bobby's just waiting for him to carry on with something really dumb like I thought *Earthquake* was really good, but then she sees Lee's eyes looking round the room and he just shrugs and glances at Bobby and they both raise their eyebrows a little bit like oh right, so this is what we've got ourselves into.

'That's good then,' said St Clair. 'Well, tell you what, why don't you two just sit down over here,' he waved at a little table set at the back of the room, behind the cameras, 'and watch what we're up to. Get a feel for how we do things round here, y'know.'

'Uh huh,' said Bobby and led the way over. Her and Lee just sat there for what seemed like hours while nothing much happened, both of them too edgy to say anything. Then St Clair walked over to the door and locked it. The lights were turned on and showtime began.

Bobby wasn't naïve. She figured she knew what to expect. After all, the Prince of Wales wasn't the Odeon, it was a porn pit. Not real porn, obviously, just innocuous crap about randy nurses. She knew; she'd sneaked in once or twice with the other kids, found out very quickly none of it spoke to her lust. She was pretty sure, though, that this would be different.

And it was. First off a couple of the lads she'd seen hanging around came on to the little set dressed in school uniform, despite being a good five years too old for it, both of them obviously trying not to laugh. She waited for the girls to come out, but they didn't; instead an older bloke dressed up as some kind of old-time teacher with a stupid fake beard on comes out and Bobby realises it's not going to be a boy-girl kind of a film. Which actually was a relief; she didn't know how she'd feel about watching that. Blokes with blokes, though, she could handle. In fact once they got going, the teacher guy starting to give his pupils the kind of lesson could get you on the front page of the *News of the World*, anyone caught you at it, she was disconcerted to find herself getting a bit turned on by it. As for Lee, his tongue was practically hanging out of his mouth. Bobby was sure St Clair wouldn't have much of a problem persuading him, he wanted to give old Lee his start in show business.

Whatever, the initial buzz wore off soon enough and the

proceedings became first comical – as the guy in the fake beard couldn't get it up – then boring – as the cameraman kept asking them to stop and do stuff again. Bobby had finished her drink so she got up, walked over to the bar and was just wondering if it would be OK to help herself to another Coke when St Clair materialised at her side.

'Not your scene, sweetheart?'

Bobby shrugged. 'Just thirsty.'

St Clair reached behind the bar and popped the lid off another bottle of Coke.

'How old are you, love,' he said, 'you don't mind me asking?'

'Sixteen,' said Bobby.

'Uh huh,' said St Clair, a flicker across his face, like he didn't believe her and was trying to figure out how old she really was. 'So where d'you live?'

'Rumney,' she said.

'Mum and dad?'

Bobby snorted with derision. 'Kids' home.'

'Oh yeah?' said St Clair and didn't say anything else about it, just left her till the filming finally finished and everyone was having a bit of a party and her and Lee were just going, and he slips up to her and asks, 'Don't suppose any of your girlfriends in the home be interested in being in one of our little films?'

And that's how it started. How she got from that – Bobby Ranger, screwed-up children's-home tomboy – to this – Bobby Ranger, top pimp, lying there in the early morning in a strange woman's sheets. And then she noticed that the strange woman was awake too and looking at her with concern and saying, 'Bobby, why are you crying?' and Bobby hadn't even noticed that she had been, and then before she knew it she was telling Kim, telling Kim all these secrets so long locked down, these secrets that had to come out before she choked on them.

16

Pete's phone rang for about the fiftieth time that afternoon. Cherri was lost somewhere near Ebbw Vale trying to find the Beaufort Theatre to interview Barbara Dickson, some idiot from the council's latest PR firm was hassling him to write something about some nautical festival they were having down the bay, the Subaru PR didn't know if she'd have a car for the weekend or not, could she let him know Friday morning, the ad manager had just rung with a couple of cancellations on page four so he'd have to dredge up some more news from somewhere and one way or another it was an afternoon of above-average hassle.

'Pete Duke,' he barked. But smiled when he recognised the voice on the other end of the line. Leslie St Clair. He'd rung up a couple of times since Pete's article had run, first to thank him for the piece, which was nice, wasn't often celebs bothered to do that.

'So what can I do for you today, Mr St Clair?'

'Les, man, for Christ's sake. I was wondering if you might like to come along to a little press conference we're having tomorrow. The WDA are hosting it, last big push for the Castle Market deal. Buffet and as much champagne as you can get down your neck. One o'clock at the St David's. You fancy it?'

'Sure,' said Pete, whose time on the *Post* had taught him never to walk away from a free lunch, and he put the phone down, already in a better humour. He worked his way steadily through the rest of the day's business, getting it all done by six, which was unusual. Now he felt like seeing someone, felt like seeing Kim, get things back on track. He dialled her number. She picked up quickly and sounded happy enough to hear from him, but she was all breathless and hyped up and busy filming something for her documentary, so she said she'd see him tomorrow which was good but didn't solve the problem of what to do now.

Pete thought about it for a moment, decided to head out into town, meet up with Randall. A quick trawl of the usual haunts failed to yield a sighting of Randall, however, which was a bit odd, so without really thinking what he was doing Pete found himself getting in the car and driving out to Whitchurch to see Viv and the kids.

Turning off Manor Way and heading up towards the close, he started to wonder if this was such a good idea after all. Viv was bound to be pissed off but he felt a real yearning to see them. Even if all they did was ignore him, they made him feel like he had some existence in the world, some solidity.

Sure enough, Viv opened the door and her face immediately turned to thunder. He could see her about to launch into a 'what the hell d'you think you're doing turning up here' rant but before she could say a word he'd slipped past her and into the kitchen where he sat down at the breakfast bar and waited for Viv to follow him in.

'Got anything to drink?'

'You what?' she said, staring at him and shaking her head. 'You can't bloody do this, you know.'

'I only asked for a drink,' he said, sounding like – who was he sounding like? – Randall he supposed, all fake innocence.

Viv shook her head again in disbelief but went to the fridge anyway, got out a big bottle of Coke, poured him a glass. Wasn't the kind of drink Pete had meant but he was getting soberer by the second and there was something achingly familiar about the glass of Coke.

'Kids in?' he said after taking a swig.

'Yeah,' said Viv. 'You mind telling me what the hell this is about?'

'Nothing much,' said Pete. 'Just thought it would be nice to see you.'

'Oh yeah, you just thought it would be nice to see us? Well, great. And how are we supposed to feel? Honoured? Look, kids, Dad's come back to see us. Well, you bastard.' She broke off, just stared at him. 'You got any idea what you've done to us, walking out like that?'

Pete looked around him, wondered if there was any evidence of what he'd done. Everything was just the way it used to be. The fridge had the same stuff inside it, the same fridge magnets on its door; the wipe-clean noticeboard had the same notices on it. A three-quarterful bottle of wine identical to the one that had been there the day he left was stood on the spotless work surface next to the cooking oil. Nothing had changed. If he let his eyes fasten on any more details he was sure he'd go mad. As far as he could see, it all just proved his point. There'd been no need for him there, the place had run perfectly well without him. Or had it? Up till now he'd repressed the idea that his leaving might have been devastating – he'd never thought himself capable of devastation. But what if the sameness of everything was not a sign of continuity but of trauma; what if that wasn't a similar bottle of quarter-drunk wine but the same bottle? What if he'd paralysed these lives that had been dearer to him than his own? What words to say then?

'You all right, love?' he said at last. Well, it was a start.

She looked at him like he was mad. 'What d'you bloody think, Pete? Your bloody husband walks out on you after seventeen bloody years, out of the blue, and you ask if I'm all right. Course I'm bloody not. And right when Becca's got her GCSEs coming up and all . . .'

Pete tuned out a bit at this point. He just had to believe that the kids were OK. They seemed OK whenever he'd visited them since. They said their schoolwork was going fine. He had to hang on to that. And he knew Viv, knew she'd try and work on his guilt. What she didn't seem to get was that it was his guilt over leaving her that was her better avenue of attack, but then maybe she was just like him, didn't think she mattered for herself.

'. . . and you leave me here stuck out in the middle of bloody nowhere . . .' exactly where you always insisted on living, thought Pete '. . . and you're off in bloody town and no doubt you got yourself a bloody girlfriend already . . .' She always said that but this time she must have noticed some reaction in Pete's face cause she stopped all of a sudden. 'Oh Christ,' she said, 'you have, haven't you? You've got a bloody girlfriend,' and then she burst into tears and Pete awkwardly tried to put his arm round her but she batted him away, just let herself sob and sob then turned to him and said through her tear-stained face, her face made ugly by crying, 'Who is it?'

'No one you know,' he said, stalling for time. He hadn't planned on telling Viv about Kim, not till he was a lot surer about it all himself. Best thing maybe would be to deny the whole thing except, bollocks, 'no one you know' kind of gave the game away.

'Yeah, well,' says Viv, half laughing, half hysterical, 'didn't think you'd be going off with Julie next door. C'mon, tell me who the bitch is.'

'Her name's Kim,' said Pete. 'She works for the BBC.'

'Well la-di-da. How old is she?'

'I dunno,' said Pete, wondering if she'd ever told him.

'Younger than me, I'll bloody bet. Have to be young to be taken in by a wanker like you.'

'She's about thirty,' said Pete, adding a couple of years on to what he guessed Kim's actual age to be. He should ask her, should find out her bloody birthday. Christ, how little he knew about her. How much he knew about the woman stood in front of him.

'Well, you want me to tell the girls, tell them about Dad's new girlfriend? Bet they'd be interested.' Viv's voice was getting louder.

'No, for Christ's sake. I wasn't even planning on telling you yet. It might be all over next week. You know what it's like . . .' Oh, why did he have to say that?

'No, I don't know what it's like; I'm stuck here with two kids. How'm I expected to know what it's like? Or d'you think I'll be hopping over the garden fence having it away with old Duncan?' She turned round, grabbed the bottle of wine, took out the stopper and poured herself a big glass. Pete watched her face carefully. If the wine had really been there for two months, no way she'd be able to swallow it. He felt a moment of idiotic relief when it seemed to go down smoothly. Life had been going on as normal. It hadn't all been paralysed by his absence.

'Look,' he said, 'I'd better go.'

'Yeah,' said Viv, 'you better had,' and then, as Pete was walking out the door, her door, their door, she shouted after him, 'And give my love to your girlfriend, tell her I'll tear her throat out I ever sees her.'

Christ, a bit of Cardiff creeping into Viv's hard-won accent. Pete drove off pondering her threat. Did it mean she still loved him? Did he want her to still love him?

17

Bobby and Jamal were in the health centre. Jamal had a bit of an earache, and Maria had a regular booked in at four, so Bobby'd taken him down after school. Jamal was sat there with a packet of crisps and Bobby was wrapped up in her thoughts, wondering what the hell had been going on in her head, blurting out all that stuff to Kim.

Anyway, she's sitting there minding her own business when this old feller comes in and sits down next to her, starts rabbiting on about the development and that, and Bobby's not paying a lot of attention cause it's not like she hasn't heard it all before about a million times, but then the feller – Noah his name was, she thought; old West Indian feller anyway – starts talking about the Big Windsor and what the hell are they doing just leaving it to rot? Heard tell they were going to turn it into a lap-dancing club – he laughs and stares at Bobby but nothing happens – and I remember when that place was jumping, all the entertainers used to come down there – and Bobby's ears prick up at this and she asks the question one more time.

'You ever hear of a singer called Troy Thursday?'

The old feller thinks about it. Bobby can see he's dying to say yes, but eventually he shakes his head and says, 'No, darlin', 'fraid not.'

Bobby just smiles and says, 'No worries.'

The old feller won't leave it alone, though. 'When was he around then? Fifties? Sixties?'

'Early Sixties,' says Bobby, her eye on the doctor's surgery door which is just opening, should be Jamal's turn next.

She can see the old feller ransacking the memory banks one more time but before he can speak the nurse calls out, 'Jamal Hughes,' and she stands up then taps Jam on the shoulder so he gets up too and they're heading for the doctor's door when the old feller finally pipes up and says, 'I know, darlin', I know who you should ask. Feller called Bernie Walters. That feller knows everyone in the entertainment business.'

'Yeah, thanks,' says Bobby, her first thought being what would I want to talk to that old cunt for, but then she thinks again and she has to face it. It's a good idea. If anyone could tell her who Troy Thursday was, it was probably Bernie Walters. Been booking acts in Cardiff since Moses showed up with the tablets. Funny she hadn't thought of him before, really – it was just that he was hooked up with Kenny Ibadulla and bloody Ken always treated Bob like she was something you'd stepped in. So, yeah, sure, Bernie Walters, but how was she going to get to him without going through Kenny?

It was a question she asked Maria later on, the three of them having their tea back at the home flat. And Maria surprised her by saying well why don't you just go round Bernie's office? It's only down on St Mary Street.

Just a little remark but it was one of those moments for Bobby, like someone just turned the lights on. Of course – that was all you had to do, look in the phone book to get his address and go round his office. What could be more obvious? It struck Bobby forcibly just how small-scale her existence was, how limited she'd let herself become by the hustling life. The world outside Butetown had become unreal to her. An outsider like Bernie Walters only really came into focus through his connection with Kenny Ibadulla.

But this one little unthinking remark of Maria's, it was like she'd been let out of prison. You just take it for granted that Kenny is the man, cause within Butetown, of course it's true, Kenny's the man. But let your horizons widen and what's Kenny? Another petty gangster whose territory amounts to a single crumbling housing estate. And if Bobby wanted to move up in the world, who was Kenny, who was anyone, to stop her?

'Ri,' she said then, 'what d'you think about moving?'

'Moving?' said Maria.

'I don't want to move,' said Jamal, suddenly tuning into the conversation, 'I'm watching *Simpsons*.'

'Not now, love,' said Bobby, ruffling his hair and waiting till his attention was focused back on Springfield's first family before turning to Maria. 'I was thinking maybe we could rent one of the other flats over the wharf, to live in, like. Be easier for work and stuff.'

Maria's eyes immediately flickered to Jamal. Bobby knew what she was thinking. Boy was nearly six now; one of these days he's going to be wondering where it is Mummy goes to work.

'Doesn't have to be the same block or anything. I was just thinking it'd be good to get away from here —' she waved her hand, not sure herself if she was referring to the flat or the street or the whole of bloody Butetown '— and they're nice, the flats, aren't they?' Christ, she sounded like she was an estate agent, trying to sell Maria the place — what was going on in her head?

'I dunno,' said Maria eventually. 'What's the point?'

And Bobby just shrugged, wondered if these changes she was going through, maybe they were going to take her away from everything. 'Fine,' she said, 'whatever. I'm going over the wharf for a bit.'

'Playing with your bloody computer again.'

'Yeah,' said Bobby, feeling once more like there was a chasm opening up between her and Maria, 'that's right.' She kissed Jamal and headed out into the evening.

On the street she turned on her mobile, listened to her messages. A couple of hang-ups, probably punters. One from the feller Pete asking for an interview. Christ, she'd have to think about that bit first. And one from Kim – you fancy coming round? Bobby grinned suddenly; she could think of something better to do than play with her computer.

She called Kim. Kim only had an hour before she had to go out but if Bobby wanted to come over like right now . . .

Bobby fancied it, all right. Fancied it like she hadn't in a long time. Fancied Kim like she fancied leaving her life behind. Hardly a word spoken between them the whole time, just hot and heavy from the moment she walked in the door. Came like a fucking train. Afterwards she did go over the wharf, played with the computer a bit, more than anything just to take the flush from her face before she had to see Maria again.

Next morning Bobby was up bright and early, made Jamal a cooked breakfast, took him to school chatting all the way there – how did he like his teacher? what did he think of the lunches? all this stuff – till the kid was looking at her like what are you on? And then she called up directory enquiries and got Bernie Walters's number, phoned it up and got an address in St Mary Street off the secretary.

She hung up and stood there for a moment, just knowing that Bernie would be the key.

Half of her wanted to stop now, go back to the flat, have a cup of tea, sort of savour the anticipation. Other half wanted to get it over and done with, plus to be honest she was nervous and she knew the longer she left it the worse she would get and before she'd realised she'd made a decision her feet were carrying her towards town.

On the way she wondered what excuse she could use to get to talk to Bernie. She'd met him once or twice over the years. Sixtyish feller but looked good on it; thick grey hair and a permanent tan, word was he owned a share of Kenny's club, Black Caesar's. She knew who he was, all right, but she doubted it was mutual. So what was she going to say? Maybe ask him about the lap-dancing, see if he was interested in her introducing some girls to him. Get a commission or whatever. Nah, she thought, as she reached the Monument and the beginning of St Mary Street, might as well go straight for it.

The secretary put on a bit of a show when Bobby walked in – like 'You want to see him today? Oh no, I don't think so' – but then she buzzed through and had a quick word, told him there was a young lady wanted to ask about an entertainer he might have represented back in the Sixties and obviously Bernie said send her right in, cause, after a little bit more fiddling about and making Bobby take a seat next to the framed photo of Dave Edmunds, the door opened and there was Bernie.

He walked over to shake her hand, clocking her as she stood up, stuck his hand out and said, 'I know you, don't I? But you're going to have to excuse me. I never forget a face, love, but I'm hopeless with names.'

'Bobby,' she said, 'Bobby Ranger.'

'Course,' said Bernie, 'Bobby Ranger . . . well, come on in.'

She followed him into the office, framed photos all over the place, everyone from Stan Stennett to Cerys Matthews. Her eyes passed over them quickly, hungrily, like she was expecting one of them to say Troy Thursday in big letters. Didn't, of course.

Bernie sat down on his desk, great big fuck-off computer on a table next to it, obviously brand new, the box was stood there in the corner. Bernie clicked on the screen and she saw a game of cards disappear.

'Nice computer,' she said.

Bernie shook his head. 'Probably. That's what my bloody nephew sold me the thing tells me. "Bernie," he says, "you got to get into the computer age, get your business on-line, get a website." So like an idiot I say yes and he sells me this stuff, five grands-worth of it, and be honest with you that was six months ago and I just about know how to turn it on, love . . . Makes me feel like I'm from out the ark. You understand this stuff?'

Bobby shrugged. 'I knows a bit.'

'Really?' says Bernie, brightening up. 'Cause I've been asking our old mate Kenny if he knows anyone could help me out and he's just been um-ing and er-ing . . .'

Our old mate Kenny. Bobby wondered who the hell Bernie thought she was. Still, now wasn't the time to set him right. 'Yeah, well,' she said, 'I'm not an expert exactly, but I might be able to help you out a bit, if you want to build a website or something. I've built my own . . .' she added, thinking why am I telling him this?

'Really?' said Bernie. 'That'd be great. If you could find some time in the next week or so. Wouldn't be able to pay you much, but . . .'

'Sure,' said Bobby, thinking Christ, looks like I'm the one getting the job. 'Sure.'

'Great. Now what was it you wanted to see me about?'

'Well,' began Bobby, 'I'm trying to trace this singer from the Sixties.'

'Oh yes?' said Bernie. 'What's the name?'

'Troy Thursday,' said Bobby, the name sounding ridiculous as ever, like she was trying to track down Scooby Doo.

'Troy Thursday,' said Bernie, frowning. 'And might I ask why?'

'Well,' said Bobby, launching into what was becoming a familiar spiel, 'I was adopted —' that was the first lie; what she really meant was I was left abandoned, unwanted '— and I'm looking to trace my natural parents and I found my mum, right, and she says my dad was a singer called Troy Thursday.'

'Hmm,' said Bernie, who'd suddenly gone all inscrutable.

'Well,' said Bobby, who frankly couldn't bear the suspense, 'you remember him or what?'

'Oh yes,' said Bernie, 'I remember the name, all right. Only trouble is there wasn't just one Troy Thursday; it's a name a few people used.' He looked up at the ceiling, frowned. 'Well, it was a name I invented, to be honest, and any time someone dropped out from a bill we'd stick Troy Thursday on instead. This was late Fifties, early Sixties, see, things were less sophisticated then: you could tell folks that Troy Thursday was a big name in London and they'd believe you. But really it'd be whoever was hanging around the office at the time – they would be Troy Thursday for the night up in Aberdare or Ponty or wherever.'

Bobby thought about this: typical of her bloody mother to get off with a guy who wasn't even real. 'You remember who any of them were?' she asked hopefully.

Bernie shrugged. 'Long time ago, you know, but I tell you what. You come back next week and have a look over the computer situation, I'll see if I can't get a little list together – how's that sound?'

'Fine,' said Bobby. 'How about if I ask my mum where the gig was she met him – would that help? You got any records or anything?'

Bernie laughed. 'Nothing that thorough, I'm afraid, but yes, if your mother can remember where it was, that might help jog the old memory bank. Amazing what sticks in there, you know. Well, to be honest, you get to my age it's easier to remember stuff happened in 1961 than stuff happened last week. So if you make an appointment with Marguerite on your way out I'll look forward to seeing you next week.'

Bobby shook Bernie's hand awkwardly and was just about to leave when something obvious struck her. 'All the Troy Thursdays, they were all black then?'

She could have sworn she saw a flicker of panic on Bernie's

face but if there was one he banished it quickly and all he said was, 'Look, love, like I say, it was a good old while ago, but yeah, quite a few of the Troys would have been black, always had a lot of docks boys on the books. And like I say, I'll get a little list together for you.'

'OK,' said Bobby, because what else could she do – beat the name out of him?, but as she walked down the stairs she reckoned Bernie Walters had a pretty good idea who her dad was.

18

Pete had slept really badly. Viv kept appearing in his dreams. Guilt coming down hard. Pete wasn't good with guilt. He couldn't bear to feel he had hurt someone else. Part of him, a big part of him, just wanted to go back home to her, put the shutters up and carry on with their nice quiet life. Kind of like those old guys who can't hack it outside prison; first thing they do when they get released is commit another crime, so they can go back to their nice comfy cell and a life without decisions.

He got out of bed before these thoughts suffocated him. He knew he was doing the right thing. Was sure that in the long run Viv would see he was doing it for both of them – saving them from a living death. Wouldn't she?

He was in work early and spent most of the day being, he suspected, a bit of a bastard. Right on everyone's case. Worked straight through lunch drawing up a three-month plan for the features pages and was just calling an arse-kicking meeting of his key writers when the phone went. Kim. And for the first time that day he felt happy. She said she wanted to meet him somewhere quiet, she had a story she wanted to tell him about, so he suggested the Conway and she said fine and just this brief exchange seemed to relax him, helped him get through the second half of the day a little more calmly than the first.

In the Conway Pete was almost at the bottom of his first pint by the time Kim showed up. As she walked towards him he wondered what Viv would make of her. She was younger than Viv – seven, eight years younger. Of course Viv kept herself in pretty good shape, a bit obsessive about it, if you asked Pete, while Kim didn't seem to care that she was carrying a few extra pounds. That was a lot of it for Pete, really; Kim just didn't seem to see life as such a bloody training course as Viv did. You could see it on her face that Kim was a girl liked to have a good time. But what would Viv think? God knows. Probably that she was a bit of a slapper. Well, thought Pete, maybe he was a bit of a slapper at heart too. He wondered what Kim saw when she looked at him. A bloke learning to relax a bit, he hoped. He'd gone back to the flat after work, changed out of his suit into jeans and a plain blue shirt from Gap. Nothing fancy but he wasn't trying to be fancy; all he wanted to be was a steady good bloke who knew how to have a bit of a laugh as well. And as Kim walked towards him and kissed him on the lips he felt sure this was a woman he could have a laugh with.

'So,' she said once they'd got a fresh round of drinks, 'you want to hear about my story?'

Sure said Pete so Kim launched into this long-winded account of how she'd done this, like, in-depth interview with this Bobby, you know the pimp, yeah, and that was all really good, yeah, really good material for Kim's documentary, but then she came out with this incredible stuff about Leslie St Clair.

'Oh yeah?' said Pete, his ears pricking up a bit.

'Yeah,' said Kim and told Pete all about the Prince of Wales and the porn movies.

'Christ,' said Pete when she finished. 'I'd heard a few rumours before. But never from anyone was actually involved. Shame she didn't come forward before I wrote my piece about him.'

'Well she couldn't have really,' said Kim, ''cause it was only reading your piece made her remember it all.'

'Wouldn't have thought you'd forget something like that,' said Pete. 'You sure she's not just making it up?'

'No,' said Kim, 'no way. She obviously just, like, repressed the memory or whatever.'

'Yeah,' said Pete, 'I guess. So what are you going to do about it? How's it going to fit with your documentary?'

Kim looked at him, shook her head. 'It's not for me, stupid. It's for you so you can do a follow-up story, expose the real Leslie St Clair.'

Pete thought about it. It was . . . well, potentially it was a great story. If it checked out, which was a big if. Controversial as hell, mind. Wales wasn't a place which liked to see its heroes taken down. So taking down Leslie St Clair wouldn't be something to do lightly. Most definitely controversial. And Graham wouldn't be keen on that. What Graham liked was good news, civic-booster stuff – under-35s vote Cardiff Britain's best city for getting completely arseholed in. 'I dunno,' he said eventually. 'Might be tricky to get it past the editor.'

Kim looked at him aghast. 'For fuck's sake, Pete, don't be such a gutless bloody wimp. Your editor doesn't want to know, take it to bloody London. Tabloids'll pay you a fortune.'

Pete thought about it some more. Yes. Well. Maybe anyway. But he wasn't at all sure that Graham would be happy to let Pete moonlight. So where would that leave him? Did he want to quit his nice comfy job and dive into the world of freelance muck-raking? Did he hell. On the other hand, he didn't want Kim thinking he was a total wimp. And anyway it was most likely just a load of ancient gossip would never add up to anything, so for the moment he figured he'd try and stick to his usual life strategy, trying to please everybody.

'Uh, yeah, of course,' he said, 'I'll check it out. You tell Bobby to get in touch with me she wants to take things further.'

'Great,' said Kim, 'great,' and Pete smiled at her and was just standing up to get another round of drinks in when there was a clap on his shoulder and he looked up and saw Randall standing there.

'Randall,' said Pete, 'what are you doing here?' which was a stupid question – like asking a dartboard what it's doing in a pub. So Randall just shrugged and Pete remembered his manners and said, 'Oh, this is Kim.'

'Robert Randall,' said Randall, sticking out his hand.

'Oh,' said Kim, 'from the paper? My nan loves your column.'

'Hmm,' said Randall, 'thanks,' not looking altogether thrilled by this information. Pete could see he still fancied himself as a bit of a ladies' man. But he recovered himself quickly and in no time was getting the drinks in. And then they were sat round the table together and it occurred to Pete that if anyone would know about St Clair and dodgy movies in the Prince of Wales, Randall would be the man.

'Oh yes,' said Randall. 'You know he used to own the Prince of Wales?'

'The old porn cinema,' said Pete. 'Yeah, I heard that.'

'Well,' said Randall, lowering his voice to conspiratorial level, 'I seem to remember there was a rumour at the time he wasn't just showing porn movies there, he was making them too, and none of your soft-core business either.'

'Yeah? So when would that have been?'

'Late Seventies,' said Randall. 'Lot of that stuff going on then. Porn stuff. There was a feller in Bridge Street used to have a trapdoor in his shop floor, let his special customers down to where he kept the hard stuff. It was all new then.'

Bridge Street, thought Pete. Heart of the old seedy Cardiff centre long since airbrushed out of existence. The new Bridge Street had a selection of multi-storey car parks and a bike shop in it; the old Bridge Street was a hundred-yard stretch of dodgy second-hand 'bookshops', smoky cafés, scrumpy pubs and 'medical supply' shops that lost half their trade when they legalised abortion. Pete used to haunt the street when he was a kid looking for *Marvel* comics, knowing he was trespassing into the forbidden world of adults. The Seventies: sin and perversion behind those doorways filled with blue and yellow streamers.

And then the conversation moved on to Kim's documentary; *The Secret World of the Lesbian Pimps* she told Randall it was called.

'Hmm,' said Randall. 'Always were a few of them around. Used to be an amazing woman in the House of Blazes, six foot tall if she was an inch. Sailors used to come in and . . .'

And Randall was off into tales of the old Tiger Bay. Kim sat there lapping them up, all this good stuff that never made it into *Randall's Rambles* – the hookers and pimps and Benzedrine addicts and blue movies made in the Prince of Wales.

Pete was happier, happier than he'd been for a while. Watching Kim and listening to Randall, he realised that a lot of the strain he found in being with Kim was they were always around her mates, who invariably made him feel straight and boring and old. Randall, on the other hand, made Pete feel like he was someone, someone dry and witty and experienced. Someone who could have a few drinks, tell a few stories.

They ended up staying in the pub till closing time. Afterwards, Pete announced he was starving, partly to try and head off a visit to the Cambrian, which was bound to be full of Kim's mates and could too easily break the evening's spell, and partly because it was the simple truth. He figured he'd walk back with Kim and pick something up from the takeaway, but instead Randall chipped in with, 'How about you two lovebirds come back to the flat for some bread and cheese and a drop of whisky?'

Pete looked at Kim and she nodded and smiled and then cooed with delight when she saw Randall's flat and turned to Pete and said why the hell haven't you brought me here before, this place is fabulous, and Pete for once didn't try to explain, just shrugged and smiled and soon they were sat in the kitchen eating bread and Brie and drinking tumblers full of single malt that tasted of peat and fog and chocolate and had one of those nights when everyone's laughing like hell and in between unburdening their deepest thoughts and no one can remember a thing about it in the morning, which is partly just as well and partly because it feels like the top of your head is going to come off.

At least that's how Pete's head felt at six the following morning. But feeling the warmth of Kim next to him helped and so did the Alka-Seltzers he fetched for them both and so did the sweaty, still half-drunk, sex that followed, allowing them both another hour's sleep, and after they'd breakfasted on strong coffee and kissed in the street before parting Pete felt great as he walked down past the stadium to work. Felt terrible but great too.

19

Bobby and Maria dropped Jamal off at school then walked over to Atlantic Wharf. Malcolm Hopkin was meeting them there at half nine to show them a potential new flat before they started work. Bobby was buzzing with ideas. She'd been on the computer half the night. First she'd finally sorted out how to upload her site on to the Net, and found a server who wasn't too fussy what kind of sites they hosted, which wasn't hard. It was starting to become obvious to everyone that there was only one sure-fire money-maker on the Net and that was sex. Funny, really, what happened to all those smart young entrepreneurial types. Six months ago they'd all been chopsing on in the papers about how their new site selling designer perfume or handbags or offering a unique service to the Jewish, lesbian, whatever community was going to take the world by storm, and now they were all busy getting their hands dirty, trying to actually generate some revenue. Well, good luck to them, but Bobby couldn't help but see the irony. She'd spent years on end being the object of general disgust – the evil pimp – and now the world was awash with cyber-pimps in Armani-framed glasses. Now she was looking forward to getting back over there, tweaking the site some more.

'Bob! Earth to fucking Bob? I'm here, you know.'

Bobby came to, looked at Maria, smiled vacantly.

'Sorry, doll, miles away.'

'You're always fucking miles away. You're living on another planet, Bob. It's doing my head in.'

'What?' said Bobby. 'You happier working out on the street? You don't think it's a better set-up we've got now?'

'No, Bob, course it's better. All that side of it, course it is. But you, Bob, it's like I don't know who you are any more. You never bloody speak to me. You're always on the bloody Internet. Jamal's complaining how you're never there at bedtime like you used to be. And I'm sick of telling him don't worry, love, Auntie Bob's building a nice website so your mum can screw more punters.'

'Christ, Ri, I'm only doing it for you. Make life easier.'

'Yeah, right, like you don't take half the money. Anyway, that's not the point; I don't want to talk about that. All it is, Bob, is I don't want a fucking website, I wants you to talk to me, I wants to have a laugh like we used to.'

Bobby didn't say anything, just hunched her shoulders up in her jacket and walked on ahead.

Maria laughed, ran after her, put her arms around Bobby. 'Christ, Bob,' she said, 'you look just like a little boy sometimes.'

Bobby rolled her eyes. She gave Maria her wintriest, oldest smile, a smile devoid of joy. 'Yeah, girl,' she said, 'never heard that before.'

'Oh, fuck off, Bob. That's exactly what I mean. You're so serious all the time. Lighten up, why don't you?'

Bobby kept her mouth shut, strode on towards the Atlantic Wharf flats. Didn't say another word till she saw Malcolm Hopkin waiting outside.

'All right, Mal,' she said and he raised his arm in greeting.

'All right, Bob,' he said.

'Yeah, not bad.' Bobby turned and saw Maria walking away, over towards the work flat.

'Something the matter, Bob?'

'Fuck knows. Time of the month? Who knows? Women, Mal. You know what I mean?'

Bobby had a good look around the new flat with Malcolm Hopkin. There wasn't anything special about it — it was pretty much identical to the one she was already renting, but Hopkin liked to haggle over money. You could see he got off on the game of it and, to be honest, Bobby found she liked being around Hopkin, liked the way he seemed to know everyone, know how to get things done, and yet he stayed in the background. She was sure she could learn a lot from a feller like that. How to survive, even. It was bothering her a lot these days. She'd wake up in the night worrying about shit she'd never even thought of before. What would she be doing in ten years' time? What would she be doing when she was old? How would she live? Suppose when you're young, you don't care about that stuff. That's why you get fucked up. But here she was pushing forty and the amazing thing really, when she thought about it, was how un-fucked-up she was. No drink or drug problems and she was fit as she'd ever been; didn't go to the gym or nothing but she walked a lot, she supposed. So she might as well face it; all the signs were she was going to be around for a bit.

'You got a pension, Mal?' she said as they left the flat, the rent agreed at a quarter of the figure she was paying for the other place ('One word you're doing any business in there, Bob, though, and you're out, right').

Hopkin laughed. 'Course I have, love.' He pointed to his head. 'It's right in here. Certain people don't look after me, I'll be writing my memoirs; well, dictating them anyway, you know what I mean?'

Bobby laughed briefly. 'Seriously, though.'

Hopkin raised his eyebrow. 'I am being serious, love. But if you're serious, I'll give you the number of a financial adviser won't rip you off too bad.' He looked at her quizzically. 'You feeling all right, Bob?'

'I dunno, you just gets tired sometimes.' Then she mustered up a smile and said, 'Yeah, well, back to work.'

Hopkin headed off to meet someone in the Wharf. Bobby headed for the work flat.

When she got there, there was no sign of Maria, just Nikki and Tanya sat in front of the telly watching MTV Base.

'Seen my girl?' said Bobby.

Nikki and Tanya looked at each other.

'She went out,' said Tanya eventually.

'Oh yeah?'

Tanya didn't say anything, apparently under the impression that 'out' was a good enough answer. Bobby let Tanya's eyes drift back to the TV, Destiny's Child high-kicking their way through 'Survivor', then bent down and yelled in her ear, 'Where the fuck did she go?'

'Christ, Bob,' said Tanya, sitting up. 'I don't know, do I? Phone rang and then she said she was going out.'

'Christ sake,' said Bobby, shaking her head. Then Nikki spoke up.

'Town, I think, Bob. She said to whoever it was she was going to meet them in town. Somewhere called Space, she said. You know where that is?'

'Space?' Bob thought about it, knew she'd heard the name, couldn't think where it was. 'All right,' she said, 'thanks, Nikki. Now, who wants to do the silly cow's one o'clock?'

'Can't, Bob,' said Tanya. 'Got an outcall over in Cyncoed.'

'I'll do it, Bob,' said Nikki. Amazing how she'd got it together since being given that talking to.

'All right, girl, nice one. It's a regular. Mr Jones, middle-aged feller, no problem. I got to go out for a minute but don't worry if I'm not back; he's all right.'

Bobby headed back outside. She wanted to be by herself for a moment to think. Where the fuck had Maria gone and who with? She called Maria's mobile number; it rang a couple of times then went on the voicemail. Bitch must have clocked Bobby's number. She called Maria's flat – nothing. Who the hell had she gone to see? She decided to go check out the flat anyway. Five minutes and she was round there. Let herself in with her key. Nobody home. Started to look through Maria's stuff for some clue as to where she'd gone, then stopped herself. What on earth was she doing? Maria would turn up later on; she was just acting like the unreliable bitch she always had been. Question was, why was Bobby taking it so serious?

Lot on her mind, that's what the trouble was. Nothing to do about it but calm down and get on with the job. She took a few deep breaths, let herself out of Maria's flat and drove back round the wharf, parked outside the pub. As she got out of the car she saw Malcolm Hopkin come out of the pub, meeting over presumably. 'All right, Mal.' She nodded her head at him.

'All right, Bob.' Malcolm waved her over and as he did so another fixture came through the doors: Malcolm's meeting. 'Bob, you ever met my friend Leslie St Clair?'

Somehow Bob got through it. Handshake, mumble. Long time, mumble. See you. She turned away and walked towards the flat. Felt like she was underwater. But her calm was well and truly shattered now. She couldn't go in, couldn't face Tanya and Nikki for a bit. Instead she waited till Hopkin and St Clair were gone then walked back past the pub to the canal.

Bobby sat by the wharf, aware that time was passing, aware that she should go back inside, take charge, make sure Tanya and Nikki were doing what they were supposed to, make sure the punters were behaving. After all, that was her job, wasn't it? Pimping. Taking control of the lives of dumb lazy girls would sooner lie on their backs than do a proper day's work. Course it was. It always had been, ever since . . . Bobby couldn't stop them coming now, couldn't stop the memories, couldn't move from her post, sitting above the dirty water, her legs dangling, a fag between her lips, her mind stuck twenty-odd years back in the past.

Late Seventies again. Coming out of the Prince of Wales that day, Bobby and Lee were in hysterics, couldn't stop laughing. You see that guy with the false beard? Laugh. Couldn't get it up, could he? Laugh and laugh. Desire kept at bay. But not for long. Ten minutes later walking up Caroline Street, sharing a bag of chips, looking at the stuff in the window of the army-surplus shop, Lee says, 'You reckon they get paid?'

'Course,' says Bobby. 'Course they get paid.'

Lee had another couple of chips. 'How much, d'you reckon?'

'Fuck should I know,' says Bobby, leaves it a beat then adds, 'Why? You thinking about having a go?'

'Fuck off,' says Lee. 'I'm not a fucking queer.'

'Course not,' says Bobby, little bit sarky, risking a punch off Lee, and when he doesn't react she knows for sure he's thinking about it. 'Anyway,' she says then, 'maybe they're not always queer films.'

'What d'you mean?'

'What d'you think I mean? Maybe they do films with girls and all.'

'What, lezzos?'

'No, are you fucking thick or what? Ordinary fucking sex.'

'Oh right, yeah,' says Lee. 'You reckon?'

'Yeah, maybe,' says Bobby, but she doesn't tell Lee what St Clair said to her about seeing if any girls at the home would be interested. She wanted to think on that a bit first.

And she did think about it and a couple of nights later when this girl called Debbie, barely sixteen, comes back to the home looking a right state and she's boasting about how she's just had sex with five boys in a tent over Butetown one after the other and

Bobby's listening to this thinking that's disgusting and then the old lightbulb goes off and she figures the girl's doing that kind of shit for free, might as well make a few quid out of it. So next day she goes up to Debbie and has a little word and next time her and Lee are up town they go round the Prince of Wales as per usual and Bobby can see Lee's a bit disappointed that things are back to normal but St Clair's there and when Lee's off playing pinball with a couple of other boys Bobby leans over and says how she has a friend might be interested in doing a film and St Clair says wonderful, wonderful, bring her along, and it works out we'll see you get a little finder's fee, yeah, and Bobby says that'd be good – oh and there's just one thing: it's got to be black boys; Debbie – I mean my mate – she doesn't go with white boys. Oh, says St Clair, black girl is she, looking a bit disappointed, and Bobby says oh no blonde as anything and St Clair says oh really and he's almost licking his lips and Bobby's sitting there feeling a bit sick to be honest but still thinking a finder's fee sounds good.

And it was too. Twenty quid St Clair slipped her after Debbie had done her thing under the lights, whole bunch of hard black boys St Clair had rustled up from somewhere, couple of faces Bobby knew from the football in amongst them. Twenty quid: best part of a week's wages back then. And it wasn't like Debbie minded; she was all over Bobby afterwards thanking her. Debbie got fifty quid, see, for doing what came naturally, couldn't thank Bobby enough, insisted on giving her a tenner out of the money. Bobby didn't feel the need to mention she'd got paid already. Second she pocketed that tenner, saw how keen Debbie was to pay her, that's when Bobby realised she had a job for life.

A job for life. Back in present time, 2001, Bobby thought about it. Her job for life. Twenty-odd years taking money off girls too dumb or lazy or screwed-up to make it any other way. And all of them grateful. Yeah, grateful. Sure, they'd all have their moments of chopsing on about how Bobby was ripping them off, how they were doing all the work, and all that. But even if they broke off with her like one or two did – only one or two, mind – they'd soon enough be hooked up with some real shark and be forking over even more than they were with Bobby. Cause they needed to. They had to give the money up; they had to be doing it for love. Otherwise they couldn't handle it. Stupid bloody slags.

Bobby hated them. Loved them, hated them. All those girls, girls like Maria. Didn't know what they wanted, ended up casually chucking their lives away. How different would it be she was living with a nice girl like Kim, didn't need to go out on the streets and give blokes blow-jobs to earn a few quid. Instead of Maria, who was doing Bobby's head in, pissing her around like this.

Or was she? Was it really Maria was the problem here or was it Bobby herself? Didn't she know deep down the way things were going? Maria would mess about one time too often and Bobby would cut her loose, like she'd cut all the others loose. When it got deep down Bobby was sure she had ice in her heart.

Bobby pulled herself together. What alternative was there? Wasn't like any civilian was going to get involved with the likes of Bobby, was it? OK, now and again a girl like that Kim might like a little walk on the wild side, but that was as far as it went.

Bobby dialled Maria's mobile again. Left a message – short and none too sweet. Phoned the flat – nothing. She had another thought, called Maria's sister Mandy, she'd know all right. Wouldn't necessarily tell Bobby what was going on, but she'd know. Bobby dialled the number. It rang and rang and eventually Mandy picked up, great wall of noise in the background. She was a DJ, Mandy, well into all this two-step stuff.

'Who's that?' she yelled into the phone.

'Bobby,' said Bobby.

'Oh yeah, hang on.' A pause while Mandy walked away from

the phone, turned the music down and came back. 'You looking for Ri?'

'Yeah,' said Bobby.

'Well, I don't know where she is,' said Mandy, a bit too pat for Bobby's liking but they were sisters, what could you do, 'but she asked if I could pick up Jamal for her.'

'Oh yeah,' said Bobby, 'and when's she planning to collect him from yours?'

A pause at the other end of the line, Mandy obviously thinking about it. She sighed. 'Well,' she said eventually, 'she said could I have him for the night, like. Thought she was going out with you, like, Bob.' The lie quickly tacked on at the end.

'Thanks, Mand,' said Bob and hung up quickly before her throat caught. The bitch was leaving her. It really sounded like the bitch was leaving her. Maybe the script had changed.

She stood up, chucked her fag into the murky water and started walking randomly, trying not to think about what it meant if Maria could leave her, just like that, trying to be strong Bobby, Bobby the leaver, Bobby the pimp, one of the boys, not giving in to Bobby the lost, Bobby the left behind, Bobby the motherless, fatherless child. Now more than ever she needed something, someone to hang on to.

20

Pete made it to the St David's Hotel for half twelve, determined to put Leslie St Clair on the spot over these porn-film allegations. Inside, the press conference was every bit as lavish as St Clair had promised. The champagne and canapés kept on coming and, nervous at the unfamiliar prospect of asking hard questions, Pete kept on going back for more.

By the time they were all herded into the conference room, Pete was feeling the worse for wear. He collapsed into a chair at the back and struggled to focus on the speeches. First some bloke from the WDA stood up and blahed on about what an exciting bid this was, how happy he was to support one of Wales's leading entrepreneurs, and there's a big round of clapping and up gets St Clair and goes into this long spiel about his community capitalism idea and how it was crucial to the rebirth of Cardiff and how proud he was to be in the forefront of it all, and there was more clapping and Pete forced himself to take some notes and that helped him sober up a bit and then they all trooped back outside — back to more champagne, more canapés.

Pete was hoping to get straight over to St Clair — couple of questions and out of there — but he could see that there was little chance of that. St Clair was surrounded by a group of cronies — the Welsh Development Authority feller; a man Pete recognised as Malcolm Hopkin, political fixer, had been around since the ark or at least the Sunny Jim days; the head of the council planning committee, pompous jerkoff in a bow-tie; and a big black guy with a crop, didn't look like a politician at all.

He hung around for another ten minutes or so, stoking up on the canapés and sticking to orange juice, doing his best to make small talk with a couple of girls from Red Dragon Radio. But there was no sign of St Clair's little group breaking up and Pete certainly didn't want to just barge in and start throwing embarrassing questions around. He decided to knock it on the head for the moment, just say a quick hello, try and fix up some other occasion to meet. First, though, time for a piss and he was just in there admiring the designer urinals when he found himself standing next to St Clair himself.

'Mr Duke,' said St Clair. 'How the hell's it going, man?'

'Good,' said Pete, 'good,' thinking this is hardly the place to start asking questions.

'Great,' said St Clair, then as they were walking out together, 'C'mon, let me get you a drink, from the private stock, like, and you can meet the boys.'

And so, within seconds, Pete was stood holding a glass of Cristal that he knew he shouldn't be drinking, being introduced to St Clair's mates. First the Welsh Development Authority feller, Dai Thompson, an instantly forgettable suit; then Malcolm Hopkin who gave Pete the professional great to see you again, butt, treatment. Next up was the council leader who Pete'd had the limited pleasure of rubbing shoulders with dozens of times over the years and who could hardly be bothered to hide his uninterest at this latest meeting.

Finally St Clair turned to the last member of the group. 'Well,' he says to Pete, 'seems like I'm introducing you to all your best mates already, but maybe you don't know Kenny Ibadulla of Ibadulla Holdings. Kenny, this is Pete Duke, finest journalist in Wales.'

'How you doing, mate?' says this Kenny Ibadulla, and sticks out a hand the size of a dinner plate, friendly enough but eyes like slate.

'All right,' says Pete and shakes Ibadulla's hand trying to figure out why he knows the name.

Pete's arrival seems to provide the catalyst for the group to break up. Immediately the council leader and the WDA bloke say their goodbyes to St Clair and head off towards the chauffeured cars waiting outside.

St Clair waits till the council leader's out the door then smiles and says why don't we all step outside on the terrace where a man can smoke a cigar in peace and next thing they're all out there looking over the bay with a bucket full of Cristal on the table and Hopkin and St Clair lighting up the Monte Cristos and St Clair is waving his arms about and saying, 'I still can't quite believe how all this has changed.'

'Tell you what, Les,' says Hopkin, 'thing I can't believe is how much it's all cost and how little we've got for it. You look around here, what have we got really? A shopping mall with no shops in it hardly, a half-dozen or so restaurants and a nice hotel. Don't seem like much of a return on a billion pounds, eh? Looks nice enough in the summer – OK, they raised the water level so you could sail your yacht over to the hotel, fair enough – but I liked it fine when the water went up and down, one day water one day mud, and I still don't see too many yachts, you know what I mean, Kenny?'

Kenny Ibadulla gives a not-entirely-hostile grunt which Pete supposes passes for approval.

'That's right, Ken,' Hopkin carries on. 'Some of us don't mind a bit of mud now and again, long as it doesn't stick, eh, Les?'

Les's turn to laugh. Pete watched his face. Didn't give away a thing. Yep, if there was one feller knew all about mud not sticking it was Leslie St Clair all right. Pete looked at his empty glass. He knew he should be getting out of there while he can still drive. Asking St Clair questions could wait.

'Listen,' he says, 'I should get going. Work to do.'

'Nonsense,' says St Clair, 'you just call your editor, pass the phone on to me, I'll sort him out for you.'

And, blame it on the Cristal, that's what Pete does. Calls Graham's number, speaks to Mags, then passes the phone on to St Clair who mouths what's his name and Pete says Graham, then St Clair's talking. 'Hi, is that Graham? Ah, right, Leslie St Clair here . . . we met at the Celtic Manor . . . Yes, yes, that's right, wonderful course, for sure . . . Now listen, Graham, I'm afraid I've kidnapped one of your staff, the irreplaceable Pete Duke . . . No, no, only joking, but we're having a bit of an extended interview here . . . yeah, yeah, that's what I thought . . . OK, I'll put him on, all the best.' St Clair winks and hands the phone on to Pete who takes it and moves over to the edge of the terrace away from the others.

'Graham?'

'Pete, looks like you're moving in rather exalted circles all of a sudden.'

'Um, yeah, listen is that all right, I'm not back for a couple of hours?'

'No, don't worry, you just get the story. You've done the page layouts already, so there's nothing the subs can't take care of.'

'Spose not,' said Pete and wound up the conversation, put the phone back in his pocket and rejoined St Clair and his mates, suddenly confronted with the dizzying prospect of being a free agent on a weekday afternoon.

More champagne was the first step, St Clair continually refilling everyone's glasses. Then any remaining illusions Pete had about the probity of public life and those in the spotlight were further dismantled when St Clair suggested they head up to the suite for a little straightener.

Again it wasn't that Pete was entirely naïve; when Kenny Ibadulla tipped the pile of white powder on to the table, Pete knew it was cocaine all right. He watched TV, he'd seen *Scarface*. It was just that somehow he thought this stuff happened elsewhere, not in Cardiff.

Kenny cut the powder into lines, took the first one himself and nodded happily like a satisfied goods taster then gestured at St Clair who, in turn, looked round at Pete and said go on my son and there he was right on the spot unable to think of any excuse that wouldn't sound unforgivably wussy in such company and next thing he knew he was accepting the rolled-up twenty from Kenny and trying hard to look like he'd done it many times before.

Pete gave way then to Malcolm Hopkin and retired to a chair in a corner of the room waiting for the heart attack that he felt sure would inevitably follow such lunatic behaviour.

But it didn't come. In fact nothing much seemed to be happening; there was a bit of a funny taste in the back of his mouth but otherwise Pete couldn't see that very much had changed at all. God knows why people paid fifty quid a gramme or whatever for this stuff. On the other hand he did feel like another drink and these were an interesting bunch of fellers so he was happy enough to stay here and chat to them.

It was only after an hour or so of chatting with rather more animation than he normally displayed, finding himself telling indiscreet stories about assorted colleagues and laughing hard at St Clair's jokes, and then seeing Kenny preparing the next round of lines and feeling considerable enthusiasm for another go of this stuff, that Pete figured maybe it was doing just a little bit more than he had realised.

After another straightener, a half hour or so later, the mood turned restive. The Cristal had run out and St Clair was clearly itching to get back out into the world, a feller who loved an audience.

'How about the Hilton? You fancy the Hilton, Kenny?'

Kenny shrugged. Even after the coke Kenny seemed to be a man of remarkably few words.

'How about you, Mal? The Hilton all right?'

'Food,' said Malcolm. 'Food would be good, Les, I reckon, first.'

St Clair nodded. 'All right then, food. What d'you fancy? Le Monde? Fish? That suit you, Pete? Fish?'

'Yeah, sure, I dunno,' said Pete, thinking that this really would be a good time to leave, but somehow unable to face the prospect of being on his own.

'Nah, bollocks to that,' said Kenny suddenly. 'We should get some serious food.'

Men of few words, when they say something people tend to listen – well, they do if they are big menacing men of few words like Kenny; men of few words like Pete just seem to fade into the wallpaper, but there you go – so half an hour later the cab dropped the four of them off outside Kenny's choice of restaurant, a nondescript-looking French place on the edge of Pontcanna.

Inside the restaurant Kenny took charge, had a word with the waiter who greeted him with effusive respect, ordered steaks all round and a couple of bottles of what looked like serious Bordeaux. No pissing about with starters, salads or mineral water; this was big-boys' food. Pete could see a few of the other punters, mostly couples looked like they were on their wedding anniversary, giving this bunch of loud blokes a quick shufti, but none of them were in a hurry to catch Kenny's eye and anyway before long St Clair was out of his seat and working the room.

Then the food came, and you couldn't fault it. You wanted steak, steak you most definitely got, and they all tucked in with relish. Pete couldn't help feeling like suddenly he was on the big-boys' team.

Steak finished, two more bottles of wine ordered, Hopkin turned the conversation to football.

'Still thinking of buying the City then?' he asked St Clair with what looked to Pete like a wink.

'Course I am,' said St Clair. 'You read the papers don't you, Mal?' He winked at Pete this time.

'Bit of a long shot, innit?' chipped in Kenny. 'Seems like the Ayatollah's doing a fair old job there.'

St Clair put his hands up. 'Yeah, fair enough, Ken, he is that.' A little pause. 'Doesn't hurt the old profile to register an interest, though, you know what I mean?'

Pete sat back in his chair, getting it and feeling pleased with himself. The Cardiff City thing was just St Clair blowing smoke, a way of upping his profile while he got on with his real business, this new development or whatever. Nice. He was enjoying seeing how the world worked.

Next step in his education came a half hour or so later. The meal done and dusted, conversation turned to where to go next. St Clair fancied a champagne bar on Mill Lane, but Hopkin was emphatic that somewhere called Cupid's Lounge was the place to go. Then Kenny said yeah the manager was a mate of his, like, and so that was agreed.

In the taxi, sandwiched between Kenny and Malcolm, Pete remembered what Cupid's Lounge was – a lap-dancing joint round the corner from the New Theatre.

Soon as they get to the club the manager greets Kenny, has a quick word and then they're ushered into a private sanctum and this time Pete's in there like Flynn just as soon as Kenny's chopped out the lines and then it's downstairs into the club proper and soon they're sat in a booth in the VIP section and there's the inevitable bottle of champagne in the ice bucket and a good view of the dance floor where, Christ, a naked girl is writhing around a pole as the DJ plays Seventies disco records and all around the room there's other women in various states of undress gyrating in front of parties of blokes, mostly twentysomething suits. And the state Pete's in, instead of looking at his shoes as he'd ordinarily be doing in such a situation, he's checking the girls out.

'She'll do, all right,' says Malcolm Hopkin, pointing over his shoulder at one of the older performers, a thirtysomething blonde who seemed to be making up for in enthusiasm anything she conceded to her colleagues in age as she shimmied around in front of a couple of junior execs who looked like rabbits in the headlights in the face of this full-on sexual display.

Soon as she finished with the execs, Malcolm was waving a twenty-pound note and the blonde who said her name was Liza gave him and Pete her full attention. All Pete's sober instincts told him not to stare at the increasingly naked woman in front of him. On the other hand, surely it would be ruder to look away; after all Liza was putting everything into it so the least a gent could do was show some appreciation. And well, blame it on the coke, blame it on the champagne, when it came down to it he really didn't want to look away. He was one of the big boys now; he could look where he liked.

One thing about big boys' games, though, is that they're played by big boys' rules. After watching a couple more dancers, Kimberley and Danielle, Pete was in the midst of an animated conversation with Malcolm Hopkin who was telling him about the old days when strippers were strippers and not entertainment consultants, when, his tongue well loosened, he saw an opportunity to ask the question he'd been working up to all day. 'Oh yeah,' he said, 'talking of strippers, wasn't St Clair involved in something like that?'

'How d'you mean?' said Hopkin. 'Don't think old Les ever used to take his kit off.'

'No,' said Pete. 'Years ago, in the Seventies, didn't he make films or something? In the old Prince of Wales?'

Hopkin paused, then looked at Pete carefully. 'Don't know who you've been talking to, son, but I'd recommend you don't believe everything you hear.'

'Oh yeah, well,' said Pete, dimly aware that probably he shouldn't be blundering on with this conversation, 'it's just someone's come forward, said Les was involved in some pretty nasty shit back then.'

Hopkin lowered his voice, focused in on Pete. 'A word to the wise, Mr Duke. You be careful when you're nosing around because you never know where your nose might take you. After all, there's some people might say the stuff you've been up to today was some pretty nasty shit.' He laughed humourlessly. 'Some people, believe it or not, don't appreciate that girls like our Liza over there are really highly skilled entertainment consultants, you know what I'm saying?'

Pete nodded slowly. A sinking in his stomach said he understood all too well. He'd just had the bill for the day's entertainment.

21

Amazing how fast five years can unravel. All weekend Bobby had been brooding on it. Two days ago, the only way she could see her and Maria splitting up was if she, Bobby, decided it was time. Bobby had been utterly sure of her control of the situation. Sure, she'd been having her little thing with Kim and, to be honest, wondering if it mightn't turn into a big thing. Yeah, Bobby had been going through some changes all right. But Maria was just the same girl she'd always been, wasn't she? Sweet if you caught her right, but vain and lazy and under Bobby's thumb like all the rest. She'd have put cash money on it.

Well, how dumb did she feel now? Hadn't she noticed the way Maria was always going out clubbing? How she never came back till the early hours? Hadn't she thought the other morning that she smelt someone on Maria and hadn't she just decided the dirty slag was losing it, not washing properly after work? Hadn't she been thinking she was so cool, nipping out for a quick one with Kim without Maria noticing? Well, guess who'd been the blind one.

Maria had told her it straight. She'd had enough of Bobby, her moods and obsessions; she'd met someone else. A bloke. At least it was a bloke. Maria'd found another woman, Bobby would have fucking killed them both. A bloke, though, you could see that was different. Didn't have to like it to see it was different.

Course the bloke in question sounded like a right peach. Macca, one of the DJs down the Hippo; Bobby knew the name, could just about put a face to it. His little brother played for the

City. Second team, no one you'd heard of. Macca'd been inside a couple of times; one of the guys, you know. Bobby didn't have to know him; she knew the type all right.

'How many kids he got then?'

Maria shrugged. They were sitting in the new flat on their own, Tanya out on call, Nikki not due in till after lunch. Bobby had been there all morning fiddling with the website, trying to think of nothing, when Maria had shown up around eleven, her mouth set hard.

'Probably doesn't know himself. How many other women he got?'

'Leave it, Bob, you don't know him. He's not like that.'

'Course not. They never are, are they? Not till you ask them for some child support anyway.'

'Fuck off, Bob — just cause you can't have kids.'

Bobby froze; the words hung there between them for a brief eternity. Then Bobby flipped, dived straight at Maria, grabbed her by the throat, started banging her head against the floor, screaming at her, not even screaming words, just the guttural gut-wrenched sounds that lie behind every bitch or cunt or fuck you ever yelled, and then Maria kicked her hard in the kneecap and Bobby relaxed her grip and Maria took her chance and ran white-faced and tear-stained out the door, Bobby lying on the ground panting hard, the sound of Maria's feet on the stairs carrying through the open doorway.

Later, maybe a half hour later, when Bobby had got her breathing back to normal and washed her face in the basin, letting the cold water pour down till her skin was numb with the cold of it, and she was sat at the table clutching a cup of tea and ignoring the ringing phone, she almost felt grateful to Maria. Cause that was it. The line was crossed, there was no going back, no making up. Over, over, over.

Over and no regrets. Over just in time before it got really

ugly. And wasn't that deep down what she wanted, to be free? Yeah, yeah, probably, but who was she kidding? She was hurting now, all right; no one wants to be the one that gets dumped, the unknowing fool whose lover has betrayed them. And suddenly she was thinking about Jamal and tears were rolling down her face. If the vindictive little bitch stopped her seeing Jamal she'd kill her. She stood up possessed by rage, then stared around blindly as if trying to sense her adversary's presence in the room, then sat down again, tried to calm herself. Of course she'd see Jamal, she'd pick him up from school, she'd buy him clothes, she'd . . .

Suddenly she knew what she had to do next. She had to go and see Bernie Walters and this time she wasn't leaving till he told her who her dad was.

Bobby was sat in Bernie Walters's office, a whole mass of computer equipment laid out on the desk in front of her, drinking a glass of wine and listening to Bernie talk about the Sixties.

She'd felt a hell of a lot calmer the moment she stepped into Bernie's office. Walking over there, she'd been well out of it. She'd called Maria's mobile three more times: cow wasn't answering. Walking past the building site where the Custom House used to be brought her to tears. Crying over some evil bloody dump full of alkies and hookers; what was the matter with her?

So, yeah, she had been in a bit of a state when she showed up at Bernie's door. Only just about held it together when she was talking to the secretary who gave her the same old bollocks about Bernie being a very busy man, but a bit more half-hearted this time, and sure enough Bernie was obviously absolutely delighted to have someone come round, stop him from playing Minesweeper on the computer. And so Bernie ushers her into the office, beaming away, and asks if she'd like a drink and Bobby says yeah – cause she wasn't that much of a drinker by and large but right then she needed one – and he opens up a little fridge, gets out a bottle of white wine and fusses around finding a couple of glasses and he's nattering away, all this stuff about how Dame Shirley used to come here all the time when she was a slip of a girl and Bernie's wife used to take her out shopping for clothes and then he starts rummaging around finding all these boxes with scanners and printers and software in them and treating her like she's a bit of an expert on this stuff and Bobby just feels liked and useful and the weight of the day starts to drop off her.

So much so that she'd been there a couple of hours, had pretty much connected up Bernie's system and installed all the soft-ware, had the scanner and printer up and running, was just trying to explain how to operate it all to Bernie, who was more interested in telling her a long involved story about Matt Monro and a hotel chambermaid while opening another bottle of wine, before she remembered what she was doing here in the first place.

So when Bernie stopped talking for a second to concentrate on pouring out more wine, she said, 'You have a think about Troy Thursday then, Bernie?'

That shut him up. He put the bottle down carefully, looked at the floor, looked at the pictures on the wall, looked at the ceiling, then finally looked at Bobby.

'Are you sure this is your father, the man who your mother calls Troy Thursday?'

'Sure as I can be,' said Bobby, hoping to hell it was true and not some stupid lie her so-called mother had made up to keep her off her back.

'And you're sure you want to know who he is? You realise you could be in for a lot of heartache if he doesn't want to know?

He might not be very happy to find you coming out of the woodwork.'

Bobby looked at Bernie, oddly touched. How often had anyone taken her feelings into account? 'Yeah,' she said, 'I want to know. Whoever it is can't be worse than all this not knowing.' That much she was sure was true; she felt like it was one of the things holding her back in life, all this not knowing who she was except for Bobby Ranger — top pimp.

'Well,' said Bernie, taking a big swig of wine and looking terribly serious all of a sudden, 'I must say I had a feeling I knew who your Troy Thursday was, as soon as you mentioned it was a black feller. But I thought I'd better check. And as far as I can see, there were only two black guys ever did a Troy Thursday gig for me. Now one of them, Lance, God rest his soul, wasn't ever likely to be getting no girls pregnant, if you know what I mean. But the other one — look, you're really sure you want to know this, cause this is a hell of a name I've got for you here?'

Bobby nodded, her throat too tight to contemplate speaking.

'OK then,' said Bernie. 'Well, the other one just used the name once or twice when he was trying out a new act and anyway, well he's a feller, whose name you'll know already. Leslie St Clair.'

Bernie paused to let this revelation sink in.

'Oh Christ,' he said as he watched Bobby faint clean away in front of him.

22

The last couple of days Pete'd felt unsettled, remembering what had happened the Friday before. It all felt unreal. It wasn't what he, Pete Duke, did – champagne, cocaine, lap-dancers. But it had felt good. And perhaps he could be a player too, he saw that now; all he had to do was learn how to look the other way from time to time. And how hard was that?

He called Kim, back at work after a weekend in London. She picked up straight away, sounded pleased to hear from him. Apparently she'd just shown her boss a rough assemblage of her lesbian-pimp documentary and it had gone down a treat.

'Great,' said Pete and told her about his day out with the big boys.

He was planning to stop short of the lap-dancing club but somehow he couldn't round off the story without it and as it happened it turned out to be Kim's favourite part.

'Well, Pete,' she said at the end of it, 'you naughty boy.' Then she lowered her voice, went all husky on him. 'They turn you on then, those lap-dancing girls?'

Pete said nothing, just turned red, glad he was on the phone.

She carried on. 'I'll bet they did. I was going to give it a try one time, you know. You think I'd be good? You fancy a little private dance later on?'

'Mmm,' he said uncertainly.

'Mmm,' said Kim. 'I'll give you mmm. Don't know why I waste my charms on you. Anyway, did you get anything direct out of this St Clair guy or was it all just good background stuff?'

'Well,' said Pete, grateful to be getting on to his reason for phoning, 'I certainly didn't get anything direct. Couldn't really just blurt it out in the middle of dinner. "Oh by the way, Mr St Clair, did you use to make porn films?" '

'Don't see why not,' said Kim. 'I would've.'

'Yeah, well,' said Pete, 'maybe you would, but I did ask one of his mates about it — said I'd heard these rumours and the guy basically threatened me.'

'Threatened you?'

'Well, kind of implied that if I tried to investigate this stuff they'd say I'd been taking drugs and all that.'

'Bollocks,' said Kim. 'You just say you were working under-cover, only pretended to take the drugs, got the story at great personal risk, you'll be a bloody hero.'

Pete thought about it. Probably she had a point. Probably if he had the guts that's what he would do — tough the whole thing out, get the story and take the consequences. Trouble was, first off, he didn't think he had those kind of guts and second he wasn't sure he wanted to do the story anyway. Some stupid idea that if he'd taken St Clair's hospitality he shouldn't shaft the guy afterwards, whatever he'd done.

'Look, Pete,' said Kim in mind-reading mode, 'you got to remember that this St Clair isn't Father Christmas, he's a seedy degenerate fraud. Those kids made those movies they were only sixteen, seventeen some of them. One or two of them might even have been under age from what Bobby says, runaways from the kids' home and that, and the whole experience traumatised a lot of their lives and he just exploited them.'

'Yeah,' said Pete, 'but . . .'

'But bastard nothing,' said Kim. 'You and me, Pete, we're going to work this story. It could be huge, you know, get both of us out of this town for ever. It's a London story, Pete, this one, a big London story.'

Pete hesitated. He could see she was right. Big London story – get out of this town for good. That what he wanted? He wasn't sure. But Kim was what he wanted, he knew that all right.

'OK,' he said at last, 'you're on.'

He put the phone down and checked his watch. Lunchtime. OK, he decided to kick off his investigation right away, before he lost his nerve. First step – find Randall. He caught up with him by the lift and said, 'You know that stuff you were telling me about Leslie St Clair? D'you know anyone might know about any of it like first hand?'

Randall frowned like he was deciding whether to let Pete in on the secret or not, then shrugged and said, 'Well, why don't we go and have a bit of a look-see?'

Randall led them off at a cracking pace across town, through the Royal Arcade, down what remained of Bridge Street, over Churchill Way and right into Guildford Crescent, past the Thai House and the Ibis Hotel they'd built where the swimming baths used to be, then down the alleyway alongside the prison wall and, for a moment, Pete thought they were going to see someone inside but instead Randall headed over the main road towards the Vulcan, a pub that Pete could have sworn had closed down years ago.

In fact it hardly looked open from the outside but Randall pulled on the door and led the way into the snug and suddenly Pete was transported back twenty years into the pubs of his youth.

The room was tiny, just three or four tables and a bar, and the minimum amount of space needed to house a dartboard. The bar itself offered the classic trinity of Brains Light, Brains Dark and Brains SA. Randall ordered himself a pint of Skull Attack; Pete took a pint of light and surveyed the clientele. Nobody under sixty. Couple of Arab-looking fellers in the corner, old-time sailors Pete reckoned; old couple by the dartboard doing the

Mirror crossword. Fat bald bloke with a big moustache, looked like an old-time wrestler, sat by himself at the table next to the door watching Pete and Randall with interest.

Randall waited for Pete to remember his role and pay for the drinks, turned round and waved to the fat bloke. 'George,' he said. 'Good Lord, man, you're looking big as a house. Fancy a drink? Young Pete here's getting them in.'

George raised his half-full pint of dark towards Pete who sighed and turned back towards the barman. 'Get him a large whisky while you're at it,' said Randall and Pete did as he was told.

They sat down next to the enormous George and Pete left it to Randall to kick things off, so the next ten minutes or so were spent discussing third parties that Pete had never heard of with unlikely old-school sobriquets like the Nailer and Jack the Hat. Then, just as Pete's attention was drifting off, wondering what on earth Randall was expecting to learn from this surprisingly camp old slugger, Randall suddenly said, 'The Brolly Man, he used to work for St Clair and all, didn't he?'

'Yeah,' said George. 'Well, now and again, like.'

'Pete here met old Les the other day, you know.'

'Oh yeah?' said George. 'Hope you checked your wallet after, son.'

Randall chuckled. 'Pete works on the paper with me. Doing a bit of an in-depth story on old Les, in fact. And he was asking me about the films Les used to make.'

'Oh yeah?' said George, still smiling but his eyes turned watchful. 'Long time ago, that was.'

Pete jumped in. 'You know about them, though?'

'Oh aye, used to work security for Mr St Clair at the time. I'd be there now and again, make sure there wasn't any trouble on set.'

'Got a bit more involved than that, George, from what I remember you telling me,' chipped in Randall.

George looked round at Pete then back at Randall. 'Well . . . it was all a bit of fun, really. Boys will be boys, you know what I mean.'

'Well, I can imagine,' said Randall, 'though I rather think I'd prefer not to. You don't know if any of these films are still in circulation, do you?'

George shrugged, 'Long time ago, like I said, butt, and it was all on, what d'you call it, Super 8? And I can't say I saw any of them myself even at the time. Old Terry used to flog them over in Bridge Street and I heard some got sent up to London, but like I said I never saw them myself, more of a doer than a watcher me, least back then I was.' George picked up his pint and took a reflective sip from it.

Pete looked at him, wondering what memories were flicking through his mind.

'You don't have any idea who might have copies, do you?'

'What, apart from old Les?' George thought about it, knocked back the whisky, looked pointedly at the empty glass. Pete took the hint, got another large one and came back to the table.

'Good man,' said George. 'Well, I suppose old Jock might still have some. He was the cameraman, like.'

'You know where we could find him?' asked Pete.

George looked at Pete, then over at Randall. 'Well, I might have an idea, but it strikes me it's worth more than a couple of whiskies to tell you fellers.'

Randall raised his eyebrows at Pete. Pete frowned. He'd made a point throughout his career of not paying people for information. True, it was less an integrity matter than a budget one, but still Pete felt it was a sound principle. On the other hand, he really did want to be calling Kim up, minute he got back to the office, telling her what a great lead he'd got.

Anyway, while he was hesitating, Randall weighed in. 'Well, George, it's hardly hot news, is it? Everyone's heard the rumours.

All this is just a bit of dotting the i's and crossing the t's, if you know what I mean. But still I'm sure Pete here would see you right for a drink, wouldn't you, Pete? Sure you've got twenty for old George.'

'Twenty?' said George in a grumbling growl, but, when Pete dug the note out of his pocket, he accepted it with the air of a man for whom twenty quid was still an amount to be respected.

'Right then,' he said. 'You want Jock, you try the Fisherman's Rest.'

'Out by the lighthouse?' said Randall.

'Out by the lighthouse is right,' said George, 'and tell you what, you get to see him, don't tell him I sent you.'

23

Bobby was still feeling shaky and spacy as she walked back to the flat. She couldn't believe she'd fainted. Never fainted before in her life but, Christ, what a shock. She hadn't really been able to say anything to Bernie; he was just looking at her all worried and his secretary, Marguerite, had been dabbing water on her face and she'd just said, 'You sure?' and he'd said, 'Yeah, that's why I checked, didn't want to lead you up the garden path on that one,' and she'd said thanks and sorry but she had to go home and she'd be in again tomorrow, sorry about leaving the computer in such a mess, and Bernie had said forget about it and she'd laughed cause she knew that wasn't what he meant but the one thing she couldn't do was forget about it. Though part of her wished she could, wished she'd never heard him say that name. All this time she'd wanted so much to know who her dad was and now she knew and shit she'd never thought she'd have wished she didn't know.

Leslie St Clair. At first, walking back, the name just kept buzzing through her mind like a tape loop she couldn't make sense of it; it was just here frying her brain. Gradually, though, she started to break down the enormity of it. Was it right? Was her mum lying? She didn't think so. It was too weird to be a lie. Did her mum know who he really was, this Troy Thursday? A harder question. One for later.

So was he her dad? Did she look like him? She thought about it. He was a fine-looking man, she was a pretty odd-looking woman, but . . . but she could see it. Her mouth, her eyes. Christ.

OK, maybe she looked a little like him – the strange-girl version. But was she *like* him? Well, there was a question she didn't want to answer.

This was really too much. She needed to talk to someone. Maria. She walked up the stairs and into the flat. Maybe Maria would be there, back waiting for her. Ha, ha. There was just Nikki sitting in front of the TV and she could hear Tanya in the master bedroom giving it some welly with a punter. Christ. She nodded to Nikki then put her headphones on and logged on to the computer, looking for distraction.

She soon found it in the shape of her email inbox which had received an avalanche of mail. Hundreds of new messages were waiting for her – 249 in all. The last few days the website had really started to take off. She'd got it linked up to the Good Sex Guide website, placed a few little mentions on the newsgroups, nothing that looked like spam, and you could see there was demand out there from the response. But 249 emails! This carried on, she'd be full time in front of the screen answering them. Just at the moment, though, she didn't mind at all.

Most of them were crap, of course. About half were one sort of spam or another; if it wasn't people trying to sell her scanners for only $29.99, it was other sex sites imploring her to watch their secret dorm-room cams. Yeah, right. Or offering free membership to increasingly implausibly named sites – finding an original name was clearly a bit of a nightmare which was why Bobby was pleased to have solved the problem with cardiffescorts.com, a site that did exactly what it said on the can. Anyway, she deleted all the spam, then started going through the messages from actual punters. Most of these were crap too, either abusive or pornographic and probably written by some fourteen-year-old in Australia. An inability to let go of the CAPS key was generally a bit of a giveaway. A few of them were genuinely pretty shocking, even to Bobby; the Net's anonymity surely did bring out the freaks. Anyway, weed out the kids and the nutters and what Bobby was left with was about twenty more or less bona fide enquiries. Which was fine. Say two of them turned into genuine punters: well, two new punters a day you were laughing. Kept on for long she'd be renting the whole bloody block. And now she felt tired of all these sad little missives from sad little lives. Had she ever felt so miserable? Where was Maria when she needed her?

She took the headphones off, turned round to talk to Nikki. 'All right, girl, how's it going?'

'All right, Bob,' said Nikki, looking alarmed, like Bobby was about to launch into her again. 'I've been trying harder, Bob. Have you noticed?'

'Yeah, Nikki, you've been doing great,' said Bobby and suddenly she felt faint again, sitting there talking to this poor dumb, frightened girl, doing her best to act like she was happy screwing whoever came through the door with fifty quid in their pocket. Jesus. Right now Bobby felt like she literally couldn't live with herself. This was unbearable. She forced herself to stand up, went into the bathroom. She looked in the bathroom cabinet: nothing there that would be any good to her. She thought quickly, made up her mind.

She came out of the bathroom and told Nikki she had to go. Her and Tanya could lock up after Tanya's punter left. Bobby left the flat, walked over to Butetown in a daze, completely oblivious to traffic or passers-by. She let herself into the old flat, Maria's flat, called out once, forlornly, 'Ri,' got no answer, went into the bathroom, found Maria's Temazepam, necked half a dozen of them and laid herself down on Maria's bed, waiting for unconsciousness to come, not caring if she ever woke again.

24

Pete and Kim were driving east out of Cardiff down Newport Road where the old Cardiff suddenly gives way to the brand-new strip-mall Cardiff, the procession of Allied Carpets and Burger King, TGI Fridays's and PC World, electrical stores and bowling alleys.

A right at the end of the strip, and Pete steered down through Rumney, nosing his way to the coast road. Never a big deal, the coastal road that threaded through the marshlands between Cardiff and Newport was now almost entirely hidden amongst the mushrooming industrial estates, so it took a couple of wrong turns before Pete found himself heading out past the car breakers and in sight of the sea wall.

The countryside. Well, of sorts. After a mile or so of ugly scrub, Kim looked out of the window and said, 'Bloody hell, Pete, where do you call this?'

Pete shrugged. 'Marshfield, I think.'

'Sounds about right,' said Kim, laughing.

They sped through a couple of villages that were doing their best to spruce themselves up, pretend they were in the Vale, but not really pulling it off, no matter how many riding stables they had. They couldn't get away from the fact that they were sited on a strip of no man's land bounded by the giant sink estates of St Mellons to the north and a horribly unappealing seafront of mud and industrial waste to the south. There was a hotel and a golf course, new since Pete had last been down there, and a thoroughly tiched-up pub-restaurant welcomed them into St

Brides, the last village on the road before it hit the Usk estuary and turned north into Newport.

Pete was looking out carefully for the turning now, trying to remember the directions he'd been given. Finally, just as the road was curving north and Pete was preparing to retrace his route, he saw a sign saying the Fisherman's Friend, breathed a sigh of relief and turned right. The road brought them out by the sea wall, and there it was, a big shabby pub, its car park home to a handful of beat-up white-trash motors. Beyond the pub the road dead-ended in a caravan site.

'Jesus Christ,' said Kim. 'People come here for holidays?'

'Funny old world,' said Pete. 'Funny old world!'

'OK then,' said Kim, as they walked round to the front of the pub. 'So we're looking for a man named Jock?'

'That's right,' said Pete.

'Any idea what he looks like?'

'Not really,' said Pete. 'I was kind of hoping he'd be an elderly and obvious degenerate wearing a kilt.'

Kim smiled up at him. 'You know what, Pete, you really are starting to lighten up.' And with that she kissed him and Pete kissed her back.

Inside it was every bit as rough and ready as the outside. There was a stage area festooned with the remnants of party decorations and a band entirely composed of short bald bearded blokes in their forties were just setting up their equipment. There were a handful of punters scattered around the place, a couple of traveller types were sat by the door, their kids running in and out, and a bunch of older blokes stood round the bar.

Pete took a deep breath, went up and ordered a pint of bitter for himself and a gin and tonic for Kim. As the barman gave him his change, he decided it was now or never and, casual as you like, said, 'I'm looking for Jock.' And just as casual the bloke said, 'Well, you've found him, haven't you,' and yelled out, 'Jock, over here'. And with that one of the fellers along the bar turned to look at Pete. Easy, he thought.

Then he got a good look at the man called Jock's teeth, all three of them. If the state of a man's mouth was any pointer to the state of his soul, then this Jock was one serious reprobate.

Teeth aside, Jock was sixtyish, six foot-plus, dishevelled, scrubby beard and a bush of hair with old-fashioned tortoise-shell-framed glasses. He gave the vague impression of a dissolute schoolteacher. He wasn't Scottish. The first words out of his mouth – 'Who are you then?' – placed him as a hundred per cent South Walian.

'You're not Scottish,' said Kim, like this might be news to him.

'No,' he said. 'Worked up there years ago. Now, you know my name but I don't know yours.'

'Kim,' said Kim.

'Pete,' said Pete, and then, 'We're journalists. We were hoping to talk to you about Leslie St Clair.'

Right then the band chose to kick off their soundcheck with a drum roll and the opening chords to 'Sweet Home Alabama.'

'Who?' said Jock.

'Leslie St Clair,' shouted Pete just as the band came to an abrupt stop.

'Easy, butt,' said Jock, 'no need to tell the whole world. Now, how about you buy me a drink and I'll sit down over there with the young lady.'

Pete nodded, ordered up a pint of Guinness for Jock and then remembered Randall's tip and added a large whisky to the round.

It didn't make much difference. Jock started out garrulous enough. Turned out he'd worked for St Clair on and off for years. He was happy to tell tales of how St Clair had set him up with work for porn mags, specialising in fake readers' wives: 'Just used a crap camera and made sure you could see the pattern on the carpet and the spots on the girl's bum.' But then, when Pete said it was the Prince of Wales days he was interested in, old Jock shut up like a clam.

'You were the cameraman on his films then?' Pete pressed.

'What films, son?' said Jock. 'Don't remember no films.'

'That's not what I've heard,' said Pete.

Jock laughed humourlessly. 'One thing I'd have thought you'd learned by now, son, in your line of work and all – people don't half talk a lot of shit.'

Kim had a go then, changed the subject subtly but effectively. 'You think I'd make a good model, Jock?'

'You, darlin'?' said Jock, giving her a good old-fashioned leer. 'You bet.'

Kim smiled like this was her lucky day. 'Really, cause it's always been like a little bit of a fantasy of mine . . .'

Both Jock and Pete were staring at her now, Jock obviously wondering if this was a put-on, but still unable to stop his mouth opening, his tongue starting to poke out.

'Yeah, you know, if it was shot by a real professional and all, something to remember when I'm old and saggy. You know what I mean?'

Jock smiled like he knew just what Kim meant.

'You're not still in the business, are you, Jock? Don't have a studio or anything?'

Jock swallowed hard. He obviously suspected he was being stitched up, but on the other hand it didn't look like he had too much else going on.

'Well,' he said at last. 'I have got a little bit of a studio set-up, as it happens.'

'Oh yeah?' said Kim. 'Is it far? Could I have a look?'

Jock frowned again, then made up his mind, knocked back

the rest of his pint and with a curt, 'C'mon then,' led the way out of the pub.

'You want a lift?' said Pete, heading over towards the car, but Jock grunted a no and inclined his head towards the caravan park. Kim walked alongside Jock, keeping up a stream of chatter while Pete followed a few paces behind, marvelling at her ability to improvise and wondering how far she was planning to take things. He wouldn't put it past her to suddenly whip her clothes off; the thought immediately made him feel just a little bit possessive and a little bit absurd too.

Jock's place was a full-scale trailer home parked right at the far end of the park backed up against a large hedge. Jock opened the door and the three of them entered what turned out to be a surprisingly spotless environment dominated by a large black leather sofa at the far end and an enormous TV in the corner. Jock indicated that they should sit on the sofa then went round the room pulling down blackout blinds over the windows and door. He fiddled with some switches and the room was bathed in bright white light.

'Ta da,' said Jock. 'Instant studio.'

'Very nice,' said Kim. 'So is there any of your work I could have a look at?'

Jock frowned at this, then walked over to a filing cabinet by the far wall. He unlocked it, pulled out a drawer and started rummaging around. As he did so Kim moved up behind him looking over his shoulder. Jock immediately withdrew a couple of magazines and slammed the drawer shut.

'There you go, love,' he said, handing Kim what looked like a bog-standard top-shelf title. 'You look at the centrefold girl in that one, blonde piece, don't know what they called her in the mag, Michelle's her real name. Anyway, I took them.'

Kim flipped the magazine open, looked at the photos of the bottle-blonde with her ankles round her neck, squinted at them hard as if imagining herself in the same high heels and garter-belt get-up, then handed it back. 'Very nice.'

'Yeah,' said Jock, 'very nice indeed. Used the old Nikkormat for that one, came out a treat, didn't they? So you ready to go, love?'

'Oh God, not now,' giggled Kim, 'but I'm definitely interested. You think it would be all right if I came over on my own sometime?'

Jock's face made it clear it would be more than all right. In no time he was scribbling a mobile number on a piece of paper and then they made their excuses and Pete stood up and led the way out.

Once they were in the car Kim could scarcely contain herself.

'He's got them, Pete. In the filing cabinet. Loads of little film boxes; you know, the old-fashioned sort, like for home movies. They were there, Pete.'

Pete leaned over and kissed her. 'Bloody hell, girl,' he said. 'You were brilliant.'

'Yes indeed,' said Kim. 'Good little team, aren't we, Pete?'

'Yeah,' said Pete, thinking I hope so, I really do hope so.

As they drove, Kim spun ever wilder plans to steal the film reels while Pete tried to raise reasonable objections.

'Anyway,' said Kim as they swung left out of the Boulevard de Nantes, heading past the castle walls, 'how about if I go round there, say I want to do the photo shoot and then get him off into the bedroom or somewhere?'

'Christ's sake, Kim, be serious.'

'I am serious,' said Kim. 'You think I can't handle an old lech like him? All I have to do is keep him out of the way for a minute or two and you nip in and get the films, then I go, "Oh sorry, changed my mind."'

Pete shook his head. 'Way too dangerous. Much simpler and safer if you just meet him in the pub, keep him in there, and I, uh, I break into the trailer and get the films.'

Kim pouted comically. 'Oh and I don't get to have the nice pictures taken.'

Pete laughed, hoping she was joking. 'You want any nude photos taken, I'll take them for you,' he said and he angled the car into the car park round the back of Randall's mansion block.

Kim laughed. Pete was just about to park when he saw another car a few spaces along still with its lights on, a big black Saab. He glanced casually across to see which of the neighbours it was and instead found himself staring straight into the face of Kenny Ibadulla.

Kenny opened his window. Behind him Pete could see three more guys. Pete opened his own window and tried a smile, got nothing back.

'You two-faced cunt,' said Kenny. 'You drink with a man one day, go sneaking about digging up ancient history the next. You think that's all right?'

'You what?' said Pete.

'You fucking heard. Now, you stop digging and we'll forget all about it. That's what Les said to tell you. I told him I should break your fucking arm, make sure you got the message, but Les said no. Next time, though . . . Well, you better make fucking sure there ain't no next time. You got that?'

Pete nodded, the power of speech temporarily lost to him, and with that Kenny closed his window and backed the Saab out of the car park before accelerating off into the night.

'Christ,' said Kim. 'Who was that?'

'A man called Kenny Ibadulla.'

'*The* Kenny Ibadulla?'

'I suppose.'

'Wow, Pete, looks like we're really stirring some shit up here.'

'Wow?' said Pete, getting out of the car, his legs trembling underneath him. 'You think this is exciting? It's not, it's stupid and it's dangerous.'

Kim got out of her side of the car, came round and put her arm in his. 'Course it's dangerous, darling. It's a big story, didn't we know that already? A big story, a big get-out-of-Cardiff story.' And Pete felt her tongue snake its way into his ear and he shuddered at his own helplessness.

25

Bobby Ranger was dreaming. She was dreaming about flowers. Lots of old flowers, a whole carpet of flowers, a whole wall of flowers, a whole world of flowers — roses, tulips, orchids, daffodils, carnations, chrysanthemums, daisies, sunflowers, poppies, violets, lilies, anemones, pinks, poppies again, flowers she didn't know the names of, flowers bright, bright colours, red, yellow, purple, flaming scarlet, yellow, blue and white, white, white, flowers everywhere, flowers left and right and up and down, flowers in her eyes, flowers in her mouth, flowers.

26

Pete couldn't sleep. It was three in the morning and Kim had left an hour or so before, left after they'd had the most intense, the most abandoned, dangerous sex of his life. From the second Kenny Ibadulla had threatened them she'd been all over him; they'd gone straight to the bedroom, her desire pervasive, sucking the air out of the room. For a moment he'd felt nauseous, afraid, sure he wouldn't, couldn't respond, but even as he was thinking that he realised he was responding, that the same cocktail of danger and transgression had its effect on him too, and then he was locked together with her, inside her, outside her, all over her, her biting scratching screaming and him feeling no pain, into her like drowning, and barely stopping at all between the first time and the second time.

And then she was gone and now it was three a.m. and Pete got out of bed and went down to the kitchen and once again thought it must be nice to smoke a cigarette at a time like this. Instead he made a cup of Nescafé and was overcome by a backwash of disgust at what he'd just done, the sex suddenly seeming not mystical and revolutionary but like too much chocolate: sickly and decadent. And as for his 'mission', it seemed sordid, pointless, grubby muck-raking, the reverse of what journalism had come to mean to him, which was order and structure and . . . and a quiet life, he supposed. Looking at his coffee in the cold of three a.m. he wondered if he wouldn't do best to run and hide, run back to Viv and the kids and beg their forgiveness.

Pete heard the front door to the flat open and then a burst of cheery whistling. Randall was home; the Cambrian must have finally tipped him out.

Seconds later Randall was in the kitchen.

'Peter, good Lord. What keeps you awake at this ungodly hour? Not woman trouble, I hope?'

'No,' said Pete, 'not that.'

'Good, good. She's a gem that one. Trouble, all right, you can see that, but worth it, I'll bet. So if it's not that, then what? Ah, you've been out adventuring, have you? On the trail of the lonesome Jock, perhaps? Did you find him?'

'Yes,' said Pete, and filled Randall in on the evening's events.

'Hmm,' said Randall when Pete had finished. 'Well, for God's sake don't rob the place yourself.'

'Who else is going to do it? Can't exactly send one of the reporters out, can I?'

'No,' said Randall, 'but you can do what people normally do when they've got a particular problem: call in the professionals. The toilet breaks, you call in a plumber; you need a burglary doing, you call in a burglar.'

'Yeah, yeah, sure,' said Pete, 'but I don't know any burglars. Don't exactly advertise in the *Thomson Local*, do they?'

'No,' said Randall, 'you just have to move in the right circles.' He checked his watch. 'C'mon, get yourself dressed. We'll go have a bit of a shufti, see who's out and about.'

Ten minutes later Pete and Randall were out on the street, skirting the Millennium Stadium and heading for the Tudor Road bridge over the Taff, Pete shivering from the cold, Randall seemingly oblivious to it. Must be all the alcohol in his system, thought Pete. The amazing thing with Randall was the way he never seemed to get any drunker. Not after the first few lunchtime pints. He seemed to have some way of gauging the optimum level of mild drunkenness and maintaining it indefinitely. A skill the youth of today could profitably learn, Pete thought, as he stepped over a pool of vomit.

Over the Tudor Road bridge they carried on into Tudor Road itself. The first couple of blocks were Cardiff's Chinatown, the next couple were a free-for-all for recent immigrants into the city: Somalis, Bengalis et al. On the south side of the street was a sari shop and a tattoo parlour and then a sign saying Tudor Pool Hall. Randall went up to the door, which looked to have been recently kicked in, and pressed the intercom. A voice said, 'Who is it?' Randall replied and the door buzzed open. 'After you,' said Randall and Pete led the way up a flight of stairs into the pool hall.

There were ten or so pool tables: half a dozen pub-sized and three or four big blue American ones. Only one of them was in use, a couple of Somali boys just setting the balls up. There was a bar over to the right with a couple of tables in front of it. Half a dozen guys, most of them Chinese-looking, were sat round one of the tables playing cards. A genial-looking bloke with un-mistakably Cardiffian mixed-race features turned to look at the newcomers.

'Randall,' he said. 'How're you doing, man?'

'Good, good,' said Randall. 'This is my friend Pete, works on the newspaper.'

'Hiya, Pete,' said the bloke, then looked at his watch. 'Bit late really, but seeing as it's you . . . what can I get you?'

'Large whisky, Naz, please and . . .'

'Bottle of Beck's,' said Pete.

Naz walked over behind the bar and got the drinks together. Randall and Pete followed him.

'So what brings you gents out this time of night?'

'Well,' said Randall, 'as it happens, my friend Pete here has need of a couple of young lads to do a little job.'

'Uh huh,' said Naz. 'Well, no disrespect to your friend, right, but why don't you and me have a little chat in private?'

'Fine,' said Randall and headed back behind the bar and into the office.

Pete stood sipping his Beck's, trying not to catch anybody's eye, saw a discarded copy of the *Mirror* on a banquette and picked it up, idly flicking through to see if there were any stories he should have picked up on. Pete in general was dead against the way that happenings in *Big Brother* or *Popstars* were counted as news even in the broadsheets, but he knew and Graham knew that you couldn't move too far away from the spirit of the times. OK, the *Post* was meant to be a bit of a fuddy-duddy paper, safe for farmers from Carmarthen to read without having apoplexy, but still. Even farmers from Carmarthen watch the soaps.

Pete suddenly looked up to see Randall and Naz emerging from the back office.

'Thank you, sir,' said Randall to Naz and then ushered Pete over to a neutral table where he passed across a scrap of paper with a mobile number and a name: Daniel.

'Not to be melodramatic or anything,' said Randall, 'but it's probably best if you just memorise it.'

Pete nodded, feeling oddly detached as he gently crashed through another ethical and legal barrier. Suborning a felony? Why the hell not?

27

Bobby woke up screaming then gagging, her fingers in her mouth trying to empty it of nothing.

'Stop it, for Christ's sake.'

Bobby looked round, her head spinning, trying to take in what was happening. She wasn't dead, she was alive, and Maria was standing over her looking furious. What time was it? Christ, what had she done? What kind of a bloody idiot had she made of herself? She started to sit up, but she still felt terribly tired and her head was aching like she'd drunk a bottle of vodka.

'Lie down, you stupid cow,' said Maria, no trace of sympathy on her face. Well, Bobby could understand that. 'How many have you taken?'

'How many what?' said Bobby, then, feebly, 'I haven't taken anything.'

'Course you haven't.' Maria waved the empty bottle of Temazepam under her nose. 'C'mon, how many?'

'I dunno,' said Bobby, feeling utterly miserable, defeated, unable to bear the switch-around of roles that was going on. 'Six or seven. Is that dangerous?'

'Well, you're not dead, are you?' Maria paced over to the window then walked back. 'You better go down the hospital anyway, get them to check you out. But I'm not bloody taking you, you already screwed my night up. I brings Macca back and he sees you snoring on my bloody bed and he pisses off just like that.'

'Sorry, Ri, I'll tell him for you.'

'Oh shut it, Bob, I'll sort it out. Anyway, why don't you give her a call, get her to take you?'

'Who d'you mean?'

'Who d'you think I mean? That BBC bitch you been screwing the last month or whatever it is. Or d'you think I didn't know?' Maria looked at Bobby closely. 'How stupid have you been taking me for all this time?'

Bobby closed her eyes, wished Maria would go away. But she was right: she'd better go down the hospital.

She told Maria the number.

'Fine,' said Maria, picking up the phone. 'What's the bitch's name?'

'Kim,' said Bobby and repeated the number as Maria dialled, thinking, Kim, just you be there, girl. I'm needing an angel right now.

Bobby was on one of those trolley beds in a cubicle somewhere in the A & E ward in Llandough Hospital, the old-fashioned one on the hill, looking back down over the bay. She was feeling really, really stupid. She was going to have to tell Kim what it was all about; she couldn't see any choice unless she wanted the girl to think she was a total bloody loser.

Be fair to Kim, she'd been magic so far. After Maria had called her, she'd come round straight away, even though it was six a.m. Hadn't freaked when Maria had given her the iceberg treatment; instead she'd sent Maria packing, got on the phone and had an ambulance round. Then she'd talked to all the doctors and that while Bobby lay there still a bit woozy, to be honest, and quite glad she was in the hospital cause it was a pretty scary idea, really, that you might just shut your eyes and never wake up again, though that didn't seem likely. Didn't seem like the doctors were too bothered at all, sounded like Temazepam wasn't really the way to go, you wanted to top yourself. Paracetamol'd be a whole lot more effective. The nurse had given her the full horror-story thing with Paracetamol you took a load of them; they might get you into the hospital and that and you'd be all right and just thinking what the hell was all that about and I must get my life back together and then day or two later your liver packs in and that's the end of you.

Bobby didn't want this to be the end of her. She just felt ashamed of herself and soon as Kim came back from making some calls or whatever, she'd tell her what it was all about and maybe Kim would have some idea what she should do. It was so nice for once to be around someone else who was, like, capable, could sort stuff out. All her life it seemed like Bobby had been the one sorting everything out, always been, like, the man, and right now she was feeling a bit sick of being the man. She was, don't laugh, feeling like a little girl. Needed a bit of looking after.

Ah, thank Christ, there was Kim now, talking to the nurse, smiling. She came up and squeezed Bobby's hand.

'Nurse here says you'll be fine, Bob.'

Bobby smiled, dragged herself up into a sitting position. 'Yeah. Does that mean I can go now?'

'Just wait till the doctor comes round,' said the nurse. 'Then he'll check you over and sign you out, I expect.'

'How long will that be?' asked Bobby, hating her voice as it came out like a whiny kid's.

'Not long,' said the nurse and moved off to the next bed, leaving Bobby alone with Kim.

'I've never done this before, you know,' said Bobby.

Kim put her hand on Bobby's. 'Don't worry about it.'

'No,' said Bobby, 'I do worry. I just want you to know: this isn't me. I'm not one of those girls always pretending like she's going to kill herself any time she don't like her haircut, it's just . . .'

'Yeah?' Kim looked at her. 'Just what?'

'Just . . . I've had a bit of a shock.'

Then Bobby told her, told her who her dad was, and Kim said fucking hell in a tone of reverence and Bobby said fucking hell is about right and they both just sat there quietly for a bit and finally Kim said, 'Well, what are you going to do?'

'I dunno,' said Bobby, telling the simple truth.

'Well,' said Kim, 'you still want to go after him over the Prince of Wales stuff? Oh God, don't answer that now.' She shook her head. 'Talk about a mind-fuck, that was your dad.'

'Yeah,' said Bobby. And then the doctor showed up and gave Bobby a bit of a lecture while Bobby bowed her head, then he said she could go home and she walked out to the car and Kim said, 'D'you want to come to mine?' and Bobby had never felt so grateful for anything in her life. 'Yes please,' she said.

28

It was lunchtime before Pete called Kim. Been a godawful morning. Cherri was off sick again, and Graham had decided to weigh in with some ideas. Graham's ideas were always things he'd picked up at some dinner party the night before and Pete would send someone off to write them up and then, likely as not, a few days later Graham would spike them all, having completely forgotten he'd commissioned them in the first place. And today Pete was really not in the mood for it. He needed his sleep, that's what Viv always said, and as with so many things she was right. That was what he missed at the moment, being with someone who knew him that well, who knew he needed his sleep – oh God, he was thinking about his mother not a lover. Maybe that was the problem? Maybe he'd treated Viv like she was his mother and now aged forty he was leaving home. God, that was a scary thought: age nought to twenty living with his actual mum, then twenty to forty, more or less, with Viv. Now was he doomed to do the whole thing all over again? Christ, he hoped not. Maybe, just maybe, he was finally a grown-up. He thought about Kim then: was she a mother figure? Not hardly.

He dispensed jobs right, left and centre, then sat back at his desk and phoned her, sure she'd be excited to hear about his adventures in burglar recruitment.

He rang her work number first, got her chirpy voicemail, then tried her mobile. She picked up on the third ring, sounding distracted.

'Yeah?'

'Kim, it's me, Pete.'

'Oh, hi Pete . . .' Then Pete could hear someone saying something to Kim and her sounding irritated replying, 'OK, OK,' then, 'Hang on, Pete, I've just got to go outside.' Sound of her footsteps then, 'Hi Pete, sorry about that. Bloody hospital won't let you use the mobile.'

'Hospital?'

'Yeah, long story, Pete. Bobby's here, you know the pimp, yeah?'

'Yes.'

'Well, basically she took an overdose – don't worry, she's all right. But, uh, basically she called me to give her a hand and I feel a bit responsible, like what with the docco and everything, like maybe I put her under a lot of pressure with the St Clair stuff and all.'

'Yeah,' said Pete, not really taking in what Kim was telling him. 'Yeah, about the St Clair stuff. Randall knows someone reckons he can get the stuff, you know, that we were talking about last night.'

'What?' said Kim. 'What are you talking about?'

'Oh, forget it,' said Pete, realising that this really wasn't the sort of thing he wanted to be blurting out on the phone while sitting in the middle of a newspaper office. 'Listen,' he said, 'how about we meet up after work and I'll tell you about it?'

'Um, yeah,' said Kim, sounding like she wasn't sure, 'except it depends a bit what's happening here with Bobby and that. I'll bell you later, right.'

'Right,' said Pete, but already he was talking into dead air. Probably got cut off. He frowned. Why was Kim helping this Bobby out at the hospital?

Her mobile seemed to be switched off all afternoon so, after work, Pete decided he'd walk round to her place, see if she was in and, if not, leave her a note.

Took him fifteen minutes to get there. He rang the bell, waited for a bit, nothing seemed to be happening. He was just starting to write a note when the door opened and there was Kim standing in her dressing gown, just like the first time he'd called round there except that was on a Sunday morning and this was a Tuesday evening.

'Hi Kim, you all right?'

'Yeah,' said Kim, looking flustered. 'I was just having a bath. What d'you want?'

'Got some news for you, you know about the films.' He inclined his head towards the stairs behind her. 'Let's go in, I'll tell you about it.'

'Uh, yeah, OK,' said Kim, 'but be quiet, yeah, cause I've got Bobby staying here.'

'Oh,' said Pete, 'right. Is she OK?'

'Yeah, she's fine, I think, just a bit shaken; you know, bit disorientated or whatever.'

Pete followed Kim up the stairs thinking she was certainly carrying through with the Florence Nightingale bit, taking Bobby home with her. It was just then that he flashed on a drunken memory of Kim snogging Bobby on the last night of the Custom House. He shrugged it aside; everyone had been well out of it. It came right back into focus, though, the minute they got inside Kim's flat and Bobby, wearing one of Kim's old T-shirts, stuck her head out of the bedroom and said, 'You coming back to bed, darlin'?' Then she saw Pete and just closed her eyes like a kid, thinking if they can't see you, you can't see them, and shut the door again quickly and quietly.

Pete just stood there staring at the closed door, then he turned to look at Kim, wondering if there was some way he could be jumping to conclusions here. Couldn't think of one. He started to speak. Kim cut him off.

'Don't start, Pete. You're not my fucking mother, you know what I mean? We have a good time together, right? So don't say a word, yeah, don't screw it up. I don't ask you what you get up to when I'm not around, you don't hassle me.'

Pete just stood there, mouth opening and closing like a goldfish. Words running through his head but none of them right. Finally he just shook his head, turned and walked back down the stairs.

Back outside, the evening now seeming not brisk but bloody freezing, he pulled up his collar against the wind and headed back towards town. As he walked he had a Wham record maddeningly stuck in his head, 'I don't want your freedom, I don't want nobody else' – maybe that wasn't right but that was what was going through his head. Thing was, he did want his freedom but he felt like he wanted Kim as well, and not on a timeshare basis either, so maybe he didn't want his freedom after all. Maybe the only kind of relationship he could consider was just a straight-ahead monogamy deal.

Shit, shit, shit, he thought. He really wished what had just happened hadn't. Cause on the one level he could handle the idea that Kim had a life outside of him; even that she might have other affairs. It was just coming smack up against the reality of it so suddenly that he was finding hard to handle. But then, as he walked, he started to feel less angry and hurt and more philosophical. Because deep down he was pretty sure he had more sticking power than most people. If he really wanted Kim he would fight and fight for her and he'd wear down the competition, he was sure of that. You wanted dogged, you came to Pete Duke. He set his face against the wind, mustered a bit of a smile. He knew what he was going to do: he was going to press on with the investigation, get on with it by himself and present it to Kim, show her what he was made of.

He got out his mobile, dialled the number Randall had procured for him.

'That Daniel? . . . Good. Yeah, I got your number from Naz, said you might be able to help me out with a little job.'

29

Bobby woke up feeling better than she had in months. Stronger, clearer. Kim wasn't in the bed. Bobby called out: no reply. She looked at the clock: quarter to ten. Kim must have gone to work. She padded into the kitchen. There was a note from Kim on the table. Make herself at home. The level of trust implied by this made Bobby feel like crying. She had a bath, a piece of toast, took her time, savoured being in the flat, let herself think once more what it would be like to have this different life.

Then reality started to crowd in. First off, she had a business to run. She hadn't been there for two days and she'd been in a right old state before that. God knows what would be going on over the wharf. Was Maria planning on keeping on working? How about Nikki and Tanya? She had to get over there, sort it out one way or the other.

She called a cab. Came five minutes later. Time was, when the old Cabbies Club was still going, she knew all the drivers, more or less . . . Now, though, she got some Sikh feller she'd never seen before, didn't say a word.

Went to her own flat first, had a shower, put some fresh clothes on, then opened the work flat up. She couldn't settle. Made a cup of tea, didn't drink it, got her website up on-screen, couldn't face working on it. Too much shit in her head. What was going on with Maria? What was she going to do about St Clair? Questions circling round and round, driving her mad.

She willed herself to act. Got out her mobile and called Maria first. Switched off. Shit. Tried Tanya next. Alleluia, she picked up.

'Tan?'

'Bob, that you? Where are you?'

'At the wharf.'

'You feeling better, Bob?'

'Yeah, yeah. You coming in this morning?'

'Just doing a bit of shopping, Bob. I'll be over soon. What time's first one?'

Bobby checked her appointment book. 'Twelve,' she said, 'but I may have to go out before that. You handle it?'

'Course, Bob. Been handling it all right the last two days.'

Bobby laughed. 'Yeah, I know, and thanks a lot, girl.' She paused, thought about something then carried on. 'Tell you what, Tan, sometime soon we should talk about you becoming a partner, like.'

'Yeah?' said Tanya. 'You serious?'

'Sure,' said Bobby, 'later, yeah,' and clicked her phone off, feeling like she was making a start. Letting go of a bit of control; it felt good. Now for the next stage, the big one.

Bobby took a deep breath, picked up her phone again and dialled Bernie's number. Thankfully he wasn't in yet. Bobby persuaded Marguerite to dig in her Rolodex and find a number for Leslie St Clair. There were half a dozen of them including a mobile number she said was written in red, which Bobby figured would be the one to go for.

Without giving herself time to think twice, she dialled the number. Two rings and there he was on the other end of the line. Leslie St Clair, corrupter of her youth and most likely her dad.

'Hi,' she said. 'This is Bobby Ranger, don't know if you remember me.'

A laugh at the end of the phone. 'Bobby Ranger! I remember you, all right. What can I do for you, Bobby?'

'I was wondering if I could come and see you about some-thing.'

'Mm hmm. What sort of something might we be talking about?'

'I'd rather not say on the phone.'

St Clair's voice hardened. 'I hope that isn't some kind of threat.'

'No,' said Bobby, 'nothing like that. It's just something, I don't know, personal.'

'How mysterious. Well, I dare say I can fit you in. You still down the docks?'

'Yeah,' said Bobby.

'Excellent,' said St Clair. 'Well, let me think, where to meet?' He laughed again. 'Tell you what. For old times' sake, how about we meet in the Prince of Wales? Twelve thirty all right with you?'

'Yeah,' said Bobby, her mouth suddenly so dry she could barely speak. 'See you there.'

She got there early. Stood on the other side of the road, outside the Cardiff Jeans Co., looking at it. The Prince of Wales. Now it looked so innocuous, all sandblasted stone on the outside, plate-glass doors and loads of signs advertising deals on drinks and food. Lot of the girls liked to go in there, she knew that. Herself, though, she'd always begged off. Too many memories she didn't want to face up to. Well, now she was going to be facing them. Big time. Bobby checked her watch: still ten minutes early but what the hell, she could have a little look around the place, prepare herself. She squared her shoulders and crossed the road then walked into what used to be the foyer. Suddenly she could smell the ammonia in the cleaning fluid they used to use, could feel the dread and excitement of twenty years before.

As before, there was a choice; head straight into the downstairs or take the stairs up. Bobby decided to start at the bottom. She headed on through the foyer into the body of the building, where the stalls used to be. The space disconcerted her at first. Where there used to be a Stygian darkness lit only by the flickering of *Swedish Dentists on the Job*, now there was a big light open space, dotted with tables and chairs, a long bar approximately where the screen used to be. She turned and looked up. Weird, they'd kept the circle more or less intact, even the upper circle, which, Christ, seemed to still have cinema seats on it.

She felt dizzy suddenly, unable to separate past from present. What was strange was the powerful nostalgia she felt for the old building, the old days. You looked round it now and it was nice enough, a big city-centre pub just starting to fill up with office boys and girls after a cheap lunch and a couple of drinks to take the edge off the afternoon in surroundings which if you didn't know looked like some lovely old theatre: the old Prince of Wales, in fact, the legitimate theatre it had been before Bobby was born, where Ronald Reagan once trod the boards. Was nostalgia completely indiscriminate? If she went back to the home they'd stuck her in, would she feel the same? She shook her head. No way. But this place, this place she felt something for. Maybe it was because this is where it had started: her life, the life. Bobby Ranger, top pimp. Gold teeth to prove it.

She had to see more, go upstairs. There was a big new staircase taking you up from the stalls, but she ignored that and made her way back to the front door. Took the old staircase up, and then headed into the circle. More seats, another bar. She looked up at the upper circle, realised it was closed off, just decorative with its rows of original seating, hopefully now thoroughly disinfected. She stood there for a moment wondering what to do next, was just going over the new walkway towards the bar when she noticed they had kept two of the boxes, one on either side. The one to her right held a couple in office junior get-up, her hands all over him, him looking bored. The box on the left had one occupant sitting there, watching her. Leslie St Clair.

He raised his glass to her, motioned for her to join him. She looked around, spotted the passageway that led to the box and followed it, her heartbeat accelerating.

St Clair stood up to greet her, kissed her on the cheek. 'Bobby Ranger. Well, well, well. You want a drink?'

Bobby shook her head, not trusting herself to speak just yet; instead she sat down at the little table they'd squeezed into the box and St Clair followed suit. She scanned his face. He was still a handsome man, all right, even at sixty-odd. Light brown skin, not much darker than Bobby's, really. Sharp regular features, a bit like Johnny Mathis or someone; his nose was a bit more Afro than hers but the eyes, his piercing green eyes – they were her own eyes looking back at her. She wondered if he had ever noticed, ever thought.

St Clair smiled at her. 'So what can I do for you after all this time?'

Bobby dived in, involuntarily closing her eyes as she spoke. 'Were you ever known as Troy Thursday?'

'Troy Thursday?' St Clair looked at her in amazement. 'It's a long time since I heard that name.'

'Thirty-eight years,' said Bobby.

St Clair sat back in his chair and stared at her. 'Thirty-eight years. That'd be your age, perhaps. Are you trying to tell me something, girl?'

'Yeah,' she said, her voice coming out as little more than a whisper. 'My mum, she said . . .'

But before she could finish St Clair was out of his seat and pulling Bobby out of hers, opening his arms to her. 'She said I'm your dad, didn't she?'

Bobby shrank back instinctively from St Clair's approach –

nothing in her memory banks welcomed such an approach from any man – but then something deeper kicked in – some primal need – and suddenly she just gave it up, all the years, all the lifetime of holding back from the embraces that were never offered, and with an audible groan she let herself go, like a vertigo sufferer giving in to the joy of falling, and collapsed into the waiting arms of Leslie St Clair.

Bobby was doing her best to keep her sense of perspective, but she could tell that she had a big stupid grin on her face and her eyes were shining as she listened to him talk. Her dad.

He'd been great so far; she could hardly believe it. No denials, no doubt; he had just opened his arms to her, pulled her in and held her.

Eventually they broke apart and St Clair ordered a bottle of champagne and they sat there in the box looking out over the ground floor of the pub and St Clair entertained her, told her showbiz stories, business stories, told her about his big plans for Cardiff, this thing called the Castle Market that was going to make him a fortune, went on about what an exciting time it was to be back in the city. More stories, stories about his childhood, the old Tiger Bay, and Bobby just sat there looking at him, looking at his skin, his hair, his eyes, thinking: my skin, my hair, my eyes.

Only little disappointment was he didn't seem to remember a thing about Bobby's mum. Oh, he talked like he did, but you could just see he was blagging it. 'Lovely girl, used to come to all the gigs . . .' he started, but then visibly ran out of steam. Well, it was no more than Bobby expected, but still it would be nice to think your conception was more than just ten minutes out the back of the Embassy Ballroom, Pontypridd. And yet that was the amazing thing: one stupid meaningless little fuck between some stupid young girl and some horny chancer and you end up with a human being. St Clair had a fit of coughing, then went off to the toilet and Bobby looked around the pub feeling a bit drunk now from the lunchtime champagne.

It was no wonder she'd never wanted kids herself, she thought. It wasn't just she was a lesbian, lot of lesbians got kids, not the point at all and she liked kids, loved Jamal, but she'd never wanted one growing inside her. Never wanted that responsibility. Weird thing was, though, when she had the hysterectomy, couple of years back, she'd cried for a week. Who'd be a woman, eh?

St Clair, Les, her dad, came back from the toilets, sat back down and lit up another fag. 'So you know old Bernie, then?'

'Yeah,' said Bobby. 'How d'you know that?'

'Oh,' said St. Clair, 'Bernie gave me a call, warned me that there might be a surprise in store, didn't want me having a heart attack on the spot.'

'Oh,' said Bobby, feeling a little cheated by this news, wondering why he'd gone through that little charade of pretending not to know, a familiar little flicker of suspicion in her mind. She looked at her watch and saw it was closing in on four. 'Time I was getting back to work,' she said.

'Work?' said St Clair, raising an eyebrow. 'What line of work are you in, then?'

'Well,' said Bobby, pausing, caught between the desire to chuck the realities of her life in the face of this never-was father and the desire to impress him, make him proud of his never-was little girl.

'Computers,' she said finally. 'Helping people set up their systems, web design, stuff like that, got my own business doing it. Doing a little job for Bernie Walters at the moment, as it goes.'

St Clair nodded, gave her a proud-father smile. 'Good line of work to be in. Lot of my business is on the Net these days. Don't suppose you'd like a job working for your old man, would you?'

Bobby looked at him, trying to keep her face neutral. 'Really?'

'Sure,' said St Clair. 'Good web designers, always a demand for them.'

'Yeah, course,' said Bobby, wondering why this all seemed a little too good to be true.

30

Pete woke up with an overwhelming sense of guilt, that awful sense that you've done something terrible the night before but you can't quite remember what.

Then he remembered. He'd phoned up Daniel. He'd met Daniel in an estate pub in Llanrumney, kind of place you really didn't want to catch anyone's eye. He'd told Daniel what he wanted and Daniel had said yeah, Naz had told him more or less. Some fucking nonce needed turning over. No problem, mate. And Pete had said yeah, but no violence, just a burglary, just these films the guy had. That'd be enough to turn him over to the law, and this Daniel had nodded and said no problem, boss, and had taken fifty quid from Pete with the promise of another fifty when the job was done and Pete had explained which trailer it was and which pub the cameraman drank in and had gone back to the flat to wait and Randall had suggested popping out for a quickie and even though Pete knew full well what a quickie was he'd said yes and gone and got completely hammered and he'd told Randall all about finding Kim with Bobby and Randall had just looked a bit embarrassed and said well that Kim she's certainly not a girl for the fainthearted and that was about the last bit of conversation Pete could remember. Till about half two walking back from the Cambrian, completely out of it, his mobile had rung and eventually Pete had managed to find it and answer it and the kid Daniel had said he'd got the stuff, when did Pete want to pick it up, and Pete had said how about lunchtime, one o'clock in the car park of the pub they'd met before, and Daniel had said fine.

And so, feeling like his life was spiralling out of control, Pete dragged himself out of bed and into work. Then he dragged himself through the morning, behaving like the original sore-headed bear, well aware that he was drawing on years of accumulated goodwill.

One o'clock Pete was in the car park. Ten minutes later Daniel turned up and jumped over the wall from the estate, a carrier bag in his hand. Pete had a quick look, saw a bunch of little white boxes with film reels inside, handed over the next fifty quid to Daniel who said thanks boss, then laughed and said served the old pervert right and all and Pete said yeah sure and drove back into town feeling like the feller from *Taxi Driver*, cleaning up the streets at whatever lunatic cost. Except Pete lacked the comfort of madness, so basically just felt out of his depth. He shook his head; what was the matter with him? He'd got the films, had an out-and-out scoop for the first time in his journalistic career. Big story, as Kim would say. Big London, get-out-of-Cardiff story.

As he pulled into the office car park, it struck him that it might be an idea to check what was on the films first, before he went in to see Graham, told him he'd got the scoop of the decade, then realised all he had was a bunch of home movies: Jock on the beach at Porthcawl.

Who would have a film projector? His dad used to have one but they'd chucked everything out when they moved. He was pretty certain Randall didn't have one. Randall seemed to have gone through life acquiring a bare minimum of possessions, a couple of shelves of books and three sets of clothing. Maybe the ex-wives had all the stuff. The BBC? Surely the BBC would be able to lay their hands on one. He took a quick deep breath and dialled Kim's number.

'Kim?'

'Yeah. Pete, that you? Look . . .' Her voice was immediately awkward.

'Yeah, it's me, and it's OK, I'm not calling about last night, leave that for the minute. Listen, I've got the films.'

'The films? Christ, Pete, how d'you do that?' Kim sounded excited.

Pete smiled. 'Don't ask,' he said – well, wasn't he the cool one? – then followed up, 'listen, have you got a film projector there, something we can watch them on?'

A pause. 'Yeah, I'm sure I can find something, but let's not watch them here. Why don't you come over to mine about four?'

'Make it five,' said Pete and rang off, feeling like he was getting back in the saddle here.

Back in the office Pete was just settling in again when Terry on the police desk passed him a little story, asked if he was interested. A caravan had been burnt out in the trailer park at St Brides, the words Fuck Off Nonce found painted on what remained of one of the walls. Nobody hurt, but a fair bit of property damage. What did Pete think? Single para, or go a bit bigger, maybe link it to all that paedophile vigilante stuff from last year?

Pete found himself staring at the story, the two paras of notes, unable to speak. This was his doing.

'Well, boss?' said Terry, impatient.

Finally Pete found his voice. 'Single para will be fine, don't want to reopen all that can of worms.' Terry said OK and walked off, giving him a little bit of a look but nothing special, and Pete sat back and wondered at himself.

His phone rang then. Pete picked up. Malcolm Hopkin. Pete was immediately on the alert and Hopkin didn't beat about the bush.

'Pete, boy, what the hell has got into you?'

Pete said nothing.

'You're running around town like Clark Kent all of a sudden. Your boss Graham there assures me you're Mr Sensible, Mr Quiet Life, and now you're trampling all over the prize rose bushes.' He paused. 'Or should I say prize caravan parks?'

Pete shuddered but managed to stay silent.

Hopkin sighed.

'OK, lad, well you obviously reckon you're on to a bit of a story here, and I suppose you're right, but what I'm asking is whether you might be able to listen to the other side. You prepared to do that, son? Listen?'

'I guess,' said Pete, guardedly.

'Good man,' said Hopkin. 'How about six o'clock at my office?'

'OK,' said Pete. 'Where's that?'

Hopkin laughed. 'The Wharf, son, pub by the dock. Six o'clock, yeah?'

'Yeah, OK,' said Pete, frowning.

31

Bobby was sitting in Bernie Walters's office, a glass of wine in her hand, her head spinning. Les – her dad – had had to shoot off on some urgent business and she'd just sat there by herself for a bit in the Prince of Wales wondering just how different her life might have been if her mum had told her, if her mum had known, if her mum hadn't given her up the second she saw what colour she was, if her mum and dad had wanted each other, had wanted her. Bollocks, this was the kind of self-pity she'd long since learnt you couldn't afford; known since she was six years old there was no one in this world you could rely on but yourself and she'd made peace with that but now this feeling that she'd had a dad all this time, a dad who did want her, who was pleased to see her, who didn't reject her, well it hurt, left her feeling scalded and raw to the world.

And that was without even thinking about the other stuff – who he was – the things that had happened all those years ago, happened right in that pub. She'd had to get out of there, stood up, realised she was well on the way to being drunk. Out in the fresh air she'd considered going home, but her head was buzzing too much and she felt like another drink, needed a bit more of a blanket between her and the world. Then she'd looked across the road, seen the light in Bernie's office and thought Bernie'll have a drink, Bernie knows my dad, and in she'd gone and it was like he'd been waiting for her. She walked in and she was just going to say hello to Marguerite when Bernie's door opened and he just gave her this big hug and led her into his office and there was a bottle open and an empty glass waiting and Bernie was smiling at her and she felt . . . cared for.

'When did you realise, Bern?' she asked him.

Bernie looked at her. 'The moment you asked if this Troy Thursday was black. Course, my apologies, I should have thought of that at once, but I'm not as swift as I once was. Anyway, moment you asked that I thought of Les and then I looked at your face and thought well, the truth's staring right back at me. But of course I had to check it out a little bit, see how the land lay, if you know what I mean.'

'You told him, didn't you?'

Bernie squirmed in his seat a little. 'Well, yes, I felt it was best, really. Didn't want you getting hurt, and I didn't want Les getting too much of a shock either, not in his state.'

'What d'you mean, not in his state?'

Bernie shook his head quickly. 'Oh nothing, he's just had a few health problems lately.'

'He didn't say anything about that.'

'No, well, probably not the main thing on his mind, not when he was seeing you. And it went all right, did it?'

'Yeah,' said Bobby, 'great, I think, but odd, you know?'

Bernie nodded. 'I can imagine. You going to see him again?'

'Yeah, tomorrow. Wants me to meet him at the Castle, show me his plans.'

'Great,' said Bernie again, beaming effusively and refilling her glass. 'Going to hear on Friday, isn't he, whether he gets it or not.' A frown quickly passed over Bernie's face but was summarily dismissed. 'Anyway, forget business, this is wonderful.'

'Yeah,' said Bobby, coasting on the alcohol high, well aware that she might be in for an almighty comedown, but just for now letting herself enjoy it.

32

Pete was round at Kim's flat. She was assembling the Super 8 projector and he was watching her. They were both being fastidiously polite to each other, skating round the huge crater that was the Bobby business.

Finally Kim had the first film threaded into the spools of the projector. Pete had closed the curtains and cleared the pictures off a white wall that would serve as the screen. Kim switched the projector to play and Pete turned the lights out.

The film started. It was colour but faded and badly lit. There was a big table and some sort of banquet in progress. There were all these older blokes sitting round the table with masks over their eyes and these younger blokes in shorts and T-shirts serving then. Very quickly and without any attempt at dramatic explanation the sex began. Pete and Kim looked at each other. Pete tried a grin like it's all right, this was all a long time ago and it's just a rather kitsch artefact now. Except it wasn't; there was still something shockingly illicit in what they were watching.

Pete tried to neutralise it by concentrating on whether any of the masked men could possibly be St Clair. He stared at the screen; the masks made it hard to be at all sure, but even so none of the older men seemed to have St Clair's colouring. He reeled back in shock then as the screen cut to a close-up of a penis entering a mouth.

'I dunno,' he said to Kim to cover his embarrassment. 'Can't see St Clair in there.'

'Must have stayed behind the camera,' said Kim, her attention not wavering from the screen, apparently unbothered by what she was watching.

'Yeah,' said Pete, 'suppose so,' hoping the film would run out soon.

'We can just keep looking through the others,' said Kim brightly. 'Maybe he appears himself in the straight ones. After all, it must be girls he's into if he's Bobby's . . .' Kim's voice tailed off.

Pete looked at her. Bobby's what? What was she talking about? Before he could ask, though, Kim let out a yell.

'Fucking hell!' She was pointing at the screen, as an acned blond youth was lying back letting a fat bloke in a mask go down on him. 'I know him.'

'Who is it?'

Kim waved his question away, eyes still fixed on the screen. She watched till the blond boy got off, then she walked up to the screen as the camera panned up to his face cracking into a big grin. Then the reel ended and the film started flapping about in the projector till Kim switched it off and turned to Pete.

'That's Lee Fontana.'

Pete looked at her blankly.

'You know. The chef. He's got his own show on HTV, has his own restaurant out in Radyr. I worked with him on *Good Morning Wales* a couple of years back.'

Pete nodded. The name rang the faintest of bells; probably the bloke had done the Dish of the Day feature in the Saturday magazine or something, wasn't like Wales was overburdened with celebrity chefs. Anyway, that was hardly the point. 'You sure?'

'Yeah,' said Kim. 'Well, ninety-nine per cent anyway.'

'Christ,' said Pete. 'Well, if he confirms St Clair was there, then . . .'

'Then we've got him, yeah.' Kim had a huge smile on her face. 'Jesus, Pete, this story just keeps on getting better and better. Lee Fontana, that is so brilliant. This could be a bloody *Panorama* special, this could. I will just be so out of here.'

Kim came over to Pete, put her arms round him from behind and whispered in his ear, 'That was one brilliant piece of work, Peter Duke. You fancy a little celebration?' She slipped her hand down his chest, found his nipple and squeezed it then turned him round to face her, kissed him hard.

Pete wanted to resist but failed completely and allowed himself to be dragged to the bedroom. Just then her mobile rang, making them both jump. She switched it off immediately but it gave Pete the opening he needed. 'Look, Kim, we've got to talk. What's going on with you and Bobby?'

She carried on unbuttoning her shirt, smiling. 'Nothing you have to worry about, Pete. She was just in a bit of a state and I brought her home and . . .' She laughed. 'You know what I'm like, Pete, terrible old tart, but it's nothing. Hardly like I'm going to go off with a lesbian pimp, am I? Be serious. But if it bothers you that much, I'll knock it on the head.'

She looked at him, all fake sincerity and sweetness, and she unhooked her bra, then gave him another smile and said, 'Or maybe you'd like to watch, that it? You one of those fellers desperate to see two girls getting it on?'

'Piss off,' said Pete, but even as he said it he was moving towards her, letting her undo his buttons, letting himself sink into it, feeling that if something was this much fun what did it matter if it was wrong, and thinking that sounded like the lyrics to a country song, maybe it was the lyrics to a country song and then he wasn't thinking about lyrics any more, wasn't thinking of anything more complex than touch and taste and sight till it was over and he was once more wishing he smoked. Then he turned to look at the clock by the bed and it was five to six and he remembered he was meant to be meeting Malcolm Hopkin in five minutes.

'Oh God,' he said. 'Sorry, look I've got to go.'

'Oh right,' said Kim, mock-outraged. 'Well, just leave the money on the mantelpiece, is it?'

'Sorry,' said Pete again. 'It's just I've got to meet Malcolm Hopkin – you know, St Clair's mate. Says he's got some information for us.'

'Like hell,' said Kim. 'He'll just be trying to buy you off.'

Pete shrugged. 'C'mon, got to get all sides of the story.'

'Yeah, well. Anyway, while you're doing that I'll try and set something up with old Lee Fontana. You want to come along?'

'Sure,' said Pete.

'Fine,' said Kim. 'Well, call me on the mobile later on . . . Oh, and you know when you meet Hopkin?'

'Yeah.'

'Well, there's any bribes going, you make sure you get one for me and all.'

Pete made it to the Wharf at half six, hair still wet from the shower. Malcolm Hopkin was sat at the bar with a copy of the *Echo* in his hand, a pint and chaser next to him.

Hopkin looked him up and down quizzically. 'You just fall in the canal, son?'

'No,' said Pete. 'Just had a shower.'

'Oh aye,' said Hopkin. 'Afternooner, was it? Married, is she?'

Pete spluttered haplessly. Hopkin clapped him on the back. 'Only joking, son. What are you drinking?'

'Pint of light,' said Pete and waited for Hopkin to get the drink and lead them over to a table in the raised area looking out over the water, near where a band was soundchecking – later on the Wharf would be packed. Any night there was a decent band on, the Wharf was full of men and women Pete's age, the kind of people who'd been squeezed out of the town pubs by the youth revolution.

The band were running through something mellow, sounded like a Bobby Blue Bland tune, and the lights from the Holiday Inn Express further up the wharf looked almost pretty.

'Did it ever strike you, son,' said Malcolm, lighting up a fag, 'that Cardiff's really like an American city?'

Pete took a pull on his pint, raised his eyebrows.

'You think about it. Listen to the music – American music, right. People been hearing that in Cardiff since for ever. Cause of all this.' Malcolm waved at the docks. 'Sailors brought the music in. And that's the other thing to remember; it's a new city, hardly more than a hundred years old.'

'Hundred and fifty,' said Pete.

'Hundred and fifty, whatever. Same age as Chicago. And an immigrant city too. People came from all over to work here. Africa, China, England. All over.'

'Uh huh,' said Pete, thinking about it. Well, the Chicago comparison was apt enough, at least when it came to the way local politics ran. Chicago – the natural home of the political fixer. 'Yeah,' he said, 'I'd have thought Chicago would be your kind of place.'

Hopkin laughed. 'I know what you're saying. But what I'm saying is this city is changing. You grew up here, didn't you, son?'

'Yeah,' said Pete. 'Well, Whitchurch way.'

'Exactly. So you know how the city was, you remember it before all this development, right? And you've seen it change, yeah?'

'Yeah,' said Pete, wondering what on earth this was all about.

'Yeah, of course you have, and let me ask you, you think it's changed for the better?'

Pete scratched his head – flashed on St Mary Street on a Saturday night, a neon strip of theme bars and blokes in

Aquascutum shirts throwing up. 'I guess,' he said. 'More jobs, more money, you know.'

'Sure,' said Hopkin. 'You're right there. No question. And I like to think I've played my part over the years helping bring the investment in. But that doesn't mean I have to like it all.'

'Yeah,' said Pete, 'I know what you mean, but I don't exactly get why you're telling me this, if you don't mind me saying.'

'Not at all, cause the reason you don't get it is cause I'm taking a bastard long time to get to the point, and that is that if you run the story that I suspect you've got about old Les and his dirty doings half a bloody lifetime ago, well, what'll happen — more than likely — is the bid will be screwed, Globalcast Holdings or whoever will nip in through the back door and you'll have another bloody drive-thru Burger King and an Allied Carpets and you'll have played your part in bringing that about.'

'Yeah,' said Pete, 'that's all well and good and, be honest, I don't disagree with a word you've said, but that still doesn't mean I can condone what St Clair did.'

'No,' said Hopkin, 'fair enough. If you've got evidence that Les did wrong — and I suspect you haven't really got much more than a load of tittle-tattle — well, fine, go ahead and print it, but let me just say that if you waited till next week, once the contract's been awarded, you'd be doing the city as a whole a big favour.'

Pete didn't say anything, just kept on looking out at the water, thinking that what Hopkin said was reasonable enough.

'Doing your bank balance a big favour and all, I wouldn't be surprised,' Pete said in the end, 'but, fair enough, the story's been waiting twenty-five years to come out, couple more days won't kill it.'

'Good man,' said Hopkin, all but sighing with relief before carrying on. 'And of course our friend Kenny will be relieved and all. Not a man you want to get on the wrong side of, is our friend Kenny.'

'No,' said Pete, kind of wishing Hopkin hadn't said that, had allowed Pete to feel like he was acting out of magnanimity and not out of fear.

33

Bobby tried Kim's mobile again around eight and finally got an answer. She seemed really pleased to hear from Bobby and sure she'd love to have a chat; why didn't Bobby meet her back at her flat in about half an hour?

On her way round Bobby found herself thinking about the Pete feller, wondering how serious it was between him and Kim. Stupid – what was she doing feeling jealous? Not like the thing with Kim could ever go anywhere, and anyway didn't she have enough on her mind already? But still she could tell she was going to have to talk to Kim about the Pete feller. In the past it didn't bother her too much a girl she was seeing was sleeping with some bloke; she always felt like the girl would see sense before long, see who gave her the best time. Yeah, well. That's how she'd always been; arrogant, y'know. Up till lately. Now all she was was vulnerable.

Then Kim opened the door and saw Bobby and gave her this big oh-dahling hug and kiss and led her into the front room and they sat on Kim's nice sofa and Bobby told her how it had gone with her dad, badly wanting, she realised, Kim's approval.

She didn't get it, though. Kim kept shaking her head and when she finished just looked at her and said, 'He's got a nerve, thinking he can just swan back into your life like that.'

'Yeah,' said Bobby, suddenly feeling apprehensive, 'maybe you're right. But I dunno, it's not like he abandoned me on purpose; he never knew I existed. And he's a nice guy really. I'd forgotten that; a real charmer, like. You don't know, you never met him, have you?'

'No,' said Kim, 'but I think you may be losing your sense of perspective a bit here, Bob. Remember how angry you were when you came to me first, told me about all the abuse you'd suffered?'

'Well,' said Bobby, 'it wasn't me who suffered it really.'

'Oh come on, he abused you all one way or another. Look, I've seen the films. Did I tell you that I've got the films?'

'No,' said Bobby, 'Jesus,' and then she realised that she'd been staring idly at a Super 8 projector, a film loaded up.

Kim followed her gaze. 'Yeah, that's one of them there. You want to have a look?'

Bobby didn't say anything. She wasn't sure if she did or she didn't. But Kim didn't wait for an answer, just turned the film on anyway.

Suddenly she was sixteen again. And she was caught exactly halfway between laughing and crying. Laughing cause it had all been a laugh back then, sixteen and without a prospect in the world, but still somehow invincible and at last amongst her people, Leslie St Clair's circus of outsiders. Crying because it was so long ago and where were they now, all those hard and pretty boys – Lee Fontana, Darren Jones, Perko and, Christ, wasn't that Rizla in the corner just sitting there watching, a stoned grin on his face? She walked up closer to the wall, trying to make out anyone else.

'Recognise anyone?' asked Kim.

'Yeah,' said Bobby. 'That's Jonesy, Darren Jones, giving the fat guy a blow-job, and that's Lee Fontana there just taking his shirt off.'

'Yeah,' said Kim, all pleased. 'I recognised him already.'

'You didn't? Lee!' Shit, she hadn't seen Lee in years, always feared the worst for him.

'Yeah, you know he's a chef now, has his own restaurant, does a lot of TV stuff.'

'You taking the piss?'

'No, it's true.'

'Well, fucking hell.' Bobby shook her head, feeling slightly happier. God, if Lee Fontana could make it . . .

'Anyone else?'

Bobby shrugged. 'Few people. You see that guy there with the little 'tache, that's Frog. I still sees him now and again.'

'Oh yeah, how's he doing these days?'

Bobby frowned. 'Smackhead. Used to be a rentboy years ago, but he got a bit past his sell by.'

'Oh yeah?' said Kim. 'That's awful. You wouldn't know how I could get hold of him, would you?'

'Dunno,' said Bobby. 'Lives up the Valleys somewhere, but he goes in the White Hart now and again. His Auntie Liz works there.'

'Thanks, great,' said Kim, 'and he goes by Frog, does he?'

Bobby laughed. 'No, not to his auntie. He's Paul, his name is Paul Richards. Why d'you want to know, anyway?'

'Oh,' said Kim, 'just been following up a bit on what you told me about St Clair – your dad, I mean.'

Bobby waved the correction away. 'Yeah, St Clair is fine, Les, whatever; not like he's been a dad to me, is it? So, what, you're making a documentary about him?'

'Oh yes, well, maybe, see how it pans out.'

Bobby stared at Kim for a moment, wondering how she felt about St Clair being exposed on the TV. Confused. That was how she felt. 'I tell you I'm going to see him tomorrow?'

'Yeah?' said Kim. 'Really? Oh, you don't think I could . . .'

She broke off but Bobby could guess what she wanted to ask, something like can I come along and film you with him, and she felt a heaviness inside her; maybe there was no straight world, maybe everyone was on their own hustle after all – TV, brothel-keeping, whatever – maybe it all came down to individuals trying to screw as much as they could get out of each other. There was a line she'd used often enough to her girls: least you know you're getting screwed with what you do, and you're getting paid for it. You try working in McDonald's, you're getting screwed there and all and you're getting four pound an hour for it. Said it once, she'd said it a hundred times, but now, looking into Kim's eyes seeing the calculations going on there, she felt its truth. She couldn't help it, her face crumbled and she was reaching out to Kim like a bloody baby.

'Don't push me,' she was saying and then Kim was putting her arms round her and saying, 'Hey, girl, I'm sorry. Always working, that's my trouble,' and Bobby didn't try to analyse that for sincerity, just took the comfort offered, and then she let Kim put her to bed, half expecting that, tired though she was, she wouldn't be able to sleep, and if she did there'd be nightmares all the way, but instead she was asleep the second her head hit the pillow and if she dreamed at all she didn't remember it when she woke up a full twelve hours later.

She woke up feeling like she was newborn, an extraordinary lightness upon her and her whereabouts utterly strange. Second by second, though, the world came back to her. First her surroundings came into focus; the clothes spilled on the chair, Kim twisting in her sleep next to her, then a rush of pleasure. She was meeting Les – her dad, Les, her dad, Les – at twelve, then a rush of fear, an old familiar lesson learned; don't get your hopes up, girl, cause that's how you get hurt.

And then it was nine am, time to go, and Kim said softly in her ear, 'Go on, Bob, you better go see your dad,' and Bobby clutched on to her hard then let go and headed out the door and down the stairs and off to meet her father.

34

Pete and Kim were driving out into the Vale, on their way to see Lee Fontana. Pete was driving his latest review car; he'd finally managed to wangle a Subaru Impreza and as they passed Culverhouse Cross heading up the Tumble Hill he put his foot down and fairly hurtled past the other motors. He looked over at Kim, saw her smile back at him but her mind was clearly elsewhere – on the story, no doubt, the big story – and he had a stabbing sense that no matter how fast a car he was driving he was never going to keep up with her.

Lee Fontana lived in a converted chapel in Llancarfan, one of the little villages off the A48. Kim had phoned him the night before to say that she was making a docco on Leslie St Clair and his name had come up and she told Pete that he'd said, 'Oh fucking hell, love, I was wondering when someone would finally dig that whole business up, why don't you come over for breakfast?'

So nine forty-five there they were, ringing on the doorbell of a very tastefully converted chapel. Seconds later the door was open and a big hospitable bloke, with a sharp suit straining a little over his ample stomach, was ushering them into the kind of place Pete had only ever seen in the Saturday magazine. All burnished hardwoods and brightly coloured Sixties-looking furniture.

'You must be Kim, then,' said the bloke, smiling, his accent dead Cardiff but camped up a bit. 'I'm Lee and you're the photographer, are you?' he asked, turning towards Pete.

'No,' said Kim. 'This is Pete, he's from the *Post*.'

'Oh right,' said Lee with a little sigh. 'Oh well, the more the merrier, I suppose. Come on in.'

They followed Lee across the open-plan interior through a living area which had Kim exclaiming, 'Wow, Lee, is that all Memphis?' and Lee saying, 'Yes, well a few bits and bobs,' but looking dead chuffed and then they were over in the eating and dining zone and there was a big plate of croissants in the middle of the table next to a pot of coffee and they each took a plate and a cup and Kim did a bit more ooh-what-a-gorgeous-place chitchat and then it was down to business.

'So,' said Pete, taking on the pro-journalist role, 'you're not denying your involvement with Leslie St Clair?'

'No,' said Lee. 'Why would I want to do that?' He frowned. 'I was wondering how you got to know about all that, though.'

'Uh . . .' said Pete, wondering how much to reveal.

'We saw one of the films,' chipped in Kim, clearly not bothered about showing their hand.

'Oh bloody hell,' said Lee, laughing out loud. 'Well, I suppose it's a compliment you recognised me. Bit skinnier back then, wasn't I?'

'A little bit, maybe,' smiled Kim. 'How old were you?'

'Oh, I dunno,' said Lee. 'Depends a bit which one you saw. Was it like a dinner party – God, it's all coming back to me now – with masks, was that the one?'

'Yeah, that's it.'

'Oh bloody hell, well do let me have a copy when you've finished with it. I've got to show it to Stefan; he'll never believe how fit I was back then. Oh God, how old was I? Sixteen definitely; you're not having me saying I was under-age.' He paused, looked from Kim to Pete and back again. 'Is that what this is about, you trying to say Les was using people were under-age?'

'Well,' said Kim, 'obviously if some of the performers were under-age . . .'

'No, no way,' said Lee. 'Absolutely no way is that what was going on there. That was the best bloody thing ever happened to me, meeting Les and his crowd. I was a right little hooligan back then, if you can believe it. Out of touch with my sexuality is what they'd say now. First person ever treated me decent was Les St Clair and once I saw what was going on I'd have bloody killed to get into those films. Well, you've seen them – did it look like anyone was forcing me to do it?'

'Well,' said Kim, laughing despite herself, 'not exactly but that doesn't mean it was appropriate.'

'Appropriate!' Lee burst out laughing now. 'C'mon, love, what the fuck has appropriate got to do with a good shag? No, you won't find me saying one word against Leslie St Clair – he put me in the films, he introduced me to people, he made all this,' Lee waved a hand at his elegant living space, 'made it all possible. Before I met Les my life was utter shit. Since then, well, it's not been all wine and roses, but there's been a hell of a lot more up than down. So if that's all you wanted to know, I've got work to do.'

And that was that, really. Kim tried to get in a couple more questions but you could see that the more Lee thought about what was going on the more pissed off he was getting and in no time they were out the door and Pete was driving them back to Cardiff.

'Well?' said Pete.

'Well what?' said Kim, sitting next to him frowning hard. 'Look, it doesn't matter if Lee bloody Fontana doesn't want to co-operate; he's admitted he was in the film, that's dynamite for starters. All we have to do now is find some of the other people who were in it and we're in business.'

'I dunno,' said Pete. 'It was a long time ago and, like Lee there said, it doesn't seem like anyone was frightening the horses exactly.'

'Pete! It's a big bloody story, all right? Network are really excited about it. I spoke to someone in London about it last night; they're ready to run with it the minute I've got a couple of witness statements. Pete, you got to keep your head screwed on here. We're talking major fucking break. For both of us. You been on to the tabloids yet, have you, Pete? *News of the World*'ll love it.'

Pete didn't answer, just revved up the car as they pulled out of St Nicholas and a stretch of open road loomed, trying to become one with the motor, miles away from the muck-raking.

35

He was waiting for her in the Louis, an old-fashioned full-service café, looked like nothing from the outside but went back about a mile once you got inside. All daily-roast specials and puddings with custard and all the waitresses looked like your nan, place Bobby had completely forgotten existed, place you walked past thousands of times without even registering it any more, and there was St Clair sitting at a table near the front, chatting to the manager, finishing up a cup of coffee. And you could tell, she was sure you could tell, that he was pleased to see her and she was pleased to see him but scared too and wary and in a minute they were out on the street and he started talking to her, talking in a different voice from any she'd heard before, a quieter, more thoughtful voice. He asked her what she knew about the history of Cardiff and she said not much and he said, 'Well I've made quite a study of it. You know there was hardly anything here two hundred years ago?'

Bobby nodded; she wasn't stupid, she knew it was a Victorian city, an industrial city.

'Hardly anything at all here till one man came along. The second Marquess of Bute. His family already owned the castle, what there was of it then, just a falling-down keep and a half-built manor house really, plus all the land around it. Then they discovered coal up in the valleys and Bute had the vision to turn his land into the biggest port in the world.

'He had the vision, the second Marquess, but he died before it all really got going. Left a baby son – the richest baby in the world, they called him – John, the third Marquess. Imagine that – you're born fabulously rich and all the time you're growing up you're getting richer and richer. Coal and shipping is making you relatively speaking about the richest man there's ever been. Can you imagine that?'

'Hardly.'

'Me either, girl, me either. You and me, we come up the other way. And yeah, yeah, before you start I know I never helped you, but how could I when I never even knew you existed? But anyway, imagine you had all that money, what would you have done with it?'

Bobby shrugged.

'Well, this feller, he built himself castles. He built this one, for starters.'

By now they were at the foot of St Mary Street, looking across the road at Cardiff Castle. Bobby found herself blinking at it, thinking how strange it was that things that were frankly pretty extraordinary, like this great big castle stuck right in the middle of town, should become so familiar that you hardly even notice them. She had to think for a moment to remember if she'd ever actually been inside. All she could recall was a school trip to the Tattoo when she was a kid, a load of soldiers firing off cannons and stuff. She'd been scared but she hadn't shown it, wet the bed in the home that night. She couldn't remember anything much about the castle itself.

Well, now she was going to see it all again. St Clair walked over the drawbridge, had a quick word with the security guard and led her into the big open space in the middle.

The castle basically had these huge walls, made a square about a hundred yards across. In the middle was the one original part, a big Norman keep. The south wall where they came in had a tower in the middle with a military museum. The east and north walls had nothing much on them. It was the west wall that had all the main buildings, a whole hotchpotch of towers linked together by galleries.

St Clair gave her a whirlwind guided tour. He led her through these rococo rooms decorated in crazed Victorian gothic style like a fairytale castle come to life.

'You've got to remember the third Marquess was only eighteen when he started building all this stuff. He found this opium-fiend architect called Burges and they built this. You see that,' he pointed at a table in the middle of what was called the small dining room, 'you see that hole in the table? He had a bloody vine growing up from the floor below, came up through the table so they could pick grapes off it at the end of the meal.'

'Right,' grunted Bobby, kind of enjoying this new side of St Clair, the historian, but also wondering what the point of all this was. Leslie St Clair wasn't a feller did things without a point.

And sure enough, after they'd whisked through half a dozen more over-elaborate rooms, St Clair led the way back outside, into the central area.

'OK,' he said then, 'one last thing I want to show you.'

She followed him past the peacocks towards the castle keep. Over the inner moat then up a steep flight of stone stairs and they were inside. Up two flights of wooden stairs then into the tower. Up a winding staircase and then they came out at the top. The whole city of Cardiff spread out before them on a cold bright spring lunchtime.

'You see this?' St Clair flung his arms out wide. 'This is our city, girl, yours and mine.'

'Yeah,' said Bobby, like yes it's Cardiff, I know.

He turned to her. 'I'm not joking, girl. This is my city now; anywhere I go people know me, people respect me. Wasn't like that when I was coming up. Back then they wouldn't serve you in the pubs in town; you was supposed to stay back past the bridge, specially at night. Ever since the race riots all those years ago we had our place, which was a great bloody slum down there – ' he pointed towards the docks and the strip of housing that separated the town centre from the docks: Butetown '– and they had all the rest of it.'

Bobby nodded. She knew this.

'Course,' he said, 'you don't need me telling you all this; point is we've raised ourselves up, you know what I'm saying?'

Bobby nodded again, her mind suddenly occupied by an image of herself, raised up all right, standing on top of a pile of girls – Maria, Tanya, Nikki and all the ones who'd gone before – and St Clair next to her on a much bigger pile.

'Now then,' said St Clair, 'look over there.' He pointed beyond the banqueting hall and the castle wall and the river to the point where Llandaff Fields dead-ended in what used to be the Sophia Gardens exhibition centre and was now a makeshift car park. 'That's where it's going to be.'

'Your new shopping mall?'

'It's not a shopping mall, girl, it's a community development – the Castle Market, loads of incentives for local businesses to get involved.' He paused. 'Fucking hell, who do I think I'm talking to? Yeah, course it's a shopping mall. I know – just what the city needs, whatever. Point is, this deal comes off it's one big bloody payday.'

St Clair turned to look at Bobby. 'You think I'm rich, girl? Well, think again; I've got the biggest overdraft you ever heard of. All the magazines are going down the pan – the computer mags are losing me an arm and a leg. Everyone thinks they must still be coining it but there's so much competition these days, and the advertising market's gone to hell. Soon as a decent accountant gets anywhere near the books he'll close down the whole shooting gallery.

'But if this comes off,' he waved once more towards the

notional new development, 'well, I'm back in business. So I'm just holding my breath till Friday. We sign the deal, then I close the whole publishing thing down and I'm into the property business big-time.'

He put his hands on her shoulders then looked deep into her eyes. She looked back into his, could see nothing there, just a blackness. 'And not just for me – for you too.'

'Oh yeah?' said Bobby, mustering up a bit of front of her own. 'Written me into the will, have you?'

Then she turned her head away from St Clair's siren voice, looked back out over the Castle Field, sure she could see the two human pyres there, his victims and hers, and then she had an awful sense that she could see figures detaching themselves from the pyres walking towards her like zombies or the undead or something, all crying out: poor bloody Frog standing outside the Glendower trying to sell his shrunken junkie body; poor bloody thick bloody Debbie on the game from sixteen, carved up by some psychotic bloody punter when she was twenty-two; and all the rest of them, all walking towards her.

36

Pete was sitting at his desk fielding phone calls from Cherri, who was waiting for Bryn Terfel to show up, finishing the layout for tomorrow's arts page, and doing a bit of work on the St Clair story which was suddenly a hot priority.

He'd gone in to see Graham after the rocket Kim had put under him earlier on and just sort of mentioned that if Graham didn't want it, would it be OK if he freelanced it to one of the tabloids, the *News of the World*, maybe? Well, he'd never seen Graham so animated. No way was Pete taking the story any-where. This was terrific principled journalism and that was what the *Welsh Post* stood for – subject to the lawyers approving it, of course.

'Of course,' Pete had said and he'd gone back to his desk feeling oddly depressed. He could see it was the right thing to do – what St Clair had done was morally repugnant, whether or not some of the participants had survived the experience apparently unscathed. But still, raking it all up now; well, he wasn't too sure who it was going to help exactly. But it would surely sell newspapers and that at the end of the day was his job so he was sitting there staring at a brand-new Word 97 document trying to assemble the facts of the story when the phone rang yet again.

'Pete.'

'Oh, he arrived yet, Cher?'

'Pete, it's not bloody Cher, it's Kim.' She sounded excited. 'I've found another witness, Pete, and this one's not going to be telling us how great it all was. Apparently he's a real fuck-up, lives near Blackwood. You up for it?'

Pete sighed; he supposed he had to be. 'Yeah,' he said. 'Where are you?'

'Beeb.'

'Right, I'll pick you up from there, front entrance in forty-five minutes. OK?'

Forty-five minutes later, right on the dot, Pete was there; another half hour and they were making their way up the valley north of Newport and they were either in Risca or Cross Keys – Pete could never figure out where one started and the other finished – and Kim was map-reading and telling Pete all this stuff she'd got from . . . Well, she didn't want to admit it but it was pretty obvious she must have got it from Bobby so Pete had called her on it and she said yeah, yeah, she had seen Bobby, but it was strictly business, Pete didn't have to worry, which of course meant he was worrying like mad cause he didn't know what it meant, didn't feel like he knew what anything meant just at the moment, and the rain was starting to come down and one slate-grey Valleys town looked the same as the next and boy could it get depressing up here, even now it was all greened over to the point you came from Mars or London or somewhere you would scarcely imagine there had ever been coal mines here, or slag heaps big enough to bury a school.

Finally they were in Blackwood, and a quick word with a passer-by who actually knew something about his town and they were knocking on this feller called Frog's door, an upstairs flat above a newsagent. A minute or so later they could hear someone coming down the stairs and then the door opened a crack. 'That you, Daz?'

'No,' said Kim.

The door opened and a desperately skinny, toothless apparition, red blotches all over his face, stood before them. 'Who are you then?'

'I'm Kim,' said Kim, 'and this is Pete. I'm from the TV.'

'Oh yeah?'

'Yeah, we're making a documentary about Leslie St Clair.'

'That bastard.'

'Yeah,' said Kim, a grin coming to her face, 'that's right, that bastard. Now is it OK if we come in?'

'Oh yeah. OK,' said the apparition, 'it's a bit of a tip, like.'

It was more than a bit of a tip; it was a sofa and a carpet and a huge pile of newspapers and all of it doubled as an ashtray and Pete was damn sure he wasn't going to sit down anywhere but just put his tape recorder on the table and stood staring out the window at the rainswept street outside wishing he was any place else. Kim, though, played the bloke like a trouper. She told him they'd seen the film and she couldn't believe such a respectable figure as Leslie St Clair, such a role model to kids, had been involved in such sordid goings-on and the bloke certainly caught on very quick and was soon agreeing that yeah, it had been terrible, traumatised his whole life, and Kim was lapping it up and Pete was thinking yeah, well the guy was certainly in a hell of a state. But then, when the guy suddenly had a lightbulb moment and asked Kim if she thought there might be any compensation available for a person who'd suffered like he had and Kim said she was sure there was and the bloke's ravaged face took on a certain serenity and the terrible details of addiction and self-destruction started to mount up, Pete started to feel sick cause God knows on one level the guy wasn't lying, he was fucked – you could see that from a mile off. But on another level you wondered whether it was all down to being in a porn film when he was a teenager and really, to be honest, in the end Pete felt like he'd rather not know about all this; it just made him feel sick and depressed and despairing of humanity and really nostalgic for his nice house and nice wife and nice kids and he couldn't stand it any more. He went outside to wait in the car and he sat for another half hour listening to Johnny Walker on Radio 2, Johnny Walker's voice reminding him of being thirteen again and listening to Mott the Hoople on Radio 1, and finally Kim came out holding Pete's tape recorder and all but hugging herself with delight. 'Bingo,' she said, 'absolute bloody bingo. We've got him on toast. I'll take a copy of the tape, play it to my boss and we'll be back up tomorrow with a film crew.' She leaned over and gave Pete a great wet kiss on the cheek, her hair smelling of fags, of junkie squalor.

'Let's go,' she said.

'Yeah,' said Pete, putting the car into gear, and was just about to add something about how glad he was to be getting out of there when he had to pull over slightly to get out of the way of a car coming fast in the opposite direction. And as he did so he saw it was a black Saab, but it was past him before he could see the driver.

He turned to Kim. 'You see that?'

'What?' said Kim, who was looking down at the tape recorder, rewinding it a little to make sure the sound quality was OK.

'Nothing,' said Pete. 'Just looked a bit like Kenny Ibadulla's car, the one passed us back there.'

'Really?' said Kim momentarily alarmed. Then she relaxed, patted the tape recorder. Well, he's too late, isn't he. We've done it, Pete. We've got him.'

'Yeah,' said Pete, 'I suppose we have,' but he didn't stop checking his rear-view mirror till they were back in Cardiff.

37

After her talk with her father Bobby had wanted to be by herself. She'd walked and walked and walked, found herself heading east, down Newport Road under the bridge where the old AA headquarters was morphing into a block of luxury flats, past the Jane Hodge Foundation and what was left of the old infirmary, past Clifton Street and Summers Funeral Home, past the Royal Oak, and a memory of Charlie Unger, the nearest she'd come till now to a father-figure, dead these past three years, past the commercial zone, past the car showrooms and over the round-about and up Rumney Hill, before she realised what she was doing: walking back to the home, retracing the footsteps that had first led her to Les St Clair those years ago, set her life on course.

She got as far as the corner, the street where the home was. Was it still there? Was it still a home? She hadn't a clue. There wasn't exactly a big old-girls' club, got together for reunions. That was it, though; she could go no further. She looked around her, saw a bench on the pavement outside a curry house, and fairly collapsed on to it, suddenly aware of how much her feet were hurting. She looked back down the hill; for the second time that day she could see the city spread out before her. But there was a difference: with Les she'd been in the centre looking out; now, on her own, she was on the outside looking in, and this was the view she trusted. After they'd come down from the tower Les had laid out his plans. He'd told her he was serious; if she wanted it, he would groom her as his heir. But then again if this big deal tomorrow didn't come off he was history.

And he was worried about the Prince of Wales stories getting around. Cat's out of the bag there, he told her. He didn't say it was her fault but she was sure he must have guessed, cause the next thing he said was obviously a message – we can keep it out the news a couple more days then it should be OK; after that they can say what they like cause I'll be back in business.

So that was what he wanted. It was almost a relief discovering that he wanted something. Only question was what she was going to do. Sat on top of Rumney Hill she pondered it. Did she owe more to Frog and poor dead Debbie and all the rest of them or to this new-found father? On the bus back into town she decided. She'd try and have it both ways. She'd put the brakes on Kim for a day or two, let Les's deal go through. After that Kim could drag the truth out into the open and che sera sera.

First thing she had to do was get hold of Kim. She called her at the flat. Got the machine. Called her mobile. Got the voicemail. Left messages on both. Then she got a call from Tanya: she was needed back at the flat.

She tried Kim's numbers every hour or so through the evening; still no reply. Finally she figured that nothing was going to happen till morning so, after she'd seen the back of Nikki's last punter for the day and replied to the last of her emails, she closed the work flat up and went upstairs to sleep.

Kim finally answered her phone at eight in the morning, sounded exhausted, said she'd been up all night working on the programme. Bobby asked if she could stop by and have a quick word about that. Kim sighed but said OK if she could get round fast.

Bobby was round there in fifteen. Kim was all power-suited up and doing her make-up and though it had been the last thing on her mind Bobby couldn't repress a thrill of desire at the sight of her, something really dead sexy about that whole Ally McBeal trip, especially coupled with Kim's curves.

She did her best to be a bit subtle, asking when the programme was coming out like she was just making conversation, but when Kim said she'd seen Frog the day before, got a dynamite interview with him and they were thinking of maybe using part of it on *Wales Today* tonight, she had to weigh in.

'Why don't you keep it back a few days till it's all finished?'

'Too much of a risk,' Kim said. 'HTV might get wind of it. Got to get something out tonight, put the marker down that it's my story.'

'How about tomorrow night?' said Bobby, thinking that the contract was being announced at lunchtime, so any time after that should be OK.

'Why?' said Kim. 'What's it matter to you?'

Bobby tried to think of a plausible lie, couldn't think of one and resorted to the truth, told her that after all this was her dad, and it was bad enough the story coming out without screwing him on his deal and all.

'Oh right,' said Kim.

'And,' said Bobby, feeling desperate now, 'you do it tomorrow I'll give you an interview and all.'

'Yeah?' said Kim. 'Really? That'd be excellent.' She paused, thought about it. 'Look, Bobby, I'll have a word with my producer, see what we can do, yeah? But, to be honest, your real worry isn't me, but Pete, you know. He saw Frog and all and we've got a bit of a deal going – I go tonight on the TV, he leads off tomorrow morning in the press. So you really want to put a lid on this till tomorrow night, you best speak to him.'

'Yeah?' said Bobby, thinking this was starting to feel like pushing water upstream. 'You think he'll listen?'

'Worth a try. He's a decent bloke. Honest, go.'

38

Pete was transcribing the tape of Frog's interview, still flip-flopping between pity and disbelief, when he got a call from reception. It was Albert, using the tone of voice he reserved for announcing obvious undesirables. 'There's someone down here,' he said, 'wants to speak to you.'

'Oh yes?' said Pete, seized with immediate dread, sure it was Kenny Ibadulla. He'd hardly slept all night, convinced Kenny would be banging his door down. He paused, waited till he felt as if he had his voice under control. 'Who is it?' Even as he spoke he was wondering what he was going to do next. Rely on old Albert to deal with Kenny? Hardly.

'Bobby Ranger, she says her name is.'

Pete experienced an immediate rush of relief, followed by bemusement, and then a lesser dread, a minor-key dread. Bobby Ranger, what in hell did she want? Better find out. 'I'll be right down.'

She was waiting in reception, a stocky woman in a big black jacket emblazoned with the name of some American sports team, staring at nothing. Then she saw him and smiled. A gold tooth caught the light, but the smile was oddly shy, nervous.

'Thanks,' she said, 'thanks for seeing me.'

'It's all right,' said Pete. 'You want to come up or . . .' he felt oddly bashful '. . . we could get a coffee round the corner.'

'Coffee sounds good,' she said.

Pete led the way over the road and into an empty

brasserie/café/bar-type place. Pete ordered a coffee. Bobby had a hot chocolate.

'So,' Pete said, 'you wanted to talk to me about something.'

'Yeah,' she said. 'Well, quite a lot of things really.' There was that shy smile again. 'Expect you do and all.'

'Yeah,' said Pete awkwardly, trying to improvise his way through a wholly unfamiliar situation. 'Well, I dunno. I suppose in the end it's not between you and me, it's up to Kim . . .'

'Yeah, no, actually, I mean you're right I suppose, but that's not why I'm here. What it is is the Leslie St Clair story.'

'Oh,' said Pete, 'right.'

'Yeah, well, I don't know how much Kim has told you . . .'

'Well,' said Pete, 'I know it was you who brought her the story in the first place and everything.'

'Yeah, she tell you he's my dad?'

'Who?'

'Leslie St Clair.'

'No,' said Pete, 'she didn't tell me that. Christ, when did you find that out?'

'Just the other day.' She shook her head, again the nervous smile. 'Well, you can imagine.'

'God,' said Pete, 'don't know if I can.'

'No, you're probably right. Anyway, thing is I know I've got no right to ask you this, really, but is there any chance you can keep the story back till the day after tomorrow?'

Pete frowned. 'Why?'

Then he listened as Bobby explained that St Clair would be completely ruined if the story came out before the deal was signed. She was just starting to go on about job losses, clearly laying it on a bit, when Pete cut her off.

'S'all right,' he said. 'I've already agreed not to run it till next week. Someone else been on to me about it already.'

'Who?'

'One of your dad's business partners, Malcolm Hopkin.'

'Mal? Should have bloody guessed.' He watched Bobby shake her head like she too only had part of the whole story.

Finally she looked at Pete and said, 'So why did Kim tell me you were going to be running the story first?'

'I dunno,' said Pete, wondering the same thing. 'I tell you what, why don't I ask her?'

He got out his mobile, called Kim's number. Voicemail. Called her flat, got the answering machine, thought about it for a moment and called the main BBC number. Got put through to her department and finally spoke to some woman with a North Walian accent said she thought Kim was out filming something for tonight's news, the big hush-hush story.

'Oh yeah?' said Pete. 'I'm Pete from the *Post*, yeah, I've been working on the story with her, yeah? You wouldn't know whereabouts she is?'

'Oh, hi Pete,' said the North Walian. 'Yeah, she's mentioned you. But I've no idea where she is; all very secretive, it is. She said something about going back to the scene of the crime, that's any help.'

'So?' said Bobby, as he clicked off the phone.

'She said she was going to the scene of the crime – that mean anything to you?'

Bobby thought about it, then grinned. 'She's at the Prince of Wales.'

39

Bobby led the way into the building. They'd parked the car round the back, next to the car park, blatant double yellow and the Pete feller was worried about it, but she told him not to be stupid. He was a funny bloke, the Pete feller, but all right; she could see why Kim liked him. He had the dependable sensible thing going. Good-looking too, though he dressed like a bit of a bank manager and listened to Radio 2 but then so did she, now and again when Maria wasn't looking. Maria! Christ, she hadn't even thought about her the last day or so, there had been so much going on. Been no calls or anything, though; no 'Oh Bob I'm so sorry I made such a mistake', so she supposed that was well and truly over. She took a deep breath as they entered the lobby. Well, if a part of her life looked like it was coming to an end, this was where it had all started.

They checked inside the pub first; no sign of any TV crew.

'Let's have a look upstairs,' said Bobby and they went back to the entrance and up the stairs. No sign of anyone in what used to be the circle either. They walked slowly back out to the first-floor foyer by the toilets.

'Must be somewhere else,' said Pete.

'I dunno,' said Bobby and looked around her, trying to figure out what was new and what was old. There was a door over by the wall, said No Admittance on it. Was that the one? She walked over and opened it. It gave on to a narrow staircase going up. That was the one, all right.

They walked up to the top of the stairs, faced another door. A chill passed through Bobby as she opened it.

Christ, it was like time had stood still. The room was exactly the same, apart from being half full of boxes. For an instant she was sixteen again, stood on the edge of adventure, of knowledge; Eve about to eat the apple of desire.

Her eyes automatically tracked left to the bar area, half expecting Leslie St Clair to be sat at his table with a bottle of wine open, his serpent's smile in place.

He wasn't there, of course. But Kim was. She didn't see Bobby at first; there was a cameraman filming her as she talked earnestly into camera. Bobby couldn't make the words out from where she was standing, just the hushed tone of TV concern.

Then Kim must have fluffed her lines because she stopped, swore loudly, turned and saw Bobby frozen there in the doorway.

'Well bloody hell,' she said. 'Give me a shock, why don't you?' She walked over, a smile – a slightly puzzled smile but still a smile – firmly in place. 'How the hell did you find me here? I thought you were looking for Pete.'

'Well, I found him, didn't I?' said Bobby, moving forward into the room as, right on cue, Pete stepped through the doorway.

'Jesus,' said Kim, giggling nervously. 'Don't tell me it's *This Is Your Life.*'

'Hardly,' said Bobby. 'More like this is my life, isn't it? Thought you said you would wait on the story.'

Kim looked at her, gave this bright brittle liar's smile, same smile Bobby had seen on a thousand lawyers and a million hustlers and on everyone who'd ever let her down. 'Oh c'mon, Bobby, it's my job, you got to understand that. I don't do the story now, someone else will do it, someone who doesn't understand you the way I do.'

Bobby felt like kicking her, couldn't find the words to express her disgust. Kim turned to Pete. 'Pete, tell her that's how it is.'

Bobby looked at Pete, wondering which way he would jump.

Hell, what was she wondering about? It was obvious. Kim and him, they were two of a kind – media people, liked a bit of a walk on the wild side maybe, but knew which side their bread was buttered on all right. Why did she ever think an ambitious girl like Kim would be seriously interested in her; what was she on? She was just a bit of rough, wasn't she? Well, they wanted a bit of rough, they could have one; least she could do was smack Kim one on her smug little Rhiwbina face. She was just winding herself up ready to throw the punch when Pete spoke.

'Christ sake, Kim, it's only a fucking story. It doesn't matter if you run it today or tomorrow. Doesn't matter if HTV get it the same time as you at the end of the day, does it? We're not God here.'

Bobby watched Kim stare at Pete in disbelief. 'Might not matter to you, Pete. That's why you've been stuck in the same shit job for twenty years. It matters to me cause I am getting the fuck out of here.'

Pete's turn then to stare at Kim like he was ready to smack her one. For a few seconds no one said anything, then all four of them jumped as the cameraman spoke up.

'Kim,' he said, 'are we shooting this or not? Cause if we're not I've got work to do.'

Kim turned round. 'We're shooting it,' she said, 'just as soon as . . .'

Suddenly there was the sound of the door below being opened and then the clumping of four large men hurrying up the stairs.

Seconds later they emerged into the room, Kenny Ibadulla in the lead.

One thing about Kenny, Bobby thought, was once he was in the room everyone knew who was in charge, especially when, like now, he was carrying his trusty baseball bat.

'Bob,' he said first, 'you a part of this?'

'Part of what, Ken?'

'Digging up a load of old shit for the TV.' He nodded towards Kim.

'Well, no, Ken, not really, like. I've been trying to get her to lay off.'

'No good telling them,' said Kenny. 'You got to show them.'

Kenny walked towards Kim who was backing away fast, staring at him in wide-eyed terror. Bobby didn't reckon he would hit her; Kenny, bastard that he was, was still a bit of an old-fashioned gangster type, didn't hold with beating up women. But obviously Pete didn't realise that cause all of a sudden he's like running at Kenny from behind and Bobby doesn't know whether to laugh or cry cause Kenny's going to lick him down in a second but it makes her think that maybe the poor sucker's really in love with Kim and – state that she's in – it brings a tear to her eye as Kenny swings the bat behind him and it goes thud into Pete's thigh and then he's down on the floor groaning and Kim's screaming bloody murder and the cameraman's looking like he's going to weigh in and the situation is just ripe to get out of hand when a voice calls out, 'Ken! That's enough of that,' and the whole room freezes and there, standing behind the bar, a door flapping open behind him, is the Prince of Wales himself, Leslie St Clair.

'Les,' says Kenny. 'Just sorting things out.'

'Yeah, I can see that,' says Les, a little bit sarcastic, which is still the most sarcastic Bobby's ever heard anyone try on Kenny Ibadulla. 'Thing is, Ken, you know how they say no publicity is bad publicity; well I've got to say I'm not sure that goes for hospitalising TV reporters. So, you don't mind Ken, I think it might be best you leaves this to me.'

Kenny stared at Les then looked round the rest of the assembled crew. 'You sure, Les, cause if this deal goes arse up tomorrow I am not going to be very fucking pleased.' He fixed

Kim then Pete with a particularly hard glare. Pete didn't seem to notice, but Bobby could see Kim flinch.

'Yes, Ken,' said Les, and Bobby could hear the tiredness in his voice, 'and nor will the rest of us.'

Kenny nodded, then did a bit of huffing and puffing to show that no one ordered Kenny Ibadulla around, but soon he was out of there and Bobby watched in reluctant admiration as her father turned his charm on to Kim. Would she like an interview? Of course she would and all of a sudden Kim was interviewing Leslie St Clair right in his old position next to the bar of the Prince of Wales. And for the next ten minutes Bobby watched, experiencing a bewildering mixture of emotions, as Leslie St Clair lied his heart out, swore black was white and rivers flow uphill. His accusers were troubled individuals with long histories of drug abuse and psychiatric illness who had sadly focused their inadequacies on the successful figure of Leslie St Clair – just an unfortunate part of the fame game, he called it, and Bobby could see Kim half believing it. Christ, she half believed it herself and she knew it was all false.

And then Kim was done and the cameraman was packing up and there were the four of them stood in the middle of the room, her and her dad and Pete and Kim and all of them awkward now.

'Right,' said Kim finally, as the cameraman made for the door, and she turned and looked Bobby in the eyes and Bobby was just fixing her face into a scowl when Kim leaned forward towards her and then they were hugging, a hug that was definitely a goodbye but a decent one, a let's-remember-the-good-times one, and, as they parted, Kim breathed a single word in Bobby's ear. 'Sorry,' she said, and Bobby breathed back, 'It's OK,' because in the end she understood her; the girl was only trying to get on, and if there was one thing Bobby had learned it was that if you wanted to get on you did what you had to.

Then Kim turned to Pete and something went on between their eyes too, and it ended with Kim smiling and saying, 'You coming then?' and Pete saying, 'Yeah, I guess,' then he turned and hugged Bobby too, awkward like she'd have expected, but nice too and real and then they were gone and she was left alone in the Prince of Wales, with her father.

'Well, Les,' she said once the others' footsteps had faded away, 'what d'you reckon?'

'Oh,' said Les (she thought she'd stick with Les from now on; he wasn't Dad — he had never held her as a child — he was Les, always had been), 'I thought it went pretty well. Plausible old bastard when I want to be, aren't I?' and he looked at her like he was expecting a pat on the back.

'Yeah,' she said, 'you always were that.'

'That's right,' said Les. 'Now, as long as Kenny gets your old friend Frog to change his mind about what he remembers, we should be all right. And he's a persuasive fellow, Kenny, as I'm sure you know.' This time the grin he gave Bobby was pure evil and Bobby couldn't bear the complicity of it, the blood-is-thicker-than-water sharing of it.

Gone suddenly was the St Clair she'd walked the Castle with; here instead was a shifty dangerous bastard: the Leslie St Clair she remembered, in fact. Not the one she'd met at first when he was drawing her in, but the one she'd met later, when she'd tried to get out.

The strange thing was that suddenly she had an overwhelming sense of relief. All the time she'd spent with him, she'd felt like it was nice but it wasn't real. This felt real.

'You fucking bastard,' she said suddenly. 'You fucking black-mailing bastard.'

St Clair looked shocked for an instant, then his eyes went reptilian. 'Don't give me your airs and graces, girl. You and me, we're the same; we do what's got to be done. You've said worse things to your girls a hundred times.'

'You what?' Bobby looked at him in horror: what did he know about her business?

'Oh,' said St Clair, 'you forgetting you're a pimp?' He dug in his pocket. 'Or isn't this your card?'

He held out a card. Bobby grabbed it: it was one of hers all right.

'Where did you get this?'

St Clair smiled. 'The Hilton. You must congratulate the lad does your distribution, gets them in all the right places. So it's a good service, is it? Been tempted to call it up myself. Like father, like daughter, you know what I mean?'

Bobby rocked at that. God knows it was true; he may not have known it at the time but he'd been a true father to her, all right. He'd shown her the ways of the world. And now at last she had her chance to throw it all back in his lying face. She'd give Kim that interview after all.

'Fuck you,' she said and waited a beat before adding 'Dad' and heading fast away from him, her fingers closing on the mobile phone in her pocket.

40

'Did you know he was ill?' Pete asked Bobby as they stood outside the crem up in Thornhill two months later.

'Well,' she said, 'not really. I mean, he had a terrible cough and you know, now you think of it he smoked a hell of a lot and he looked a bit red round the eyes, but no, I didn't have a clue.'

'You think you'd have done anything different if you'd known?'

'What? You mean the interview with Kim?' Bobby thought about it. 'Nah,' she said finally. 'Anyway, he'd told me he was dying, I wouldn't have believed him. Didn't believe he was dead now, till I went round the funeral parlour and looked in the coffin.'

'You didn't?'

'Yeah.' She smiled at him then, the shy smile he'd come to see as the real Bobby Ranger, the one lived inside the tough girl. 'I suppose I wanted to say goodbye to him by myself, like. I hate these things.'

'You been to a lot of funerals then?'

'One or two, you know. First time it's ever been a family one, obviously.' Bobby tried a weak smile but her mind was going back to the last funeral she'd attended. Debbie's. Nearly fifteen years ago now but the thought of it still freaked her out. Well, it had freaked everyone out, of course, what happened to her – carved up by some psycho punter in a derelict house over by Tindall Street. Bobby shivered, watching a couple more motors pulling into the car park, flash ones again; amazing how many friends old Les had now he was dead.

She felt responsible of course, when Debbie died. Wasn't pimping her herself or anything – Debbie always found some right charmer to do that for her – but she'd played her part in turning Debbie out there, she knew that. Her and Les St Clair both. No, that wasn't fair on her; she could see that now. She'd only been sixteen herself; it was St Clair was at the root of it. It wasn't even like there was any malice or whatever in it, thinking about it now, waiting for his body to be turned to ash; she couldn't see him as evil exactly, just without any moral sense at all. And there was something so charming about that, that it corrupted practically everyone he ever came in contact with. And that was why she was glad he was dead.

She hadn't been glad when she heard. 'Cancer?' she'd said to Bernie when he'd called her up and given her the news. 'He didn't have bloody cancer. He didn't tell me.' And then she'd cried buckets partly cause he was dead, partly cause he hadn't told her. And partly, yeah, partly cause she'd felt guilty. There wasn't any big reason to be guilty on one level; he'd been diagnosed six months before. But still the speed it had taken him at the end there, she couldn't believe there was no connection with what had happened. First the scandal fuelled by Bobby's testimony. The Welsh Development Authority had put the Castle Market deal on ice right away, and the day after that Les's associates, Malcolm Hopkin and the rest, had cut him loose. Week later the magazines went into liquidation. The whole house of cards had come tumbling down.

She saw a familiar car pull into the car park, a black Saab. She touched Pete on the arm, pointed. They watched as Kenny Ibadulla emerged from the driver's side, then the passenger's side door opened and out got Malcolm Hopkin.

'Jesus Christ,' said Bobby, 'don't know how they've got the nerve, the way they dropped him.'

Pete looked at her and gave an apologetic sort of smile. 'Well,' he said, 'I suppose some people might say the same about you.'

'No,' said Bobby, 'no way. First, he was my bastard father so I got a right to be here whatever. Second thing, it's not the same . . .' She tailed off. How wasn't it the same? What the hell made her any better than Kenny Ibadulla or Malcolm Hopkin, these fellers who knew how the world worked and how to make a profit out of it?

'Tell you why it's not the same,' she said. 'You see me, right, you take one look at me and you know who I am, always been that way. All the time I've been a pimp – and yeah, yeah, don't worry, that's all finished with more or less – but all that time anyone asked I told them, I'm a pimp. But you see Mal over there, you see Kenny – thing about people like that, they want to have it both ways. And in the end you ask me, that's the thing you've got to learn in life; you got to make choices sooner or later – no such thing as having it both ways.'

Pete thought about this. He knew she was right, could feel the truth of it in his own life. The only problem was knowing what to give up – the cake or the eating. Kim had got what she wanted. Her documentary unmasking Leslie St Clair had been – well, not a huge success or an artistic triumph or anything, but it had got her noticed. Got her a job offer from a company up in London, did those *Ayia Napa Uncovered*-type documentaries, one step from porn movies themselves far as Pete could see but still. Anyway it paid lots more money than she'd been making at the Beeb and she'd taken it. Moved up to London within a month.

He was still seeing her, though. In fact the funny thing was, since she'd been in London she seemed to need him more, like she was a bit scared of the pace and the ambition, needed Pete's stability to stop her from going under. So they'd seen each other most weekends and it was good and everything but . . . but what? Well, seeing the hard time Kim was having, adjusting to the pace, just confirmed what he really already knew – no way was he, Pete Duke, moving up to London. The St Clair story had given him plenty of Brownie points with Graham, his job was about as secure as any job in journalism ever was and frankly he couldn't see himself leaving. And maybe in turn that was why he'd been seeing more of Viv. He wasn't sure really which one of them had initiated it but gradually they'd got into the pattern of him taking the kids out for the afternoon or whatever then afterwards him and Viv would go for a drink and a bit of a chat and catch up on how things were going and, well, the other day they'd got on so well that he'd suggested going back to the house after and Viv had said God no, what about the kids, but he'd given her a lift back anyway and they'd ended up parking up on Caerphilly mountain and doing it in the back of the car like a couple of kids. And now really he didn't know what to think and he was going to see Kim at the weekend and he was really going to have to make his mind up, but deep down he had a feeling that his mind was made up already.

'Yeah,' he said to Bobby, 'you're right there,' and then he looked up, saw another car pulling in, a four- or five-year-old Lexus. Bernie Walters climbed out.

'How's the job going?' Pete asked her then.

'Good,' she said. Bobby was enjoying working for Bernie. He'd taken her on three days a week at first, setting up his website, sticking the details of all his acts online, then administering it. Wasn't that much of a culture shock, specially when it came to booking the lap-dancers who were probably the steadiest-working section of Bernie's talent roster. But it wasn't all strippers; there were plenty of singers and dancers, even a couple of magicians. 'Got a couple of cruise-ship bookings this week via the site, so that was good.'

'Oh right,' said Pete, 'good.'

'Yeah,' said Bobby, feeling a definite sense of pride. It was amazing how her skills had translated to the showbiz world. Bernie noticed her then and came over, his face creasing into a sympathetic smile.

Bobby hugged him. She felt easy around Bernie these days and now they walked for a little while in silence, Bernie looking at her, gauging her mood before starting to talk.

'You know,' said Bernie, 'and maybe this is just the kind of bullshit that people talk at funerals cause they're trying to be nice, I was thinking about old Les today and all this trouble, and it made me think about the city as a whole and the way things are changing. Specially I was thinking about the place it all happened; you know, the Prince of Wales.

'Now, you remember how people used to say it was an eyesore. Well, I don't know about you and maybe I'm biased, but I kind of liked it being there. You close down all the dark and seedy places, what you're left with is a fake. It isn't real any more, it doesn't sweat and bleed like it used to. I suppose what I'm saying, Bob, is the thing about the Prince of Wales, places like that, you only ever miss them when they're gone. And that's kind of what I think about old Les too. Does that mean anything to you or am I just burbling on like an old fool?'

'No,' said Bobby, 'I kind of know what you mean . . . You got a fag, Bernie?'

He frowned at her. 'Thought you quit, young lady?'

'Yeah well, give me a break all right, not today.'

'Your funeral,' said Bernie, then clapped his hand over his mouth and Bobby couldn't help laughing and then, before she could light up, the funeral director started ushering everyone in, so Bobby stuck the fag in her pocket and went inside to bury her father.

Afterwards a few people came up, the few who knew about her and Les, said how sorry they were, but really she couldn't wait for them all to go. She'd held firm all the way through the service but now she wanted to be alone.

Last to go was Pete. He asked her if she wanted a lift and she said no thanks she'd walk and he said you sure and went off with Mikey Thompson in tow, and she smiled cause any time you saw Mikey you ended up smiling, but then they were all gone and she was left in peace to mourn.

She went round the side of the crem to where the wreaths and flowers were laid out. She looked at the labels – couldn't help but be struck by how none of them seemed to be from anyone really close to Les. You never really noticed it in life because he was always surrounded by people, but now you could see he was a loner at heart. Even when he was making those films he was never really involved; he certainly never took part. She'd read his obituary in the *Post* that morning. Amazing how much she hadn't known about him. She sat down overcome by self-pity for a moment. Truly fatherless now; motherless and childless too. Lord, it wasn't St Clair she was mourning; it was herself.

And then it was gone. She was watching a big black crow fly over the cemetery and she had that song that goes I'm like a bird I want to fly away in her head, but then it passed and instead she felt like the bird was carrying St Clair's soul off and with it the dark part of herself. And she knew these moments are never for ever, that the darkness once touched always returns, but for now as she turned and walked down the hill, the city of Cardiff once more laid out before her, she felt as light as she ever had.

A Note on the Author

John Williams lives and works in his
hometown of Cardiff. The author of four
other books, he also writes screenplays and
journalism.

TEMPERANCE TOWN John Williams
£9.99 0 7475 70981

'This is Brit crime fiction at its best. John Williams' obsession with his home town of Cardiff has spawned several novels and short story collections, and this is the best yet' *Independent on Sunday*

Take three guys. Mikey's a shoplifter. That's when he's not working on his true vocation as a ladies' man. The Colonel's a man of leisure. Well, these days he is. Deryck's a copper. And he's back in the last place he ever wanted to be. That's Cardiff, Wales. *Temperance Town* follows three guys, their lovers, their kids and their mates, all trying to make sense of their lives in a world that makes less sense every day.

'Pacey, well plotted and shocking, it has a thrilling denouement and impressive psychological depth' *Mail on Sunday*

'Williams does what only the wonderful writers can do – he convincingly and vibrantly brings to life characters most of us would never know otherwise' Daniel Woodrell, author of *Ride with the Devil*

To order copies from our online bookshop visit www.bloomsbury.com/johnwilliams
Telephone order line: +44 (0)20 7440 2475 between 9.30 am and 5.00 pm (GMT).

bloomsburypbks

www.bloomsbury.com/johnwilliams